SUNS
WILL
RISE

ALSO BY JESSICA BRODY
& JOANNE RENDELL
Sky Without Stars
Between Burning Worlds

SUNS
WILL
RISE

SYSTEM DIVINE: BOOK III

JESSICA BRODY & JOANNE RENDELL

SIMON & SCHUSTER | BFYR

NEW YORK   LONDON   TORONTO   SYDNEY   NEW DELHI

SIMON & SCHUSTER BFYR

An imprint of Simon & Schuster Children's Publishing Division
1230 Avenue of the Americas, New York, New York 10020

SIMON & SCHUSTER BOOKS FOR YOUNG READERS and related marks
are trademarks of Simon & Schuster, Inc.
For information about special discounts for bulk purchases, please contact
Simon & Schuster Special Sales at 1-866-506-1949 or business@simonandschuster.com.
The Simon & Schuster Speakers Bureau can bring authors to your live event.
For more information or to book an event, contact the Simon & Schuster Speakers Bureau
at 1-866-248-3049 or visit our website at www.simonspeakers.com.
Interior design by Michael Rosamilia
The text for this book was set in Adobe Caslon Pro.
Manufactured in the United States of America
First Edition
2 4 6 8 10 9 7 5 3 1
Library of Congress Cataloging-in-Publication Data
Names: Brody, Jessica, author. | Rendell, Joanne, author.
Title: Suns will rise / Jessica Brody, Joanne Rendell.
Description: First edition. | New York : Simon & Schuster Books for Young Readers, [2021] |
Series: System Divine ; book 3 | Audience: Ages 12 up. | Audience: Grades 10-12. |
Summary: Three months after the Patriarche was beheaded,
Laterre seems to be flourishing under General Bonnefaçon, but as dangerous
rifts threaten the peace, Alouette, Marcellus, and Chatine reunite.
Identifiers: LCCN 2020057264 | ISBN 9781534474437 (hardcover) |
ISBN 9781534474444 (paperback) | ISBN 9781534474451 (ebook)
Subjects: CYAC: Space colonies—Fiction. | Soldiers—Fiction. | Revolutions—Fiction. |
Cyborgs—Fiction. | Science fiction.
Classification: LCC PZ7.B786157 Sun 2021 | DDC [Fic]—dc23
LC record available at https://lccn.loc.gov/2020057264
ISBN 9781534474437
ISBN 9781534474451 (ebook)

For all those who have
marched,
protested,
rallied,
spoken up,
sung out,
danced,
written,
painted,
created,
donated,
legislated,
barricaded,
struggled,
voted,
and fought
against inequality, oppression, and injustice.

This book is for you and inspired by you.

Ce qui fait la nuit en nous peut laisser en nous les étoiles.
(Whatever causes the darkest night in our hearts
may also grant us the brightest stars.)
—Victor Hugo

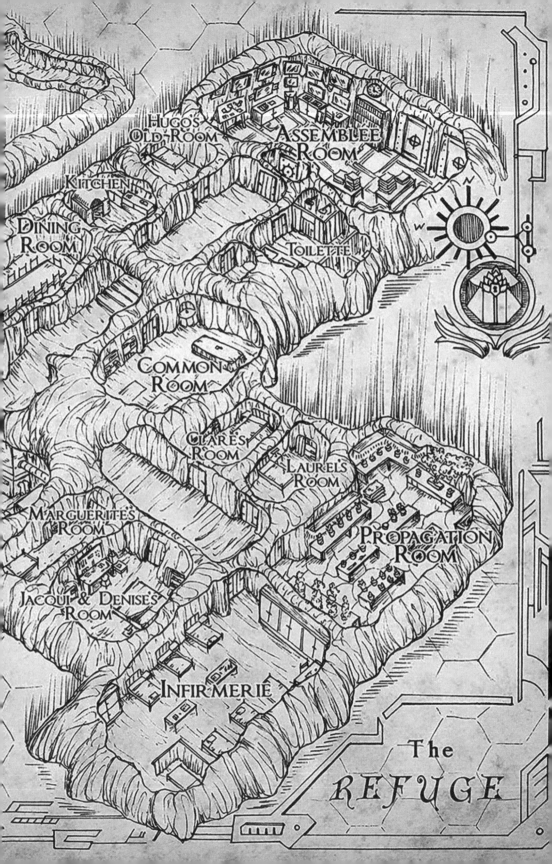

OVERVIEW OF BOOK 2,
Between Burning Worlds

PRIMARY CHARACTERS

Marcellus Bonnefaçon: Grandson of General Bonnefaçon and son of Julien Bonnefaçon. Once a commandeur-in-training with the Ministère, now a Vangarde rebel. Traveled to Albion to track down a weapon developed by his grandfather that would allow the general to control the Third Estate (via their Skins) and use them to murder the Patriarche.

Alouette "Little Lark" Taureau (aka Madeline Villette): Raised by Vangarde rebels and her adoptive father, Hugo Taureau. Recently revealed to be the daughter of the Patriarche. Saved the Third Estate from the general's weapon by using her DNA to access the Forteresse, which houses a kill switch for the Skins. Last seen outside the Paresse Tower, where she was knocked unconscious by an unidentified attacker.

Chatine Renard (aka Théo): Daughter of con artists, former resident of the Frets (slums), and escapee from the prison moon of Bastille. Lived with the Défecteurs while recuperating from injuries. Infiltrated the Ascension banquet with Marcellus, Alouette, and Cerise to stop the general from using his weapon. After riots broke out, she and Marcellus sought refuge at the Vangarde base, where Chatine was reunited with her long-lost brother, Roche.

THE VANGARDE

A rebel group believed to be dead after attempting to free their leader from Bastille. They formerly communicated via devices disguised as devotion beads, but had to shut down the network to convince the Ministère they had perished. Their base is located in the underground Refuge, where the primary members (aka the Sisterhood) protect the Forgotten Word, the First World library, and the Chronicles.

Citizen Rousseau: Former leader of the Vangarde and the Rebellion of 488. Believed by all of Laterre to be dead, but recently revealed (to Marcellus and Chatine) to be alive and recuperating in the Refuge.

Sister Denise (aka Vanessa Collins): The Vangarde's technical expert and a former cyborg who worked on the top-secret Forteresse project (a DNA lock that protects the kill switch for the Skins and can only be opened by a direct Paresse descendant). She is currently being held in a secret facility run by the general.

Sister Jacqui: Responsible for maintaining the Refuge library, and Alouette's favorite sister. Currently being held in a secret facility run by the general.

Sister Laurel: The Refuge's healer and a maternal figure to Alouette.

Principale Francine: Head of the Refuge and responsible for updating the Chronicles.

Roche (aka Henri Renard): An Oublie (orphan) and former messenger for the Vangarde. Recently revealed to be the long-lost brother of Chatine, who helped him escape from Bastille. Now living in the Refuge with the Vangarde.

Julien Bonnefaçon: Father of Marcellus and son of General Bonnefaçon. Wrongfully imprisoned for a deadly bombing during the Rebellion of 488.

Mabelle Dubois: Undercover operative and former governess to Marcellus Bonnefaçon. Killed on Bastille during the mission to break out Citizen Rousseau.

THE MINISTÈRE

The division of the Regime responsible for maintaining law and order on the planet of Laterre.

General Bonnefaçon: Marcellus's grandfather and head of the Ministère. Conspired with the Queen of Albion to develop an update to the Third Estate Skins that turned them into weapons so he could seize control of Laterre.

Inspecteur Limier: Cyborg and former inspecteur of Vallonay. Found unconscious after trying to capture Hugo Taureau in the Forest Verdure, where he was shot by Alouette. Last seen recuperating from a brain injury and memory damage in the Ministère headquarters.

Directeur Gustave Chevalier: Directeur of the Cyborg and Technology Labs in the Ministère headquarters and father of Cerise Chevalier.

Inspecteur Chacal: Former sergent and then inspecteur of the Policier who brutalized the Third Estate. Killed by Chatine at the Ascension banquet.

Warden Gallant: Warden of the Bastille prison.

Apolline Moreau: Laterrian Spaceforce capitaine who led the combatteur attack on Bastille during Citizen Rousseau's attempted escape.

Commandeur Michele Vernay: Close friend of General Bonnefaçon and former commandeur of the Ministère. Killed on a failed mission to assassinate the Queen of Albion.

DÉFECTEURS

A community of people who have chosen to live off the Regime's grid in the Terrain Perdu. Stealth technology (fueled by zyttrium) keeps their camp and ships concealed from detection. Their numbers have dwindled in recent years due to General Bonnefaçon's roundups. They helped the Vangarde break Citizen Rousseau out of Bastille.

Etienne: An experienced pilot and spacecraft builder who lost his father in one of the roundups when his community set fire to the chalets in an attempt to scare off the droids and Etienne went back inside for a lost toy. Rescued Chatine from Bastille.

Brigitte: Mother of Etienne and former cyborg who worked on the Forteresse project with Sister Denise. Now a healer.

Marilyn: Etienne's handmade ship, who has a very "sexy" voice.

Gabriel Courfey: Former thief from the town of Montfer and now honorary Défecteur. Traveled to Albion with Marcellus, Alouette, and Cerise to track down the general's weapon. After being gravely wounded by a cluster bullet, he was left in the care of Brigitte.

FIRST AND SECOND ESTATES
The "upper" estates who enjoy a privileged life of luxury. Most live in the climate-controlled Ledôme in the capital city of Vallonay.

Patriarche Lyon Paresse: Direct descendant of the founding Paresse family and former leader of Laterre. Recently revealed to be Alouette's biological father. Beheaded by the Red Scar.

Matrone Veronik Paresse: Former Matrone of Laterre and wife to Lyon Paresse. Originally from Reichenstat.

Premier Enfant Marie Paresse: Daughter of the Patriarche and Matrone, who was murdered by a poisoned peach just before her third birthday.

Cerise Chevalier: Daughter of Directeur Chevalier, skilled hacker, and a self-proclaimed sympathizeur of the Third Estate. She intercepted a message sent through an abandoned space probe that revealed details about the weapon the general was developing with Albion. Later, while infiltrating the Ascension banquet, she was captured by her father, who scheduled her for a cyborg operation.

Grantaire: Son of the Montfer Policier inspecteur and part of the sympathizeur network. Helped Marcellus and his friends sneak onto a voyageur and break into Ledôme.

THIRD ESTATE

Consisting mostly of ferme, hothouse, exploit, and fabrique workers, these Laterrians are the poorest of the planet and live in slums like the Frets. Until recently they were tracked and monitored by the Skins (screens implanted in their arms).

Maximilienne "Max" Epernay: Leader of the violent Red Scar rebel group. Responsible for many attacks, including the bombing of a hothouse and the execution of the Patriarche.

Jolras Epernay: Member of the Red Scar. Sister of Maximilienne and Nadette Epernay. Began to have doubts about Max's violent plans and tried to warn Marcellus of her intentions.

Nadette Epernay: Former governess wrongfully executed for the Premier Enfant's murder. Sister of Maximilienne and Jolras Epernay.

Lisole Villette: Alouette's mother, who died when Alouette was very young. A former maid at the Grand Palais who was fired after her affair with future Patriarche Lyon Paresse was discovered. Faked baby Alouette's death to protect her from the Ministère and gave instructions to Hugo Taureau to bring her to the Refuge.

Hugo Taureau (aka Jean LeGrand): Alouette's adoptive father, former resident of the Refuge, and escaped convict, who fled to Reichenstat after being pursued by Inspecteur Limier.

Monsieur and Madame Renard: Con artists and parents of Chatine, Azelle, and Roche. Constantly evading arrest, they were last seen at the Défecteur camp in the Terrain Perdu, where they posed as "Fabian and Gen" in an attempt to steal the camp's zyttrium.

Azelle Renard: Oldest child of the Renards and sister to Chatine and Roche. Died in the Red Scar bombing of the TéléSkin fabrique, where she worked.

The "Capitaine": Trader in illicit goods and old acquaintance of Chatine who lives secretly amid the first estate.

THE PLANET OF ALBION

Of the twelve planets in the System Divine, Albion is the most similar to the First World and Laterre's longest-standing enemy. Despite its superior weapons development program, the planet recently lost dominion over Usonia (and its supply of titan) during the War of Independence.

Queen Matilda: Current ruler of Albion. Plotted with General Bonnefaçon to develop a weapon in exchange for help winning back control of Usonia.

Admiral Wellington: Admiral of the Albion Royal Space Fleet who commandeered the voyageur carrying Marcellus, Alouette, Cerise, and Gabriel en route to Albion.

Lady Alexander: The Queen's High Chancellor. Escorted Marcellus and his friends to the Royal Ministry of Defence complex, where the general's new weapon was being developed.

Dr. Edward Collins: Father of Sister Denise and a neuroengineer who helped develop the weapon for General Bonnefaçon. Killed by a cluster bullet while helping Marcellus and his friends escape Albion.

- PART 1 -
ORDER OF THE SOLS

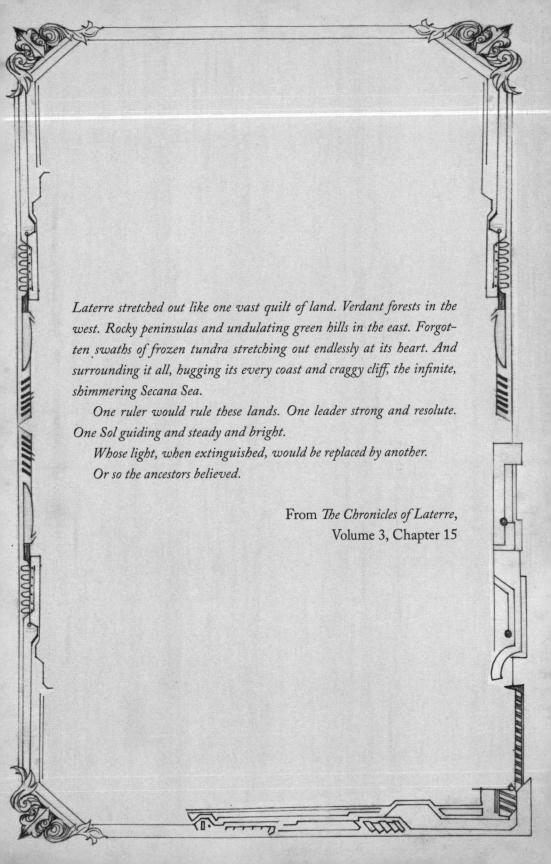

Laterre stretched out like one vast quilt of land. Verdant forests in the west. Rocky peninsulas and undulating green hills in the east. Forgotten swaths of frozen tundra stretching out endlessly at its heart. And surrounding it all, hugging its every coast and craggy cliff, the infinite, shimmering Secana Sea.

One ruler would rule these lands. One leader strong and resolute. One Sol guiding and steady and bright.

Whose light, when extinguished, would be replaced by another.

Or so the ancestors believed.

From *The Chronicles of Laterre*,
Volume 3, Chapter 15

CHAPTER 1

ALOUETTE

ALOUETTE IMAGINED IT WAS LIGHT FROM THE SOLS. Beautiful flares of cobalt blue, golden white, and scarlet red. As the blinding spark pierced her vision, she bit back a scream, reminding herself that it was an illusion, a trick of the brain, nothing more than electrical signals telling her this was even worse than the last time. It was all in her mind. The light. The pain. The fire that burned her face. That's why they did it. They were trying to break her mind. But they would not. The last thing Alouette would allow them to break was her mind.

The scream broke instead.

It charged out of her like a voyageur breaking atmosphere, like a planet exploding. Until all she could hear was that scream and all she could see was that light and all she could feel was that fire.

Then, she vomited. And it was over.

For now.

The inspecteur lowered the device and took a step back while Alouette caught her breath. She knew to take her time. It was the only reprieve she had—these precious moments between being unable to speak and being expected to.

"Where is he?" asked the cyborg in that chilling monotone. Even though it was the same question the inspecteur asked every day, it still sent a shiver of fear through Alouette. She wasn't afraid of more pain. She'd almost gotten used to the pain. It was the fear that her body would eventually betray her. Her tongue would move on its own. Her lips would foolishly give away the only thing that was keeping her alive.

"Where is Marcellus Bonnefaçon?" the inspecteur said, raising the device again and waving it ominously toward Alouette's neck. Alouette flinched and immediately reprimanded herself for it. The circuitry embedded in the left side of the cyborg's face flickered with satisfaction. "This can all be over. This can all end tonight. All you have to do is tell us where he is and the pain will stop."

Alouette gritted her teeth. The device moved closer. Alouette pressed her toes against the tops of her shoes and her wrists against the metal restraints, bearing down.

"Relax," came a familiar voice in her mind. *"The pain is worse when you fight it."*

The sharp prong of the device brushed her skin, and Alouette let her body fall limp against the chair. She heard a sizzle as the electricity hummed through her skin, locating the nerve at the base of her jaw.

And then it happened.

Her forehead exploded in flames. A million tiny daggers stabbed at her eyes. Her cheekbones felt as if they were being crushed by a droid's unyielding metal fist. And inside her mouth, her tongue turned to scorching molten lava.

This time, however, Alouette was somehow able to contain her scream.

And the meager contents of her stomach.

The inspecteur stepped away, taking the pain with her. "Where is the general's grandson?" she asked. If she was getting tired of the same routine day in and day out, she didn't show it. Then again, cyborgs rarely showed any emotion.

"Don't let them see the truth," the voice reminded her. *"Or they'll have no reason to keep you alive."*

Alouette closed her eyes, gripping desperately to the clarity and comfort the voice brought her. She was so grateful to have it back in her life, even if she had to use her imagination to make the words sound real.

"Give it to me," someone snarled from the other side of the room, and Alouette's eyes shot open to see a figure emerging from the shadows. Had it been there the whole time? Watching?

"This farce has gone on long enough," the figure said. "Who is running this facility, Inspecteur Champlain? You or her?"

The cyborg looked momentarily stunned by the rebuke. "I'm sorry, Monsieur. I've been trying. Every day. But she won't talk."

The figure snatched the device from the inspecteur's hand and stepped into the single shaft of light affixed over Alouette's head. But Alouette didn't need the light to recognize him. She would recognize him in a dark room, with her eyes sewn shut, and her ears covered. She would recognize the *feel* of him. His energy was unlike any she'd ever known. It filled every centimètre of the room, forcing out all of the air.

"Perhaps it's because she doesn't *actually* know anything," General Bonnefaçon said, his cool hazel eyes focused intently on Alouette. "Perhaps she's been playing us for fools this whole time."

And then, he was there. Towering over her. Glaring down at her like a hungry lion standing over an injured lamb.

No, Alouette reminded herself. *I am the lion. He is the prey. He is more afraid of me than I am of him. That's why I'm here.*

The inspecteur took three paces back, as though Alouette might implode and she was afraid of getting hit by the debris. The general lowered himself into the chair opposite Alouette, his eyes never leaving hers.

She hadn't seen him since the night he'd found her at the base of the Paresse Tower. She remembered the blow that came to her head, extinguishing all the stars in the sky. Then, she'd woken up here, in this dark place that knew no stars, no light, no hope of rescue. They were on an island not drawn on any maps, not marked on any TéléComs, invisible even to satellite imagery due to Laterre's thick cloud coverage. Up until a few months ago, she hadn't even known it existed.

"Madeline Villette," the general began in a cold, chilling tone. It was the name her mother had given her. An unfamiliar name. A name that conjured up a past of running, hiding, of pretending to be someone else without even knowing it. "I am not pleased to be here today. There are so many other worthwhile things I would rather be doing. I had hoped this little problem would have been solved by now." He flashed a look at Inspecteur Champlain, who was now hiding in the shadows. "And yet, here we are, more than three months later."

Alouette felt something heavy and ominous slink into the pit of her stomach. If the general was here, if *he* was the one holding that device, that meant it was all over. She had strung them along for months and now her time was up.

"Sometimes," the general went on, straightening the cuffs of his pristine white uniform, "it's the small pebble in your shoe that ends up causing more disturbance in your life than the largest of boulders. You have been an inconvenience since the day you were born. And I see now that time hasn't changed you at all."

He stood up and began to pace behind his chair. "You should be resting with the Sols right now. You know it and I know it." He stopped and snapped his gaze back to her. "But I think Inspecteur Champlain has underestimated you. I think you know *exactly* what you're doing and why you're still here."

The chill of his words sent shivers of dread through Alouette. It *was* all over. He was onto her. Somehow Alouette had been able to fool the inspecteur all this time, but she couldn't fool the general. Not anymore. He knew now that she didn't have the slightest idea where Marcellus Bonnefaçon was. He knew that every well-timed hesitation and subtle hint she'd given the inspecteur over the past three months had all been a ruse to keep her useful. Keep her alive.

Because Marcellus Bonnefaçon was a dangerous threat. He was one of the few people left who knew the truth about the general and what he'd tried to do at that banquet. With those Skins. And every day that Alouette pretended to know his whereabouts was another day she got to live. Another day she got to rot away in this cell, thinking about Marcellus, and all the other people she prayed were still alive. Still safe. Chatine and Gabriel and Cerise.

Cerise.

Alouette's chest squeezed at the memory of the last time she'd seen her. Fighting, screaming, twisting in the grip of those guards who had dragged her down the hallway of the Ministère headquarters. Had she managed to escape them? Or was she now . . .

Alouette shoved the thought from her mind. She had to keep hold of her hope, no matter how thin and flimsy it had become. It was all she had left in here.

That and the voices in her head.

"So, how about we make this clean and simple?" the general said. "No more pain. No more games. Do you actually *know* where my grandson is?"

Alouette said nothing and the general gestured to Inspecteur Champlain, who hurried over with a hologram unit and switched it on.

Seconds later, Alouette's face was bathed in light of every color: the warm browns of the Bûcheron Mountains, the inky dark blue of the Secana Sea, the luscious greens of the Forest Verdure, and the stark whites of the Terrain Perdu. The whole of Laterre spread out before her, a world unfurling. And Alouette saw her home. Not just the Refuge she grew up in or the exploit city she was born in. But all of it. It was all her home. A planet that lived in her blood and pumped through her veins. A people whom she'd set free. This was the hope that breathed inside of her. That kept her from giving up.

"I'm giving you one last chance," the general said. "Tell me where he is, and I might even be merciful and let you live out your days on Bastille."

"*Lies,*" said the voice in her mind.

As Alouette stared at that hologram map of the planet—*her* planet—it was like she was staring at a blank page of the sisters' Chronicles, just waiting to be written upon. Just waiting for the next page of history to be recorded.

And she would have a say in that history if it was the last thing she did. Even if it killed her.

Alouette glanced up from the map and forced herself to hold the general's steely gaze. Then, in a voice ragged with time and neglect, she said, "The people will never follow you. They will never trust you. And as long as Marcellus Bonnefaçon is still out there, he will make sure you never win."

The general's jaw tensed and his grip around the metal-pronged device tightened. Alouette braced herself for more pain. But the general only laughed. "Stupide girl. You've been in here a long time. The planet is a different place than you left it. A *better* place."

He rested his hands on the back of his chair and leaned toward her, close enough that his energy, his menacing presence, was everywhere, covering her, chilling her, seeping deeper into her nerves than any torture device. "They already trust me. They already follow me." Then, after glancing over his shoulder to ensure the inspecteur was out of earshot, he whispered, "It's better than following the daughter of a worthless blood whore, just because her father is the Patriarche." His mouth broke into a sinister smile as his hazel eyes flashed in the single shaft of light. "Sorry. *Was* the Patriarche."

The general turned and stalked toward the door of the cell. All the while, Alouette's mind was spinning, struggling to make sense of this new information.

Is the Patriarche dead?

But her thoughts came to a jarring halt as something sparked across her vision. At first, she thought it was the device again, sending blinding, searing light through her skull. But she felt no pain. That's when she realized the light was coming from Inspecteur Champlain. Something was happening to her circuitry. It was flickering erratically, like someone had hacked the signal. And her face had gone deathly still, her jaw hanging slightly ajar and her eyes fixed on the empty space in front of her. Alouette glanced at the general, but he didn't seem to notice.

"Inspecteur," he said brusquely as he reached the door.

The word seemed to free the cyborg from whatever was happening to her. The flickering stopped. Her eyes snapped into focus. "Yes, General?"

"Don't make me regret giving you this promotion." He thrust the device back into her hand and nodded dismissively to Alouette. "Make sure this is taken care of, or you'll be back rounding up scum on the streets of Lacrête."

"Yes, General," the cyborg replied. She clutched the device in her hand and stepped toward Alouette, the metal prong glinting in the overhead light.

Alouette winced, once again bracing herself for the pain. But again, the pain didn't come.

"Forget that," the general barked as he yanked open the door of Alouette's cell. "She doesn't know anything. It would seem the decision to keep her alive has been a waste of time." His gaze settled on Alouette once more, and she could see the finality in his eyes just as clearly as she could hear it in his voice. "Obviously, she's worth more to me dead."

CHAPTER 2

CHATINE

THERE WAS NO RAIN IN THE MARSH TODAY. A CLOAK OF gray clouds hung above the bustling marketplace, but there wasn't a drop of moisture to be found.

He's even somehow managed to improve the weather.

Chatine Renard scooted forward on the exposed metal beam she was straddling, trying to identify one thing about the scene below that felt familiar. She couldn't. She'd been living underground for more than three months, and it was like she'd emerged onto an entirely different planet.

Every stall in the marketplace bore a brand-new canopy, made of blue, yellow, or turquoise canvas, and as they flapped and billowed in the soft breeze, it was as if the whole Marsh had transformed into a vast rainbow sea. On the tables below, great pyramids of gleaming fruits sat next to huge baskets of vegetables that appeared so fresh and vibrant it was as if they were made of plastique. Not a single loose chicken pecked or squawked or flapped amid the mud and trash. Because there was no longer any mud or trash. The walkways between the stalls looked as if they'd been scrubbed clean, slat by metal slat. And there was a freshness in the air—a sharp cleanliness that stung Chatine's nostrils. It was almost more pungent than the stink that used to cling to the city like a drenched jacket.

But the most unsettling sight of all was the flickering images that danced in the air, populating every corner of the marketplace and the Frets beyond. The holographic projections stood taller than a Policier droid, and their dizzying loops of bright, flashing color kept snagging at the periphery of Chatine's vision, constantly sucking her into their shimmering displays.

How did he manage to do all of this in only three months?

"Are you keeping watch?" said the thirteen-year-old boy balancing next to Chatine on the high rafter. His hand was shoved into a joint that connected two support beams of what was left of the old cargo ship that now served as the Third Estate marketplace. "You have to warn me if you see anything."

Chatine rolled her eyes. "I know."

That was another thing that was vastly different about her trip to the Marsh today. Chatine was *not* used to having a partner. Especially one who gave her orders. Even if it was her little brother.

"And whatever you do," Roche said, twisting his fingers deeper into the joint, "if you spot trouble, *don't* be a hero."

She snorted. "When have I *ever* tried to be a hero?"

"Pretty much every moment since the first time I met you."

"Hey," Chatine shot back. "If it weren't for me, you'd still be on Bastille."

"If it weren't for you, I never would have been *sent* to Bastille."

Chatine bit back the reply that came instantly to her tongue. He *might* have a point. Ever since she'd met Roche, the homeless Oublie with no parents, she'd somehow always found herself trying to save him from dire situations. But maybe that was just because he was always stupid enough to get himself *into* those dire situations.

"Just keep watching," Roche told her. "Don't move your eyes in one fluid motion. Instead focus on object to object. You'll see more that way."

"I lived in the Frets for ten years, remember? I know how to keep a lookout."

With a huff, she turned and focused back on the swarms of people below. They felt no more familiar than anything else in this place. She was used to sitting on this very perch and gazing out at a sea of crocs and hustlers and con artists. Her kind of people. Or what *used* to be her kind of people. But now, no one was stealing. No one was sleeping off a bad weed-wine hangover in the alleyways between stalls. No one was fighting over the size of a chou bread loaf. People were being . . . civil to one another. Even *nice*. Wrapped in warm wool coats with shiny new boots on their feet, they moved carefully and politely around one another on the walkways, sometimes stopping to greet a friend or smile at a rosy-cheeked baby in a mother's arms. Everyone seemed to have a lightness in their gait and a hop in their step. The hunger and misery that used to weigh them down, Chatine realized, was nowhere to be found. And neither were the three-mètre-high droids that used to patrol the streets like metal monsters.

The sisters had warned her that things would look different now, but she'd never expected anything like this. The whole thing was creepy. She almost preferred the droids. At least with bashers, she knew what to expect.

"Can you hurry up, please?" she said with a shiver.

"Got it!" Roche yanked his hand out of the joint, revealing a tiny black sphere clutched between his slender fingers.

Chatine leaned in for a better look. "That's it? That's what we're out here risking our necks for?"

"Don't forget," Roche reminded her with a smirk, "you're the one who *begged* to come on this mission."

"I didn't beg. I asked. Politely." Then, after a look from Roche, Chatine was forced to add, "A few times."

"This is one of the Vangarde's primary cams," Roche explained, gesturing to the crowded marketplace below. "Just look at this placement. You can see almost the entire Marsh from up here. The sisters have been practically blind since this cam went offline. Obviously, it's an important mission."

Chatine didn't doubt it was an important mission. She just doubted the sisters' judgment in sending a thirteen-year-old kid to do it. The truth was, she *had* begged. She'd begged them not to send him. It was too dangerous. He was too young. And when they'd refused to listen, that's when she'd begged to go with him. She'd assured the sisters she could be an asset, a lookout. But really, she couldn't breathe at the thought of him being out here alone.

Roche pulled his récepteur from his pocket and flipped it open to reveal a numeric keypad and a small screen inside. He held down one of the keys and then spoke quietly into the barely visible microphone. "I've extracted the faulty cam."

"Good work," came Sister Marguerite's response a moment later through the device's tiny speaker. "Install the replacement cam and return to base immediately."

"Roger that," Roche said officiously, and snapped the récepteur closed.

Chatine watched on as he pocketed the old cam and pulled out the replacement that Sister Marguerite had given him earlier this morning. After blowing twice into the joint to chase away the dust, he leaned forward and concentrated hard on positioning the new cam between the two beams, his tongue peeking out from the corner of his mouth, making him look like the little boy he would always be in Chatine's mind. No matter how old he got or how tall he grew or how many missions the Vangarde entrusted him with, he would always be Henri, the precious baby she'd lost, and then, by the grace of the Sols, found again.

"Chatine, you're doing that creepy staring thing again," Roche reprimanded her, and it was only then she realized he was right.

"Sorry," she muttered, and returned her gaze to the Marsh. Sometimes she just couldn't believe he was back.

"You need to stay focused. The sisters are counting on us."

"I know the stakes," she said impatiently. She might be grateful to have her little brother back, but that didn't mean she liked taking orders from him.

Chatine drew in a deep breath. It was a relief to feel fresh air in her lungs again. To be back in a dark hooded coat and comfortably worn pants, instead of those weird tunic things the sisters made her wear. The Refuge—buried ten mètres below the ground—was a good place to hide, but it seemed to be growing smaller by the day. And the circulated air that pumped through the hallways by archaic humming machines left a stale, bitter taste in Chatine's mouth. When Principale Francine had *finally* agreed to let Chatine accompany Roche to the surface today, Chatine had nearly leapt for joy.

That is, until she saw, firsthand, just how much the surface had changed in the past three months. Everything about this place was unnerving her. And the longer they were out here, exposed, the more she just wanted to get Roche safely back underground.

"Bonjour, Laterre!" Music suddenly flooded the air, causing Chatine to lose her balance. She gripped the beam and glanced around at the multitude of hologram projections, all displaying a bright-eyed, big-haired woman standing in front of what looked like the Vallonay docklands. But they, too, were no longer recognizable. They were too clean, too shiny, too *perfect*.

"It's Month 3, Day 9, 506, and another day in Laterrian paradise," the woman said with a voice that made Chatine want to punch her. "I'm Desirée Beauchamp, the host of your daily TéléCast. As you can see from the glorious view behind me, Vallonay's rebuilt docklands are a spectacle to be admired."

The footage zoomed in closer to show a stream of smiling Third Estaters crossing the gangway onto a brand-new bateau whose deck rails and vast anchors glittered and gleamed in the daylight.

"Thanks to the generosity and goodwill of our provisional leader, General Bonnefaçon," the obnoxious host continued, "these newly reopened docks are yet another bright and shining mark of progress on our beautiful planet."

Chatine snorted again and was about to yank her gaze away when she noticed the crowds of people below. They had all stopped what they were doing, freezing in place like someone had pressed pause on a playback. Every single person in the marketplace was staring upward, basking in the glow of the holograms, absorbing every single word this chipper woman was saying to them. As if her voice was coming straight from the Sols.

"Are you done yet?" Chatine asked Roche. "This place is giving me the creeps."

Roche scooted closer to the support beam, stretching his arm up so that his entire hand nearly disappeared into the joint. "Almost . . . there . . . ," he said through gritted teeth.

"We're so grateful to General Bonnefaçon."

Chatine's attention snapped back to the hologram. The bright-eyed woman was no longer standing in front of the docks. She was now interviewing a man dressed in a dark brown fabrique uniform, sitting with other workers at a long table overflowing with trays of crispy potatoes, bubbling gravy, and piles of steaming broccoli.

"The Patriarche's death was a travesty, to be sure," the man continued. "But the general has been good to us. We have food in our bellies and warm clothes on our backs. My bébés haven't cried from hunger in months. As far as I'm concerned, the System Alliance can just appoint the general as leader and I'd be happy as a chicken in a cornfield."

Desirée Beauchamp turned back to the cam, resuming her rosy-lipped artificial smile. "Of course, we still have to wait a little while longer to find out who will be chosen as Laterre's permanent leader. For the first time in our history, the System Alliance has been forced to invoke the contingency clause of the Order of the Sols, which states that in the absence of a legitimate heir, or if the heir is deemed unfit to rule, the Alliance shall appoint the next leader of Laterre. The general has been in talks with the delegates who represent the twelve planets of our glorious System for weeks now and, as of yet, a decision has not been made, although we expect the official vote and appointment to be announced any day now. Speculations on who the delegates of the System Alliance will choose have spread across the planet. The most popular rumors among Second and Third Estaters alike have been, of course, that the System Alliance will nominate the closest living relative to the departed Patriarche, putting his three cousins, Élisabeth, Alphonse, and Philippe Paresse, at the top of the list and earning them the nickname of 'the Favorites.'"

Chatine watched on, sickened, as the footage of the fabrique's cantine dissolved into an image of the soaring Paresse Tower, backdropped by the vast blue TéléSky of Ledôme. Underneath the enormous clawed feet of the tower stood a slender, coiffed woman in a flowing apricot-colored gown.

"Obviously, I would be honored to be appointed," said the woman Chatine recognized as Élisabeth Paresse. Her stiff upper lip barely moved as she spoke. "And as the Patriarche's oldest cousin, I do believe it is my duty to step up in this time of our planet's greatest need."

The footage morphed again, this time to a man—Alphonse Paresse—sitting beside a sparkling blue pool behind the largest manoir Chatine had ever seen. "I'm certain whoever the Alliance appoints will be the right choice. I trust in the delegates of our beloved System. And should they appoint me, of course, I will do my very best to serve this planet and ensure that we *all* continue to live in glory." As he winked at the cam, Chatine felt a clench in her stomach.

The Vangarde better figure out what the fric they're doing. And fast. Otherwise one of these buffoons is going to be moving into the Grand Palais.

"Done!" Roche announced, withdrawing his hand from the joint. He kept it poised under the beam, ready to catch the cam in case it fell back out. But it held.

"Great," Chatine said, anxiously licking her cold lips. "Let's go."

"Not yet," Roche said, squinting into the crevice between the beams. "Sister Marguerite told me I had to wait for the green light. That means it's online."

Chatine sighed. She wasn't sure if it was the chill in the air, that Desirée woman's tinkling voice echoing off the surrounding Frets, or just the stark, unsettling difference of this whole place, but she was starting to get a bad premonition deep in her gut. As a Fret rat, she'd learned to trust those intuitions. They were usually right.

"We, of course, will be giving you live updates as we continue to monitor the System Alliance's fateful decision," said Desirée Beauchamp. "Until next time, au revoir and Vive Laterre!"

The host's beaming face faded away, leaving behind the shimmering emblem of the Ministère—two rayonettes crisscrossed over the planet—and a smooth, friendly voice crooning, "Glory for *all* of Laterre," which was apparently the Ministère's new motto.

Chatine tapped her fingers anxiously on her leg, glancing between a group of sergents who were patrolling nearby and Roche, who was still peering into the joint. The sight of those somber gray Policier uniforms uneased her, and even though she was confident the two of them were well hidden up here in the rafters, she still pulled her hood low across her brow, covering her dark hair that was now just long enough to tuck behind her ears. Sister Marguerite had warned her about the repercussions of getting scanned by a cyborg or the TéléCom of a passing sergent. Since the Vangarde had erased her profile from the Communiqué, Chatine Renard officially no longer existed in the eyes of the Regime. But she definitely still existed in the eyes of the general. And he would undoubtedly be looking for her. And Marcellus. After what they'd done at the Ascension banquet three months ago, she wouldn't be surprised if the general had tasked the most brilliant of his lackeys with tracking them down.

"Success!" Roche whispered beside her, pulling her attention back to her brother. "We have a *working* cam."

"Fantastique," Chatine said hurriedly, preparing to crawl across the beam to the nearest exit. "Let's go."

"Wait a minute." Roche's attention was suddenly focused on something in the distance. "Is that . . ." He rummaged around in the sac strapped to his chest and pulled out a bulky contraption that looked like a pair of detached droid eyes. He held the gadget up to his face and peered through it.

"What?" Chatine asked, trying to follow the direction of his gaze.

"It is!" Roche exclaimed. "Sols! What the fric is he doing here?"

"Who?" Chatine's anxiety ratcheted up three notches as she glanced between the crowd below and her brother, who was still peering through the strange contraption. It somehow seemed too big for his little head. "Give me that." She snatched it out of his hand and held it up to her own eyes. The world magnified in an instant, making her so dizzy she nearly fell off the beam again. "Whoa," she said, steadying herself. "What is this thing?"

Roche huffed. "The sisters gave it to me. It's called a binocular. Or binoculars. I forget. Anyway, it's a First World relic, so be careful with it."

"What did you see?" Chatine asked, ignoring him.

Roche pointed straight into the distance. "Over there. At Monsieur Ferraille's junkyard stall."

Mindful of her her balance this time, Chatine peered through the strange droid-like eyes, marveling at the level of detail she was able to perceive. She could see the soft fuzz of golden apricots being delivered from the hothouses, the glint of the metal coins the Ministère had minted to replace digital tokens as they passed between buyers and sellers, and even the corner of a darkened, inactive Skin peeking out from the cuff of a sleeve. If only she'd had one of these binocular things back when she was a thief. She could've spotted a gullible Second Estater from kilomètres away.

Finally, Chatine located the stall, and the familiar details of Monsieur Ferraille's wares came into focus. But it wasn't the rusted pots, spools of wire, or scraps of mismatched fabric that interested Chatine. It was the man rummaging through it all, his eyes darting anxiously around as though he were being followed.

He wore the same pristine coat as everyone else in the Marsh, the same gleaming new boots. But it was the flowing curls and high, almost regal brow that made him recognizable. And those pale, intense eyes.

Chatine shuddered. The last time she'd seen those eyes, she'd been standing in this very Marsh, moments before she'd watched Maximilienne Epernay, the leader of the Red Scar, stand on a platform and call for the Patriarche's death. Moments before she'd watched the blue laser of the Blade slice through Lyon Paresse's neck.

No one had heard from Max or any of the Red Scar since that night. They'd all fled into the darkness the moment the droids had arrived. Most people hoped they were gone for good.

And up until a few seconds ago, Chatine had been one of them.

But now, as she watched Jolras Epernay, Maximilienne's brother, riffle through a pile of engine parts at Monsieur Ferraille's stall, she wondered if they'd all been foolish to hope.

The man plucked a rusty power cell from the pile and turned it around in his hands. It was clear he was only *pretending* to study it because his gaze kept bouncing around the marketplace.

What was he doing here? In broad daylight? Was he on his own? Or was he back to working for Max?

"As soon as he leaves that stall, we move."

"Move?" Chatine lowered the binoculars and turned back to her brother. "You mean, go back to the Refuge?"

"No, imbecile. We follow him."

Chatine nearly lost her balance for a third time. "Whoa, whoa, whoa. No way. Too dangerous. We're not following him."

"We have to figure out what he's doing here," Roche said with a twinge of impatience.

"No," Chatine said sternly. "*We* don't have to do anything. *You* were assigned to replace the broken cam. Which you did. And *I* was assigned to protect you."

"After you begged."

Chatine threw up her hands. "It doesn't matter! Sister Marguerite just told us to return to the Refuge, which is what we're going to do. We'll tell the sisters what we saw, and they can figure out what to do about him."

"But by then he might be gone again. What if this is our only chance to find the Red Scar?"

"You don't even know he's still *with* the Red Scar. He told Marcellus that he wanted nothing to do with Max anymore."

"And you believe that?"

Chatine squirmed under her brother's scrutiny. The truth was she wasn't sure what to believe. Jolras had always given her confusing vibes. But she didn't want to supply Roche with any more ammunition. She could tell he was already forming one of his infamous "hunches." He'd been driving her up the wall with them. The general had poisoned the water supply. The Matrone hadn't escaped to Reichenstat, as everyone had been told, but was, instead, hiding out on a sheep ferme in Delaine, pretending to be a ferme worker. The rusty machines from the old blood bordels that the general had shut down were being used to make the Ministère's new coins. And now, Jolras Epernay was on some secret, undercover mission for a terrorist group that had vanished months ago.

"I don't think we have enough information to make this decision," Chatine replied diplomatically. "And I don't think we should stray from our assignment. Remember the sisters can track us wherever we go." She gestured to the pocket where Roche had stored the Vangarde's récepteur.

"If you're afraid, you don't have to come," Roche said, jutting out his chin defiantly. "I can do it by myself."

Chatine felt a growl building in her throat. "I'm not afraid, I just—"

"Good, then on my count. One, two . . ."

Chatine's gaze darted back to the stall, where Jolras was handing Monsieur Ferraille a shiny new coin in exchange for a rusty pair of old pliers.

"Roche!"

"Three!"

Suddenly, Roche was moving, leaping to a nearby support beam and sliding toward the ground. Chatine released a final grunt of protest before letting her body tip forward.

It was like she'd never left. Her muscles remembered every move, every turn, every loose pipe, as she spun around the metal beam and somersaulted down to the ground. The force of her landing knocked the hood off her head and she scrambled to yank it back up, desperately scanning their surroundings for anyone nearby with a TéléCom, but thankfully, there wasn't a sergent or officer in sight.

Roche slid to the ground beside her and they were off, two former Fret rats moving in perfect synchronicity through the crowd, communicating only in glances and subtle gestures, as though they'd been doing this together their entire lives. As though the Renard blood that ran through both of their veins connected them by some invisible force.

All the while, Chatine kept Jolras Epernay in her sights, following his movements easily, effortlessly, watching his flowing curls bob through the crowd. As much as she despised Roche's disobedience, she couldn't deny the thrilling adrenaline that was surging through her veins. She'd forgotten what it felt like to track, to chase, to hunt. She felt like a wild animal who'd been locked in captivity for too long, and now she was finally allowed to do what she did best. For the first time in three months, Chatine Renard felt *alive*.

- CHAPTER 3 -
CERISE

"INCOMING DOWNLOAD FROM SURVEILLANCE SECTOR 01.09.63. Please accept."

Cerise Chevalier paused the footage on her screen and turned to her tertiary monitor. "Accept," she replied, and the display began to populate with thousands of images.

"Downloading," said the smooth voice through her audio interface. "Five percent . . . ten percent . . . fifteen percent . . ."

Cerise's long black lashes fluttered softly as her left eye performed a rapid initial scan of the download. She already knew from the metadata that it was originating from the Third Estate marketplace in Vallonay, captured by hologram module 63. But she wouldn't know how useful the surveillance would be until the download was complete and she could examine it more thoroughly.

She turned back to her primary monitor and resumed playback on the footage she'd been analyzing.

"Take a closer look. Think really hard before answering. Now, tell me, have you seen this man?" The sergent on the screen shoved his TéléCom closer to the stall owner's face. The woman swallowed hard and focused her flitting gaze on the image.

"I told you already," she said shakily. "I-I-I haven't seen him. Not since the general broadcast his arrest warrant a few months ago."

"Look again!" the sergent shouted, causing the woman to whimper and cast her gaze back down at the screen. "Take your time. This is extremely important to the general. And he will be *very* pleased if you give him the information he wants."

"I . . . ," the woman began, her fearful eyes watering.

"Yes?" the sergent prompted.

"I . . . *might* have seen him."

"Where?" he demanded.

The woman's throat bulged as she swallowed. "In the Marsh. A few days ago. He was buying vegetables. Potatoes and leeks. Maybe for a stew?"

Cerise tapped on her control panel and paused the footage. As she zoomed in on the stall owner's frozen face, Cerise could see the flicker of her own embedded circuitry reflected in the screen of her monitor, flashing in rhythm with her neuroprocessors. Her cybernetic eye diligently captured images of the woman's lips, cheekbones, forehead, and the skin around her eyes, until Cerise could decrypt the true meaning behind the stall owner's response.

Lie.

Cerise marked the footage as a dead end and clicked to the next interview in her queue.

This was the weakness of humans, Cerise had quickly discovered after her operation three months ago. They gave away their secrets without knowing it. Their true thoughts and feelings and struggles were displayed right across their faces. If you had the right software, it was easy to decrypt their real emotions. And Cerise had the right software. She'd programmed it herself, using a modification to her internal facial recognition scanners.

Now Cerise could decrypt it all.

Well, 99.999 percent of it all. She was still working on perfecting the code.

But it was this ability, to analyze humans so efficiently, that had earned her a permanent job in the Ministère's Bureau of Défense, her own cubicle in the front row of the primary operations room, and the general's very special assignment. His *top*-priority assignment.

"Have you seen this man?" The next footage in her queue had started to play, and Cerise watched the same sergent present the same image to a group of workers loitering around the entrance of a hothouse. "His name is Marcellus Bonnefaçon and he is wanted for treason."

"Is there a reward?" asked one of the men. "Because then, yeah, I've seen him."

Lie.

Cerise fast-forwarded to the next response.

"Sorry. I don't know where he is," the worker mumbled.

Truth.

As the footage played on, Cerise's hands flew deftly across her control panels, pausing on each face long enough for her left eye to capture the image and decrypt the response. It was the nanosecond after a lie was told when it was the easiest to detect. And thanks to her cyborg surgery, Cerise Chevalier now saw the world in nanoseconds. She saw the world in nano-everything. Molecules and bytes of data. Milli-centimètres and microscopic pixels. She'd never realized the universe could be so detailed and so beautiful.

It was like she'd been living her entire life with a blindfold on, only seeing the world in slivers and stolen shafts of light. But now she saw *everything*.

And she had the Ministère to thank for that.

They had saved her. Saved her from a pitiful, frivolous existence. Saved her from herself.

"Download complete," said the voice in her audio interface, and Cerise swiveled seamlessly back to her tertiary monitor. She activated the first batch of clips, and her screen morphed into a grid of hundreds of tiny moving images. She focused her glowing, cybernetic eye on the screen, letting it capture the data so her internal processors could sort through the myriad of faces. All it would take was one slipup on his part, and she would have him. Marcellus Bonnefaçon would be as good as caught.

Oftentimes, when she lay awake in her sleep pod in the cyborg dormitories, she would imagine the look on the general's face when Cerise announced that she'd accomplished his most critical objective. When she handed his traitorous grandson to him on a titan platter. She imagined the praise, the accolades, the commendation. Maybe even a promotion or the Medal of Accomplissement to wear around her neck, announcing to everyone that Cerise Chevalier, the former shame of the Chevalier family, the former traitor to the Regime, had single-handedly captured one of the Ministère's most-wanted fugitives.

And then she imagined the look on her father's face. Not just the pride that was sure to be sparkling in his eyes. But the last traces of disappointment finally being washed away.

The surveillance footage from the marketplace continued to flicker across her screen: thousands of Third Estaters going about their day, buying, selling, conversing with friends, all completely oblivious to the cams that were installed in every hologram module across the planet.

It was one of General Bonnefaçon's more brilliant tactics. Now that the planet was stable again, thanks to him, initiatives had to be put in place to keep it that way. But without the Skins, the Ministère had lost their ability to comprehensively monitor the Third Estate. And since the general had significantly reduced the number of droids patrolling the cities—in favor of a friendlier, more peaceful atmosphere—there simply wasn't enough footage available for the Ministère to do its job and protect the people. The hologram modules, which both projected and captured, was the next best thing to an implanted device, especially when the general announced that they would eventually be installed inside every Third Estate dwelling and workplace as well.

It also created the need for an entirely new division in the Bureau of Défense, of which Cerise was now a part and which spanned the entire fifth floor of the Ministère headquarters. Sparse cubicles in long, curving rows filled the room, all of them facing toward a set of large monitors up front and a vast glowing hologram that projected Laterre's new thirty-hour-a-day TéléCast feed. Cerise's cubicle was at the end of the first row, and if she pushed back from her desk and peered out of a nearby window, she could just see the Grand Palais and the gushing sparkle of a fountain in the distance.

"Halt," she called out, and the hundreds of moving images on her screen paused mid-playback. Her hands flew over the controls, isolating the footage that had snagged her attention.

It was a girl. A girl who, up until a nanosecond ago, had not been visible on any cams. It was as though she'd just fallen from the sky. And the moment she landed, her bulky black hood fell back, giving Cerise a momentary glimpse of her face.

It was a face that tickled at the edges of Cerise's mind.

Where had she seen that girl before?

Normally, Cerise's memory was faultless. Flawless. The database in her brain was nearly as vast as the Communiqué itself, and her cyborg implants had given her the gift of perfect recall. But, for some reason, this girl's painfully familiar features could not be recalled.

Why not?

The levels of cortisol in her body started to rise, and Cerise could feel her neuroprocessors firing up, fighting against her body's natural response to stress. An easy calm flowed through her and she relaxed back in her chair, observing the still-frozen footage with a detached curiosity.

She magnified the image of the girl's face and uploaded it to the Communiqué. If her own facial recognition software failed her, the Ministère's central database certainly would not.

"No results found," replied the voice in her audio interface, causing Cerise's head to tilt in fascination.

Not in the Communiqué? Not in her memory?

Who was this girl?

Keeping the frozen image up on one monitor, Cerise dragged the source footage to another and continued the playback. She tracked the girl in the black hood as she maneuvered deftly and stealthily through the marketplace. She was clearly on the hunt for something. Maybe even following someone. When the girl moved out of range of hologram module 63, Cerise quickly accessed the footage from module 64, matching the time stamp to the millisecond so she could pick up the girl's trail again.

It was not until she neared the center of the marketplace and Cerise paused the footage again that she was able to identify whom the girl was following. And this was a face Cerise certainly *did* recognize.

A face anyone in the Bureau would recognize.

Jolras Epernay. The brother of Maximilienne Epernay. If there was anyone higher on the general's most-wanted list than his own grandson, it was Maximilienne. The Ministère had lost all traces of the Red Scar the night of the Patriarche's murder. It was as if they'd simply vanished off the face of the planet.

Suddenly, the image of the Medal of Accomplissement hanging from Cerise's neck swelled and expanded in her mind. The Red Scar was the Regime's greatest enemy. Possibly even more dangerous than the Vangarde had been when they were still alive. If Cerise were to single-handedly locate the Red Scar *and* its leader, she would be a hero. No longer would anyone be able to see her as Gustave Chevalier's sparkle-headed daughter who had been naïvely hoodwinked and manipulated by a known traitor. No longer would anyone be able to see her as the foolish, stupid girl who had helped Marcellus Bonnefaçon break into the Grand Palais three months ago and attempt to assassinate the general.

Her slate would finally be wiped clean. Her reputation would finally be untarnished, and she would be redeemed.

"Ah, very good!" said a deep voice behind her. "Excellent find, Technicien."

Cerise calmly turned and peered up at the man of the hour. The celebrated hero who had saved Laterre from the brink of destruction and returned it to all of its former glory . . . and then some.

"Good afternoon, General." She nodded her head in salute and followed the general's gaze back to her monitors, assuming the "find" he was referring to was Jolras Epernay. But his eyes were incontrovertibly directed at the frozen image of the girl in the black hood. Flickers of recognition danced once again on the periphery of Cerise's mind. "Do you know her?"

"Yes. And so do you."

"I do?"

"Her name is Chatine Renard." The general cocked one of his dark, immaculately groomed eyebrows, as though he expected this might trigger something for Cerise.

"Chatine Renard," she repeated, turning back to the screen and waiting for the name to spark a connection in her neuropathways, but once again, it just gave her a frustrating sense of impenetrability. "I have the perception that I have seen this girl before. But for some reason I cannot access her in my memory."

The general's brow fell, and when he spoke again, Cerise could hear disappointment in his voice. "Perhaps because Chatine Renard reminds you too much of your own betrayal."

Heat flooded through Cerise's face, causing her circuitry to spark.

"It appears," the general continued after clearing his throat, "we have found yet another memory that has fallen prey to the unfortunate side effect of your surgery."

Cerise's head fell into a rueful nod. "It appears so, sir."

She knew she had been an integral part of Marcellus Bonnefaçon's treasonous plan to assassinate the general, but only because she had been told so. Not because she remembered any of it. In fact, she had so few memories of her life before the surgery. Sometimes she would experience fleeting glimpses of strange images—like a voyageur rocketing through space, a planet with radiant blue skies, and two men with bloodied faces, locked behind a wall of clear plastique. But these images never made any sense to her.

Her father had determined that it was a known but rare side effect of her cyborg procedure. Her newly implanted neuroprocessors had deemed certain human memories to be inefficient and disruptive in her role of serving the Regime—namely, any memories that marked her as a traitor of that very Regime—and these memories had been relegated to less accessible parts of her brain. No matter how hard Cerise tried to conjure them up, they simply wouldn't come to her. Not when the general had interrogated her for days on end about the details of Marcellus's plan, not when she lay awake at night and commanded her brain to remember. And because human memories were not downloadable and viewable like cyborg memories were, Cerise found herself held hostage by her own human weaknesses.

"Chatine Renard is an excellent lead on my grandson," the general said, pulling Cerise's attention back to the screen, where he was tapping a finger

on the face of the girl frozen there. "She has always had a special relationship with Marcellus. And, like you, she was an integral part of the mission
to infiltrate the Grand Palais and assassinate me."

Cerise wanted to look away. She wanted to hide her shame and disgrace
behind one of these monitors, but her programming would not allow it.

"Which means," the general concluded, "she might still be working
with him."

"Yes," Cerise replied evenly. "That makes sense."

"Keep an eye on her," the general said. "She might lead us straight to
Marcellus."

"Yes, General." Cerise felt the immediate increase of dopamine in her
bloodstream. "That is an excellent idea."

The general turned to leave and Cerise's gaze fell back to her monitors.
"Excuse me, General?" she called out. "May I ask you a question?"

The general nodded. "Of course."

"I have also recently located Jolras Epernay in surveillance sector
01.09.64. I am requesting your permission to add Monsieur Epernay to
my tracking queue with the objective of obtaining intelligence about the
Red Scar."

The general's brow furrowed as his unflinching stare traveled back to
Cerise's secondary monitor and lingered on the pale-eyed man currently
paused on the screen. For a moment, something unreadable flashed across
the general's face, and Cerise felt the sudden urge to capture the expression and run it through her neuroprocessors in an attempt to decrypt it.
But once again, her programming held her back. That programming was
stronger than any urge. It stemmed from the most profound part of her,
the most deeply wired neurons in her brain.

General Bonnefaçon is the provisional leader of the Regime.
He cannot be questioned.
He cannot be analyzed.
He cannot be doubted.

"Request denied," replied the general. "The Red Scar are a top priority,
to be sure, but we already have plenty of personnel assigned to tracking
them. I need you to be focusing all of your efforts on locating Marcellus.

I recently lost an important lead on his whereabouts. We can't afford to lose any more. Please log the footage you found of Monsieur Epernay and send it directly to my TéléCom. I'll make sure it's distributed to the right techniciens."

Cerise blinked as his response processed. She was certain she was perfectly capable of tracking two suspects at once without losing any bandwidth, but she was also certain the general knew best.

"Understood, sir. I will continue my efforts in locating Marcellus Bonnefaçon. I am confident he will be found quickly."

"Good," said the general, "I am confident too. My grandson is smart. But he's not a criminal mastermind by any stretch of the imagination. He's sure to slip up. And that's when we'll find him."

As the general walked away, Cerise could once again see the reflection of her own circuitry in her monitor. It was flashing rapidly now, her mind desperate to make another connection that felt just out of reach.

Criminal mastermind.

There was something exasperatingly familiar about that phrase. She longed to search through her hazy memories until she located the right one. But she also remembered what the general had told her moments ago. All of her efforts were to be focused on locating Marcellus. And if this was another human memory that had been marked as treasonous, then perhaps her neuroprocessors were right to block it. As it would only distract her from doing her job.

She turned back to her secondary monitor and directed the frozen footage to play again, following the black-cloaked figure of Chatine Renard as it snaked and skidded through the marketplace.

Marcellus Bonnefaçon was still out there.

And Cerise Chevalier would stop at nothing until he was found.

- CHAPTER 4 -
MARCELLUS

MARCELLUS BONNEFAÇON ENJOYED MEALS IN THE REFuge because of the silence.

"Grateful Silence," the sisters called it. Long stretches of time filled with nothing more than the quiet clank of spoons against bowls.

Marcellus did not, however, spend these moments thinking about gratefulness as he was meant to do—thanking the Sols for the food in his bowl and the solid roof of bedrock over his head. He spent them thinking about Alouette.

For the past three months, she had occupied all of his thoughts. All of his dreams. All of his nightmares. Every available molecule of space in his brain was dedicated to finding her. And now, any minute he might discover if his obsession had paid off.

He peered at the clock on the wall. It had been thirty-two hours since Sister Nicolette and Sister Noëlle had left on yet another mission to find her, and twenty-eight hours since their récepteurs had gone out of range. Marcellus sighed and glanced around the dining room's long table. There were far too many empty chairs for his liking. With Chatine and Roche in the Marsh on one mission and Nicolette and Noëlle on another, the Refuge felt off-balance. *He* felt off-balance.

Marcellus felt a soft nudge on his arm and looked up to see Principale Francine peering at him with clear gray eyes that were both sharp and compassionate at the same time. She knew how much the mission to find Alouette meant to him. How much it meant to all of them. But a subtle nod of her head toward his bowl of stew reminded him that there were still two components to this meal: the silence and the food, which Marcellus had yet to touch.

He glanced down at the stew sitting in his bowl and his portion of burnt bread on the table. None of it looked appealing. But it wasn't the food. He could be sitting back in the banquet hall of the Grand Palais, staring down titan platters towering with every gourmet dish from here to Samsara, and he would still have no appetite.

He was almost glad Chatine wasn't there to scold him again.

"You need your strength," she'd say to him now. *"You're no help to Alouette dead."*

He took a tentative bite of stew—which was now cold—and forced it down with a sip of water. It almost immediately came rushing back up. He swallowed hard and glanced at the clock again. There was still ten minutes left of the meal, but he didn't care. He couldn't just sit here waiting. He needed to do something. Research something. Read something. He felt his fingers itch to be back within the soft, worn pages of the Chronicles, searching, scouring, looking for any hint, any clue that might reveal where his grandfather was keeping her.

Marcellus pushed back his chair with a loud scrape that drew every pair of eyes in the room to him. He looked into the steady gaze of each of the sisters and felt his face flush with embarrassment.

"Sorry," he muttered as quietly as he could. "I just . . ." He peered back at his barely touched stew, wondering if he should sit back down and endure the wait. But then the smell of cooked vegetables and savory broth hit his nostrils and he knew the answer. "Can't."

He turned away from the table and ducked under the low-arched doorway before making his way toward the library. He needed to work. It was the only way to unravel this twisted knot in his chest.

As he turned right off the main corridor, he stopped and glared at the small metal hatch cut into the wall on the far end. His stomach did its usual flip. There wasn't a day that passed when he didn't lurch to a halt and stare at the glinting, circular doorway nestled in the uneven bedrock wall. The Refuge's back door.

It felt like ages since the sisters had closed the front entrance in the vestibule, the one hidden beneath an empty mechanical room in Fret 7. Marcellus and Chatine had knocked on that door three months ago, bloodied and bruised from the riot at the Ascension banquet. The sisters had let them in, welcomed them, given them a place to sleep, food to eat, tasks to keep their minds from idling, a cause to fight for.

Then, the general's renovations had begun. The Frets were cleaned up. Couchettes were given proper locks and unbroken windows. Empty, unused mechanical rooms were no longer empty. And the sisters had been forced to seal off the grate that led down to the Refuge's front door and to reopen the *other* entrance. The one Marcellus hadn't even known about until the heavy wooden bookshelf had been shoved aside, revealing a small, circular hatch cut into the bedrock wall.

"When the founding sisters first built the Refuge, they needed a way to transport the books that had been rescued from the First World," Principale Francine had explained to Marcellus and Chatine as she stood before the mysterious new door. "The books had been smuggled on the original freightships and hidden in couchettes, under floorboards, and inside secret rooms around the planet, until a more secure place could be found. For two years, workers dug through the bedrock, carving out a passageway large enough to transport thousands of rescued books but small enough to go unnoticed by the Regime."

Francine had swung the small metal hatch open then, and Marcellus had peered inside to see a piece of his planet's history he'd never known before. A dark and endless tunnel stretched out before him. A dark and endless tunnel stretched out before him, barely tall enough to stand in. The walls were rough and imperfect, as though someone had carved them with a dull exploit pick.

"Is it safe?" Marcellus had asked, eyeing the low ceiling and ancient foundation, which appeared moments away from collapsing.

"It's our only option," Francine replied with a grimace. "The main entrance is no longer operational. From here on out, this will be our only access to the above-ground world."

"Where does it end?" Chatine asked, and Marcellus could tell that she, too, was doubting the integrity of the passageway.

"Far enough away to keep us safe," was all Francine had said at the time, before pulling the hatch door shut with a *bang*.

Marcellus stared at that door now, willing it to open. Willing Sister Noëlle and Sister Nicolette to burst through it with Alouette following closely behind.

But the hatch stayed firmly and defiantly shut.

With a sigh of frustration, he continued down the hallway into the library. His desk in the far back corner sat undisturbed from how he'd left it before lunch. He took in the stacks of books—each lying open to the last page he'd read—the long pages of notes written in his unsteady hand, and the countless maps he'd searched and analyzed until he couldn't keep his eyes open. They were all still there, waiting for him. But he couldn't bring himself to sit down. He paced in front of one of the bookshelves, wringing his hands, and darting glances at the clock on the wall.

Thirty-three hours.

Where were the sisters? What was taking them so long? He wished Sister Marguerite could track their récepteurs, but the new network the Vangarde had been forced to build from scratch was frustratingly limited. The signal had to be passed between archaic First World antennae hidden across the planet, and there just weren't enough of them. The trackers could be out of range for hours at a time.

His mind raced with panicked thoughts of capture. Torture. How would he live with himself if they, too, had fallen into the ruthless clutches of his grandfather? And all because of *his* suggestion?

He stared again at the messy pile of maps on his desk, zeroing in on the long peninsula that jutted out from the southeast corner of Laterre's single landmass and the city that rested at its tip. Céleste. The water surrounding it had been his most recent hope. Visions of secret islands hidden in the mist had danced before his eyes. But it had only been a hunch. He hadn't had any evidence to back it up. Laterre's constant cloud coverage made even satellite imagery useless. Had it been foolish—selfish, even—to send the sisters on such a dangerous mission based on only a hunch?

The sound of a heavy metal hatch sealing shut stopped his thoughts dead in their tracks. Every follicle of hair on the back of his neck prickled as he listened to the footsteps hurrying down the hall, coming closer.

Two sets, Marcellus quickly identified.

Chatine and Roche?

Or . . .

Marcellus saw two figures in dark woolen coats sweep past the door of the library. He hurried to the hall and followed behind them as they disappeared into the Assemblée room, where the rest of the sisters were now gathered, having finished their meal.

As always, the room buzzed and chattered with noises from hidden speakers. The myriad of monitors on the walls—showing views from surveillance cams all over Laterre—cast a blue-white glow over the desks, cabinets, and twisting cables on the floor. Every surface and pinboard and shelf heaved with carefully organized notes, paper files, and neatly stacked books.

As Sister Noëlle and Sister Nicolette stood before their fellow Vangarde leaders, Marcellus tried not to analyze the drawn, defeated looks on their faces. He told himself to wait. Wait for words. Wait for the truth to spill from their lips. Only then would he allow himself to admit defeat. Only then would he allow his body to shrivel up on itself and vanish into nothing.

Principale Francine was the first to speak, an audible tremble in her usually stern and unwavering voice. "Did you find her?"

Marcellus looked to Noëlle, his favorite of the sisters. She was a petite older woman with a personality as bright and hopeful as Sol 1. But today, it was as though it had been eclipsed by the dark shadow of an asteroid headed straight toward Marcellus's heart.

Noëlle's eyes met Marcellus's, and for a moment her gaze lingered on him, as though she wanted to make sure he was the first to know. The first to understand that all of his hard work, all of that research, had been for nothing. That small sliver of hope that he'd uncovered, that had sent two of the sisters out on this dangerous mission, had turned out to be another false lead.

Noëlle gave the smallest, most imperceptible shake of her head, just moments before Nicolette announced, "We searched every centimètre off the coast of Céleste. There was so sign of an island. We found nothing."

- CHAPTER 5 -
ALOUETTE

OUTSIDE HER CELL, THE WET WIND HOWLED LIKE A frightened child. Alouette sat in the corner, her knees pulled up to her chest, her lips moving ever so slightly as whispered words slipped into the air.

"The System Divine offered hope. Hope to the inhabitants of a dying world."

Today, she was back to the beginning of Volume 1. She'd cycled through every volume of the sisters' Chronicles ten times now, trying her best to recite each chapter from memory. Some days the lines came to her crisp and clear and vibrant, as though she were sitting in the warm Refuge library, reading them straight from the page. Other days, trying to remember one word was like trying to pinpoint a single star through a cloud-filled sky.

"With its three beautiful Sols and twelve habitable planets, the miraculous system would become a new home. A new start."

She wasn't sure what it was about today that made the words flow so easily to her lips. Perhaps that's what happened when you were face-to-face with death. The clouds that once blocked all light simply vanished and everything became clear.

She lifted her hand and rapped softly on the heavy stone wall. Then, she waited, holding her breath, listening. But nothing happened.

Alouette closed her eyes and continued where she'd left off. "A place where twelve powerful families could begin again. The Paresse family was one of those families and Laterre was their new planet."

A shiver passed through her, causing her teeth to chatter. Ten times she'd been through this chapter and she still got caught up on the name. *The Paresse family.*

Her family.

Would that ever fully sink in? Would she ever be able to hear her real name and feel like it truly belonged to her?

Madeline Paresse.

The daughter of the Patriarche.

The heir to the Regime.

No. She wouldn't. At least not this time around. Maybe the next time. Except she knew there wouldn't be a next time. That had already been decided. Madeline Paresse and General Bonnefaçon could not exist in the same universe. At least, not the universe that the general envisioned for himself. That was why he'd killed the other heir, Marie Paresse. Why he'd plotted with the Queen of Albion to kill the Patriarche. Why he had ordered Alouette to be killed too.

And yet, almost a full day had passed since General Bonnefaçon had ordered her execution, and she was still here. Every moment that ticked by, she waited to feel the fear of death. The shadow of its clutches whispering down her spine. But she felt none of it. Three months in this place had prepared her for this moment. Three months waiting for this day had dulled all the precarious edges of her own mortality. The only thing that still felt sharp was the question of why?

Why hadn't Inspecteur Champlain completed her gruesome task? Why was Alouette still alive?

She shook the thought from her head and focused back on the Chronicles.

"High on the hill, the family built their Grand Palais under a vast climate-controlled dome. And in the flatlands below lived their chosen people. The magnificent ships . . ."

Pain pulsed through the back of her neck. Alouette winced and reached up to gingerly touch the raw, festering wound that had formed from months and months of contact with Inspecteur Champlain's "device." It was a constant reminder of what her life had become. Even in the breaks between the pain, there was pain.

She gritted her teeth and forced herself to keep going. "The magnificent ships that had once carried these workers across the galaxies became their homes. They were the lucky ones. At first."

Once she'd come to the end of the chapter, Alouette turned and tapped again on the wall of her cell, this time heavier, with more urgency.

But there was still no response.

She took a deep breath and pulled another chapter from the dark corners of her memory, whispering the words into the cold, damp air.

"Way out in the darkness, two Sols spin in the infinite silence. One red. One blue. But they are not alone. Together the twin stars loop around another Sol. A burning white Sol around which twelve beautiful planets orbit and twirl. It's the beautiful, endless dance of the System Divine."

As she spoke, Alouette started to rock back and forth, partly to keep the chill away, partly to soothe herself. She had become very good at that over the past three months, sitting alone in this cell with no one to cling to, no one to squeeze her hand and tell her it would be okay, no one to speak to except the voices in her wall. But even they had fallen silent tonight. As though they were keeping vigil, mourning her death before it even occurred.

She reached the end of the next chapter and rapped again. The silence that followed felt like it was invading her. Maybe they were gone too. Maybe that's what was keeping Inspecteur Champlain. . . .

Alouette let out a squeak of fear as tears instantly filled her eyes. She could accept her own death. But not theirs. She swatted at her cheeks and continued to rock and whisper, faster and faster.

"Volume One, Chapter Five. She stepped out. The sole of her boot kissing the soil for the very first time. Making a first muddied impression on a virgin land. A land of promise and new beginnings. A land that she and her fellow workers would toil and tend and terraform—"

TapTapTapTap.

TapTap.

Alouette stopped rocking. A gasp of relief broke free from her lips and she spun toward the wall, spreading her arms out wide as though to embrace the cool stone.

"Thank the Sols," she whispered.

She raised her knuckles to tap back the message she'd been longing to send since the moment the general had walked out of her cell and the clock on her life had begun to tick down. But just before touching the wall, her hand fell still.

What good would it do to tell them? What good would it do to worry them?

What could they do? What could they say? The plan to string the inspecteur along had stopped working. The general had run out of patience. She had proven to be no use to him alive. What could they possibly tell her to do next? Alouette knew it was silly to hope that the voices in her wall would have some miraculous solution. Some plan of escape that they'd been concealing until the final hour. There was no escape from this place. They were trapped on an island in the middle of the Secana Sea, kilomètres away from any civilization, and light-years away from any hope. Up until hours before she was taken here, Alouette hadn't even known there *were* any islands on Laterre. Every map she'd ever studied—every sketch in the Refuge library—showed only a single landmass, surrounded by water. Who would even think to suspect that something might be hidden out there in that water?

No one.

Which was why, when she finally heard the careful measured footsteps of the cyborg echoing down the hallway outside her door, there was only one thing to say.

TapTap.

Tap . . . Tap . . . TapTap.

Tap . . . Tap . . . Tap . . .

I love you.

Then, there was a low hiss as the biometric lock disengaged and the door to her cell slid open.

- CHAPTER 6 -
CHATINE

IT WAS OBVIOUS THAT JOLRAS EPERNAY WAS HEADING IN the direction of the Thibault Paresse statue. Chatine and Roche followed a safe distance behind, weaving and speeding through the Marsh like a pair of swooping combatteurs zeroing in on their target. They ducked under canopies, hopped over shopping sacs, scooted around kids playing on walkways, keeping those distinctive curls in their sights.

But Jolras was not an easy mark to follow. He'd clearly had experience evading trackers. He threaded through the maze of stalls and people, cutting corners and taking unexpected detours. He passed right through one of the towering hologram projections—now showing a view of a hothouse with a riot of colorful, plump fruits growing inside—and turned left around the statue. Roche caught Chatine's eye and signaled with two fingers, indicating they should split up and meet on the other side. Chatine nodded and veered to the right. As she rounded the base of the statue, she tried to ignore the feeling of the founding Patriarche's eyes glaring down at her, judging her, judging *all* of them for what had transpired in this very place three months ago. When his distant descendant had been murdered at the hands of the Red Scar. At the hands of that man's sister.

Chatine still didn't like the thought of Roche out here, in the open, vulnerable to probing eyes and Policier scans. But it was too late to go back now. They were committed. The target was in sight. And she had already tasted the sweetness of the chase. It tickled her tongue and roused all of her senses. She had deprived herself for too long, and the flavor of it was far too intoxicating. Weed wine didn't stand a chance against the power of Chatine Renard with a mark.

Emerging from the shadow of the statue, Chatine picked up the pace, darting through people perusing the well-stocked stalls. She spotted three sergents up ahead and instinctively ducked her head and veered to the left, her blood pressure spiking at the sight of them.

At least, she reminded herself, she didn't have to worry about running into Chacal. That was somewhat comforting. She'd heard the sergent-turned-inspecteur had been given a proper Second Estate funeral after the Ascension banquet, his coffin blasted into space on a one-way trajectory to Sol 2. But she often wondered what the médecins had done with the high-heeled shoe that had been impaled into his neck. Chances were, it was locked in a forensic lab somewhere at the Ministère headquarters, being analyzed for fingerprints.

Her fingerprints.

With the sergents safely behind her, she lifted her head, only to freeze a second later when she realized Jolras was no longer in sight. She spotted Roche directly to her left, standing next to a stall selling fresh pears, and watched as he stood on tiptoes, trying to see above the crowd. He had lost him too.

As Chatine continued to scrutinize the dizzying sea of faces that swam and blurred in her vision, she felt a strange mix of defeat and relief. She didn't like to lose. She didn't like to fail. Especially at something she used to be so good at. But maybe now she could convince Roche to give up and return to the—

A blinding light flashed in Chatine's eyes. She looked up just in time to see a massive transporteur crashing through the nearest hologram projection and barreling straight toward her and Roche. She shoved her brother out of the way and dove to the right, just before the enormous hovering vehicle lumbered past and continued to glide down the street.

For a moment, she couldn't move. She was mesmerized by the vehicle. Not the sight of it—transporteurs were often seen hovering through the Marsh—but by the people's reaction to it.

There was a growing buzz of excitement as bodies converged around the transporteur, like bees around a honeypot. They followed closely in its wake until it finally parked itself near a stall and a man in a green foreman's uniform hopped out of the front compartment. He was swarmed almost instantly, forcing him to fight through the fast-expanding crowd.

"Back up! Back up!" he shouted. "Form a line! Don't worry. There's enough meat for everyone."

Meat?

The general was giving the Third Estate meat now? No wonder there hadn't been a single riot in three months.

There was a crash as the canopy of a nearby stall was accidentally knocked to the ground by people jostling to form a line behind the transporteur. Chatine blinked out of her trance and glanced around for Roche, her pulse skyrocketing when she realized he was no longer there.

"Fric," she swore under her breath, and pushed her way toward the nearest exit. He'd go back to the Refuge, right? He wouldn't go following after a member of the Red Scar on his own, would he?

But a tightening in her gut told her that she couldn't be sure. He tended to follow his own code. His own rules.

Just like me.

She groaned and picked up the pace, searching for a beam or scaffolding she could climb to get a better view. Her gaze landed back on the Thibault Paresse statue and she quickly changed course. But just as she neared the base and readied herself to climb up one of the former Patriarche's legs, she felt a large hand clamp down on her shoulder.

There was something eerily familiar about that hand. That touch. The steady, even breath of the dark figure standing behind her.

But most familiar of all was the shiver that ricocheted down her spine as she slowly turned and looked into the glowing orange eye of Inspecteur Limier.

CHAPTER 7

MARCELLUS

"IF NO ONE ELSE IS GOING TO SAY IT, THEN I WILL. IT'S time to call off the search."

Everyone in the Assemblée room turned to Sister Léonie, some with expressions of shock, others with somber shadows of resignation.

Marcellus, who had been up until this moment sitting at one of the workstations, trying to ease his still-pounding heart, leapt to his feet. "What? No! Are you insane?"

"Actually," Léonie replied calmly, "I think I'm the only sane one in this room. Or at least the only one willing to accept the reality of the situation. That this might be a lost cause."

"Breathe," whispered a warm voice behind Marcellus. He didn't have to look back to know it was Sister Noëlle. He knew all the sisters by the sound of their voices, the swish of their tunics as they walked, even their energy as they entered a room. They were as different and as unique as the planets themselves. "In through the nose, out through the mouth."

Marcellus tried to follow her instructions. They usually worked. At least for a few minutes. But not now. Not with the horrific words coming out of Léonie's mouth.

"It's not a lost cause," Marcellus vowed. "She's still out there. And we can find her. I'll go back to the library. I'll look at the original settler maps again. There's got to be something that I missed."

"We can't keep spending time and resources looking for her," Léonie said. "We have to remember what our primary objective is here."

"Exactly!" Marcellus shouted. "I thought *she* was the primary objective. She's the Lark. The one who can take down my grandfather and overthrow the Regime."

"The primary objective is to rally the *people*," corrected Léonie. "To demand change peacefully."

"But you can't just give up on her!"

"We can't keep risking our lives and our operatives for her either," Sister Léonie said, casting a glance at Nicolette and Noëlle.

"She's right," agreed Sister Clare in a voice so small, it was as though she was frightened of hearing her own words. "The Vangarde cells have been waiting for our next move. They've been doing everything we've asked them to do: recruiting in secret, building up their numbers, setting up surveillance, helping us expand the new communication network. They're waiting for a revolution to start and we're just sitting here."

Dread swirled dangerously in Marcellus's stomach as his gaze pivoted between the sisters. They couldn't give *up* on her, could they? He reached into his pocket and ran his fingers over the cool, metallic surface of Alouette's devotion beads. She *had* to come back. They *had* to find her. He'd kept these beads safe for her all of this time. When Sister Laurel had come back from Ledôme the night of the Ascension banquet and revealed she'd found the beads on the ground outside the Paresse Tower, Marcellus had told himself it was a sign. Alouette had dropped them for a reason. She was trying to tell them something.

Don't give up on me. I'm coming back.

"But what about our plan?" asked Sister Laurel. "Alouette was supposed to be the symbol of unity. Paresse and Vangarde together. Someone the people would follow."

"The people will follow Citizen Rousseau," came Léonie's swift reply. "That was *always* the plan. That was why we risked our lives three months ago on Bastille. Yes, Alouette would have been an asset, she would have helped bring people to our cause, but we don't have a choice. We have to move forward without her."

Marcellus felt a warm hand on his arm and once again knew that it was Sister Noëlle. Of all the sisters, she was the one who understood him the most. Understood his frustrations and the way his anger would twist inside of him until he no longer felt like himself. She was the one who always seemed to be able to steady him when he wavered. But Marcellus didn't want to be steadied. He didn't want to be calmed. He just wanted to find Alouette.

Léonie must have felt the animosity radiating off him because she turned to cast him an apologetic look before continuing. "This is our moment. Laterre has no leader. The planet is in flux. There's a power vacuum. This is the best time to dismantle the Regime and convince the people that there's another way. That luck of birth should not determine who lives in luxury and who starves in the street, toiling away in the exploits and fermes and fabriques for goods they will never enjoy. We still have hope of bringing about a peaceful revolution. Just as we always imagined. But we have to act now before the System Alliance appoints some Paresse cousin, or worse, *General Bonnefaçon*, to take control of the Regime. Let's announce Citizen Rousseau's return and let her lead the people. She did it once before. She can do it again."

For the first time since he'd entered the Assemblée room, Marcellus allowed his gaze to drift to the back corner. To the place where a woman sat, quietly listening and observing, just as she always did. She was dressed like all the other sisters in a gray tunic, and her hair snaked down from the nape of her neck to below her ribs in a single, shimmering silver braid. On her long and gracefully angular face, a myriad of lines crisscrossed and fanned out like a tapestry of stories and secrets. Her mouth held something that was almost a smile. But not quite.

And then there were her eyes, which shone with an even more silvery glimmer than her hair.

Two ocean pools, infinite and deep and reflecting.

"It's too risky," Sister Laurel affirmed, pulling Marcellus's attention back to the discussion. "It's been more than seventeen years since anyone's even heard from Rousseau. There's a chance the people won't follow her again."

Marcellus couldn't help but agree. Even though Citizen Rousseau's physical appearance had vastly improved in the past three months, she was still just as silent as she'd been lying on that bed in the infirmerie, breaths away from death. She hardly ever spoke. How was she planning to rally the people to the Vangarde's cause? With nods and mysterious smiles?

Now the face of the woman in the back of the room bore the same composed yet attentive expression it always did. Like she was content to simply listen to what the world around her had to say but felt no compulsion to reply. In her lap, she gripped and tweaked the one thing Marcellus never saw her without—a peculiar cylinder of cardboard with a rotating top that her slender fingers constantly turned around and around.

"Laurel has a valid point," said Sister Marguerite. "Especially after all the lies the general has spread about Rousseau. About *us*. Half of this planet still thinks we're terrorists after the Rebellion of 488. We need Alouette. She's the Paresse heir, for Sol's sake. If she comes forward as a member of the Vangarde and stands beside Citizen Rousseau as an ally—"

"We don't even know if she's still alive!"

Everyone turned toward Sister Léonie, whose outburst had shocked them all into silence. She blew out a breath and pushed back a strand of her ash-brown hair. "I'm sorry," she said, composing herself. "I know this is not what we all want to hear or believe. But we *have* to consider the fact that she might already be dead. That every moment we spend looking for her, instead of acting, is time wasted."

The coldness of her words seemed to spread through the Assemblée room like a plague. Marcellus could feel it tickling his skin and the back of his neck, until he couldn't stop shivering.

As much as he knew it was a possibility, he couldn't believe it. *Wouldn't* believe it. He reached into his pocket and felt for Alouette's devotion beads again.

Don't give up on me. I'm coming back.

"She's alive." Marcellus barely recognized his own voice as it broke through the silence. He may not have been an official member of this Refuge. He may not have had the experience of a long-term Vangarde operative or the sisters' flare for political strategizing. But this was a question he could speak to with authority. Because this was a question that he knew the answer to, not in his mind, but in the very core of his being. "She's out there. She's alive. I know it. I *feel* it."

He didn't miss the subtle look of impatience that passed over Léonie's face, nor the pity in her voice when she replied, "Marcellus, I know you're hurting. I know you *want* to believe that—we all do—but we must move beyond our hopes now and focus on the facts—"

"My grandfather needs her alive," Marcellus fired back. "That's a fact. I know him. I know how he thinks. You might all be experts on the minds of the people and the history of this planet, but I'm an expert on General Bonnefaçon. He hoards things he believes might be useful. It's why Jacqui and Denise disappeared from Ministère custody all those months ago. He knows I'm still alive and that I know the truth about him. About what he's done. About his special relationship with Queen Matilda, the weapon they built together, and his promise to help her win back Usonia. And he also knows that Alouette and I infiltrated that Ascension banquet together to try to stop him. Which means he will try to use Alouette to find me. He will extract every last gramme of information out of her. As long as I'm still harboring his secrets, she is more valuable to him alive than dead."

The room slipped back into another heavy silence. This one was as suffocating and noxious as the riot gas that helped put an end to the Vangarde's last rebellion. Marcellus glanced again at Citizen Rousseau, surprised to find her looking straight back at him with an almost intrigued expression. He quickly looked away. Just as he always did. Not because she wasn't radiant in her serenity and magnetic in her poise, but because she *was*. Almost too much. Sometimes it felt like looking at her was like staring directly at a Sol. For one blissful second, it was beautiful and glowing and magnificent. And then, it was just blinding.

But there was another reason Marcellus kept his distance from the woman who had led the most famous rebellion in Laterre's history.

Shame.

He had spent seventeen years condemning her name, believing his grandfather's lies about her, swearing his oath to a Regime who would have kept her locked up until her last days.

He wasn't worthy of that glow.

It was Principale Francine who finally spoke next. "It is time to take a vote."

Marcellus nodded and dutifully retreated to the corner of the room. He crossed his arms, like he was trying to stop his heart from beating right out of his chest. It was out of his hands now. He had said all he could say. Now it was time for the sisters to decide.

"All in favor of calling off the search and moving forward?" Francine asked.

Marcellus held his breath and forced his eyes to stay open as he watched the hands of Léonie, Nicolette, and Clare rise into the air. He was devastated but not surprised. It was the fourth vote, however, that gutted him the most. Principale Francine offered him a sad smile as she slowly lifted her hand, and Marcellus couldn't help but think that she was signing Alouette's death warrant.

"All in favor of waiting?"

Marcellus's gaze darted anxiously around the room, landing on Noëlle, Laurel, Marguerite, and eventually Muriel.

It was a tie. Four to four.

All eyes fell on the deciding vote.

The woman at the back of the room stood up, and this time, Marcellus forced himself to look at her. To keep looking at her until she said yes. Until she proved she was the faultless leader everyone claimed her to be.

Citizen Rousseau twisted the top of the cylinder in her hands as she looked at all of her fellow sisters in turn, before her eyes landed back on Marcellus. For the life of him, he could extract no answers from those eyes. She was the one sister in the Refuge whom he could never read. Could never predict. And who always managed to surprise him.

She took a step forward, preparing to speak, but she was never given the chance.

"Wait a minute," said Sister Marguerite, who had been monitoring the Vangarde's myriad of surveillance cams. "I think you should all see this." She reached for her console to turn up the volume and pointed to the monitor that was currently showing a view from high above a crowded marketplace. "There's a problem in the Marsh."

CHAPTER 8

CHATINE

"GOOD MORNING, INSPECTEUR."

Chatine fought to keep her voice light, her smile innocent, and the screams in her head from echoing out of her ears. Her heart was racing a thousand kilomètres a minute as the inspecteur's blazing orange eye bore down on her, scanning her face.

"Is there a problem?" she asked sweetly, searching the cyborg's expression for a hint of recognition.

Limier's circuitry blinked once and then fell quiet. "For some reason I'm having trouble locating your profile in the Communiqué."

Chatine shuddered at the sound of that voice again. All fritzers had a blank, monotone inflection, but there was something about Limier's that had unnerved Chatine more than others. She hid her reaction behind a shrug. "I have no idea why. Could be an error, perhaps?"

It wasn't an error. The sisters had made sure of that. But what about his memory? Marcellus had told her the unsettling tale of Inspecteur Limier. How his circuitries had been scorched after Alouette shot him in the face with a rayonette. How his cyborg memory files had been damaged, possibly beyond repair. How no one at the Ministère was even sure he'd ever be back on the streets again.

And yet, here he was.

But how much of his memories had been restored?

"Perhaps," Limier said after a long pause. "Where are you going in such a hurry?"

She refreshed her smile and gave a nonchalant wave of her hand. "The meat transporteur, of course. Can you believe the general is giving us meat now? Isn't it amazing? I've never tasted anything so delicious."

Chatine nearly gagged at the sound of her own voice. It was high and pitchy, reminding her way too much of her sister. There was no doubt in her mind that if Azelle were still alive today, she'd be first in line behind that transporteur. First in line to smile up at one of those holograms and sing the general's praises.

Azelle had always been far too gullible for her own good.

But that didn't stop Chatine from missing her. Every Sol-damn day.

"Yes," Limier said vacantly. "It is quite generous of the general." He continued to study Chatine with that sinister cyborg eye. "But the line for the meat is the other way."

Chatine swallowed. For a moment, she considered running. She'd escaped Limier before. Many times. And without his army of bashers to give chase, she liked her odds. But she couldn't risk drawing unnecessary attention to herself. Or Roche. Wherever the fric he was.

"What is your name?" Limier asked, and Chatine felt her entire body tingle with relief. He didn't recognize her.

She stood up taller and racked her brain for an alias. "Eponine. Nice to meet you, Inspecteur."

Limier glared at her. "You haven't been stealing, have you?"

"Don't be silly, Inspecteur," she replied with a lighthearted chuckle. "I know better than to steal from the hand that feeds me."

The moment the words were out of her mouth, she regretted them. They were too familiar. She'd used them before, she knew it. And the inspecteur knew it too. Something shifted on Limier's face. His circuitry started to flicker erratically as his mind processed, as his cybernetic implants fought to rebuild connections that had been severed long ago.

"Théo Renard," Limier whispered, and the Marsh fell deathly quiet. Despite the chaos and movement still bustling around them, it was as though they'd been transported into their own little universe. Their own little planet.

A planet of the past.

Back before there was talk of revolutions and dead Patriarchs and whispers of whom the System Alliance would appoint to take over the Regime. Back when Chatine was nothing more than a self-serving Fret rat—a thief—and Limier was nothing more than a dogged inspecteur, on the hunt for a Renard.

There was a moment, as Chatine looked into Inspecteur Limier's unwavering eyes, when they both acknowledged the truth. But then that moment ended and Chatine did the only thing she could think to do next.

She giggled. Loud and obnoxious. "What did you call me? Silly inspecteur. You must have me mistaken for someone else. I do get that a lot. I have one of those faces, I guess. I wouldn't beat yourself up about it, though. It's an honest mistake. Maybe you should get that memory of yours checked, huh, Inspecteur? Go in for a little checkup at the cyborg labs. Make sure everything is functioning properly."

She told herself to stop babbling like an idiot, but there seemed to be a disconnect between her brain and her mouth. Limier continued to watch her, with an almost amused expression.

"Well then," he said. "Since you're not showing up in the Communiqué, why don't I bring you into the Precinct, so we can figure out *exactly* who you are?"

Chatine felt all the blood in her body drain to her toes. Now was the time to run. Before he could ship her back to Bastille. But just as she was scanning her surroundings for something she could use to create a diversion, a scream shot through the marketplace. It was horrific and blood-curdling, like someone coming face-to-face with death.

The inspecteur's eyes snapped up, tracking the source of the sound instantly. When Chatine followed his gaze, she found herself staring at the newly arrived meat transporteur.

That's when the scream grew louder and somehow more textured, until Chatine realized it wasn't just one scream but many. It was spreading. Like a contagious disease. Jumping from host to host until the entire marketplace was infected.

Inspecteur Limier took off toward the transporteur. Chatine knew she should use this opportunity to flee. But she still didn't know where Roche was. What if he was somewhere near that transporteur? What if he was part of whatever was happening?

She shoved her way through the crowd, following in the footsteps of Inspecteur Limier, until she finally penetrated the tight circle that had formed around the vehicle.

The loading ramp of the transporteur hung open like a giant mouth. At first, Chatine saw nothing but the murky inside of the yawning cargo hold and the shadows of a few sheep carcasses hanging on their meat hooks. But then she spotted the blood, trickling down the vehicle's ramp onto the ground.

It looked fresh.

Red and glimmering and warm.

"Oh my Sols!" someone shrieked.

The crowd around her was growing. More people screamed and cried out as Chatine was shunted farther forward. She pushed and elbowed back, trying to keep her footing. And this time, when she looked up into the yawning mouth of the transporteur, she saw it all clearly.

Two pairs of polished leather boots.

A pair of dainty velvet shoes.

Tailored suits and crisp white shirts.

A silk gown stitched with ribbons and pearls.

A necklace studded with jewels that twinkled in the half-light.

And coating all of this finery . . .

Blood.

Rivers and oceans of blood, streaking the fabric, blotching the shoes, staining the sky-white shirts, and trickling amid the sparkling gemstones.

Chatine's stomach clenched as her mind desperately tried to fathom the awful sight in front of her. These were not carcasses of sheep, coming to be carved up and distributed in the marketplace.

On these hooks hung three bodies.

Three *people.*

"Is that them?" someone called out from behind her.

"It's them!" another person said through frantic sobs. "It's the Favorites."

While the crowd continued to shove and shout and gasp at the horrifying scene, Chatine forced herself to look at the faces. The terrible distorted faces, drained of blood, and hanging at odd angles, thanks to the meat hook jammed into each neck. The makeup of the woman had smeared from her eyes and mixed with the streaks of blood on her cheeks. Her once-intricate curls now hung like limp, dead snakes around her shoulders. And on the next hook, the man's neatly trimmed snow-white beard was soaked with blood, while his lips hung open as if he were still crying out a final plea to be spared.

But worst of all were the gashes on each face. Two long, intersecting wounds that traveled diagonally from jawbone to forehead, forming a gruesome and bluntly carved *X*.

Crossed off the list, Chatine thought with a horrifying lurch of her stomach. These were the three First Estaters rumored to be the System Alliance's top candidates to lead the Regime. And it was as if someone had erased them from existence. Exed them out of contention.

"But why?" cried a woman next to Chatine. "Why would anyone do this?"

Third Estaters pushed and jostled in tighter around the transporteur, as if magnetized against their will by the bloody horror in front of them. Constricted among the crowd, Chatine felt bile rise up in her throat. She'd witnessed a lot of horrible things in this marketplace: the death of an innocent girl, the execution of a revered leader, countless riots and fights.

But this was something else.

Unable to stomach the sight any longer, she angled her face away, trying to find anywhere to look but into those dead, glassy eyes. And that's when she caught sight of the open window. Five floors above her head, in the center of Fret 2, a man stood gazing out at the spectacle below. It wasn't abnormal for Third Estaters to peer out from their couchettes at the bustling marketplace. But the man standing in the window, pointing what looked to be a TéléCom down at the commotion, wasn't a normal Third Estater.

He was the answer to the question that had just been asked by the woman standing next to Chatine. The question everyone in this Marsh was now asking themselves.

Why would anyone do this?

As Chatine stared up at the shadowy form in the window, she felt her teeth clench with rage. Roche had been right. Jolras Epernay wasn't here to buy junk from Monsieur Ferraille's stall.

CHAPTER 9

ALOUETTE

ALOUETTE PROMISED HERSELF SHE WOULDN'T CRY. SHE wouldn't beg. She wouldn't scream. She might be on death row for being a Paresse, but she would die like a Vangarde. Like a sister.

Inspecteur Champlain slipped inside her cell and waved her rayonette, gesturing for Alouette to stand. There was no use fighting. She knew the voices in her wall would have told her that. Not that she had the strength to fight anyway. After three months of being cooped up inside this tiny cell with barely enough food to survive and muscles bruised and atrophied from the torture, her Tranquil Forme was useless to her now. She could barely raise her hands above her head, let alone perform an *Orbit of the Divine* worthy of taking down an armed cyborg.

Once steady on her feet, Alouette met the cool brown gaze of the inspecteur's single human eye and waited for her next instructions.

How will she do it? Alouette wondered as beads of sweat began to drip down the back of her neck. *Torture? Suffocation? A lethal paralyzeur pulse to the head?*

She'd read a book once about an entire First World family who had been locked in a room and shot to death one by one because of the blood in their veins.

Just like her.

She wasn't being murdered because she was a rebel. She was being murdered for her name. A name she learned about only a few months ago.

She was being executed because she was a Paresse.

With a flick of her rayonette, the inspecteur motioned for Alouette to sit in the chair in the center of the room, where she secured the clamps around Alouette's ankles and wrists.

Alouette watched with calm yet curious eyes as the cyborg turned around and pulled something from the small sac she had brought with her. It wasn't until Alouette saw the flash of the needle in the cell's dim light that she finally understood.

Lethal injection.

Alouette kept a close watch on the needle as the cyborg approached. She'd seen one just like it months ago at a blood bordel in Montfer. Just moments before it was plunged into her neck and her head filled with clouds. She'd been wanted for her blood then, too.

She felt a sharp pinch as the needle sank into a vein in her arm, delivering the toxin that she hoped would work fast and painlessly.

Little Marie Paresse's death had been messy. Gruesome. Asphyxiation from a poisoned peach. The poor innocent girl had suffocated to death. Alouette prayed that she would at least fall asleep first.

She closed her eyes and conjured up the faces of everyone she cared for and who had cared for her in return: Hugo Taureau, Marcellus, Cerise, Gabriel. Even Chatine Renard, whom she'd lived with as a child and who had saved their lives in the Terrain Perdu. She pictured the faces of the sisters who had perished on Bastille. Even in death, they were her lifelines, her symbols of strength and wisdom and hope. One by one, they paraded through her mind. Francine, Muriel, Léonie, Noëlle, Marguerite, Laurel, Nicolette, and Clare. And of course, she pictured her beloved Jacqui and Denise.

Then, she thought of the voices in her wall. The ones that had kept her sane and safe all of these long months. They would be listening right now, wondering what was happening.

And *that* was the real reason Alouette would not scream.

She would not put them through that. She would not allow that to be the last thing they heard from her. She would grant them the gift of knowing that she had died peacefully. Honorably. With the strength of the sisterhood in her heart.

She felt another pinch in her arm and sucked in a breath. But when she opened her eyes, a moment later, she saw the cyborg was no longer standing next to her. She was back across the room, rifling through her sac.

Alouette's gaze fell to her arm, where a minuscule puncture wound was visible just behind her elbow. She stared, confounded, at the small pinprick of blood bubbling on the surface.

Was it over? Was the poison already working its way through her system?

She heard a sharp intake of breath, and her attention snapped back to the inspecteur, who was now staring at the screen of her TéléCom. It was clutched in one hand while the other held tightly to a small crimson vial. Any tighter and Alouette feared the plastique might crack.

"It's true," said Inspecteur Champlain, and Alouette immediately recognized the shift in her tone. It wasn't the usual affectless drone that was common among cyborgs. There was a hint of emotion in it. As though, for just a split second, her cyborg tendencies were shoved aside by an even stronger inclination.

A *human* inclination.

She sounded stunned.

Alouette struggled to make sense of what was happening, but her mind felt dull and muted. From the injection? From lack of food and sleep? Or this festering wound on the back of her neck that she was sure was poisoning her slowly? The inspecteur pocketed the vial and stalked menacingly toward her, a fierce determination in her eyes the likes of which Alouette had never seen on a cyborg.

Alouette squirmed against her restraints. All of her former resolve and dignity vanished in an instant. She was now fully prepared to scream. But before a single sound could escape, the cyborg's hand clamped over her mouth as her chilling cybernetic eye bore down on Alouette.

"Shut up," she whispered urgently. And once again, her voice was so un-cyborg-like, it rendered Alouette temporarily silent.

The inspecteur removed her hand from Alouette's mouth and dropped it hastily to her restraints. Alouette heard a hiss, then a small click, and suddenly her wrists were free. Followed by her ankles.

Still too dumbfounded to move, Alouette gaped at the inspecteur, who stepped back, away from the chair, as though wanting to give Alouette room.

"I'm sorry," the cyborg said, averting her eyes to the ground. "I didn't know. If I had known, I never would have—" Her voice broke off, like there was an error in her verbal programming. "I'm sorry, Madame Matrone."

A shiver whispered its way down Alouette's spine.

"W-w-what did you call me?"

"I wasn't one hundred percent certain I could believe it," Champlain replied, still staring at the grimy floor. "What the general said. I needed proof." She nodded to the TéléCom still clutched in her hand. Alouette's gaze drifted toward the screen. She was fairly certain of what she would see, but she had to look anyway.

There they were again. The two entwined snakes, coiling around each other in a spinning waltz.

Her DNA.

The needle in her vein. The cyborg hadn't been injecting, she'd been withdrawing. She'd been testing.

Alouette's mind fluttered back to the general's words to her yesterday, just before he left her cell.

"It's better than following the daughter of a worthless blood whore, just because her father is the Patriarche."

He'd whispered those words for only her to hear, but clearly Inspecteur Champlain had heard too. In the general's frustration with Alouette, he must have forgotten that cyborgs have enhanced senses. Alouette had never known the general to make a mistake. But she supposed he was only human. And humans err.

The inspecteur walked to the door and placed her palm flush with the scanner. The lock disengaged with another hiss, and the door slid open.

But Alouette was still too stunned to leave. Her legs felt numb and useless. "You're . . . letting me go?"

"I am programmed to follow the laws of the Regime and the Order of the Sols," Champlain said stiffly, her usual cyborg cadence having now been fully restored. "And according to that Order, set forth by our founding Patriarche and maintained by the Ministère, as the direct and only descendant of Lyon Paresse, you are now the true and rightful leader of Laterre. If I were to keep you here, even under the general's orders, I would not only be willfully disobeying my programming but committing a crime punishable by death."

Alouette eyed the door, wondering if this was a trick. Was the inspecteur toying with her? Would she shoot her in the back of the head as she tried to leave?

But she knew cyborgs didn't think that way. They were rational beings. Programmed for efficiency, not cruelty.

She took a step, then another, keeping her vigilant gaze on the inspecteur the whole time. The woman didn't move. Her head was bent low, almost as though she were displaying deference.

Alouette shivered again. Even though she had used her DNA to access the Forteresse and shut down the Skins, there was a small part of her that still clung to the doubt. The sliver of belief that this had all been some kind of misunderstanding. Her biological father had been a simple fabrique worker, or a Palais guard, or one of the men who hauled in the fishing nets at the docks.

Not a Patriarche.

But that sliver of belief was shrinking with every step she took toward the exit. With every second that the cyborg didn't tackle her to the ground.

She reached the door and stepped outside. The hallway was low-ceilinged and sparse, with just a few naked lights glowing over the bare walls, and Alouette realized she had no idea how to get out of here. She turned back to the inspecteur, who was already at her side, gesturing for Alouette to follow her. "The general is on his way here now. He wants to ensure his orders were carried out. He'll be arriving through the front gates. I have a cruiseur waiting out back in the loading bay."

But Alouette didn't move. Her eyes fell to the locked PermaSteel door just to the left of her cell. She thought about the voices in her wall. She'd never expected to see their faces again. She had been convinced she'd die with the memory of only their soft, rhythmic taps against the stone. But now, hope surged through her. Incredible, impossible hope. It lifted her heart and filled her lungs.

"Wait!" she called out to the inspecteur, who was already moving briskly down the hall. "Aren't you going to let them go too?"

Champlain turned around and that glowing orange eye bored into Alouette once again. Alouette tried to focus on the other eye, the human one that seemed to crackle with life and something she couldn't quite pinpoint. Hesitation, maybe?

"Those prisoners are enemies of the state," the inspecteur replied robotically. "They have committed treason against the Regime. I am unable to release them."

In an instant, Alouette's hope deflated. She couldn't just leave them. They had been through this whole ordeal together. They were a part of her. They were her family. She stepped up to the heavy door and pressed a single palm against the cool surface. She wanted so badly to tap out a message in their secret code, begging them to give her advice, just as they'd done for the past three months.

Tell me what to do.

The inspecteur was suddenly beside her, urging her to move. "We must leave now. Before the general arrives and kills us both."

And that's when Alouette realized she already knew what to do. She didn't need the voices in that cell to tell her. Their wisdom was inside of her. Their strength was a part of her. And their power ran in her veins.

"Open this door," Alouette said with a sternness that surprised even herself.

The inspecteur's circuitry began to flicker softly.

"Now," Alouette added.

"But Madame Matrone," the inspecteur began. "These prisoners are—"

"These prisoners are now under my jurisdiction." The words came with a burst of vitality and purpose. The numbness that had coated Alouette's skin for three whole months was fading away, and she felt like she was finally waking up. "And as the sole heir to the Regime and rightful leader of Laterre, I order you to release them."

Now it looked like someone had plugged the cyborg directly into an active power cell. The circuitry in her face was alight with confusion and hesitation, her neuroprocessors working overtime to make sense of conflicting inputs and outputs.

"*Now*," Alouette repeated.

The circuits gave one final flash and then fell silent. Champlain stood up straighter, like a droid powering on. Her limbs moved with intent, her stride mechanical, as she approached the door and swiped her palm against the lock. With a hiss the door slid open and Alouette peered inside.

They were barely recognizable.

Just two brittle shapes tangled up in ragged clothes.

But it was them.

Her beloved sisters. And they were alive.

"Little Lark?" came a whisper. It was Denise. But the months of neglect and darkness and torture had turned her voice into ash.

Alouette burst into the cell and kneeled down before the two women. She wanted so badly to throw her arms around them, to squeeze them to her, but they were so frail, so fragile, she was afraid they would shatter to dust at a single touch.

"It's okay," she said hurriedly, brushing the tears from her eyes. "It's me. I'm here. You're safe now. We're going to get out of here. Can you stand?"

Denise nodded and, with Alouette's help, rose shakily to her feet. But her gaze immediately fell back to Jacqui, who had not moved. She was staring vacant-eyed at the wall to Alouette's cell, as though she were still waiting to hear another sequence of soft, rhythmic taps.

As though she barely noticed Alouette at all.

"Sister Jacqui," Alouette said urgently, shifting around until her face was directly in front of Jacqui's. Until the sister was forced to look at her. But still, Jacqui didn't see her. She looked straight *through* her, her eyes locked on that wall.

"What's the matter with her?" Alouette asked. "Is she okay?"

"She . . . ," Denise began hesitantly, as though she was searching her once-sharp-and-brilliant brain for the right words, the *accurate* words, but finding nothing. "No."

More tears sprang to Alouette's eyes as she looked back at Jacqui. The sister's cheeks had sunk inward, like two deep caves. Her lips hung open and were chapped, as if nothing had passed between them in weeks. Or months. And her hair, which had once been chaotic and lively, now sagged forlornly against her temples, shot through with streaks of gray that weren't there before.

For the past three months, Alouette had clung to the belief that the two of them were fine. They were alive. Never once in their long conversations, played out in Denise's secret code of taps and knocks, was it ever revealed that something was wrong.

Denise.

Alouette glanced up at the dark-haired woman. The intricate scars, where Denise's cyborg circuitry had once been, looked deeper, more shadowed and sorrowful somehow. And in her eyes, which had never been the most expressive of the sisters', Alouette could now see the grief that she'd been holding on to for so long. Bearing all by herself.

Of course. It was *Denise's* secret code. Alouette was the only other person she'd ever taught it to. Alouette had always assumed the messages were coming from both of them. The voices belonged to *two* sisters. But all this time, Denise was the only one who had been speaking to Alouette, answering all of her questions, sending her messages of love and strength and courage. And all this time, she'd been hiding the truth from her. Truth of what the general had done.

The general . . .

"We have to get her up." Alouette positioned herself behind Jacqui. "We don't have much time." Denise scurried over to help, and together, the two lifted the sister to her feet. Jacqui's body was nothing but skin and bones, yet somehow her limpness made her feel surprisingly heavy, and the moment they hoisted her to her feet, she began to tip forward, sagging like someone drunk on weed wine. Alouette dove to catch her and for an instant, in Jacqui's eyes, she swore she saw a flicker of recognition. Like a tiny milligramme of zyttrium flashing blue from beneath a layer of heavy Bastille rock.

It gave Alouette strength and resolve.

Her beloved sister was still in there. Somewhere.

She draped one of Jacqui's arms around her shoulders, and Denise did the same.

"Come on, let's go," Alouette said as they maneuvered awkwardly toward the door. "The general is on his way here and we have to—"

"Halt," said a clear, mechanical voice, and Alouette looked up to see Inspecteur Champlain standing in the doorway, her rayonette raised. She pointed it at Jacqui, then Denise, then back to Jacqui, as though she couldn't make up her mind who was the bigger threat.

"Inspecteur," Alouette said with a twinge of impatience. "I told you to let these prisoners go."

The cyborg's circuitry began to flicker erratically again, and her cheek twitched. "I . . . c-c-cannot . . . let . . . them . . . g-g-go." Her speech was stilted, snagging on every word.

"I *command* you to let them go!" Alouette shouted. The numbness was completely gone now, and all that was left in its place was desperation. She had to get them out of here.

A strange clicking sound emerged from the cyborg's mouth, as though her brain were playing tug-of-war with her tongue. Her finger snapped against the toggle on the rayonette, shifting the weapon into lethal mode and Alouette's heart into palpitations.

"I . . . c-c-cannot . . ." Champlain began to repeat the same juddering phrase, but this time, she never reached the end. Because something very strange was happening to her. Her circuitry was a dizzying display of flashing color and sparking light. Her entire body began to seize, the rayonette shaking in her grip, her finger twitching dangerously against the trigger.

Alouette didn't know what was happening. Or what to do. If they took another step, she was certain the cyborg would fire. Either on purpose or at the whim of these strange spasms that seemed to have overtaken her entire body.

Then, without a word, Denise carefully untangled herself from Jacqui, leaving the sister to sag heavily against Alouette's side, and began to approach the convulsing inspecteur.

"What are you doing?" Alouette asked, terrified. "Denise. Don't." She tried to lunge for the sister, but Jacqui's body was too heavy, and she nearly collapsed under its weight. "Stop!"

But Denise did not stop. She kept walking, slowly but steadily, toward Inspecteur Champlain. Alouette watched the cyborg tense and her grip on the rayonette tighten with every step that Denise took.

Alouette wanted to shut her eyes. After everything they'd been through, months of torture, she could not watch Denise die right in front of her, steps away from freedom. She eyed the door of the cell, fully expecting to hear the general's footsteps thundering down that hallway at any moment.

The cyborg's circuitry continued to flash and sputter, illuminating the walls of the dark cell with waves of dancing light.

"D-d-d-d-d-d-d . . ." Champlain tried to speak, but no words would form now. She was beyond speech. Beyond everything. This cyborg was melting down in front of them, and Alouette had no idea how to stop it. Or if it even could be stopped.

She'd never read anything in the Chronicles about malfunctioning cyborgs. But that was clearly what was happening here.

Inspecteur Champlain was *malfunctioning*.

Right before their very eyes.

And Denise was walking straight into the blast zone.

She stepped up to the inspecteur and stood on tiptoes to reach the woman's right ear. Then, with whispered words that Alouette had no hope of hearing above the stuttering and sparking and trembling, Denise spoke. Her lips moved rapidly but assuredly, as though she'd been practicing. As though she'd been waiting her entire life to say these words.

Everything fell still.

The room. The walls. Alouette's shallow, frightened breath. The whole island.

All of the circuitry on the cyborg's face stopped flashing. Her body stopped convulsing. And her tongue stopped clicking uselessly against the roof of her mouth.

Until all that was moving—seemingly for kilomètres—was the inspecteur's left eye. Where there was once a glowing orange cybernetic sphere, there was now—for just a split second—a flash of brown.

A flash of human.

It happened so fast, Alouette could almost convince herself she'd imagined it. But then, the cyborg blinked, as though waking up from a bad dream, and her hand holding the rayonette slowly lowered.

Her head clicked toward Denise, who was still standing by her right ear. The sister gave the inspecteur a subtle yet reassuring nod and then, to Alouette's utter disbelief, Inspecteur Champlain handed over the weapon.

Sister Denise carefully eased it out of the woman's grip. Alouette watched the whole exchange in fascination and shock. She knew the sisters were secretly members of a rebel group, but this was the first time she'd ever seen any of them holding a weapon. And the ease and expertise with which Sister Denise maneuvered the toggle back to paralyze left Alouette slightly breathless.

"What—what just happened?" Alouette asked once the rayonette was safely in Denise's control.

But Denise didn't respond. Instead, she aimed the weapon at the inspecteur's right leg and fired. The cyborg went down silently. As though she'd been expecting it. Then, Denise tucked the rayonette into her waistband, rushed back to Jacqui, and, in a decisive tone, said, "Let's go."

- CHAPTER 10 -
CHATINE

A LOW HISS EMITTED FROM THE OVEN, FOLLOWED BY A puff of smoke. Chatine spun away from the mountain of potatoes she was peeling and stared in panic.

That can't be good.

Ovens weren't supposed to hiss, were they?

Clutching two pot holders, she eased open the door and immediately broke into a fit of coughs as noxious smoke surrounded her like mist in the Tourbay. She grabbed a towel from the nearby counter and began to fan at the plumes, chasing them away until she could finally see what was left behind.

Fantastique.

Another burnt loaf of bread. What was she doing wrong? She'd followed the sisters' instructions exactly this time. At least, she *thought* she had. She squinted at the piece of paper that held Principale Francine's neat block handwriting. Chatine was still learning to read the Forgotten Word, and she often got letters mixed up.

"What is that smell?"

She turned to see Roche standing in the doorway of the Refuge kitchen, munching noisily on one of her raw, half-peeled potatoes. Even though it had been hours since she'd finally located him in the Marsh, the sight of him standing there, safely back in the Refuge, still made her chest squeeze with relief.

"Yikes, that looks bad." He nodded toward the bread.

"I know," she muttered, pulling the burnt loaf from the oven. She snatched up a knife and began to scrape carefully at the exterior. The burnt flakes fell to the countertop like black snow.

"What happened?" Roche jumped up on the countertop and began to swing his legs back and forth.

"What happened is," Chatine growled as she continued to scrape furiously at the blackened crust, "the sisters put me in charge of cooking for an entire Refuge when I *should* be doing something more worthwhile with my time."

"Cooking *is* worthwhile. We have to eat, right?"

"Yes, but why do I have to be the one to do it? I'm the least qualified person on the planet for this job." She let out a grunt as the knife slipped off the edge of the bread and nearly took off her fingers. "Argh. This is hopeless."

Roche took another noisy bite of his potato. "Sister Clare says everyone in the Refuge has a unique yet equally important purpose, and without everyone working together, the whole community would collapse."

Chatine rolled her eyes. She'd heard this speech *many* times before. But it wasn't the words themselves that annoyed her. It was the emotions they conjured up. Reminders of another community. Another group of people working together. Far, far away from here.

Far enough away to keep them safely from her mind.

Except when they managed to creep back in.

"That's why Sister Laurel tends to the propagation room and the infirmerie," Roche was still babbling. "Sister Marguerite maintains the communication networks, Muriel and Clare clean and mend all of our clothes—well, it's mostly Clare these days, with Muriel being ancient and all—Léonie and Nicolette keep the Refuge and the founders' tunnel from falling apart, Sister Noëlle helps Francine manage the Refuge, I wash the floors, and you . . ." His gaze fell onto the black brick on the counter. "Burn the bread."

"Exactly!" Chatine said, forcing her rebellious thoughts back to the task at hand. "We've been reduced to servants. Just like the Third Estate scum that we are."

"The sisters don't think like that," Roche said adamantly. "They want equality for everyone on Laterre. They're trying to get *rid* of the estates."

"And yet, notice the Oublie and the thief"—she pointed to Roche and herself respectively—"the two *Fret rats* are the only people never invited into that Assemblée room. We should be in that room right now with the sisters. The Red Scar killed *three* First Estaters today. And I'm in here cooking dinner."

"What would you rather be doing?" Roche challenged her.

Chatine glanced around the small Refuge kitchen. It was littered with dirty pots and pans, the mangled carcasses of badly chopped vegetables, and of course, now her half-scraped loaf of burnt bread. "I don't know. Anything but this. When we were tracking Jolras through the Marsh earlier, I felt something. I felt useful for the first time in months. It was the same thing I felt when Marcellus and I snuck into the Ascension banquet. Like I had special skills that no one else had and they were needed. I just thought when I joined the Vangarde, it would be more like that. I thought I'd be plotting a revolution. Not feeding it. If I wanted to work in a kitchen, I could have stayed at the inn in Montfer. But I guess the Vangarde don't have much other use for someone like me. I don't even know what they're doing in there!" She flung her arm in the direction of the Assemblée room.

"I know what they're doing."

Chatine turned to her brother. "No, you don't."

"Yes, I do. They're analyzing the intel I delivered."

Chatine dropped a lid on the pot with a snort and turned back to her potatoes. "What intel?"

Roche gave an innocent little shrug. "I don't know. Maybe just the récepteur I *might* have dropped into Jolras Epernay's pocket when we were tailing him."

"What?" Chatine screeched.

"I'm a pickpocket. It works the other way around, you know?"

"That récepteur is property of the Vangarde. It was given to you to keep us safe."

"And to keep tabs on us," he reminded Chatine. "I simply repurposed it. Now, thanks to my quick thinking and flawless reflexes, the Vangarde are tracking Jolras Epernay as we speak."

Chatine stared speechlessly at her little brother, unsure whether or not she should be furious or impressed. She decided on the former.

"You can't just make those decisions! You can't just change the assignment whenever you see fit and start dropping Vangarde tech into the pockets of terrorists."

"He's working with *her* again," Roche fired back. "That's why he was in the Marsh today. It has to have something to do with the attack on the Favorites. You know the Red Scar are behind that. And now we have a shot at figuring out not only where Max has been hiding for the past three months, but what she's been up to."

"I don't need a tracker to do that. Obviously, she's killing off anyone rumored to be appointed by the System Alliance. Just like she killed off the Patriarche."

The memory of those bloody red *X*s carved into the faces of the dead Favorites made Chatine visibly shudder. She'd been doing her best to banish those images from her mind, but they were too powerful. Too gruesome to be ignored.

"And how did they manage to accomplish that?" Roche asked. "How did they even get access to the Favorites? Or know where the Patriarche was going to be when they kidnapped him? Aren't you a little bit curious? That's why the Vangarde are tracking Jolras as we speak. Hoping he might lead us to some of these answers."

Chatine's stomach tightened. She did not like the idea of the Vangarde tracking anyone involved with the Red Scar. Those people were dangerous. They were terrorists. They had killed her sister, Azelle, in that TéléSkin bombing. And if Roche kept acting on his hunches and inventing his own spur-of-the-moment assignments, she worried he'd find himself with the same fate. And that was something her heart certainly could not take.

A loud *bang!* broke into her thoughts, startling them both. Chatine peered over at the stove, where the lid had exploded off the giant metal pot and now thick brown stew was bubbling over the rim and cascading down the side.

"Fric!" she swore, diving to turn down the heat.

"Wow, you really *are* bad at this."

Chatine shot her brother a look as she snatched up the spoon and began to stir again.

"Maybe I'll just take another one of these," Roche said, reaching across the counter to grab one of the half-peeled potatoes.

She shooed him away. "No! I'm saving those for tomorrow. Get out of here. You're distracting me."

"But I have to talk to you about something."

Chatine grabbed a stack of bowls from the shelf above the stove and searched for some free counter space. Finding none, she finally shoved the remnants of her chopped vegetables aside and spread out the bowls. "What?"

"When we were in the Marsh, did you notice something strange?"

Chatine began to ladle servings of stew into each of the bowls. "You mean, besides the fact that there were dead bodies hanging in a meat transporteur?"

"I mean before that. Did you notice anything strange about the *people*?"

"They were clean. Too clean for my taste."

"Exactly!" Roche exclaimed, as though he had led her right where he wanted her to go. "But where was everyone else? Where was *our* kind?"

"What do you mean *our* kind?" Stew distributed, Chatine turned back to the bread. There was no use trying to remove the rest of the burnt bits. She would just have to cut it up, and the sisters would have to deal with it. She reached for the knife again.

"I mean the crocs! The Fret rats! The Oublies!"

"Principale Francine told me the general rounded them all up and they were either given jobs or sent to Bastille." Chatine sawed mercilessly at the bread, but it was like trying to cut through stone. Eventually she gave up with a sigh, plopped the entire black loaf on a plate, and stabbed the knife into the center so that the handle stuck straight into the air.

"Nuh-uh." Roche shook his head. "No way. The Oublies would never go to a Ministère-assigned job."

"Then they're on Bastille," Chatine said impatiently, glancing at the clock on the wall. Dinner was supposed to be on the table five minutes ago, and Principale Francine did not like disrupting the Refuge's sacred schedule.

"But what if they're not?"

Chatine loaded the bowls of stew and the bread onto a tray and headed for the dining room. "Look, Roche, I would love to chat Fret-rat politics with you, but I have a group of rebels to feed." She carefully positioned the bowls around the table and the bread in the center before walking over to the meal bell on the wall and giving the rope two sharp tugs. As soon as she heard the door of the Assemblée room creak open, she grabbed one of the bowls from the table, slipped a spoon into her pocket, and disappeared into the hall, kicking out the hem of her tunic as she walked. Even with the extra clips and knots she'd fashioned over the thing, it was still too big, and she was always tripping over it.

"I'm just saying." Roche suddenly appearered behind her and picked up where he left off, "I have a bad feeling about it."

"This is General Bonnefaçon we're talking about. You *should* have a bad feeling about it."

"No, I mean, there's something else going on. Something bigger."

"Yes, a revolution." Careful not to spill the stew, Chatine slowly made her way toward the library with Roche close at her heels.

"I think we should go back to the Marsh and investigate."

Chatine rolled her eyes. *Here we go again.* "No."

"Here's my plan," Roche began, ignoring her. "We wait until the sisters have returned to the Assemblée room and sneak back into the tunnel. Then, when we get to the Marsh, we casually start asking stall owners if they've seen—"

"Roche," Chatine snapped, stopping in her tracks so suddenly, bits of hot stew sloshed over the rim of the bowl and onto her hands. "Stop. I'm not doing any of that and neither are you."

"But you just said you wanted to do something *more*."

Chatine relinquished a sigh and kept walking. "Yeah, well, chasing after wild conspiracy theories is not what I had in mind."

"It's not a conspiracy theory!" Roche argued. "I know the Oublies. I *was* one. There's something else going on here."

Chatine shook her head and nudged the library door open with her shoulder, leaving Roche alone in the hallway. The library was Chatine's least favorite room in the Refuge. Not because the light seemed dimmer here and the walls seemed more uneven. It was the books that bothered her. There were just so many of them. And it always felt like they were taunting her, mocking her slowness. While the sisters used big words and quoted First World scholars she'd never heard of, she was still trying to read one line of text without fumbling and giving up. Even Roche had managed to master the Forgotten Word in the short time he'd lived here. He was already writing full pages of text, scribbling daily in a little book called a "journal."

Chatine had had to look up the word in an even bigger book called a "dictionary." (Another word she'd had to look up.) When would it ever end? Back when she was a thief and the streets of Vallonay were her refuge, she thought she knew all the words. At least the ones she needed to survive. But now, living here, she realized she hadn't even scratched the surface.

And she'd never felt more stupid in her life.

The little wooden table at the back of the room looked the same as it did every day. Piles of books were stacked chaotically with their yellowy brittle pages held open by yet more books. Scraps of paper and unfurled maps teetered and dangled off the sides of the table, and writing implements lay everywhere, like windblown sticks in the Forest Verdure.

In the middle of the storm sat Marcellus, dark hair disheveled, eyes rimmed red from another sleepless night, hunched over the table with his fingers pressed against his temples, like he might squeeze the solution to his singular obsession right out of his head.

Chatine clutched the bowl of stew tighter in her hand, trying to extract warmth from its surface. There was always a temporary moment of shock every time she came in here and saw him like that. But today, it seemed to hit her harder, run deeper, until she could feel the tremors in the tips of her toes.

He was so far from the Marcellus Bonnefaçon she'd met in the morgue all of those months ago. Under his mop of dark hair, now as chaotic and unruly as his desk, his brow bore deep, anxious lines. His cheekbones jutted out below his wearied eyes like two dangerous arrows, and his cheeks had sunk inward, dark and cavernous. The shirt he was wearing hung from his shoulders as if there were nothing beneath it except a spindly coat hanger. And even though she couldn't quite see it now, she knew he'd punctured his belt with fresh holes to account for his shrinking waistline.

Chatine cleared her throat, announcing herself so she didn't startle him. But he didn't even blink. She approached slowly, like one might approach an injured animal, and set the bowl of steaming stew down on the table next to one of the open books.

"You need to eat," she told him, annoyed at how much she sounded like a mother. Not *her* mother, of course. But a normal mother. One who didn't sell her baby son to pay off a debt and then tell her daughter that their four-year-old ward had killed him.

Marcellus didn't move.

Chatine had spent her entire lifetime purposefully concealing herself behind hoods and dirt, hiding in the shadows of Frets, but she had never felt more invisible than she did right now.

She pulled the spoon from her pocket and dropped it onto the table with an angry clank. Marcellus flinched but didn't look up.

"Eat," she said again, pushing the stew closer.

"Look at this!" Marcellus yanked one of the massive parchments out from under the bowl.

Chatine angled her head to get a better look. She could now see that the paper contained a hand-drawn map of Laterre. It was rougher and less detailed than the digital versions she'd seen on holograms, but she could still make out the rocky cliffs of the Southern Peninsula, the grassy knolls of the Northern Région, and the mountainous terrain around Bûcheron in the southwest.

"It's a map," Chatine said blankly.

Marcellus let out a huff of frustration and jabbed his finger against the page. "No, right here. What does that look like to you?"

She leaned in to get a closer look, but her gaze was momentarily distracted by the silver ring on his finger. His mother's ring. The sight of it still made her stomach flip. It felt like years since that ring had been on *her* finger.

You only had it because you stole *it,* she was quick to remind herself. *Not because he gave it to you.*

"Do you see that?" Marcellus asked, wrenching her focus back to the map. She squinted at the dark blue emptiness that surrounded his fingertip.

"The Secana Sea?" she asked.

"No, that little dot *in* the Secana Sea. Does that look like an island to you?"

Chatine leaned in closer still, until her nose was almost touching the paper. Marcellus tapped his finger again. "Right here."

Finally, the infinitesimal dot came into focus and Chatine's heart sank. She reached out and scraped at the dot with her fingernail until it came loose from the page. "That's stew from *last* night's dinner."

She watched Marcellus's reaction carefully as she held up the hardened speck of food for him to see, waiting for the realization to hit: *This obsession is driving me to the end of my wits.* But it never came. Marcellus shook his head and returned his attention to the map, dragging his fingertip across the parchment in slow, meticulous lines.

"Why don't you take a break and eat," Chatine suggested, trying to sound lighthearted, and not at all as worried as she felt. "If you spill, you'll have something to get excited about tomorrow when you find it on the map."

Marcellus shot her a sharp look.

"Sorry," she muttered. "Bad joke."

"It has to be an island!" Marcellus exclaimed, shoving the map aside and pulling down one of the heavy, clothbound books from a nearby stack. Hastily, he thumbed through the withered pages, his eyes wide with desperation, until he found what he was looking for and pointed to the page. Chatine didn't even dare try to read it. The handwritten words were way too small and close together. With just one glance, she could already see the letters rearranging themselves, like her mind was playing tricks on her.

"This entry from the original settlers' journals clearly describes an island off the coast of Laterre," Marcellus went on. "Shortly before landing, Remy Arnaut wrote, 'The cloud layer was thick, blinding, and uninterrupted. . . . '" He faltered slightly over the words as he read aloud. Chatine glanced down at the page and tried to follow along.

But when our freightship finally broke through, an ocean spread out below us, vast and gray and choppy. Before the large landmass emerged on the horizon, I spied an outcropping of what appeared to be small rocks, like a trail of lonely punctuation marks in the midst of the immense gray, squalling sea. . . .

Marcellus frowned down at the page. "Unfortunately, it doesn't say which coast they were flying toward. Or how far off the coast they were."

Chatine nodded like this was all very fascinating, even though she'd heard every single word of it before. Marcellus had been talking about this infamous entry from the settlers' journals for weeks. It's what had inspired Sister Nicolette and Sister Noëlle's mission to explore the coast of Céleste. Because Marcellus had had a hunch that the general's secret facility might be there. It had been a complicated, dangerous mission, complete with false identities, elaborate disguises, and a stolen cruiseur. But it had yielded nothing. Just like all the other search parties they'd been sending out for months.

Chatine wanted to find Alouette just as much as anyone, but she was starting to worry that Marcellus's obsession was putting everyone in danger. And although she'd never say it aloud, she was starting to think that it might be a lost cause.

What if she's already dead?

"The other problem is," Marcellus was now saying, "I've scoured every volume of the settlers' journals, and Remy Arnaut's account is the only one that mentions anything that could be interpreted as an island."

"Maybe he was drunk and imagined it," Chatine suggested, which prompted another unamused look from Marcellus.

He flipped the book closed and collapsed into his chair. "It's just . . . I know my grandfather. I know how he thinks. If he's going to build a secret facility somewhere, he'd build it on an island."

"But the Secana Sea is huge! Even if an island did exist, how would you ever find it? You'd have to fly over the whole thing!" Chatine had meant for this to come out gentle and patient, but she was running out of both qualities these days.

Regardless, her outburst seemed to spark an idea in Marcellus. "Yes!" He leapt out of his seat and scurried to a shelf on the other side of the library. "The original flight paths of the freightships!"

Chatine sighed. She had to change the subject. Distract him. She had to get him to eat something. He was one skipped meal from vanishing completely. "Have the sisters made a decision yet? About what the next step is?"

She was careful *not* to mention Alouette's name, even though she knew her return was pivotal in the Vangarde's original plan.

"No," Marcellus said distractedly as he ran his fingers across the spines of the books. "The vote was interrupted before they could come to a decision. And now the return of the Red Scar has thrown a wrench into everything. They don't want to move forward with any plans until they figure out what Max is up to. We're waiting to see if Jolras can lead us to more information."

Marcellus located the book he was looking for and carried it back to his table. As he thumbed desperately through the pages, Chatine noticed sketches of vast spacecrafts with rows and rows of tiny portholes and long, sleek hulls that looked as if they could cut through galaxies, like knives through water. She doubted something so massive and majestic could ever have existed. Yet, at the same time, there was something vaguely familiar about these crafts.

"Are those the ships that became the Frets?"

"Here it is!" Marcellus ignored her question and pointed to the page now open in front of them. "This table has the coordinates of every freight-ship flight path from the First World, including where and when they accelerated to hypervoyage, their entry point into Laterrian atmosphere, and their approach to Vallonay. Now all I have to do is cross-reference this table with the settlers' journals. If I can determine which of the twenty freightships Remy Arnaut was on, I can pinpoint *what* he was flying over when he wrote that entry!" Marcellus immediately started shoving aside maps and documents, searching through the clutter. "Where did I put that passenger manifest?"

Chatine eyed the untouched stew on the table, and her jaw clenched. "Marcellus, how about you take a short break to—" But her words were cut off when Marcellus lifted a large sheet of parchment, and her gaze fell on the device concealed beneath it. The breath emptied from her lungs. The blood evaporated from her veins.

No bigger than her palm, the box was metallic and slightly rusted with a crooked antenna protruding from its top. On the side, a clunky button shone out as bright and fiery and red as Sol 2.

"W-w-what is that?" she asked in a shaky voice.

Marcellus glanced up from his search long enough to see what she was staring at. "It's an old First World radio. Undetectable by the Ministère. It's what the Vangarde have been using to communicate with the Défecteurs—" He cast an apologetic look at Chatine. "Or whatever they call themselves. According to Principale Francine, they gave the Refuge that radio when they first started planning Citizen Rousseau's breakout."

Despite her efforts to stop it, the memory shoved its way into her mind. The first time she saw one of those bulky devices. It was after she'd been rescued from Bastille and woken up inside the cockpit of a ship flown by a rogue pilot named—

"Why do you have it?" The question exploded out of her, stopping the memory in its tracks.

"I was trying to check in on Gabriel." As he lifted up one of the heavy books, his eyes lit up. "There it is!"

Chatine remembered the lanky, long-haired man who had been brought to the camp with Marcellus, Alouette, and Cerise. He'd been half-dead from an Albion cluster bullet. Brigitte had been able to remove the bullet and save his life, but he had still been in recovery when they'd left. They'd been forced to leave him behind when they went to break into the Ascension banquet.

But he wasn't the only one they'd been forced to leave behind.

The difference was Gabriel had never been given the choice.

"And?" Chatine compelled herself to ask, even though she wasn't sure she could handle the answer. "What did they say?"

If the desperation was evident in her voice, Marcellus was the last person to pick up on it. He was far too preoccupied with the list of names he was currently scanning with his fingertip, his lips moving silently as he sounded out the letters, just as Chatine had been taught to do.

"Nothing," he muttered. "We haven't heard anything from them since we left."

Now it wasn't just the books. Everything about this room was making Chatine feel uneasy. The walls seemed to be closing in. The lights appeared to be flickering, but that might have been her vision clouding over—it was hard to tell.

"Why not? Did something happen? Are they okay? Was there another roundup?"

Marcellus looked up and for the first time since she'd entered this room, he seemed to see her. Not just glance at her, not just acknowledge her presence with hasty, dismissive replies, but actually *notice* her. His gaze softened into what could only be described as pity. Normally, that would annoy Chatine—she'd spent her entire life trying to avoid other people's pity—but it was the most she'd gotten out of Marcellus in weeks. She'd take it.

And *that* was pitiful.

"I don't know," he said softly, almost gently, as though he was afraid of crossing that invisible line they'd drawn between themselves three months ago. "But with everything that's been happening on this planet lately—the Patriarche's murder, the general's cleanup efforts, and now this thing with the Favorites—it would be smart of them to go silent for a while."

She swallowed hard, trying to take solace in his answer. He gave her a slight nod, and for a moment, their eyes locked, a million silent words streaming between them. Words as deadly as cluster bullets and far too dangerous to say aloud.

The door to the library creaked open, severing the fragile connection between them. Citizen Rousseau stood in the doorway. Her long braid glowed like polished PermaSteel and snaked its way over her shoulder and down the front of her gray tunic. She was looking intently toward Chatine and Marcellus with those eyes of hers. Those silver and shining and contradictory eyes, which in one moment were like the points of two ice picks and in another, a pair of dazzling stars.

It had been three months and Chatine still hadn't gotten used to the sight of her. Sometimes she would see her gliding through the corridors or seated at the dining room table and Chatine would do a double take, convinced she was seeing a ghost. A lifetime of being told the woman was as good as dead was hard to overcome.

Chatine wondered what she was doing here, but Marcellus seemed to know instantly. "Is he moving?" he asked.

Citizen Rousseau gave a single, distinct nod, and Marcellus immediately dropped the paper he was holding and scurried toward the door.

"Wait, what's happening?!" Chatine shouted after him, her frustration finally boiling over like that pot of stew on the stove.

He barely even slowed as he hastily called back, "Jolras! He's been camped out in the Frets all day, but he's finally on the move. We need to see where he goes."

And then he was gone, leaving Chatine alone with the books and his untouched bowl of stew growing cold on the table.

You couldn't have stopped him from leaving, she told herself. And even though she knew it was true, it still stung. She couldn't stop him from doing anything. Because she *wasn't* his mother. She wasn't his keeper. In fact, she wasn't sure what she was to him anymore. A nuisance? A distracting reminder of the past? A servant who brought him food that he refused to eat?

All she knew was, she would never be his obsession.

CHAPTER 11

ALOUETTE

ALOUETTE HADN'T UTTERED A WORD SINCE THEY'D boarded Inspecteur Champlain's cruiseur. Despite the questions rattling around in her brain, she was still too terrified to speak. Terrified the vehicle would hear her. Terrified the inspecteur would change her mind and come zooming after them. Terrified they would be shot down in a swarm of combatteur explosifs and go plunging into the squalling Secana Sea below. She sat on one of the plush leather banquettes, curled up against a sleeping Sister Jacqui, listening to the soft hum of the cruiseur's engine as it took them far, far away from that awful place.

But when the coastline of Laterre's large landmass finally began to loom up ahead of them, like a shadowy ghost in the darkness, she couldn't keep her voice trapped inside any longer.

"Where are we going?" she asked Denise, who sat opposite Alouette, next to the cruiseur's complex navigation system.

The sister had immediately taken control the moment they'd left the facility, ordering them all into the idling vehicle and rattling off a string of coordinates that Alouette hadn't even tried to focus on. She'd been too grateful to follow someone else's lead. She was tired. Her head ached. Her heart was still pounding from the encounter with the inspecteur. And the wound on the back of her neck was throbbing with a ferocity she'd never felt before. But mostly, she had just been relieved to feel like a child again. A child who only had to follow the guidance of her beloved sisters and she would be safe.

"We need to land," Denise replied. "It will only be a matter of time before General Bonnefaçon puts a trace on this cruiser, if he hasn't already."

Fear bubbled back up in Alouette's chest at the mention of his name. At the image of him walking into that facility to find his inspecteur on the floor with a paralyzeur pulse in her leg and her three captives gone.

The cruiser banked slowly, and Alouette peered out at the sprinkling of lights that were just coming into view on the horizon. She glanced at the map on the navigation display and saw they were far north of Vallonay, past even the outermost exploit complexes, veering toward a small inlet cut into the craggy coastline.

"Coquille," she said softly, recognizing the location at once. She'd spent so many years poring over maps in the Refuge library, running her fingertips over sketches of cities and towns she never thought she'd see. And yet, in only a few short months, she'd traveled the Secana Sea, crossed the Terrain Perdu, wandered the streets of Montfer, and now she would be landing a stolen cruiser on the banks of a small fishing village.

"It's the closest town with an active cell," explained Denise. "We need to make contact with the base."

Alouette ripped her gaze from the display and stared at Denise.

The base? Does she mean . . . ?

Guilt and dread coated Alouette's stomach. Three months they'd been tapping on that shared cell wall. Three months they'd been talking in secret, coded conversations. Alouette had told Sister Denise everything—about the general's secret alliance with Queen Matilda to build a weapon out of the Skins, about her voyage to Albion with Marcellus, Cerise, and Gabriel to try to stop him, about meeting Denise's father, Dr. Collins, and his steadfast bravery right until the moment he'd died, about the Ascension banquet and the Forteresse and Alouette using her Paresse DNA to shut down the Skins.

But there was one thing Alouette had left out.

One detail she just couldn't bring herself to tell them. Because it was too crushing. Too devastating. Too much. Alouette hadn't been able to find the strength nor the words. It was as though Denise's secret code simply didn't have a translation for this kind of tragedy.

But now, she had no choice. She had to tell them. Because Sister Denise was expecting to make contact with the Refuge. She was expecting to reunite with her sisterhood. A sisterhood that was all dead.

"Denise," she began, but just then something hard hit the bottom of the cruiseur, sending Alouette flying off the banquette. Sister Jacqui's eyes fluttered open.

"What was that?" Alouette asked as the cruiseur continued to judder and sway before finally coming to a stop.

"Just a rock," Denise announced matter-of-factly. "The Secana Sea is very rough in these parts."

Alouette glanced outside the window. The lights from the cruiseur illuminated a long stretch of beach, and all around them, tiny stones and expanses of wet sand were being sucked, rolled, and pulled by the beating waves. "But why are we . . ."

Once again, she wasn't able to finish the thought. Denise was already on the move. With the touch of a button, the doors of the cruiseur were gliding open. Denise reached for Jacqui, helping her down onto the pebbly sand. As soon as Alouette jumped out, a strong sea wind grabbed at her curls, fierce ocean droplets spattered her cheeks, and her shoes immediately filled with water as a wave lapped up the beach and broke over her feet.

Hunkering down against the cold gusts and stinging spray, Denise and Alouette walked Jacqui up the darkened beach to drier land. With every step, the wet sand sucked at their feet, making it difficult to move.

"Keep hold of her," Denise commanded in a stern voice. "Don't let go. And take this." Denise pulled out the inspecteur's rayonette and tucked it into Alouette's waistband.

"Wait, why?"

But before Alouette could make sense of anything that was happening,

Denise was gone. She'd released Jacqui's other arm and was now running back through the darkness toward the cruiseur.

"Denise!" Alouette called out, but her voice was drowned by the squalling wind.

Alouette's heart began to riot in her chest as she watched the sister scramble back through the open door of the cruiseur. Then, the vehicle began to move. Its headlights bobbed and flashed as it drifted backward, out into the buffeting sea, until they were nothing more than pinpricks in the darkness. Alouette wanted to throw her body into the ocean, swim out to the retreating vehicle, and cling to its side, refusing to let go. But Jacqui's weight against her side held her in place.

"Denise!" she called out again, but again her pleas were snatched up by the cruel, thieving sea.

The almost infinitesimal glow from the cruiseur's headlights finally vanished into the ocean mist. Either that, or Alouette was crying so hard, she could no longer see them. "Please!" she whimpered, gripping tighter to Jacqui, who felt like she was one breath away from crumbling to the ground.

Somewhere in the distance, Alouette heard a splash. She squinted into the darkness, trying to make out remnants of the headlights, but there was no longer any trace of them. Not even their shimmering reflections in the rough waves.

Inspecteur Champlain's cruiseur was gone.

Alouette felt her knees give out. She could no longer support Jacqui's weight plus her own. She started to collapse, until the sound of wet, spongy footsteps on the sand yanked her gaze up the beach, where a figure was emerging from the swirling mist.

Alouette's heart pounded harder. It was too short to be a droid. And too sluggish to be a sergent on patrol. The footsteps grew closer and the first thing Alouette's eyes focused on, when she could see through the gloom, were the scars. Those familiar, twisting rivers on the left side of her face.

"Denise!" she called out, beautiful relief filling her lungs. "What did you—where did you—"

Denise put her finger to her lips. "Shh. The night is our only disguise right now. We need to get somewhere safe."

"But the cruiseur?" Alouette whispered.

"Won't be found." Denise took hold of Jacqui's other elbow and nodded toward the faint lights of the village that sprawled out before them. "This way."

As they walked, Alouette's head was still swimming with questions. She had known for more than three months now that the sisters were leaders of a famous rebel group called the Vangarde, but she'd never actually witnessed them *being* the Vangarde. She'd never seen the sisters behave as anything more than sisters. Scholars. Teachers. Protectors of the Forgotten Word.

But now, it was like she'd stepped into another dimension. Another reality. Sister Denise wasn't just the Refuge's technical expert. She was flying them to small villages in the middle of the night, disappearing stolen cruiseurs, defusing malfunctioning cyborgs with loaded rayonettes. And Alouette still didn't know what was going on.

All she knew about the town of Coquille was what she'd read in the Chronicles. That it was built to house the workers who fished oysters from the gravelly, shallow waters of Vallonay's north shore. The meat from the shells was a delicacy for the First and Second Estates, while the precious pearls adorned the soft necklines and uncalloused fingers of the ultrarich. Was it also some secret rebel stronghold?

They weaved their way through the narrow passageways on the docks. Sharp winds tore past them, rattling tarps and swaying the shadowy oyster baskets that hung from shuttered storefronts.

When they eventually reached the cluttered main street with its row of small huts and the sharp scent of seafood in the air, Alouette's feet dragged to a halt and she let out a quiet, strangled gasp.

Everywhere she looked, there were dazzling images dancing in the air. Hundreds of them. And they were enormous. As tall as the buildings themselves. There was barely a nook or dark corner that wasn't filled with the looping, glowing footage. Alouette saw fabrique workers devouring hearty meals, passengers boarding sparkling bateaus, and men in hothouses picking plump red tomatoes from an abundant vine.

They all looked so . . . happy.

But where were the images coming from?

Alouette turned to Denise, whose eyes were not trained on the startling visions in the air, but rather, on something near the ground. Alouette followed her eyeline until she could make out a small module affixed to the side of one of the nearby shacks. And from it, a brilliant shaft of light fanned upward and outward.

Projecting.

It was a hologram.

They were *all* holograms.

The thought made Alouette shiver.

"Come on," Denise urged quietly. "It's right up here."

Alouette stumbled forward through the glow, trying to ignore the blindingly bright images as she concentrated on putting one foot in front of the other. Finally, Denise stopped before one of the small huts that lined the far end of the street, and that's when Alouette saw it.

At first, she was certain she'd imagined it. Or it was simply a coincidence. But after blinking twice to refocus her vision and staring down at the doorstep again, she was fairly certain the two angled lines sketched in wet sand across the hut's front stoop were quite purposeful.

The letter V.

It was, Alouette soon realized, the only thing that distinguished this hut from the endless row of them that looked identical.

Denise reached out and knocked twice on the door before pausing for three seconds and then knocking once more.

There was a long silence, during which Alouette grew more and more convinced that the hut was empty. But then, she heard soft, padding footsteps coming from the inside and the door creaked open.

From the darkness, a gray-haired man with an unkempt beard peered out at them. His gaze scanned Alouette first, then Jacqui, before finally landing on Denise. The smile that overtook his face revealed crooked teeth and darkened gums, but there was true joy in it.

"My Sols," he swore in a gruff voice. "I never thought I'd—"

"We might have been followed," Denise said, and the man's smile instantly vanished.

"Come in, come in." He ushered them all inside and shut the door behind them before tugging at the already-closed curtains.

The house was sparse and dark inside, and the briny smell of salt, fish, and ocean wind hung in the air. A small lamp on a table offered the only source of light, and a set of bare wooden stairs led up to a neat loft bed above. An open doorway to the left revealed a tiny galley kitchen, where a faucet dripped into a sink and battered cooking pots hung from a wall.

Alouette and Denise eased Jacqui onto a sagging couch in the corner of the main room. She stared vacantly ahead for a few seconds, like there were beautiful stars in front of her that only she could see, before curling onto her side and drifting into a peaceful, oblivious sleep.

"You look dreadful," the man said, switching on another lamp. "I'll get you something to eat."

Alouette hadn't even realized how hungry she was until she heard those words.

"Merci," Denise said. "But first, we need to send a message to the base and let them know where we are."

And suddenly, all of Alouette's hunger curdled in her stomach.

"Of course," the man said before turning and hobbling into the kitchen. He began to rummage through drawers and cabinets, and Alouette knew she could wait no longer.

"Denise," she began in a shaky voice. "There's something I haven't told you. About the sisters."

Denise, who had been silently watching Jacqui sleep, looked up at Alouette.

Alouette swallowed hard and forced herself to hold the sister's gaze. She would not look away. She would not take the easy way out. Denise deserved her strength and her courage. She'd, after all, been one of the women to instill it in her in the first place.

"There was a problem when the Vangarde tried to break Citizen Rousseau out of Bastille. Their ship was . . ." Alouette faltered but quickly recovered. "Shot down by the Ministère." She took one final deep breath. In. Out. "We are all that's left of the sisterhood."

Alouette watched Denise's expression carefully, waiting for a reaction.

Waiting for *something*. But there was nothing. Not even a hint that the sister had heard her.

"I'm sorry I didn't tell you earlier," Alouette rushed to say. "I just couldn't bring myself to do it. I couldn't bear to break your heart that way. And I honestly didn't think we were ever getting out of that place, so I . . ." She let out a shuddering breath. "Denise, did you hear me? They're gone. They're all gone. The Refuge is empty."

But still, Denise did not even so much as flinch. And Alouette started to wonder if maybe these months in captivity had taken their toll on Denise, too. She knew the sister had never been one to readily display emotion, but she'd expected a little more than *nothing*.

"Sister Denise, do you understand what I just—"

"I understand," Denise said in a flat tone. "I just wouldn't be so sure."

Alouette blinked in confusion, now certain that the sister *had* lost some of her mental faculties in that prison. "Denise," she began again, keeping her voice tempered and even. "I'm sure. We intercepted a conversation between the general and Directeur Chevalier, who analyzed your devotion beads and discovered that they were part of a communication network. And when the Ministère traced the other signals from that network, they found that they had all gone silent on Bastille. And Marcellus said the ship carrying Citizen Rousseau never—"

"There's something you must understand about the Vangarde, Little Lark," Denise interrupted once again. The tone of her voice immediately brought Alouette back to the days of her lessons in the Refuge. Denise sounded like she was about to lecture Alouette on the mechanics of some First World communication device. "We are trained to hide in the shadows. We have spent the past seventeen years making the planet think we were nothing but ghosts."

Baffled, Alouette glanced between Denise and the sleeping form of Jacqui. "What are you talking about?"

"We're very good at *pretending* to be dead."

The words sank deep into the corners of Alouette's mind, threatening to light a fragile ray of hope that she had extinguished long ago. But before she could even begin to process their meaning, the man returned from the kitchen carrying a very aged and ripped piece of paper in one hand and a short, stub-nosed pencil in the other. "Here we are."

"Merci." Denise took the writing instruments and bent over the side table, where she hurriedly scribbled out three lines of text that Alouette couldn't make out, before hastily folding up the note and handing it back to the man. Without a word, he shuffled toward the front windowsill and switched on another lamp. This one, however, had a distinctive blue tinge to it, reminding Alouette of the stories she'd read in the Chronicles about the season of the Blue Dawn, when the nights glowed the color of dark sapphires.

"It should only take a few minutes," he told Denise. "I'll get you something to eat."

The man disappeared back into the kitchen and returned with plates of dried fish on crackers. Alouette removed the bulky rayonette from her waistband, set it aside, and sat down on the floor to eat. The fish was overly salty and the crackers were stale, but Alouette was too hungry to care.

"So," the man said to Denise, jutting his chin toward Alouette. "Is this the Lark?"

"Yes," said Denise, reaching for a cracker. "The general had her in custody for three months. We just escaped."

Alouette glanced between Denise and the gray-haired man. It felt peculiar to have one of the sisters talk about her so openly to a stranger. "You know about me?"

The man nodded. "You've been mentioned in a few communications between the cells." He smiled. "I'm Prouvaire. I head up the effort here in Coquille. Been here since 488."

"Nice to meet you," Alouette said meekly between bites.

Prouvaire turned back to Denise. "So the general knows who she is?"

"We think he only kept her alive to try to get information out of her."

"He asked me about Marcellus," Alouette put in, not knowing if she was being helpful to this cryptic conversation, or just intrusive. "His grandson."

"Makes sense," said Prouvaire. "He's trying to tie up all the loose ends. Anything that might spoil the illusion."

"What do you mean?" Alouette asked uneasily.

Prouvaire cut his eyes to Denise before replying. "The planet has changed in the past few months. It's not the same Laterre you once knew. The Matrone has fled back to Reichenstat. The general is in charge now. He cleaned everything up, the Frets, the fabriques, the med centers. There are no more Ascensions because there don't need to be. People are content. Happy, even."

Alouette thought about those hundreds of projections she'd seen outside. The glittering images. The smiling faces. "And now he's broadcasting his triumph on those holograms?"

"Exactly," said Prouvaire. "It's called the TéléCast. The general's own little propaganda machine. He covered the entire planet with those Sol-forsaken things. I hear he's already started putting them in the couchettes in Vallonay." He peered around his quaint hut with a sigh. "Pretty soon there'll be one in here, too. And he took credit for shutting down the Skins."

Alouette gasped. "The general? How?"

"He just did." Prouvaire shrugged. "That's the way things are now. He's a hero. General Bonnefaçon speaks and the people believe. He told them the riot at the Ascension banquet was just a fluke, started by an embittered Third Estater who didn't win and tried to crash the party. There are few people left who know what really happened that night. Marcellus is one of them. And the general needs to deal with him before the System Alliance makes their appointment."

"What appointment?" Alouette asked.

Prouvaire let out a weary breath, as though this was all too much for a man his age. "The contingency clause has been invoked."

Alouette racked her muddled, sleep-deprived brain, recalling the familiar term from the Chronicles. "You mean, from the Order of the Sols? But that's only used in the case of a leader who is deemed unfit to rule or . . ."

"A dead Patriarche with no heir," Prouvaire finished the thought for her, sending another shiver down her spine. His gaze lingered on her for far too long and with far too much significance.

Two knocks came at the door, but they may as well have been rayonette pulses from the way Alouette jumped out of her skin. She looked to Denise, who was looking at Prouvaire. He waited, silently counting the three seconds until a third knock sounded.

Biting her lip, Alouette watched the old man hobble toward the door. He eased it open barely a crack, just enough to slip Denise's note into an unseen hand on the other side, before closing it tight again.

"Now what?" Alouette asked.

"Now," Denise said with a sigh that seemed as rough and powerful as the savage sea air outside, "we wait."

- CHAPTER 12 -
MARCELLUS

WITH EVERY FLASH OF THE BLINKING RED LIGHT ON the hologram, Marcellus felt his muscles tighten. He glanced around the silent Assemblée room. All eyes were trained on the luminous three-dimensional map, as though the moving dot at its center held the future of the planet in its tiny red pixels.

The tracking signal from the récepteur was traveling rapidly south through the Forest Verdure, making sudden turns, and crossing kilomètres in a matter of minutes. Which meant Jolras Epernay was probably on a stolen moto.

Marcellus squeezed his crossed arms tighter against his chest as he watched the signal disappear from range on the edge of the Terrain Perdu, only to pop back up minutes later, heading west. The blinking dot weaved deftly around the foothills of a small mountain range, like Jolras was purposefully *trying* to mislead them. Or perhaps he was trying to mislead everyone. Policier and Ministère. Did that prove he was back with *her*? Back to working for his murderous sister, whom he'd sworn he wanted nothing to do with?

Marcellus ripped his gaze from the map just long enough to study the tall, silent figure of Citizen Rousseau. She was focused intently on the tracking signal like all the others, but her face—which glowed in the soft light of the hologram—held an expression of complete serenity and calm. The only thing moving was her long fingers as they turned the end of her cardboard cylinder round and round and round, a repetitive motion that obviously soothed her. She hadn't said a word since they'd reassembled to track Jolras Epernay. And once again, Marcellus found himself wondering if the passionate, charismatic woman who'd led the Rebellion of 488 all those years ago had never come back from Bastille. If she'd died on that moon and this silent, fragile, white-haired figure was her ghost.

"He's slowing," Marguerite reported.

Marcellus glanced over at the sister, who was positioned behind her busy workstation that held a series of flickering panels and monitors. She jabbed at one of her screens, and the hologram in the center of the room instantly bloomed and brightened as the map zoomed in.

The blinking red dot was, indeed, slowing down, and the sisters and Marcellus watched in rapt silence as it finally came to a halt a few kilomètres from the town of Bûcheron.

"What's out there?" asked Francine.

Marguerite's fingers maneuvered swiftly across her workstation, and, a few moments later, a hologram map zoomed even further into the landscape until Marcellus could make out what looked like a cluster of dilapidated wooden cabins surrounded by messy piles of rotting lumber.

"Looks like an old logging camp," replied Marguerite.

"One that clearly hasn't been used in a while," added Laurel.

"Activate the audio," Francine directed, and Marguerite tapped on her screen. A moment later, the Assemblée room filled with the sound of voices, tinny and distorted through the microphone of the ancient device still hidden in Jolras's pocket. There were so many people talking at once, Marcellus couldn't even begin to make sense of the noise.

Until one voice silenced them all.

"You . . . gone . . . long . . . what . . . you?"

The words came out choppy and disjointed, some of them lost altogether. The récepteur was too far from any of the Vangarde's hidden antennae. But Marcellus still recognized the voice. And it sent chills ricocheting through every vertebra of his spine.

"We . . . getting worried . . . thought maybe . . . decided . . . abandon me again, brother."

It was Maximilienne Epernay. The leader of the Red Scar. The woman who hadn't been seen or heard from in three months and who Marcellus had prayed was gone for good.

But now she was right there. Her voice in his ear.

". . . can't . . . be . . . this . . . you . . . was it?"

Marcellus strained to hear what was being said, but the words were becoming less and less recognizable.

"Can we get a stronger reception?" Francine asked Marguerite.

Marguerite tapped at her controls. "I can amplify the nearest antenna, but we have to be careful. Any further and the Ministère could detect our signal."

"I thought you said they don't have the technology to recognize the new network," Sister Nicolette said.

"They don't," Marguerite replied. "But I also don't want to give them any reason to try." She pressed something on the screen, and the voices instantly grew louder. And much clearer.

"After your little stunt with the meat transporteur, the whole place was swarming with bashers. I had to wait until it was safe to leave."

Marcellus recognized this voice too. It was Jolras.

"*Our* little stunt, brother," Max corrected him. "We all worked together to achieve this. This is a shared victory. Isn't that right, my camarades?"

Her question was met by a rallying cheer that nearly knocked Marcellus off his feet. It sounded like the battle cry of an *army*.

"How many followers does she have?" Sister Clare asked, her face sick with dread.

"Too many," replied Francine.

Marcellus's stomach clenched. The last time he'd seen the Red Scar, during that ghastly spectacle in the Marsh, there had been eight, maybe ten of them. How had they managed to multiply their numbers so quickly?

"Unlike our dearly deceased Patriarche," Max continued, "I don't take credit for the efforts of others."

"It was *your* idea to murder a bunch of innocent people. I told you I wanted nothing to do with it," Jolras spat back, and even though Marcellus was hundreds of kilomètres away, hidden in a bunker beneath the Frets, he still felt his muscles coil in anticipation of Max's reaction.

"Innocent?" Max repeated with a heavy, grating laugh. "You think Élisabeth, Alphonse, and Philippe Paresse were innocent? First Estaters? Favored to become the next leader of Laterre? The next corrupt, gluttonous villain to take advantage of us and steal from us and enslave us."

Silence followed and Marcellus glanced again at Rousseau. Her eyes were closed, but her face was alert, listening intently.

"Do you have the footage you captured in the Marsh?" Max asked, and Marcellus heard a shuffling sound as people and items were rearranged. He wished they could see what was going on out there. But they were forced to rely only on the scratchy audio feed from the récepteur in Jolras's pocket. "I want to see how *our* little stunt played out."

Then, not a minute later, Marcellus heard the sound of screams. They were so real, so horrific, he almost jumped.

Max let out another unsettling chuckle. "It's perfect! Look at how scared they all are. As they should be. The Third Estate should be scared of this Regime. Of more of the same."

"They're scared of dead bodies hanging in a meat transporteur," Jolras snapped.

"The bodies are a symbol," replied Max calmly. "And the people should be screaming in terror at the idea of any of those Paresse idiots ruling us. *We* are the ones who keep this planet functioning. We make the bread in the bread fabrique and process the milk in the dairy fabrique. We manufacture the cloth in the textile fabrique and slaughter the sheep in the meatpacking fabrique. *We* should choose how this planet is run. Not some lazy pomps who just happened to be born with a single drop of Paresse blood in their veins. They have no idea what it's like to work our soil and chop our trees and manufacture our goods. They have no idea what it means to be a Laterrian."

Marcellus could hear a few murmurs echoing through the speakers. Max's followers voicing their agreement.

"Let's hope this news reaches the members of the System Alliance before their next session is called," Max went on. Her voice was traveling now, moving farther away from Jolras and the device sitting at the bottom of his pocket. "Antoine has left to gather more intel for us in Ledôme. He'll let us know if any other names start surfacing as possible contenders for the System Alliance appointment."

Intel? Marcellus's heart started to pound. The Red Scar had a spy inside Ledôme? Was that how they were able to get to the Favorites? Was that how they knew where the Patriarche would be when they kidnapped him and dragged him to the Marsh to be executed by the Blade?

Max's voice came closer again, like she was pacing. "Those System Alliance wretches are so desperate to put a Paresse in the Palais, they'll root out every last third cousin and great-uncle the Patriarche ever had." There was a heavy, sinister pause, during which Marcellus swore he felt the bedrock shift beneath his feet. "And we'll be ready for *all* of them. By the time the System Alliance is done, there won't be any First Estaters left." She let out another gruff laugh.

Marcellus's throat went dry as, once again, he checked on the reaction of the sisters. Noëlle had her hand over her eyes, like she was too scared to look. Léonie stood with her arms crossed, her mouth an angry, unmoving line. And Principale Francine sat next to Marguerite, cracks of fear breaking through her stoic façade.

"Well, you can count me out," Jolras said, a fire of determination now burning in his voice. "I'm not participating in any more of your murder sprees."

"Jolras," Max said in a soothing tone, which reminded Marcellus of a mother condescendingly coddling a small child. "You know you don't mean that."

"I mean it," Jolras snapped. "You can get one of your other lackeys to be your eyes next time. I'm out."

"No, you're not."

Marcellus could hear the smile in Max's voice. It made him want to throw up.

"You've made that threat too many times now, brother. It's no longer credible. You always come running back to me. Just like the last time. Because you love me. We shared a womb. That's too strong of a bond to break. And because you loved Nadette. And you want retribution for her."

"I think we've done enough retribution for Nadette," Jolras spat. "The Patriarche is dead. An eye for an eye. A life for a life. Isn't that what you've always said?"

"It's not enough!" Max's words were suddenly hot, enraged, as wild as her fierce gray eyes on the night Marcellus had first seen her speak in the Jondrette. "This isn't just about Nadette anymore. This is about all of us. Every single poor, downtrodden, miserable Third Estater on this planet. When our sister was killed, it might as well have been *all* of our heads under that blade. Because that's how little the Regime cares about us. Killing one of them, or even ten of them, is not enough. And it won't be enough until the estates are dismantled, Ledôme is ripped apart, the Grand Palais is demolished brick by brick, and the people control their own destinies. Not a Paresse. Not the System Alliance. Not the general. But the *people*."

Marcellus stole another glance at Citizen Rousseau and noticed something that almost resembled a smile tugging at her lips.

". . . and if we have to kill every First and Second Estater on the planet to make our dream a reality, then hand me the rayonette," Max went on, her voice building with intensity and passion. "You can't kill the snake until you cut off its head. That means every First Estater and *anyone* who supports this oppressive Regime must die. We will put them all under the Blade if we have to, we will hang all of their bodies from meat hooks if we must, but they will be punished for their silent complicity. They will suffer—"

"Turn it off," a voice said behind Marcellus, and he spun to see Sister Laurel holding her head in her hands. "I think we've heard enough."

Marguerite looked to Francine, who nodded, and a moment later, the voice of Maximilienne faded to silence. Marcellus felt a rush of relief. He wasn't sure how much longer he could have listened.

"She's lost her mind," whispered Noëlle. "She's—"

"She's playing right into my grandfather's hands." Marcellus didn't realize he'd said that aloud until he noticed every pair of eyes in the room looking at him. He sighed and clawed his fingers through his hair. "The general's goal has always been to rid the planet of the First Estate, whom he thinks of as the 'fat to be trimmed.' And the Red Scar are inadvertently *helping* him. With every First Estater they kill, his grip on the planet will tighten. As long as the Red Scar are out there, causing trouble, the general will continue to look like a hero."

"But do you think he was planning to use them all along?" asked Sister Clare, and when Marcellus pinched his brow in confusion, she added, "I mean, he must have known about the contingency clause, right? That's why he killed the Premier Enfant, so there would be no heirs left to inherit. But why would he go through all of that trouble if he knew the System Alliance would just appoint another First Estater to take control?"

"First of all, we don't know if the System Alliance was planning to appoint any of the Favorites," Nicolette pointed out. "That was just a rumor being streamed on the holograms, which, remember, the general controls. What if he's spreading that rumor himself so that the Red Scar will do exactly what they're doing?"

"Or maybe this is evidence that the general has been forced to swerve," suggested Francine. "Maybe he assumed the System Alliance would appoint him all along, and then when he got wind that he might be upstaged by one of the Patriarche's cousins, he used his new TéléCast feed to make sure the Red Scar knew about it."

"Either way," Marcellus said, "he's manipulating them. He's *using* them. And I guarantee you, Max has no idea."

"And she's far from done," Sister Laurel whispered hauntingly. "She's going to keep killing."

"What are we supposed to do?" Sister Léonie asked. "We can't fight her *and* the general *and* the Regime. We don't have the resources. We have to choose our enemy."

"But if the Red Scar are going to keep spreading fear and violence, we'll never accomplish anything," said Sister Clare before casting a sorrowful look at Marcellus. "Even if Alouette returns tomorrow, even if we're able to continue as planned, put her in front of the people, present her as a symbol of unity, the Red Scar will undermine us at every turn. Not to mention, the moment they find out she's a Paresse—the *rightful* Paresse heir—they'll try to kill her, too."

The weight of this truth left everyone momentarily speechless.

"Well, we can't take on Maximilienne Epernay," Sister Marguerite finally said. "You all heard her just now. She's unstable and unhinged and—"

"Not wrong," said a quiet, composed voice. Everyone—including Marcellus—turned toward Citizen Rousseau.

"Excuse me?" asked Sister Léonie, echoing Marcellus's disbelief.

"Maximilienne is angry, yes," replied Rousseau. "She has been done a great injustice by the Regime. But if you listen to the words and ideas beneath her anger, they are not too dissimilar from our own. She wants change. She wants a better future for Laterre. She wants an end to a corrupt system. Just like us."

Marcellus peered again around the room. He saw a mismatch of reactions, ranging from disbelief to confusion to adoration.

"She's simply approaching it with a different strategy," Rousseau concluded.

Léonie snorted. "I'll say."

"It's true," Sister Laurel said with a weary sigh. "Max shares many of our same ideals. Our same vision for the future."

"She's just willing to kill every First and Second Estater on the planet to get it," muttered Léonie under her breath.

"Even if it is true," Marguerite began hesitantly, "what are we supposed to do about it? How does that help us defeat her?"

"We don't defeat her," Rousseau said, once again attracting every pair of eyes in the room. "We work *with* her."

"WHAT?" Léonie spat.

"We have the same enemy," replied Rousseau. "We shouldn't also be fighting each other."

And then, all the sisters were speaking at once. Marcellus fought to sort through the cacophony of voices, but they all seemed to blend together.

". . . she's a madwoman . . ."

"... what other choice do we have ..."

"... can't be trusted ..."

"... hear her out ..."

"... worked this hard just to throw it away ..."

"... have an open mind ..."

Marcellus squeezed his temples with his fingertips. Pressure was building in his head. From the voices. The stress. The image of that abandoned logging camp still visible on the hologram map.

It was only now he noticed, amid the noise, that one of the Assemblée room monitors was flashing with an alert.

Incoming message.

He recognized the notification from the Vangarde's new communication network. It was most likely coming from one of the cells. The sisters received at least a dozen messages a day, asking what the plan was. What was the next move? What were they all waiting for?

We're waiting to deal with a madwoman who has a thirst for Paresse blood, Marcellus thought bitterly. There was nothing they could do until this Red Scar issue was resolved.

Marcellus tore his gaze from the flashing alert and focused back on Citizen Rousseau. Despite the heated discussion that still waged between the sisters, she had fallen silent again. And Marcellus worried she wasn't going to intervene. That once again, she was going to opt out of the decision altogether and then slip back into one of those deep, contemplative trances he so often found her in.

"Silence!" Francine called through the storm, and Marcellus was grateful when he could hear the familiar, comforting sounds of the Assemblée room again: machines humming, surveillance feeds softly chattering, the sound of the sisters' gradually steadying breaths.

"No matter what we do about Maximilienne Epernay," Francine went on, "we cannot let her turn us into something we are not. We cannot let her divide us and turn us against each other. That's exactly what her strategies are built around, creating chaos."

A few of the sisters nodded while others looked slightly ashamed.

Out of the corner of his eye, Marcellus noticed the incoming message alert was still flashing, still demanding attention. But all of the sisters were far too preoccupied to notice.

Francine turned back to Rousseau and gave her a small nod to continue.

"I recommend we request a meeting with Max and try to negotiate an alliance between the Red Scar and the Vangarde," Rousseau said, and Marcellus swore the room would erupt in debate again, but no one spoke. "We must explain to her that her violent actions are not helping the situation. In fact, they are only playing into the general's hands, as Marcellus said. Like us, Maximilienne wants freedom. Like us, she wants the unjust estates to end. Like us, she wants change on Laterre. But we must convince her that this change cannot come about through murder, destruction, and hate. As the First World showed us, as Laterre has shown us, blood only ever leads to more blood. We must persuade Max that peace is the only way to true change. We must persuade her to work *with* us."

Marcellus glanced around the room once more and saw the power of Rousseau's words play out on every single face. He saw fear melt away. He saw disbelief turn inside out. He saw confusion dissolve until all that remained was a shining, shimmery layer of pride.

There was no vote necessary.

The decision was unanimous.

"Very well," said Francine with a definitive clasp of her hands. "Sister Marguerite. Can you activate the speaker on the récepteur in Jolras's pocket?"

Marguerite's hands flew across her controls. "Activating now."

A moment later, a single green button illuminated on a nearby panel. Just waiting to be pressed. Just waiting to send an impossible question across the vast landscape of Laterre, bouncing from secret antenna to secret antenna, all the way to that forest on the outskirts of Bûcheron.

With sweat pooling underneath his collar, Marcellus turned back to Rousseau, waiting eagerly for what was to happen next. But, to his surprise, she was staring right back at him.

"Marcellus," she said in that cool, even tone of hers. "You know Jolras better than any of us."

He felt the color drain from his face. "What? N-n-no I don't," he stammered. "I only met him once. And that was months ago."

"But he trusted you enough to warn you about what Max was planning. He will trust you now."

Marcellus backed slowly away. As though he was preparing to run from the room. As though he could possibly escape any of this. He glanced anxiously around at the eight other sisters, who were now staring at him with so much expectation in their eyes. So much hope.

He had already failed them once this week. He had sent Noëlle and Nicolette on a dangerous mission across the planet, based on a stupide hunch that turned out to be wrong. He knew he could not fail them again.

This was what it meant to be a member of the Vangarde. To follow in his father's footsteps. Fear hadn't been an option for Julien Bonnefaçon, and it was not an option now. It was only a distraction.

In one decisive motion, he leaned forward and pressed the glowing green button on the control panel. "Jolras. This is Marcellus Bonnefaçon. We need to talk."

- CHAPTER 13 -
ALOUETTE

IT WAS THE FIRST TIME ALOUETTE HAD FELT WARM IN months. The walls of Prouvaire's tiny hut in the village of Coquille enveloped her like a cocoon. She had a soft pillow under her head, a thick blanket wrapped around her, and a constant stream of heat chugging from the small heater, chasing away three months of chill and pain.

And yet, Alouette still couldn't sleep.

There were too many thoughts crowding her mind. Too many questions still unanswered. Too many fears still lurking just below the surface.

The Patriarche was dead. Dead without an heir. The contingency clause had been invoked. Which meant the System Alliance would soon be appointing the next leader of Laterre.

Unless another heir came forward . . .

And on top of all that, hours had passed, and no reply had come from Denise's message. Denise had been so certain that the sisters were still alive. But Alouette couldn't help fear that she had been right all along. That the sisters really were gone.

"Try to sleep, Little Lark," came a quiet voice in the darkness. Alouette turned on her side to see Sister Denise's eyes were open too. She was lying next to her on the floor of the hut while Sister Jacqui slept soundly on the sofa. "Morning will be here soon. And you'll need your strength."

"I can't," Alouette whispered back. She expected Denise to argue with her. To tell her to count her breaths until she fell asleep. The way she would have done when Alouette was a child and the Refuge was still just a Refuge and the sisters were still just sisters. But Denise didn't say anything at all. She simply reached out and took Alouette's hand in hers, squeezing it gently. The gesture surprised Alouette. Denise didn't like human contact. Normally, Jacqui was the only one allowed to touch her. Sister Laurel had been the one Alouette learned to go to for a reassuring embrace or a tender kiss on the cheek or a warm snuggle on a cold night. Sister Denise's comfort came from her stoic silence and gentle looks and knowing half smiles.

But as Alouette stared into Denise's eyes now, she no longer saw the sister who had raised her. All she saw was a stranger. A skilled Vangarde operative who had outsmarted the general and led them to safety. She still couldn't seem to wrap her mind around anything that had happened tonight.

"How did you convince the inspecteur to let us go?" Alouette whispered.

Denise turned onto her back and stared up at the ceiling, blinking slowly as though trying to access the memory in her mind. "I was once in her place. I knew what she was experiencing."

"You mean, because you were a cyborg?" Alouette clarified, desperate to understand.

"Because I was a cyborg who experienced a glitch."

"Glitch?" Alouette repeated the word, thinking about Inspecteur Champlain's chaotically sparking circuitry. It was the perfect description for what Alouette had seen. It had looked like someone had cut the wrong wire in the cyborg's brain and the entire system had errored out. "Is that what was happening to her?"

Denise nodded and peered over at Sister Jacqui, whose eyelashes were fluttering softly with dreams. "Yes. When she realized you were the Patriarche's daughter, and therefore, the rightful ruler of Laterre according to the Order of the Sols, her mind was able to make the connection, but her internal programming was slower to update. Essentially, her brain was arguing with itself. The conflicting orders she was receiving from you and the general were causing her circuitry to malfunction."

"So, what did you tell her? To stop the glitch?"

"I told her I would make it look like we escaped."

Alouette's head started to pound. She still wasn't following.

"Cyborgs are complicated beings," Denise went on, sensing Alouette's frustration. "On the one hand, they're programmed to be rational to a fault; their human emotions are tamped down so as not to interfere with their jobs. On the other hand, they're programmed to follow the laws of the Regime and to never question authority. Ninety-nine percent of the time, these two programs work harmoniously together. But then there's that tiny one percent, the rare occasion when rationality no longer goes hand in hand with the law. This was one of those moments. She was trapped in a rationality loop. Releasing two prisoners the Regime had marked as traitors and terrorists was punishable by death, but so was disobeying the rightful leader of Laterre. As a cyborg, it's almost impossible to escape from a rationality loop. I offered her a way out."

Alouette fought to make sense of what Denise was saying, but it kept coming back to the same question. "And this happened to you, too? This glitch?"

She tried to imagine Denise as the cyborg she once was. Her face alight with twinkling filaments, her left eye glowing a vibrant, penetrating orange, her emotions bound and shackled by lines of code. She tried to imagine Denise experiencing what had happened to the inspecteur earlier tonight. Twitching, spasming, stuttering. But it was far too painful a picture to hold in her mind.

"Yes," Denise whispered. "That's exactly what happened to me. Except my glitch was left unchecked. It got worse. I experienced more frequent symptoms, more spasms, more circuitry malfunctions. There are only three ways to resolve a cyborg glitch. The first is reprogramming. If the Ministère catches the problem early enough, they can fix it with an adjustment to the cyborg's operating system. This is most likely what will happen to Inspecteur Champlain when they find her. The second, less conventional way is for the cyborg to wake up."

"Wake up," Alouette repeated the phrase with reverence.

"It's when a cyborg is able to break free from their own code."

"That's what happened to you, isn't it? You woke up?"

Even in the darkness, Alouette could see a grim shadow pass over Denise's face. "If I hadn't, I'm not sure I would be alive today."

"What do you mean?"

Denise let out a slow breath. "The third solution for a cyborg who has glitched—and the far too common solution—is *self*-correction."

Alouette sucked in a breath. "You mean . . . suicide?"

"It can feel like the only rational way out. Especially for a cyborg."

Jacqui made a small chuffing sound, and Alouette looked over to see the sister's eyes were now open again, staring into nothing. Alouette sat up and positioned herself in front of her. "Jacqui? Can you hear me? It's Alouette. It's Little Lark. Can you—"

"She doesn't speak," Denise said quietly.

"At all?"

Denise shook her head, moisture pricking at the corners of her eyes. "Not in months."

Alouette felt like a knife had been plunged into her rib cage. How could Jacqui just *not* speak? She was the most eloquent, most passionate, most opinionated of all the sisters. Her thought-provoking questions and perspectives had filled Alouette's childhood with joy and curiosity and wisdom. Her voice had been the soundtrack of Alouette's life.

A world without Sister Jacqui's words was like a world without light. A canvas without paint. A galaxy without stars.

"B-b-but she will . . . ," Alouette struggled to say, holding back a flood of tears. "She will speak again, right?"

Denise looked away. "I'm not sure. We'll have to wait for Sister Laurel to examine her before we know anything more."

The knife plunged deeper at the mention of the sister's name. There it was again. That hope that Denise had dangled in front of her ever since she'd told her that the sisters might not be dead. That hope that Alouette was far too terrified to grab on to.

Two sharp knocks cut through the silence, startling Alouette. Denise sat bolt upright and stared at the door. Alouette could tell she was count-ing. Waiting for that ever-important third knock.

It never came.

Instead, there was a voice. "This is Commandeur Apolline Moreau of the Ministère. Open up."

Alouette's heart leapt into her throat. *Commandeur?*

"Quick!" Prouvaire whispered urgently, scrambling down from the loft ladder. "You must hide." He pushed back the coarse handwoven rug that Alouette and Denise had been lying on, revealing an uneven square cut into the wooden floor.

"Open this door! Or we will use force!" the woman shouted from out-side.

Digging his nails into the groove, Prouvaire wrenched up the loose floorboards to reveal a narrow, dusty stairwell leading to a shadowy cham-ber below. "Get in."

Alouette and Denise each took one of Jacqui's arms and helped her down the rickety steps. The light coming from the room above barely illu-minated the tiny basement, but Alouette could just make out a workbench, covered in an assortment of tools and disassembled devices, and a small shelf filled with what looked like a row of handmade journals and note-pads.

The floorboards closed above their heads with a soft click, and they were plunged into an engulfing blackness. A swishing sound from above told Alouette that Prouvaire was replacing the rug. Then, she could hear nothing but the sound of her own heart pounding in her ears. She fought to keep as still as possible. There was a creak as the front door opened and three pairs of footsteps entered: one human, two definitely *not* human.

In the darkness, she could see the whites of Denise's eyes mirroring her own fear back at her. Alouette found Jacqui's hand and squeezed it.

"Commandeur Moreau? In our little village. What an honor. What can I do for you?"

Even with the sound muffled by the floorboards, Alouette could hear the impressive steadiness in Prouvaire's voice as he spoke.

"A Ministère-commissioned cruiser went off-line not far from the shores of this town," said the crisp voice of the woman called Commandeur Moreau. "The Communiqué identifies it as belonging to an Inspecteur Champlain, who was recently attacked by known and wanted criminals. Do you have any information about this?"

Alouette's heart pounded harder.

"No, Commandeur," came Prouvaire's convincing reply. "I'm only just hearing about this now."

There was a pause. Alouette stared straight up at the ceiling, as though she could see right through the floorboards. Heavy, clomping footsteps echoed above her head. The droids were moving around. Scanning, no doubt. Looking for evidence.

"I see," came Moreau's delayed response, and there was something in her tone that sent a shiver through Alouette. Something dark and disbelieving. "So, then you have no idea why surveillance footage of this sector showed three figures knocking on the door of *this* hut earlier tonight."

Surveillance footage?

Alouette struggled to make sense of this. The Ministère had cams hidden in the street of this tiny village? But where would they—

The answer came to her like a clap of thunder. She looked over to Denise, who seemed to be piecing together the same conclusion. They shared a knowing look before Alouette mouthed, *The holograms?*

Denise nodded and another shiver shot through Alouette.

Of course. The general no longer had Skins to keep tabs on the Third Estate. So he'd replaced them with something else.

"Oh yes," said Prouvaire casually. "Those were some friends of mine from the docks. They'd come over for a cup of weed wine."

"In the middle of the night?" Moreau asked dubiously.

"It's long hours out on those oyster bateaus," Prouvaire explained. "Sometimes the middle of the night is our only time to relax."

"Friends who leave behind Ministère weapons?" Moreau asked, and Alouette heard the distinct sound of metal scraping against wood. She peered again at the ceiling, remembering, with sickening dread, the rayonette she'd placed on the floor earlier. *Inspecteur Champlain's* rayonette.

Her pulse skyrocketed. Alouette spun around, her eyes desperately struggling to see through the darkness. She searched for something—*anything*—they could use to defend themselves, when suddenly she realized there was another option. Because there, in the back corner of the basement, was a single pinprick of light. A window.

She nudged Denise and pointed to it. Denise nodded once before gripping hold of Jacqui. Alouette understood. She released Jacqui's hand and slowly, carefully crept her way toward the window.

"Search the hut!" Moreau shouted, and Alouette heard more footsteps, followed by a series of creaks and bangs as the droids started to tear the little dwelling apart. Guilt ricocheted through Alouette's stomach. This was what Prouvaire got for helping them. His home destroyed. His life turned inside out.

But she knew, if they didn't get out of here soon, a few broken dishes would be the least of his problems.

She reached the window and gently pushed aside the heavy curtain that was blocking it. The basement instantly brightened as light from the street lamps streamed inside. Climbing onto a nearby bench, Alouette peered out at an abandoned alleyway. The window was at street level, which meant if they could somehow get it open, they could shimmy through. But there was no latch anywhere to be found. The window was just a solid piece of plastique embedded in the frame.

Alouette spun back, searching the room. Her gaze landed on a small screwdriver lying on Prouvaire's workbench. Using the droid's footsteps from above to shield the sound, Alouette hopped down and snatched up the tool. She immediately went to work trying to pop the window from its frame. But after three futile attempts, the screwdriver slipped and clattered to the ground with a magnificent crash.

The barrage of searching footsteps overhead stopped.

Alouette froze and looked up again, waiting, her heart hammering now. She listened carefully for a voice, anything to give her a hint of what was happening above.

But it turned out, she didn't need a voice.

A second later, she heard the familiar sound of wood scraping as the trapdoor hidden in the floorboards creaked open. Light from the upstairs flooded the small basement. Alouette grabbed the screwdriver and started to bang violently on the window with the metal tip, hoping to break through the plastique, but it was too strong.

"I don't remember seeing a basement on the floor plans of these huts," said Moreau.

"There's nothing down there but rats," Prouvaire said, and now Alouette could hear the tremor in his voice. All of his former steadiness was gone.

"Pretty noisy rats," remarked Moreau, and again, that cold mocking seeped into her tone. "Get down there," she barked with a snap of her fingers. "Shoot anyone you see on sight."

Alouette bit back a shriek as an enormous metal droid foot appeared from the gash in the ceiling and landed with an alarming thud on the first step. She jammed her shoulder against the window, feeling pain splinter through her collarbone from the impact. But the plastique wouldn't budge.

Another ground-shaking thump thundered through the basement as the droid's second foot appeared on the stairs.

Alouette yelped, staring desperately between the window and Denise and the massive metallic feet. She didn't think her heart could beat any faster.

That is, until the droid clunked down another step. And then another. But it seemed to be moving unusually slowly, as though it was having trouble fitting through the opening.

Commandeur Moreau let out a grunt of frustration. "Get out of there!" she bellowed. "Let me do it."

There was a monstrous ripping sound as the droid worked itself free from the trapdoor, taking half of the flooring with it. Dust and wood particles sprinkled down around them. Alouette turned and banged on the window again, slowly coming to terms with the fact that Commandeur Moreau was coming down those stairs, armed, and there was no escape.

Alouette felt her muscles coil as that familiar sensation passed through her. The memory of the ten Tranquil Forme sequences flashed through her mind. She was still weak, but she knew she would not go easily. She would not allow herself or her sisters to be taken without a fight. She looked to

Denise, who had lowered Jacqui onto the bench and was now standing with her feet slightly spread, her arms raised in what Alouette recognized as the first move of the *Sols Ascending* sequence. She was ready to take on whatever came down those stairs. They both were.

The basement walls started to shake as a woman in a crisp white uniform came charging down the steps.

"Halt!" called Moreau, and then Alouette heard something shatter as a burst of electrified air rushed past her left ear and the wall beside her exploded. Another rayonette pulse came a split second later, and Alouette braced herself for either intense pain or a quick death. She wasn't sure which.

And yet, it was Commandeur Moreau who slumped to the ground, her paralyzed arm dropping her rayonette. Alouette's eyes darted back to the window, blinking in disbelief when she noticed the plastique had been completely blown away. But it wasn't until a face appeared through the gap, a familiar pair of deep-brown eyes, that she realized what had happened. And her heart exploded with hope and relief and joy and terror all mixed together in a single detonation.

"Sister Laurel?"

- CHAPTER 14 -
CERISE

IT WAS THE MIDDLE OF THE NIGHT IN THE CYBORG DOR-
mitories of the Ministère, and quiet and darkness had descended like a
thick blanket. Only soft blue lights glowed from the exterior of the sleep
pods, which were lined up in long, neat rows throughout the room. Occa-
sionally, a slight snore or sleeping murmur was audible through their plastique hatches. But mostly it was the ventilation units that could be heard
as they maintained the optimal temperature and humidity for each pod.

Cerise wasn't quite asleep yet, but the nodes attached to her forehead—
refreshing and replenishing her circuitry for a new day—vibrated softly
like a lullaby. For a moment, as dreams and darkness tugged at her, she
wondered how she'd ever slept peacefully before. Without these crisp
sheets beneath her. Without the calming flicker and buzz of her circuitry
being recharged. Without being tucked into this sparse white cocoon,
with all her fellow cyborgs fast asleep in their pods around her.

It was no wonder she was never troubled by fitful nights or bad dreams.
Only delicious . . .

Quiet . . .

Restful . . .

Just as sleep started to slip its gentle fingers around her, tugging her down, the lock on her pod clicked loudly. Cerise jerked awake and when her eyes snapped open, she saw her father standing outside.

She scrabbled out of her pod and stood quickly at attention. "Directeur Chevalier. Good evening. Is everything all right?"

"Apparently not," her father replied rigidly, running a hand over his chin, which bore an uncharacteristic layer of stubble.

Cerise felt a sudden spike of cortisone in her system. "What is it?"

The directeur cast his gaze around at the quiet, glowing pods, as though checking to make sure everyone was asleep, before lowering his voice. "The general has asked to see you."

More of the stress chemical flooded her system. "Me? Now?"

The directeur nodded once and stepped out of the dormitory while she dressed. Cerise opened her locker, which contained her only possessions. Cyborgs didn't need much. All of the equipment they required for their job was provided by the Ministère, as well as their food, personal supplies, and uniform. She quickly slipped on her standard-issue gray cargo pants, neatly pressed shirt, and technicien coat that bore the same silver stripes and silver collar as the shirt beneath.

As she followed the directeur swiftly and silently down the corridor toward the elevator, Cerise scanned her processors for a logical reason as to why the general would be asking to see her at such an hour. The most probable conclusion was her failure to track the suspect identified as Chatine Renard with any success. Cerise had lost her in the crowd during the Red Scar incident yesterday and had been unable to find further traces of her in any surveillance footage since.

But would General Bonnefaçon really be summoning her in the middle of the night to chastise her for a lost lead? That seemed highly irrational, even for a human.

The directeur stepped into the elevator, followed closely behind by Cerise. But to Cerise's unprecedented surprise, her father did not direct the elevator to the floor for the Bureau of Défense as she was expecting. Instead, the elevator deposited them on the ground floor, and the directeur walked straight out of the Ministère headquarters.

The night air, which was controlled by Ledôme's powerful climatization systems, had just the right amount of chill. Not enough to warrant a thick jacket, but enough that the breeze nipped pleasantly at the skin.

As they walked down a paved path, through the illuminated Ministère gates, and along an avenue lined with shadowy cypress trees, it didn't take Cerise long to deduce where they were going. She waited for her father to provide more information, but he was silent. And all she could hear in that silence was disappointment.

Cerise had been programmed with an innate drive to please her superiors. And, because he was the head of the Ministère's Cyborg and Technology Labs, that included her father. But there was something that ran deeper than just her programming when it came to Gustave Chevalier. A determination not only to please but to prove. Despite all of the progress she'd made since her surgery—her job assignment, her title of technicien, her clearance level—there was something in her father's eyes every time he looked at her that still resembled disapproval.

Cerise couldn't remember much about the days leading up to her operation. Her neuroprocessors had catalogued the memories as traitorous and therefore inefficient. But the one thing she did remember—that she knew she'd never be able to *un*remember—was the look in her father's eyes as the médecins wheeled her into the surgery center. It was her last human memory and the only one that seemed to stay vivid and fresh, despite her enhancements.

"Papa," she'd said quietly from the gurney, reaching out a hand for him. "I'm sorry. I'm so sorry."

But he'd said nothing in response. He'd simply torn his weary gaze away from her and looked to the médecin pushing the gurney. "Fix her," he'd said with a gruff, unforgiving tone. "I want a daughter I'm not ashamed to introduce to my friends."

Tears had leaked out of the corners of her eyes as she was pushed through a set of metal doors and her father disappeared behind them. The médecins must have already sedated her by then because the next thing she remembered was drifting to sleep.

And then . . .

"Technicien Chevalier," came her father's deep voice, and Cerise blinked to see they had reached their destination. Glinting under the nighttime TéléSky, hundreds upon hundreds of windows lined every wall of the Grand Palais, dozens of decorative columns held up the immense roof, and above the vast entrance doors, the rearing lions of the Paresse crest glowed through the darkness. "The general has requested you proceed to his private study in the south wing."

"Yes, Direct—" Cerise began to reply, but her father had already turned away and was hurrying up the stone pathway back to the Ministère.

Cerise pushed her shoulders back and continued to the large set of double doors that had just been opened for her by two Palais guards. She'd never been inside the Grand Palais before, but she knew from the blueprints stored in her memory files that the general's study was on the second floor. She ascended the left side of the curving double staircase and walked briskly down the corridor to the south wing, passing titan-framed First World paintings on the wall, decorative vases displayed on sculpted pedestals, vast woven rugs imported from Samsara, and a marble bust of the former Matrone, Veronik Paresse, who was now back with her family on Reichenstat.

When Cerise reached the door of General Bonnefaçon's private study, she knocked quietly and waited.

"Come in," said a voice a moment later, and Cerise entered.

In the midst of the vast, oak-paneled room, General Bonnefaçon sat at a large desk, his TéléCom glowing in front of him. Cerise cast a quick glance around the room, taking in the head of the First World beast affixed to the wall, the framed painting of what appeared to be a blurry nightscape complete with stars the size of Sols, and a Regiments game set up on a table with ornately carved marble pieces standing ready for battle.

Cerise knew the rules of the game, but cyborgs weren't allowed to play against humans because of their unfair advantage. She didn't understand the inclination to play anyway. There were so many other, more worthwhile endeavors with which to make use of one's mental capacities.

"Merci for coming, Technicien Chevalier," said the general. "And apologies for the late-night invitation, but this simply could not wait."

Cerise swallowed and took a step forward. "It is my honor to serve you, General."

"Will that be all, General?"

Cerise startled at the third voice coming from behind her. She spun around to see that the general was not alone in his study. Apparently, she wasn't the only recipient of a late-night invitation.

"Yes, merci, Inspecteur," replied the general. "I will be in touch with any further developments."

Inspecteur Limier bowed his head before stalking toward the door. He stopped only long enough to lock eyes with Cerise for a brief yet tense moment. Cerise felt her circuitry flicker with unease. There was something about the inspecteur that hadn't been quite right since he'd been released from Reprogramming a little over three months ago. The hue of his cybernetic eye was just a tad too orange. The flutter of his circuitry a tad too sluggish. And his posture didn't match the rigid authority that he had been known for in his glory days as Vallonay's prized Policier inspecteur.

There had been much speculation around the Cyborg and Technology Labs on the subject of Inspecteur Limier's return to service. After he'd recovered from a paralyzeur pulse to the head with only some of his memories intact, Directeur Chevalier had advised the general against reinstating the inspecteur to his previous position, suggesting that it was too much responsibility too soon. But the general had ignored the directeur.

And now, here he was. Standing before Cerise in General Bonnefaçon's private study in the middle of the night.

"Good evening, Technicien," Limier said with a curt nod.

"Inspecteur," Cerise returned the greeting before Limier vanished into the hallway and the door sealed shut behind him.

The general swiped off his TéléCom and gestured for Cerise to take a seat. "I was hoping you could assist me with a special project," he said once she'd stiffly lowered herself into the leather chair across from him.

"Of course, sir. I would be honored."

The general nodded but didn't continue straightaway. Cerise's circuitry began to hum with pride and anticipation. She was 94.25 percent certain that this "special project" must be in relation to the recent attack. The Red Scar were the primary suspects behind the murder of the Favorites.

Perhaps, given the severity of the situation, the general was finally going to allow her to track the rebel group.

"This is a highly unique matter," the general continued, pressing his fingertip against a single speck of dust on his desk and then flicking it away. "One that I would prefer be kept in the strictest confidence."

"I am incapable of betraying your confidence, sir."

The general looked up and pinned Cerise with a long, probing stare, as though he was searching for signs of weakness. Of deceit. He would not find any, as she was also incapable of both.

"Right. Exactly," he said before pushing his chair back and standing up. "Which is why I chose *you* for this assignment. You might be one of the younger techniciens in the Bureau, but you are certainly one of the most capable."

"I appreciate the compliment, sir."

"And thanks to your surgery, I assume that any remnants of your former"—the general paused, his eyelashes fluttering slightly—"*behavior problems* are a thing of the past."

Cerise was grateful her body had been built to hide most physical reactions, but she could still feel her circuitry humming more rapidly in an attempt to distill the familiar and unwelcome sensation of shame that was spreading through her.

"Yes, sir," she replied. "As you know, even though I can't remember most of them, I have been made fully aware of my unfavorable actions in the past, and I assure you, they are no longer a threat to my loyalty. Not only am I incapable of betraying the laws of the Regime, but I no longer want to."

"Good," said the general. "But there is one more reason I chose you for this project."

Cerise straightened in her chair. "Yes?"

He yanked open a drawer and rifled around inside until he scooped up a small object, which he kept concealed in his large hand. "I need a hacker."

Cerise's eyes snapped up from the mysterious object. "A hacker, sir?"

"You were once the best, were you not?"

"I . . ." Cerise's neuroprocessors failed her. She truly did not know how to respond. She had been told that it was her hacking abilities that had allowed Marcellus Bonnefaçon to infiltrate the Ascension banquet three months ago, but that was precisely the behavior problem the general had just referred to.

General Bonnefaçon raised an eyebrow, encouraging her to finish her half-formed response.

"I . . . presume that I was, indeed, extremely qualified in the field of illegal technology manipulation."

The general gave a snort of laughter. "You cyborgs never can make a quick point, can you?"

Cerise only blinked back at him, failing to understand the mechanics of what was clearly a joke.

"You managed to hack into my security system and sneak my grandson onto the Palais grounds. I assume that kind of talent does not just *vanish* because of a few enhancements made to your brain."

Cerise's circuitry burned red-hot. She commanded her neuroprocessors to stabilize her body temperature. "I . . . ," she began, once again, floundering for the right words. "I have never tested that theory."

The general nodded, looking satisfied. "Well, let's test it now." He opened his hand and deposited the small object onto the desk. It landed with an almost imperceptible clank. Cerise trained her cybernetic eye on the petite, glinting box, taking in its finely wrought titan and its delicate engraving. Just like the Paresse lions had glowed over the Palais doors earlier, the same lions—although a thousand times smaller—now twinkled up at Cerise from the box's tiny lid.

"What is it?" she asked.

"It belonged to the Patriarche. I found it in his rooms after the funeral." The general gingerly lifted the lid of the box and Cerise peered inside to see, nestled on a bed of soft, purple velvet, two interwoven strands of hair—one a vibrant auburn, the other a rich dark brown. She still didn't understand.

"This contains vital information." The general dug his fingers inside and lifted up the swatch of velvet fabric to reveal what Cerise immediately identified as a microcam. It was a much older model, however, one that had been decommissioned years ago. "About a girl named Madeline Villette."

The name swept through Cerise's mind, her neuroprocessors desperate to link it to a memory, a profile, an image, a face, something.

But she came up blank. Was this another memory her brain had chosen to block?

"I don't know a Madeline Villette," she replied flatly. "Should I?"

"No," the general said. "Actually, no one knows her. She's been living in hiding for the past seventeen years. But late last night, I received word that she's"—he paused again, his tongue clucking against the roof of his mouth—"no longer in hiding."

"Is she connected to the Red Scar?" Cerise asked, still clinging to her previous conjecture of why she was summoned here.

"No," the general replied. "She's even more important than the Red Scar."

"And the information on that microcam?"

"I believe it might be proof of her true identity."

Cerise suspected she still did not have all the necessary information to make sense of this situation. Her mind was struggling to link facts together that seemed to be missing integral connections.

"What is her true identity?"

The general waved his hand in front of his face, resembling a hothouse worker trying to shoo away a bothersome fruit fly. "That's not really important right now. What *is* important, however, is that we gain access to the information on this microcam. Unfortunately, it's protected with an advanced encryption. One that I assume the former Patriarche hired someone to develop."

"A technicien?" Cerise asked. If a cyborg had encrypted the data, certainly there would be a log of the encryption key in one of the Ministère's archives.

The general pursed his lips. "Probably not. Given that my usual decryption software was unable to crack it, I would imagine this is the work of a skilled hacker." He leaned forward, resting his hands on his desk as he held Cerise's gaze. She could almost see her orange cybernetic eye reflected in his clear hazel ones. "And that, Technicien Chevalier, is why I need you."

- PART 2 -
THE HEIR

They weaved across and through, down and deep, snaking under the fabriques, the Frets, and the fields. In their dank chambers once ran the waste of the city. But amid the dark hollows and twisting bends, criminals hid and thrived. Secret messages wound their way. And in the gloomy shadows, rebels connected and conspired.

Until finally these old sewers were sealed off.

In hope that mutiny and defiance would never flow there again.

From *The Chronicles of Laterre*,
Volume 12, Chapter 46

CHAPTER 15

MARCELLUS

MARCELLUS PACED THE HALLWAY OUTSIDE THE INFIR-merie, wearing tread marks in the Refuge's bedrock floors.

She's back.

The thought had been rumbling around in his brain for the past two days, and it still didn't seem real. Even though Alouette Taureau was now just a few mètres away, right behind this closed door, he couldn't bring himself to believe it was true. She still felt lost on that island.

Marcellus reached the end of the corridor and turned back, kneading his hands restlessly.

It *had* been an island. He'd been right. He'd been so close and yet still so far away. Months of reading and researching and scouring endless reports and hand-drawn maps, and now it was all over. He'd begged to go with Laurel on the rescue mission, but the sisters had insisted that he stay. That he was too emotionally invested to be of any use. Which was probably true. He hadn't taken a single deep breath since they'd received that message from the Vangarde cell in Coquille. And every time Marcellus thought about how he'd first ignored it—how after everything he'd done to find her, he hadn't even paid attention when she'd called right out to him—he felt sick to his stomach.

What if they'd been too late?

The door opened and Marcellus jolted to a stop, standing up so straight he suddenly felt like he was an officer back under his grandfather's watchful command. "How is—"

"Better," Sister Laurel said, closing the door behind her. "Much better. She had a nasty infection on the back of her neck—probably from some kind of device . . ." Marcellus flinched and Laurel, thankfully, changed course. "The point is, she's going to be fine."

"Can I see her yet?"

"Soon," Laurel said kindly. "She's still sleeping. They all are."

Marcellus blew out a breath. They'd all been rushed to the infirmerie the moment they burst through the Refuge's back door two days ago, and Marcellus had barely caught more than a glimpse of Alouette's face. He'd been dying to see her, touch her, know that she was real. That this wasn't just a cruel dream that he'd be forced to wake up from.

"There's nothing you can do for her in there," Laurel said, clearly reading the torment playing out on his face. "She just needs to rest now."

Laurel gave his hand a squeeze and slipped back into the infirmerie. Marcellus resumed his pacing. Up and down. Up and down.

She's back, he told himself again.

Why, then, did he still feel so anxious and fidgety? He'd had a million fantasies about this moment, and in each one, he felt nothing but elation, exuberance, triumph. But that's not at all what he felt now.

He just felt . . .

Paralyzed.

Helpless.

Because even though she was back, he knew she still wasn't safe.

The thought was enough to snap Marcellus into action. He turned on his heel and stalked down the hallway to the dining room, where the rest of the Refuge was gathered for dinner.

Laurel was right. There was nothing he could do for Alouette *here*, but he could do something to keep her safe out there.

"Take me with you tonight," he said, stopping in front of Citizen Rousseau's chair.

The quiet sounds of spoons clanking against the bowls fell still, and all eyes turned toward Marcellus. He could feel the inquisitive stares of Roche and the sisters, and the dagger-like stare of Chatine burning a hole in the side of his face. But the only eyes he cared about right now were Rousseau's. They shone back at him, bright and silver and frustratingly inscrutable.

"Please," he added, his voice cracking ever so slightly. "I can be an asset to the mission."

After Jolras had agreed to the meeting on behalf of the Red Scar, there had been a great discussion about who would go. It had ended swiftly and resolutely when Citizen Rousseau had insisted that *she* be the one to talk to Maximilienne Epernay. Marcellus hadn't even considered the option that he might go too. Until now. Until Alouette had walked through that door.

"Marcellus," Francine said from the head of the table. "It has already been decided that Sister Noëlle shall accompany Rousseau tonight."

"I know," Marcellus said, nodding respectfully to Francine before turning back to Rousseau. "But you said so yourself, Jolras trusts me. I'm the one who set the meeting. He'll be expecting to see me there. And if we're going to convince Max to stop the violence, we'll need Jolras on our side."

The sisters exchanged cryptic looks and quiet murmurs across the table. Marcellus held his breath as the memory of those bloody red *X*s carved into the faces of the Favorites shuddered through his mind. Those were mere *cousins* of the Patriarche. Imagine what Max would do when she discovered he had a *daughter*.

"Very well," said Francine, speaking for the group. "But I suggest you start preparing now."

Something warm flooded through him. It wasn't relief, exactly. It was more frenetic and feverish than that. But it still eased the clutch in Marcellus's chest just a little.

"Merci," he said hurriedly to the sisters before turning and darting from the room.

Flinging open his bedroom door, he headed straight to the closet cut into the back wall. He pushed aside the old valise that was stored on the top shelf and pulled down his above-ground coat.

This room used to be Hugo's, Alouette's adoptive father, and Marcellus had always found something comforting about this small space he'd once occupied. Maybe it was the uncluttered orderliness, the bare walls, the single chair, and the unadorned lamp beside the narrow bed. Or maybe it was the fact that Marcellus felt a special kinship to Hugo Taureau now. They were both wanted men, with a desperate yearning to protect the same girl.

"Don't do this."

The voice cut through his thoughts like a knife. He turned to see Chatine standing in the doorway, an almost sickly expression on her face. How long had she been there?

"You don't have to do this," she implored. "You don't have to be a hero, Marcellus."

He snorted. "I'm not doing it to be a hero. We both know Maximilienne has to be stopped."

"The woman is a murderer. She killed the Patriarche. In front of everyone. She delivered three mutilated bodies to the Marsh. She killed my sister in that attack on the TéléSkin fabrique."

"And she'll kill Alouette, too, the moment she finds out who she really is," Marcellus snapped. He could immediately tell it was too harsh, from the way Chatine flinched. She'd been doing that a lot lately. Either he had become angrier, more intimidating, or she had lost some of that Fret-rat nerve she used to have.

Chatine folded her arms across her chest. "And what makes you think *you* are the person who can stop her?"

"Citizen Rousseau thinks we can talk her down and convince her to work with us in leading a peaceful revolution."

"Wake up, Marcellus. Since when do the words 'peaceful' and 'Red Scar' fit together?"

"I'm trusting Rousseau." Marcellus turned back to the closet and snatched a flashlight from the shelf before stuffing it into the pocket of his coat. "If she thinks we can do this, then I have to believe that."

Chatine leaned against the doorjamb. "Did you ever stop to think *why* Max agreed to this meeting? What possible reason would she have for meeting with the Vangarde?"

The question gave Marcellus pause. He'd been so preoccupied with what the Vangarde hoped to get out of the meeting, he honestly hadn't given any thought to why Max had said yes. "Maybe she recognizes that the Vangarde have resources and a strong reputation. Maybe she does want to team up with us."

"Or maybe she just wants to kill you," Chatine fired back. "Slice up your face with a big red *X* and hang you in a meat locker."

His stomach turned again at the memory. "That's . . . unlikely. She seems to be targeting members of the First Estate. Those who would be favored to inherit the Regime."

Which is now Alouette, he thought with another shudder.

Chatine scoffed. "You think she'll stop with the First Estate? Are you forgetting the hothouse superviseurs she branded and then blew up? She despises all of the upper estates, which in her mind still includes *you.*"

Marcellus felt a flush of indignation. "We don't have a choice."

"But why does it have to be *you*?"

Marcellus noticed an uneven stack of shirts on a nearby shelf and began to straighten them. But it immediately reminded him of something his grandfather would do, and he knocked them over with a flip of his hand. "I just told everyone. Because Jolras trusts me. I'm the one he warned about the Patriarche's execution, remember?"

"Or," Chatine challenged with a raise of her eyebrows, "maybe because if you don't go, you won't know what to do with yourself."

Marcellus blinked at her. "What?"

Chatine rolled her eyes. "You think I don't know? You think I can't see? Whether you realized it or not, I've been here the whole time. I watched you disappear into that library for days and days without coming out. Alouette is back now. Which means *you* have nothing to do. Nothing to obsess over. Nothing to stop eating and sleeping for. So now you're putting your life in danger because you're incapable of doing nothing."

Marcellus ran his fingers through his hair, trying to let her words bounce off him. They weren't true. They couldn't be true.

The problem was, Chatine had been seeing right through Marcellus from day one. From the moment they'd first met in that morgue. He'd always been a sheet of thin plastique to her. While she'd always been a solid brick wall to him. It was one of the things that he liked about her. And one of the things that drove him up the wall.

"The sisters wouldn't have agreed to it if they didn't think I was a good choice," Marcellus said dismissively.

Disappointment flashed in Chatine's eyes. "Does Max know Citizen Rousseau is alive?"

Marcellus hesitated. "Not . . . yet. All Max knows is that she's meeting with Vangarde operatives."

"So you're just going to send the most famous rebel in Laterre's history into a den of terrorists?"

"She'll be protected," Marcellus said, but the words brought him no comfort. It was as though Chatine had climbed into his head and was echoing all of his doubts aloud. "We'll have guards with us."

"I still think it's a stupid idea," Chatine muttered.

"If Citizen Rousseau can convince Max—"

"Oh, so she's actually going to talk now, is she?"

Marcellus scowled at her. "What?"

"I keep hearing all of these stories about how persuasive she was. How she turned the planet on its head with just her voice. And yet, I can count the number of words I've heard her say on two hands."

Marcellus swallowed as, once again, Chatine voiced the very fears that were trampling through his mind. Ever since they'd come to live in the Refuge, he'd seen little evidence of the loquacious, effervescent woman who had once been capable of rousing a crowd with just the power of her words. The Citizen Rousseau who now lived under this roof was quiet and withdrawn, like she was constantly lost in her own thoughts.

Maybe her mind was still trapped in that cell back on Bastille.

Maybe the woman she used to be was still trapped there too.

Maybe this mission was destined to fail before it even began.

"What if you get out there," Chatine went on, "and she says . . . *nothing*?"

Someone cleared her throat behind Chatine and they both pivoted toward the doorway, where Principale Francine was standing, her cool gray eyes glaring disapprovingly at Chatine. How much had she heard?

"We need to brief you for the mission," Francine said to Marcellus. "And then, Laurel has agreed to let you see Alouette before you leave."

Marcellus gripped his coat tighter before pushing past Chatine to the hallway. He could sense her watching him the whole time and it made his skin burn.

He glanced back for just a moment and her gaze slammed into his, feeling like a punch in the gut. In her eyes he saw something so rare, he swore he was imagining it.

He saw *her.*

Not the thousands of faces she wore. The kilogrammes of brick she hid behind. But her. The real Chatine Renard.

He hadn't seen anything like it since the night she'd pushed back her hood, uncoiled her long, dark hair, wiped the dirt from her face, and pleaded with him to truly see her.

And now those same eyes were pleading with him again.

Don't go.

Don't do this.

Stay.

But he couldn't say yes. To any of it.

That had always been the way with him and Chatine, hadn't it? It was always no, and never yes. There was always something, someone, standing in the way. His grandfather. The Vangarde. A revolution. He could never be the person she so clearly wanted him to be.

"I have to go," Marcellus said, his throat thick with regret.

He watched Chatine visibly deflate. Then, with heavy, thudding footsteps that felt painfully uncharacteristic for Chatine, she pushed past him, pausing only long enough to lock onto his eyes once more and mutter, "Good luck, Marcellus."

But all he could see in those eyes now was that Sol-damn brick wall.

- CHAPTER 16 -
ALOUETTE

ALOUETTE'S SKIN WAS ON FIRE. HER WHOLE BODY WAS being consumed by flames. She tried to scream, but no sound came out. She tried to pound out the flames, but they only seemed to grow and spread and burn, until everything around her was ablaze. She tried to breathe through it. Just as the sisters had always taught her.

In. Out. In. Out.

But the smoke charred her throat and lungs until she was choking, gasping for air.

"Little Lark," said an achingly familiar voice, and she spotted a figure in a dark, hooded coat making its way toward her. Through the dancing flames, the figure seemed to flicker. As though it were not quite real. Not quite solid.

It drew closer, its lumbering frame moving quickly, desperately, until finally, Alouette could see his face. And she felt every emotion she was capable of bubble up inside her at once. Fear, elation, regret, joy, grief, love, and then . . . *panic.*

"Papa!" she tried to cry out through the smoke. "No! Go back! It's too dangerous."

But Hugo Taureau did not retreat. His warm, determined eyes found hers through the flames and she knew. She knew he would walk straight into this fire. She knew he would let himself burn.

He would die saving her.

Alouette sat up in bed with a jolt. She touched her arms, her neck, her face. Her skin was cold and clammy.

Not burning.

Not on fire.

Not real.

She let out a whimper and collapsed back against the pillow as the dream skittered into the back corners of her mind. She tried to catch her breath. Her bedsheets were tangled and damp with sweat.

"It's okay," said a calming voice. "It was just a nightmare."

Blinking through the dim light, she saw the familiar shapes of the Refuge's infirmerie—the narrow beds with their crisp white sheets, the rows of medical supply cabinets along the walls, the grooves and bumps in the low ceiling—and finally Sister Laurel's kind face hovering over her. Alouette let out a shudder of relief. It seemed like every five seconds her mind forgot. And then, every sixth second, it blissfully remembered again.

The sisters were alive.

The Refuge was not empty. It was full of life and light.

And she was back.

She was safe.

The thick bedrock walls were wrapped around her once again. She was back among the women who'd raised her. And their love radiated off every surface.

"I was burning . . . ," Alouette whispered, fragments of the nightmare coming back to her. "I was on fire."

Laurel pushed the dark, damp curls from Alouette's face and placed a cool hand on her forehead. "That was the fever. It looks like it's finally broken."

"Fever?"

Laurel nodded and walked over to a nearby tray covered with syringes, rolled-up bandages, and a glinting pair of tweezers. She began to organize the contents. "Yes. You came back with quite a nasty wound on the back of your neck. It was horribly infected. Another few days in that place, and I'm certain you would be dead."

Dead. The word echoed in Alouette's mind. *Just like the general wanted.*

She was not dead, though. She had escaped. She had *won.* This battle, at least. But she knew the general too well to believe he would simply give up. There would be more battles to come. More mind games. More of his brilliant tactical maneuvering, Alouette was sure of it. If there was any- thing she'd learned about César Bonnefaçon, it was that he *never* gave up.

"Thank the Sols you were able to escape," Laurel continued. "You'll be okay. The médicaments are working, but you need your rest."

Alouette swallowed. Her throat felt scratchy and sore. Somehow Sister Laurel knew because a moment later, a glass of water materialized in front of her. Alouette drank deeply. As the familiar taste of the Refuge's filtered water ran across her tongue, a thousand safe and happy memories trickled through her mind. Like the water was magic, with the ability to chase away not only her thirst, but the past three months as well.

She wiped her mouth on the sleeve of her fresh, clean nightgown and glanced around the infirmerie, the memory of the other night coming back to her in short, disorienting bursts. She remembered climbing through Prouvaire's basement window, Sister Laurel leading them to an await- ing transporteur. The man behind the contrôleur—what was his name? She couldn't remember—Laurel had said he was another member of the Vangarde. Alouette had pleaded for him to wait. "We can't leave without Prouvaire!" But the painful look on Laurel's face as she gave the final order to depart told Alouette the old man would not be escaping with them.

Then what?

They'd come back here. But not through the entrance. Through a long, dark passageway underground. "The old founders' tunnel," Laurel had explained. The one that Alouette had heard stories about as a child but had never seen, because she'd always been told it was too dangerous. Con- demned, even. As she'd stumbled down the Refuge hallway to the infir- merie, faces had blurred in and out of her vision. She could have sworn one of those faces belonged to Marcellus.

Marcellus?

Why would he be in the Refuge? With the sisters?

And what happened to Jacqui and Denise?

She blinked her surroundings back into focus and felt another rush of relief as her gaze fell to the two beds on the far end of the infirmerie, where she could see the sleeping forms of the sisters.

"How are they?" she asked groggily.

Sister Laurel followed her gaze and smiled. "They're fine. I gave them a strong tincture to help them sleep. Something you should be doing as well."

"And Sister Jacqui?" Alouette asked. "She's going to be okay?"

"Yes. Of course. She's just . . ." Laurel flashed her another smile—this one much too bright to be real. "She just needs time."

"I thought . . ." Alouette tried to rub the bleariness from her eyes and her mind. "I must have been imagining it, but the other night, when we came back, I thought I saw Marcellus."

Laurel chuckled. "You weren't imagining it. He came to us after the Ascension banquet. With Chatine Renard. They've both been living here."

Alouette couldn't contain the smile that took over her entire body. He was alive. They all were. It was more than she could have ever hoped for. More than she'd ever dared allow herself to hope for. "Can I see him?"

Laurel smiled. "Of course. He'll be in soon. For now, you need to rest."

Alouette nestled back against the pillows as Laurel straightened out her sheets and blankets.

"In the meantime, I brought someone else to see you," Laurel said, her voice taking on a singsong quality that reminded Alouette of the bedtime stories Laurel used to tell her when she was little. "Someone who is *very* happy that you're home."

Laurel reached into a small cupboard beside the bed and pulled out a plastique doll in a faded yellow dress. "Katrina!" With a smile, Alouette took the doll from Laurel and turned her around in her hands. "You're . . ." Her brow furrowed as her gaze landed on Katrina's left arm. *"Whole."*

"What?" Laurel reached over Alouette to tuck in the other side of the sheets.

Alouette squeezed the plastique arm through the sleeve of the doll's dress.

"She has two . . ." But Alouette's voice trailed off as she caught sight of something shiny dangling from Laurel's neck. She reached out and caught the metal tag between her fingers, reading the engraving etched into the side.

Sister Laurel.

"I thought all of your devotion beads went offline," she whispered.

Laurel glanced down at the tag. "They did. Most of us still wear them anyway."

Alouette shook her head. "I'm still so confused. Happy, but confused. Marcellus swore your ship was shot down on Bastille. And then the beads went offline. I was so convinced you were all gone."

Laurel lowered herself onto the edge of the bed. "I know. And I'm so sorry you had to experience that kind of loss, Little Lark. It was not our intention to deceive you. That was an unfortunate consequence of a highly necessary measure. When Jacqui and Denise were captured, we had to take drastic steps to cover our tracks. The network that these beads were connected to was shut down permanently. We had to make it look like we were dead, but we also had to make sure our devices couldn't be traced back to us. Sister Marguerite has been instrumental in setting up a new communication network for us, one that we're confident the Ministère can't track. But it's extremely limited, based on an old First World technology. That's why when you arrived in Coquille, Prouvaire wasn't able to send a message to us directly. He had to deliver it to someone who could get close enough to one of our antennae. And even then . . ." Tears began to leak from her eyes again. "We almost missed it. We were distracted by . . ." She glanced down at Alouette's concerned expression and seemed to change her mind about whatever she was going to say. "You know what? It doesn't matter. You're here. You're safe." She tucked Katrina under the covers with Alouette and gave the doll an affectionate pat. "You're all safe. For the first time in more than seventeen years, the sisterhood is complete."

Complete.

Up until a few months ago, she hadn't known that the sisterhood had been *in*complete. She hadn't known that one of them had been rotting away on Bastille for almost two decades. That every day the sisters had gathered in their Assemblée room, there was a person missing. That every time they'd sat down at that dining room table, there was a vacant seat.

"You're talking about Citizen Rousseau," Alouette said numbly, feeling the weight of that name bear down on her like the weight of a planet.

"Yes."

"She survived."

"Yes," Laurel said again, and Alouette could not ignore the light that seemed to radiate from the sister's face. It reminded Alouette of the day she'd first heard that name. When she'd learned the truth about the sisters. Principale Francine had told her about Citizen Rousseau and their plan to break her out of Bastille. Her face had lit up then too.

There was something about this woman that inspired the sisters. That lifted their hopes and their hearts. Alouette could feel it in the air now.

But she could not feel it in her own heart.

She could only feel that same twist of resentment.

"Citizen Rousseau is our top priority," Francine had said to Alouette that day. *"Jacqui and Denise understood the risks when they agreed to the mission."*

That woman was the reason Jacqui and Denise had been captured, imprisoned, tortured. That woman was the reason the Vangarde hadn't been able to devote more resources to rescuing them. That woman had stolen the light from Sister Jacqui's eyes and her voice from the world.

And she was the reason Alouette had believed everyone in this Refuge was dead.

"Do they . . . ," Alouette began uncertainly. "Does the Ministère know she's back?"

"No one knows," Laurel said, kneading her hands as if this question made her uncomfortable. "Not yet, anyway. As far as the Ministère is concerned, we're all dead. Rousseau has had a long road to recovery. It has not been easy. But she is ready. Our moment is finally here."

At these words, Alouette felt a shiver of something work its way down her spine. She couldn't quite identify what it was, though. Excitement? Fear? Lingering anger at being kept in the dark for so long?

Ever since she'd unlocked the Forteresse with her DNA and shut down the Skins, ever since she'd solved Denise's riddle—*When the Lark flies home, the Regime will fall*—she'd wondered what role the Vangarde had imagined for her. Why had they offered her and Hugo refuge here? What had they been planning all of these years?

Now she would finally know the whole truth. She would finally hear the words the sisters had kept from her for thirteen long, dark years.

"Who am I?" Alouette asked in a voice so steady it surprised even herself.

Laurel blinked, like she'd misheard the question. "You're the Lark. The little bird that sings so brightly, bringing hope for a new morning. A new dawn."

"Yes, but what does that mean?" Alouette demanded. "Who am I to *you*? To all of you? To *her*? Who did you raise me to be?"

Laurel smiled knowingly. "Of course you have questions. But you're still in a very fragile state and I don't want to overwhelm you. I think it best that we wait until you feel well enough to—"

"No," Alouette said forcefully. "I feel well enough now. I'm done waiting. I've waited thirteen years. Tell me now. Who am I?"

Laurel's shoulders sagged in resignation. She angled her body toward Alouette but for a long moment didn't look at her. Then, as she sighed, her dark brown eyes flickered upward and latched on to Alouette. "You are a symbol."

Alouette's brow crinkled. "A symbol? Of what?"

"Of what this planet could be. You were born with Paresse blood, but you are no different than anyone else. You have been raised outside the Palais walls, and you have been brought up to be kind and nurturing and respectful of *all* life. You are proof that the estates are a construct, an illusion. That the will of the Sols is not for anyone to be placed above anyone else. That the corrupt and cruel Regime of the past is not the way of the future. That there is hope for change. Hope for a new way. A better way."

Alouette blinked back the tears that were forming in her eyes. Laurel's words had stirred something deep inside of her. Something that had already started to blossom and grow, ever since she'd descended that elevator from the top of the Paresse Tower, ever since she'd discovered that she was the daughter of the Patriarche.

It was the feeling of purpose.

For three long months, though, that feeling had fallen dormant. It had wisped away to almost nothing. But now, it was waking up again, chasing away every other emotion, until all she could feel was a beautiful resolve breathing through her like oxygen. Like life.

"I want to join you," Alouette said, sitting up straighter in her bed. "I am ready. What is the plan? When do we start? What do I do?"

Laurel let out a tinkle of laughter that sounded just the slightest bit forced. "Never you mind that right now. I told you, you need to rest."

"And I told you, I'm fine. I want to help."

Ignoring her, Laurel pulled the covers up to Alouette's chin. "How about something to help you sleep?"

"Tell me what's happening!" Alouette demanded, losing her patience. "Prouvaire said that the Patriarche is dead and the contingency clause of the Order of the Sols has been invoked. He said the System Alliance will be appointing a new leader soon. That means we have to move quickly, right?"

Laurel reached for Katrina, who had been lost under the covers, and tucked her back under Alouette's arm. "The only thing you have to do right now is rest."

"Stop telling me to rest!" Alouette shouted, tossing the doll aside. "I'm not a child. I don't need protecting from the truth anymore. You have to stop coddling me and start trusting me. What is the Vangarde's plan?"

Laurel closed her eyes and took a deep breath, as though summoning strength from another place. A far-off place. When she opened her eyes again, she looked pained, almost distraught. "Our plan was to reveal you both. Together. Side by side. Citizen Rousseau, the Vangarde's long-lost leader, and Madeline . . . *Paresse*. We thought that if the people saw you— the rightful heir—standing up for a different life, standing up for their freedom, they would come to our side. They would protest with us and demand change with us. We thought that, with you as the symbol of unity, we could bring about a revolution. *Peacefully*. But . . ."

Her voice trailed off and suddenly, she wouldn't meet Alouette's eyes.

"But what?"

The sister stood and started to rearrange the instruments on her tray again, and for a long time all Alouette could hear was the soft clink of metal on metal.

"Laurel," Alouette said, her throat constricting, her skin tingling. "You said the plan *was*."

Laurel dropped the tweezers she was holding onto the tray. And that's when Alouette could see that the sister's hands were trembling. "Things have changed."

A coldness seeped into Alouette's skin. "Changed how?"

This time, when Laurel didn't answer, Alouette pushed back the covers and stood up. Her legs were still wobbly, and her mind was still woozy from the médicaments, but she walked to Laurel and rested a hand on her arm. "What happened?"

The sister flinched at Alouette's touch and lowered herself down onto one of the empty beds. "It's the Red Scar," she whispered.

Alouette felt a thump behind her rib cage at the mention of that name, and all the horrific memories that came with it.

A blue laser aimed at Cerise's left wrist.

A hothouse vaporized.

A single boot left in the mud.

"What did they do?" Alouette asked.

"They were the ones who killed the Patriarche," Laurel said. "And now they've murdered three of his relatives as well. We don't know how they did it, how they even got close to them. They've proven to be more dangerous than we originally thought, and we have reason to believe their numbers have grown significantly."

Lowering herself onto the bed next to Laurel, Alouette began to shiver. She was suddenly chilled to the bone. "Why did they kill them?" she asked, even though she was certain she already knew. It was written all over Sister Laurel's face.

Laurel grabbed for Alouette's hand and squeezed it. In that one, simple gesture, Alouette could feel a thousand promises being made. Each equally reassuring and crushing at the same time.

We promise to keep you safe.

We promise to keep you hidden if that's what it takes.

We promise to protect you.

"Because of their blood. Their *Paresse* blood."

CHAPTER 17

MARCELLUS

"SHE'S STILL WEAK. TRY NOT TO UPSET HER."

Laurel pushed open the door of the infirmerie and gestured for Marcellus to enter. As he stepped inside, his entire body was buzzing with nerves. Even though he'd prepared himself for the worst, what he saw was like a punch to the gut. Tucked in the corner of the room, Alouette was sitting up in bed, her eyes fixed on something in the distance. Her face was gaunt, marred with deep shadows and bruises. Beneath her cotton nightgown, her body was frail, starved, and he wondered if she was even able to stand.

But all of that seemed to vanish the moment her eyes blinked and focused on him.

"Marcellus!" She was out of her bed in an instant, running to him, colliding with him. He grunted from the impact, surprised by its strength, and stumbled backward before righting himself with a chuckle.

"I missed you," she whispered as she embraced him tightly, much tighter than he would have thought her capable of.

He tried to squeeze her back, but his arms suddenly felt weak, hesitant. "I missed you, too."

She must have heard the wrongness in his voice, because she pulled back and examined his face with those round, inquisitive dark eyes of hers. "Are you okay?"

He nodded. "I'm fine." But once again, the words came out stiff. Distant. Like they were coming from too far away. A parallel universe where words had no meaning.

She collapsed against him again, burrowing her face in his chest. "I wasn't sure I'd ever see you again."

"I know. I . . ." He stopped, frustrated by his lack of poise. His lack of everything. "I never . . . I mean, I hoped . . ."

Alouette drew back again, this time with creases between her brows. "What's the matter?"

Marcellus dropped his gaze to the floor, unable to look into that penetrating stare any longer. Because the truth was, he didn't know. Maybe it was the upcoming meeting with the Red Scar weighing on his mind, maybe it was the deep shadows under her eyes, but this wasn't the reunion he'd imagined for so many sleepless nights as he'd sat in that library, poring over maps and settlers' journals. This wasn't the conversation of two friends coming back together, at least not from his side. He felt more like he was meeting her for the first time. It was the same sensation he'd had on the voyageur to Albion, the last time he'd been alone with her. When they'd stood in the flight bridge and looked out at the endless sea of stars. He'd wanted so badly to feel the same connection he'd felt with her at the fireside in the Forest Verdure. And in the hallway of Fret 7 the first time they met.

But he hadn't.

It had felt like they were starting over from square one. And now, frustratingly, it felt like they were doing it again. Even though Marcellus was standing less than a mètre away from her, there was still a gap between them as wide as the Secana Sea that had separated them for months.

"You should sit down," Marcellus said, guiding Alouette back to her bed and pulling closed the thin curtain around it. He could still hear the quiet sleeping breaths of Jacqui and Denise on the other side of the infirmerie, but the curtain provided some privacy.

Still, Marcellus struggled to think of what to say next. He reached into his pocket. "I . . . um . . . kept these. For you. In case you . . . you know . . ."

Alouette let out a tiny gasp as Marcellus withdrew the long string of metallic beads. He held them up so the low light of the infirmerie bounced off the metal tag, causing the engraving of her name—Little Lark—to shimmer.

"How did you—"

"Laurel found them," Marcellus rushed to explain as he sat down on the bed next to her. "Near the Paresse Tower. Where you . . ." Once again, his voice trailed off. He felt like a faulty cruiseur engine that kept starting and dying over and over again.

"Merci," Alouette whispered, placing the beads around her neck. The metal tag settled against her chest with a small *clink*. And then, there was that silence again. That distance that seemed to shove them apart even when they were finally so close together.

"So," Marcellus said, desperate to fill it with something. Anything. "You're the Patriarche's daughter." He said it with a chuckle, aiming for a light joke, but immediately, he realized it was the wrong thing to say. A flame seemed to extinguish inside Alouette as her entire body sank under the weight of his words.

"Yes. But it doesn't really change anything, does it?"

Marcellus nearly choked. "Are you kidding? It changes everything!"

"I mean," she said quietly, almost self-consciously, "it doesn't change anything between us?"

Marcellus ran his fingers anxiously through his hair. He wanted so badly to tell her that it didn't. To assure her that nothing had changed. But he knew that was a lie. He could feel it from the moment he'd walked into this room.

"I . . . ," Marcellus said. "I don't know. But I think it does."

More silence descended between them, and Marcellus feared this would be it. For the rest of their lives, this silence would define them. Follow them. Be ready and waiting to drag them back whenever they crept too far away from it.

"Let's pretend that it doesn't," Marcellus blurted, once again desperate to fill the empty space. Desperate to cling to the version of this moment that had lived in his mind for so long.

Alouette's eyebrows knit together. "What?"

"For just a second. Let's pretend that it doesn't change anything. That you're just you, Alouette, and I'm just me, Marcellus."

"Okay." A smile quirked the corners of her mouth. It was adorable. And it immediately set his mind at ease.

"Let's pretend you've just come back from being away for three months," Marcellus said, the energy in his voice building. "But not in a top-secret facility run by a power-hungry monster. Just a regular trip."

Alouette's smile widened. "Where was I?"

"You can decide."

"Samsara," she said instantly. "I've always wanted to see those beaches I read about in the Chronicles."

Marcellus nodded, his own smile growing. "Yes. I can see the Sol-light has done wonders for your complexion."

Alouette giggled. "And now what?"

He bit his lip, thinking. The numbness inside of him had been replaced with a nervous flutter. The good kind of flutter. "And now, um, you're back and we're very happy to see each other." He paused and then rushed to add, "I mean, because you've been away for so long. Enjoying the beaches of Samsara without me." He pulled his face into a mock frown that caused Alouette to laugh. Bright and full.

It was a beautiful sound.

"Okay," Alouette said. "And what do we do?"

Marcellus cleared his throat, the flutter intensifying. "Well, what do friends do when they greet each other after a long time?"

"They hug. Which we already did."

Marcellus nodded one too many times. "Yes. Right. I guess they do. . . ." His voice trailed off and he fidgeted with the hem of the blanket on her bed. "Or they could, um, do something else."

Alouette fell silent again and he was terrified he'd said the wrong thing. Pushed the game too far.

But then, in a tiny voice, she whispered, "You mean, like kiss?"

All the thoughts in Marcellus's mind evaporated at once. "Y-y-yes," he said hurriedly, afraid if he didn't get the word out fast enough, his engine would stall again, and he'd never be able to say it.

Alouette ran her fingertips over the metal tag hanging from her beads. "Right. Yes. I suppose they *could* do that. If they were really good friends."

"Or more than friends?"

"Or more than friends," Alouette agreed, meeting his gaze with her own clear, confident one.

"Maybe they don't quite know what they are," Marcellus said, feeling the truth of his words thrum through him. "And that's why it's been hard for them. Because they've never really had a chance to figure it out."

"Right. Yes. Maybe."

"But maybe," Marcellus went on, feeling himself pick up steam, feeling the chasm between them shrink with each passing second, "they *need* to figure it out. Because it's been weighing on them for too long. And maybe this is the only way they can do that."

"Right," Alouette said again. "That makes sense."

"Doesn't it?" Marcellus asked, relieved.

"So, they just need to do it. So they can see."

"Exactly."

"Okay."

"Okay?" Marcellus's eyebrows rose.

Alouette nodded, the smile still playing at her lips. "Yes. Okay."

"Okay," Marcellus said again before scooting closer to her on the bed. He nervously fidgeted with his hands, unsure where to put them. "Right. So I'm going to, um . . . yeah."

Marcellus leaned forward. Alouette met him in the middle. His arms wrapped loosely around her back. Her eyes closed. And, as his lips touched hers, Marcellus felt his eyelids flutter shut.

He could feel the closeness of her. He could smell the scent of the Refuge's homemade laundry soap on her nightgown. He could hear the clock on the wall of the room ticking far too slowly. Like time was dragging this moment on forever.

He pressed his lips harder against hers and she reciprocated. Leaning deeper into him, but it just felt like they were trying to knock each other over with their lips. Marcellus let out a soft moan, but it was boorish and forced.

And also, apparently, *hilarious*.

Alouette broke into giggles and pulled away, leaving Marcellus to stare at the top of her head as she dropped her gaze and covered her mouth with her hands.

"Sorry," she offered, still refusing to look at him. "It's just that was—"

The door of the infirmerie creaked open and a moment later, the curtain swished to the side, revealing Sister Laurel standing there with a tray of food. "It's time." She cast a pointed look at Marcellus before setting the tray down next to Alouette's bed.

"Right." Marcellus leapt to his feet. Despite how eager he'd been to see Alouette, he suddenly felt anxious to get out of this room.

"Time for what?" Alouette looked suspiciously between Marcellus and Laurel.

Marcellus opened his mouth to respond but, after another sharp look from Laurel, remembered her earlier warning. A meeting with the very people who wanted Alouette dead was sure to upset her. "Time for you to get some more rest," he said, trying to make his voice sound breezy. But between the lingering uncertainty of that kiss and his terrible acting skills, he doubted he was very convincing. "I'll come visit you again soon."

He prayed this was the truth. He prayed Chatine was wrong and Max wouldn't put a rayonette pulse in his head the moment she laid eyes on him.

"Okay." Alouette would only meet his eye for a moment before looking away again.

Marcellus pulled the door of the infirmerie closed behind him and rested his head against the wall, trying to arrange his thoughts. What had just happened in there? He couldn't even begin to sort it out. But whatever it was, it had only made things feel more uncomfortable between them. Which was the opposite of what he'd been trying to do.

He turned back and reached for the door handle, determined to set things right. Or at least, *talk* about what had happened. But he was interrupted by urgent footsteps padding down the hallway. When he looked up, Sister Noëlle was moving toward him, her gray tunic swishing around her ankles. For one horrifying second, he thought she was coming to tell him that the sisters had changed their minds. That he would not be accompanying Citizen Rousseau to meet with the Red Scar. But instead, she peered up at him with a grim expression, worry deepening her already-lined face, and said, "You realize that this mission is more important than ever now, right?"

Thoughts of kisses and Alouette's averted gaze instantly vanished from his mind. "I do."

"Remember, Maximilienne preys on fear. She preys on anger. You can't afford to lose your cool out there."

A tidal wave of emotions rushed through him, but somehow, he managed to swallow them all down. "I know."

Noëlle closed her eyes, as though summoning strength. When she opened them again, there was a fierce determination burning, the likes of which Marcellus had never seen from the even-tempered sister. "Good. Alouette is safe now. You've done your part to bring her back. But in order to *keep* her safe, you can no longer rely on your desperation or your frustration or your anger. The only thing that can protect her now are your words. Use them."

- CHAPTER 18 -
CHATINE

CHATINE HAD READ THE SAME LINE SEVEN TIMES, AND it still didn't make any sense to her.

The . . . Sys . . . tem Di . . . Di . . . vine off . . . er . . . ed hope. Hope to the in . . . in . . . hab . . . i . . . tants of a dy . . . dying wo . . . rld.

The words wouldn't connect in her mind. They were too long, too complicated. By the time she finished sounding one out, she'd forgotten how it started. And the letters kept rearranging themselves on the page, like rebellious children who refused to stand in a straight line. Why couldn't these Chronicles be written normally? Simple words in a simple order. The way people spoke. This just sounded like gibberish to her.

Anxiously, she glanced up at the clock on the wall. Only two minutes had passed since the last time she'd checked. She dropped her gaze back to the open page. The first chapter of Volume 1 of the sisters' Chronicles stared unflinchingly back, like it was challenging her to give up. Technically, it wasn't even the first chapter. It was the third. The first two chapters had been lost to time, vanished somewhere in the 150 years since the founding sister Bethany had written them. Sometimes Chatine found herself wishing the other chapters would vanish as well. Just so she wouldn't have to feel this crushing sense of defeat every time she looked at them.

She was beginning to give up hope that she'd ever get a handle on this Forgotten Word stuff. Maybe there was a reason the whole thing had been forgotten. Because it was stupid and pointless. Why write something down when you can just say it?

With a huff, she shut the cover of the heavy book and leaned back in her chair. She'd thought that practicing her reading might help her pass the time, but it only seemed to make it drag by slower. Marcellus and Rousseau hadn't even been gone a full hour, and already she felt like she couldn't breathe.

Peering around the empty library, Chatine spotted Marcellus's desk in the back corner, where his research was still scattered chaotically across the surface. Piles of papers and open books and half-rolled maps. Months and months of time and effort searching for Alouette.

What would he obsess over now that she was back? What would he lose sleep and weight over if he had no missing heir to search for?

That is, *if* he returned from this mission.

Chatine quickly scolded herself for the thought. Sister Noëlle always said to think positive. It was a foreign concept to Chatine: expecting the best when the Sols had always given her the worst.

Not always, a voice inside her head reminded her, and she felt her anxiety simmer. The voice was right. The Sols had brought back Henri, and she would never stop being grateful for that.

Chatine scooted her chair back and stood up, anxious to move. But as she paced around the shelves of the library, wringing her hands, she longed to be doing *more*. She longed to be up there with Marcellus, trying to talk sense into the Red Scar. Or roaming around the planet, erecting antennae for the Vangarde's new network. Or even delivering messages like Roche used to do in the Frets. She knew it was all dangerous work. She knew it could land her back on Bastille, like that old man, Prouvaire, who had helped Alouette and the sisters in Coquille. But even that had to be better than being cooped up here.

She'd never felt more useless in her life.

But what else was she supposed to do? She wasn't the Patriarche's long-lost heir, or the general's grandson. She could barely even read the language of the Vangarde. She was a Fret rat and a former thief. Maybe the sisters had gotten it right sticking her in the kitchen. What other place was there for her?

Eventually, just as she knew she would, she found herself standing in front of Marcellus's cluttered desk, staring down at the scattering of books and documents. One by one, she pushed them all aside, until the small device buried underneath was visible.

She picked up the old First World radio and, as she brushed her thumb over the clunky red button on the side, the memories showered down on her like pounding rain. Memories that she'd tried to keep penned in, locked out. But they just kept coming all the same.

Brigitte walking her through a graveyard of stones.

Little Astra proudly connecting a newly built chalet to its power source.

Etienne placing a radio just like this one into her hand.

"Radio me when you change your mind and want me to come get you."

If she'd allowed her heart to make the decision, she would have pushed this button days ago, when she'd first found this radio buried beneath the rubble of Marcellus's obsession. She would have called Etienne and told him she'd changed her mind. *Please come get me.*

Which was exactly why her heart wasn't allowed to make decisions.

Because it always chose wrong.

Her gaze fell to the hand-drawn map pushed off to the side of the wooden table, and she recognized it as the one Marcellus had been scouring in hopes of finding a missing island and a missing heir. Her fingertip traced around the edges of the landmass, over rugged coastlines and steep inlets, until finally crossing over to the small, jagged peaks of the frozen tundra that separated Laterre's east and west coasts. A long trail of handwritten letters stretched across it. Letters that should be familiar after all the hours of studying she'd done in this very room.

She squinted, forcing her vision to focus, as she sounded them out, one by one, just as the sisters had taught her to do. "T-t-err-ain. Per-du."

The no-man's-land that had briefly felt like home. That had felt like a place she could actually belong in. But now that place seemed more lost to her than ever.

Anger and longing swirled together in her stomach, creating a danger-ous concoction that no good could ever come out of.

"Etienne made his choice," she muttered to herself, shoving the map away with the tip of her finger. "And I made mine."

And, as she took one last look around the empty library, filled with books she couldn't understand, information she didn't know how to use, and the stacks of paper that had consumed Marcellus's every waking hour, she told herself, for what felt like the five hundred thousandth time, that it was the right choice.

CHAPTER 19

ETIENNE

ETIENNE COULDN'T IMAGINE ANYTHING WORSE THAN not being able to fly. The camp-wide ban on flights had hit him harder than the other pilotes. Flying was his life. His heart. His escape from thoughts of *her*.

But when his community had decided to ground all the ships after the announcement of the Patriarche's execution, it had felt like Etienne's head was the one under that blade.

"Primary stabilizeurs look good. Power converteur converting properly. Zyttrium processors operational." Etienne closed the maintenance panel on the side of Marilyn's hull and gave it a quick buff with the rag hanging from his belt loop. He took a step back, admiring the shine on her sleek, silvery surface. "How do you get more beautiful every day? It's uncanny, really."

The ship seemed to shimmy in response and Etienne smiled, even though he knew it was just a trick of the light.

Probably.

It had been three months of this quarantine. He wouldn't be surprised if Marilyn sprouted legs and walked right out of this hangar.

Etienne sighed, dabbed his rag with a few drops of the camp's homemade emberweed oil, and rubbed it into the side of the left cooling duct. "I know, baby. I hate it too. We'll be out of here soon, though. I can feel it. Any day now those gridders will figure out what the fric they're doing, choose their stupid new leader, and everything will go back to normal. We just have to wait a little longer."

The lockdown had been hard on the whole camp. Not just because their zyttrium stores were depleting by the day. It took a lot of it to keep the camp concealed from the rest of the planet, and no flights meant no missions to replenish the stock. But ever since it had been decided that there was to be no outside communication until the Regime was stable again, the community had been lingering in a state of unease and uncertainty. As much as they prided themselves on living off the grid, unaffected by the Regime's laws and rulers, they still needed the rest of the planet to function, in order for the camp to function. In other words, they needed there to be a grid so that they could live safely off it.

Now it just felt like they were all waiting for something to happen. Waiting for someone to take control. Etienne knew very little about Laterrian politics. All he knew was that the Patriarche was dead, leaving behind no heir, and now the gridders were without a permanent leader. But if all that was required to lead the planet was Paresse DNA, surely they could rustle up a cousin or aunt or half brother who could do the job.

Surely, it didn't take *three* whole months to decide who was going to lead a bunch of gridders.

That's why Etienne preferred the way things were done around here. When something important needed to be decided on, the whole community assembled together in the lodge and didn't leave until a decision had been reached that everyone found acceptable.

Although it had taken Etienne the longest of any of them to accept *this* particular decision. Even though, deep down in his gut, he knew it was the safest choice—the best way to protect the community—he still itched to be up in that sky. Just him, Marilyn, and the endless gray clouds. Where he could empty his mind of everything. Thoughts. Memories. Reminders of *her*.

Being in this hangar was the next best thing. He often came out here at night when the rest of the camp was asleep. It was the best time and place to be alone.

"Let's check on that thruster again, shall we?"

Etienne lowered himself down on his mechanic's roller and slid beneath the small ship, immediately feeling comforted by her shadow. Holding a flashlight between his teeth, he prodded gingerly at the side of the main thruster with the tip of his finger. "Seems to be holding." He gave the underbelly of the ship an affectionate pat. "You're healing nicely, baby."

The accident had happened shortly after she left. Etienne hadn't been able to contain his anger, and his maman had suggested he take a flight, to clear his head and gain some perspective.

She'd been right, of course. She was always right about things like that. But then, as he'd been coming in for landing, he'd caught sight of a piece of blue prison uniform stuck to the jump seat and he'd lost it all over again. The landing had been rough. He'd nicked the edge of the thruster against the side of an ice patch, causing the whole part to crack. And, despite his relentless efforts to repair it, it wasn't the same as it used to be. He still blamed *her* for the injury.

"I know," Etienne cooed to the ship as he buffed the thruster's soldered scar. "She hurt you. I'm sorry. We won't let her in ever again. I promise."

It was the same vow he'd made to himself every single night for the past three months. Every single night since he'd watched her board a transporteur with that shiny-haired gridder and vanish from his life forever.

It was her choice, he reminded himself. *She made hers and I made mine.*

And for what felt like the five hundred thousandth time, he told himself that it was the right one.

"That's it! They're goners. They have to be. It's the only explanation." A whiny voice echoed through the hangar, crashing into Etienne's thoughts.

With a sigh, he slumped against his roller as a pair of barely visible feet danced anxiously across the floor. *So much for being alone.*

"Bonjour, Gabriel," Etienne muttered, searching for something on the underside of the ship to busy himself with. Did this generateur look wobbly? Etienne was certain it looked a little wobbly. He would have to tighten that.

"Why else wouldn't they come back for me?" Gabriel asked. Etienne could tell from the way his voice traveled that he was circling the hangar. "Why else would they leave me here in the middle of this frozen wasteland?"

"It's not a frozen wasteland," Etienne murmured under his breath. "It's our home."

"What?" Gabriel called out from the back of the ship. "Where are you, anyway?"

Ignoring the question, Etienne fit his screwdriver into the bolt holding the generateur and began to twist. It was pointless to hope that if he was just quiet long enough, Gabriel would eventually give up and disappear. Because if there was one thing he'd learned about Gabriel Courfey over the past three months, it was that he never *ever* disappeared.

Nor did he give up.

"It's just that I'm going out of my mind with this radio silence," Gabriel ranted, his feet still shuffling around the perimeter of the hangar. "I can't eat! I can't sleep! What if they're trying to get in touch with me? What if they're trying to contact me and I'm not answering? What if they think *I'm* dead? Ah! There you are."

Gabriel's head suddenly appeared beneath the ship, causing Etienne to flinch. Gabriel dropped down onto his belly and scooted in next to Etienne, tilting his head at an awkward angle to peer up at the generateur. "What are you doing, mec? You're going to strip that bolt."

Etienne's hand fell still. It was only now he realized how aggressively he'd been twisting his screwdriver. Over and over and over.

He dropped the tool and slid out from under the ship. "I'm just having some *alone* time with Marilyn." He'd hoped his emphasis on the word "alone" would be enough of a clue for Gabriel, but of course it was not.

"The main thruster is looking good," Gabriel called out. "Healing nicely."

"Thanks," Etienne said, wiping his hands on his rag.

"You can barely even tell you broke it over a girl." Gabriel snickered and Etienne felt his fists clench.

He *would* have been able to keep his promise to himself and forget she ever existed . . . if it weren't for Gabriel.

"But seriously, mec." Gabriel scrabbled ungracefully out from under the ship. "Aren't you worried about her? Aren't you worried she might be dead too?"

The ground shifted slightly beneath Etienne's feet. He grabbed on to a storage locker for balance. He wished Gabriel would stop using the word "dead."

"If there's one thing I've learned, it's that she can take care of herself."

"Her name is *Chatine*," Gabriel said in a voice that felt like he was a child curiously prodding an open wound.

"I know what her name is."

"Really? Because you never say it, I'd just assumed you forgot."

"I didn't forget."

He could never forget.

"Good," Gabriel said, snatching up a cartridge of emberweed oil from a nearby shelf and twirling it in his hands, "because Brigitte says trying to forget things that aren't ready to be forgotten is like swallowing a drop of poison every single day and hoping it won't kill you."

Etienne rolled his eyes. That sounded *exactly* like something his maman would say. But for some reason, hearing it from Gabriel—his mother's newest disciple—made it less helpful and more just . . . *annoying*. He grabbed the cartridge from Gabriel and set it back down on the shelf. "Don't play with that. It's highly flammable."

"Brigitte also said that if you want to fight your own internal monsters, you can't hide from them. You have to face them every day. Which is why I started a scrapbook."

Etienne abruptly spun around. "A what?"

"It was your maman's idea. I find things that remind me of Cerise, and I glue them to pieces of paper to create a book." He paused to scrutinize Etienne's reaction. "It's a First World object that—"

"I know what a book is," Etienne snapped.

Gabriel threw up his hands in surrender. "Okay. You just looked a little confused for a moment there. Anyway, Perseus and Astra are helping. They let me borrow some of their craft supplies. Yesterday, I found this piece of black fabric that looked just like the fabric of her cute, little beret, and I—"

"Wait a minute," Etienne said skeptically. "Is this the same beret that you were ranting about just last week? The one with the diamonds? You said it was—and I quote—'another representation of her overprivileged, sparkle-headed life.'"

"I know!" Gabriel reached out to slap Etienne playfully against the chest with the back of his hand, and Etienne fought the urge to punch him. "This is what I'm talking about. Your maman is a genius. Last week, just the thought of that beret sent me into a spiral of rage, and now . . ." He breathed in deeply and let out a long, slow exhale. "I feel okay about it. I even *miss* it."

Etienne scoffed. "A hat? You miss a hat?"

"It's a *beret*."

"Okay."

"Anyway, my point is, you gotta face up to these things. You gotta fight these monsters head-on or they'll destroy you."

"Right." Etienne reached into his toolbox and pulled out a pair of pliers, which he waved in Gabriel's face. "I'll get right on that."

Gabriel fell silent. Etienne walked over to the cooling module on Marilyn's side and popped open the panel before systematically checking the integrity of each wire.

"So, is this what you do all night when everyone is asleep? Spend time with a ship?"

Etienne supposed it was too much to hope for that Gabriel's silence would last more than a minute. He almost liked it better when he was recovering from his cluster bullet wound. At least then, he'd been sedated.

"Yes." Etienne closed the panel and opened the adjacent one. He grabbed a fresh rag from his back pocket and began to wipe down the power cells inside.

"Do you really think that's the best use of your time?"

"Marilyn needs me," Etienne replied dismissively. "Plus, I have to keep up with her maintenance, so she'll be ready the minute the flight ban is lifted."

"And then what?" Gabriel asked. "Where will you go?"

Wherever the fric I want, Etienne thought, but instead replied, "Wherever the community wants me to go. Probably on a mission to replenish the zyttrium stores."

"Ooh, titanique. Can I help? I'm really good at stealing stuff. I could be your first mate or whatever. We could be a team! People would call us the Blue Bandits. You know, because zyttrium is bl—"

"I work alone," Etienne quickly replied. "And besides, aren't you itching to get out of this 'frozen wasteland'? As soon as the flight ban is lifted, I could take you anywhere you want to go."

And leave you there.

"Right," Gabriel said, sounding slightly disappointed. "Yeah, sure. I've got lots of places I could go. I mean, like *tons*."

"Good," Etienne said as he closed the panel.

"Good," Gabriel repeated, but his face was twisted up like he was bracing for a crash. "Uh-oh. It's happening again."

Etienne shot him a skeptical look. "What's happening?"

"I'm having those *feelings* your maman talks about. You know, it's kind of panicky, like your heart is racing but you feel sluggish and maybe a little nauseous. Definitely the monster. I think I should talk this through. Get it out in the open."

Etienne felt a flash of the same panicky feeling come over him. "Right. Yes, you should definitely wake up my maman and talk to her about—"

"It's probably my abandonment issues." Gabriel hopped up onto a nearby workbench and leaned back on his hands. "My parents died when I was young, and I was on my own for a long time, living off whatever I could steal. Ever since then, I've been very sensitive about people trying to get rid of me. And now every day that they don't come back for me, I start to wonder if—"

"Stop!" The word escaped from Etienne before he could catch it. But now that it was out, a hundred more tumbled after it. "Just stop. They're *not* coming back for you. You need to let it go. You need to just accept the fact that they're gone. Maybe they *are* dead. Or maybe they've just forgotten about you. About *all* of us. Which means we should forget about them."

Gabriel fell quiet again, and Etienne immediately felt a rush of remorse. He could see the hurt registering on Gabriel's face already. He shouldn't have done that. He should have kept his frustration locked inside. Or at least waited until Gabriel was gone and taken it out on another bolt screw.

But then, Gabriel's expression shifted ever so slightly, and he leapt off the workbench and walked over to rest a hand on Etienne's shoulder. "I know you miss her, mec."

"What?" Etienne blinked. How did this become about him? "No, I don't. I—"

"I never met the girl, but I can tell from the look in your eyes that she was something special. And that's hard."

Etienne ground his teeth together. "I told you, I don't—"

But he never got the chance to finish. Because the door to the hangar slammed open, and Etienne heard the scuffle of urgent footsteps. He hurried around the back of the ship, nearly colliding with his mother.

"Maman?" Etienne asked, taking her in. She looked shaken. Her braided hair sprang out from a hastily made bun, and her eyes burned with an alarming black intensity. Even the scars on her forehead and cheek, from where her cyborg circuitry had long ago been removed, seemed deeper, angrier, and more distressed. "What are you doing up? What's wrong?"

Brigitte fought to catch her breath. "There's been a break-in."

"What?" Etienne felt the air leave his lungs.

Gabriel sidled up next to him, his body rigid. "Here? In the camp?"

Brigitte nodded and tried to speak, but her voice was drowned out by a tiny sob.

"Maman," Etienne said quietly but forcefully. He couldn't take the anticipation any longer. It was squeezing his chest. "What happened?"

"They've taken it." She finally got the words out, but Etienne immediately wished she had held them in, swallowed them down, kept them locked away forever. "They've taken it *all*."

CHAPTER 20

MARCELLUS

THE RAYONETTE STRAPPED TO MARCELLUS'S BELT FELT heavy and clunky. With every step he took down the craggy, dimly lit tunnel that led out of the Refuge, he could feel it clanking against his hip. Did he really used to carry one of these things around with him all the time?

When Principale Francine had cranked on the round handle of the Assemblée room's tall metal cabinet and the shelves of books had winched backward to reveal a dark chamber behind it, Marcellus had lost the ability to breathe. For a rebel group that claimed to want to bring about a peaceful rebellion, they sure had a lot of weapons stashed away.

"For protection," Francine had said in response to his reaction, before plucking one of the familiar shiny rayonettes from its hook and guiding it into Marcellus's hand. "Yours and hers."

Marcellus glanced at the woman walking silently beside him, hunched slightly to avoid the low, rough ceiling above. Under the dull yellow glow of the emergency lights that dotted the old founders' tunnel, Rousseau's silvery eyes glinted like frozen rocks in the Terrain Perdu.

She had said nothing since they'd left the Refuge. None of them had.

They were a synchronized unit of silent, swishing cloaks.

Two armed Vangarde operatives kept pace with Marcellus and Rousseau, one in front and one behind. Six more would meet them at the end of the tunnel, making a total of ten Vangarde representatives. That had been the arrangement. Ten from each side.

No more. No less.

The Vangarde had kept their end of the bargain. He just prayed Max would as well.

The passageway narrowed up ahead, and they had to crouch down and pass through single file. As Marcellus ducked under the low archway, he held his breath and instinctively rested his hand on his rayonette, like it could possibly protect them from being crushed to death. The unstable bedrock walls, lined with multicolored wires and the Vangarde's tiny surveillance cams, seemed to rain down dust and debris with every step he took through the narrow crevice. Marcellus could now understand why this tunnel hadn't been used for hundreds of years. It felt like it was one wrong footstep away from collapsing around them.

Finally, the passageway widened again, as did Marcellus's lungs. He couldn't gauge how far they'd walked. The Refuge already felt kilomètres away. He thought about what was waiting for them on the other end. Another army. Most likely armed as well. He shivered and, unable to stand the silence any longer, blurted out, "What happens when we get there?"

Rousseau answered his question with a silent raise of her brow.

"I mean, do we have a plan or anything? For convincing Max to join us? What do we say?"

"We don't say anything," replied Rousseau.

Marcellus's stomach swooped. "Nothing?"

"First, we listen. It's impossible to know what to say until we do."

"Right." He nodded like he was following. "So, that's what you were doing the other day? When the sisters voted on whether or not to stop searching for Alouette. You said nothing. Because you were listening?"

"Yes . . . ," Rousseau replied easily, but there was an unfinished quality about the word, as though it were a trail she wanted Marcellus to follow.

"The decision came down to you, but you never got a chance to vote. What would you have said?"

A small, knowing smile flickered across her face. "It doesn't much matter now, does it?"

Marcellus felt a twinge of frustration. He could not let this go. He had to believe that Citizen Rousseau was on his side. On *Alouette's* side. "I know it doesn't. Because she's back. But you couldn't have possibly known that she would come back. So at the time, you must have had an opinion. You must have been ready to vote yes or no."

"Nothing is that black and white, Marcellus. Nothing is just yes or no. There is always another way. A *third* way. A variable that hasn't yet been considered."

Rousseau fell quiet again as the tunnel curved and fanned out slightly. Marcellus had the sinking suspicion she wasn't going to continue. She was just going to slip back into one of those deep, contemplative silences he so often found her in.

But then, in an almost wistful tone, she said, "I spent a long time on Bastille. A long time with nothing to keep me company but my own thoughts and my own regrets. And I soon realized that regret is a wasted emotion. It works under the assumption that another outcome could have been achieved, if we'd just fixated hard enough on it."

Marcellus's brow furrowed as he struggled to unpack her words. It was like she was speaking in riddles. Puzzles that needed to be flipped around, examined from multiple angles until the true meaning became clear. If the true meaning *ever* became clear.

But he was tired and hungry and drained. He had no brain power left for puzzles. "What does that mean?"

"It means there is no what could have been. There is only what is."

The words sank deep into his subconscious as his mind conjured up all sorts of disturbing images. He didn't like the "what is" any better than he liked the "what could have been."

The "what is" was his grandfather cleaning up the Frets, playing the hero, turning the people to his side.

The "what is" was a violent rebel group determined to kill anyone with a single drop of Paresse blood in their veins, unknowingly playing right into the general's greedy hands.

The "what is" was that Alouette still wasn't safe.

"The exit is just up ahead," Rousseau announced, pulling Marcellus from his spiraling thoughts. The last few emergency lights shone through the darkness, revealing a round metal hatch embedded in the rough bedrock wall, identical to the one that led out of the Refuge. Its thick handle and circle of hexagonal bolts glinted in the half-light.

Marcellus reached for it but was held back by the operative in front. "Wait. We need to make sure it's clear." She approached the door and gave three firm knocks on the surface—two close together, the third coming after a long moment of silence. They waited. Seconds passed that felt like hours. Until finally, eight tinny beeps echoed from an electronic lock on the other side and the hatch wheezed open.

The smell hit Marcellus instantly, strong and painful and foul, like the stench of the old Frets before the cleanups. The operative crouched down and stepped through the opening, disappearing into the darkness.

"Come on," she called back, and with shaky hands, Marcellus pulled himself through.

They were met on the other side by six more operatives, dressed in woolen coats and sturdy boots. In the bobbing glow of their flashlights, Marcellus caught sight of a familiar face in their midst and gaped in surprise.

"Grantaire?"

The young man gave a sheepish shrug in return. "Hello again, Officer."

"What are you doing here?"

"I joined up a month ago. The Montfer cell recruited me shortly after I snuck you and your friends into Ledôme."

"*And* onto a voyageur in Montfer," Marcellus reminded him, shivering at the memory.

"The ice box. How could I forget?" A smile quirked at the corner of Grantaire's mouth. "I told you I would work to earn your trust. Maybe tonight will be the night."

Marcellus started to say more, but one of the operatives waved for them to keep moving. "This way."

Marcellus kept pace behind two of them, his boots splashing through the remnants of filthy water. The old sewage chamber was cold and damp, but much wider and taller than the hand-built founders' tunnel. Darker, too. Marcellus pulled his flashlight from his coat pocket and switched it on. As he moved the beam around, taking in the rusting walls, the flitting shadows of rats scurrying out of the way, and the small puddles at his feet, he was grateful this archaic sewer system was no longer operational.

"How are you?" Grantaire asked, falling into step beside him. "When I didn't hear anything from you after the Ascension banquet, I assumed the worst."

Marcellus nodded. "It didn't go quite the way we'd planned." He glanced up at the sewer ceiling, as though he could see all the way to the Grand Palais and the malicious man still sleeping within its walls. "I've been in hiding ever since."

"And the others? That were with you?"

Marcellus swallowed. He knew Grantaire wasn't asking about the fate of Gabriel or Chatine or even Alouette. He was asking about the one fate Marcellus didn't know. "I'm sorry. We haven't heard from Cerise."

Grantaire nodded like he'd been hoping this wasn't the answer but expecting it all the same. "Me neither. For a moment I thought she'd . . ." His voice trailed off. "Well, it's probably not true."

"What's not true?" Marcellus asked.

Grantaire looked down at the beam of his flashlight bobbing across the floor and sucked in a sharp breath. "After I didn't hear from any of you for a while, I searched for her in the Communiqué and her profile said she was now a technicien. In the Bureau of Défense."

"A technicien?" Marcellus's stomach twisted. "But techniciens are . . ."

"Cyborgs, I know." He chuckled. "Can you imagine? Cerise Chevalier? A cyborg?"

Marcellus shook his head. He could not even begin to imagine that.

"That's why I convinced myself it couldn't be true. It's probably just one of her hacks. Knowing Cerise, she's cooking up some kind of plot. That girl has kept me on my toes from the moment I first met her."

"Yeah," Marcellus agreed uneasily. "Me too."

The procession slowed to a stop, and Marcellus shone his flashlight up ahead to see they had reached a PermaSteel ladder bolted to the side of the old sewage chamber. He peered upward where the ladder disappeared into the gloom, and spotted the faintest of glows: three dull slits of light in the darkness. The exit point.

Grantaire and one of the other operatives led the way up and Marcellus followed. The pressure in his chest as he ascended from the depths of the sewage chamber felt a lot like accelerating into hypervoyage. Except this sensation was not the result of traveling at light-blurring speeds—it was the result of his heart rioting in his chest, staging a formal protest for what they were about to do. *Whom* they were about to face.

At the top of the ladder, a heavy grate had been pushed aside, and Marcellus heaved himself out into the shadowy depths of a large, circular room. He'd never exited the Refuge this way before, but he knew from Principale Francine's pre-mission briefing that they were inside a decommissioned grain silo in the outer ferme-lands of Vallonay. The very same grain silo the sisters had used to sneak Citizen Rousseau back into the Refuge after they'd broken her out of Bastille. In the glow of his flashlight, Marcellus could make out the murky shapes of broken machinery, rusting tools, and an old, abandoned moto lying on its side in the corner.

Outside, a light drizzle fell from the sky, and a breeze kicked and blustered around them. Night had descended and the darkness made even the most innocuous of shadows feel ominous. Marcellus pulled up his hood as he and Citizen Rousseau followed the operatives into a vast field stretching endlessly into the distance. Thousands upon thousands of towering plants stood guard all around them, like a great battalion of droids. Their overgrown and tangled leaves slapped at Marcellus's face and snagged at his clothes like tiny claws.

Wheat-fleur, he thought, recognizing the long stems and blade-like leaves of the genetically enhanced hybrid crop. The plant had been designed by Ministère cyborgs to thrive in Laterre's rainy climate. It had been harvested and ground up to make bread for the poor. The Third Estate called it "chou bread."

But now that the general had made *real* flour available to everyone, the crop had been abandoned. Left to grow, uninhibited and unharvested. Each plant now loomed taller than Marcellus.

Headlights broke through the blanket of dark clouds above, and one of the guards ordered everyone down. Marcellus hit the ground, shivering, as the blustering wind howled, and tiny raindrops nipped at his skin. The distant vehicle—a cruiseur from the looks of it—seemed to be traveling straight toward them. Marcellus held his breath, certain the mission was over before it had even begun.

But then, the headlights veered left, back in the direction of the silo, and everyone dusted themselves off and rose to their feet. The encounter, however, had left them all jumpy. As they trudged through the maze of crops, loud cracking noises jabbed the air, causing Marcellus to flinch and the guards to draw their weapons.

"Stay behind me," Grantaire told Marcellus and Rousseau, his fingertip primed against the trigger of his rayonette, as though expecting an ambush at any moment. From the Red Scar or the Ministère, Marcellus couldn't be sure. And, at this point, he honestly didn't know which one he feared more.

Marcellus reached for his own rayonette and tugged it from the holster. The weapon felt awkward in his hand. The last time he'd held one had been the night of the Ascension banquet, when he'd flicked the toggle to lethal mode and pointed the barrel straight at his grandfather's chest.

And then chosen *not* to pull the trigger.

Now, more than ever, he wondered if that had been the right decision. What would the planet look like if he had simply fired? If the general had died that day, the way he was supposed to.

Maybe Rousseau was right and there *was* no use in obsessing over the past if you couldn't change it. If it was set in PermaSteel and not even the strength of a droid could bend it. But, as they stole through the shadows of the towering crops, toward an awaiting army of red-hooded terrorists, Marcellus knew, without a doubt, that if faced with the same choice tonight, he would not hesitate again. He would pull the trigger.

CHAPTER 21

CERISE

"DEVICE ENCRYPTED. CONTENTS UNVIEWABLE."

Cerise glared down at her TéléCom and swiped her fingertip across the screen, dismissing the alert. It was the tenth one she'd received in the past hour. The brute-force attack she was waging on the contents of the Patriarche's old microcam was proving ineffective. The general had granted her access to the Ministère's most powerful processors to help with the task, and still, she couldn't view anything that was stored on the device. Whatever hacker had encrypted it had done too good of a job. Even for Cerise.

She lifted her gaze and focused on the darkened scenery streaming past the window of her cruiseur. The sleek silver craft cut through the starless night, speeding over seemingly infinite fields of ferme-land. In the darkened plastique, Cerise caught sight of her own reflection. The circuitry embedded in the left side of her face was twinkling with frustration.

The general would not be pleased if she couldn't decrypt the contents of that microcam. Since handing it over to her two nights ago, he'd already AirLinked her seven times to check on her progress. And each time she'd had to tell him that she was still working on it, her cortisone levels had skyrocketed.

Failure had a straining effect on a cyborg's neuroprocessors. It was difficult *not* to obsess over it. Cerise knew this from the popular case study of Inspecteur Limier, whose obsession over an escaped ex-convict had almost gotten him killed, before eventually landing him in Reprogramming.

"Arrival at destination in two minutes," the cruiseur reported.

Cerise leaned back in her seat and ordered herself to focus on the current task. There was nothing more she could do about the microcam except wait for the decryption processors to do their job. And, rationally, she knew that could take days. Until then, she still had another assignment to focus on. Her original assignment: locating Marcellus Bonnefaçon.

That assignment, she at least had made *some* progress on.

"Navigational display," she commanded the cruiseur, and a moment later, a vast hologram map spread out before her. Her gaze zeroed in on the solitary orange line that was overlaid across the landscape of Laterre, leading from the Marsh all the way out into an abandoned wheat-fleur field.

Three days ago, she'd lost her only lead on Marcellus Bonnefaçon when she'd lost track of the girl named Chatine Renard. None of her previous searches of the surveillance footage from the Marsh had resulted in any matches. But fortunately, just this morning, Cerise had realized her mistake. She'd been searching for all the wrong criteria. Chatine Renard, as a single variable, was too nondescript, her clothing too plain and her face always shielded by a hood, making it impossible for the facial recognition scanners installed in the hologram units to make a positive identification.

However, what Cerise had failed to notice at first was that Chatine Renard was not alone when she came into the Marsh three days ago. After going back to study the footage again, Cerise had identified a second hooded figure walking close enough to Chatine for Cerise to postulate with reasonable certainty that they were traveling together.

This discovery had opened up a whole new set of search algorithms.

When Cerise had queried the archived surveillance footage for *two* people dressed in dark hooded coats, both with a small, wiry build, walking roughly a mètre apart, the search had revealed two figures leaving the range of the surveillance cams, traveling southeast on a single trajectory.

This trajectory.

"Arrival at destination in one minute," reported the cruiseur.

Cerise released a breath and closed her eyes. She didn't enjoy riding in cruiseurs. She disliked how fast the landscape blurred by. It was too many sensory inputs coming at her at once and it overloaded her circuitry, making her dizzy.

She couldn't believe there used to be a time when she would ride in a cruiseur for *fun*.

Minutes later, Cerise felt a pull in her stomach as the vehicle slowed and the door yawned open. She scooped up her TéléCom and stepped out into the drizzling darkness, anticipation humming like tiny fireflies through her circuitry. The moment she glanced at her surroundings, however, the humming stopped, and her mouth fell into a subtle frown.

There was *nothing* out here for kilomètres but open fields. Her triangulation program had marked this as a possible destination along Chatine Renard's trajectory, but unless the girl had burrowed under the soil like a rodent, this couldn't be right.

Cerise unfolded her TéléCom and pulled up the map. Deftly maneuvering her fingers across the screen, she zoomed in on the path she had just followed, until a shadowy shape began to appear at the end of it.

She peered out at the darkened ferme-lands again, trying to identify the object that should have been right in front of her. "Nocturnal mode," she commanded. A second later, her cybernetic eye blinked twice and everything around her brightened, as if the Sols themselves were shining down on this very spot.

And that's when Cerise saw it. Through the drizzle and the gloom, she could make out the crooked shape of an old silo sitting slumped in the mud.

Curiosity tickled at her neuroprocessors. She double-tapped on the identical object on her screen. "Requesting location marker."

The TéléCom was silent as it pinged the request across the AirLink network back to the central Communiqué database before returning the result less than a second later. "Grain silo. Decommissioned in 462."

"Reason for decommissioning?" she asked the TéléCom.

"Reason unknown."

Cerise's internal processors began to spark with suspicion. While humans had to rely on fickle intuition to make decisions, cyborgs were given flawless deduction capabilities. Their processors meticulously logged and stored past experiences and knowledge to provide a stunningly accurate assessment of any situation. And a decommissioned grain silo that was not logged in the Communiqué was definitely a situation that warranted further investigation.

She turned her focus back to the silo's shadowy profile. Although still perfectly round, the abandoned building now sagged into the ground. A decrepit ladder with missing rungs clung to one side, and through the gloom, Cerise could make out an old drainage pipe jutting precariously from its pointed roof. Her cybernetic eye focused in on it, sensing the slightest traces of heat radiating off the metal.

And then, a strange, high-pitched squealing sound tore through her right ear, making it feel like someone was scraping at her eardrum.

Her processors sparked again. She was *definitely* on the right track.

After deactivating her nocturnal mode, Cerise darted inside the cruiseur and rifled around in one of the many compartments until she found the small kit she'd borrowed from the Ministère's Bureau of Innovation. Inside was a single contact lens, which she affixed over her cybernetic eye, and a swatch of synthetic flesh, a product her father had been developing for undercover operations. It was still a prototype, but when Cerise pressed the patch to the left side of her face, it fused to her skin flawlessly. She nearly started at her reflection in the cruiseur window. With two brown eyes and her circuitry no longer visible, she looked so different. So *human*.

She didn't like it. She looked too much like *her*. The traitorous girl who had disappointed her father and betrayed her entire planet. But she had no choice. She couldn't risk being spotted from the glow of her enhancements.

After checking to make sure her disguise was secure, she swiped at her TéléCom to extinguish the exterior and interior lights of the cruiseur, shrouding herself and the surrounding landscape in a black cloak. Then, she pulled the rayonette from the pocket of her cargo pants and stepped carefully and quietly out of the cruiseur.

As best she could, Cerise kept to the narrow aisles between the crops. The towering wheat-fleur plants provided optimal concealment, but their overgrown state made it hard to pass through. She felt a burst of frustration every time her black boots crunched on a mess of dried leaves or her stiff gray cargo pants scraped noisily against a snarl of giant stems.

Slowly, she approached the silo and pressed herself against the rusting metal wall, listening for voices inside. She was expecting to hear *something*: soft murmurings, even the quiet breath of sleep. If this was where Marcellus Bonnefaçon had been hiding for months, surely there would be a sign of life inside.

But she heard nothing.

Cerise pushed herself from the wall and crept around the silo until she located a weather-beaten door, which squeaked and crunched as she pulled it open and slipped inside. The stress chemical began to filter through her blood again, bringing with it that uneasy feeling of panic. She could not be wrong about this. She had to have *something* to bring to the general. If not the contents of the Patriarche's microcam, then at least this.

But it was clear from a single glance that the interior was just as dead and abandoned as the structure itself. There wasn't any indication that a fugitive had been living here, hiding here, or doing anything here, for that matter. Not a single sign of life or movement.

Except for that.

Cerise's gaze suddenly snagged on a small indentation in the dirt, toward the back of the silo. With the contact lens obstructing her enhanced vision, she'd almost missed it. She crept closer, her brain processing the shape of the marking at superhuman speed.

Footprint.

Correction: footprint*s*.

There were several clustered together, all different sizes and varying shapes. She counted at least seven distinct patterns. Cerise lined up her own black boot next to one of the prints and pressed. Then, she bent down and compared the shapes. The edges were nearly identical. Sharp and defined and . . .

Recent.

With a steady flicker of confidence, she followed the prints through a maze of rusting machinery, old tools, and an abandoned moto collecting cobwebs until the footprints stopped at the edge of a corroded metal grate cut into the ground.

Drainage, Cerise identified, quickly downloading Vallonay's utility grid and overlaying it across her vision. Now, when she looked down at the ground, she could see a complicated network of abandoned sewage pipes fanning out below her feet.

Was that where he was hiding?

But the footprints had been leading *away* from this part of the silo.

Cerise backtracked, following the indentations in the dirt until she was outside again, surrounded by darkness and the soft rustle of wind through the crops. She pulled out the contact lens and scanned the horizon, her cybernetic eye taking in every detail, every subtle shift, until she saw exactly what she was looking for.

Far in the distance, in another vast field of abandoned wheat-fleur, the tall, entangled plants snapped and wavered. The movement was far too strong to be a gust of wind or the skittering of a rodent.

As she charged up the rickety ladder attached to the side of the silo, Cerise reactivated her nocturnal mode and focused on the field, where she could now see a cluster of moving figures. She zoomed in and her facial recognition scanners made the identification almost instantly.

Marcellus Bonnefaçon. Wanted fugitive. Highly dangerous.

Adrenaline chugged swiftly and determinedly through Cerise's bloodstream. She jumped down from the ladder and was about to run in the direction of the field when something pulled her up short. A warning signal pinging through her processors.

Cerise had been enhanced with basic tactical skills, just like all cyborgs. But unlike an inspecteur tasked with policing the streets of a city or town, she did not have any advanced field skills. Which meant she was not the most qualified Ministère representative to capture a wanted, highly dangerous criminal. The task was out of her jurisdiction.

With a flush of irritation, she reluctantly pulled out her TéléCom and initiated the AirLink. "This is Technicien Cerise Chevalier from the Bureau of Défense," she whispered. "I am requesting assistance in the apprehension of a top-priority fugitive. Prepare for transmission of coordinates."

- CHAPTER 22 -
MARCELLUS

MARCELLUS COUNTED TEN OF THEM. ALL DRESSED IN their signature red. The color of blood and death and mourning. Maximilienne stood in the middle of the small clearing, next to her brother, Jolras, as the drizzling rain whipped and swirled around them. Her hood was thrown back, her arms hanging loose and relaxed at her sides while those fierce gray eyes blazed out across the field.

Marcellus hadn't forgotten those eyes. They haunted him while he slept. And now, with the memory of those three bodies hanging from hooks like slabs of meat, they haunted him while he was awake, too.

"Do the Sols deceive me," Max said as Marcellus and Citizen Rousseau stepped into the clearing, flanked by their eight operatives, "or am I actually in the presence of the infamous Vangarde?"

Marcellus looked to Rousseau. Her face was still shielded by her hood, which snapped and buffeted in the sodden wind. She gave a small nod and they continued forward, across the uneven mud, the slippery puddles, and the windblown leaves from the abandoned wheat-fleur crops nearby.

"When my brother told me you wanted a meeting, I thought it was a joke. The Vangarde are dead, I told him. Gone. Vanished. *Poof.*" Max made a small explosive gesture with her fingers, and as she did so, Marcellus noticed a strange series of red slashes on the backs of her hands. They looked permanent, deeply scored into her skin like . . .

Scars.

"And yet here you are," Max continued, sharing a sneer with her brother. "Or what's left of you. I can't imagine it's *much*."

Marcellus opened his mouth to tell her she was wrong. The Vangarde were stronger than ever, building their numbers in secret, ready to make their next move. But he felt Citizen Rousseau's hand rest on his, gently urging him to stay quiet. Apparently, they were still *listening*.

"I'm honored, really," Max went on. "That you wanted to meet with me and my humble little group. After all, you're the all-powerful Vangarde. I was only eleven when you failed at your last rebellion, but I grew up being taught to fear your name and rue the day you would return." She let out a small chuckle that set Marcellus's nerves on edge.

This woman was mocking them. Mocking the greatest rebel group in Laterre's history. Mocking the cause his father gave his life to.

"*Have* you returned?" Max asked, cocking an eyebrow. "Is the Vangarde making a grand comeback?" She clapped her hands together. "How delightful."

Marcellus heard another soft crunch. His gaze flicked to the left and that's when he saw it. Through the drizzling gloom. Like pinpricks of blood sprinkling the tall husks that surrounded them. More red.

More of *them*.

Max had broken their agreement. She'd brought far more than nine people with her. Around him, Marcellus could feel the Vangarde operatives stiffen. He glanced at Citizen Rousseau, who must have seen it too, but her face was as calm and peaceful as ever.

Maybe after a lifetime in solitary confinement on Bastille, nothing scares you anymore. Even an encroaching army of bloodthirsty terrorists.

"Are you going to speak or are we just going to smile at each other from across an abandoned field?" Max asked, and once again, Marcellus looked to Rousseau. But still, her expression remained unreadable. And her lips remained sealed.

"Marcellus Bonnefaçon."

He shivered at the sound of his name on Max's lips.

"My brother told me you had joined the Vangarde."

Marcellus cut his gaze to the man standing directly to Max's left, but Jolras wouldn't meet his eye.

"I'm not surprised, given who your father was," Max continued. "A Second Estater. Who killed a lot of people. Innocent Third Estaters who were mining copper for *your* decadent lifestyle."

"My father—" Marcellus snapped.

"Was taking a stand, I know," Max said, raising her hand to stop him. "I admire someone who takes a stand. Despite what the Regime told us, I never believed Julien Bonnefaçon acted on behalf of the Vangarde. The Vangarde were too weak and too soft to pull off a feat as big as the bombing of an entire copper exploit. I always figured he went rogue."

"You're wrong," Marcellus said with a familiar rage simmering inside of him. "My father was framed. It was the general and Patriarche Claude who orchestrated that bombing."

At that, Max let out a throaty laugh. "Now, that makes much more sense. But you see, that is exactly why the Vangarde's last rebellion failed. They were never a viable enemy for the Regime. They were too weak. Too hesitant to do any real damage. The Regime will never hesitate to push a button and destroy our lives. They'll never hesitate to murder. Which is why we must not hesitate either."

"The Vangarde weren't hesitant!" Marcellus fired back. Sister Noëlle's warning to him flashed briefly through his mind—*"You can't afford to lose your cool"*—but he couldn't help himself. "And they weren't weak. They were trying to bring about change peacefully. Just as they are now."

Max snorted. "Because it worked so well the last time?"

Marcellus clenched his fists at his sides, reminding himself to breathe.

"You see," Max said, pointing at his balled-up hands, "you're angry, Marcellus. You have every right to be angry! Your grandfather is a monster. He raised you to be a monster too. But you've broken free and now you're trying to tamp down that anger. I see it. You're trying to push it back. When it can't be pushed back. It can't be tamped down. It must be *used*. Your anger is a gift. A weapon. And until the rest of the planet feels that anger and uses that weapon, we will not be free."

"I don't . . ." Marcellus hesitated. Noëlle had told him to use his words, but he couldn't find them. He wanted to stay true to what the Vangarde believed—what his father believed—but Max was making too much sense. He scuffed his boot against the ground and mumbled, "I don't believe that."

Max shook her head and flashed a melancholy smile. "Actually, I think you do. I think, deep down in your angry, bitter heart, you know that if we want to see change on this planet—real change—we can't just ask for it nicely. We have to *fight* for it. We have to be willing to *kill* for it. Die for it. And I think most of the Third Estate are. Your precious Vangarde had their chance. Seventeen years ago. They failed and nothing changed. In fact, things only got worse. It's time to do things a different way. My way."

"Don't you see you're only playing into the general's endgame?" Marcellus finally exploded. "The more First Estaters you kill, the higher he rises in the line for the Regime. The more anarchy you create, the more he looks like the savior. You're pushing the planet right into his hands."

"Oh, don't worry, Officer. We have plans for your grandfather, too. General Bonnefaçon is not the only one with spies on this planet."

Another shudder ricocheted through Marcellus as he remembered what they'd overheard three days ago, from the récepteur hidden in Jolras's pocket. His gaze shifted uneasily between each of the Red Scar guards flanking Max, searching for the man who could be the one she'd called Antoine. The one who was feeding them intel from Ledôme. But they all looked the same to him. Faceless figures in red hoods. Although, it was only now that he noticed they all had matching red marks slashed into their hands.

"Is that how you knew when the Patriarche fled?" Marcellus asked, forcing himself to focus back on Max. "Is that how you captured him? And the Favorites? With the help of your *spies*?"

Max's lips tugged into a coy smile, but she said nothing. Once again, Marcellus glanced at Rousseau, but she showed no intention of stepping in. He huffed and tried a different tack, turning to the man next to Max.

"Jolras. What happened? I thought you said you wanted to stop this. Stop the killing, the violence—"

"Jolras and I have worked out our differences," Max cut in, reaching out to grab her brother's hand, as though she was reminding him of where he belonged. "We are linked by blood and nothing can come between that. Not you or the Vangarde. We only have each other. We are all that's left of our broken family. Only death will part us now."

Marcellus flicked his gaze back to Jolras, but once again, he would not meet his eye. He only nodded and stared at the ground.

"Jolras knows, as you will soon too," Max continued, "that death is a natural consequence of war. The Regime doesn't bat an eye at the thousands of Third Estaters that fill the morgues each year. We cannot be afraid of getting blood on our hands if it's for the right cause."

Then, Max pushed back the sleeves of her coat and held up her hands so Marcellus could see the red slashes on the backs more clearly. Some looked sickeningly fresher than others. "This one is for the Patriache," she said, pointing to a jagged, fading scar before moving on to the three wounds that had just started to scab over. "And these are for the Favorites." She lowered her hands and locked eyes with Marcellus. "But there's plenty room for more."

"Is that what your mother would have wanted?"

The voice was clear and even, ringing out across the night. For a moment, Marcellus couldn't pinpoint who had spoken. That is, until he tracked Maximilienne's fierce gaze back to the woman standing next to him with her face still shielded behind her hood.

"Who are you?" Max snapped.

Citizen Rousseau flashed a cryptic smile in return. "Just an old friend of the Vangarde."

"You knew my mother?" It sounded like an accusation.

"I did."

"So, you know she wasted her life for the Vangarde."

"Carra Epernay was a beautiful, brave woman," Rousseau said, her voice turning slightly wistful. "Full of grace and conviction. She desired a better world. As you do."

"My mother was delusional. Just like that repulsive leader of yours. Citizen Rousseau." Max practically growled the name. "Maman worshipped that woman. Like she was a Sol in the sky. Citizen Rousseau and the Vangarde brainwashed her into thinking she could change the planet without pulling a single trigger. Too bad they couldn't convince the Regime to do the same."

"Your anger is understandable," Rousseau said evenly. "You've lost a lot of people you love to this battle. And the people who promised to save you from it all only let you down. But your anger is *not* your only weapon, Maximilienne." The way she pronounced the name felt like she was consecrating it. "That is a misconception that leads to far too much bloodshed. You have a powerful voice. People listen to you. They follow you." She nudged her chin toward the shadowy red figures dotting the periphery of the field. "*That* is your gift. And we've come here today to offer you a choice. Will you use that gift to bring about more death or will you use that gift to change people's minds and sway people's hearts?"

Max stared at Citizen Rousseau for a long moment, like she was trying to see past the hood, past the shadows concealing her face. "So, what?" she said with an amused chuckle. "You want me to *join* you?"

"We do."

Max flinched, as though she wasn't expecting that answer. Or at least, not put as bluntly as that. "Right. Me join the Vangarde. Follow in darling Maman's footsteps. Rattle off endless drivel about peace and a better life and another way."

"There *is* another way," Rousseau said.

"This is war!" Max shouted and pointed in the vague direction of Ledôme, its vast curving top invisible behind the shroud of mist. "And they are the enemy."

Marcellus tensed, his fingers twitching against the rayonette still clutched in his hand. In one swift motion, Max could be dead. This could all be over. But then, he reminded himself of the guards that surrounded them, hiding among the overgrown forest of crops. He would barely be able to take aim before this turned into a massacre.

"They have enslaved and murdered us for hundreds of years." Max's eyes were blazing again. "Violence is the *only* answer. The *only* way because it's the only thing the Regime understands. *They* started this war, and therefore we must fight them with their own weapons."

Citizen Rousseau made a soft tutting noise with her tongue, but her whole demeanor radiated so much serenity and warmth, it was as if even the fine rain evaporated before it settled on her long coat. "If we allow anger to flourish and bitterness to rage out of control, if we turn to violence and hate, then the new Laterre that we create will be nothing but a copy of the old."

"So what do you suggest we do instead? Knock on the Palais door and ask politely that they pay us back for five centuries' worth of theft, murder, and injustice?"

Rousseau barely faltered. "For a start."

Max let out a sharp, vitriolic laugh. "Well, good luck with that. Meanwhile, we will be exacting some real change."

"Real change *can* happen," Citizen Rousseau maintained. "But only through peaceful means." Max tried to interrupt, but Citizen Rousseau held up a hand with an abruptness that made even some of the other Red Scar guards startle. "On the First World, oppressed people threw off their oppressors without raising a fist. Without lifting a weapon. They stood together, united and peaceful and strong, and their freedom came to pass. They freed themselves. They unshackled their nations. They found their promised lands." Citizen Rousseau paused and shook her head. "It is not a weak method. When a person can stand up to violence and hate and not retaliate with violence and hate, *that* is strength. That is power. And if we come together, we can change Laterre in the way we *all* want it changed. Unity is the greatest need of this time. If *we* can unite—the Red Scar and the Vangarde—then the people will be united too. And with the people beside us, we can achieve anything. If we unite *in peace*, Laterre can reach its promised land."

Suddenly there was a sound of quiet murmuring among Max's guards. And Marcellus understood why. It wasn't just Citizen Rousseau's words that were stirring. It was the voice and passion and conviction behind them. They were as strong as the words themselves. They didn't just make you feel powerful. They made you feel infinite. A world of meaning and promise in every syllable.

Max snapped her fingers sharply to silence the guards and then turned back to Rousseau, her eyes narrowing with suspicion. "Who did you say you are?"

But Rousseau didn't answer.

Max gave a dismissive snort. "Well, that's a lovely theory. And maybe in fantasyland, that plays out nicely. But it won't work on Laterre. And it won't work on me." She shared a glaring look with her brother before returning her fiery gaze to Rousseau. "Because *I*, unlike my mother, am not delusional. I can't be brainwashed with fancy words and empty promises of peace. I remember the day Maman came home from her first Vangarde rally. Citizen Rousseau had spoken in an abandoned building in the Planque. Maman was so energized. So hopeful." She scoffed. "And then I remember the day she didn't come home at all. She died at one of the Vangarde's *peaceful* rallies. 'Complications from exposure to riot gas,' my helpful Skin informed me. Little Nadette was just five years old. Jolras and I had to raise her on our own. And Citizen Rousseau . . ." Max took a small step forward. The Vangarde operatives reached for their weapons. Rousseau held up a hand to stop them. Max's eyes latched on to Rousseau's, and Marcellus could almost feel the boiling, hot rage radiating off them. "She miraculously escaped from the rally without a scratch. Imagine that."

Without a word, Citizen Rousseau reached up and slowly pushed back her hood, revealing a face that was too memorable to forget. Too recognizable to stay hidden for long.

Every tiny raindrop in the windswept clearing appeared to freeze in the air.

Every breath hitched.

Every gaze snapped toward her.

The gusting wind yanked at Rousseau's hair, making it flap and twist around her like a million writhing silver snakes. Her eyes blinked and sparkled as if they were two ancient and insistent stars beaming from the darkness of the galaxy.

Max didn't so much as flinch.

"You've been through a lot," Rousseau said gently. "Your mother—"

"Don't talk about my mother!" Max spat, her composure slipping once again in this endless tug-of-war with her temper. "You *killed* her. Just like you killed so many others with your talk of peace. Throw a rock and you'll find thousands just like me. Children of your failed rebellion. Oublies left behind by your pitiful attempts at peace."

Marcellus's blood was pumping hard and fast through his veins now. He felt like he was standing on a land mine. One wrong step, one wrong word, wrong noise, could set Max off and end them all.

"It is true." Citizen Rousseau lowered her head. "I have been locked in a cell on Bastille for many years, and every second of every minute of every hour of every day and month, I remembered and grieved for each one of our losses."

"You should have fought." Max's eyes flamed again. "You should have met their brutality with your own."

"We will lose many, many more if we meet violence with violence." Citizen Rousseau looked Max straight in the eye. "On the First World, they had a saying, 'He who lives by the sword dies by the sword—'"

"This is not the First World!" Max bellowed. "Wake up and take a look around you. This is Laterre. Things are different here, so we need a different way. And if you're not with us, we have no choice but to treat you as another enemy."

"But we are not your enemy!"

Everyone's gaze snapped toward Marcellus, looking as startled by his outburst as he felt. He swallowed down the growing lump in his throat and forged on. "We should be working together. Not against each other. Just like she said. We're on the same side here. We have the same goal."

"No," Max said with a note of finality. "We don't. You want to hold hands and chant until a combatteur comes along and blows your head off, and I want actual *change*. Now is the time to act. To strike. Before the System Alliance can nominate another useless leader to dictate our lives. I did not kill Lyon Paresse just so another rich pomp in a fancy outfit could swoop in and take control."

Marcellus opened his mouth to speak, but it was Citizen Rousseau who stopped him, resting another gentle hand on his. It took only one look at her face for him to know that she was resigning. That she was marking this down as another Vangarde failure. That she was giving up on Maximilienne Epernay.

"Good luck with your chanting," Max said with a derisive chuckle. "If you decide you want to join a *real* revolution, you obviously know how to get in touch with me."

Out of the corner of his eye, Marcellus saw a rustle of movement in the surrounding field. Max clearly saw it too because her gaze darted to the left, then back to Rousseau. A look of fury passing over her face. "Did you—"

But she never got a chance to finish, because just then, the unmistakable whoosh of a rayonette pulse sizzled through the air. Marcellus raised his weapon, assuming it was the Red Scar who had fired, but then, a body dressed in a red coat tumbled out of the nearby towering crops and collapsed into the clearing.

The field exploded in a chaos of pulses, whizzing every which way. Marcellus didn't even have the chance to aim his rayonette before someone shouted, "Policier!"

The Red Scar guards scattered like a flock of frightened birds, yanking rayonettes out of holsters as they went and firing with abandon into the wheat-fleur fields. Until the only one left standing in front of Marcellus and Citizen Rousseau was Max. Her eyes smoldered like the making of a terrible storm.

"You will pay for this treachery," she warned.

"What?" Marcellus gasped, glancing anxiously around as more shots rustled through the air and more bodies fell. "No, Max, we didn't—"

"Run!" Grantaire shouted, and Marcellus felt a tug at his sleeve. He stumbled forward, struggling to put one foot in front of the other. As he glanced back, he saw Max disappearing into the overgrown crops, just as a swarm of Policier sergents and droids charged into the clearing.

- CHAPTER 23 -
CHATINE

CHATINE POUNDED ON THE CLOSED DOOR AT THE END of the hallway. A moment later, it opened a crack and Principale Francine stuck out her head, looking disapprovingly down at Chatine through her half-moon spectacles.

"Any word?" Chatine asked, trying to keep her voice even.

The sister shook her head. "Not yet. The tracking signal from their récepteur still hasn't moved."

Chatine's stomach gave a nasty twitch. "But it's almost Sol-rise. Surely it doesn't take that long to walk to the wheat-fleur fields, have a quick chat with a murderer, and come back?"

Francine frowned at Chatine's flippant tone. "We are monitoring the situation closely."

"But what if something is wrong? We need to send someone, right? To check on them? I can—"

"You can stay right here. We will let you know if there is any movement."

Chatine blew out a ragged breath. "Well, can't you at least make contact?"

"That would be unwise at this juncture. If, for some reason, they are trying to stay hidden, making contact could jeopardize their safety. And ours."

"But—" Chatine tried to argue but was once again cut off.

"Idle hands make for idle minds, Chatine."

Chatine's forehead crumpled. "Huh?"

Francine glanced back into the room before letting out an impatient breath. "If you are looking for something to occupy your thoughts, perhaps you can get started on breakfast."

The door closed in Chatine's face before she could protest. She balled her hands into fists and stomped toward the nearby kitchen, all the while muttering under her breath. "Perhaps you can get started on breakfast, Chatine. It's time to make the bread, Chatine. Chatine, the sisters are getting hungry. Chatine, we're all going out to fight the revolution. Can you have dinner ready by the time we get back?"

She chuckled darkly at that last one, amused by her own impersonation of Principale Francine.

Chatine was about to turn into the kitchen when, at the end of the long hallway, she spotted a pair of dark canvas shoes peeking out from the vestibule that led to the Refuge's decommissioned front entrance. Curious, she crept toward them, and when she reached the shadowy alcove and peered inside, she saw Roche standing on his tiptoes, studying the monitor attached to the wall.

"What are you doing?" she asked.

He jumped and spun around to flash her a guilty smile. "Nothing."

Chatine snorted. "How did you manage to survive on your own in the Frets for so long being such a terrible liar?"

"I wasn't on my own. I had my bébés."

"Your what?"

Roche jutted out his chin. "Léopold and Adèle. They're Oublies like me. I looked after them. Took care of them. Showed them the best places to steal food and which stall owners wouldn't whack you if you got caught."

"What happened to them?" she asked before realizing what Roche had just done. "Hey! Don't change the subject."

He smirked. "Does that answer your question? Of how I survived in the Frets?"

Chatine rolled her eyes. She hated being conned by anyone. Especially her own flesh and blood. "What are you doing back here?" She narrowed her eyes at him. "Why aren't you in bed?"

Roche rocked back and forth on his toes. "I couldn't sleep. So I thought I'd just . . . " He gestured toward the monitor on the wall. "Keep a lookout."

She peered at the screen, which showed a view of the Fret 7 mechanical room ten mètres above their heads. Chatine remembered the days it used to be a run-down, Sol-forsaken place that no one ever ventured into. Now it was clean, shiny, and stripped of all the old, rusting machinery.

"A lookout?" she repeated suspiciously. "For what? This entrance is sealed off." She pointed at the monitor, to the place where the old access grate used to be. Now there was only a solid concrete floor. "See? No one is getting in this way."

"It doesn't mean we shouldn't be keeping watch," Roche said in an admonishing tone. "What if the general is using the mechanical room as a secret lab to develop biological weapons?"

Chatine groaned. "I highly doubt he's doing that."

"You don't know," Roche maintained. "He could be—"

Just then, a scream boomeranged down the long hallway, cutting off Roche midsentence. Chatine looked back, into the shadowy depths of the Refuge, and waited, her heart hammering in her chest. A second scream ripped through the air and Chatine took off, charging in the direction of the sound.

Her first thought was of Marcellus and Citizen Rousseau. What if the sisters had gotten word that their mission had failed? What if Max had added their heads to her growing collection of war trophies and—

The thought stopped dead as Chatine found herself in the doorway of the infirmerie, staring in shock at Alouette. Her whole body was trembling violently under the bedsheets, and her black curls coiled and uncoiled across her pillow as she shook her head from side to side.

But her eyes were closed.

She was having a nightmare.

Alouette gave another violent thrash, knocking the covers clear off the bed. Sister Laurel had warned Chatine not to enter the infirmerie. Alouette, Jacqui, and Denise needed to rest and recuperate. But Chatine couldn't take it anymore. She charged into the room and reached for Alouette, ready to shake her from her sleep, ready to rescue her from her own mind. But just as she reached the bedside, Alouette let out a tiny whimper and then fell still again. Restful. Her eyelids stopped fluttering and her breathing returned to normal.

Chatine lowered her hand and began to back slowly and quietly out of the room but stopped when she felt someone watching her. Her head snapped to the left, and through the dim light of the infirmerie, she saw a pair of dark, inquisitive eyes staring back at her.

"Sorry," Chatine whispered. "She was . . . I was just going to . . . I'm leaving. . . ."

"You're the Renard girl, aren't you?" Denise asked, and Chatine felt a familiar shudder at the mention of her family's name. For years, she'd tried to escape that name. Escape the reputation and disgust that came with it. But it seemed to follow her wherever she went.

Chatine nodded.

"Sister Laurel has been telling me about you."

"I'm sorry," Chatine muttered because it was all she could think to say.

"For what?"

"For whatever Laurel said about me. I'm sure it was bad."

Denise's eyes crinkled in amusement and, in the low light of her bedside table lamp, Chatine caught sight of her circuitry scars. "On the contrary. She told me about your bravery at the Ascension banquet. And Alouette told us how instrumental you were in shutting down the Skins."

"Alouette shut down the Skins. I just wore a stupid dress and got the snot kicked out of me."

Denise's forehead crumpled, and for a long time she didn't say anything. Chatine wondered if she should rephrase. Maybe the sister didn't understand the expression. "I mean—" Chatine began.

But Denise cut her off. "Every conductive pathway is necessary for a motherboard to function."

"What?" Apparently, *she* was the one having trouble understanding.

Alouette started to thrash again, pulling Chatine's attention to the bed on the other side of the infirmerie.

"She will be all right," Denise said, as though reading the concern in Chatine's eyes. "Young minds are resilient. As *you* well know."

Chatine wanted to ask what Denise meant by that, but she was too focused on Alouette, whose violent tossing and turning suddenly settled into quiet murmurs. "He tortured her, didn't he?" she asked, feeling like tiny spiders were crawling up and down her arms.

There was silence behind her before Denise finally replied. "Yes. He tortured all of us."

Chatine pulled her gaze away from Alouette and directed it toward the third occupied bed. The one next to Denise.

As much as the general had ruined Chatine's life, it was nothing compared to what he'd done to them. His mark was visible on all three of them. In the anguished flutters of Alouette's eyelashes as she dreamed. In Denise's bruises. In the empty, motionless stare of Jacqui.

Chatine felt her blood grow hot. They had to find a way to break through this glossy façade the general had pulled over the planet and the eyes of the people. They had to find a way to make the Third Estate see that it wasn't real. It was an illusion built to pacify them and quiet them and dull them.

He had to be stopped.

Alouette let out another whimper, causing Chatine to flinch, before falling still again.

"Don't worry," Denise said. "If it becomes too much for her mind to take, she will wake herself up."

Chatine's gaze flicked back to Denise and, once again, settled on the scars running down the side of her face. "Is that what happened to you? It became too much for your mind to take and you woke yourself up?"

Denise seemed to understand instantly that Chatine wasn't referring to a normal nightmare. She raised her eyebrow in a silent question.

"The cyborg sleep," Chatine whispered, almost immediately hearing the voice that had first uttered those words to her. But she quickly pushed away the thoughts of Etienne before they had a chance to take hold of her again.

"Ah, so you've met Brigitte," Denise said knowingly. "She's the only other person I know who ever used that phrase."

"She saved my life," Chatine said, feeling a small prickle of longing well up inside of her. She may have been purposefully trying to rid her mind of thoughts of him, but she didn't want to do the same for his mother. Brigitte had become important to her. Like the maman she'd never had.

"And mine," said Denise with a rare twinkle in her eye.

"You were friends, right?" Chatine confirmed, but Denise didn't answer right away. She seemed to get lost in her own thoughts.

"Not at first."

"Really?" Chatine lowered herself onto the small chair next to Denise's bed.

"We were bitter rivals at the start, always competing for the top marks, the top assignments, the top praise. We entered the Cyborg Initiation Program around the same time, back when I went by a different name."

"Vanessa," Chatine remembered aloud.

Denise flinched slightly at the name. "Yes. Eventually the Patriarche put us on the Forteresse project together. It was rocky at the start. We couldn't seem to put aside our relentless rivalry. It was prohibiting our progress. When they turn you into a cyborg, they repress many of your human emotions, particularly the ones that will hinder you from doing your job well. Ambition is not considered to be one of those hindering emotions. In fact, they consider it to be an asset to a cyborg. But for Brigitte and me, it was not. We clashed at every turn, every decision. To this day, I still believe the moment we became friends, the moment we were able to put aside our ambition and connect to each other, was the moment the glitch started. In both of us."

"The crack," Chatine echoed dully, her mind involuntarily flashing back to Etienne's words that morning in the lodge, when he'd first revealed this piece of his mother's past.

"She said it was because her soul finally caught up to what her mind was doing, and it broke her in half."

"I guess you could call it that. Brigitte and I have had many discussions about it. She believes the crack is there from the start, patched up by the Ministère's circuitry and drowned out by the numbing drone of their programming, just waiting for you to remember it."

"And you don't believe that?" Chatine asked, completely absorbed. She liked talking to Denise. There was a simplicity about her, a stark honesty that reminded her of Brigitte. So many of the sisters talked in riddles and codes. Denise seemed like the kind of person who didn't have time for riddles.

"I don't know," she admitted with a weak smile. "When you're a cyborg, your mind is so sharp and awake, but your humanity is asleep. It's difficult to connect the two and make sense of things because that connection has been purposefully severed."

"So, how do you wake yourself up if you don't even know you're asleep?"

"That's the question, isn't it?" Denise replied. "That's the glitch in the whole program. And if the Ministère could find it, I imagine they would have fixed it by now. For me, it started small. A niggling doubt in the back of my mind. It would pop up from time to time as I was working on the Sovereign gene for the Forteresse. At first, I was able to push it down. My cyborg programming fought against it like an immune system attacking a virus. But eventually the doubt got bigger, harder to ignore. The crack grew wider and wider, until it split me in half. My cyborg self and my human self started to war with each other, and that's when I knew I had to decide."

Chatine leaned forward in her chair. "Decide what?"

Denise's dark, determined gaze latched on to hers. "Which side would win."

CHAPTER 24

CERISE

"DUE TO THE QUICK THINKING, BRAVERY, AND INGENU-
ity of Technicien Chevalier, we were able to capture and arrest nineteen members of the Red Scar terrorist group, including Jolras Epernay,
Maximilienne Epernay's second-in-command."

Cerise's circuitry hummed softly with pride as the briefing room broke
into raucous applause. She stood tall and regal on the stage next to Commandeur Apolline Moreau, feeling a warmth flowing through her. She
knew it was just the serotonin pumping through her veins. Nothing more
than a chemical reaction in her brain, but she still reveled in the sensation,
all the same. Especially when she glanced out into the crowd gathered for
today's briefing and saw her father, Directeur Chevalier, beaming back at
her. If he'd had circuitry embedded in the left side of his face, Cerise was
certain it would be humming too.

"Merci, Technicien, for your service to Laterre." The commandeur
turned toward her and proffered forth the shiny titan medal. The small disk
with its engraved symbol of the Ministère—two crisscrossing rayonettes
guarding Laterre—shimmered on a bed of soft velvet. Cerise couldn't
help the hint of a smile that tugged at her lips. She'd seen the Medal of
Accomplissement in broadcasts and archived footage. And of course, in

her mind's eye as she drifted to sleep at night. But never in person. And never right in front of her, about to be placed around her own neck.

You don't deserve it.

The thought came so swiftly, so unexpectedly, she didn't have time to filter it from her consciousness. She tried to focus on the shiny medal before her and push the thought from her mind. But it pushed back. Just as resilient and determined and *logical* as all of her thoughts.

You still failed to achieve your primary objective.

Marcellus Bonnefaçon is still out there.

"In addition to this Medal of Accomplissement," Commandeur Moreau continued ceremoniously, "I am also pleased to announce your promotion to spécialiste. You are a valuable asset to the Ministère and our glorious planet. Please bow to receive your well-deserved commendation."

Cerise bent forward and felt a tingle shoot down her spine as the strap settled around her neck. When she rose up again, to the sound of more applause, she was a different person. She knew it. She was no longer Cerise Chevalier, the disappointment. Cerise Chevalier, the failure. Cerise Chevalier, the girl who associated with traitors but couldn't even conjure up a single memory to help catch them.

She was now *Spécialiste* Chevalier, savior of the Regime, banisher of the Red Scar, pride of the Ministère.

It was not her fault that Marcellus Bonnefaçon was still at large. And everyone in this room knew it. Commandeur Moreau included. Cerise had sent the coordinates. She'd delivered the intel to the proper authorities, just as she'd been trained to do. The local Vallonay Policier were the ones who'd let him get away. Not her.

"The general—who, unfortunately, could not be with us, as he's currently meeting with the System Alliance—also sends his congratulations and appreciation, Spécialiste," the commandeur said before pushing back a strand of her immaculately cropped dark hair and turning her attention to the awaiting audience. She took a moment to gather herself, before clearing her throat and resuming her briefing. "The arrest of Jolras Epernay and the eighteen other Red Scar members was made this morning, at 02.32, System Standard Time. Based on reports from Spécialiste Chevalier and

Sergent Zabelle, whose team was dispatched to the scene, we believe that at the time of the arrest, the Red Scar was attempting to recruit known fugitive Marcellus Bonnefaçon. This is consistent with Bonnefaçon's criminal profile, given that his father, Julien Bonnefaçon, was a prominent member of the Vangarde, and Marcellus was, of course, discovered to have also been affiliated with the Vangarde while they were still in operation. Marcellus Bonnefaçon, unfortunately, is still at large."

Almost instantly, Cerise felt the hum of her circuitry taper off. She hadn't even realized Marcellus was on his way to meet with the Red Scar when she'd tracked him to the wheat-fleur field. The news that the Red Scar operatives had been arrested because of her intelligence was a pleasant surprise, but it was also creating a vexing conflict inside of her processors. She had unknowingly orchestrated the capture of nineteen criminals and, in the process, lost her only lead on her primary objective.

"Although we still have a long road ahead of us in the quest to make our planet safe from terrorism," the commandeur went on, "this has been a huge step forward. I can't emphasize enough how much sounder I will sleep at night knowing so many of those criminals are now in the custody of the Vallonay Policier Precinct and awaiting transport to Bastille. We are so much closer to the peace and stability that we all work so hard to instill on Laterre every single day. Of course—"

The room broke into more applause, which seemed to startle the commandeur, but she composed herself quickly and waited for the clapping to die down.

"Of course, we cannot rest until every member of the Red Scar is in custody. And we will continue to devote a large portion of our resources to finding Maximilienne Epernay and ensuring that she pays for her crimes against our planet, our First Estate, and our former Patriarche, may he rest with the Sols." Moreau gave the hem of her crisp white uniform a subtle tug, which caused her new titan commandeur's badge to glint in the overhead lights. "That concludes my briefing. Are there any questions?"

Cerise felt a pull at the sleeve of her uniform and was ushered away by an aide who had hurried onto the stage. As Cerise took her place in the audience, alongside the rest of her department, she felt the last hum of her circuitry twinkle out. Her moment in the spotlight was over. All eyes were back on the commandeur.

"Officer Giraud." Moreau called on a man in the front row who had just raised his hand.

"Merci, Commandeur, and may I congratulate you on your recent promotion."

Moreau nodded her head in response and the officer continued. "You mentioned Sergent Zabelle had been dispatched to the scene. Is there a reason why Inspecteur Limier was not present?"

The commandeur took a sip of her water, and Cerise noticed the tiniest nano-droplet splash down the front of her uniform. "At the time the Air-Link came in, Inspecteur Limier was tending to a special assignment for the general, so one of his sergents was dispatched instead."

"Can you tell us more about the search for Maximilienne Epernay?" said an imperial advisor in a dark green robe. "Have there been any leads to her whereabouts?"

The commandeur gave a tight nod. "Yes, actually. Upon his arrest, Jolras Epernay was found with a device in his pocket that we believe might be used for communication. It will be analyzed by the Bureau of Défense, and we're hopeful this will provide us with intelligence leading to the capture of Maximilienne Epernay. . . ."

Moreau's words faded into the background as a ping echoed through Cerise's audio interface. She reached into her pocket for her TéléCom, intending to dismiss the alert, but froze when a voice in her ear announced, "Decryption successful. Device decoded."

Cerise stood up straighter, her circuitry flickering with excitement. *The Patriarche's microcam.* The general's special project. She'd done it. She'd hacked into it.

Ignoring the hum of the continued chatter in the room as questions were asked and answered, Cerise opened her TéléCom, clicked on the notification, and swiped across the screen until the contents of the device were visible.

There was only one file.

Cerise could tell from the look of it that it was some kind of footage. She tapped to reveal the metadata.

"Captured on Month 4, Day 35, Year 488," her TéléCom recited in her ear.

The date rumbled around in her brain, trying to find significance. But there was none. She thought about the general's words to her as he'd shown her the microcam.

This contains vital information. About a girl named Madeline Villette.

Cerise hovered her fingertip over the screen, desperate to push play, but the steady thrum of her programming held her back. The general had given her strict orders *not* to view the contents of this device, but instead to turn it over to him immediately. In person.

"Any other questions?" Commandeur Moreau asked, and as more hands rose into the air, Cerise eased away from the crowd and made her way toward the door of the briefing room, the adrenaline of a new victory pumping through her blood.

"I was the first to interrogate the arrested members of the Red Scar after they were taken into custody. One of them claimed that Maximilienne Epernay was actually meeting with the Vangarde when the arrest took place, and that Citizen Rousseau was among the participants of that meeting. Is there any way this could be true?"

Cerise froze halfway to the door and spun around to pinpoint the woman who had asked the question. It was a young officer by the name of Tolbert, and all eyes in the room were now pivoting between her and the commandeur at the podium.

Moreau let out an uneasy laugh. "Citizen Rousseau? The woman who died more than three months ago on Bastille? Was he meeting with her ghost?"

Nervous chuckles permeated the room, but no one looked particularly mollified, despite the fact that they'd all seen the footage in the official Ministère report. Just as Cerise had. When the Vangarde had tried to free Citizen Rousseau from prison, their ship had been shot down by a Ministère combatteur as it was taking off from Bastille. It was Commandeur Moreau herself, back when she was Capitaine Moreau, who had fired the fatal explosif.

"Obviously, this is a ploy," the commandeur said, resuming her serious demeanor. "A vain attempt to try to divert blame and split our focus. If we're off chasing down ghosts, we'll have far fewer resources to devote to the real threat at hand: Maximilienne Epernay. Which, I imagine, was exactly the intent behind these blatant lies that the Red Scar are attempting to spread."

Cerise let out the breath she'd been holding, feeling relief flood through her system. This was logical. This made sense. Most of the humans in the room seemed to agree because, one by one, Cerise watched the same relief play out on their faces. No one wanted to deal with the threat of the Vangarde again. Especially not with the leader of the Red Scar still out there.

But there was one face that caught Cerise's attention. Namely, because it didn't exhibit the same calm as everyone else. Cerise zeroed in on the broad-shouldered woman standing behind the podium and watched a single bead of sweat form at the base of Commandeur Moreau's hairline.

Something unnerving danced at the outer edges of Cerise's consciousness. She activated her cybernetic eye and kept it trained carefully on the woman's face as the commandeur took another sip of water and fielded the next question.

From somewhere behind Cerise, a voice asked, "Is there a chance that Citizen Rousseau *did* escape and—"

Moreau held up a hand, stopping the question in its tracks. "Officer, I spent twenty years on the Laterrian Spaceforce. I've witnessed a lot of things, flown a lot of missions. Some successful, some not. I am versed in every type of explosif there is. Their trajectories, their destruction capabilities, the likelihood that someone could survive the blast radius. I was there the day when Citizen Rousseau attempted to escape from Bastille. I dropped the explosif that destroyed her ship. It was a direct hit. And so, I can say with absolute certainty that Citizen Rousseau, and any other Vangarde leaders aboard that ship, are dead."

Cerise's neuroprocessors worked quickly, analyzing and decrypting every centimètre of the commandeur's face, cataloguing every minuscule twitch and blink. But it wasn't until she was out of the room, safe from the blast radius of her own conclusion, that she allowed herself to process the results of the scan.

Lie.

CHAPTER 25

ALOUETTE

ALOUETTE AWOKE TO A BANG. IT SOUNDED LIKE A CLAP of thunder. She sat bolt upright in bed, blinking her surroundings into focus. The relief washed over her in gentle waves. She was still in the Refuge infirmerie. She was still safe.

Another nightmare?

When would they end? When would she stop trying to escape General Bonnefaçon in her dreams? Perhaps when she stopped trying to escape him in real life.

She glimpsed at the clock on the wall. It was already the afternoon. She could see the quiet, sleeping form of Sister Jacqui on the bed across the room, but Sister Denise's bed was empty.

And then, she heard the voices. Hushed and frantic.

She stood up, fighting back a wave of dizziness. Her head was still groggy from the sleeping tincture Sister Laurel had given her earlier. Pulling a sweater over her nightgown, Alouette slipped out of the dark infirmerie, turned the corner, and followed the sound of the voices down the hallway, toward the door at the end. The one that had been closed to her for thirteen long years. But now it was wide open. Like an invitation.

She crept closer to the Assemblée room but froze just outside the entrance when she heard Marcellus say, "The Policier came, the field was flooded with droids. We had to run."

Alouette's chest squeezed. Policier? Droids? Where had Marcellus been? She felt the familiar embers of anger start to flare up again. He had lied to her.

Eager to hear more, she squeezed herself behind the open door and peered through the crack.

"Thank the Sols, you're all right," said another voice. It was Sister Laurel. "Are either of you hurt?"

Marcellus grunted in response. "No. We got out just as they started shooting. One of the operatives hid us in a wheat-fleur field until it was safe. We couldn't risk leading anyone back to the silo."

Alouette pressed herself against the cool bedrock wall to get a better angle into the room, but all she could see were slivers of Francine, Noëlle, and Marguerite, who was wringing her hands. Everyone else—including Marcellus—was out of sight.

"And Maximilienne?" asked Francine in her usual clipped tone.

"She got away," said Marcellus. "A handful of her guards were arrested, including her brother, but we saw her flee."

All the blood seemed to drain from Alouette's head, making her woozy. She grabbed on to the doorjamb for balance. *Maximilienne?* As in Maximilienne Epernay? Marcellus had been meeting with the leader of the Red Scar?

"And?" prompted Sister Noëlle, who was now standing on the very tips of her toes, something she often did when she was nervous.

There was silence in the room, sending Alouette's mind spinning to keep up.

"We tried," Marcellus finally said, his voice smaller than a child's. "Rousseau was brilliant. We did everything we could, but Max . . ." He never finished the sentence, but it soon became apparent that he didn't have to.

"It was a long shot," said Francine sensibly. "We all knew that."

"We need to deactivate the récepteur," said Sister Denise. "If Jolras still has it on him and the Policier search him—"

"I doubt the Ministère will even know what to do with it," replied Sister Marguerite. "They certainly won't have the technology to trace the signal."

"Agreed. But we can't take any chances," said Denise.

Sister Marguerite nodded. "I'll take care of it."

"What on Laterre are we supposed to do now?" asked Sister Laurel in a voice shattered by fear. "We can't very well send her out there like a lamb to the slaughter! The Red Scar will murder her the moment she steps foot outside this Refuge."

"We won't," replied Francine in a tone that left nothing to be negotiated. "Of course we won't. As long as Maximilienne is still out there, we will keep her here. We will keep her identity hidden. It is the only way to ensure she is safe."

"Perhaps we should ask Alouette how she feels about this," said a calm, unfamiliar voice.

Alouette flinched at the sound of her own name and pushed her face farther against the crack in the door, trying to see who was speaking. But all she could make out was the tattered, dirty hem of a coat and a pair of slender hands. They gripped a small cardboard cylinder and twisted its top round and round and round.

"No," said Laurel, shaking her head. "She is too young. She is too inexperienced. And Maximilienne is too dangerous. This isn't Alouette's decision to make."

Something dark and bitter started to bloom inside Alouette. She was so tired of hearing Laurel insist she wasn't ready when she *was* ready. How long were they going to stand there and talk about her like she was a child who needed to be taught not to touch a hot stove? How long before they started treating her like an adult? Like a *real* member of this sisterhood? And not the Little Lark they'd kept caged and protected her whole life?

"I agree," said Sister Léonie. "The risk is too great. We must move forward without her. The Red Scar now know that Rousseau is alive. We can't delay any longer. We must reveal her. She can lead the people on her own, just as she did seventeen years ago."

There was a pause as Principale Francine seemed to be looking to each of the sisters one by one, before she said, "Very well. Tomorrow we will make contact with the cells to discuss the details of Rousseau's unveiling."

Quiet murmurs of assent spread through the room. Alouette reached for the devotion beads hanging from her neck, expecting to feel something, a moment of contentment, of serenity. Yet, all she could feel now was that bitterness.

She wasn't a real sister. Had she ever been? Or were the beads just a ruse? A way to track her. To keep tabs on her. To protect her. Even when she didn't want to be protected anymore.

"For now," Francine continued, "I suggest we retire. It's been a very long day, and I think we all could use some rest."

As the sisters filed out of the room and disappeared down the corridor to their respective bedrooms, Alouette pressed her back against the bedrock wall, trying to make herself invisible. Once the coast was clear, she stepped out of her hiding place, but stopped a second later when she noticed someone peering back at her through the gap in the door.

Her first instinct was to startle, but then a surprising calm washed over her. Alouette had never seen eyes quite like that. Not on a human and not on a cyborg. They seemed to glow on their own accord, brighter than any lamp in the Refuge.

She quickly glanced down at the woman's long fingers, still wrapped around the small cardboard cylinder, and then back up at her face. Her lips were curved into a mysterious smile, as though she were guarding a secret bigger than the universe itself.

It was Citizen Rousseau. Alouette knew it instantly. And the sight of her—the memory of all the pain she'd caused—only fueled the bitterness growing inside her.

Alouette opened her mouth to speak, but the woman never gave her a chance. She swept out of the room and didn't look back.

After three long breaths, Alouette stepped tentatively into the Assemblée room. It was only the second time in her life she'd been inside, and the shock of seeing it all again hit her like a slap in the face.

Her gaze crawled over every centimètre of the space, taking in every spine of every book, every button on every console, every screen showing feeds from every hidden cam. She recognized some of the views—the Marsh bustling with midday activity; the docks of Montfer, where a herd of travelers disembarked from a moored bateau—while others were foreign to her—giant machines spinning out rolls of cloth in a fabrique; a busy spaceport; a group of workers in Delaine corralling a herd of sheep into a rustic building.

It was a world cast in darkness. A world that knew nothing about her. And, based on what she'd just overheard, would continue to know nothing about her.

When the Lark flies home, the Regime will fall.

It was a lie. She was home. She was ready. She was the Lark they had rescued and kept safe for thirteen years. But she would not be the one to bring down this Regime.

Because the sisters weren't going to let her be a part of this. They weren't going to allow her to be the symbol they had raised her to be. She would continue to be their secret, locked up in this Refuge forever, like one of their First World books. Too fragile for this new world.

Someone cleared his throat and Alouette jumped, turning to see Marcellus standing in the corner. The shock of his appearance hit her all over again. She still couldn't believe how different he looked. She'd been picturing his face for three months. Those chiseled cheekbones. That dark, wavy hair that, even when combed, always looked just the slightest bit tousled. Now he was so . . . *thin*. Almost sickly.

But behind the gaunt skin and frail frame, she could still see them.

The eyes she remembered. The man who had crossed the System Divine with her. He was still in there. She wanted so badly to run to him again. To embrace him. But the memory of what had happened in the infirmerie last night kept her legs shackled in place.

"Are you okay?" she asked, pointing to the rip in his shirtsleeve.

He waved this away. "I'm fine. A pulse glanced my shoulder as we were escaping, but it was just a paralyzeur. The numbness has already worn off."

Alouette tried to catch his eye, to tell him it was okay. He could talk to her. He could say anything to her. But he refused to look at her. He kept his gaze trained on the ground.

Obviously, the kiss was still on his mind. She admitted it wasn't what she'd built it up to be in her head. She *had* thought about it before, lying awake in her cold, damp cell. But it had been so different in reality. Maybe that was because *they* were so different in reality. Maybe there would always be another version of Marcellus that lived in her mind. And another version of her that lived in his. Maybe those two versions had a chance to live happily ever after. In a different life. A different story.

Because Marcellus was right. Her being the Patriarche's daughter *did* change things. It changed everything. She and Marcellus didn't exist in a vacuum. They weren't variables she could pull out and study on their own. It was all connected. The dead Patriarche. The general. The Vangarde. The Red Scar.

There was no them and her now.

There was no difference between her life and everyone else's.

Her story and Laterre's.

"Just for the record," he said, crashing into her thoughts, "I think the sisters are making the right decision."

She blinked up at him. "What?"

"I think it's too dangerous for you to step forward as the Paresse heir."

"Well, maybe it's not up to you," Alouette said, the animosity blooming again. "*Any* of you."

Marcellus breathed out a sigh. "You don't understand how dangerous she is. Maximilienne. You didn't see what she did to the Patriarche, or those other members of the Paresse family. She carves the deaths into her hands, like conquests. If she knows about you, she will stop at nothing until she sees your head lying on the ground next to your father's. And your death scarred right into her skin."

"Is that why you went to see her? Without telling me? Is that how it's going to be now? You and the sisters will just continue to make decisions about me without consulting me at all?"

For a moment, Marcellus looked chastised before his eyes burned with a fresh dose of determination. "You don't know how much we went through to bring you back. How much *I* went through. I'm just . . . so relieved that you're safe." His voice broke, and as Alouette watched the pain and agony play out on his face, she began to understand.

Was *she* the reason for those shadows under his eyes? Those hollow cheeks? The collarbones visible through his skin?

"I can't lose you again." Marcellus let out a shaky breath. "And I don't think they can either. You have to know that . . ."

His voice trailed off as his gaze was captured by something on one of the screens. Alouette turned to see a face had suddenly appeared on the center monitor between the myriad of views of Laterre. It was the face that had populated all of Alouette's nightmares. And, she guessed, all of Marcellus's as well.

Marcellus dove for the controls, turning up the volume just as General Bonnefaçon began to speak. "Bonjour, fellow Laterrians."

Alouette felt the air in the room drop ten degrees. She placed a hand over her mouth. To keep from screaming, or throwing up, she wasn't sure.

"I come into your homes and towns and cities this fateful day to deliver news of a very interesting turn of events."

"What is this?" Alouette asked Marcellus, her throat dry.

"It's the TéléCast," he replied without looking away from the screen. "The general's new network to replace the Skins. It's being broadcast to every hologram on the planet."

"As you know," the general went on, "for the past few months, I have been spending countless hours meeting and deliberating with the delegates of the System Alliance in an attempt to resolve this unprecedented situation we now find ourselves in. Namely, the absence of a clear inheritor of the Regime."

Alouette glanced back at the surveillance footage from the Marsh. It was as though time had come to a standstill. Everyone in the marketplace had frozen and was now staring up at the nearest hologram projection in wonderment, hanging on the general's every word.

"I, along with the majority of the delegates, solemnly believe that the Regime should be inherited by a direct descendant of the late Patriarche Lyon Paresse, as it is decreed by the Order of the Sols and as it has been our custom and tradition for the past five centuries." The general's voice continued to ricochet around the room, like it wasn't coming just from one screen but from every corner, every crevice, every molecule of air. "But due to the unfortunate and untimely death of poor Marie Paresse, the brutal attack on our Patriarche by the Red Scar, and now the gruesome and tragic murders of his closest relatives, for the first time in five hundred years, our Regime finds itself without an obvious choice for its next leader."

Alouette felt ill. She wanted to run back to the infirmerie. To escape that voice. Those eyes. That face, which now loomed over this entire planet, like a chilling foreshadow of everything to come. But she couldn't move. She was paralyzed with fear and dread.

"Fortunately," the general continued, "it seems a solution may have presented itself."

"This is it," Marcellus whispered, pulling at the sallow skin of his cheeks. "He's going to do it. He's going to claim the Regime for himself."

Alouette's gaze darted back to the view of the Marsh, then to the docks of Montfer, the fabrique, the workers in Delaine, the spaceport. The size of the crowds in each location seemed to have doubled in the past few seconds. Hundreds of thousands of people stared up at their nearest hologram. Alouette could see lips moving, people murmuring to one another as answerless questions pinged back and forth.

The general continued, "It has come to my attention that prior to his marriage to Veronik Paresse, the Patriarche bore another legitimate child. A true heir to the Paresse line."

There was a small, strangled sound, but Alouette wasn't sure if it had come from her or Marcellus.

"Once this information was brought to my attention, I took it upon myself to research its validity. And I can now confirm that, nearly eighteen years ago, on Month 4, Day 35, 488, Lyon Paresse was married in a secret ceremony to a woman named Lisole Villette."

Alouette swore she could hear a hush fall over the planet, even from way down here, ten mètres below the surface. Suddenly she was no longer inside her body. She was hovering above the Refuge, above the Frets, looking down at herself, and at every shocked face and speechless stare that filled every street of every town and every city.

"Sols," Marcellus swore, his gaze still trained on the TéléCast feed. When Alouette managed to refocus her vision, she saw something that made her certain she was still dreaming. Still locked in the hazy hold of one of Sister Laurel's tinctures, conjuring all of this up in her mind.

The general's face had evaporated away and was replaced by two glowing figures. Under an arch of pink and white roses, a man and woman stood face-to-face, smiling and staring and adoring each other. The young man wore a crisp shirt and dark suit that accentuated his auburn hair, while the young woman's soft golden dress fluttered in a breeze. A simple tiara made of tiny flowers and glittering sequins snaked through her hair. Hair that was as dark and full and abundant as Alouette's own.

Alouette sucked in a sharp, stunned breath as she felt herself being pulled into the screen, into this moment trapped in time.

The couple's fingers entwined together like lace. Their eyes sparkled as brightly as the sequins in the woman's hair. And when the man leaned forward and whispered something into her ear, she threw back her head and laughed. A dazzling, beautiful laugh that seemed to come straight from the Sols.

"Lisole bore one child from the union," the general continued, his face breaking through the dream-like scene, until the image of the laughing couple was nothing but a wisp of vapor. "Her name was Madeline Villette, but she now goes by Alouette Taureau."

Alouette slammed back into her body. Every single centimètre of her skin was on fire. Blazing. Burning. Scorching. And General Bonnefaçon was holding the smoking match.

"That clever wretch," Marcellus whispered, and Alouette startled, forgetting for a moment that he was standing next to her. "He's exposing you."

"Why?" Alouette's voice trembled. She could not follow the reasoning. Could not fit pieces together in her mind. Everything around her was now debris of her exploded life, floating aimlessly, with no hope of making sense again.

But then, she saw the TéléCast feed flicker. The general's face faded away, and in its place a new image began to form. Even on the sisters' small monitor, it felt huge. And crystal clear. It made Alouette feel like she was back in that locked cell, with jolts of electricity ricocheting through her body.

It was *her*.

She glanced back at the surveillance feeds, and this time she knew that the strangled sound was coming from her. Because her image now filled every corner of Laterre. Every spare centimètre of space in every fabrique, exploit, ferme, fishing town, terminal building, and marketplace. Her face was mirrored back at her across the entire planet. Like she was being haunted by her own reflection.

"That's why," Marcellus said, his voice strained.

And suddenly, Alouette understood.

"This girl is our rightful leader and the heir to the Regime," the general announced with an unsettling gleam in his eye. "And I am not one to stand in the way of five hundred years of history and tradition. The only problem is, she is missing. I have searched everywhere for her, but she is nowhere to be found. It is my sincere hope that by broadcasting her face to all of you and by updating the Communiqué with her image and biometrics, you can help me restore her to her rightful place as our new Matrone."

The surveillance feeds of the cities were suddenly bubbling with activity as people chattered animatedly and studied the faces of their neighbors with new, inquisitive eyes.

Every single person on this planet had now been turned into a spy for the general.

A population of hunters.

And Alouette was the prey.

"However," came the single warning word, pulling everyone's attention back to the general's broadcast. "If Alouette Taureau—our rightful heir—is not found or she does not wish to come forward, then we must find someone else to lead this planet."

The general paused, letting all of this sink into Alouette's mind like a pile of rocks.

"But we do not have the luxury of time. The future of our planet cannot be put on hold forever. Which is why I am giving Alouette Taureau—Alouette *Paresse*—five days to come forward and claim her title and her birthright. Otherwise, the System Alliance will have no choice but to appoint someone else to lead in her place. And I'm incredibly pleased and honored to announce that just this morning, in a unanimous decision, the delegates of our twelve great planets have elected me to be that leader."

CHAPTER 26

ETIENNE

ETIENNE HAD NEVER SEEN THE LODGE IN SUCH CHAOS. The entire community had gathered. Grandmothers, fathers, daughters, grandfathers, mothers, brothers, sisters, and sons squeezed together around every table. Every chair was taken, and some of the community had to stand along the walls or gather near the large heating stove that glowed a radiant violet color from the emberweed oil burning inside. Little children crawled and darted through the room, while all the adults seemed to be talking at once.

Questions and speculations were zooming around the room like flies.

"How did they do it?"

"They must have known about it."

"But who would have use for so much?"

Etienne stood in the back of the lodge, surveying the scene in a state of numb shock, while Astra, his four-year-old sister, weaved between his legs, pretending she was a spaceship.

"Hush!" someone shouted, and Etienne looked up to the center of the room, where Mentor Ava was standing on a table to get everyone's attention. The mentorship had only recently cycled to her, and she was still getting used to her temporary role as the community moderator.

Finally, the room settled down and all eyes peered upward.

"Merci," Ava said, slightly breathless. "We will *never* get anywhere if we all talk at once. Now, let's review the facts. And then we can decide on a course of action. Here's what we know." She tugged back a lock of her ice-white hair and cleared her throat. "Last night, an outsider entered our camp and stole our primary supply of zyttrium."

Someone began to speak, but Mentor Ava raised her hand, preempting the question. "No, the backup reserve is safe. The intruder obviously didn't know about it. We have no idea who the perpetrator could be. They've left no evidence. No demands. No leads. But because nothing else in the camp was disturbed, we can surmise that it has to be someone who knew about the zyttrium store to begin with. Someone who knew exactly which chalet to raid."

Ava cast her gaze around the room, and Etienne could see the fear behind her dappled green-brown eyes. It was the same fear that had been thrumming through Etienne since the moment his maman entered the hangar with the news.

But there was something else thrumming through him too. Something much darker. Something he didn't even want to identify. But he had no choice.

Guilt.

Because he knew exactly who had done this.

"Zoom! Zoom! Zooooom!" Astra whispered as she made another rotation around Etienne's feet. "Watch out for the asteroid channel!"

"Shh," Etienne cooed, gently patting her head.

"Clearly, this has massive repercussions on our way of life," Mentor Ava continued. "Without zyttrium—"

"We're doomed!" someone shouted, but their voice was lost in the crowd, and Etienne couldn't pinpoint who had spoken.

Mentor Ava looked like she was holding on to her last scraps of patience. Etienne wouldn't be surprised if, shortly after this meeting, she passed the rest of her term on to the next member in the mentorship cycle.

"It's not ideal," she agreed with a hard swallow. "Without zyttrium, we will be unable to keep our camp concealed from passing crafts and detection scans and, of course, unable to power the stealth management systems on our ships. Brianne." Ava turned to the woman standing closest to the table. She was a member of the team who handled resource allocation. "How long do you estimate our backup reserve will last us?"

Brianne shifted uneasily on her feet. "Not long. A week, maybe."

The room erupted in chaos again.

"What are we supposed to do?" Laurent set his granddaughter down on the ground, and she scurried off to play with Perseus and a few other kids who were building chalets out of blocs.

"If the Ministère finds us, we're finished!" cried Caroline, a fellow pilot.

Etienne's chest lurched. Was this all his fault? Should he have spoken up sooner? He'd thought the threat was dealt with. He didn't think they would find their way *back*. But clearly he'd underestimated them.

"It's that gridder, Gabriel!" shouted Bastien. "He told me he used to be a thief. He said it was how he survived."

Etienne felt a growl rise in his throat. As much as the gridder drove him up the wall, he knew Gabriel wasn't capable of conning the entire camp. He'd been too busy scrapbooking and sharing all of his innermost thoughts with anyone who would listen. When would he have had time to organize a zyttrium heist? Etienne opened his mouth to speak, but his maman beat him to it.

"Gabriel is harmless. He hasn't left the camp since he arrived. He is my charge, and I will vouch for his innocence."

Etienne's gaze darted toward the door of the lodge. He was certain Gabriel was still on the other side, freezing his pants off and pacing anxiously. The injured look on his face as Brigitte told him the meeting was for permanent community members only and that he should wait in his chalet had *almost* made Etienne feel sorry for him.

"And let's not forget the code," Brigitte went on. "We don't judge people by their pasts. Otherwise, we are all suspects here."

"Exactly!" called out Jordane as she bounced baby Mercure in her arms. "The *code*. It says we keep to ourselves. We don't get involved. We've been letting far too many gridders into this camp lately. And this is where it's gotten us."

Another thunderbolt of guilt shot through Etienne's chest. He needed to speak up. He needed to set the record straight. But they were *so* angry. What if they turned on him? What if they thought he was an accomplice in all of this? He was, after all, the one who'd escorted the perpetrators out of the camp the night they'd been caught. He'd secured the blindfolds and flown them in dizzying circles until he was certain they couldn't find their way back.

And yet, they had.

What if Etienne revealed all of this now and the community decided to kick him out of the camp? Or worse, banned him from flying . . . permanently.

"Three, two, one, liftoff!" Astra launched her arms in the air and reached toward Etienne. Familiar with this game, he bent down and scooped her up. He positioned her against his left hip as she continued to gurgle engine noises in his ear.

"If you want to point fingers at anyone, point them at Marcellus Bonnefaçon," said Mercure's father, stepping up beside Jordane. "He was here only a few months ago, along with an entire crew of possible accomplices. And he has the most direct connection back to the Regime."

"Yes, but what would the Regime want with zyttrium anymore?" asked Castor from the other end of the room, where he was adding more of the camp's homemade emberweed oil to the heating stove. The brilliant violet flames inside sparked and roared as he shut the door. "We were told the Skins were deactivated."

"And besides," added his new partner, Saros, "if the Regime knew where we were, the whole camp would be gone right now. Not just the zyttrium."

"Plus, Etienne blindfolded them all," Brigitte said. "And we checked their devices for trackers. They were clean. It's most likely someone *outside* the Regime."

"Another planet?" suggested Laurent.

"Could be," Mentor Ava replied.

"ARGH! Am I the only one who's going to say it?" The outburst came from the front of the room, and everyone swiveled to gaze upon the towering frame and scowling black eyes of Sylvain.

"Ouch!" Astra complained, squirming in Etienne's arms. "Too tight! Too tight!"

"Sorry." He loosened his grip.

Just hearing Sylvain's gruff voice set him on edge. He'd never liked the man, ever since they were kids and he threatened to douse Etienne's chalet in emberweed oil and set fire to it. Then, he accused Etienne of not being able to take a joke when he started bawling his eyes out.

"I suppose I *am* the only one who's going to say it," Sylvain said, casting a fleeting glimpse at Etienne, as though he knew whatever was coming next would set him off.

And he was right.

"It was that Chatine girl. I never trusted her. I saw her sizing up the storage chalet with a gleam in her eyes numerous times. The pieces are all there, right in front of us. We just have to put them together. Etienne picked her up on *Bastille*." Sylvain turned and, this time, gave Etienne a long, hard glare. "She's a criminal. She conned the Regime. And she conned all of you, too."

"That's a lie!" Etienne could no longer keep his voice trapped inside.

"Ouch!" Astra said again, holding her hands over her ears.

Etienne hastily lowered her to the ground and glared back at Sylvain. "You don't know what you're talking about."

"Don't I?" Sylvain retorted. "Or are you just too blinded by your feelings for her to see the truth?"

Something hot and fiery and numbing exploded behind Etienne's eyes. "It was her parents!" he shouted, feeling instant relief from the burden of his words.

"Her parents?" Sylvain spat back, sharing a confused look with Bastien. "Who on Laterre are her parents?"

Etienne sighed. This was it. There was no turning back. With a grit of his teeth, he murmured the two names that he knew would send the lodge into another cacophony of noise. "Fabian and Gen."

The reaction was instantaneous.

"What?" cried Jordane. "Have you lost your mind?"

"You *have* been blinded by that girl," said Sylvain.

"I miss Fabian and Gen," little Astra whimpered by his feet.

"Fabian and Gen wouldn't hurt a butterfly!" shouted Saros.

"You're all wrong," Etienne seethed. "That's how good they were. They deceived every single one of us. Their real name is Renard. They are Chatine's parents. They were planning to steal the zyttrium and sell it to the highest bidder. When they were out 'looking for their lost children,' they were actually securing a buyer."

A few eyes swiveled to Caroline, the pilot who had taken them on that journey.

"Is that true?" asked Bastien.

Caroline shook her head, looking dumbfounded. "I . . . I don't know. They left me with the ship. They were gone for a while. I suppose they could have. . . ."

The outrage morphed into hushed whispers of shock and disbelief.

Etienne raised his voice to be heard. "Chatine *saved* this camp."

"How do we know that?" Sylvain fired back. "She could have easily been working with them."

Etienne shot a scathing look at Sylvain. "Because I was there when she confronted them and convinced them to leave. I flew them out that very night. I used all the proper protocols, blindfolds, indirect routes, but . . ." He let out a breath that felt as heavy and dense and dark as the Laterrian sky. "Apparently, they found their way back anyway."

"And you never thought to *tell* us about this?" Jordane shouted, startling baby Mercure, who began to wail. Jordane passed the baby to his father and continued to glower at Etienne. "You just decided to keep this to yourself?"

Etienne felt sick. Because she was right. He shouldn't have kept it to himself. He should have told someone. His maman, at least. But . . .

The truth suddenly barreled into Etienne like a speeding combatteur.

He *was* blinded by his feelings for Chatine. And he knew if he'd told the camp, they would have turned against her. Just as they were turning against her now.

"I thought . . . ," Etienne began forcefully, but his voice seemed to lose momentum with every word. "I thought I had taken care of it."

"Clearly, you were wrong," Sylvain snarled.

"That's enough," said Mentor Ava, sounding more sure of herself than she had during this entire meeting. "What's done is done. We must stop passing blame and start making plans. Who would like to put forth the first proposal?"

A few hands were raised, but Etienne couldn't handle it. He knew how this process worked. The community would deliberate for hours, maybe even all day. Proposals would be made and discussed and dismissed. More ideas would be circulated until finally a solution was reached that was acceptable to everyone. And although Etienne had every right to be a part of the process, he couldn't stand to be in this room for any longer. He needed air. Space. A place to think.

He grabbed his coat and started for the door but stopped when he felt a hand on his. He turned to look into the warm chestnut eyes of his maman and quickly lowered his gaze.

"I'm sorry," he whispered as the din of the first discussion rose up around him. "I messed up. I made a hasty, selfish decision. Just like the night of the—" His voice broke, and he stopped himself before the tears could come.

"Shh," Brigitte cooed as she planted a soft kiss on his cheek. "I'm proud of you."

Surprised, he looked up. "What? Why?"

"You chose to protect her. That's not selfish. That's brave."

Etienne felt his cheeks warm. Of course his maman could see right through him to the truth. She knew him better than anyone. Sometimes, it seemed, better than he even knew himself.

"I'm going back to the hangar," he said before nodding in the direction of the tables with a half-hearted smirk. "Don't let them kick me out, okay?"

Brigitte smiled, causing her cyborg scars to ripple like gentle waves across her cheek and forehead. "They'd have to kick me out too, and then, let's see what happens when they try to heal themselves."

Etienne allowed himself a chuckle before squeezing his mother's hand and slipping out the door.

As predicted, Gabriel practically pounced the moment he appeared.

"What took you so long? I've been freezing my pants off out here!"

"You could have waited inside your chalet," Etienne pointed out.

"And miss something? No way. What'd they say? Do they know who did it? What are we going to do? How long before the Ministère finds us? Oh Sols, I cannot go to Bastille. That has been my motto from day one: Don't get caught. Don't go to Bastille. It's freezing up there. I mean, it's freezing here, too. But at least here we have clothes and food and ember-weed oil to fuel the heating stoves—"

"Gabriel," Etienne said sternly. "Stop."

Gabriel fell quiet. But it only lasted a second. "Wait. Where is everyone else?" His gaze bounced between Etienne and the door.

"They're deliberating," Etienne said, and then, when Gabriel's face crumpled in confusion, he added, "It's what we do when a decision needs to be made. Everyone has to agree on a proposal before it's acted upon."

"And that works?"

Etienne shrugged. "Yeah. Pretty well, actually. It stirs up more ideas than anyone could ever come up with on their own. And instead of a few people getting their way, we all try to find a solution that everyone likes, or at least can live with."

"Huh." Gabriel glanced at the door again, then back at Etienne. "So why aren't *you* in there, you know, deliberating?"

"I don't know." He pulled on his puffy silver coat and yanked the hood over his head to try to stave off the cold wind that was whisking through the camp. "But I'm going to wait in the hangar."

Gabriel followed him up the covered walkway into the building and was surprisingly quiet as Etienne busied himself with maintenance checks on Marilyn. He'd already completed all of the same procedures just last night, but he didn't know what else to do with himself.

As he opened compartments, poked and prodded, and Gabriel passed him tools, he felt his anxiety ease just the slightest. If they kicked him out, so be it. He would find a way to smuggle out Marilyn and take his maman and all of his siblings with him. They'd start a new community. Somewhere far away from Laterre. Maybe on an asteroid. He might even let Gabriel come.

"Etienne? Are you in here?"

Etienne stumbled out from under an open hatch to see Mentor Ava standing in the doorway of the hangar. His throat went dry. It was too early. Too soon. The community had been deliberating for barely a full hour.

"Can we talk?" Ava asked.

With a heavy sigh, he stepped outside, into the crisp air. "Look, I just want to say—"

But Ava held up a hand to stop him. "Can you find them?"

Etienne blinked, not following. "Excuse me?"

"Can you find Fabia—" She stopped herself. "Can you find these Renards?"

"What do you mean?"

"The community feels that the best course of action is to try to get the zyttrium back, and it was suggested, since you were the last to see the perpetrators who stole it, that you be the one to attempt to track it down."

Something broke free in his chest. Something that had been penned up for far too long. He shot an incredulous look back into the hangar at Marilyn. The community was giving him a mission? He was going to get to fly again?

"Of course, you can say no," Ava reminded him.

"Yes!" came a desperate voice behind them. "And I can help!" Gabriel sidled up next to Etienne and threw his arm around his shoulder. "Etienne and I are a team. Some even call us the Blue Bandits."

Etienne stiffened and flung Gabriel's arm away. "Gabriel. I told you, I work alone."

Gabriel snorted. "Not this time, mec. You might be able to fly that hunk of junk, but if you're looking to track down criminals, *I'm* your man."

"Marilyn is not a hunk of . . . ," Etienne began at the same time as Mentor Ava said, "Do you accept this mission, Etienne?"

A gust of wind tore through him, biting at his cheeks. "Yes." He didn't have to think about it. "I accept."

Ava nodded, looking relieved. "Very good. Then, I suggest you depart as soon as possible. Take only enough zyttrium from the reserve as you need. Use cloud coverage instead of stealth whenever possible. In the meantime, we will prepare the rest of the camp for departure."

Etienne's stomach lurched. "Departure?"

Ava cast a sorrowful gaze at their surroundings—the hangar, the chalets, the roofed walkways that crisscrossed between the buildings. Years of hard work and collaboration. "The location of our camp has been compromised. We are no longer safe here. Good luck, pilote."

She turned and headed back in the direction of the lodge. Gabriel let out a tiny whoop and began to dance up and down the walkway.

As Etienne watched Mentor Ava disappear around the corner, a flame of hope ignited in his chest. He could do this. This was his chance to make amends for his mistake. He would find the Renards, steal back the zyttrium, and save his community.

There was just one problem. Where would he even begin to look for these people?

And suddenly, the flame in his chest was snuffed out again as he realized there was only one place to begin. He had only *one* lead.

CHAPTER 27

CHATINE

CHATINE SLAMMED THE DOUGH DOWN ON THE counter, causing a puff of flour to bloom into the air. She had probably kneaded this bread enough by now, but she was far from done. She peeled the wet loaf from the countertop and squeezed it mercilessly in her hands like she was strangling something. Normally, she despised making bread. It was messy and sticky, and she was always finding flour in strange places for days afterward. But today, she was quite enjoying the outlet.

BANG!

She threw the dough onto the counter with the force of a basher and plunged her hands into it. Pushing. And shoving. And crushing.

General Bonnefaçon had put a target on Alouette's head.

BANG!

She had three more days to step forward.

BANG!

And if she didn't step forward, *he* would be appointed the next Patriarche of Laterre.

BANG! BANG! BANG!

After she'd beaten the bread into a pulp, she set it aside in a baking dish to rise and got started on the soup for dinner. As she chopped and poured and stirred, she kept Marcellus's face in her mind. It was the only face that inspired her to keep going. Keep cooking. He needed to eat. He'd been looking even frailer than usual. Had he eaten *anything* since returning from his meeting with Max?

With the bread finally in the oven and the soup simmering, Chatine wiped her hands on her apron and shuffled out of the kitchen to look for Roche. He'd been acting so strangely the past few days. This morning, Chatine had found him in their shared room, which used to be the old office. He was scribbling something in his journal, and when Chatine asked about it, he stuffed the whole thing—pen and all—under the mattress. She had the sneaking suspicion he was hiding something from her.

Oh, who was she kidding? He was a *Renard*. He was most certainly hiding something from her. And she was determined to find out what it was.

With Marcellus and the sisters locked away in the Assemblée room strategizing with the leaders of the Vangarde cells, and Alouette still resting in the infirmerie, the Refuge was quiet. As soon as Chatine reached the intersection of the two main hallways, the soft light seeping from under the library door snagged her attention.

"Hello?" Chatine called as she stepped inside and glanced around. A few small reading lamps glowed on nearby tables, illuminating the rows and rows of books huddled on a myriad of shelves. "Roche?"

There was no reply.

She was about to switch off the lights when a flicker of movement caught the corner of her eye and she spun back around. A woman was slinking between the bookshelves.

"Hello?" Chatine called out again.

Still nothing.

Curious, Chatine made her way toward a tall shelf and peeked around its corner. There, in the middle of the aisle, staring up at the shelves as though she'd never seen books before, was Sister Jacqui.

Her short, dark hair was combed neatly to the side, but a lone silver lock sprang outward behind her ear. Above her gaunt, sunken cheeks, the sister's eyes—the color of Sol-rise through the clouds—gaped, wide and glassy. They didn't move. They didn't blink.

"Aren't you supposed to be in the infirmerie?" Chatine tried to keep her voice quiet so she didn't frighten her. She'd heard the other sisters whispering in the hallways. She knew Jacqui was in the worst shape of any of them. According to Sister Léonie, Jacqui had come back from that island "broken."

But Jacqui didn't reply. She just continued to stare at the books. Was she *looking* for a particular one? Perhaps "broken" meant she had lost parts of her memory. Maybe she didn't remember what books were.

"Do you need help?" Chatine tried again, but once again, the sister acted like she wasn't even there.

It certainly wouldn't be the first time. Chatine was used to feeling invisible. In fact, there was a time in her life when she actually relished it.

"Okay," Chatine said awkwardly, "well, I'll leave the lights on for you." She turned and started for the door again but was stopped a moment later by a loud *crash!* Chatine raced back to see a slew of fallen books on the floor. Sister Jacqui was huddled in the middle of them, her hands covering her head like she expected more to fall.

And she was trembling.

Chatine hurried over but soon realized she had no idea what to do. The woman was clearly having some kind of traumatic episode. But was Chatine supposed to comfort her? Touch her? Hug her?

That felt wrong.

She barely knew the woman, and Chatine had never been much of a hugger.

So instead, she did the only thing she knew how to do. She bent down and started to gather up the fallen books and return them to the shelf. The woman continued to shake and whimper. Chatine picked up the pace, scooping up books and tossing them on the shelf. When she reached for the last one, however, she felt Jacqui's hand encircle her wrist.

Chatine let out a small shriek and nearly dropped the book. Not because her grip was strong. It wasn't. The woman had the strength of a butterfly. But because, up until this moment, the sister hadn't even acknowledged

Chatine's existence. Now, though, she was staring right up at Chatine. And her eyes, which just moments ago had looked glassy and unfocused, were clear and warm and kind.

Jacqui didn't have to speak. But Chatine still understood.

"You're welcome," Chatine said with a small smile before turning to place the final book on the shelf. But when she turned back to Jacqui, she noticed her expression had changed. Where, a split second ago, Chatine had seen gratitude, she now saw only distress.

Confused, Chatine glanced at the shelf where she'd haphazardly placed the fallen books. Darting another quick look at Jacqui, Chatine began to straighten the shelf, making sure the books were pushed all the way back and their spines were straight.

But Jacqui's troubled expression did not change. And her gaze did not leave the shelf.

With a spike of determination, Chatine rearranged the books from shortest to tallest, once again making sure the spines were straight and flush with the wall. When she looked back to the sister for approval, Jacqui was pointing at a book on the shelf.

"This one first?" Chatine asked, plucking it out.

Jacqui's chin dipped ever so slightly in a nod.

Shoving the other books aside, Chatine slid the chosen volume into the correct place, before turning back to the sister, who was already pointing at another spine.

"Then this one?" Chatine confirmed.

Jacqui nodded again.

It wasn't until the tenth and final book was placed that Chatine noticed the pattern. The first letter of each of the spines followed the same order that Francine had taught her for the letters of the Forgotten Word.

Huh.

Chatine ran her fingertips over the spines, feeling a faint tingle. As though the books were speaking to her. Thanking her.

When she spun around, Jacqui was back on her feet, pointing at another one of the shelves. Chatine leaned in closer to study the spines, immediately seeing the discrepancy. "They're out of order."

Something that resembled the beginnings of a smile appeared on Jacqui's lips.

Chatine immediately got to work, slipping books in and out of place, all the while quietly singing the song Francine had taught her to help her remember the order of the letters. She admitted the work was starting to soothe away the remnants of her anger and helplessness. It was methodical, and there was a sense of satisfaction with each book that she placed.

She heard a rustle of movement and glanced over to see Jacqui was organizing the neighboring shelf, her lips moving silently as she worked. There was something about the way she touched the spines—with reverence and love—that made Chatine smile.

"This was your job, wasn't it?" she asked.

Jacqui nodded again.

"But since you've been gone so long, no one was tending to the books?"

A shadow passed over the sister's face, and Chatine berated herself for saying something so stupid. She should have just kept quiet. She grew up with the Renards—you would think she'd know when to shut her mouth.

But the longer Chatine and Jacqui worked, the farther they moved through the library—sorting and organizing—the more Jacqui seemed to settle. Her shoulders fell away from her ears. Her face relaxed. Her speed and dexterity picked up. Sister Laurel might have bandaged her wounds and injected her with healing tinctures, but it was clear to Chatine that *this* was the real treatment center.

"I wish they had assigned me this job," Chatine muttered to herself as they made their way through a collection of dark crimson spines with gold lettering. "It's much better than working in the kitchen."

Jacqui glanced out of the corner of her eye at Chatine, and even though she still said nothing, Chatine could see the challenge in her gaze.

"I know, I know." Chatine blew out a breath. "Principale Francine already gave me that lecture. 'Every job has honor in it.'" Her Francine impersonation brought back that ghost of a smile on Jacqui's face. "But honestly, how are you supposed to feel honorable when you're covered in flour and scraping burnt bits off the crust?"

She turned back to Jacqui, but the sister was no longer there. Startled,

Chatine scurried around the corner to find Jacqui plucking a small, thin book from one of the higher shelves. She pushed it into Chatine's hands.

"What's this?"

But once again, the sister said nothing. She just dropped her gaze to the book, then peered back up at Chatine, her golden eyes glimmering with something Chatine couldn't interpret.

Chatine turned the book around in her hand, examining it from all sides like it was an unfamiliar object salvaged from the heap of junk at Monsieur Ferraille's stall. When she glanced back up again, the sister was already slipping out through the library door and disappearing into the dimly lit corridor beyond.

Chatine knew she should check on her bread, but her curiosity got the better of her.

She lowered herself into a chair at one of the tables hidden between the stacks and flipped the book open to the first page. Immediately she could spot the difference between this book and the countless others she'd tried to slog through. She felt her body relax. The letters were larger, and the sentences were spaced farther apart, making it so much easier to follow them with her eyes. And the words were shorter, simpler, made up of three or four or five letters instead of a hundred.

She smiled to herself as she began to read, but before she could even turn the page, she was startled by the sound of heavy footsteps echoing down the hall. A moment later, through the gaps between the shelves, she saw Marcellus trudge into the library, looking lost and aimless.

Chatine's stomach flipped at the sight of him: skin ashen, eyes hollowed, hair mussed like he'd been running his fingers through it relentlessly.

She rose from her seat and followed Marcellus to his desk in the back corner. He didn't seem to notice her as he glared down at the scattering of books and maps on his desk for a long time before something snapped inside of him and he began to hastily gather everything up. Chatine had an inkling it wasn't so much because he wanted to clean, but because he wanted something to do with his hands.

She knew the feeling.

It took a good five seconds before she compelled herself to speak. "What happened?"

Marcellus startled at the sound of her voice. He spun around and for a long time just stared, like he was trying to make sense of her.

"He . . . ," he began, and Chatine noticed the shakiness in his voice. He sounded as haunted as he looked. "My grandfather . . . ," he tried again, but he couldn't finish. Instead, he focused back down on the desk and, seemingly irritated by the state of it, went back to work, rolling up a sheet of fragile, aged parchment and gathering up scattered notes. He tried to arrange them into a neat pile, but his hands were shaking and some of the pages slipped right through his fingers and floated to the floor.

Chatine waited, fighting the urge to scream, *Just tell me already!*

Marcellus bent down to pick up the fallen notes, but his gaze seemed to catch on something on one of the pages and he stopped, staring numbly down at his own handwritten letters. As though this one, these words, were too big of a burden. Too much to take. With a quiet whimper, he dropped heavily into the chair and, to Chatine's shock and disbelief, started to cry.

Chatine could only stare, once again, unsure what to do. Why was everyone choosing to break down in front of *her* today? She was the *least* capable person she knew of dealing with these kinds of outward displays of emotion.

"The coronation ceremony has been scheduled." Marcellus buried his face in his hands. "He's really going through with it. Three days from now, my grandfather will be Patriarche."

Chatine's stomach flipped. "But I thought the sisters were working on a plan."

"They have a plan," he said darkly. "They're going to reveal Citizen Rousseau during the ceremony. As a kind of protest. They're hoping they can hijack the event and stop it from happening."

"And Alouette?"

Marcellus shook his head. "They still agree she should be kept hidden. Thank the Sols. But I just can't help thinking that without her . . ."

"It's a lost cause," Chatine whispered, leaning on the desk to steady herself. The anguish that was streaming off Marcellus in great, undulating waves felt like it was going to knock her over.

"He's always three steps ahead," Marcellus cried into his hands. "If she reveals herself as the heir, there's a chance the Red Scar will kill her. If she doesn't, there's a chance the Vangarde won't be able to stop the coronation and then . . ." He shuddered visibly at the thought of what came next.

Chatine sighed and maneuvered herself between the desk and Marcellus, kneeling down in front of him. "Maybe . . ." She knew he wasn't going to like what she was about to say, but someone had to say it. "Maybe Alouette *should* come forward."

Marcellus sniffled and blinked at her, aghast.

"Just hear me out," she pleaded. "Everyone's so terrified that the Red Scar will kill her, but what if they don't? I mean, if there's a chance that she can stop this coronation from happening, shouldn't we at least entertain the option?"

"No," Marcellus said adamantly. "Absolutely not. You saw what they did to the Favorites."

"But those were a bunch of pomps!" Chatine fired back. "Whose only skill was lounging around pools. Alouette is strong. Stronger than you think. She brought down the Skins, remember? And you told me about what she did on the voyageur to Albion. How she stood up to that admiral and his guards. She also saved Gabriel's life. The sisters have taught her a lot. Maybe . . ." She struggled, trying to find the right words, but that had never been her strong suit. "Maybe you all need to have a little more faith in her."

Marcellus's jaw tightened, and he looked away. "Well, it doesn't matter anyway. The sisters won't allow it. And if it were up to me, neither would I."

"Fine. Just forget it." Chatine sighed and stood up, but Marcellus reached out and grasped on to her hands, like he was drowning in the Secana Sea and she was the lifeboat.

Chatine glanced nervously between his bloodshot eyes and her hands clutched in his. The whole situation was making her uneasy. Not because she didn't like being this close to Marcellus. But because she *did*.

Too much.

For too long.

With too many consequences.

"I'm sorry," he muttered. "I just . . . the whole thing makes me so angry."

She nodded weakly. "I know."

Marcellus let out a shaky breath. "I know you know. Because you know me better than anyone. What would I do without you, Chatine?" His voice was so broken and yet so earnest. "You've been my rock. The ground beneath my feet. The planet to my moon. When I thought I'd lost you on Bastille, I went insane. I was racked with guilt and grief. I don't think I ever got a chance to tell you this, but *merci*."

Chatine felt the air vanish from her lungs. She couldn't think. She couldn't see. And breathing was certainly out of the question. "Merci?" she croaked, trying to keep her voice light. Humorous. That's what she and Marcellus were good at, right? Keeping things light. Making jokes. Building safe distances between themselves. "For what?"

"For surviving up there!" he exclaimed, obviously failing to catch on to her signals because his voice was kilomètres away from light. "For saving my life at that Ascension banquet. For being here with me now."

Chatine let out a silent curse under her breath. How did this always happen? How did he always manage to pull her in even after consistently pushing her away? And why could she never fight it? Why did she never *want* to?

Marcellus continued to stare up at her, his eyes shimmering with something she hadn't seen in a long time. And for a split second, she wondered if he felt it too. If he'd been trying just as hard to resist it. If pushing her away, ignoring her, pretending he couldn't even see her when she was standing right in front of him, had just been his way of coping. *Fighting*.

Because, for the first time in three months, when she let her gaze fall to his, when she let herself really *look* at him, he didn't look away. He didn't get pulled into a map or a book or another rambling rant about a lost island in the Secana Sea. He kept his eyes steadily, earnestly, *obsessively* focused on her.

Like he really did mean those words. Like she really was the planet to his moon. Keeping him turning. Keeping him moving. Keeping him close.

"I . . . ," Chatine began awkwardly. But she didn't know how to finish. Because what on Laterre do you say to all of that? It didn't matter, though. Her words had never been enough before, and they certainly wouldn't be enough now.

Because suddenly, Marcellus was on his feet. His lips were crushed against hers. His hands were wrapped around her waist and he was pulling, pulling, pulling. Until she couldn't possibly get any closer. Until the moon overtook the planet with its gravity. With its desperation.

Chatine now fully understood the shock Marcellus must have felt on the roof of the textile fabrique so many months ago, when she'd let down her hair, revealed her true identity, and kissed him.

Because right now, she felt exactly the same way. Like Marcellus had turned into a different person right before her very eyes. And yet, they were both the same. They were back on that rooftop, heat and electricity streaming through them like a thunderstorm about to break the sky.

And his kiss, it was so hungry, so urgent. Like he was trying to extract so many things from her lips: redemption, salvation, assurances that everything was going to be okay.

Chatine knew those were promises she couldn't make. Those were things her lips were just too feeble to offer. And yet, she couldn't bring herself to pull away. She couldn't stop making those false promises. Because she knew, with certainty, that she, too, was trying to pull impossible things from Marcellus's kiss: purpose, usefulness, validation that she'd made the right choice by being here. With him.

Instead of . . . somewhere else.

And then, suddenly, that somewhere else was here. In this very library. Crowding this tiny space.

"Is anyone there? Can anyone hear me?" A familiar voice flooded the room. It sounded crackly and distant. But it was clear enough to fling Chatine halfway across the library. "Hello? Does anyone copy? If you can hear me, please respond!"

Etienne?

Chatine's heart pounded as her gaze darted around the room, searching for the source of that voice. Until, finally, she found herself staring incredulously at the bulky device still sitting on Marcellus's desk, tossed haphazardly next to his straightened pile of maps and books.

Panicked, Chatine looked to Marcellus, who was still trying to compose himself from the interruption. And . . . what had happened *before* the interruption.

He seemed to shake himself out of a trance before lunging for the radio. "Hello? Yes, we can hear you. We copy."

There was a long, weighted pause before the voice spoke again. "Who is this?"

Chatine heard the same traces of bitterness that she'd seen so clearly on Etienne's face the day she'd left the camp. With Marcellus.

"This is Marcellus Bonnefaçon. Who is *this*?"

Another pause. This one seemed to last a lifetime. Long enough for Sols to die and be reborn. For solar systems to realign. For moons to find another planet to orbit.

"This is Etienne. I need to talk to Chatine."

Just then, the smell of smoke bombarded Chatine's nostrils and her gaze snapped to the door, where Sister Clare stood holding a very black and very burnt loaf of bread.

CHAPTER 28

ALOUETTE

THE AIR IN THE PROPAGATION ROOM WAS SUFFOCATing. It was hot and damp. Clammy and intruding. It made Alouette's tunic stick to her neck and the backs of her knees, and it tasted heavy and metallic on her tongue.

Normally, Alouette loved the propagation room. With its rows of potted seedlings growing under strips of purple light. The tangles of berry bushes and trimmed grapevines snaking up the uneven walls. The narrow aisles and network of workbenches for potting plants and holding grow trays. The herb beds that released a cacophony of beautiful scents. And those pails of soil, rich and dark and ready for planting.

But today, as she paced in tiny circles in front of Laurel's tool cupboard, she felt trapped. Like the vines on the walls would soon come for her next. Wrap around her neck. Pin her to the wall so she couldn't leave. Couldn't fight.

No room in this Refuge was safe anymore.

Because every room had become her prison.

That was the way the sisters wanted it. They wanted her locked up. Hidden away. And ironically, that was exactly what the general wanted too. He wanted her to feel trapped. He wanted her to feel hopeless. That broadcast was a warning and a prison sentence all at once.

Leave this Refuge, show your face anywhere on the planet, and most likely die.

Or stay in hiding forever and live.

Either way, the general gets what he wants.

Alouette's balance shifted at the thought, and she grabbed on to one of the workbenches to right herself.

Never mind that she was ready to fight. The sisters had made up their mind. There was no way she could change it. The general's announcement had doomed her to a life underground. A life lived in secret. A life wasted.

"I forgot how good it smells in here," came a wistful voice.

Alouette spun around and froze. She'd thought all the sisters were locked away in the Assemblée room, discussing their plans for the upcoming coronation ceremony. But apparently, not *all* of them.

The tall woman in the long gray tunic strode gracefully into the room. Her hair glimmered like titan, and the glow from the propagation lights reflected in her eyes, turning them into pools of shimmering violet. Alouette was suddenly unsure where to direct her gaze, where to put her feet, how to stand up straight.

"Laurel tells me that you've been a big help to her in here during my absence. Merci."

Alouette opened her mouth, but no sound came out. She expected to feel differently in Citizen Rousseau's presence. She expected to feel the same flashes of rage and resentment she'd felt in the infirmerie, when she'd thought about how many lives had been endangered for this woman. How many of Alouette's beloved sisters had nearly died trying to break her out. But there was something about her—this *stranger*—that immediately knocked Alouette off guard. Words fluttered through her mind—some fierce and angry, some calm and rational—but she couldn't seem to organize any of them into a coherent sentence.

Citizen Rousseau took a long, deep breath and gazed around the room. "I used to work in here, you know. Laurel was my apprentice. In fact, I built this room."

"You did?" Alouette blurted without thinking.

"I did." Rousseau reached out and lovingly touched a flowering tomato plant. "It was one of my first projects when I came to live in the Refuge nearly thirty years ago."

The words slammed into Alouette. *Thirty years.* She'd been a member of the sisterhood for far longer than Alouette had. Which meant, she wasn't a stranger. Not really. The sisters knew her. They trusted her. Did that mean that Alouette should automatically trust her too?

But then Alouette thought about Sister Jacqui's silent, vacant stare, and Sister Denise's bruises, still healing from months of torture and neglect. And every gramme of that borrowed trust dissolved right into the damp, humid air.

"What are you doing here?" Alouette demanded sharply, even though she knew, from what Rousseau had just told her, that she had no valid claim on this propagation room. But she didn't want anyone else's voice in her head right now. She just wanted to be alone.

Rousseau looked more amused than offended. "I came to talk to you."

"Why? I don't even know you."

"I don't know you either," Rousseau said, as though that settled it.

"Well, you can't just expect me to trust you. You might be *their* leader, but you're still a stranger to me."

Rousseau flashed Alouette a cryptic smile. "I don't."

Alouette balked, once again caught completely off guard. "So, you came here to gain my trust? So you could convince me the sisters made the right choice to keep me hidden? That it's for my own protection?" As soon as she said the words, the fury and frustration behind them came surging back.

Citizen Rousseau didn't answer. She bent down to examine a small cluster of green beans dangling among their vine's protective leaves, and then turned to Alouette. "Will you walk with me?"

Curious, Alouette glanced around the small room. *"Where?"*

"I often used to walk up and down the aisles in here when I couldn't sleep. Or when I needed to think. I find the plants calm me." Rousseau began walking down the narrow aisle that traced the perimeter of the room. Hesitantly, Alouette caught up with her, matching Rousseau's pace.

She waited for the sister to speak, to answer some of these rambling questions in her mind. To her surprise, however, Rousseau was silent. And

Alouette found herself listening way too closely to the sound of their canvas shoes padding across the slate tiles of the propagation room.

They'd already weaved through the room three times before Rousseau finally said, "I didn't know about you until three months ago. After the sisters rescued me from Bastille." Her voice was hushed and quiet, yet steadfast and melodic at the same time. "In fact, I didn't even know about the rescue mission they'd been planning for years. Because of my solitary confinement, I have been kept entirely in the dark. Much like you." The Vangarde leader turned to flash Alouette an apologetic half smile. "But unlike you, I *chose* to enter this world. I chose to become a revolutionary."

"Why?" The question slipped out of Alouette before she even knew she was asking it. But as soon as it was there, hanging in the damp air, she realized she really did want to know.

Rousseau raised an eyebrow. "That's an extremely good question. Because I could bear it no longer. The injustice, I mean. The inequality of this planet. The way everyone on Laterre is divided into those that have nothing and those that have too much." She shook her head, and her braided hair—a metallic serpent snaking over her shoulder—twinkled in the purplish glow of the propagation lights. "Nature never intended for people to be separated. The three estates of the Regime are unnatural. They will never work. As long as we are divided, there will always be unrest."

She stopped walking and turned toward one of the vast grow trays that held Sister Laurel's jungle of herbs. "It's the same with plants. In their most natural form, they are all mixed together. They flourish from each other. Under the surface, their roots intertwine and mingle and support each other in one vast network. It was humanity that started to separate them, for efficiency of production. We created fermes and hothouses and orchards, isolating the different species from each other and forcing them to live in regimented rows and fenced sections. They can grow that way, yes. But it's not how they *want* to grow. Which is why ferme workers always have the task of maintaining, weeding, separating." Citizen Rousseau lovingly touched a nearby sprout that was just breaking the surface of the soil. "But if you let them grow how nature intended, they will thrive."

Alouette was rendered nearly speechless as she watched the woman stare wistfully at the trays of intermingled herbs. She recognized the expression on Rousseau's face. It was the same loving gaze with which Hugo used to look upon Alouette, and it filled Alouette with a burst of nostalgia and longing. "How do you know so much about plants?"

With a slow exhale, Rousseau began to walk again. "My parents were assigned to work in the Vallonay fermes. They were both very talented botanists."

"Did you live in the Frets?" Alouette asked, feeling her curiosity begin to peek out from under the surface. Just like that tiny seedling in the grow tray.

"Yes," Rousseau said. "I grew up in Fret 15. My parents used to grow herbs in secret inside our couchette. Mostly herbal remedies and homeopathic cures outlawed by the Regime. I learned all of this from them." She gestured around the propagation room with a look of pride before turning her intense silver gaze back on Alouette. "When I was about your age, they put me in charge of delivering the herbs and remedies to our customers. I spent a lot of time in the sewers," she added with a chuckle.

Alouette's eyebrows shot up. "The sewers?"

"Back then, they weren't just for waste. They were like a network. A place for people to move about undetected. Anyone doing anything that the Regime would disapprove of went down to the sewers—to trade, to pass information, to connect. I'm told, after the Rebellion of 488, the Regime cracked down on this. They shut down and boarded up most of the sewer systems and moved to a self-composting system."

"So, you and your parents used the sewers to carry and trade your herbs and remedies?" Alouette tried to imagine Citizen Rousseau when she was young. Before her hair had turned silver. Before her skin had been hollowed and beaten and lined. Before so much of her life had been stolen away in a solitary prison cell on Bastille.

"Exactly," said Citizen Rousseau. "There was a grain silo near my parents' ferme that had a well-placed entrance to the sewers, through a drainage grate in the floor. It used to hold grain for bread. Not the good kind of bread that the First and Second Estates ate. Chou bread for the poor. When my parents discovered the access point, they released an herbal toxin into the silo that contaminated the grain, making it inedible. The Ministère didn't want to cause a panic, so they quietly decommissioned the silo, without logging the event in the Communiqué, and it became one of our primary entry points for the sewer system. It was through the sewers that I came to discover the Refuge."

"The founders' tunnel," Alouette said with sudden comprehension.

"Yes," Rousseau said. "Back then, the sisterhood was just a group of women who had chosen to live off the Regime's grid, to protect the books of the First World. At first, they were our customers. They bought my parents' herbs and tinctures and I delivered them. It wasn't until much later that I convinced them to become something else."

"*You* turned them into the Vangarde?" Alouette asked, stunned.

Rousseau smiled. "The sisters taught me how to read and write, and soon I devoured every one of their books, consuming everything I could about the First World—its upsides and downfalls. And I, in turn, taught the sisters how to be brave and to use their sacred protected knowledge to change the planet. 'What good is all of this wisdom you've been protecting,' I used to say, 'if you don't share it and use it to make the planet a better place?'"

Alouette smiled. "So, the sisters were your first followers?"

"You could say that. But they also gave me my name."

"'Citizen Rousseau'?"

She nodded. "The sisters were the ones who introduced me to the stories of the First World. The leaders and thinkers and artists who were brave enough to fight for change."

"But how did you come to *live* with them?"

Suddenly, the smile ebbed from Rousseau's face, and she reached into her pocket and pulled out that strange cardboard cylinder Alouette had seen through the crack in the Assemblée room door. Rousseau began to turn the rotating top, round and round. It reminded Alouette of the way some of the sisters would thread their devotion beads through their fingers when they were contemplating something. And for the first time, Alouette saw a hint of grief on the woman's face.

"The point is," Rousseau said, clearly dodging the question, "I was raised by rebels. Just like you. And I decided to use that rebellious spirit that my parents instilled in me to try to change the system. That was my hope for the Rebellion of 488. My path was so clear to me. I made a choice. All of the sisters did. But you, Alouette, you were never given that choice. You were brought into this world of the Vangarde without having any knowledge of it and without having ever been asked. I'm not sure I agree with the strategy the sisters have taken, keeping your identity and their purpose a secret from you all of these years, but I do understand it. They have been trying to protect you. To keep you safe." Rousseau stopped walking and turned to face Alouette. "Just as they are doing now."

At this reminder of the sisters' decision, the anger came crashing back down around her. "But I want to help," Alouette insisted. "I want to fight. I was *raised* to fight. I don't want to stay hidden anymore. I don't care if it's dangerous. I don't care if the Red Scar find me. I can't just stay locked up in here and let the general win. You're right. I was never given a choice. And I'm *still* not being given one. *You* got to decide your own fate. You knew the risks and you led that rebellion anyway. Why am I not allowed to do the same?"

"You are."

Alouette felt as though she'd been running full speed only to be stopped short. "So," she began reluctantly, afraid to say the hopeful words aloud, afraid they might be popped like fragile soap bubbles before ever lifting off the ground, "you *didn't* come here to convince me to stay hidden?"

There was a long, heavy silence before Rousseau replied, "No. I didn't."

Dizziness overtook Alouette. Maybe she'd walked in one too many circles around this propagation room. "Why did you come here, then?"

"To find out who you are."

The simplicity of the statement ironically uneased Alouette. "What do you mean?"

"Like you said, we don't know each other. I don't know anything about you. I don't know who you are." Rousseau paused to twist the cylinder in her hand two more times. "Do you?"

"I . . . ," Alouette faltered, her mind rushing back to that image of her parents on the hologram feed, standing beneath the archway of roses, gazing so lovingly into each other's eyes. Lyon Paresse and his Third Estate bride. "Yes. I'm the daughter of the Patriarche. Which makes me the last of the Paresse name. The only heir. I . . ." Suddenly, Laurel's words to her in the infirmerie solidified in her mind, along with her resolve. "I'm the symbol. Of unity. Of a planet without estates. Of everything you just said you wanted for Laterre."

Rousseau nodded, considering her answer, like she was trying to figure out if she liked it.

Frustrated by her silence, Alouette kept going. "That's why the Vangarde took me in. Why they raised me to be one of them. So that I could grow up to play a part in this revolution and help them change the planet. That was their plan all along, wasn't it?"

"Yes," Rousseau said. "I suppose it was."

"Then, I don't understand why any of that should change. I'm not scared of them. Any of them. The general. The Red Scar. I want to do what I was raised to do. I want to fulfill my duty to this cause. I have Paresse blood in my veins. That is a weapon. A source of power. And it will be wasted—all of their sacrifices will be wasted—if I'm forced to sit within these walls like a . . . like a . . ." She waved her arms around. "Like one of these plants. Protected from the outside world until I wither away to nothing."

Rousseau studied her as her fingers continued to rotate the top of her cardboard cylinder. "So that is your why?"

Alouette blinked, once again knocked off guard by this woman's labyrinth-like train of thought. "What?"

"You asked me why I chose to become a revolutionary. It's an important question. Possibly the most important. Because the why is what will fuel you. Drive you. Protect you. It's what lights the path even in the darkest moments. If your reasons aren't clear, aren't pure, your path will quickly become obscured and you will lose your way."

A shiver passed through Alouette as she stared numbly at Citizen Rousseau, feeling her words sink deep down into her bones, her marrow, her blood. Her *Paresse* blood.

"Yes," she said, the certainty coming to her in thick, powerful waves. "That is my reason. Because that is who I am. Who I was born to be.

When I brought down the Skins with my DNA, I felt it. I knew this was my purpose. I knew this was why the sisters had taken me in and raised me to believe in a better world. A just world. I am the heir. I am the Lark. And I can help bring about the fall of this Regime."

"Very well," Rousseau said conclusively, as though she'd completely forgotten about the bigger issue here.

"So, you'll go back to the sisters and tell them?" Alouette asked. "You'll convince them to let me join you? To stand beside you?"

Rousseau flashed Alouette a small smile. "I don't think I can do that."

Frustration rushed back to her, chopping up her words again. "But . . . you just said . . . I can't convince them. They won't listen to me. They'll listen to *you*."

Citizen Rousseau gazed wistfully around the propagation room. "Have you ever noticed how effortlessly plants adapt? It's impressive. Their ability to live in different environments, different climates. It's why they will surely outlive us as a species."

Alouette dug her fingertips into her palms, trying to keep up. But it was like chasing after a dust mote caught in a breeze.

"But we can learn from them," Rousseau continued, her eyes tracking one of the long, winding vines that had split off from the rest. "The most effective leaders on the First World were the ones who adapted. Who ventured beyond the obvious and found new ways of thinking. New ways of approaching a problem. Even if it diverged from what others thought was the right way."

Alouette followed her gaze to the ceiling of the propagation room, where the rogue vine twisted and stretched its way up, up, up, toward the nearest grow light. As though it would break right through the bedrock, right to the surface of Laterre. As though it were reaching not for the grow light at all, but for the Sols.

"There is *always* another way," Rousseau said. "The question is whether or not we are brave enough—whether our convictions are strong enough—to reach for it."

Another shiver passed through Alouette, and she turned to gape at the enigmatic woman standing next to her, still staring up at the ceiling. Was she really saying what Alouette thought she was saying? Was she really telling her to—

"This is not the cage you think it is," Rousseau said, her eyes drifting back down to meet Alouette's. And in those eyes, in those shimmering, endless pools of silver, Alouette got the answer she was looking for. "And larks can fly."

- PART 3 -
THE
CORONATION

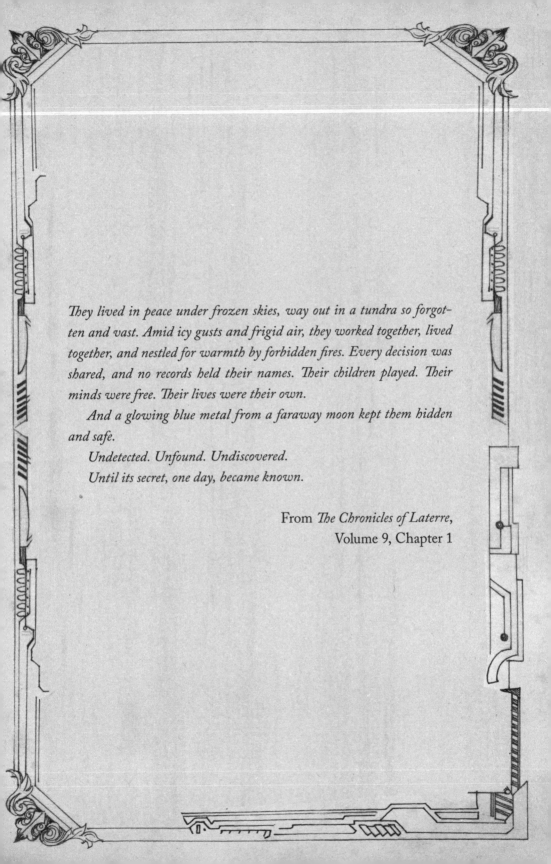

They lived in peace under frozen skies, way out in a tundra so forgotten and vast. Amid icy gusts and frigid air, they worked together, lived together, and nestled for warmth by forbidden fires. Every decision was shared, and no records held their names. Their children played. Their minds were free. Their lives were their own.

And a glowing blue metal from a faraway moon kept them hidden and safe.

Undetected. Unfound. Undiscovered.

Until its secret, one day, became known.

From *The Chronicles of Laterre*,
Volume 9, Chapter 1

CHAPTER 29

CERISE

"IT'S ANOTHER EVENING IN LATERRIAN PARADISE! I'M Desirée Beauchamp, the host of your daily TéléCast, coming at you *live* from the capital city of Vallonay on the eve of General Bonnefaçon's historic coronation. As you can see from the view behind me, preparation crews are hard at work setting the scene for tomorrow's festivities."

Cerise momentarily peered up at the enormous hologram that stood tall and regal at the front of the Bureau of Défense's now-empty technology labs, where she had been working nonstop for the past thirty-two hours without sleep. The footage showed the Marsh filled with transporteurs unloading supplies, workers clearing the pathways between stalls, and a series of vast tables being hammered and bolted together.

"It has been four days since General Bonnefaçon made his fateful announcement to the planet that there was, in fact, another heir to the Paresse line possibly still alive somewhere," Desirée Beauchamp continued. "Of the more than two hundred people who have come forward since the announcement, claiming to be Alouette Taureau, none of them have proven to be legitimate. Facial recognition scans performed by Policier droids and compared to the Communiqué have confirmed that the real Alouette Taureau has not yet been found."

Cerise felt her circuitry start to flicker with irritation. She promptly blocked the sound of Desirée's voice and focused back on the device in front of her. Or rather, what *used* to be a device and was now a carefully organized assortment of disassembled parts laid out across her workstation.

No matter how hard she tried, how deeply she buried herself in her work, she could not escape that name.

Alouette Taureau.

Cerise still hadn't fully recovered from the shock of what the general had revealed to the planet. She was certain the footage of the Patriarche's secret wedding to a woman named Lisole Villette was the very footage she'd decrypted from the microcam. And the implications of it were still reeling through her mind.

The Patriarche had another daughter. And her face, just like the face of Chatine Renard, felt frustratingly familiar to Cerise. A glimmer of something just out of reach. A piece of her traitorous past that her brain had deemed dangerous and distracting.

But if Alouette Taureau was the rightful ruler of Laterre, why would her brain choose to block that out? There was something about this that didn't add up.

And Cerise Chevalier did not like it when things didn't add up.

"Energy in the marketplace is already starting to build as people await this historic moment. Never before, in our history as a planet, has a Patriarche been crowned who was not a direct descendant of Thibault Paresse—whose statue still stands behind me now as a tribute to the founding family. And never before has a coronation ceremony taken place outside Ledôme, among the very people the Patriarche is being called forth to lead."

Desirée waved one of her manicured hands around at the crowd that had gathered in the Marsh to watch the preparations. "It's clear that General Bonnefaçon is sending a very different kind of message with this choice: I am a people's leader. I am here to serve the people. Not myself."

Cerise gripped the tweezers and got to work reassembling the various components spread out across her workstation. The device she was working on had been found in Jolras Epernay's pocket at the time of his arrest, and Cerise had volunteered to analyze it for two reasons: (1) she was certain she was the most qualified cyborg in the Bureau to do so, and (2) she believed it might lead her to Marcellus Bonnefaçon, who was last seen with the Red Scar.

But so far, the device had only perplexed her. It was, by far, the strangest thing she'd ever come across. Its surface was an ugly matte gray, its hinges large and unwieldy, and the metal shell of the whole boxy contraption, now stripped from its inner components, felt oddly chunky and heavy in her palm.

After sliding the final pieces into place with tiny, satisfying clicks, Cerise pressed down on what she'd gleaned was some kind of power activation button and waited, her circuitry flashing eagerly with anticipation. A moment later, the small screen illuminated with a soft green glow and then . . .

Nothing.

No images. No sounds. No connections.

"Any progress?" someone asked from behind her. Recognizing her father's voice, Cerise dropped the tool in her hand and stood at attention.

"Directeur Chevalier. Good evening, sir. I have conducted a thorough analysis of the device. The mechanics are intricate and well-made. But it's definitely not Ministère technology."

"Does it work?"

"Not completely, sir. At first, I was unable to turn it on. I deduced that it had been remotely deactivated somehow. Even though I was eventually able to power on the device with new firmware, unfortunately, I've been unsuccessful in my attempts to connect it to any network."

"Hmm," the directeur said, running his hand across his chin. "Have you tried any of our nonoperational networks?"

"Yes," Cerise said. She'd tried *everything*. Every network under the Sols. But the device had still done nothing. It hadn't even seemed to *recognize* a signal. As if it were a newborn baby who simply stared blankly at anyone attempting to speak to it.

Directeur Chevalier picked up the device and studied it, flipping the lid open and closed. It reminded Cerise of an oyster shell, the inside revealing not a pearl but a set of twelve squat buttons and an impossibly small screen.

"How did Jolras Epernay wind up with a device that doesn't connect to any of our networks?" her father asked.

"I don't know, sir." Cerise had been asking herself the same question. How did a group of scruffy, red-hooded terrorists like the Red Scar manage to construct a piece of technology that Spécialiste Chevalier, recipient of the Medal of Accomplissement, couldn't understand?

Unless it wasn't the Red Scar who had developed it.

Cerise immediately rejected the idea. It was unprompted and unfounded, and she didn't have time to entertain such notions. The Red Scar were the enemy here. There was no other enemy. All other enemies were dead and gone.

Despite whatever doubts Commandeur Moreau had.

The directeur placed the device back onto her desk with a sigh. "So, you're saying we still have *no* leads on the whereabouts of Maximilienne Epernay and the remaining members of the Red Scar?"

Cerise felt her processors flood with frustration. She had tracked Marcellus Bonnefaçon to the wheat-fleur fields and then lost him due to the incompetency of the Vallonay Policier. And now she was failing at this, too.

She cleared her throat. "I can try reconfiguring the firmware again. As soon as the device connects to a network, we can trace the signal back to its source. I am confident this will lead us to the Red Scar and potentially Marcellus Bonnefaçon as well."

She watched her father's face carefully, waiting for him to exhibit some hint of reassurance, trust that she would succeed, that she was the cyborg he wanted her to be. But he simply gazed around the technology labs with a look of defeat and said, "Well, that will have to wait. The coronation ceremony is tomorrow, and you should be well rested. Have you chosen a dress?"

"Chosen a dress?" Cerise repeated, the question not computing in her mind.

The directeur gave her a quick once-over and chuckled. "Did you honestly think you were going to attend the ceremony wearing that?"

She glanced down at her neatly pressed cargo pants and shirt with its spotless silver collar and stripes on the sleeves. "This is my uniform."

"And this is a *coronation*," her father replied. "As the most recent recipient of the Medal of Accomplissement, you have the honor of representing the Ministère and the Regime. It would be disrespectful for you to not look the part." He gave a tight nod toward the door. "I'm sure you can find appropriate attire in your closet back home."

Home.

The word rippled through her processors like a faulty line of code. This building was her home now. But she knew her father wasn't speaking of the Ministère headquarters. And the thought of going back to that place filled her with a sense of dread.

"Can't I do it in the morning, sir?" Cerise asked. "Certainly, the choosing of a dress doesn't take longer than a few minutes?"

The directeur raised an eyebrow. "Oh, how much you have changed, Cerise."

The cruiseur doors sealed with a *whoosh* and the craft lifted into the air. As the Ministère headquarters disappeared behind her and she sped along the bustling Grand Boulevard, Cerise spotted the familiar landmarks of Ledôme. The towering and ornate columns of the Opéra gave way to the grand marble staircase outside the Musée of the First World. And after the cruiseur swept around the gigantic base of the Paresse Tower, the sculpted turrets and stained-glass windows of the Maison de Valeur came into view. There was usually a large crowd of Second Estaters waiting in long, snaking lines to look upon the imperial jewels and Paresse family treasures kept within its walls. But tonight, the entrance was empty. It was late and, according to the TéléCast, Laterre's ceremonial crown had already been transferred to a fortified transporteur to be delivered to the coronation ceremony tomorrow afternoon. It was the first time in over two years that the priceless, gem-laden artifact had been released from the vault. The last time was when Lyon Paresse was crowned.

Cerise snapped her gaze from the window. She didn't understand why the coronation of a new leader required so much extravagance and circumstance. Her own promotion had been a simple update in the Communiqué.

A few taps on a screen, and she was given a new title and a higher clearance level. That was all that needed to be done. But all of this preparation and work and fanfare felt like a waste of the planet's time and resources.

The cruiseur finally pulled to a stop in the porte cochère of a magnificent manoir with a majestic bubbling fountain in front. Cerise took in the striped pillars, the ornate pediments, the grand and glinting rows of windows, and felt her stomach turn over.

It was the first time she had returned to her family's manoir since her surgery. She'd had no reason to come back. Everything she could ever want was provided at the Ministère: a sleeping pod perfectly acclimated to her body temperature, meals prepared with the ideal macro nutrient balance for her enhanced brain, and a job that fulfilled her and gave her a sense of purpose.

The only thing this house had ever given her was a sense of failure.

She didn't want to do this. Her processors were pulsing in protest, once again trying to protect her from the painful truth of her past. But she knew she had to do it. Her father had given the order. And, as the Medal of Accomplissement recipient, it was part of her official duties to attend frivolous Regime functions like the coronation.

Inside, the manoir was empty and silent. Her mother was currently vacationing on Novaya, and her father spent most of his nights in his private office suite at the Ministère headquarters, where he could be on call whenever the general needed him. As Cerise climbed the elegant, curved staircase to the second floor, she could hear hazy echoes of her father's words reverberating off the marble steps, off the titan-gilded frames on the wall, the tiny crystals that bloomed from the chandelier overhead.

"When are you going to do something worthwhile with your life?"

"How did I end up with such a silly, sparkle-headed daughter?"

"You can't keep running away from your future, Cerise. I've rescheduled your operation for tomorrow morning. . . ."

Cerise stopped in front of the double doors at the end of the hall and stared down at the ornately carved handle, promising herself she would do this quickly. She would go in, she would grab a dress, and she would leave. She would not linger. There was no reason to linger.

Bracing herself, she pushed open the doors and stepped inside her old bedroom. But surprisingly, the sensation that came over her was not what she expected. She felt . . . *nothing*. She was a scientist observing the natural habitat of a typical Second Estate teenage girl. She walked around, examining the immense four-poster bed with remote interest and the mountains of multicolored cushions with cool detachment. She ran a fingertip across the impossibly smooth marble nightstand like she was checking it for remnants of dirt. She gazed out the vast arched windows at the moonlit pool below like she was taking mental notes for an upcoming manoir sale.

But then, she stepped into the closet.

And it was like a tsunami crashing down around her. Hazy, half-formed memories were attacking her from all angles. She could see an endless parade of fancy fêtes and giggling girls preening themselves in mirrors. She could see herself prancing down the Grand Boulevard, carrying linen sacs filled to the brim with clothes. Clothes that now hung in this very room.

Her eyes tracked to the far back wall, which was constructed entirely out of shoes. Shelves upon shelves that stretched all the way to the ceiling. How could one person possess so many shoes? Cerise couldn't comprehend the purpose.

But there was something about these shoes that intrigued Cerise. For some reason, she couldn't stop looking at them. One pair in particular snagged her attention. They bore heels like knife blades and small jewels encrusted in the toes. She felt an illogical yet overwhelming urge to look closer. And the moment she did, a beam of light shot out from one of the tiny red jewels and swept across her right eye. Startled, she scurried backward, out of its reach, but evidently not quickly enough because just then, an ethereal voice from some undetermined location said, "Biometric scan complete. Access granted."

Access? To what?

The unmistakable sound of a lock disengaging pinged through the closet, followed by a low whirring hum. Then, the rows of shoes in front of Cerise began to shudder and split apart. A blue light shone from within, like the season of the Blue Dawn arriving six years early. The crack grew and grew as the two rows of shelves disappeared into the surrounding walls. Finally, the whirring stopped and Cerise found herself staring at a whole other closet.

A secret, *hidden* closet.

And that's when she realized that these expensive clothes that surrounded her weren't the end of her shameful past. They were just the beginning.

Because before her, where moments ago there had been a wall of shoes, floor-to-ceiling shelves now stood, holding all the evidence of her past life. Boxes and boxes of devices big and small, some stolen, some handmade, all of them illegal. All of them marking memories her brain had been wise to block out.

Her breathing started to grow shallow. It had been a mistake to come here. To this place that only reminded her of the traitor she used to be. A traitor who hid her crimes behind a false wall with a biometric lock disguised as a shoe. Every single device on these shelves was something that could easily send a hacker to Bastille. Cerise knew because she worked in the department that was tasked with catching them.

She almost turned around. She almost ran straight back to the Ministère to divulge everything. The Bureau could have a team of forensic spécialistes here within minutes.

But then, something in her peripheral vision stopped her short. Her gaze snapped to the left, where a TéléCom, which had been very deliberately propped up on the middle shelf, flickered to life. Like it had been triggered somehow. The screen lit up to reveal a face Cerise knew all too well. She let out a sound that was half scream, half gasp, and one hundred percent human.

Because it was *her* face staring back at her. But it was also *not* her face.

The girl's left cheek and forehead were completely smooth, void of any circuitry. Her eyes sparkled out from the screen, fierce and determined, and both of them as warm and brown as the rich mahogany shelves that lined this closet. And when she spoke, there was absolutely nothing monotone about her voice.

"Bonjour, Cerise. If you're watching this, it means we failed."

CHAPTER 30

CHATINE

THE REFUGE WAS QUIET WHEN CHATINE CREAKED OPEN the door of her bedroom and peered out. The heavy PermaSteel door at the end of the hallway was closed. Tomorrow was the general's coronation, and Marcellus and the sisters had been locked away in the Assemblée room all night, preparing to save the world.

It was a fight Chatine now knew she was not a part of.

At least not here.

At least not with them.

Here, she was just a servant. A cook. The Third Estate Fret girl who burned the bread. But out there . . .

She let out a shudder of a breath as the thought that had been batting around in her head all night finally coalesced in her mind.

Out there I'm needed.

She pulled the bag she'd packed earlier—flashlight, food, water, and those strange binocular things Roche had used in the Marsh—onto her shoulder and glanced back at the young boy sleeping on the bed in the corner of the room, next to Chatine's unmade cot. For the hundredth time, she reminded herself why she could not take him with her. Why he was safer here. Why this was the right choice. Even if it made her feel like a weight as heavy as a droid was crushing her chest.

She turned around and started to walk toward him but stopped herself. It was better if she just left. Easier. Cleaner. Plus, she'd always been wretched at good-byes.

It's not good-bye, she quickly reminded herself. This was temporary. She would see Roche again. She would see all of them again. She was sure of it. She just didn't know *when*.

Her ribs started to crack under the pressure.

Just go, she told herself. *Turn around. Don't look back.*

She took a deep breath and spun toward the door, her heart hammering with every step she took.

"Are you running away?" The sleepy voice caused the small fissure in Chatine's ribs to grow and spread, until the brittle bones were one twitch away from crumbling.

She painted on her best breezy smile and turned back. "What? No. Of course I'm not running away."

She marveled at the irony of it all. The last time she'd left in the middle of the night, she'd been leaving to look for *him*. It was Etienne who'd convinced her to stay. Now she was leaving Roche to find Etienne. Would her life ever stop being so Sol-damn complicated?

Roche sat up and rubbed the sleep from his eyes. "Then what are you doing?"

"I'm just . . . ," Chatine fumbled. "Going to get some water."

"With a sac?"

Chatine glanced down at the bag hanging from her shoulder and mentally kicked herself. She used to be better at this. She used to be able to lie through her teeth to anyone. But Roche was different. He'd always be different.

A knowing smile crept its way across his face. "Ohhhh, I know where you're going."

Chatine's own smile collapsed. "You do?"

He nodded and a twinkle flashed in his eye. "Yup. And I'm coming with you." He pushed away his covers and began to stand. Chatine rushed over to him.

"No, no, no. You stay right here. You're not going anywhere." She pushed on his shoulders until he fell back down.

His lips tugged into a petulant scowl. "But they're *my* bébés. I should help find them."

For a moment, Chatine could only gape. "What?"

"You're going to find the missing Oublies, right?"

Chatine struggled to connect the dots. "Roche," she said gently, searching around the blankets for his hand. She gave it a squeeze. "I'm not going to look for the Oublies. I'm sorry."

The look on his face was the end of her. It wasn't her ribs anymore. Every bone in her body seemed to shatter to dust.

"But Léopold and Adèle," he said in a cracked voice. "What if something has happened to them? What if they're scared and alone and they have no one to tell them it's going to be okay? They're afraid of the dark, you know? When we used to sleep together in the Paresse statue and the Marsh would fall quiet and the Darkest Night would come, I would keep my Skin on for them all night long. I had to stay awake and keep tapping it so it wouldn't shut off. I told them the glow from the screen was the Blue Dawn coming early, lighting up the dark. What if they're in the dark now and there's no one to keep the light on?"

Chatine exhaled a heavy breath and cast her gaze down to the bed. She couldn't stand to watch the tears forming in his eyes. "I'm sure they're safe," she told him, searching for some untapped well of conviction she might have stashed away in her mind somewhere. "In fact, I bet the reason there are no more Oublies on the streets is because they've all been taken in by families."

Roche sniffed, and in his voice she heard a glimmer of hope. "You think?"

She nodded and forced herself to meet his eyes again. "I do. I mean, it makes sense, right? You saw the Marsh. You saw how people were dressed. How happy and healthy they looked. They have more food now. More largs. They can afford to take in children and feed them and clothe them and keep them safe."

She watched the comprehension play out on Roche's face, his Fret-rat mind knitting together the threads of her spun tale. Maybe it was true. It certainly *could* be true. But what mattered most was the look of relief in Roche's eyes as he nodded and scooted back down under his covers. "You're probably right," he said, fatigue creeping back into his voice. "They're probably with a family now."

"Definitely," Chatine agreed. "A nice family who gives them real bread to eat and keeps the lights on for them all night long."

"Mm-hmm," Roche said dreamily as his head sank deeper into the pillow and his eyes began to close. Soon, his chest was rising and falling with the restful breath of sleep.

And as Chatine crept out the door and down the hallway toward the tunnel hatch, she was eternally grateful that Roche had forgotten to ask her again where she was going.

Because she wasn't sure she could lie to him twice.

With her coat wrapped tightly around her, Chatine reached for the circular handle on the hatch and gave it a firm twist. The old passageway stretched out before her, dark and dank and ominous. She didn't like the tunnel. It reminded her too much of the exploit shafts buried beneath the surface of Bastille. And despite the sisters' efforts to stabilize it, the walls felt like they were on the verge of collapsing. Then, of course, there were the old sewers at the other end, with just enough remnants of their former use to make your nostrils sting. But the front entrance had been sealed off, leaving the tunnel as her only option.

With shaky hands, she pulled the flashlight from her sac, flicked it on, and stepped into the darkness before pulling the heavy, round hatch closed behind her.

For some reason, however, it wouldn't shut all the way. It was as though something—or some*one*—was pulling at it from the other side.

"What the fric?"

The door slowly swung back open, and there stood Marcellus, his skin sallow and his dark hair tousled again. A single rebellious strand curled across his forehead.

"I can't *believe* you're doing this," he said in a low hiss.

She painted on the same breezy smile she'd doled out for Roche. "Doing what?"

"Don't play stupide, Chatine. It doesn't suit you."

She blew out a breath. "Fine. I'm going to meet him, okay?"

"Why?"

"Because he needs help."

"And why are *you* the one to give it to him?"

She threw up her hands in frustration. "Because I can!"

"You don't even know what he wants," Marcellus fired back, still keeping his voice low. This was the first time either of them had said a single word to each other since Marcellus had kissed her in the library two days ago. And the conversation was going about as well as Chatine had expected.

"He insisted on telling me in person," she explained. "But I know he contacted me for a reason. Which means he thinks I can help."

"What about this?" Marcellus gestured to the quiet corridor behind him.

"What about *what*?"

He rolled his eyes. She was playing stupide again and they both knew it. "This! The Refuge. The sisterhood. The Vangarde. The *revolution*. We're unveiling Citizen Rousseau *tomorrow*."

"The revolution doesn't need me," she muttered.

For a moment, the frustration faded from Marcellus's face, replaced with confusion. "What are you talking about? Of course it needs you. *We* need you. You're an integral part of this whole thing."

"Open your eyes, Marcellus," Chatine whispered angrily. "The Vangarde has no real use for me. I agreed to live here with all of you because I *did* want to be a part of something. I wanted to help people and change this planet. But I'm not the general's grandson or the Patriarche's daughter or a famous rebel who's been locked in prison for two decades. I'm just a Fret rat whose skills have no place in this world of your pomp revolutions. But now . . ." Her voice trailed off as her gaze drifted back down the long, snaking tunnel into the darkness. Into the unknown. "Now there's a chance my skills *are* needed. There's someone who believes I *can* help. And so I will."

For a long time, Marcellus didn't speak. But he didn't look at her either. His eyes were locked on the floor. On that narrow threshold between the

Refuge and the tunnel. Between in here and out there. Between safety and unknown dangers.

"I had no idea you . . . ," he started to say, but quickly changed his mind. "Fine." With a huff, he turned on his heel and stalked away from the hatch. But instead of continuing down the hallway, back toward the Assemblée room, he threw open the door to the utility closet and disappeared inside.

Chatine rolled her eyes and followed behind him, watching Marcellus open locker doors and rummage around in various bins. "What are you doing?" she asked in annoyance.

But Marcellus didn't answer. His eyes looked wild, almost frenzied, as he pulled a sac from a hook on the wall and started to fill it with seemingly random items: wire clippers, a screwdriver, and a strange piece of filament that looked like cyborg circuitry. His lips moved silently, as though he were reciting directions to himself. The lack of sleep and food had clearly gone to the boy's head.

"Marcellus," she said in a warning tone. "What are you—"

"I'm coming with you."

Chatine balked. "What?"

He continued to toss things into the sac. "I want to find out what this mec wants. And it's not safe for you to go out there alone."

"Marcellus, I don't need your help."

He closed the sac and swung it over his head. "Clearly you do."

"What's that supposed to mean?"

But Marcellus was already on the move, striding briskly but quietly back down the corridor. Chatine knew she could not let him accompany her. He was too tired. Too stressed. He would only be a liability. This was the work of a Fret rat. Not a pomp, spoiled former Second Estate officer.

"Those coordinates he sent are deep in the Forest Verdure. How exactly were you planning on getting there?" Marcellus asked over his shoulder.

"I was going to walk," Chatine said, no longer as confident in her plan as she was two minutes ago.

"Exactly," said Marcellus, as though this settled it. But it certainly did not settle it.

Chatine rolled her eyes again. "Are you saying you have a better idea?"

"As a matter of fact, I do." Marcellus reached the hatch of the tunnel and swung it all the way open, gesturing for her to go first. "We're going to steal a moto."

- CHAPTER 31 -
CERISE

CERISE LEANED FORWARD, CAPTIVATED BY THE GIRL speaking on the screen. It wasn't just her face that was shocking. It was everything about her. The way her black hair seemed to glisten. The way her dark eyes danced. The way she talked like every word was as sparkling as a star.

"The Ascension banquet starts in a few hours. The others are getting ready now, but I couldn't leave without capturing this message. Without leaving something behind. Just in case . . ."

Information streamed through Cerise's processors, almost too rapidly for her to keep up. This footage was captured three months ago. Right before her former self helped Marcellus Bonnefaçon infiltrate the Grand Palais. Right before Cerise committed treason against the Regime.

"We have a plan. It's a good one and I told the others I was confident it would work, but . . ." The girl on the screen paused, glancing over her shoulder into the empty closet. The same closet Cerise was now sitting in. "But I have to admit to someone that there's a chance it might not. Something could go wrong. My father could be alerted that I'm back in Ledôme. He could track me down. He could have me arrested and sent to Bastille. But most likely, he'll put me in a very different kind of prison."

The girl touched the left side of her face, as though trying to commit its smooth, unblemished surface to memory.

Cerise reached up and did the same, delicately tracing the tiny nodes embedded in her skin. The feel of them usually filled her with a sense of calm and purpose. But now, she was almost startled to find them there.

"I guess if you're watching this, that's exactly what happened." The girl on the TéléCom gave a small laugh that was filled with more sadness than joy. "But my father turning me into a cyborg is not the worst thing that could happen tonight. The worst is that we fail to stop the general."

Cerise's circuitry sparked frantically to life. This was it. This was the evidence and testimony she'd been unable to provide on her own. The memories that had been held prisoner in her mind were captured right here. On this TéléCom. She grabbed for the device, still perched so precisely—so *purposefully*—on the shelf, and slid to the floor of the closet, clutching it in her hands.

"Cerise, I need your help. If General Bonnefaçon—"

"Hello?" a voice called from somewhere behind her, and Cerise leapt to her feet, fumbling to turn off the TéléCom and return it to the shelf. "Is anyone in here?"

Cerise grappled along the wall of the closet, searching for a panel, a switch, a trigger, something to seal the wall back up, but she found nothing. So, when a dark-haired girl in a blue-and-black cleaner's uniform walked into the closet, the shelves full of contraband were exposed for all to see.

"Oh! It's you." The girl stopped short and gaped at Cerise, before lowering her gaze as though embarrassed to be caught staring. "I'm sorry. I didn't know you were—no one ever comes here anymore." She fidgeted nervously with one of the pockets of her uniform. "I was just . . . doing some last-minute cleaning."

Lie.

Cerise's processors decrypted the girl's expression almost immediately. But before Cerise could confront her, she burst out, "I'm sorry, that's a lie. I wasn't cleaning. I was just . . . it's so nice and warm in here and the house is always empty, so I thought it would be okay if I just hung out for a little longer. I promise I won't do it again!"

"Who are you?" Cerise asked, doing her best to shield the wall of contraband with her body. But she knew that was a futile effort. The wall was too large, and she was too small. But if this cleaner was at all shocked to see the illegal devices behind Cerise, her facial expressions did not register that emotion. They only registered confusion.

"It's me," she said, as though this were the determining variable that Cerise had overlooked. "Lucie." And when Cerise didn't reply, the girl added, "I've been cleaning your house for two years now. Remember? You used to make me gâteau and we would talk. For hours."

Cerise's circuitry flickered with suspicion. Nothing about any of these words felt familiar to her. Which meant this girl was yet another part of Cerise's questionable past that her mind had chosen to obstruct.

"I apologize," said Cerise. "Some of the memories from my former life have been . . ." She filtered her vocabulary for the best word. "Compromised."

The girl—Lucie—still looked confused. Cerise pointed to the implants on the left side of her face. "It's a known but rare side effect of my cyborg operation."

"B-b-but," the girl stammered, "you *have* to remember. We spent all that time together. I even gave you some of my uniforms for one of your 'secret missions.' That's what you used to call them. You seemed to have an outfit and a special device for each one." She pointed at the wall behind Cerise. "Remember?"

Cerise snapped her gaze between Lucie and the shelves. "You know about this?"

"Of course." Lucie chuckled weakly and stepped past Cerise to pick up one of the devices. The sight of it in the girl's hands made Cerise's nerves flutter. "This is what you used to use to hack my Skin every time they released a new update."

"I used to hack the Skins?" Cerise asked incredulously.

Lucie seemed to find this amusing. "Not just the Skins. You hacked *everything*. TéléComs, cruiseurs, holograms, motos, voyageurs . . ."

Cerise darted a look at the illegal TéléCom still sitting on the floor, and her own words echoed hauntingly in her mind.

"If you're watching this, it means we failed."

"Wait, is that what you're doing here?" Lucie asked, pointing again to the exposed wall behind Cerise. "Are you hacking something?"

"No," Cerise said hastily, bending down to scoop up the TéléCom before returning it to the shelf. "I came here to choose a dress. For the coronation ceremony."

Lucie's eyes lit up like exploding stars. "Oh my Sols! You get to go? That's so soop! I wanted to go, but I have to work. They let the fabrique and exploit workers off and the ferme and hothouse workers, too, I guess. But not me. Do you need help?"

"With what?" Cerise asked.

"Choosing a dress."

"No," Cerise said automatically before her brain processed the overwhelming selection of garments that filled the closet. "Yes."

Lucie laughed again and quickly stationed herself in front of the rack of dresses. "Okay, so this is a coronation, kind of a big deal. We should definitely go big or go home." She was already sorting through hangers at nearly the same speed with which Cerise sorted through incoming surveillance footage. "What do you think of it all, anyway?"

Cerise opened her mouth to ask for a clarification, but Lucie kept talking.

"I mean, it's whacked, right? This whole thing with the general and Alouette Taureau and the Patriarche's secret wedding." She plucked out a soft turquoise dress with a hem of tiny embroidered flowers and held it up in front of Cerise, tilting her head and pursing her lips before evidently deciding against the selection and returning it to the rack. "A lot of people think she's dead. Otherwise, why wouldn't she have stepped forward by now? I mean, who wouldn't jump at the chance to be Matrone? All of those clothes and jewels. Not to mention the crown!" Lucie sighed and pulled out another dress, before quickly ruling that one out too.

All the while, Cerise kept stealing glances at the TéléCom on the shelf, her mind wandering back to the footage.

"Cerise, I need your help."

"I don't know, though," Lucie went on as she continued to slide hangers across the rack. "I really like the general. He's pretty soop. Papa had the rot a few months ago. We thought he was going to die. But then, one day, médecins just showed up at our couchette out of the blue, said they were there on the general's orders, and they cured him. Oh, this one! For sure!"

Cerise blinked down to see the girl had pulled out a dark purple dress with complicated shoulder straps, a sleek bodice trimmed with gems, and layers of silk pluming from its waistband. She eyed it skeptically. It did not look like something one could easily maneuver in. "This is what I should wear?"

"Absolutely," said Lucie, hanging the dress from a hook on the wall. "With your coloring, you'll look titanique."

Cerise felt a strange warmth flood through her. "Merci."

Lucie grinned. "No problem. Why don't you try it on, and I'll wait out here."

Before she could reply, Lucie was closing the door behind her, leaving Cerise alone in the closet. Alone with that TéléCom. She knew she should turn it in. Preferably now. She'd seen enough to discern that it was a valuable piece of evidence and may even include intelligence about Marcellus Bonnefaçon's failed attempt to assassinate the general.

But the longer she stared at the darkened screen, the more an overpowering curiosity seemed to thrum through her, circumnavigating her programming like a virus designed to evade detection. It was almost as if the device were calling to her. Summoning her. Despite the hangers and hangers of bejeweled dresses and sequined garments, that TéléCom was the shiniest thing in this closet.

She walked toward it, feeling the pull grow stronger the closer she got. There was only one valid reason to press play: to review the entire contents of the message so that she could properly log it into evidence. She couldn't very well turn it in without knowing everything it contained.

Glancing back over her shoulder to ensure the closet door was still closed, Cerise slowly reached out and tapped on the screen.

In a heartbeat, the girl was back. With her shiny, dark hair and unblemished skin. "Cerise, I need your help," she began again. "If General Bonnefaçon is in control of the Regime right now, then Laterre's worst nightmare has come true. You can't trust him. The general is not who you think he is. I won't tell you what he's done because I know you won't believe me. If you're what I think you are now, you will need to see it for yourself. You will need proof. I can help you get that proof."

Cerise flinched as the programming buried deep within her brain began to protest, alerting her of the threat, of the treachery of these words. And yet, Cerise could only feel entranced by them. Her former self—the way her eyes shimmered, and her voice bounced, and her energy radiated through the screen—captivated Cerise in a way she couldn't comprehend. Couldn't process.

"On this TéléCom is something I've been working on for months. It's a program that's able to trace unregistered networks. Networks invisible to Ministère scans. I know it works because I recently used it to uncover a First World signal that was being broadcast through an abandoned space probe."

Silence filled the closet, as though the girl who had captured this message had known exactly how her words would affect Cerise. Had known how violently her hands would tremble, how quickly her breaths would come, how erratically her circuitry would flash.

A pain started to pulse deep within her skull. Something strange was happening inside of her brain. Like tiny fireworks exploding, sending fleeting sparks of light to places that were once dark, once forgotten. Blurry images flashed across her vision.

A voyageur cutting through the stars.

A picturesque blue-green planet looming in the distance.

Spatters of blood on a plastique wall.

With shaking hands, Cerise just managed to reach out and pause the footage, letting her processors scan the girl's face, letting them decrypt every centimètre, every crevice, every line, until the result she didn't want to admit came charging back at her.

Truth.

The girl was telling the truth.

She reached toward the screen again, trying to find the strength to shut the TéléCom off. But it was like she was fighting against an invisible force guiding her hands, a new set of programming controlling her movements. All she could do was press play.

"The general sends all of his AirLinks over a secure network. An *unregistered* network. Because he doesn't want anyone at the Ministère to know what he's really doing. I was never able to get close enough to trace the signal. But now you can. If you run the program while he's on an AirLink, you can trace the signal back to its source. To his private, encrypted server. There you'll find all the proof you need of who he really is." The girl leaned closer. Her eyes were no longer sparkling. They were now as dark and penetrating as deep space. "Please, Cerise. You must do this. For the sake of the planet. For all of us. At this point, you might be the only one who can stop him."

"How does it look?" came Lucie's chipper voice through the door. It was finally enough to snap Cerise from her trance. She dove forward and shut off the TéléCom, silencing the voice of her former self. The quiet that followed was anything but comforting.

"Does it look amazing?" Lucie asked. "Can I see?"

"One moment!" Cerise called out, running her hands along the back side of the shelves, once again searching for a button or trigger. Finally, her fingertips slid across a flat, smooth panel, and Cerise felt a hum of relief as the rows of shoes began to protract from the surrounding walls, gliding toward each other before seaming together with a low hiss and a decisive click. And just like that, the TéléCom, her former self, and all of her treasonous words were locked away again. Hidden behind an innocent wall of shoes.

Cerise exhaled and reached for the dress.

- CHAPTER 32 -
MARCELLUS

MARCELLUS HAD FORGOTTEN HOW GOOD IT FELT TO ride. To see the ground blurring beneath him and hear the wind rushing past his ears.

Stealing the moto had been more complicated than he'd thought. He'd stumbled upon the hack in one of the sisters' books a few weeks ago in his relentless search for Alouette. The diagrams and instructions had made it *look* easy—a few clipped wires and a spark—but it hadn't been easy. The abandoned moto that Marcellus had noticed in the grain silo, when he'd passed through with Citizen Rousseau, looked like it hadn't been ridden in years. And once he'd finally managed to locate the right wires to cut and threaded them through the small piece of filament, the moto had been hesitant to get going. It took three sparks before the bike finally awoke from its long slumber and sprang to life.

Marcellus gripped the handles tighter and banked into a sharp turn as the coordinates of their destination flashed across the console. He felt Chatine's arms wrap tighter around his waist for balance.

He'd insisted on driving, but now realized that might have been a mistake. He hadn't considered what it would do to him—his heart, his mind, his focus—to have her so close to him. Her body pressed so tightly against his.

He tried not to think about it.

But it was like trying not to think about warmth when you were freezing in the middle of the Terrain Perdu. Something he personally had experience with.

I never should have kissed her, he muttered to himself for what seemed like the hundredth time. It had been rash and impulsive and just . . . wrong. He'd been distraught over the general's coronation and the Red Scar and Alouette. He'd felt hopeless. And so incredibly lost.

And Chatine had been right there.

Looking just as lost and distraught and hopeless as him.

For just a moment, he'd wanted to feel something. Something other than frustration and helplessness. For just a moment, he'd wanted to clear his mind of thoughts of missing heirs and General Bonnefaçon and Maximilienne Epernay.

And for just a moment, he had.

He'd felt . . . *everything.*

The coordinates flashed again on the console, and a voice in his audio patch directed him to turn right. Marcellus steered the moto toward the Forest Verdure, and as they charged into the trees, branches snagged and grappled at his hair while leaves whizzed by in a gloomy blur. Under the moto, brambles and bushes snapped and creaked as Marcellus accelerated over them.

"Almost there," he called back to Chatine, but she didn't respond. Maybe she couldn't hear him over the rushing wind. Maybe she was still ignoring him. Just like she'd been doing for the past two days. He couldn't lie and say he wasn't relieved. The last thing he wanted to do was rehash that kiss.

Especially now.

The coronation ceremony was scheduled to begin tomorrow at 16.00. Which meant, in less than eighteen hours, everything would change. Citizen Rousseau would be unveiled to the planet. General Bonnefaçon would be crowned Patriarche. Unless the Vangarde could stop it.

The moto swerved, and behind him, Marcellus heard Chatine gasp. He tightened his grip on the handles and forced himself to focus. As they rode onward, the forest grew denser. And darker. Ahead of them, Marcellus could see nothing but branches like a great horde of dangling, shadowy fingers and a blanket of leaves so thick it cut out any glimpse of the night sky above. The beam from the moto was nearly the only light in this seemingly endless forest of darkness.

Finally, the coordinates blinked red on his console and Marcellus careened to a halt, keeping the moto idling so its beam lit up the small clearing in front of them.

"What the fric was that?" Chatine bellowed, jumping from the bike as though the seat were on fire.

Confused, Marcellus glanced back into the thicket of trees. "What?"

"You call that driving?" In the moto's light, her eyes glimmered with a mix of fear and fury. "You almost killed us! Multiple times."

"I did not."

"That low branch nearly took my head off." She started counting on her fingers. "The moto was a centimètre away from tipping when you rounded that tree. And when you hopped the stream, I thought I was going to fly right off the back."

Marcellus snorted. She was clearly exaggerating. Finding reasons to scream at him. Because lately it seemed like something she enjoyed doing.

"Look," he said tightly as he dismounted the moto and moved toward her. "I'm sorry if you're too delicate for my driving, but—"

"Delicate? Seriously, you want to go *there*? You get queasy at the sight of a hangnail."

"I do not."

"You passed out at the Ascension banquet, and I had to practically carry you back to the Refuge."

"I was shot by a lethal pulse."

Chatine scoffed. "And I was attacked by a deranged cyborg with a metal baton!"

"Who I shot."

"And missed!"

Marcellus huffed. This was not helping his frustration. "Whatever. I got you here, didn't I? You're alive, aren't you?"

"Barely," Chatine muttered under her breath as she grabbed her hood and yanked it up over her short, windswept hair.

Marcellus glanced around the small clearing. In the glowing light from his moto, he could see it was completely empty and utterly silent. There was no human sound for kilomètres.

"So where is your darling Défecteur boy?"

"We're early," she said miserably. "And he's not *my* Défecteur boy."

Marcellus cocked an eyebrow. "Oh no?"

Chatine collapsed down onto a pile of leaves and started to thread one between her fingers. "No."

Marcellus leaned against a nearby tree, trying to look more casual than he felt. "Are you trying to tell me that you spent all that time out there in the freezing Terrain Perdu with this mec and *nothing* happened?"

Chatine opened her mouth to speak but seemed to quickly change her mind and looked away. Marcellus felt a knot form in his chest. He tried to relax, but there was just something about seeing that Défecteur again that was setting him on edge. He'd always had a bad feeling about him. Like he couldn't bring himself to fully trust him.

"So, what?" Marcellus asked. "We're just supposed to sit here and wait?"

"No one asked you to come. You volunteered."

"For how long?" Marcellus asked, and he swore he noticed Chatine gulp.

"I don't know. It could be hours."

His thoughts began to scramble as he, once again, glanced at the trees, then back at Chatine. What were they supposed to do out here? *Alone?*

Marcellus started to speak, but Chatine got there first. "And let's not forget about the time I saved your life in the Jondrette."

"What?" Marcellus blinked, trying to catch up.

"*And* in the Marsh. If it weren't for me, that statue would have fallen right on your head."

"What are you talking about?"

"I'm just saying, if there's anyone here who's delicate and needs saving, it's *you.*"

Marcellus snorted. "Please. I've saved your life plenty of times."

"Name one."

"Bastille," he said, jabbing a finger at her.

Chatine rolled her eyes. "Name *two*, then."

"I think Bastille should count twice." He folded his arms across his chest.

"Of course you do."

Marcellus cut his gaze to her. "What's *that* supposed to mean?"

"Never mind," Chatine muttered.

"No, not never mind. What did you mean by that?"

Chatine pitched her voice down into what Marcellus assumed was meant to be an imitation of him. "I'm Marcellus Bonnefaçon. I'm special and important because I'm the general's grandson. Which means anything *I* do counts double."

"I . . . ," Marcellus spat, anger flaring up inside of him. "That's not true."

"Isn't it?"

"No! If anything, it's the opposite!"

This seemed to stump Chatine. Instead of sending a fiery remark ricocheting back through the forest at him, she fell silent and looked up at him with those intense almond-shaped gray eyes of hers.

Marcellus kneaded his hands together, wishing he'd just kept quiet. He lowered himself to the ground and rested his head back against the tree. "If anything, I *have* to count what I do twice because nothing I do matters."

Once again, Chatine didn't reply. But her eyes still stared unblinkingly at him, willing him to continue.

"Do you have any idea how hard it is to keep up with you?"

"Me?" Chatine croaked.

"Yes, you. You and all of your skills. There's nothing *you* can't do. There are a zillion things *I* can't do."

Chatine stared at him like he was speaking another language. Some ancient First World dialect that died out hundreds of years ago.

He kicked at a small tangle of sticks. "You think *you* don't belong in this revolution. How do you think I feel? I had one job. To find Alouette. And I couldn't even do that." There was a long pause as his admission hung in the air, thick and suffocating. He sighed. "I'm just so relieved she's not going out there tomorrow." He'd actually been surprised by how easily Alouette had agreed to stay in the Refuge. To stay hidden. He'd expected her to put up more of a fight.

"You care about her a lot, don't you?" Chatine asked after a while, her voice noticeably softer.

Marcellus slowly slid his eyes back to her. For a moment, he was convinced he knew what he would see in her cat-like eyes. It would be the same thing he felt in his chest whenever he heard her utter that Défecteur boy's name. But when his gaze connected with hers, he saw something else entirely. Something pure and untarnished and innocent.

"Yes," he replied. "I do. I think . . ." He drew in a breath and then slowly released it as the truth finally came tumbling out. "I think I would die to protect her."

Chatine nodded and dropped her head. As though the weight of his words were too heavy. Too monumental. Too big for just one little person to process.

When she finally spoke, her words were jittery and rushed. "That makes sense. I mean, she is the Patriarche's daughter. I guess that makes her pretty important, doesn't it? I suppose we should all be willing to die—"

"Chatine," Marcellus said, stopping her rambling in its tracks. She turned back to him, looking embarrassed. He held her gaze. Tightly, like her arms wrapped around him on the moto. Boldly, like every word she'd ever screamed at him. Resolutely, like the Sols had already decided. "I—"

A twig cracked and Marcellus looked up. Straight into a beam of a blinding white light pointed right at his head. He shielded his eyes and blinked, trying to force his vision to focus. But the light was too strong.

"Marcellus Bonnefaçon," said a deep, droid-like voice. "By order of the general, you are commanded to halt."

Marcellus scrambled to his feet, searching the clearing for more light. More droids. Could they make it back to the moto before they were surrounded?

"You are under arrest for the harmful neglect and reckless abandonment of one criminal mastermind by the name of Gabriel Courfey," the voice continued.

Marcellus flinched and peered back into the light. "What?"

"According to our intelligence, you and—" The droid's voice cracked and, after a quick throat clear, continued. "Excuse me. I've been getting over a little cold. We bashers are actually very susceptible to human disease."

"Gabriel, cut it out," said another voice, and suddenly a second flashlight appeared through the trees, illuminating a tall, shaggy-haired man standing in front of Marcellus with an enormous grin on his face.

"Gabriel?" Marcellus said.

"Long time no see, mec!"

Marcellus closed the small gap between them and threw his arms around Gabriel's neck. "Oh my Sols, it's good to see you!"

Gabriel chuckled and patted Marcellus roughly on the back. "It's good to see you, too. But I meant what I said about the reckless abandonment part. You left me out there in the Terrain Perdu to rot."

There was a groan beside Gabriel, and then the man with the second flashlight stepped into view. Marcellus recognized him at once and his body stiffened.

Etienne.

Just the thought of his name made Marcellus want to throw something.

"I wouldn't call three meals a day and all the hot chocolat you can drink *rotting*," the Défecteur said irritably.

"I've been waiting three months to dole out this guilt trip," Gabriel spat back. "Can you just . . . you know . . ." He put a finger to his lips and then turned his glare back to Marcellus. "Seriously, mec. What gives? Why didn't you come back for me? And where's Cerise? Is she okay? Is she safe? Is she dead? You can tell me if she's dead. I'm mentally prepared for it." He closed his eyes and took a deep breath. "Okay, tell me."

Marcellus tried to speak, but the Défecteur cut him off.

"What are *you* doing here?" He did little to hide the disapproval in his tone. "Where is Chatine? She said she'd come alone."

Marcellus turned back to the spot where Chatine had just been sitting, but it was empty.

"I had no choice," she replied, stepping out from the shadow of a nearby tree. "He insisted on coming. And stealing that." She pointed at the moto.

The Défecteur's eyes went wide as he finally seemed to register where that massive beam of light was coming from. "Are you out of your mind? You hacked a Ministère moto? Are you trying to get us all killed?"

Marcellus instantly felt his hackles rise. "I'm sorry. Did you want her *walking* across open ferme-land where any Policier patroleur could pick her up?"

"So, instead you'd rather just lead them right to her? Ministère motos have tracking devices, you know."

"I *know*. I've been riding them my entire life. Which is how I know how to deactivate their trackers. But this one is over a decade old. I doubt it's even registered anymore."

The Défecteur snorted but said nothing. And Marcellus felt the tiniest gleam of satisfaction.

Gabriel let out a long, low whistle. "Yikes. This is colder than the place we just left."

Marcellus and Etienne shot him matching looks, and Gabriel took a cautious step backward. "Soooo," he said, elongating the word, "where did we land on the whole Cerise thing? Dead? Not dead?"

Marcellus glanced at Gabriel and felt a sudden stab of guilt. He'd been so preoccupied with his own obsessive fears, he hadn't even considered that Gabriel might have some of his own.

"She's . . . ," Marcellus began, but trailed off a second later. He didn't quite know how to say this. He lowered his gaze.

"Dead!" Gabriel bellowed. "I knew it! I just knew it. Oh Sols, I'm not prepared for this. I'm not ready to say good-bye! She was so young. So young." Tears welled in his eyes, and he tipped his head back and stared up at the sky. "Why, Sols? Why?"

Marcellus leapt forward. "Gabriel. No. Stop. She's not dead."

Gabriel blinked back at him, hope illuminating his features. "She's not?"

Marcellus exhaled heavily. He wasn't sure the truth was going to be much better. She may as well be dead. Maybe it would be easier for Gabriel to take. "She's . . ."

"She's what?" Gabriel pressed.

Marcellus glanced at Chatine, who gave him an encouraging nod. "Although we haven't been able to confirm it, we're pretty sure she works for the Ministère now."

Gabriel's eyes lit up. "As a Vangarde spy?"

"No." Marcellus shook his head and forced himself to meet Gabriel's eye. "She's registered in the Communiqué as a cyborg."

"What?"

Marcellus was startled to discover the reaction came not from Gabriel but from the Défecteur. Then he remembered that the woman who had helped Gabriel after he'd been shot was a former cyborg. *And* Etienne's mother.

"I'm sorry," Marcellus said, turning back to Gabriel. But Gabriel didn't seem affected at all by the news. In fact, he actually started *laughing*.

"Yeah, right. Cerise? A fritzer? No way. She'd never volunteer for the operation. She hates cyborgs." He flashed Etienne an apologetic look. "No offense, mec."

Marcellus felt another pang of guilt and struggled to keep talking. "I don't think she volunteered, Gabriel. Alouette said she was captured by her father when we infiltrated the Ascension banquet. We think the operation might have been performed against her will."

Gabriel fell very quiet, and Marcellus shared another anxious look with Chatine, who had her bottom lip caught between her teeth. Then, as though coming to a decision, Gabriel shook his head. "Nope. Don't buy it. That girl is as stubborn as they come. There's no way the Ministère would be able to turn her into one of their mindless minions." He let out a snort. "I'd like to see them try, though. I know Cerise. If she's working for the Ministère, then she's up to one of her schemes again. I'm sure she's got them all fooled."

"Gabriel," Marcellus said gently. "I really don't think—"

"We need to go," the Défecteur cut him off, and glanced sharply at Chatine. "The ship is nearby, but I can't leave her idling for long."

"Hold on a minute," Marcellus said, stepping in front of Chatine. "First, you have to tell us what's going on. Why do you need her help?"

"I don't *have* to tell you anything," the Défecteur replied sharply. "I'm not under your command, *Officer*. Chatine offered to help." He sidestepped Marcellus and beckoned to Chatine. "We need to go now. We couldn't use stealth mode, so the ship might be visible through the trees."

"Wait, why couldn't you use stealth—" Chatine started to ask, but Marcellus took another menacing step toward Etienne, cutting her off.

"She's not going anywhere with you until you tell me what this is about."

The Défecteur let out a deep belly laugh. "Ah, so I see. Now you're her father? Shall I start calling you 'Monsieur Renard'?"

Marcellus felt his teeth clench. He was about this close to socking this mec right in the eye.

"Chatine can take care of herself," the Défecteur growled.

"Excuse me!" she said. "I'm standing right here."

"It's not *Chatine* I'm worried about," Marcellus fired back, ignoring her.

The Défecteur opened his mouth to reply, but Gabriel blurted, "Someone stole all the zyttrium!"

Marcellus, Chatine, and Etienne all turned toward Gabriel at once.

"What?" Chatine gasped at the same time as Etienne barked, "Gabriel!"

Chatine stepped out from behind Marcellus and faced Etienne. "Is that true?"

He nodded once.

But Marcellus was still trying to catch up. "Why do you have zyttrium?"

Everyone ignored him.

"It's nearly all gone," Etienne murmured, and for the first time, Marcellus saw behind the mask of irritation he'd been wearing since they arrived. "The storage chalet was raided in the middle of the night. We have only a small emergency reserve left."

Marcellus turned to Chatine, but she was clearly already three steps ahead of him. "My parents," she said softly.

Marcellus's eyes widened. "What do your parents have to do with this? And can someone please tell me what the Défecteurs"—Marcellus heard a low growl and quickly corrected himself—"sorry, whatever you call yourselves, are doing with stores of zyttrium?"

"They use it for stealth mode," Gabriel whispered behind his hand, but if he was trying to keep from being heard by everyone in the clearing, he failed miserably.

"Gabriel," Etienne warned. "Will you please stop talking?"

Gabriel pressed his lips together and mimed turning something and then throwing it over his shoulder. He leaned into Marcellus again and whispered, "That was a key. They use them to lock the storage chalets. But apparently, it's not foolproof."

The Défecteur sighed impatiently and focused back on Chatine. "We were hoping you could help us find them."

Chatine visibly shuddered. "My parents?"

"Yes. If we can find them, we might be able to track down the zyttrium and steal it back."

Marcellus watched Chatine's reaction carefully. She wouldn't agree to this, would she? The last thing in the world she would want to do was come face-to-face with her parents again. But the longer he studied her, the less convinced he became.

"Chatine," Marcellus said urgently, pulling her out of earshot of the others. "You can't do this."

"Why not?" she challenged.

Marcellus felt that same infuriating sense of helplessness well back up in his chest. "Because don't you think there are more important things going on right now? Like the coronation ceremony tomorrow?"

Chatine sighed. "I told you. The Vangarde don't need me for that. They don't need me for any of it. That plan is going to happen whether I'm there or not." She glanced back at Etienne, and Marcellus could feel the strange mix of anguish and desperation radiating off her. "The camp can't survive without zyttrium. And right now, I'm their only hope."

"Chatine—" he began to argue, but she cut him off.

"I'm going, Marcellus. You can come with me if you want, but—"

"You know I can't do that!" Marcellus blurted out. And it was true. He had to get back to the Refuge. He had to help the Vangarde protect Citizen Rousseau at the coronation. He couldn't abandon them at a time like this.

He just didn't want Chatine to go either.

"Are you coming or not?" Etienne called out, and Chatine nodded and took a step toward him. But once again, Marcellus pulled her back.

This time, however, he didn't know what to say. He wasn't going to be able to talk her out of this—that much was clear. But he couldn't just let her leave without saying *something*.

"Look," he began tentatively, haltingly. "I . . ." He let out a deep, burdened breath. "About what happened in the library—"

"It's okay," Chatine rushed to interrupt. "You don't have to say it. I *know*."

Marcellus's brow furrowed. "You do?"

"It didn't mean anything," she uttered in a bleak, inflectionless voice, like she was reciting from a rehearsed script. "You wish you could take it back. It was a moment of weakness. And you're sorry. Right?"

Marcellus gaped at her, unable to organize his thoughts. "I . . . ," he began, but no matter how hard he tried, no other words seemed to come out.

Chatine gave him a tight nod. Like he'd just unknowingly confirmed something she'd believed for a while. "Adieu, Marcellus. Go back to the Refuge. Go risk your life for . . ." Her voice trailed off, and Marcellus felt an icy chill run down his spine.

For a long, tense moment, they stared at each other, in some kind of silent challenge. A silent dare to speak.

It was Chatine who was brave enough to take it. Always Chatine.

"For the revolution," she finally finished. But they both knew it wasn't what she meant.

CHAPTER 33

ETIENNE

ETIENNE WAS STILL HAVING A HARD TIME BELIEVING she was here. As his hands maneuvered the contrôleur of the ship, he kept having to steal furtive glances at Chatine out of the corner of his eye, just to make sure he wasn't dreaming again.

He honestly hadn't expected her to say yes. Once he'd seen that shiny-haired gridder in the forest with her, he'd fully expected Chatine to turn him down and walk away, just like she'd done in the Terrain Perdu all those months ago.

Yet here she was. Sitting beside him in the cockpit, with her dark hood pulled up over her head. This ship had once felt spacious and comfortable and safe. But now it felt impossibly small and cramped.

"So," Gabriel said, nudging Etienne with his elbow. "This is cozy, huh?" Etienne tore his gaze from the window long enough to see Gabriel wink at him and then jut his chin toward Chatine. "Just the three of us. Flying high, staying dry. One might even say it's *romantique*."

Etienne felt another nudge on his arm, which he promptly ignored, and focused on his control panel.

"Actually, I was thinking it's feeling a little tight," Chatine said, cutting a glance at Gabriel.

"Me too," Etienne muttered back.

"Hey!" Gabriel said, raising his hands in surrender. "I can take a hint. If you two need to, you know, sort some things out"—he flashed Etienne another wink—"I can just hang out in the cargo hold for a few minutes." He glanced between them. "Or *more* than a few minutes."

Etienne gruffly cleared his throat. "Where exactly are we going?"

"Just a little farther," Chatine replied, and Etienne immediately noted smugness in her tone. It was the third cryptic answer she'd given him since they'd left the Forest Verdure. She was doing it on purpose. She knew he didn't like being out of control—out of the know—and she was milking it for all it was worth.

"I would start descending soon," she told him.

"Not until you tell me where we're going," he fired back.

"Do you want to find your zyttrium or not?"

"Not if it means having to deal with your power trip."

"I'm just trying to help."

"You're just trying to annoy me."

"I don't have to *try*," Chatine said with another smirk. "Your buttons are displayed right across your face."

"Fric." Gabriel let out a low whistle. "If I'd known it would be like *this*, I would have gone with fire boy."

"Fire boy?" Etienne and Chatine asked at the same time.

Gabriel swatted the question away. "There was this old inn. He kind of burned it down . . . never mind. Long story."

"Descend now," Chatine commanded, and Etienne blew out a breath and eased forward on the contrôleur. Because the truth was, he didn't have a choice. As infuriating as it was, Chatine was their only option. Their only hope.

And she definitely knew it.

As they dipped toward a layer of clouds, Etienne reluctantly activated stealth mode, cringing as he watched the zyttrium gauge dance on the edge of the yellow zone, hovering precariously close to the red. He rarely ever flew Marilyn long enough to even leave the green zone. But now that red color was taunting him, reminding him of just how close they were to having no stealth power left at all. To being completely visible and vulnerable.

"Just remember we have to conserve our zyttrium," he told Chatine. "We can't just land this thing in the middle of—"

"I don't need lessons from you on how to hide from the Ministère," she snapped.

Etienne bit his tongue against the reply that bubbled to his lips and eased the contrôleur downward. As they disappeared into the clouds and the world around them turned a moody shade of gray, the ship gave a violent lurch of complaint, followed by a sputter. Then, for a second, they were free-falling.

Chatine gripped her seat.

Gabriel screamed.

Etienne punched a button to reengage the thruster and the ship righted itself, juddering slightly until they were descending smoothly again.

"What the fric was that?" Chatine yelped.

"Just a little problem with one of the thrusters. Nothing I can't handle." It felt good to be the smug one for a change.

Chatine narrowed her eyes. "What problem? I don't remember a problem with the thrusters."

"Oh, it happened after you left," Gabriel said. "Etienne freaked out and crashed the ship into—"

"It's fine!" Etienne cut him off. "It was just a small crack. I fixed it."

"Clearly *not*." Chatine finally released her grip on the edge of the seat.

"Marilyn is *fine*."

Chatine snorted and turned to Gabriel. "Can you believe this mec named his ship?"

"I know, right?" replied Gabriel. "Who names their ship?"

"Exactly."

"Plenty of people name their ship!" Etienne shouted. "And if you two don't stop blabbing over there, I'm going to name you both 'Lost in the Terrain Perdu.'"

"Oh, we're nowhere near the Terrain Perdu," Chatine said, and nodded out the cockpit window, where the clouds were finally starting to break apart and Etienne could see where she had led them.

Perched on top of its majestic hill, Ledôme appeared in all its gleaming and glinting glory. Its massive arching shell and the radiating glow from within made it seem like a vast Sol fallen from the sky.

"Are you out of your mind?" Etienne bellowed, immediately yanking back on the contrôleur. The ship began to ascend again. "We can't go to Ledôme!"

Chatine rolled her eyes. "Calm down. Do you really think I'd take you to Ledôme? We're going over there." She pointed beyond the great biodome to a nearby ridge of mountains.

Etienne eased up on the contrôleur and evened out the ship. "What's over there?"

"It's our best chance of finding your zyttrium."

He narrowed his eyes at Chatine, trying to see through her veil of confidence. Was she really so sure she could get it back?

All he knew was that he had to try. He still couldn't shake the feeling that this whole thing was his fault. He was the one who had flown the Renards out of the camp. He was the one who had chosen not to tell anyone else in the community. If he had, would things have turned out differently? Would they still be packing everything up right now, preparing to leave? That camp had been his home for the past fourteen years. He couldn't believe it would all be gone by the time he got back.

The mountain ridge split apart, revealing a wide valley between two craggy peaks. As the ship slowed and they descended through the drizzling air, a vast complex unfolded beneath them—a patchwork of windowless, corrugated buildings. Surrounding them were gargantuan, sprawling heaps of something Etienne couldn't quite identify.

At least not yet. But as they swooped closer, the answer suddenly came to him in a surge of disgust.

"Is that trash?" Gabriel asked, squinting through the rain-splattered window.

Chatine ignored him and gestured to a small building at the far edge of the complex. "You can hide the ship over there."

Doubt rippled through Etienne, but he eased off the throttle and carefully steered down to the ground, maneuvering Marilyn between a small ramshackle shed and the perimeter fence. It wasn't the best hiding place in the world, but it wasn't the worst, either.

Etienne disengaged the hatch, and the three of them stepped out onto the muddy, uneven ground. The stench hit him at once, invading his nostrils and overwhelming all his other senses. It was a heady mix of rotting onions, burning rubber, and rancid meat.

"Holy fric!" Gabriel said, pinching his nose between his fingers. "It smells like sheep's butt out here!"

"Had a lot of experience in that area?" Chatine asked with a smirk, and Etienne had to bite his lip to keep from laughing.

"You know, I don't like your tone, mademoiselle," Gabriel said with a sniff of arrogance.

"And I don't like your hair," Chatine fired back.

Gabriel self-consciously touched his shaggy locks, looking insulted. "What's wrong with my hair?"

"Can you please tell me why we're looking for zyttrium at a garbage dump?" Etienne cut in.

Chatine pushed past him. "Do you trust me or not?"

"Trust is a—"

"Two-way street," Chatine finished the now-familiar phrase. "I know." She flashed him a steely look and kept walking.

Up ahead, a large transporteur swept down from the sky and circled over one of the massive trash heaps like an oversized insect. Then, in a blast of light from its cargo hold, it released a shower of garbage. The debris tumbled and fluttered and gushed onto the mountain below before the transporteur snapped its cargo doors shut again and disappeared from the valley.

"Hey," Gabriel said with sudden comprehension. "I know what this place is. I've heard stories about it all the way back in Montfer. It's the waste management center for Ledôme, isn't it?"

Chatine gestured grandly at the mountain of trash to their left like she was an official tour guide for the facility. "Welcome to crocs' paradise!"

Etienne grimaced, still breathing exclusively through his mouth. "Paradise?"

"Yes!" Gabriel said, rushing over to the mangled, stinking mess of garbage and plucking out an ornate mirror with a broken handle. "Oh my Sols, is this real titan?"

Chatine shrugged. "Probably. First and Second Estaters throw away a lot of good stuff."

"Whoa!" Gabriel said, reaching back into the heap. "An actual bread box. I've never seen one of these in real life. Do people actually have enough bread to fill an entire box? Wait a minute! Is that a jar of pâté?" Gabriel looked ready to dive headfirst into the trash.

Etienne quickly intervened. "Can we stay focused here?"

Gabriel held up the jar. "But it hasn't even been opened!"

"Let's go." Etienne yanked him by the shirtsleeve.

Following behind Chatine, they darted between endless heaps and hills of garbage. It seemed like there was nothing that didn't end up here. Etienne spotted broken TéléComs, empty champagne bottles, discarded leather purses, glittering shoes with broken heels, decomposing peaches, rusting gâteau trays, twisted chandeliers, and shredded ball gowns fluttering in the wet breeze.

But most surprisingly of all, there were the people. People in ragged clothes and scuffed boots who were clambering amid the refuse like sheep on pastureland in Delaine.

Etienne eyed them warily, like any moment one of them would pull out a rayonette and fire. But they didn't even seem to notice the three new-comers who had just entered the facility. Wet and forlorn, they just kept picking their way through the First and Second Estates' waste, pocketing items they deemed worthy and, now and again, hungrily stuffing a moldy tomato or apple core into their mouths.

Something twisted in Etienne's stomach. He knew there were a lot of people on Laterre who starved and froze and lived without so many things he took for granted. But he'd never actually seen it happening in front of him. "People really come here to . . . *eat*?"

"This is nothing," Chatine said as they walked. "Before the general took over, there were a hundred times this many. My father used to send me here to search for scraps of food or trinkets he could sell, and I would have to fight through the hordes of people searching for the exact same thing."

"So, the general is what?" Gabriel guffawed. "*Feeding* people now?"

"Actually, yeah."

This seemed to shut Gabriel up for once. He walked in silence beside Chatine.

"Why are people still here, then?" Etienne asked.

"Maybe they don't know about the general's handouts," Chatine said, her gaze lingering on a father and his son picking through scraps of rotting meat. "Or maybe they're smart enough not to trust them."

They continued walking toward a cluster of buildings up ahead. The stench was still strong in the air, but it didn't bother Etienne quite as much. Probably because his mind was too busy trying to process this place. There was so much wrong with it—he couldn't even sort the offenses in order. As he watched a young girl dust off a filthy piece of bread and put it in her mouth, he finally had to avert his eyes.

"Gives new meaning to the word 'déchets,' doesn't it?" Chatine asked, and Etienne realized she had slowed to walk next to him and was now watching him.

"Déchets?" Etienne repeated the unfamiliar word.

Gabriel slapped him on the back. "Yeah, you know. Garbage. Trash. Scum. Third Estate. Whoa!" His gaze snagged on something and he darted toward a tangle of broken crates to dislodge a small object, causing a landslide of trash to skitter to the ground. "Score!" Gabriel placed the object in one of his pockets, both of which Etienne noticed were now bulging.

Etienne rolled his eyes and was about to reprimand Gabriel again for losing focus when his attention snagged on something on the ground near his feet, shaken loose from the avalanche.

It was shinier than the one he used to have. Larger, too. But the shape was the same. The rounded body. The fluted crown on top. The tapered tip on the bottom where, once released, the little toy top would spin and spin and spin.

Etienne shut his eyes tight, trying to block out the sound of the screams that suddenly filled his mind. And smoke. So much smoke. He was choking on it. It was snatching the air from his lungs. It was stinging his eyes.

"Etienne! Don't go in there!"

"Etienne! Come back!"

"Papa! Help!"

Rough hands shook his shoulder, and his eyes shot open.

"You okay, mec?" Gabriel asked, his forehead furrowed. "You went a little whacked there."

"I'm fine," Etienne said quickly, stepping over the abandoned toy and hurrying to catch up with Chatine, who was now a good ten paces ahead of them.

When they reached a set of buildings huddled around a deserted and messy yard, the deafening sound of banging, whirring, and crunching filled the air. Etienne peered into the gaping doors of one of the sheds and caught sight of an enormous, unmanned machine that glinted ominously as it chewed on piles of garbage like a hungry caged beast.

"So," he said, clearing his throat to chase away the memories of smoke still clinging to his lungs. "Your parents live here now?"

Chatine snorted. "Wouldn't that be fitting?"

"You mean, they *don't* live here?"

"I have no idea where my parents are."

Etienne stopped walking. "What? But you said—"

"I said I could help you find your zyttrium," Chatine said sharply. "And I will."

Once again, Etienne felt a kick of frustration at being two steps behind. Literally. Chatine was walking way too fast, and he had to practically jog to catch up again. "So, are you going to tell me what the fric we're doing in a—"

Chatine put a finger to her lips before stopping in front of a smaller building at the far end of the yard. The shed had no windows and one door that was unmarked and firmly closed. Etienne fell quiet, apart from his heart hammering behind his ribs. Where had this girl led them? What were they about to get themselves into?

After readjusting her hood around her head, Chatine raised a hand to the door. Concentrating hard, she knocked four times, once in each corner. A moment later, the door swung open and the three of them tumbled inside a small space filled almost to the ceiling with broken crates, mangled bed frames, and stacks of corroded ferme tools.

And in the center of it all, perched on a throne made entirely of trash, was a man with a face like Etienne had never seen before. His cheeks were etched with deep grooves, and angry red notches pebbled across his forehead. They were nothing like his maman's scars, which felt purposeful and almost logical. The entire left side of this man's face looked like it had been randomly and chaotically rearranged.

"We're here to meet an old friend," whispered Chatine.

CHAPTER 34

CHATINE

"THÉO!" THE CAPITAINE CALLED OUT AS HE HALF ROSE from his throne to greet Chatine.

She flinched at the sound of her old name echoed back at her, and the haunting memory of Inspecteur Limier's grip on her shoulder. But she smiled anyway. It was good to see the old man after so long. "Bonjour, Capitaine."

Beside her, she felt Etienne stiffen. It was evident from his exaggeratedly neutral expression that he was doing what everyone did when they first met the Capitaine—trying not to react.

Gabriel, on the other hand, was a different story. "Whoa, mec. Those are some serious battle wounds you got there."

But the Capitaine was too focused on Chatine to notice. "Where have you been all of these months?"

Chatine shrugged coyly. "Here and there."

"I thought I'd lost my best customer for good. I'd assumed you'd finally found your way to Usonia."

Chatine shivered at the reminder of her abandoned dream. She couldn't believe she'd ever wanted to live there. Especially after what she'd learned from Marcellus about his trip to Albion. About Queen Matilda's secret bargain with the general to try to win Usonia back.

She forced a chuckle. "Nah. Never did end up getting there. Thought I'd hang around this dump of a planet for a bit longer."

The Capitaine cracked a knowing smile. "So, what kind of trouble have you been up to?"

"Oh, you know, just getting sent to Bastille, escaping from Bastille, getting half of my leg blown off by a combatteur explosif, infiltrating Ledôme, killing maniac inspecteurs with my shoe, take your pick."

The Capitaine laughed heartily. "I'd expect nothing less. And welcome back. How'd you find me?"

"Let's just say I've been living with some people who know things." She glanced appreciatively around the room. "I like your new office."

The Capitaine rolled his good eye. "Well, it's certainly fitting, anyway. Operating amid the waste of the upper estates. After General Pompfaçon decided to make the Frets an extension of the Grand Boulevard, I had to relocate my place of business. What I do doesn't really fit with the general's cleanup efforts." He leaned forward. "So, what can I do for you?"

"We're looking for some stolen zyttrium," Chatine said.

"Zyttrium?" The Capitaine let out a low whistle. "Who have you been hanging out with that deals in zyttrium?"

Gabriel opened his mouth to reply, but Etienne cut in. "We'd rather not say."

"Ah, so your friend speaks," the Capitaine said with a gruff laugh toward Etienne. "Well, I'm sorry, kids. I don't know anything about any stolen zyttrium."

Chatine noticed Etienne's hands ball into fists. "Come on," he muttered, grabbing her by the sleeve. "This was a waste of time. Let's go."

She shook herself free and gazed up into the Capitaine's good eye. "We can pay."

"What are you doing?" Etienne whispered.

"What I agreed to do," she shot back.

The Capitaine sat up straighter in his seat, suddenly much more interested in the situation. "How much?"

Chatine knew how this worked. She'd been dealing with people like the Capitaine her whole life. They did nothing for free. "Worth your while, I assure you."

"How. Much?" the Capitaine repeated.

"Chatine," Etienne hissed in her ear. "I don't have any—"

"Fifteen percent," Chatine said.

"Thirty," the Capitaine countered.

"Thirty of what?" asked Etienne.

"Fifteen," Chatine repeated with authority. "As you probably know, the planet is not exactly stable right now. Who knows who will be in charge tomorrow. The general? The Red Scar? A random Patriarche cousin? Not the time to be taking risks, is it?"

The Capitaine stared her down, considering. "Fair point."

"Hold up," Etienne shouted, stepping between Chatine and the Capitaine. "Someone has to tell me what's going on here. Fifteen percent of *what*?"

Gabriel grabbed Etienne by the arm and pulled him back. "Of the zyttrium we recover, idiot," he whispered. "Try to keep up."

"What?!" Etienne exclaimed. "I never agreed to that."

"So, do we have a deal?" Chatine pressed, ignoring Etienne.

Etienne gaped at her. "He doesn't even know where it is. He just said—"

"If I were you," the Capitaine said, folding his hands across his lap, "I'd take a little trip to the Vallonay spaceport."

Etienne fell quiet. Gabriel stepped up to stand beside Chatine. "What are we looking for there?"

The Capitaine acknowledged the shaggy-haired boy for a split second before turning back to Chatine. "Lots of activity recently on the southwest launchpad."

"The one they shut down two years ago?" Chatine confirmed, the adrenaline of the hunt starting to build inside of her.

The Capitaine nodded. "That's the one. I have an old acquaintance who works the cargo port nearby. He mentioned there's been quite a few shipments lately that aren't registered in the flight logs."

Chatine nodded. "Got it. Merci." She turned to Etienne and beckoned for him to follow. "Come on. Let's go."

"Wait a minute," Etienne argued. "He didn't even say—"

"Let's *go*," Chatine repeated through gritted teeth. She was starting to wish she'd left him back with the ship.

"I have to say," the Capitaine said as they reached the door. Chatine looked back to find a rare smile on the man's face. It was such a stark difference from his usual smirks and sarcastic sneers. "I sure have missed you, Théo."

Chatine couldn't help the smile that snuck onto her face as well. "Actually," she said before pushing her hood back and letting her short, dark hair fan out around her face, "I go by Chatine now."

The Capitaine fell still, staring at her with an undeniable sense of wonderment, like he was retracing moments of time in his mind, trying to pinpoint the second when all of his assumptions went off track. But it wasn't the Capitaine's reaction that intrigued Chatine the most. It was Etienne's. There was something about his eyes as they traveled over her hair and face like they were seeing them for the first time. For a second, they softened, chasing away all traces of the resentment that had flashed there only moments ago.

Then, the Capitaine let out a gruff laugh, pulling Chatine's attention back to the man seated on his déchet throne. "You never cease to amaze."

- CHAPTER 35 -
CERISE

THE DRESS WAS A DISTRACTION. ITS TINY GEMS KEPT twinkling in Cerise's peripheral vision, and the crisscrossing straps tickled her shoulder blades. Not to mention her hair—which one of the Matrone's former handmaidens had teased and tugged and styled into an elaborate knot—made her head feel off-balance and uncalibrated.

In short, as she climbed into her father's cruiseur the afternoon of the coronation ceremony, she didn't feel at all like a Medal of Accomplissement–adorned spécialiste. She felt like an impostor. A performer at a fête.

"I'll also need a full diagnostic analysis of Inspecteur Champlain's neuroprocessors," Directeur Chevalier was saying into his TéléCom as Cerise situated herself on the leather banquette. That, too, was a challenge, as the dress was twice as wide as she was and never seemed to stop spilling out of her like a broken faucet.

Her father paused his AirLink long enough to direct the cruiser to their destination, before turning back to whoever was on the other end of the connection. "We have to figure out what went wrong with her in the first place. Inspecteurs don't just let prisoners go free for no reason."

Cerise stole a glance at her father out of the corner of her eye. She'd heard from a recent Ministère broadcast that Inspecteur Champlain had been sent to Reprogramming for breaking protocol and defying her programming, but the details of the breach had been classified above Cerise's clearance level. Even as a spécialiste.

"Absolutely," Directeur Chevalier said to the screen. "But it's my fear that the error might go deeper than that. That it might be an early sign of a system-wide malfunction." Directeur Chevalier cut his gaze to Cerise, as though wanting to gauge her reaction to this phrase.

She had no reaction. Sometimes cyborgs malfunctioned. It was a basic rule of programming. Any code had the possibility of glitching and erroring out. Inspecteur Champlain would be reprogrammed and that would be it. She'd be good as new.

But then, Cerise thought of Inspecteur Limier, and how he hadn't quite been himself since his own reprogramming. Was it possible for a cyborg to malfunction *beyond* repair?

"Merci," the directeur said. "And let me know when you have the results of the diagnostics." He ended the AirLink and set his TéléCom next to him on the seat. The sight of it made Cerise's circuitry flicker with frustration. She hadn't been permitted to bring her own TéléCom to the coronation ceremony, because her father had insisted she didn't need it and had ordered her to leave it behind at the Ministère headquarters.

But fortunately, he hadn't said anything about the Red Scar communication device she'd been working on.

The bulky object that had been found in Jolras Epernay's pocket was currently tucked into the bodice of Cerise's dress, making the impractical garment even more unbearable. She still hadn't been able to connect the device to any network, but she was determined to succeed. It was currently her only lead on finding Marcellus Bonnefaçon. She didn't know how long this event would last, but she saw no reason why she couldn't sneak off somewhere and work on the device when everyone's attention was preoccupied with the ceremony.

"I trust Inspecteur Champlain is doing better," Cerise said cordially as she nodded toward her father's TéléCom.

Directeur Chevalier let out a small grunt. "As best as can be expected from a malfunctioning cyborg. The médecins in the Reprogramming Department are confident she will make a full recovery."

"That's good news."

Her father cut her another glance. "It is. We just need to find out what rationale would have provoked her to ignore her programming in the first place."

Cerise felt her circuitry begin to flash again. This time, not with frustration, but with the same uncertainty that had been plaguing her since last night. Since she'd accidentally stumbled upon her former self's secret lair. And that illegal TéléCom stashed inside.

"If General Bonnefaçon is in control of the Regime right now, then Laterre's worst nightmare has come true. . . ."

"You will need to see it for yourself. You will need proof. . . ."

"It's a program that's able to trace unregistered networks. Networks invisible to Ministère scans. . . ."

At first, she'd been certain that the correct course of action was to report the incident and log the entire lot into evidence. The contraband in that closet was illegal and therefore the possession of it was illegal too. But then, a conflicting logic had arisen. *She* was the one who had possessed it. Or at least some former version of her.

"Directeur?" Cerise began as the cruiseur silently glided to a stop at the main gate of Ledôme.

"Mmm?" Her father was already distracted by something else on his TéléCom.

"What is the proper protocol when new evidence is discovered on a closed case?"

The directeur looked up, pensive. "Was the suspect originally found guilty or innocent?"

The word "guilty" brought a flutter to Cerise's stomach. She swallowed. "Guilty."

"Was the suspect effectively punished?"

Through the window, the security shield shimmered to nothing, and the cruiseur swept out of the gate into the gray, drizzly air. Even though the vehicle was airtight and climatized, Cerise still swore she could feel the internal temperature drop.

"My father could be alerted that I'm back in Ledôme. . . . He could have me arrested and sent to Bastille. But most likely, he'll put me in a very different kind of prison."

Cerise nodded. "Yes."

"And does the new evidence change the outcome of the case?"

Cerise considered the question carefully and thoroughly. If she alerted the Ministère about the contraband in her closet, did it make her less guilty? Less of a disgrace to the Regime and the Chevalier name?

The answer pinged back immediately.

"No."

It only made it worse. It only made her past more shameful. It only made her *more* of a traitor. And there was nothing on that TéléCom that the Ministère didn't already know. No new intelligence about Marcellus Bonnefaçon's break-in at the Ascension banquet, or her own assistance in that break-in.

Her father's gaze dropped back to his TéléCom screen. "Then, I would say the new evidence is probably not worth the Ministère's time and resources. We're already spread thin as it is, and we have enough criminals to catch without bothering with the ones we've already caught."

Cerise's circuitry gave a single satisfied flash before she turned toward the window. "That was my conclusion as well."

Outside, the landscape of Laterre blurred dizzily past, and Cerise forced herself to focus on the outline of the Frets growing closer with each passing second. She thought once more about the hacked TéléCom hidden in her closet and the desperate voice that had emerged from it.

"Cerise, I need your help."

And then, with the same finality in which that fake wall had sealed before her eyes, Cerise felt another wall sealing shut in her mind.

No, she replied to any remnants of her former self that might still be lingering deep within her. *You are a traitor. A disgrace. I will not help you.*

The cruiser glided past the dairy fabrique, the bread fabrique, the textile fabrique, and the droid fabrique before weaving through the towering structures of the Frets. The closer they got to the center, the thicker the swarms of armed sergents, officers, and Policier droids. They formed a solid wall around the Third Estate marketplace and the Vallonay Policier Precinct positioned at its north end.

The cruiseur was waved through the barrier and eventually came to a stop at the back entrance of the Precinct. Cerise reached for the door release, already preparing herself for the task of maneuvering out of the vehicle in this dress, when her father stopped her.

"One more thing," he said, opening up a storage compartment and reaching inside. "I'd like you to wear the prototype today."

As Cerise's gaze fell to the familiar box that the directeur was now holding, something in her chest began to throb. "The synthetic flesh?"

"And the contact lens, yes," he said, proffering forth the same kit Cerise had brought with her when she'd tracked Marcellus to the wheat-fleur fields. "Early tests have been extremely positive," the directeur continued, "and this is a prime opportunity to show off the prototype to some of the most prominent members of the First and Second Estates. The final product will have tremendous benefits for the future of undercover operations. Both for cyborgs and humans."

Cerise took hold of the box and eased open the lid. The familiar swatch of intricately programmed nanoparticles looked like nothing in their current state. But she knew, because she'd already felt them on her face once before, that they were not nothing. They were a disguise. Just like this dress. A way to conceal yet another part of her.

And as she affixed the patch to her left cheek and forehead and felt the particles fuse seamlessly with her skin, erasing all evidence of her circuitry, all evidence of the cyborg she had become, she couldn't help but wonder if this was her father's attempt to erase her, too.

- CHAPTER 36 -
MARCELLUS

THE MARSH WAS A RIOT OF COLOR AND SHIMMERING light. The canopies on every stall had been replaced with bright, iridescent canvases. Long strings of colorful flags fluttered overhead, and thousands of tiny twinkling lights snaked up and down the walkways and around the metal beams that hugged the edges of what was once nothing more than a massive cargo hold of an old freightship.

Marcellus took in the coronation festivities from his hiding place with a mix of apprehension and awe. The center of Vallonay's Frets had been transformed from the drab, desperate marketplace he remembered to what could only be described as a carnaval.

In among the color and glitter were swarms of people, filling every space and every nook. They laughed and shouted and greeted one another with merry slaps on the shoulders. Children ran and shrieked around the stalls, stopping only to try their hand at one of the myriad of games that had been brought in or to gaze up at the trapèze performers who leapt from towering ladders and swooped above their heads like looping, iridescent birds.

Gone were their ragged, dreary clothes and dirty faces. Today the Third Estaters wore smart woolen coats, starched white shirts, and polished boots. Some of the men had bright-colored scarves tied at their necks, and women wore ribbons knotted in their hair. They jostled around vast tables that had been set out all over the Marsh, laden with every food and delicacy imaginable. Roasted meat sizzled amid platters of baked potatoes, marinated vegetables, and bubbling boats of gravy. Gâteaux towered over trays and trays of frosted sweet breads. Great wheels of cheese and mountains of freshly baked loaves of bread topped every table. And in the center of it all, a fountain hurled fizzing champagne high into the air. Crowds of Third Estaters playfully pushed and shoved around it, trying to catch the golden liquid in their glasses. Or, for some, straight in their mouths.

Marcellus faded back, trying to slow his pounding heart.

Suddenly, everything about the Vangarde's plan felt hopeless. How could they possibly compete with this? The general had done exactly what he'd promised to do. He'd cleaned up the planet. He'd fed and clothed the Third Estate. They looked happy and content. How was Citizen Rousseau going to convince the people to abandon General Bonnefaçon and follow the Vangarde instead?

The general had a track record now.

He had a Sol-damn advertising campaign running thirty hours a day on every hologram unit across the entire planet.

"Today is the day, my beautiful Laterrians!" a high-pitched voice echoed around the marketplace, pulling everyone's attention to the nearest projection. Marcellus nervously adjusted the hood around his head, remembering the sisters' warning before they'd left the Refuge. *The holograms don't just project. They capture, too.*

He glanced up at the massive projection that glowed over the marketplace like a Sol. A woman's face had appeared, her teeth dazzlingly white as she smiled down at the crowd. "I am Desirée Beauchamp, coming to you *live* on Coronation Day!"

The image then zoomed out to reveal the woman was actually standing somewhere in the Marsh. She was pointing toward the Vallonay Policier Precinct, looming tall and formidable behind her.

The crowd erupted in shrieks and applause. People jumped up and down and cheered. There was anticipation in the air, an excitement that was palpable. And every sudden movement and piercing shout made Marcellus jump.

Maybe Chatine had been wise not to participate in this mission. Wherever she was, whatever she was doing with that Défecteur boy, it had to be safer than being here, with the perimeter blocked by sergents and droids, and the general's holograms capturing every angle, scanning every face.

He tore his eyes away from the projection and tried to relax, reminding himself of what Sister Denise had said when they were laying out the details of today's plan.

"The holograms are not our downfall. They are our advantage. We can use them."

If there was one thing that the Vangarde were good at, it was using the Ministère's own tech against them. Marcellus had seen it happen on Bastille, and he would see it happen again today.

If the plan worked.

"In just a few short minutes," Desirée continued, pulling Marcellus's attention back to the nearest hologram, "we will witness history in the making. It is not in all of our lifetimes that we get to witness an actual coronation of a new Patriarche, and *none* of us have witnessed one quite like this before. This is definitely a reason to celebrate. I'm told General Bonnefaçon has already arrived from Ledôme with Commandeur Moreau, who will officiate in today's ceremony. As you may or may not know, it is traditionally the general of the Laterrian Ministère who performs the coronation duties for the new Patriarche, but that's what makes today, once again, such a historic and unprecedented event. Not only in the way the ceremony will be performed. But in its location, here among the people."

The cheers grew louder. Third Estaters danced and twirled and bounced eagerly on their toes. A high-pitched shriek came from Marcellus's left, followed by a series of pounding footsteps. Marcellus instantly reached for the rayonette tucked into his waistband, fingertip poised on the trigger. Until he heard the squealing giggle of a child.

"Halt, you dirty croc!" a small boy boomed in a droid-like voice.

"You'll have to catch me first, basher!" screamed another boy as he darted behind a bouquet of festive balloons.

The two children streaked past him, and Marcellus let out a shaky breath and unwrapped his fingers from the holster of his rayonette. Everything about this place was setting him on edge.

"The energy here in the marketplace could not be any higher right now," said Desirée with a little shimmy of excitement. "People have poured in from all over the planet to join these celebrations. And of course, we will be broadcasting the entire coronation ceremony live to all of Laterre on the TéléCast feed, so you don't miss a single—oh my Sols. Will you look at *that*!"

Every pair of eyes shot skyward, up at the vast dark cube of a building that loomed over the marketplace. On the very top floor, the Policier Precinct's sheer black façade was splitting apart, revealing a shaft of light that grew like the first ray of an Albion Sol-rise. When the sleek walls had pulled all the way back, a platform unfurled from within, creating a brilliantly lit balcony.

"All primary operatives report your status," a voice whispered in Marcellus's audio patch, causing him to startle again. "Alpha?"

"In position at the south trapèze tower," came Francine's quiet response. "Sigma?"

"In position at the champagne fountain," replied Nicolette. "Epsilon?"

Marcellus reached into his pocket and pressed number 2 on the keypad of his récepteur. "In position at the junkyard stall."

On and on it went, through every name, every Vangarde leader who was concealed in this crowd. Until finally, Denise asked, "Lambda?" And a shiver tingled down Marcellus's spine as he darted a glance toward the base of the Thibault Paresse statue.

The silence that filled his audio patch seemed to go on forever. Until finally, Sister Laurel whispered, "Omega and I are almost in position."

And then, Marcellus saw them. Two women in dark, hooded coats, weaving through the crowd, slowly making their way toward the platform steps. And his heart seemed to leap into his throat.

"All primary operatives stand by," Denise reported. "We are waiting for visual confirmation on the general."

"This is it!" cried Desirée, yanking Marcellus's attention back to the hologram, where the bright-eyed host was practically jumping up and down. "We are now counting down the *minutes* until the man of the hour makes his appearance right up there and ushers our glorious planet into a new dawn and a new future for each and every single one of us."

The crowd erupted in celebration. Every cheek radiated color and life, and every pair of gray, brown, or hazel eyes glimmered and danced in the festive lights. Marcellus glanced around, his uneasiness growing as he took in the countless Third Estaters who had no idea what they had signed up for when they arrived in this marketplace today. No idea that they were standing in the center of a tinderbox about to ignite.

"Well, then, I think there's only one thing left to say at this point." Desirée Beauchamp winked at the cam. "Vive Laterre!"

And a thousand voices echoed "Vive Laterre!" in return.

- CHAPTER 37 -
CERISE

"VIVE LATERRE!"

The shouts from the marketplace below could be heard all the way up on the sixth floor of the Vallonay Policier Precinct, where Cerise stood in the midst of a bustling observation lounge.

The room was a dizzying mishmash of color and chatter. Silk waistcoats and satin dresses of every hue and shade flashed and glimmered under the bright lights, and it seemed everyone was talking at once. An army of waiters threaded through the room with trays of canapés and clinking crystal glasses balanced in their hands. The pop of a champagne bottle ricocheted through Cerise's ears like a gunshot from an antique hunting rifle.

Backing herself into a corner by the window, Cerise tried to access poise and confidence, the two things that were expected of a medal-adorned spécialiste attending an event of this caliber. But she could find none of those attributes. All the noise and color and swishing fabric made her twitch.

Everyone in the room—directeurs, officers, superviseurs, and advisors—seemed much more at ease here, sipping champagne and participating in idle chatter.

"Have a drink!" exclaimed a man who, judging from his off-kilter stance and sour breath, had already consumed several. Cerise's processors identified him as the newly appointed admiral of the Masséna spacecraft carrier as he shoved a flute of fizzing gold liquid into her hand. She took it only to avoid it crashing to the ground and shattering.

Once the man's back was turned, Cerise placed the glass on a nearby table and pressed her hand to the bodice of her dress. The bulky communication device tucked against her skin instantly brought a stream of relief flooding through her.

She was glad she'd chosen to take it with her from the Ministère headquarters. Now she just had to find the right time to slip away and get back to work on it.

Another unified cheer rose up from the marketplace, and Cerise turned and peered out the large floor-to-ceiling windows at the festivities below. Thousands of Third Estaters were gathered there. They swarmed like one teeming mass, all of them jammed so close that barely a centimètre of unoccupied ground could be seen between them. Even the stalls with their glaring colored canopies and the glowing holograms dotted around the market seemed smashed and swamped by the bustling crowds. The size of them would make it difficult to discern individual faces in the surveillance footage, but Cerise still longed to be back at her workstation in the Bureau, sitting in front of her monitors analyzing the files streaming in from those holograms, rather than looking at the view live.

"Cerise." Her father appeared from behind a group of tipsy officers talking and laughing way too loudly. "What are you doing over here by yourself? You must mingle."

"Mingle?" she said, trying on the word, and just like the dress she was wearing, it didn't seem to fit right.

"Yes, you know, circulate. Talk. Drink. Enjoy yourself."

Beneath the synthetic flesh, Cerise felt her circuitry flash. Enjoy herself? Surrounded by so many people? Did her father not understand the meaning of "enjoy"?

"The old Cerise would have been right in the center of that group." He pointed to the officers. One had obviously just finished telling a joke because the others were guffawing and patting one another on the back.

The old Cerise.

Suddenly that face was back in her mind. That flawless skin and sparkling hair. That traitorous voice.

"*. . . you might be the only one who can stop him.*"

"I—" she began to say, but the single syllable got stuck in her throat.

"Look, there's the general. Why don't you go congratulate him on his imminent coronation?"

Cerise peered across the room where a velvet rope was blocking off the entrance to an opulent balcony beyond. General Bonnefaçon stood just in front of the rope. His white jacket and titan epaulets gleamed, and the high polish on his black boots seemed to reflect every light in the room. Surrounding him, like planets around a Sol, were Commandeur Moreau, Warden Gallant, Inspecteur Limier, and a few members of the First and Second Estates.

"The general has not initiated an interaction," Cerise told her father. "It would be against protocol to approach him unprompted."

Directeur Chevalier waved this away. "This is a celebration! Forget protocol!"

"Forget protocol?" she repeated, confused. Hadn't he just sent Inspecteur Champlain to Reprogramming for that very offense?

The directeur's eyes flickered with impatience. "Fine. Spécialiste Chevalier, I order you to congratulate the general on his coronation. There. Now it's official protocol."

Cerise felt the familiar warmth of her neuroprocessors lighting up with purpose. She gave a tight nod to her father and began to make her way to the group. She walked slowly, with measured footsteps, stopping only when she caught sight of her reflection in a large, titan-framed mirror hanging on the wall. Another reminder of how out of place she felt and looked. The synthetic flesh was smooth against her cheek. Just like that face on the TéléCom. The contact lens had turned her orange cybernetic eye to a dull shade of brown. And this construction of hair atop her head looked like a statue that belonged in the Grand Palais foyer.

She reached up and rooted around for the pins holding it in place before yanking them out one by one. Her obsidian-black hair tumbled down around her shoulders and settled against her back. It wasn't a complete reversal, but it restored a smidgen of familiarity. Enough to renew her confidence and straighten her posture.

She approached the group surrounding the general. They were deep in conversation about the state of the Bastille prison.

"Why exactly are the prisoners rioting?" asked a First Estate woman dressed in a violet floor-length gown.

"Zyttrium," Warden Gallant replied before swallowing a hefty sip of champagne. He coughed. "Now that the Skins are down, they don't understand why they have to keep digging."

"Neither do I," said Commandeur Moreau. All eyes in the group turned to her. Some even laughed, assuming she was joking, but her voice remained stoic. "Why *are* we still digging for zyttrium after you've shut down the Skins, General?"

But it wasn't the general who replied.

"Zyttrium is a very powerful element," explained Directeur Fareau, who was in charge of the energy labs. "We're only beginning to fully understand its properties and everything it's capable of."

Cerise wasn't sure how to properly insert herself into the conversation, but she was eager to complete this assignment as quickly as possible so she could locate a secluded place to work on the Red Scar device.

"Is that so?" replied the First Estate woman with mild interest. "I had no idea. Well, by all means, Warden. Get those prisoners under control." She chuckled.

The warden attempted a reply but choked on another ambitious gulp of champagne.

The general patted him on the back. "I have full confidence in the warden's ability. We're sending more droids as we speak, and they've all been updated with the Ministère's new hive-mind technology."

"What is this?" asked the First Estate woman, turning back to the general. "Hive what?"

"Hive-mind technology," the general repeated. "Spécialiste Ducard of the Bureau of Défense has been spearheading this promising new development. Improved droid performance, allowing them to learn from each other's experiences and respond to threats faster and more efficient—"

"Congratulations, General Bonnefaçon."

Everyone turned toward Cerise, their faces bearing matching displays of shock at the interruption. Cerise's neuroprocessors chugged out every possible chemical they could conjure up all at once. Then, as if the group had rehearsed their synchronicity, they all turned toward the general, their eyes wide in anticipation of his reaction.

Cerise swallowed and kept her shoulders back, grateful that her circuitry was not visible at this moment. It would certainly have given away her anxiety.

Finally, the general let out a hearty bark of laughter. The rest copied him. "Very good, Spécialiste Chevalier." General Bonnefaçon peered at the others and gestured toward Cerise. "This cyborg has the right idea. It's a fête. A celebration for all of Laterre. We shouldn't be talking about such serious matters." He shot a sharp look at Moreau. "That goes for you, too, Apolline. Have a drink."

"I don't drink, sir."

The general cocked an eyebrow. "Then have a canapé. Several of them."

"She's a cyborg?" the First Estate woman whispered to Warden Gallant. "But where is her . . ." She pointed disapprovingly toward her own cheek.

"Isn't it magnifique?" announced Directeur Chevalier, sidling up to the group. "A new prototype we've been working on in the Bureau of Innovation. Synthetic flesh."

"It's uncanny," said the First Estate woman, leaning in way too close to examine Cerise's face as though she were a rare First World gem on display in the Maison de Valeur. Cerise instinctively backed away.

"Merci for your well wishes, Spécialiste," the general said to her with a congenial pat on the back. "But I don't require any congratulations. All praise should be directed at the Regime. Laterre is the one that should be congratulated today. It is a momentous occasion for our glorious planet."

"Yes, General," Cerise replied dutifully. "Congratulations to Laterre."

"And to you, as well. Commandeur Moreau has briefed me on all of your fine work recently. Well done."

Cerise thought of the medal that was now hanging in her locker back in the cyborg dormitories. "Merci, General. It is my honor to serve and protect the Regime."

"As is mine."

"As is all of ours!" cheered Warden Gallant with his champagne flute raised high. "To Laterre!" The rest of the group raised their glasses too, while Commandeur Moreau flashed a flimsy smile and Cerise dropped her gaze to the floor. The sharp clinking of crystal was making her twitch again.

"General. Commandeur. It is time to start the preparations." Inspecteur Limier gestured to the velvet rope behind him and the balcony that lay just beyond it.

"Very well." General Bonnefaçon nodded toward Commandeur Moreau. "Apolline, after you." Then, he turned back to the group. "Please, enjoy yourselves. Drink. Eat. Be merry. And Vive La—"

The general's voice cut off again. This time, not by Cerise, but by a loud squawking sound coming from the front of her dress.

All eyes cut back to her, including the general's. No one spoke as the silky fabric let out another high-pitched screech, this time followed by a strange muffled sound.

The First Estate woman leaned back toward the warden. "Is that her . . ." She gestured again at her own cheek.

The warden shook his head. "I don't know."

Meanwhile, everyone continued to gape at Cerise as she fumbled awkwardly with the fabric of her bodice, feeling the clunky device hidden inside. Just then, an earsplitting barrage of static poured out of her dress, overpowering every other sound, until the room fell quiet, and all heads pivoted toward her.

There was no more chatter. No more clinks of glasses and scrapes of serving spoons against titan platters. The only sound in the room was coming from Cerise's dress.

She barely managed to utter out an apology before she was darting toward the door to the toilettes and locking it behind her. Once alone, she pulled the squawking device from beneath her bodice and fumbled with the buttons on the side until the volume mercifully lowered. Breathing out a sigh, she collapsed onto the sateen chaise next to the sinks and stared down at the object in disbelief.

Where the screen had once been frustratingly blank and empty, there was now a small symbol in the center. Two lines angled away from each other but coming to a connected point at the bottom. Like a downward-facing arrow.

The static continued to hum out of the tiny speakers, and Cerise pressed it closer to her ear. But a high-pitched screeching sound in her eardrum caused her to leap back. It was that same mind-numbing squeal she'd heard when she was standing outside the decommissioned grain silo. Like some kind of interference. But with what?

Braving the noise again, she raised the device back up and listened, struggling to sort through the scratchy, distorted layers.

And then, she heard it. The unmistakable sound of a voice.

". . . visual confirmation . . . general is in view . . . wait for . . . signal . . ."

Cerise's circuitry nearly exploded as she struggled to keep the device in her hand. She stared down at the tiny screen in shock, unable to believe what her processors were telling her.

The device had finally connected to a network.

CHAPTER 38

MARCELLUS

"WE HAVE VISUAL CONFIRMATION ON THE GENERAL. I repeat, general is in view. Wait for my signal to proceed."

Marcellus's whole body was thrumming as the sound of triumphant trumpets, rejoicing strings, and a cacophony of drumbeats boomed and rippled through the air. Everyone looked up. Those who couldn't see as far as the Policier Precinct kept their gazes locked on the nearest hologram. Because the once-empty balcony was no longer empty.

General Bonnefaçon appeared like an illusion.

In a dazzling burst of light and sound and fireworks.

Over his traditional uniform, a vast purple robe draped from his right shoulder and flowed down to his ankles. The edges were trimmed with immaculate silver fur, and thanks to the thousands of stars and planets hand-sewn into its rich velvet expanse, the robe glittered and gleamed like it had been plucked straight from the nighttime TéléSky. A swarm of tiny cams hovered around him, capturing his grandeur from all angles and broadcasting it to all of Laterre.

He was everywhere.

On every shimmering hologram projection. He surrounded this Marsh. These Frets. This entire planet. Filling up every available space.

Every molecule of air. Until Marcellus couldn't take a breath without feeling like he was breathing him in too.

The music faded.

A reverent hush fell over the crowd.

And then, he spoke.

"Welcome, glorious people of Laterre! We have gathered here today, at the sacred site of our ancestors' historic landing, to celebrate this magnificent planet we call home. We have gathered here today, in the presence of the Sols, to demonstrate our love and passion for the people who bring this planet glory every single day. But most of all, we have gathered here today to usher in a triumphant new era for Laterre."

The crowd exploded in cheers and applause. Heads swiveled from the balcony on the top of the Policier Precinct to the holograms to the colorful fireworks still crackling in the sky. Like they didn't know where to look. Like they didn't want to miss a thing.

Marcellus felt a shiver whisper down his spine. He hadn't seen his grandfather in person in over three months. But now it felt like he'd never left the Palais. Never escaped those watchful eyes, that judging stare. And up until this moment, Marcellus hadn't quite brought himself to believe that this was all real. That this was actually happening. That a Second Estate man—his own grandfather—had plotted and schemed and murdered his way to the pinnacle of a planet.

"The hologram signal is coming through," Denise reported in his ear. "I'll be able to override it in three minutes. Lambda, are you ready for activation?"

"Affirmative," Laurel replied.

Marcellus stole a glance at the platform underneath the statue of Thibault Paresse, where Sister Laurel was positioning a small silver case. The Vangarde's weapon of choice.

Sweat began to pool beneath the collar of his hooded coat. His body had never felt more alert. His muscles had never felt more coiled and ready to spring. He reached under his coat and rested his hand on the rayonette tucked into his waistband, hoping the feeling of the cool metal would reassure him.

But it did not.

Would he ever feel reassured again? Would there ever come a day when he didn't wake up with his stomach in knots and his lungs gasping for breath?

For the thousandth time that day, he thanked the Sols that Alouette was locked away in the Refuge. That she had agreed to stay hidden. Stay safe.

"And now," the general said, his eyes twinkling from the nearest hologram projection, "we begin the ceremony." He gestured grandly to the woman standing on the balcony beside him, dressed in a brilliant white jacket with its Sol-shaped buttons and gleaming epaulets on each shoulder. Her commandeur's insignia, pinned just above her left pocket, glittered and winked at Marcellus almost like a taunt.

Marcellus had only met Apolline Moreau in person a handful of times, but her voice would haunt his memories forever. Because he would always associate that voice with Bastille. With the explosif that had stolen away the life of Mabelle, his former governess and a prominent member of the Vangarde. Moreau had been the capitaine of that mission. And now she was commandeur of the Ministère, following in the footsteps of the great woman who had come before her, Michele Vernay, and claiming the position Marcellus had been so close to calling his own.

The new commandeur stepped forward and raised her hands to address the crowd. More hologram cams soared up to capture her from all sides. "Bonjour, fellow Laterrians," she began. "We are assembled here on this most auspicious day to witness and celebrate the dawn of a new leader. A new Patriarche who, like a Sol himself, will soon shine over and protect our great planet. Our beautiful and wondrous and prosperous home of Laterre . . ."

"Transmission override in two minutes," Denise reported, and Marcellus had to remind himself to breathe.

"The general shall now perform the sacred rite of the fleur-de-lis." Moreau beckoned to a nearby advisor in a dark green robe. He stepped forward carrying a box made of polished mahogany with ornate, fluted hinges.

Moreau flicked open the clasps and lifted the lid. The crowd let out appreciative sighs and whispers as the hologram cams closed in on the sculpted fleur-de-lis lying in a bed of purple velvet. Each of its three titan leaves was inlaid with tiny, sparkling gems: deep blue sapphires on the first, brilliant rubies on the second, and the last with blinding white diamonds.

"César Bonnefaçon," Moreau continued in a shaky voice. "With this act of unbinding, will you honor the great Laterrian leaders of the past and release them back to the Sols?"

"I will." The general reached toward the box and picked up the shimmering fleur-de-lis. Delicately, he began to unbind its three lily leaves. The ragged bootlace that held them together slipped easily away.

Moreau held up the unbound lace for all to see. "By taking up this lace, this humble bootstring that belonged to the first worker to ever set foot on Laterre, do you promise to honor our ancestors and the men and women who built our great planet?"

"I promise to do so." As the general held out his hands, looking like a humble peasant begging for food, and Moreau gently laid the threadbare bootlace across them, Marcellus's mind unwillingly drifted back to the last time he'd witnessed this sacred act. When his grandfather had officiated the coronation ceremony for Lyon Paresse. The man who had been slaughtered by the Red Scar a stone's throw away from where the general now stood.

"Transmission override in less than one minute." Denise's voice cut into Marcellus's thoughts. "Lambda, be ready to activate on my call and be sure Omega is in position."

"Copy," said Laurel.

Marcellus pushed his way forward to get a better view of the platform under the Paresse statue, where he could see Sister Laurel delicately flipping open the clasps of the small silver case. And the second hooded figure who stood close by, ready for her cue.

Moreau cleared her throat and continued. "In your binding of the three leaves of the fleur-de-lis, will you honor our three estates and the three Sols above us?"

"I will." The general's fingers did not falter or waver once as he gathered up the jewel-encrusted leaves and began to rebind them. Around and around the ancient lace twirled, almost hypnotically. He gave a subtle but purposeful yank on the string to secure the twinkling fleur-de-lis into place, and the crowd broke into apprehensive applause.

Marcellus's gaze darted between the balcony and the platform, his heart feeling like it might beat right out of his chest.

"With this binding," Moreau announced, quieting the spectators once more as she held up the newly bound fleur-de-lis and the swarm of hologram cams zoomed around it, "César Bonnefaçon has made his sacred commitment to honor our past leaders, our ancestors, and our three glorious estates. And now . . ." She took an uneasy breath. "Please kneel."

Hurry, Marcellus thought.

"Delta?" came Francine's voice through his audio patch. "Are we almost there?"

But there was no response from Denise. Panic corkscrewed through Marcellus as he peered back at the balcony, where Moreau had already removed the imperial crown from its case and was now holding it above the general's head.

"Delta!" repeated Francine. "Do you copy?"

"Our network has been compromised!" Denise's voice barreled back into Marcellus's audio patch, causing him to flinch and stagger into a man, who shot him a nasty look.

"What?" asked Nicolette in a strangled voice.

"There's another récepteur online. Shutting down all communication now."

There was a violent screech in Marcellus's ear before his audio patch fell quiet.

"With the responsibility of this crown," Moreau began stiffly, "César Bonnefaçon will lead us with virtue, fairness, and strength."

Marcellus spun back toward the platform. From her position at the base of the steps, Laurel stared back at him, looking just as confused and flustered as he felt.

"Understanding the legacy of this crown, he will continue the tradition, greatness, and values of those Patriarchs and Matrones who came before him."

Desperately, Marcellus darted his gaze back to the balcony, where the ceremony was coming swiftly and definitively to an end.

"Great Sols of the sky, we entreat your blessing. Before you today, under your mighty powers and light, we crown your humble servant, César Bonnefaçon, as Patriarche of—"

Moreau's voice cut out. The holograms flickered off. For thousands of kilomètres across Laterre, everything went deathly silent. Still. A ticking clock about to run out. An explosif about to fall.

There was a buzzing in Marcellus's ears that he soon realized was not, in fact, his brain about to explode from the pressure in his head. It was the Vangarde's hologram cams. Laurel had released them from the silver case, and they were now swarming around the base of the Paresse statue, ready to capture the face of the hooded figure who was, at this very moment, mounting the steps of the platform and taking her position in the center.

Then, in a burst of light and confusion, the holograms flickered back on, and a single pair of bright, silvery eyes shone out from every single projection. It was the same pair of bright, silvery eyes that were now peering out from the platform in front of Marcellus.

Whispers of shock and disbelief permeated the crowd as the woman pushed back her hood, revealing a face that had been burned into all of their memories.

When she spoke, her voice was clear, steady, yet pulsing with electricity. And Marcellus knew that no matter what happened next, the planet would remember this moment forever.

"Fellow citizens of Laterre. I am so pleased and honored to be speaking to you again, after seventeen years of forced silence."

CHAPTER 39

CERISE

CERISE HAD NEVER HEARD SUCH SILENCE IN HER LIFE. The observation lounge that, only moments ago, had been alive and sparking with energy and excitement had fallen motionless.

Through the open balcony door, she could see General Bonnefaçon—not yet Patriarche Bonnefaçon—kneeling in his coronation robes, flanked by Commandeur Moreau, who was still holding the crown above his head. The general had not moved a centimètre since the woman's clear, crisp voice had shot across the marketplace like a ship traveling at hypervoyage speed, bending space around it, pulling every pair of eyes in the Marsh toward it.

And now, it was speaking again.

"I have gone by many names. Traitor. Terrorist. Prisoner 40102. But you know me best as Citizen Rousseau." The woman paused and stared out across the marketplace with a piercing gaze. "And yes, I am alive."

Cerise looked down at the device still clutched in her hand, her circuitry sparking with sudden understanding.

It wasn't a Red Scar device.

It was a *Vangarde* device.

That's who she had heard crackling from the speakers. Operatives of the Vangarde.

They were alive. *Citizen Rousseau* was alive. She was standing down there right now. Every hologram projection—from here to Montfer—was now broadcasting her face and her voice, which had lulled the murmurings in the crowd to an anticipatory silence.

"Contrary to what you've been told, I did not die on Bastille. Thanks to the brave actions of my fellow Vangarde leaders, I was able to successfully escape. Which now, I suppose, makes me a fugitive. But despite what this Regime wants you to believe, I am not the most dangerous criminal on this planet."

Somewhere in the distance, Cerise heard a muted crack as someone dropped a flute of champagne and the crystal shattered into pieces on the marble floor.

"Get that woman out of there!" the general roared. He was now back on his feet, shouting into the observation lounge through the open balcony door.

And suddenly, the room was no longer still. People were scrambling, pulling out TéléComs and barking orders. A servant came to mop up the glass and spilled champagne.

But Cerise didn't know what to do. She had no TéléCom. She had no way of contacting the Bureau. She blinked uselessly down at the communication device in her hand. It was silent now. The signal had gone dead shortly after she'd started listening. That's when she'd burst out of the toilettes, hoping to warn someone of the potential threat to the ceremony, only to find she was too late. The ceremony had already been hijacked.

Far below, Citizen Rousseau's voice continued to reverberate through the powerful speakers in the hologram modules. "Just like you, I was born into the Third Estate. And just like you, I was mistreated, looked down upon, spat on, manipulated, used, and underappreciated. General Bonnefaçon has led you into a fool's paradise. He has—"

Her voice was abruptly drowned out by the sound of a commotion coming from the outskirts of the marketplace, followed by a series of screams. Cerise darted to the window and looked down just in time to see an army of droids trampling their way through the crowd, the weapons embedded in their arms already glowing. With the new hive-mind technology running through their operating systems, they moved faster and more efficiently than ever before, sharing one mind, one goal, one purpose.

Cerise's circuitry flashed rapidly as she watched one of the droids take aim at the woman standing beneath the statue of Thibault Paresse. Three officers crowded next to her at the window, gazing out, their bodies stiff, their breathing rigid.

The whole marketplace seemed to freeze in anticipation of the sound.

The pulse that would ripple through the air.

The snap that would accompany a body hitting the ground.

But no such sound came. Instead, a voice spoke.

"Halt! All droids are ordered to stand down."

It was strong, commanding, authoritative. It took Cerise's processors longer than normal to recognize that it was not coming from Citizen Rousseau but rather from a second figure that was now mounting the steps of the stage. She wore a long woolen coat and her face was concealed behind a dark hood, preventing Cerise from being able to use her facial recognition software.

"Who is that?" whispered the officer standing next to her.

But no one answered. Because no one knew.

Then, the figure threw back her hood, unleashing a riot of wild, unhindered curls that fanned out around her head like a crown. When she spoke, her voice sent tremors through the very depths of Cerise's processors.

"My name is Alouette Taureau. I am the daughter of Patriarche Lyon Paresse and the rightful heir to the Regime. My command outranks all other previous commands. And I order all droids to stand down immediately."

No one moved. No one breathed. The droids in the marketplace stood frozen on the spot, like they'd been paralyzed by their own rayonettes. Cerise was part human and part machine, but in this moment, she shared a deep connection with those droids. They were all paralyzed by their own programming.

Cerise watched with hitched breath as the droids performed their required scan. Their piercing orange eyes roamed unflinchingly up and down Alouette. Cerise knew all there was to know about droid processors.

Their scan would capture every curve of her face, every recognizable molecule of her skin, every strand of hair. And then, those details would be compared against every piece of information now available in the Communiqué.

Just as Cerise was doing at this very moment.

The crowd remained silent as everyone's gaze continued to snap back and forth from the droids in their midst to the young woman on the stage claiming to be the Patriarche's daughter. Not even whispers percolated the Marsh now. But Cerise could see it in their eyes. They were performing scans of their own, taking in Alouette's face and comparing it to the face that had been shown to them less than a week ago.

By the general himself.

It seemed as though they all arrived at the result at once. The droids, the crowd, and Cerise.

It was a match.

- CHAPTER 40 -
ALOUETTE

IT WAS LIKE LOOKING OUT INTO A FIELD OF STARS. EVERY pair of blinking eyes staring back at her filled Alouette with light and a deep sense of wonder. They saw her. They accepted her. They *believed* her.

For thirteen years, Alouette had lived underground, shielded from this brilliant light. For thirteen years, Alouette had been kept a secret. From all of them. From herself.

But now the secret was in front of them. And they were in front of her. And she soon realized, with a sickening swoop of her stomach, that they were waiting for her to *speak*.

"I . . . ," she began, but in a heartbeat, her brain had emptied. Her lungs went limp. Back at the Refuge, this had seemed like a good idea. Alouette had been so certain this was where she was meant to be—on this stage, next to Citizen Rousseau, with the eyes of the planet trained on her. But suddenly, there was so much more to those eyes. Far more than she'd anticipated.

A buzzing sound filled the air as the Vangarde's hologram cams swarmed around her. They flashed and blinked into her eyes, and under their whizzing and dizzying scrutiny, her skin grew clammy. She tried to focus on a single hovering cam, but it was like trying to focus on a single drop of ocean. It moved too quickly. It slipped out of her grasp.

"I . . . ," Alouette began again, but still, she could not conjure the right words. Or any words. The very things that she'd sworn to protect, to guard from being completely forgotten, were failing her now.

She turned to Rousseau, her face pleading for help. Seeming to understand, Rousseau took a step forward and Alouette relaxed. She would not have to speak. Her part was done. She had unveiled herself. She had stood beside the Vangarde leader as an ally. She had stopped the droids. Now Citizen Rousseau could continue her speech. Continue to rally the people to the Vangarde's cause.

But instead, Rousseau leaned forward and whispered into Alouette's ear, "You can do this."

Alouette shook her head. "I can't."

"You can," said Rousseau. "Remember who you are. Remember your why."

For a moment, the twinkle of the sister's eyes soothed her. Calmed her galloping heart. But then Alouette peered back out at the sea of faces, visible through the swirling cams, and her resolve started to slip again. The crowd was growing antsy. The silence now punctuated with murmured questions and whispered doubts. And when Alouette's gaze landed on the nearest hologram projection, she suddenly understood why. She flinched at the sight of her own face staring back at her, larger than life. She looked terrified. Out of place. Not like a symbol of unity, of what this planet could become. More like a symbol of everything this planet was now: uncertainty and turmoil.

But I'm still there, she realized with a shiver. Her face was still on that projection. Because Denise still had control of the TéléCast feed. She was still broadcasting.

The thought gave Alouette strength. She could not waste this moment. This was what they had raised her to do. This was why they'd taken her in, why they'd protected her, why they'd chosen *her.* She could not let them down now.

She scanned the crowd, searching for a familiar face. She found Sister Laurel first, standing off to the side of the platform. And just as expected, her expression was a tangle of confusion, betrayal, and most of all, fear.

"I'm sorry," she said in a desperate voice, causing the crowd to quiet again. "I know you weren't expecting me to be here today. I know this must come as a shock to you."

Her words echoed across the entire marketplace, across the entire planet, but she kept her eyes locked on Sister Laurel. She spoke only to *her*. Because she needed to make her understand, make them all understand, why she had betrayed them. Because she knew in her bones that she'd made the right choice. And she would prove it to them now.

"The thing is, I've already been kept a secret for too long. I'm tired of being hidden away. Protected for my own good. I can't do it anymore. Not when I know that my very existence can help save this planet."

More murmurs rippled through the marketplace, capturing Alouette's attention. She finally looked up, away from Laurel, and focused on the crowd. "What the general told you is true. I am the only surviving heir to the former Patriarche. My father was Lyon Paresse, and my mother was a woman named Lisole Villette. They were married in a secret ceremony eighteen years ago. Two young hearts—one First Estate, one Third Estate—who had fallen in love, against all odds, against all divides."

Alouette heard a commotion coming from the balcony of the Policier Precinct behind her, but she didn't dare look back. No doubt the general was ordering around his minions, trying to figure out how to get her off this stage. Or at least get the TéléCast to broadcast *his* face again.

But still, Denise's override held.

Alouette took a deep breath and kept speaking, letting the words come to her in smooth, confident waves. "When my grandfather Claude Paresse found out about the union, he banished my mother from the Palais and told my father she was dead. My mother feared for my life and sent me to live with people she knew would protect me and keep me safe." She glanced at Citizen Rousseau and offered her a subtle nod before turning back to the crowd. "The Vangarde."

All around the stage, the murmurings grew to an unsettling hum. Alouette forced herself to keep going, picking up speed as she went. "Lyon Paresse never even knew I existed. No one knew I existed. Except for General Bonnefaçon. And that's where the lies begin."

"Lies?" she heard someone whisper from the front row.

"Why would she say that?" asked another voice.

"The general wouldn't lie to us."

The prickles of doubt began to creep back in. Alouette's legs grew wobbly beneath her. She looked back at Laurel, needing something familiar to cling on to, but the sister wasn't there anymore.

And that's when she caught sight of two hazel eyes staring back at her.

Her spirits lifted and her heart sang.

It was Marcellus.

He was staring at her with such an intensity, she honestly couldn't determine if he was furious or proud. Either way, it was just what she needed.

The words came to her in a wild rush, and she had to stop them from all tumbling out at once. She forced herself to speak slowly, deliberately. "Despite what the general has told you, he *did* know of my existence. He's known for years. Which is why he's spent the past seventeen years searching for me, tracking my blood, my DNA, across a planet, waiting for the day that I would resurface. Because he knew that my existence would only inhibit his plans."

The crowd grew more restless. Fidgety. Loud. Alouette could feel their energy shifting right in front of her, like any minute now, they might rush the stage. But she was not finished. She had not yet accomplished what she'd come here to do.

Reveal the truth.

Unmask the true enemy.

Stop the general.

"Everything General Bonnefaçon has done on this planet, from the tokens in your pocket to the bread on your plate to these holograms broadcasting my face, has been for his own gains. For his own thirst for power. For his own rise to the top. It was for this reason he needed me to be found. So that he could get me out of the way. So that he could kill me." She now was able to focus on a single cam that hovered around her. She locked eyes with it, peering into its quivering gaze with a ferocity that was mirrored back a thousand times, on every hologram in this Marsh. "Just like he killed the Patriarche's other daughter, little Marie Paresse."

"THAT IS A LIE!" the general's voice boomed across the sky like a mighty crack of thunder. Suddenly, all eyes in the Marsh pivoted upward, toward the balcony where the general was leaning forward, his hands clenched around the railing.

Still, Denise's control of the TéléCast feed held firm, keeping only Alouette's face displayed on the projections.

But the general didn't need the cams to amplify his voice or broadcast his face.

His anger was enough.

"This girl lies to you!" the general shouted from the balcony. "Do not believe a word she says. Do you see who she stands beside? Do you see what allies she keeps? She admitted it herself. This girl has pledged her allegiance to a group of traitors. A group of criminals. An escaped *convict*."

The effect was instantaneous, as though the general's words were a toxic gas that spread through the Marsh, rendering Alouette's efforts useless. People were shouting at her now, telling her to get off the stage.

"Crown the general!" someone called out, and like a rallying battle cry, more spectators cheered.

"The general saved us!" shouted another. "We're better off now than we ever were!"

"No!" Alouette cried out, her voice wavering again, her confidence vanishing with every hammering heartbeat. "He's lying to you. He's been plotting against our planet from the beginning. He plotted to kill the Patriarche!"

But the chanting was too loud. The wave of doubt that was undulating through the crowd was too strong. It was as though the world had stopped listening. She couldn't make them understand.

Alouette found Marcellus again in the crowd. His gaze was burning with the same intensity, the same unreadable resolve. But this time, she saw something else, too. A ferocity that she'd witnessed countless times before, a determination to bring down the man who had destroyed so many lives. Who had imprisoned her and tortured her. Who had ordered her death right in front of her.

"Crown the general!" the crowd chanted. They were a simmering pot about to boil over. Alouette spotted three droids moving toward some of the more rowdy spectators.

And it was then that Alouette realized she didn't need to make them understand. She just needed to end this. And she alone had the power to do it.

She spun to face the man on the balcony. "General Bonnefaçon," she said in a clear, unwavering voice. "You have committed countless heinous and unspeakable crimes. You are guilty of treason against the Regime and must be brought to justice." She peered back into the crowd, sending her words out to every droid, officer, and sergent in this marketplace. "Arrest the traitor."

- CHAPTER 41 -
CERISE

"ARREST THE TRAITOR."

The words slammed into Cerise's mind like a pulse hitting an invisible force field. Sparks showering every which way, light bouncing, the world warping before her very eyes.

Arrest the general?

She couldn't do that. Could she? He was the general. He was the highest-ranking member of the Ministère.

But the order had come directly from Alouette Taureau. Alouette *Paresse*. The confirmed and rightful ruler of Laterre, according to the Order of the Sols.

Her mind began to spin. Sending her vision and thoughts and balance into disarray. She reached out to steady herself and locked her hands around the back of a nearby chair. All the while, Alouette's accusations continued to race through her mind. Like archived footage stuck on triple speed, running backward and forward and backward again.

"*. . . guilty of treason . . .*"

"*. . . heinous and unspeakable crimes . . .*"

"*. . . plotted to kill the Patriarche . . .*"

Something painful exploded at the base of Cerise's skull, as those frustratingly hazy memories fought to break through again. She could see flashes of a plastique cube, a lab, two men bloody and battered circling each other, something implanted in their arms glowing red.

Cerise gripped harder to the back of the chair. It felt like the ground was breaking beneath her, cracking open, threatening to pull her down into the fiery red-hot core of the planet.

Meanwhile, people were staggering aimlessly around her, unsure where to go, what to do, whom to listen to. In the flurry of activity and noise, Cerise's attention snagged on a desperate, wild-eyed girl staring back at her from across the room and she let out a shriek.

It was her! The girl from the illegal TéléCom in her closet.

"Cerise, I need your help. . . ."

Shakily, she walked toward her, reaching out for that smooth skin and glossy hair until her fingertips touched something solid and she leapt back. It was a mirror. She was looking into the titan-framed mirror on the wall.

That was *her* face.

Panicked, she clawed at her cheek and forehead, ripping the synthetic flesh from her skin. The cool air rushed across her overheating circuitry, stabilizing her pulse and her breath. But when she reached back up and pulled the contact lens from her left eye, strangely, the color did not change. It was still an unsettling brown. A *human* brown.

She stared into the mirror, incredulous. Why was her cybernetic eye—

She blinked and, all of a sudden, it was orange again. Like she'd imagined the whole thing.

Meanwhile, more memories began to push their way into her mind. Blurry human ones that she'd been told had been blockaded by her own brain. For her own protection.

She saw a sleek silver voyageur.

A shaggy-haired boy with an infuriating smirk.

An army of soldiers dressed in crisp red uniforms.

"Cerise!"

With a jolt, she was back. The memories disintegrated like dust particles in a stiff breeze. Sensory details streamed back through her neuroprocessors, and she saw her father standing before her, his neat hair slicked back, his eyes roving over her face.

"Papa—Directeur Chevalier," she said, snapping to attention. She peered at her reflection in the mirror again. Everything looked normal. Circuitry humming softly. Cybernetic eye glowing a solid, vibrant orange. Her mind raced to piece back together the last thirty seconds. But she couldn't do it. It was like she'd been kicked out of her own mind and the door had been locked behind her.

"What are you doing?" her father asked.

"I . . . ," Cerise began, but her voice trailed off as her gaze drifted to the balcony, where the general still stood, glaring down at the girl on the platform who had just ordered his arrest. Cerise willed her feet to move, to walk toward him, but she was still dizzy, disoriented, as though the whole Precinct had turned upside down.

But then, Inspecteur Limier came stalking through the room, moving purposefully toward the balcony. Cerise watched, her circuitry flashing wildly in anticipation. She waited for the inspecteur to draw his weapon, to press the general against the wall, cuff his hands behind his back.

But Limier did none of those things. He stopped in front of the general, and the two seemed to speak in silent words. Nothing but a nod was exchanged. But the inspecteur apparently understood.

"I will take care of it, sir," said Limier before pivoting and striding back off the balcony. He pushed past Cerise, making his way toward the door of the observation lounge. She struggled to make sense of what was happening. Why wasn't he arresting him? Had he not heard the command? From the rightful *Matrone*?

Limier stopped at the door and placed his hand against the biometric lock on the wall. With a ping, the door slid open and, as the inspecteur's hand fell away, Cerise caught sight of something red and fleshy hidden beneath the left cuff of his uniform sleeve. Her cybernetic eye zoomed in, but before she could capture it, Limier was gone. And the sound of a commotion pulled her attention back to the open balcony door, where she saw, six floors below, in the marketplace, an army of droids was mustering. The same ones that had been sent for Citizen Rousseau were now rerouting, barreling through the crowd toward the Policier Precinct. Coming for the general.

In one swift motion, General Bonnefaçon was no longer on the balcony. He was stalking through the observation lounge, toward the door. No one dared to move. Everyone just stared at him. Some of the officers twitched, as though trying to decide whether or not to apprehend him. The general met each of their eyes with a challenging glare. And their decision was made.

No one moved a muscle.

Except Cerise. Determination flooded through her. She could hear Alouette Taureau's command pulsing in her ears.

"Arrest the traitor."

But if the general was a traitor, wouldn't that make Cerise a traitor for following his command? And she couldn't be a traitor again. The general reached the door and pressed his hand against the scanner. But it didn't open.

The lock had already been reset. His biometrics had already been reregistered in the Communiqué. Most likely by members of *her* Bureau. Cyborgs like her following the rightful chain of command. She didn't know how she would single-handedly overpower General Bonnefaçon, but she knew she had to try. She stepped forward, only to be held back by her father, who gave a slight shake of his head as his grip tightened around her arm.

She began to protest but was cut off by a booming voice. "Someone open this Sol-damn door NOW!"

Three officers sprang into action, tussling to be the first to the door, the first to help the traitor escape. Cerise cursed their weakness, their humanness.

The general vanished into the hallway, and everyone watched the door for several minutes, as though they expected him to come back and turn himself in.

But that didn't happen.

Another commotion from outside the window drew Cerise onto the balcony. She stared out over the railing at the marketplace below and the

Frets beyond. Everyone was now pointing to the sky, where a lone cruiseur was ascending from the roof of the Precinct.

More people streamed onto the balcony, watching the general's craft soar higher and higher, until it was barely visible through the clouds. But Cerise's cybernetic eye was no longer focused on the general.

It had zeroed in on a face lost in the crowd.

A pair of hazel eyes partially shielded by a dark hood.

The same eyes she'd been searching for, hunting for, scouring countless hours of footage for.

Marcellus Bonnefaçon was there. In the Marsh. A mere six floors below her. Determination revved up inside of her once more, fueling her processors and her steadily beating heart. Regardless of whether the general was in command of the planet or not, that man was still a wanted criminal. A threat to the Regime. A Regime that Cerise had sworn to protect at all costs.

And this time, she would not let him escape. She would not let the incompetent Policier stand in the way of her primary objective again.

Because this time, she would go after him herself.

- CHAPTER 42 -
ALOUETTE

THE CRUISEUR DISAPPEARED INTO A BANK OF THREAT-
ening clouds, leaving Alouette with a darkness blooming in her chest.
A sickness spreading through her. He was gone. After everything she'd
done—betrayed the sisters, lied to Marcellus, left the Refuge on her
own—the general had gotten away.

The agitation of the crowd instantly returned. Any shocked silence that
had followed Alouette's call for the general's arrest had shattered, and now the
chant that had sent splinters through her heart resumed, louder than before.

"Crown the general!"

It quickly caught on, spreading through the Marsh like wildfire, until
another voice cried out, "But she's a Paresse! She's our rightful leader!"

"Crown the Matrone!"

"Crown the general!"

The world was splitting in two. All these shouts. All this anger.
Directed at her. It was too much.

"Please," she tried to say, but her voice came out barely a whisper. Every
gramme of determination and resolve that she'd come here with—that
she'd betrayed the sisters with—was evaporating in the mist that started
to drizzle through the air.

Nothing had gone the way it was supposed to.

Everything was falling apart.

"Please," she tried again, but the buzzing sound of the hologram cams screeched through her ears. She could feel them still circling her, little glowing orbs capturing her face from every angle. Every crevice. Every strand of hair.

Every *mistake*.

This had been a mistake.

"Crown the general!"

"Crown the Matrone!"

The chants continued to rip through the heavy, wet air. Clashing against each other like explosifs colliding.

Alouette's heart was galloping in her chest. She dropped her gaze, unable to look out at the crowd. Unable to see so much disappointment etched into some and so much false hope into others. And that's when her eyes landed on a single piece of wood. It looked just like any other plank that made up this stage, but Alouette knew this one was different. Because her mind suddenly drifted back to the last time she'd been here, the last person she'd seen standing in this very spot.

It had been a young girl named Nadette Epernay. With hair that shone like copper and a face as innocent as a child's.

She'd been killed so the general could be here today.

So they could *all* be here today.

The thought gave Alouette strength. Nadette's tearful, pleading eyes gave her resolve.

"Crown the general!"

"Crown the Matrone!"

"I am not your Matrone!" The words shot out of Alouette like a pulse from a rayonette. Steady and straight and powerful. And enough to break through the voices in the crowd.

The chanting died down, but there was a fragile edge to its stillness. As if any moment, it might crumble completely. Alouette looked to Rousseau, who gave her an affirming nod.

She cleared her throat and continued. "Yes, as the Patriarche's daughter,

I am the rightful heir to the Regime. But I did not come here to take the general's place. Nor to follow in my father's footsteps and disappear behind the walls of the Palais."

The stunned hush continued. The only sound was the raindrops that had started to fall from the sky.

"I did not come here to be crowned as your Matrone. I came here today to stand beside you, not above you."

"Do you really expect us to believe that?"

The angry voice startled everyone. It was loud and echoing. Not coming from the holograms, the stage, or the balcony, but from somewhere else. Heads swiveled in every direction. Gazes hunted. Ears listened. Breaths hitched.

"This girl attempts to deceive you all. Alouette Taureau—Alouette Paresse—is not the solution. She is the *problem*. She has the blood of murderers in her veins. If you follow her, the only place it will lead is to more oppression. More death. More chains."

Alouette spun back to Rousseau, hoping she understood what was happening, or at least, *where* that voice was coming from, but the Vangarde leader looked like everyone else in the crowd: eyes roving, face lined with shock.

And then, Alouette saw it.

It was like watching wisps of red smoke slither through the air. Pinpricks of blood bubble up and trickle across the skin.

The men and women in red hoods oozed through the crowd. Spreading. Infecting. Positioning themselves strategically throughout the marketplace.

Every muscle in Alouette's body tensed. She felt the energy in the Marsh shift, uneasiness simmering and rippling once again. Even the rain, which was falling harder now, pounding on faces and flags and stalls, seemed tinged with the color of death.

CHAPTER 43

MARCELLUS

MARCELLUS HAD STOPPED BREATHING. STOPPED MOV-
ing. Stopped feeling the sting of Alouette's betrayal and the rage over his
grandfather's escape. It all just came to a juddering standstill with the
first glimpses of those terrifying red hoods snaking through the crowd.

It didn't matter anymore if Alouette had lied to him, if she'd ignored
the sisters' decision and defied all attempts to keep her safe. Because Marcellus's worst nightmare—his *only* nightmare these days—was coming
true. Because even though his whole world had stopped, he knew he didn't
have the power to stop *them*. To stop *her*.

"Alouette Taureau is not your savior. She is your enemy. Just like her
father and her father's father. All the way back to the statue of the man she
now stands beneath."

No, Marcellus thought desperately, his gaze ransacking the marketplace, pulling it apart, searching for the source of that voice he knew all
too well. That voice that was both harrowing and powerful at the same
time. He'd heard it in the Jondrette all those months ago. He'd heard
it in this very marketplace, while a quavering, shivering Patriarche had
mounted the steps of his own undoing. He'd heard it in the wheat-fleur
fields as it swore an oath to blood and violence. And Marcellus had done

everything in his power—the sisters had done everything in *their* power—to make sure that voice never came near Alouette.

Yet here it was.

And Marcellus knew that what he'd said in the Forest Verdure last night was true. He would die to protect her.

Keeping one hand firmly on the rayonette in his waistband, he began to maneuver his way closer to the stage.

"Alouette is a symbol!" shouted Citizen Rousseau, who had stepped forward to speak again. Blustering rain kicked and squalled all around her. "A symbol of a new start. Of our unity as one people. As *citizens* of this great planet. Her father was First Estate, but her mother was Third Estate. She has the blood of leaders *and* the blood of the people running through her veins."

Marcellus tried to breathe again. Tried to trust in Citizen Rousseau's words and her ability to sway hearts and minds with them. But it was as if she were building a wall out of whisper-thin paper. And that other voice kept puncturing holes through it.

"Don't be fooled by fancy speeches and empty promises. They are only designed to twist your mind into knots until you can't see the truth any longer. You saw how quickly, how easily, this girl commanded the droids to do her bidding. Today, she sends them after the general. But tomorrow, she will send them after you. If five hundred years of history has taught us anything, it is that we cannot trust a Paresse. They will fill our heads with hope, while simultaneously draining our blood of nutrients, stealing our power and our voices, poisoning us slowly. The only way to be free of their lies and their chains is to fight them to the death."

More red-hooded soldiers streamed into the marketplace. They seemed to come in a never-ending wave. They were everywhere Marcellus looked. But he kept going, kept plunging forward through the rain, through the sea of people.

Meanwhile, the officers and sergents stationed throughout the crowd began to move toward the platform as well, their weapons primed.

They'll protect her, Marcellus told himself. *She's the rightful ruler now. They have to protect her.*

But their presence and the Red Scar's presence was only making the crowd more nervous. More restless. More confused.

"Citizens!" Rousseau called out, desperate to be heard over the growing din in the Marsh, desperate to keep that paper-thin wall intact. "Please stay calm. Remember that peace is the only way to change. We don't need weapons. We need only our words."

"Words are not enough!" replied the invisible voice. "Words have gotten us nowhere. That's why they've been forgotten. Because they don't work. Only your anger works. Use it. Feel it. Let it fuel the fire burning inside of you."

And suddenly, the voice was no longer invisible. It belonged to the woman who had just climbed the ladder of one of the trapèze towers and was now clinging to its uppermost rungs, high above the crowd, drawing all eyes upward, including Marcellus's. She, too, was dressed in red, but her hood wasn't pulled up like the others. Instead, it was thrown defiantly back to reveal her crisply shaven head, her prominent cheekbones, and her ferocious eyes the color of storm clouds. Around her neck, Marcellus spotted a small amplificateur that was broadcasting her voice to the far reaches of the Marsh.

"This is the same fire they stole from us centuries ago," bellowed Maximilienne Epernay. "When they stole everything else. Our freedoms, our rights, our dignity. The anger you feel is resonating five hundred years across time. It is the anger of our ancestors who touched down on this very ground, at this very site, only to find they'd been tricked. Deceived. Only to find they were brought here as slaves. And *she* is the link that connects it all. *Her* ancestors are the ones who enslaved us. We owe it to our ancestors and to ourselves to fight!"

"Yes!" shouted Rousseau as rivers of rain streaked down her face. "But we must fight *peacefully*. Together. With our words as our weapons, our hope and passion as our ammunition, and our unity as our strength. We have more power in our strong feet and beating hearts and urgent voices than the Ministère has in their entire arsenal. With your determination and every gramme of courage in your bodies, we can pave the path toward a new Laterre. Without shedding a single drop of blood."

"Impossible!" retorted Max from her perch above the crowd. "As long as the blood of the First and Second Estates still flows through the veins of this planet, there is no path toward a new Laterre. We must shed all of it. We must drain this planet of its manipulators and murderers and oppressors. We will never be free if they live."

It was like a single rip in the paper-thin wall. A single tear in its fragile material. But it was enough. The roar mounted, the uneasiness grew, bodies began to push against one another, like they had suddenly discovered they were packed too closely together.

Marcellus surged forward, fighting to get to Alouette and Rousseau. But the officers and sergents who had traversed the marketplace now shuffled into position around the base of the stage, forming a protective barrier between the crowd and their rightful ruler. Marcellus was blocked, unable to get through. And as the red-hooded soldiers continued to weave around him and circulate through the Marsh, something shiny and metallic caught his eye. He sucked in a sharp intake of breath, suddenly realizing what they were doing. Why they were spreading.

Horrified, Marcellus watched as one of the Red Scar guards removed a rayonette from beneath a hooded coat and shoved it into the hand of an unsuspecting bystander. The young woman, who looked no older than sixteen, stared down at the weapon in her hand like it was a bloc of pure titan. She'd never held something of such significance—such power.

The sight of it in her hands spurred Marcellus on. He had to find another way onto that stage. He darted to the left, shouldering his way through the crowd, scanning the human blockade for gaps or holes.

"This is our moment!" Maximilienne cried out. "The general has fled. This is our chance. To take control of *our* planet. Not hand it over to yet another inept Paresse heir. We can fight for the life that we want. And we can win it. Right here. Right now."

"Violence will not achieve anything!" Rousseau called out. "It will only lead to more violence. It didn't work on the First World and it won't work here. Peace is the only way to peace."

"But this is *not* the First World!" bellowed Max. "This is *our* world. And we want it back!"

And then, Marcellus heard it. Even through the shouting and chaos and the now-torrential rain. It felt as though, along with his breath and limbs and thoughts, time stopped too. Laterre no longer spun on its axis. No longer orbited around Sol 1.

Every sound for kilomètres switched off, drowned out, silenced, until all Marcellus could hear was that single rayonette pulse whooshing through the air.

One of the officers standing in front of the stage hit the ground, dark smoke blackening his white uniform from the lethal wound in his chest.

And that was all it took.

The paper-thin wall crumpled.

Anarchy erupted. More shots reverberated around the marketplace. The crowd surged forward—some zeroed in on the Policier sergents and Ministère officers standing guard, some turned on each other, while others tried to reach the platform where Alouette and Rousseau still stood. Marcellus felt himself shoved from all sides.

The droids stationed on the perimeter of the Marsh charged into action, clobbering their way through the crowd, tazeuring, paralyzing, attacking anyone who showed signs of aggression. Bodies were falling faster than the rain from above. They cried out as they fell and then trembled on the sodden ground.

"Halt in the name of the Matrone," one of the droids thundered as it shot down a man who had tried to rush the stage.

Marcellus felt a sickening mix of dread and relief. They were protecting her. But at what cost?

"Stop!" a fragile voice shouted from the stage, and Marcellus looked up to see Alouette staring at the fallen man with tears prickling her eyes. "Please stop!"

But her voice was quickly drowned out by the noise. A new chant had broken free, like birds from a cage, flittering wildly through the air.

"Take it back! Take it back! Take it back!"

Then, someone broke through the perimeter of officers and charged onto the platform. Marcellus's vision blurred and his lungs emptied as he watched the figure in the dark coat move toward Alouette. Marcellus tried desperately to get to her, clawing and shouting and shoving. But it was no use. There were just too many Sol-damn people.

He watched the figure grab on to Alouette's arm and drag her away before finally catching a glimpse of the rain-soaked face behind the hood. Delicious air poured back into his lungs. It was Sister Laurel.

She pounded down the steps of the platform, using the glowing weapon in her hand and a few well-placed elbows to clear an opening for Alouette and Rousseau, who followed closely behind her, hoods pulled back up over their heads.

Marcellus rerouted, jostling his way toward them. A body slammed into Alouette, knocking her onto the slick and muddy ground, and he ran to help her up.

"Marcellus!" Alouette cried. There were tears in her eyes. "I'm sorry. I didn't think. I didn't mean to . . . I only wanted to—"

"Later," Marcellus said urgently, and turned to Laurel. "We need to get them both out of here."

"But what about the others?" Alouette peered desperately into the mayhem. "The sisters. We can't just—"

"They'll be fine," Laurel assured her. "They have rayonettes and they know how to defend themselves. Come on."

With their heads bent low and raindrops cascading over their hoods, the four of them charged forward, fighting as one as they maneuvered through the crowd, through the torrential downpour, searching for a way out. But it was quickly becoming evident that all paths back into the Frets were clogged. Between the assailants attacking the sergents on the perimeter of the Marsh and others just trying to flee to safety, bottlenecks had formed at all exits.

Then, another swarm of people rushed toward them. Marcellus grabbed Alouette's hand, but when he spun back to find Citizen Rousseau, she was gone, swept away in the turbulent, undulating crowd.

Alouette started after her, but Marcellus held her back.

"What are you doing?" Alouette shouted. "We have to find her!"

"No!" Marcellus called out over the confusion. "We have to get back to the—" But his voice was cut off by another shot fired from nearby.

Marcellus had no idea where it came from. All he could do was hear it. And then, all he could do was smell it as the lethal pulse buried itself into flesh. Marcellus saw a blur of movement, too fast to even track, and then a body slumped to the ground in front of him. Alouette opened her mouth to scream as the remains of the pulse that was clearly meant for her smoked and steamed up from the center of Sister Laurel's chest.

- CHAPTER 44 -
ALOUETTE

"ALOUETTE!

"Alouette!

"Alouette!"

She didn't recognize the sound of her own name. The voice was coming at her from a long, dark tunnel, slowed down until every syllable was mushy and languid and nonsensical. Random sounds strung together in no order. Random letters that had nothing to do with her.

Alouette continued to thrust the heels of her hands against Sister Laurel's chest. Over and over and over.

"One and two and three and four and . . . ," she whispered through her tears. *Thirty compressions. Then breathe.*

With shaky hands, she pinched Laurel's nose and bent down, blowing desperate puffs of air into her lungs. Her chest rose but then fell still again.

"No," Alouette whimpered. "No."

She started again.

"One and two and three and . . . please! Laurel! Please!" She tried to ignore the wound that was staring back at her from the center of Laurel's chest. The skin around it was unlike anything she'd ever seen before. Blackened and ashy, smelling of burnt meat.

After tending to Gabriel's cluster bullet, Alouette had been convinced she'd seen it all. But she hadn't seen this. She hadn't seen a lethal pulse from a Laterrian rayonette bury itself into the chest of her dear, beloved sister. A lethal pulse that had been meant for her.

"Thirteen and fourteen and fifteen and . . ."

The tears were coming faster now, blurring her vision. All around her there was noise. Commotion. Feet stomping. Voices shouting. Rayonette pulses whizzing through the air. But Alouette could hear none of it. Just like that deep, sluggish voice shouting her name from somewhere, the noise was too far away. Too distorted to be real. It was a dream.

Yes, that was it. A dream. And the blood starting to seep out and stain Alouette's fingers wasn't real. This wound wasn't real. Sister Laurel wasn't actually lying on the ground in the center of the Marsh. She was in her propagation room. And Alouette was asleep in the infirmerie, tangled in her damp sheets from another nightmare.

Wake up. You're dreaming. Wake up, Alouette!

"Alouette!"

Her eyes shot open as the voice reached her. As a pair of hands tried to grab her, but she pushed them away and kept compressing.

"Twenty-eight and twenty-nine and thirty."

She leaned over and blew two more urgent breaths into Laurel's cold lips. "Breathe!" she shouted, no longer desperate, now just angry. Why wasn't she breathing?

"Alouette! We have to go! Now!"

"Start again," Alouette said, positioning her hands over Laurel's heart. "One and two and—" But she was suddenly yanked to her feet. "No! I have to save her!"

"She's gone!" came the voice. It was no longer coming from the end of a tunnel. It *was* the tunnel. It was pulling her deep down into it. It was consuming her in darkness. "Alouette, she's gone."

She spun around and stared into the wild, bloodshot eyes of Marcellus, barely able to focus on him. His face streaked with dirt. His hair tousled and blood splattered across his cheek.

"We have to get out of here," he said. "Get back to the Refuge."

The Refuge. Yes. Get her back to the Refuge. Alouette could save her there. She had the right equipment and the right herbs and—

She felt a rough tug on her hand and then she was stumbling forward, away from Laurel. "No!" she cried out, reaching back. "I can't leave her here! Laurel, wake up! Please wake up!"

"She's gone!" Marcellus said again, stepping in front of her. He was blurring in and out of focus. Nothing about him was making any sense. His words. His face. They were all just jumbled bits of information that couldn't, wouldn't, compute in her mind. She felt another tug on her hand and then, "Alouette, you have to let her go. We have to get—"

Marcellus's words were suddenly drowned out by another sound. The same sound Alouette had heard only moments before Laurel slumped to the ground in front of her.

The whistle of molecules shifting. The bending of air. Another body fell and Alouette shrieked, certain that when she looked down, Marcellus would now be lying before her with the same terrible wound in his chest.

But the woman at her feet was a stranger. And when Alouette looked up, she saw an officer in a crisp white uniform holding the weapon. Had he just saved her life?

"Bonnefaçon!" the officer shouted at Marcellus. "Get her out of here. Protect the Matrone."

The words echoed in Alouette's mind, seeming to bounce off the walls of her consciousness forever.

Protect the Matrone.

Protect the Matrone.

Protect the Matrone.

But she wasn't the Matrone. That's what she'd been trying to tell everyone. She hadn't come here to claim her title. She wasn't just another Paresse like Maximilienne had said. But no one seemed to listen. No one seemed to understand.

"Vive Laterre!" An angry roar broke into her thoughts, and she looked up to see a man in a red hood barreling toward her, a rayonette clutched in his hands.

There was no reaction. There was no time. Alouette's mind woke up on its own. Her limbs moved on their own. Her body knew what to do even before her thoughts could catch up. She spun around, arcing both arms high above her head. In one fast, fluid motion, the man was on the ground, writhing from the force of *Pushing Tides*.

It had been months since she'd had the strength to use her Tranquil Forme, but her muscles remembered the movements flawlessly. Like they were now a permanent part of her, never to leave, never to be forgotten.

When she turned back to the officer, he was staring wide-eyed between her and the man.

"I'm not the Matrone!" Alouette shouted over the noise. "And I can protect myself."

She grabbed Marcellus by the arm and dragged him into the crowd. Moving through the current was near impossible. All around them, bodies were colliding as shots were fired and fists were swung and weapons were fashioned hastily out of banner poles and wooden planks and empty gâteau plates.

Alouette kept her gaze trained on the towering form of Fret 6. Right now, it was their best chance at escape. They could cut through the inside of it and then sneak out from the alleyway in the back. They moved quickly, keeping to the shadows of the stalls like rats dodging the light. All the while, the clangs, shrieks, and thuds of the riots rang out around them.

As soon as they found themselves at the dimmed entrance of Fret 6, Alouette's muscles began to relax, to uncoil. The Fret was relatively quiet. So far, the fight had been contained to the marketplace. But as they stole down the corridor, toward the back entrance, Alouette could feel the general's presence everywhere. He'd left his mark inside the Frets as well as out. All the lights had been fixed and now shone brightly, erasing any hope of a shadowy corner. The doors were all properly secured, with functioning biometric locks that glowed orange. And there wasn't a single broken pipe to be found.

This isn't over, she reminded herself. *He'll be back. He won't just give up.*

A set of footsteps broke through the silence and they both froze. Alouette spun around, prepared to defend herself against another attacker, but the hallway was empty. She shared a wary look with Marcellus, who was gripping his rayonette. Neither of them was certain whether to run or hide. And that's when they heard it.

The tiny, infinitesimal *click* of a lever. It echoed through the long corridor as loud as a shiver tracked its way down Alouette's spine. Her experience with weapons was limited, but she was fairly sure that was the sound of a rayonette being toggled.

From lethal to paralyze?

Or the other way around?

But still, she could see no one in the hallway.

She turned to Marcellus, whose narrowed, cautious eyes were scanning every centimètre, every door, every well-lit floor panel.

The footsteps resumed and Alouette felt her muscles tense again. This time, it was clear there was more than one. Marcellus spun around as five figures emerged from a nearby stairwell. All of them wore red hoods and carried rayonettes. But it was the one who was pointing his directly at Alouette's head that she recognized first.

"Jolras?" Marcellus asked, dazed. "How did you—you were arrested! I saw them arrest you."

Jolras sneered. "It helps to have friends in high places."

"What?" Marcellus swung his rayonette toward him just as another one fired. Alouette yelped as the pulse ricocheted off Marcellus's weapon and buried itself in a couchette door. The rayonette clattered to the ground. Marcellus bent to reach for it but was stopped by Jolras.

"Don't." He waved his weapon menacingly. "Just hand over the Matrone and I won't be forced to hurt you."

"I'm not the Matrone!" Alouette fired back. "Why can't you understand that? I want nothing to do with my name or my title. I want what you want. I want change."

Jolras tilted his head to the side, causing one of his springy curls to fall across his forehead. "That's cute. But forgive me for not trusting the daughter of a murderer."

"If you won't trust her, then trust me," Marcellus snapped.

Jolras pulled his gaze from Alouette and settled it back on Marcellus. "And why should I do that? When you're the one helping her escape."

"Because I thought we were friends."

Jolras snorted at that. "We were never friends."

"Fine. But I thought at least we were on the same side. Isn't that why you tried to warn me about Max? Because you wanted to stop her. And now look at what she's done." He pointed in the direction of the Marsh, where the sound of riots could still be heard. "She's turned this planet upside down. What happened? I thought you wanted nothing to do with her anymore."

Jolras visibly twitched, like he'd been shocked by Inspecteur Champlain's torture device.

"You don't have to do this," Marcellus went on gently, coaxingly. "You are your own person. She doesn't control you. She doesn't own you. You can still break free from—"

"Shut up!" Jolras screamed, his voice trembling now. "You don't know anything!" His grip on the rayonette tightened, and he took a step closer to Alouette. "Now hand her over. I'm sure my sister would love the honor of killing the last of the Paresse name herself."

Marcellus stepped in front of Alouette. "No. You'll have to kill me—"

WHOOSH!

Alouette heard the pulse before she felt it. It whistled past her ear like a stiff wind, finding its target in one of the Red Scar guards. His body crumpled. Jolras whirled around, trying to figure out where to point his weapon. But after a second pulse brought down another one of his guards, he and the two others scattered like mice, retreating back into the stairwell, and Alouette turned to see a girl in a dark purple gown stepping out from her hiding place in an adjoining hallway.

From this angle, she could see only one side of the girl's face, but it was enough to release every taut muscle and every molecule of trapped air in her lungs. She felt her body sag with relief and her eyes well with tears at the sight of the girl's familiar stature and long jet-black hair falling down her back.

"Oh my Sols! Cerise!" Alouette began to run toward her but was suddenly yanked backward by Marcellus. At first, she didn't understand. Why was he holding her back? This was *Cerise*. This was their friend.

But then, the girl turned to face them.

And Alouette had to stifle the gasp that rose up in her throat.

It was exactly as she'd feared. She'd spent nights in her cell in the general's facility haunted by the thought of this moment. Imagining the precisely crafted filaments, the careful pattern of embedded circuitry spreading from forehead to cheek.

The lights.

They flickered now with fierce determination.

But it was the girl's glowing cybernetic eye that unnerved Alouette the most. She forced herself to focus on the other eye. The dark brown *human* one. The only part of Cerise that still felt familiar.

"Cerise," Alouette said again, trying for a milder tone. A calming tone. "Merci, you saved our lives."

Cerise ignored her and raised the rayonette in her hand. "Marcellus Bonnefaçon. You have been charged with treason against the Regime. I am placing you under arrest. I will now take you into Ministère custody. If you resist, I will have no choice but to shoot."

Alouette shuddered at the sound of that chilling, inflectionless tone. Gone was the bubbly, melodic lilt of the Cerise she knew. Gone was the stylish hacker who had ambitions to save the world. Gone was the sympathizeur.

There was nothing sympathetic about that voice.

"Cerise," Alouette cried, all traces of calm vanished. "Don't do this. You don't have to do this." She took a step toward her. Cerise flinched slightly and flicked her rayonette toward Alouette, but immediately seemed to think better of it and aimed it back at Marcellus, who was surreptitiously reaching for the weapon that had been knocked out of his hand earlier.

"Halt!" Cerise called out without a single hint of emotion. Marcellus froze again. "I do have to do this. Marcellus Bonnefaçon is an enemy to the Regime. He must be apprehended."

"He is not your enemy," Alouette said, taking another cautious step toward her. "He is your friend, remember? We both are. We saved your life in the Jondrette. With Gabriel. Remember Gabriel? The criminal mastermind?"

Cerise's circuitry began to flicker faster, and Alouette felt hope rise in her chest. Was it possible that there was a part of the old Cerise still left in there? A trace of the girl they once knew?

She kept talking. "Cerise, please put down the rayonette. You don't want to hurt him. You don't need to arrest him. He—"

"I must arrest him." Cerise's circuitry flashed once and then fell still. "I must fulfill my duties to the Ministère and the Regime."

Alouette's hopes plummeted. The more she stared at this girl who used to be her friend, the more she couldn't see her friend at all. She couldn't see the girl who had snuck them onto a voyageur, who had argued with Gabriel over a game of Regiments, who had tried and failed to bake a gâteau. All she could see was that unnerving, twinkling circuitry. And the vibrant orange eye that roved over Alouette like a droid eye.

This was not the same girl they'd traveled across the System with.

This was a product of the Ministère.

And she would not back down.

Alouette's gaze darted between the Red Scar guard lying on the ground and the weapon responsible for his death, still clutched in Cerise's hand, pointed straight at Marcellus's chest. And she knew what she had to do. It wasn't the way she wanted this to end. But she didn't have a choice.

"Cerise Chevalier," Alouette said in the most authoritative voice she could muster. "Merci for your service to the Regime. I am Matrone Alouette Paresse, and I release you from your duties and command you to stand down."

Cerise's circuitry hummed back to life, and her gaze flickered uneasily between Alouette and Marcellus, the directive clearly taking a second to process through her brain.

"But . . . ," she began slowly. "I have been ordered to—"

"Who ordered you?" Alouette shot back. "General Bonnefaçon? He is not in charge anymore. He is a traitor and he does not outrank me. I am the rightful ruler of Laterre. And I'm ordering you to abandon all prior directives."

And then, something happened. Something Alouette had seen only once before in her life. When she'd stood in a dank cell beside Sister Jacqui and Sister Denise and ordered Inspecteur Champlain to release them.

Cerise's circuitry exploded in a frantic tempest. Bright lights flashed and flickered across her cheeks and forehead like a chaotic firework display. Her eye, that terrible soulless orange eye, sparked on and off. On and off. From a glowing cyborg orange to a dark, human brown.

And then, as if someone had yanked the connection to a power supply, it all suddenly ceased. Cerise's circuitry stopped flashing, her winking eye snuffed out like the last trace of a flame, and Cerise's face emerged, blank and vacant. Her mouth hung open, as if a word had formed on her lips but never made it out in time.

Slowly, Cerise lowered the weapon. Marcellus didn't hesitate. He darted toward his fallen rayonette and scooped it up before aiming it shakily at Cerise.

"No," Alouette said, gently pushing down on his arm until it rested back at his side. She kept her eyes firmly locked on Cerise, watching her crumple to the ground, like the weight of her own mind was too heavy to hold up.

"C'mon," Marcellus said. "We need to go. Now. Before Jolras comes back with more of them."

Alouette wanted so badly to go to her. To comfort her. To try again and again and again to coax back the girl she once knew. Keep trying until she could look into those eyes and see her friend again. But she felt the rough tug of Marcellus's hand on hers, and eventually she gave up and allowed herself to be dragged down the hallway. Not before casting one last, lingering look at Cerise on the ground. Her head bent low, her left hand wrapped around her rayonette, and her circuitry flickering the sad rhythm of defeat.

CHAPTER 45

CHATINE

"THIS WAS A MASSIVE WASTE OF TIME." ETIENNE STOOD up and began to pace the cockpit of the ship, which wasn't a huge space. Each lap was made up of about five steps before he had to turn around again.

"Will you *please* sit down?" Chatine crushed her temples between her fingertips.

"We should just go," Etienne said. "There's no ship. There's no secret cargo being loaded out of here. That trash man lied to us."

"His name is the Capitaine and he doesn't lie."

"There!" Gabriel said, causing Chatine to flinch. He leaned over her to peer out the cockpit window, holding the binoculars Chatine had brought up to his eyes. "Is that something landing?"

Chatine groaned and pushed him away from her. "No. Once again, *that* is the light from Ledôme in the distance."

They'd been staking out the Vallonay spaceport for nearly a full day, hidden behind a decommissioned warehouse, and the interior of Marilyn had gotten way too claustrophobic with three people in it when it was barely built to hold two.

Out the cockpit window, night had fallen again, and the vast complex spread out before them like a tiny city. A multitude of buildings and warehouses formed grid-like patterns, and a series of launching and landing pads lit up with dazzling rows of tiny white lights. A crisscrossing network of transparent tubes led from a collection of massive cargo hangars to the center of the port. Inside, conveyor belts whisked hundreds of crates across the complex, filled with goods and products arriving from and departing to the far reaches of the System Divine.

"I still don't trust him," Etienne grumbled. "He didn't even *say* that he knew there was zyttrium being flown out of here. He just said there were shipments that weren't registered on the flight logs. That could be anything!"

"This is how it works," Chatine explained, trying to grasp on to any remaining tendrils of her patience. At first, being this close to Etienne, being in this cockpit again breathing the same air as him, had made her slightly dizzy. But now, after almost twenty-two hours, every word he uttered—every word *either* of them uttered—seemed to grate on her nerves. "That's just how mecs like him operate. They don't say exactly what they mean. It's a croc's code."

"A what?" Etienne asked.

"Never mind," Chatine muttered. "I've known the Capitaine since I was a kid. You may not trust him, but I do. And you trust me, so . . ." She let her voice trail off. Mostly because she was waiting for Etienne to contradict her. The question of trust between them was still up for debate.

But he didn't respond. He just kept pacing, stopping every few seconds to glance out the cockpit window at the nearby launchpad, which looked like it hadn't been used in years. The tarmac was spotted with potholes, and there were no lights to illuminate the forgotten warehouse that Etienne had parked Marilyn behind, making the heaps of discarded cargo crates and broken machines look like monsters in the dark.

Finally, Etienne threw up his hands and blurted, "Every minute we wait out here is more time we could be using to chase down other leads." Then, under his breath, he added, "*Good* leads."

"Relax," Chatine told him. "We're well hidden. We're not using up zyttrium. We just need to wait a little longer."

"She's right," Gabriel said, lowering the binoculars. "I knew mecs like the Capitaine back in Montfer. They're shady as sheep's turd, but their information is almost always good."

"How do you know this *Capitaine* didn't send us here on a fool's errand?" Etienne asked, directing his question at Chatine and ignoring Gabriel. He'd been doing a much better job of that than Chatine had. She found the shaggy-haired croc infuriatingly hard to ignore.

"Because he doesn't get paid unless we find the zyttrium!" Chatine said with a sigh. "He has every incentive to give us good information."

"And about that," Etienne said, reaching the end of the small cockpit and spinning on his heel to pace back the other way. "Since when do you have permission to start offering up percentages of *my* community's zyttrium?"

"Since you asked for my help."

"Yeah, and what a mistake that turned out to be. We've been sitting here all day, waiting for some mythical cargo ship that is not coming. We've officially reached a dead end."

"Hey, mecs?" Gabriel tapped Chatine on the shoulder. "I think I see something."

"You don't," Chatine and Etienne said at once.

"No, that's definitely a ship landing. Yup. It's getting closer." He positioned the binoculars back over his eyes. "Oh, never mind, it's Ledôme again."

Lowering the binoculars, Gabriel reached for a handful of dried fruit from the dwindling stash Etienne had brought and popped an apricot into his mouth.

"Fine!" Chatine said, standing up and making a show of reaching for the button to open the hatch. "If you don't need me anymore, I'll just go."

"Fine!" Etienne said, crossing his arms.

"Fine. I'm going."

"Good! Go!"

Chatine paused with her hand hovering over the button. They both knew she wasn't going anywhere. She'd already made this threat three times in the past twenty-two hours.

"I'm doing it. I'm really leaving this time." She rested her fingertips against the hatch release.

"Say hi to Officer Boy for me."

With a growl, Chatine plunged down on the release.

"Hatch open," announced Marilyn in her usual sexy voice.

"Adieu, Etienne. It's been nice knowing you." She stalked toward the unfurling stairwell. The blast of cold Laterrian night air hit her face like a slap. She took one step down the stairs before she heard someone inside let out a begrudging, "Wait."

Turning back, Chatine painted on an innocent expression. "Yes?"

Etienne looked like he'd just caught a whiff of the waste management center again. "Don't go. I still need your help." Every word came out chopped and tense.

It took all of the strength she had left not to smile as she turned back into the cockpit. "Okay, fine. If you want me to stay, I'll stay."

"So, now that you two have finished your strange mating ritual, can we shut the hatch? It's freezing in here!"

Chatine's happy mood vanished in an instant as they both turned to scowl at Gabriel. He reached out to press the hatch release to seal the door, but Etienne slapped his hand away. "Hey, hey, hey, what did I tell you about rule number one?"

"But she got to touch the button!" Gabriel whined.

Etienne sighed and closed the hatch before lowering himself back down into the capitaine's chair. The ship fell quiet again as they all directed their gazes at the only safe place in the cockpit: out the window.

Chatine relished the silence. Her nerves were on edge from the lack of sleep and being crammed into this tiny ship. She rubbed at her eyes and massaged her cheeks, trying to keep herself awake. As her vision cleared, something caught her attention on the far left monitor of the flight console. She squinted at the screen, which was showing a live feed from the cargo hold. She swore she'd seen a flicker of movement just a second ago, but as her eyes adjusted, she realized it was just a trick of the light. Or a trick of her fatigue. All that she could see now was the soft blue glow from the crates holding what was left of the community's paltry supply of zyttrium.

She blew out a long breath and tried to focus on the launchpad. But that stupid light from Ledôme kept distracting her.

"What do you think's going on out there?" she asked.

Etienne yawned. "Out where?"

Chatine nodded toward the sprawling spaceport complex and the city of Vallonay beyond. She could just make out the shadowy outlines of the Frets in the distance. "The coronation was today."

"Why should I care about that?" Etienne asked, and Chatine felt a stab of that old frustration at his indifference. His obstinate vow to "not get involved." She was out here risking her life for *him* and *his* people. Would it kill him to show even a gramme of concern for hers?

"Because it affects you, too," Chatine snapped. "If the general is the Patriarche now, that's not good for your community."

Etienne shrugged. "It's gridder problems."

"Wait a minute," Gabriel said. "Why would the general be crowned? Why not a relative of the Patriarche?"

"Because they're all dead," said Chatine.

"What?" said Gabriel and Etienne at once.

"Well, not all of them, but the three that were favored to be appointed by the System Alliance. The Red Scar killed them."

Gabriel sucked in a sharp breath. "That Red Scar is *bad* news."

"Who are they?" Etienne asked.

"They're the people who murdered the Patriarche," said Chatine, shuddering at the memory of being in that marketplace with Marcellus, watching the blue laser of the Blade slice right through the man's neck, like it was made of nothing stronger than a twig.

"And blew up a hothouse," said Gabriel, starting to count on his fingers. "And a TéléSkin fabrique."

And killed my sister, Chatine added in her mind but didn't dare say aloud.

"*And* kidnapped my dearest Sparkles." When no one said anything, Gabriel added, "I mean, Cerise. They nearly branded her with a laser. Fortunately, though, I swooped in to save her life. All by myself. With no help."

Etienne cut a glance at Gabriel, as though trying to decide whether or not to negate his statement. Finally, he just said, "What do they want, though? Why are they instigating so much violence?"

Chatine shrugged and sat back down in the jump seat. "I guess they want what we all want. Change."

"I don't want change."

Chatine and Gabriel both turned and stared at Etienne.

He held up his hands in a defensive gesture. "What? I don't. I just want everything to stay the same. I hate that the community has to move. I hate that we're being forced out of our homes. Life was good for us. We stayed out of everyone's way. We kept to ourselves. I don't see what was wrong with that."

Chatine snorted. "Are you kidding? There's a million things wrong with that."

Etienne crossed his arms over his chest. "Like what?"

"Um, how about we start with the reason you *have* to keep to yourselves?" Chatine fired back. "Because if the Ministère knew where you were, they'd round you up in a heartbeat just like they did to your . . . " With a bolt of panic, she slammed her mouth shut and dropped her gaze to her lap. She was far too much of a coward to even brave a glance in Etienne's direction.

"Just like they did to who?" Gabriel asked.

"Nothing. No one," Chatine rushed to say. She could almost feel Etienne's glare on her. He had trusted her with that secret. And she'd almost given it away, just like that, in a fit of annoyance. She had to derail the conversation and fast. "Even though I don't agree with their methods, I think the Red Scar are onto something. The planet can't keep going the way it's going. It's the same thing the Vangarde are trying to achieve . . . obviously, in very different ways. They want something different. A planet where everyone is equal, and no one is labeled First Estate or Second Estate or Third Estate."

Gabriel snorted and gave Etienne a chummy elbow to the ribs. "That'd be nice, right?"

"I'm not Third Estate," Etienne said, and flicked his hand toward Gabriel's left wrist. "And might I remind you, neither are you anymore."

Gabriel's eyes fell to the scar on the inside of his arm and seemed to linger there for a long time, as though he were just now remembering what used to be there. "Huh. I guess I never thought about it like that before." He traced the outline of his former Skin with his fingertip. "What estate am I, then?"

"None," Etienne and Chatine said at the same time. Their gazes caught, and just when Chatine vowed to be brave enough not to look away, Etienne did.

"None?" Gabriel echoed in what sounded like panic. "But . . ." His voice trailed off for a moment as he seemed to let this sink in. "Okay, okay, that's a lot of change coming at me at once, but I just need to process it one step at a time. Like Brigitte says."

Etienne let out a chuckle that, to Chatine's relief, sounded more amused than irritated. "You do that." He stretched out his legs and leaned back in his chair, shutting his eyes. "In the meantime, I'm going to just rest my eyes for a minute—"

"There!" Gabriel shouted, making Chatine flinch again. He raised up the binoculars. "There's a ship! I see it! It's landing."

Etienne didn't even open his eyes. Chatine blew out a breath. "No, Gabriel," she droned. "It's just the light of . . ." She squinted through the window. "A voyageur!"

Etienne's eyes flew open. Chatine launched out of her seat and leaned forward, practically pressing her nose against the window. The heavy gray clouds were parting, and through them, something sleek and glinting plummeted downward. A burst of light and heat followed it like a burning tail.

It was definitely a ship. And it was definitely landing.

Etienne snatched the binoculars from Gabriel and peered through them. "That's not just any voyageur. That's a Courrier-class voyageur, used almost exclusively for cargo."

"I *told* you," said Gabriel.

The voyageur circled, slowing with an unwavering ease before finally descending gracefully onto the potholed landing pad just in view behind the warehouse. Then, in an eruption of steam and bright yellow light, its loading doors glided open.

"Look!" Etienne said, pointing off into the distance where the headlights of a large transporteur could be seen gliding across the deserted tarmac. He handed the binoculars to Chatine and she watched, transfixed, as the vehicle swooped closer and came to a hovering halt right beside the voyageur. In its own puff of steam and light, the transporteur's cargo hold opened and a short ramp unfurled, connecting the vehicle to the large spacecraft. It was difficult to see amid the lingering steam and bright lights, but Chatine leaned forward and ratcheted the dial on the top of the binoculars as far as it would go, until she could just make out what looked like feet shuffling across the adjoining walkway, into the awaiting ship.

"I thought you said that was a cargo ship," she said, her fingers tingling with dread.

"It is," Etienne said, and his dark, vacant tone made her certain that, even without the binoculars, he was seeing the same thing she was seeing: a parade of slowly moving feet crossing the short distance from the transporteur to the voyageur.

"Maybe they're all ramp workers," said Gabriel, but he sounded as convinced as Chatine felt.

Then, as the steam cleared and her eyes adjusted to the light, Chatine saw something else. Something that made her stomach clench.

Flashes of unkempt clothes. Dirtied skin. Yellow, rotting teeth. And finally, a pair of feet far too small to belong to a ramp worker. The binoculars slipped from her eyes. Time seemed to slow. The endless chain of shuffling feet dragged on and on, until suddenly, everything clattered together in her mind.

"They were clean. Too clean . . ."

"Where was our *kind? . . . The crocs! The Fret rats! The Oublies!"*

"I think . . . ," Chatine said, struggling to get the words past the lump growing in her throat. "I think those people *are* the cargo."

A huge crash thundered through the cockpit. Chatine spun around, fully preparing to face a pack of bashers. But there was no one there. That's when her gaze snagged on the far left monitor again. Where she'd sworn she'd seen a flicker of movement earlier. Now an entire shelf of medical supplies was scattered across the floor.

"There's someone in the cargo hold!" she cried.

Etienne and Gabriel both cut their eyes to the monitor. "I'm on it," Gabriel said, darting toward the stairs.

Chatine's gaze bounced anxiously between the ship in front of them, still being loaded with an endless chain of people, and the monitor showing the view of the cargo hold.

"Nothing to worry about!" Gabriel called from the lower deck. "It's just a kid!"

A kid?

Chatine was halfway to the stairs when she heard the all-too-familiar voice bellow, "I'm *not* a kid!"

She froze in her tracks. Her breath stopped.

"And you're hurting me! Let go!"

"Get up there, you little croc."

There was a scuffling sound, followed by a string of curse words from Gabriel, before finally two bodies spilled out from the stairwell and onto the cockpit floor.

All the breath came back to her at once, and she used every single gramme of it to shout, "Roche?! What the fric are you doing here?!"

"Roche?" Etienne said, confused. "Who is Roche?"

"Wait, you know this kid?" Gabriel asked, mussing Roche's hair.

Roche swatted at his hand. "I told you, I'm not a kid!"

Chatine gritted her teeth. "Yes, he's my brother." She glared at him. "Did you follow me?"

Roche folded his arms across his chest. "So what if I did?"

"How?" Chatine asked.

"You think you're so smart," Roche sneered. "Sneaking off like that. But I'm smart too, you know. I have my ways of getting information."

All at once, the realization hit her, along with a sharp stab of betrayal. "Marcellus told you, didn't he?"

Roche deflated for a moment before puffing himself up again. "Yes, well, he only told me that you went on a mission to find some stolen zyttrium. *I'm* the one who figured out you'd go straight to the Capitaine. And I was right. I saw you getting into this ship at the waste management center, so I decided to hop aboard and see what you were up to."

"But how did you get out of the Refuge?" Chatine asked.

Roche ignored her and instead took the opportunity to glance around the interior of the cockpit. "Wow. Nice ship! A little rough around the edges, but I like that. Definitely *my* style."

"See?" Etienne said, giving Chatine a sharp look. "He likes my ship. He clearly has better taste than you."

"Your ship?" Roche snapped his gaze to Etienne and immediately stood up straighter. "You *own* this ship?"

Chatine could see Etienne start to glow with that infuriating pride of his. "I do. Built her myself."

"No way!" Roche raced toward the console to get a better look at the controls. "Soop!"

"Her name is Marilyn," Etienne said.

"*Great* name," Roche approved.

"Isn't it?" said Etienne, casting Chatine another look.

"Very First World. I like it."

Chatine grabbed on to her brother's sleeve and yanked him back. "Can we return to the subject of how you snuck out of the Refuge?"

He continued to run his eyes approvingly over the control panel. "Same way you did. I used the founders' tunnel." He shivered. "Sols, that place is creepy when you're by yourself. Reminds me way too much of the exploit tunnels on Bastille. But as you pointed out, the main entrance is a no-go. Completely sealed off."

"Wait," Chatine said. "Is that why you were looking at the monitor? In the vestibule?"

He shrugged, as though her question was of very little consequence. "I wanted to go find the missing Oublies."

"So you were just going to leave?" she shrieked. "Without telling me?"

But Roche ignored her again. "Wait a minute. This ship looks familiar. I've been inside one like this before." He spun back to Etienne, studying his face like he was trying to place him. "You're the other pilote."

"What?" Gabriel asked, glancing between Etienne, Chatine, and Roche, clearly trying to keep up. "What other pilote?"

Roche turned to Gabriel, sizing him up the way only an Oublie who'd lived on the streets his whole life could. Gabriel must have passed the test because Roche said, "His friend saved my life. She was flying the extraction ship to Bastille. The one that rescued Citizen Rousseau. And me." He turned back to Etienne. "Faustine told me about you. She said you were a mighty fine pilote." His face grew somber. "I'm sorry the sisters couldn't save her."

Etienne nodded. "Merci."

"Well, Capitaine," Roche said, clearing his throat and giving Etienne a hearty salute. "It's an honor to be on board such an esteemed vessel, sir."

Etienne's lips twitched with the makings of a smile.

"Roche," Chatine warned, struggling to keep her temper in check. She was not going to fall for his Fret-rat diversion tactics again. "You have to go back to the Refuge. Now."

"But you did it!" Roche said, pointing through the cockpit window where the procession of passengers was still boarding the awaiting voyageur. "You found the Oublies! And the crocs! I *told* you something was going on."

Chatine blew out a breath, hating to admit that he was right. But he was. Something *was* going on. The only problem was, she had no idea what.

"What Oublies?" Gabriel asked, clearly still trying to keep up. "What do all those people have to do with zyttrium?"

"Obviously, *nothing*," Roche said, as though this was the most stupide idea he'd ever heard. He shared a look with Etienne that clearly said, *Who invited the idiot?*

"He's right," Etienne agreed. "Whatever is going on out there clearly has nothing to do with my community's zyttrium. Like I said, this was a fool's errand."

"Well, it doesn't matter anymore." Chatine marched up to the flight console and reached to activate the thrusters. "Because we're leaving right now and taking Roche back to the—"

"Hold up," Etienne said, blocking her hand. "First of all, who is the capitaine here?"

"You are, sir," said Roche dutifully, giving another salute.

Chatine rolled her eyes and yanked his hand down. "Be quiet."

"Secondly, no one touches these controls but me."

"That *is* rule number one," Gabriel reminded her.

Spinning away from the console, Chatine turned her glare on every single infuriating face in this cockpit.

"I say, when that voyageur leaves, we follow it!" Roche launched his hand in the air to simulate a ship taking off.

"No," Chatine said sternly.

"But they're stealing *people*!" Roche argued. "Oublies like me! And sending them off to Sols know where!"

"We don't know that they're stealing them," Chatine said, trying to keep her voice steady. Rational. "They could be . . . I don't know . . . taking them on a trip."

"Yeah, a nice beach vacation on Samsara," Gabriel said before sharing a look of disbelief with Roche.

Chatine felt her muscles tensing. Panic was building in her chest. Whatever shadiness was going on at this launchpad, there was one thing for certain: Roche would *not* get involved with it. She'd already saved him from enough life-or-death scenarios. She was not about to add another to the list.

She finally swiveled back to Etienne and did her best to muster up an expression that passed for pleasant. "Etienne," she began evenly. "I've been thinking. And I've decided that you're right. This *was* a waste of time. We can't just follow random ships out into the ether. We need to start searching for a new lead on the zyttrium. So, I suggest we take Roche back to the Refuge and—" Roche opened his mouth to argue, but she clamped her hand down over it. "And then we can reconvene and come up with a new plan."

She watched Etienne for a response, saying a silent prayer that he would not make this more difficult than it had to be. But it soon became evident that he wasn't even looking at her. His gaze was trained out the cockpit window again.

Chatine spun to see what had caught his attention, and her heart plummeted into her stomach. There went all of her arguments, all of her rationale. There went all hope of turning this ship around and taking Roche back to safety. She watched it all disintegrate before her very eyes.

Because where there had once been an endless train of people boarding the voyageur, there was now a huge conveyer ramp, chugging massive crates from the shadowy depths of the transporteur into the ship. And she certainly didn't need her binoculars to spot the light emanating from every single container. A light that snuck out of the crevices between their slats. A light that glowed bright and iridescent and unmistakably blue.

- CHAPTER 46 -
CERISE

THE HATCH OF THE SLEEP POD EASED SHUT AND darkness enveloped Cerise. She waited for the reprieve. Normally, the pitch-black silence was a pleasant release from the long days of flashing screens, flickering circuitry, and the artificial Sol-light of Ledôme.

But not tonight.

Tonight, the darkness felt dangerous. Unstable. Alive. It was no longer a place of rest. It was a place where her perfect recall could not be controlled. Where her crystal-clear cyborg memories taunted her mind. Where there was nothing to distract her from what she'd done.

Not even the small nodes attached to her forehead, sending soothing vibrations through her circuitry, could chase the uneasiness away. Because the moment her eyes closed, the scene started again. Like archived footage on a TéléCom screen, programmed to repeat over and over and over.

She saw herself holding the rayonette. She saw herself aiming the rayonette. And then, with a throb in her chest, she saw herself lowering the rayonette.

"He is not your enemy. He is your friend, remember? We both are."

With a jolt, Cerise's eyes snapped back open. This was pointless. She jammed her finger against the release and the hatch slid open again.

Weaving through the neat rows of glowing blue pods, she whisked out of the cyborg dormitory, down five flights of stairs to the ground floor of the Ministère headquarters, and slipped into the night.

The air of Ledôme was only a few degrees cooler than her optimized pod temperature, but it felt crisp and refreshing. Cerise breathed in deeply as she walked the long, manicured pathway.

Overhead, the vast TéléSky was still dark. An inky blackness that seemed to stretch on forever. It was programmed to emulate the orbit of Laterre, and the planet was still six years away from the season of the Blue Dawn, when the nights would glow azure from the distant light of Sol 3. Now the TéléSky glinted with a million tiny stars, each one placed in precise alignment with the real stars that glowed far above the roof of Ledôme. When she was little, Cerise taught herself all about those stars—their names, their distances from Laterre, even the nebulous shapes they supposedly formed.

But when she looked up at the sky now, she saw nothing but randomly scattered pinpricks of light. There were no men with axes, women riding on the backs of flying beasts, or pots of bubbling stew.

Constellations, she'd learned soon after waking up from her surgery, were another human invention. A desperate attempt to give meaning to something that was supposed to be meaningless.

When Cerise reached the towering, ornately sculpted gates, she peered through the spirals of titan at the grand structure stretching out before her. Hundreds upon hundreds of windows lined each wall, dozens of decorative columns held up the immense roof, and above the vast front doors, a Paresse crest glinted in the starlight.

But just as she expected, the interior of the Palais was silent and dark. As though it, too, were waiting. Waiting to be lit up from the inside with an answer. Waiting in darkness.

Just like everyone else on this planet.

Cerise pulled her TéléCom out of her pocket and swiped on the screen to check for new broadcasts. She knew there wouldn't be any, and yet, she still felt her pulse elevate just the slightest bit at the anticipation of being wrong.

But, of course, she was rarely ever wrong.

The screen refreshed and Cerise stared dejectedly at the last archived broadcast, time-stamped hours ago. Even though she'd already memorized every word, she still found herself clicking on the footage again, silently mouthing the words right along with a mournful-looking Desirée Beauchamp.

"Six hours have passed since the disrupted coronation ceremony of César Bonnefaçon, and Laterre finds itself in the precarious position of having no confirmed leader."

The TéléCast host was standing inside the Maison de Valeur. The building's famous stained-glass windows twinkled in the artificial moonlight from the TéléSky, and the vault that stood just behind her was no longer empty. Beneath its clear plastique, the bejeweled crown sparkled almost tauntingly.

"The imperial crown was returned to its case shortly after the general fled from the Policier Precinct, and the coronation ceremony ended in violent riots, instigated by the appearance of Citizen Rousseau and Maximilienne Epernay. Fortunately, the Ministère and local Policier were able to subdue the riots shortly after they began, but *un*fortunately, more than fifty lives were lost in this uprising and both the Vangarde and the Red Scar are still at large. Even more disconcerting is the fact that no ruler was crowned today."

Cerise's circuitry gave a powerful flash as once again, the memory barged its way back into her mind.

Her rayonette raised. Armed. Ready.

Then, lowered.

"Opinions around the planet—and even within the Ministère itself—seem to be greatly divided on the subject," continued Desirée. "While some believe that Alouette Taureau's appearance on the day of the coronation validates her as the rightful heir and therefore the legitimate Matrone of the Regime, others maintain that because she pointedly expressed her desire to *reject* the title and because she also fled the scene and has yet to be heard from since, her claim to the Regime is not valid. Meanwhile, General Bonnefaçon, Laterre's provisional ruler, is missing and Commandeur

Moreau has ordered all Third Estaters to stay in their homes for their own safety and to only leave for the purposes of going to work. She has assured us all that, until a solution is found, the planet will continue to operate as normal—"

Cerise paused the playback and shook her head.

"Operate as normal."

She had spent the entire night trying to rationalize those words in her mind. But it was an illogical statement. From an illogical woman. The kind only humans seemed capable of holding in their heads. Nothing was normal. Nothing was operating the way it should. Including Cerise's own brain.

What would she do tomorrow? And the day after that? And the day after that? How would she sit down at her workstation in the Bureau of Défense and "operate as normal"? She couldn't go back to analyzing surveillance footage in search of Marcellus Bonnefaçon. She'd already found Marcellus Bonnefaçon. *Twice.* Today, she'd had him in her sights. In her *aim.*

And she'd let him go.

Because he'd been her friend? Like Alouette Taureau had claimed. *No.* Cyborgs didn't have friends. They had colleagues. They had collaborators. Friends were another inefficient human invention. A waste of time.

She'd let Marcellus go because Alouette Taureau had told her to. She was the rightful ruler of Laterre. She had to be. It was decreed by the Order of the Sols. That order had been hard-coded right into Cerise's neuroprocessors, into *every* set of neuroprocessors. Every droid, every cyborg, every piece of technology on this planet, was programmed with the information that a direct Paresse descendant shall inherit the Regime upon the death of the current Patriarche or Matrone.

The only exception to that rule, as stated in the contingency clause, was in the case of no direct heir, or if the heir was unfit to rule. But there *was* an heir. Her identity had been confirmed by every droid in that marketplace. Cerise had scanned Alouette's face herself.

Whether she accepted the title or not, Alouette Taureau *was* the Matrone.

Which meant Cerise had only been doing her job. She'd only been following orders. She'd been serving the rightful ruler. Just as she'd been programmed to do from the moment she'd awoken in that operating room with these tiny nodes implanted in her face and this flawless, superior brain that now would not shut up.

Alouette Taureau was the Patriarche's legitimate daughter. Which meant, she outranked the general and all of his commands.

Didn't she?

The circuitry in Cerise's forehead began to flicker faster, until she felt slightly woozy and had to grab on to the gate to steady herself.

This was all so unclear. So uncertain. So unprecedented.

But cyborgs were not built for unclear and uncertain and unprecedented. They were built for precision. For clarity. For certainty. And Cerise could find none of those. Not in the night TéléSky. Not in the darkened windows of the Palais. And certainly not inside the Ministère headquarters, where everyone was told to "operate as normal."

Glaring at the vast structure before her, Cerise scanned the windows of the south wing until she reached the general's private study. Where, just over a week ago, Cerise had sat. An esteemed technicien. The one the general had trusted with his most confidential assignment.

"Where are you?" she whispered to the darkened window. "Where have you gone?"

Cerise pressed play on the broadcast again and Desirée Beauchamp concluded her report, her final words hanging in the air like a too-bright star without any hope of finding a constellation. "And as the Sols set on this fateful, uncertain day of our planet's history, the question on everyone's mind remains: Who is the ruler of Laterre?"

PART 4

THE EMPEREUR

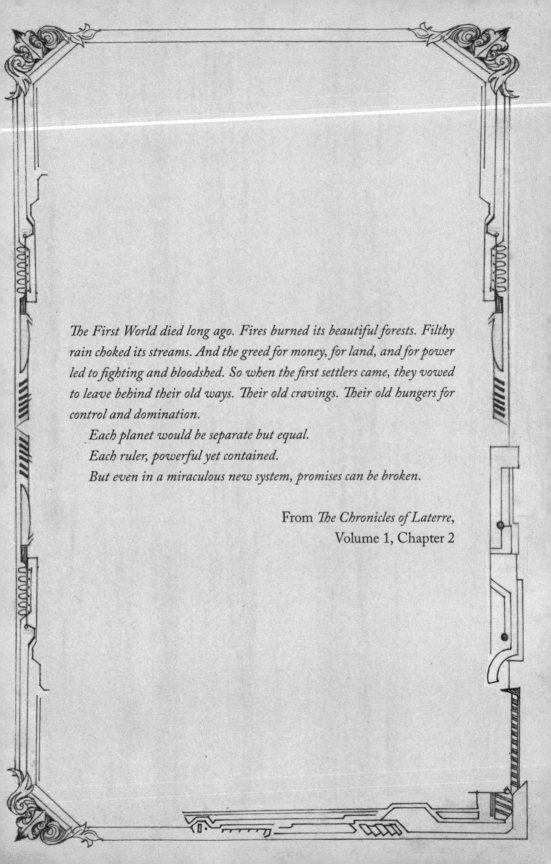

The First World died long ago. Fires burned its beautiful forests. Filthy rain choked its streams. And the greed for money, for land, and for power led to fighting and bloodshed. So when the first settlers came, they vowed to leave behind their old ways. Their old cravings. Their old hungers for control and domination.

Each planet would be separate but equal.

Each ruler, powerful yet contained.

But even in a miraculous new system, promises can be broken.

From *The Chronicles of Laterre*,
Volume 1, Chapter 2

CHAPTER 47

ETIENNE

"IS IT SLOWING?" ASKED GABRIEL. "I THINK IT MIGHT BE slowing."

"It's not slowing," replied Chatine.

"Well, it has to slow down *some*time. What are they planning to do? Just fly them out into space until they reach a black hole?"

Chatine scoffed. "Wouldn't surprise me."

"Etienne. Please tell me the ship is slowing." Gabriel approached the capitaine's chair, only to be blocked by Roche with crossed arms and a determined stare.

"The capitaine is not to be disturbed. Tracking a ship at supervoyage speed is dangerous work that requires all of his attention. Please step back."

Gabriel rolled his eyes but complied.

Roche nodded at Etienne. "I got your back, Capitaine."

Etienne flashed him a weak smile in return. "Merci." The truth was, Marilyn was doing all the work. Etienne had just been obsessively watching the zyttrium gauge for the past three days. It was deep into the red zone. Dangerously deep. They had maybe twelve hours of stealth left at the most. They'd used the last stores of the camp's emergency supply of zyttrium to track the voyageur undetected, but now he was realizing what a foolish idea that was. They had no clue how far this ship was traveling, where they were taking these "crocs," as Roche kept calling them, always with a tinge of pride in his voice.

The destination certainly wasn't Bastille, as they'd all originally believed. The moon had come and gone long ago, and still the ship showed no sign of decelerating out of supervoyage. It could be taking those passengers to Usonia, for all Etienne knew. And they *definitely* didn't have enough zyttrium to keep them hidden all the way to the outer reaches of the System.

"We're nearly to the Asteroid Channel," Roche said, pointing to one of the navigation screens.

"Maybe he's going to dump them on one," suggested Gabriel. "I heard some of them are habitable."

"You can't live on an asteroid," said Chatine.

"I heard that too," Roche said to Gabriel before taking a large bite out of a turnip he'd been slowly eating away at for the past hour. That was another thing they were running low on: food. Roche had brought a supply with him from the Vangarde base, but he hadn't packed enough for four people, and Etienne hadn't anticipated tracking a Laterrian voyageur into space when he'd filled his stores.

If that voyageur didn't reach its destination very soon, they'd either be spotted and shot out of the sky by combatteurs or starve to death. Etienne couldn't decide which was worse.

"How would you even survive on an asteroid?" Gabriel asked.

"You'd need some kind of climatized suit," Roche said knowledgably between noisy chews of his turnip. "None of the asteroids are terraformed."

"What is 'terraformed'?" asked Gabriel.

Roche's eyes lit up. "It's when you take a planet that you can't live on and make it livable."

"How?" asked Gabriel.

"You know, you change the atmosphere, make it breathable, make the temperature warmer, plant trees and stuff. Basically you make it more like the First World. It's how the Human Conservation Commission was able to settle on so many planets of the System Divine."

"But what about Usonia?" Gabriel asked. "Don't they live in plastique bubbles?"

"They're called biodomes," Roche said. "And Usonia is too far away from Sol 1 to be terraformed, so the original settlers had to build the domes. They're a lot like Ledôme."

Glancing at the stealth gauge again, Etienne tried to block out their voices. There was no way that ship was going to an asteroid. And the only other planet on their current trajectory was Albion, but that was still days away. Not to mention an enemy planet. He was starting to think he would never see his community's zyttrium again.

"How do you know all of this stuff?" Gabriel asked Roche before turning to Chatine. "Are your parents techniciens or something?"

"Hardly," Chatine muttered.

"I read it in the sisters' library," said Roche.

Chatine groaned. "The only thing he would have learned from our parents is how to cheat someone out of their cut."

"At least you got to meet them," Roche said. "They're my parents and I wouldn't even know them if I saw them on the street."

"Consider yourself lucky, then. Trust me, you were way better off an Oublie than living with the Renards."

"Easy for you to say," Roche argued. "You didn't have to sleep in the mud."

"And *you* didn't have to sleep next door to a father who stole all of your stuff in the middle of the night."

"You didn't have to beg for your food," Roche challenged.

"And you didn't have to rob dead bodies for yours."

"I've robbed plenty of dead bodies!"

"Or be used as basher bait."

Roche took a step forward until the two siblings were standing face-to-face with determination flashing in their matching gray eyes. "Well, at least *you*—"

"Okay, okay!" Gabriel mercifully stepped between them. "Congratulations, you both had a miserable childhood. Join the club. How about we focus back on tracking the ship that doesn't show any signs of slowing?"

"Actually," Etienne cut in, his gaze swiveling between the zyttrium gauge and the speed indicator, "I think they *are* slowing."

Three bodies converged around him, crushing him from all sides as they fought for the best view out the front window. Before them, an immense cluster of glowing rocks swirled and danced through the blackness. Some looked as if they were as small as grains of sand. Others looked the size of Ledôme. Each one bore jagged edges and sharp protrusions, like they had been chipped from some vast quarry way off in deep space.

"Where could they possibly be going?" Chatine asked, peering at the navigation screen, which showed a vast stretch of deep, empty space. "There's nothing out there."

"Nothing but a bunch of rocks," Gabriel muttered.

"That's not just a *bunch of rocks*," Roche said. "That's the Asteroid Channel."

"I *told* you," Gabriel said. "They're going to dump everyone on an asteroid."

"No," Etienne said quietly, focusing in on something in the distance. "I think they're heading there." He pointed out the window at the seemingly endless field of tumbling rocks. Except one of them wasn't a rock. It was a hulking, gargantuan shell of shimmering PermaSteel. As it loomed closer, Etienne could see rows and rows of white dots glowing along its sleek sides, and a great tail fin—sharp like a razor—jutting from the back of its intricate, angular form.

"What the fric is that?" Gabriel asked.

"It's not an asteroid," Chatine said smugly.

"I know what it is," Roche said, and Chatine and Gabriel both spun to look at him.

"You do?" Gabriel asked, impressed.

"Sure, I do." Roche took another bite of his turnip, clearly enjoying the attention. "I saw a drawing that looked a lot like that in one of the sisters' Chronicles."

"It's a spacecraft carrier," Etienne said, glancing again at the zyttrium gauge.

"Hey!" whined Roche. "I was gonna tell them."

"*That's* a spacecraft carrier?" Gabriel asked. "But it's so huge."

"I know," Etienne muttered. It suddenly felt like the gravity simulator onboard had malfunctioned and his heart was floating right up into his throat. "It's way bigger than any of the ones I've ever encountered in the past."

They all watched, transfixed, as the doors of the carrier's gargantuan landing bay yawned open, and the voyageur they'd been following glided steadily inside, looking like a tiny fly being swallowed by a hungry metallic giant.

"What is it doing way out here?" Chatine asked, her voice hollow and haunted.

"I was wondering the exact same thing," said Gabriel.

"There's only one reason to hang out in the Asteroid Channel," Etienne said grimly as the landing bay doors of the carrier sealed shut. They all turned to stare at him again as he pointed at the navigation screen, still showing nothing but empty space. "To stay hidden."

CHAPTER 48

ALOUETTE

THE TINY SEEDLING CURLED AROUND ALOUETTE'S fingertip, as though clinging on for dear life, before wilting back into the dirt. Dead. Gone. So many beautiful plants just withering away. Alouette reached for another.

"Come on," she said, coaxing it with a gentle prod of her finger. "You can do it. You can . . ."

But the plant gave up before she could finish her pleas.

With a sigh, Alouette glanced around the propagation room with its rows and rows of grow trays, the smell of fresh-cut herbs in the air, and the purplish-blue grow lights that ran in strips across the ceiling. Normally, this place made her feel hopeful and full of possibility. Like she, too, was a tiny seed buried beneath the soil, just waiting to sprout, waiting to show the world what she could do. But today, all she could feel was the death of this place. The hopelessness. The sorrow.

The plants were mourning their lost mother.

And Alouette her lost sister.

They were bonded in their grief.

This wasn't the first time Alouette had lost one of the sisters. Three months ago she'd thought she'd lost them all. She'd thought they'd all perished on Bastille, trying to break out Citizen Rousseau. Back then, there'd been so many tears, she thought she'd drown in them. But now, there were none. No tears. No uncontrollable sobs or body-wrenching shudders. There was just this hollowness in her chest that seemed to be spreading by the day, threatening to swallow her whole.

And Alouette wanted nothing more than to curl up like that little seedling and recede back beneath the surface of the ground, never to be seen again.

"Forestberry for colds, bitterbark for fevers, silkfleur for stomachaches," Alouette recited as she pointed to each herb, just like she used to do when she was a child in her wellness lessons. Sister Laurel had taught her to identify every single species of plant in this room by its shape, color, smell, *and* what medicinal purpose it served. "Dragonne root, menthe de mer, hivernoir."

She did it now, not to practice, or impress the sister, but to keep her mind occupied and her thoughts from wandering off. They tended to do that lately. Like a moth to the fire that burns it to a crisp, her thoughts always went straight back to the Marsh. To Sister Laurel dying before her. Dying for her. Dying *because* of her. The way her eyes had widened with fear and pain as the lethal pulse buried itself into her chest. The way her body had fallen still. Like someone had flipped the switch on the beautiful, glowing, motherly light inside of her.

The way she'd felt in Alouette's arms.

Cold. So very cold.

"Where do the plants go when they die?" she'd once asked Laurel after she'd watched the sister uproot a wilted, brittle-leaved tomato plant from the soil and lovingly wrap it in cloth before depositing it into the mulching bin.

"We turn their leaves and roots back into soil for the other plants," Sister Laurel had explained. "They go back to where they started."

"But what about the insides?" Alouette had asked.

"The insides?"

"The living part," Alouette had tried to explain, her limited six-year-old vocabulary making it difficult. "The part that makes them stand up, instead of flop over like that." She'd pointed to the dry, wilted leaves of the crop lying at the top of the mulching pile.

Sister Laurel had seemed to understand then and smiled down at her. A tender, bright-eyed smile that Alouette hoped she'd always associate with memories of Sister Laurel. "It's impossible to know that, Little Lark. Some people think the living part just changes into something new, becomes other new plants or minerals. Others believe that part goes to live with the Sols."

"What do you believe?"

Sister Laurel hadn't answered right away. She'd turned toward her favorite tray of thornwood flowers and gently touched the petals. "I don't know. But that's what makes it beautiful, right?"

The answer had confused Alouette then, and it still confused her now. It seemed that even though she was eleven years older, with the words of a thousand books in her mind, she still craved the same answers she'd craved as a child.

"I thought I might find you in here." The voice startled Alouette out of her reverie, and she turned to see Citizen Rousseau standing in the doorway, holding the little cardboard cylinder she always carried.

"What was your first clue?" Alouette asked numbly.

"Well, the fact that I looked everywhere else." Rousseau tried for a smile. It didn't work. She still looked just as haunted as she had when she'd slipped through the back door of the Refuge four days ago, her silver hair matted and her cheeks mud-stained from the riot. For several painful hours, as the rest of the sisters appeared one by one through the tunnel hatch, Alouette and Marcellus had questioned whether Citizen Rousseau would return at all. Whether Alouette would have to forge this revolutionary road alone.

She'd already decided that she wouldn't. She couldn't. Rousseau was the voice of this revolution. That much had become clear at the coronation. Rousseau was the mind. Alouette was just the blood. The symbol. Something for the people to cling on to. And it seemed they didn't even want to do that.

Alouette was still reeling from how fast they'd turned on her. Rejected her. She'd tried to speak to them. But they didn't want to listen. And then, Max had appeared, and they'd all been so eager to hear her. To follow *her*. Alouette's feeble voice had been quickly drowned out. Her useless words lost in the noise and the rain.

"They just need a little water and a little time," Citizen Rousseau said, and it took Alouette a moment to realize she was talking about the rows of plants in varying stages of decline.

"They need *her*," Alouette corrected.

Rousseau nodded and gave the end of her cylinder a slow turn. "They do. But they won't always."

Alouette's eyes flicked angrily to her. "What are you saying? That they'll learn to forget? They'll eventually stop missing her?"

"Oh no," Rousseau replied. "They'll never stop missing her. But eventually they'll learn to grow without her. Just like we all must do at some point in our lives. The question is never *will* we grieve, but *how*."

The small wave of fury that had flared up inside of Alouette gradually receded. To be honest, Alouette was relieved to feel it. To feel anything at all. "Right," she said with a sigh. "Now comes the time when you tell me that I must use my grief and let it fuel me and let it spur me on to continue the work we started."

"I would never tell anyone how to use their grief."

Alouette threw up her hands. "Then what are you here to tell me?"

"That it's not your fault." The response came so quickly, and so unexpectedly, Alouette felt like she'd been slapped.

"H-h-how did you—" she began to stammer, but apparently, she didn't need to finish.

"My mother died the same way."

Alouette glanced up into those calm eyes. "In a riot?"

Rousseau shook her head. "From a lethal pulse. When the Ministère discovered that my parents were selling illegal herbs out of their couchette, the Policier came to arrest them. Instead of going quietly and willingly, they fought back. I was out on a delivery run when it happened. I came back just in time to watch the Policier inspecteur fire his rayonette at my mother's head. She died instantly."

Alouette's stomach clenched as she reached out and allowed another seedling to wrap itself desperately around her finger. She knew it would only be a matter of time before the plant realized it wasn't the right finger. It wasn't *her* finger.

"I'm sorry." Her voice was now soft and guilt-stricken. Of all the sisters, Laurel had been the most like a mother to Alouette. She was the one who had nursed Alouette back to health when she was sick, stitched up her knee when she fell, taught her how to grow things, birth things from nothing but soil and water and seed. She'd been so wise and lovely and full of life. And now that life was just gone. Uprooted from existence before her leaves had even had a chance to turn brown and brittle.

"Merci," Rousseau said, but it sounded more polite than genuine. "Anyway, that's when I ran. I didn't know where to go and I knew I couldn't stay in the Frets. I spent years roaming around, thinking of all the ways I could have changed that outcome. If I had just gotten home sooner. If I hadn't stopped to talk to a friend in the Marsh. If I had taken the shortcut through Fret 8 instead of going the long way. If I had only convinced my parents to stop selling herbs years before. No matter which way I turned it in my head, it was my fault and I could have stopped it."

Alouette watched her intently, studying the way the details of the story bounced around in her eyes like flecks of light.

Rousseau gave her cardboard cylinder another gentle turn. "I traveled from town to town, exploring every centimètre of this planet. But no matter how far I went, I couldn't find a tunnel back to the past. What I did find, however, was almost as healing." She paused and glanced up at a strip of grow lights on the ceiling, looking like someone basking in the Sols. "It wasn't just Vallonay that was experiencing the injustice of this Regime. It was everywhere. Everyone. We were all victims. And I realized I could either choose to be angry and sad about it, I could wander around blaming myself for it, or I could do something about it. Every time I thought about my mother dying in that couchette, *fighting* back, I became more and more resolved to do the same. That's when I returned to the Frets and tracked down Francine, who had been my contact with the sisterhood when we used to sell them herbs. They invited me into the Refuge, and I invited them to fight with me."

Alouette felt another wave of anger rise up inside of her. "Maybe they all would have been better off if you hadn't."

She expected to see a flinch of something on Rousseau's face. Hurt, guilt, anger of her own. But the Vangarde leader's expression never changed. Never shifted. Even for a second. "Maybe," she allowed. "But that was their choice. They understood the risks."

"Exactly!" Alouette cried. "And that's why they told me not to do it. That's why they told me to stay here, stay hidden. Because they knew it was dangerous. But I defied them. I betrayed them. I broke their trust. I understood the risks too. Honestly, I did. I just never thought—"

"You never thought you were risking someone *else's* life. Only your own."

Once again, Rousseau had climbed up into her mind and read her thoughts as plainly as if they'd been scribbled in the ink of Principale Francine's fountain pen.

When Alouette said nothing, Rousseau continued. "Most people think of power as an opportunity. They think of all the things they'll gain from it. But power is not just an opportunity. It's a burden as well. You lose just as much as you gain. Sometimes more. The choice is never just about our lives. Our consequences. Our pain. It's about how much we're willing to lose for what we believe in. What we stand for."

Rousseau clutched the small cylinder in her hand, like she was trying to commit it to memory. "When I asked you *why* you wanted to join this revolution, do you remember what you told me?"

Alouette huffed. "Yes. I told you it was because I was the Paresse heir, and the sisters had raised me to be a symbol." She could almost hear her own eager voice echoing back at her from within these walls. The reminder of how foolish she'd been, how naïve she'd been. It brought another tidal wave of guilt crashing down around her.

"The sisters raised you to be important," Rousseau agreed. "That's for certain."

"Well, that's over now, isn't it?" Alouette muttered.

"Is it?" asked Rousseau.

"What else are we supposed to do? What *can* we do while the Red Scar are still out there? While the general is still out there?"

"As long as the people are still in chains, there is much to do."

Alouette peered up at the woman whom everyone called Citizen Rousseau, the woman named after an age of light and change. And, for the first time, Alouette felt like she could peer inside her mind as well. She could read her thoughts. Translate her hopes.

She wanted so badly for Alouette to stand up, push her shoulders back, and declare that she was ready to keep fighting. That she still *believed*. She wanted so badly for Alouette to be *her*.

But Alouette wasn't her. She was just a girl with the right blood. She was just a seventeen-year-old child who had lost not one but *two* mothers. Who was not cut out to carry such a burden. Who could not stand to lose any more.

"What are the sisters planning?" Alouette asked, feeling the numbness seep back through her skin.

Rousseau sighed and glanced almost wistfully around the propagation room. "The sisters are deeply divided. They have been in deliberation with the cells for several days. In the absence of a confirmed leader on Laterre, Commandeur Moreau has taken control of the Ministère. She's enacted strict curfews and lockdowns. No one is allowed out of their homes except to go to work. Social gatherings are prohibited. The droids are back on the streets in full force. Moreau is clearly terrified of another uprising."

Alouette shivered at the thought of all those people locked up. Locked away. Back under the PermaSteel fist of the Ministère. She'd tried to help them. She'd tried to stand up for them. But they'd turned her down. They wanted nothing to do with her and her blood.

"Some of the Vangarde believe we should be out there right now, continuing to spread our message of peaceful change," Rousseau continued. "Others think it's too dangerous. That there's too much tension under Moreau's Policier state, and a single spark could ignite more violence. *Worse* violence. And some believe . . ." She paused and took in a breath, darting a look at Alouette as though she wasn't sure if she should continue. "Well, there's an idea floating around the cells."

Alouette peered up, her dark eyes wary. "What idea?"

Rousseau exhaled. "That you should step forward and take the crown. Claim your title of Matrone. And that it's what you should have done all along."

"What?" Alouette felt her legs go wobbly. "B-b-but that's the opposite of what the Vangarde raised me to be. That goes against everything they stand for. Equality regardless of blood, regardless of birth."

"It would be a temporary solution. Just until the planet is stable again."

Alouette's eyes narrowed and she took a tentative step toward Rousseau. "Is that what you think I should do?"

But as she so often did, the Vangarde leader ignored the question. Instead, she slipped something into Alouette's hand, and Alouette looked down to see Rousseau's cardboard cylinder balancing delicately between her fingers.

"It's called a kaléidoscope," she said. "Children on the First World used to play with them. Go ahead, take a look." Rousseau pointed to a small keyhole-shaped opening on one end of the cardboard tube, and Alouette peered inside.

Her first reaction was to gasp and look away. She'd never seen anything quite like it before.

"Aim it toward the light," Rousseau told her, and she did. This time, when she peered through the keyhole, she saw magic.

A thousand tiny crystals twinkled out at her in a seemingly infinite geometric design. Glowing blue hexagons interwove with dazzling red triangles. Vibrant pink diamonds interlocked with purple rectangles. And threaded through them all, zigzagging slithers of glimmering silver.

"Now, here's the best part," Rousseau said as she reached out and gently turned the rotating top.

In an instant, everything changed. Transformed. And bloomed into a whole new glittering, glowing design. Now violet triangles connected with azure octagons. Gleaming orange squares were hitched to iridescent pentagons.

Alouette's breath skittered, and for just a moment, she was lost in the colors. In their dazzling, changing light. She reached out and spun the top again, marveling at the shift, at the interconnected shapes, at the radiance.

"I keep it with me at all times," Rousseau said. "As a reminder that there's always another way to look at something. That even just a simple turn, a centimètre, and the exact same fragments of light tell a whole new story."

Alouette slowly lowered the kaléidoscope. Rousseau was already looking at her with those shimmering silver eyes of hers, like she was trying to convey a deep secret that Alouette couldn't grasp.

But it didn't matter. Because just then, the door to the propagation room slammed open and Marcellus charged inside, his face flushed and his hair tousled.

"You need to come. Now," he said breathlessly.

Alouette and Rousseau exchanged a look, and Alouette was grateful when Rousseau was the one to ask, "What is it? What's happened?"

Marcellus latched his gaze on to Alouette, and in his eyes, she saw her same hollowness and defeat reflecting back at her. "My grandfather is on the holograms."

CHAPTER 49

MARCELLUS

"MY FELLOW LATERRIANS," THE GENERAL BEGAN IN HIS clear, clipped accent. "I am sorry for leaving you in your time of need."

Marcellus stood in the center of the Assemblée room, bathed in the light from the largest monitor, trying to figure out where his grandfather was broadcasting from. The image streaming through the planet-wide TéléCast signal was zoomed in, cropped tightly on the general's hard-lined face and cold hazel eyes, making Marcellus feel like the general was standing too close. He had to keep reminding himself that the cool breath he felt on his face was only his imagination.

"No doubt my hasty departure from the coronation ceremony has left uncertainty in your mind regarding the future of our glorious planet. No doubt you have many questions."

When Marcellus squinted, he swore he could make out pinpricks of light in the dark background behind the general's left ear. Was he on a voyageur? Traveling to another system, never to return?

Wouldn't that be nice?

"And I'm pleased to finally be able to bring you some definitive answers to those questions." The general paused to build up his breath, and the suspense. "For the past four days, I was en route to the planet Kaishi."

The floor dropped out from beneath Marcellus's feet.

He can't.

They wouldn't.

Not when there's a legitimate heir . . .

"I have met with the System Alliance," the general continued, as though making a point to dismiss Marcellus's silent protests. "And we all agree that Laterre currently finds itself in the midst of very unprecedented circumstances. Circumstances far beyond my ability to navigate alone."

The cam zoomed out slightly and Marcellus felt light-headed. He suddenly understood the scenery. The darkness and its million pinpricks of light. His grandfather was *at* the System Alliance headquarters right now. He was broadcasting from the infamous skytower, a vast needle-like structure that swooped toward the sky and crescendoed into an enormous disk at its summit. Within this rotunda hovering amid the clouds, hundreds of meeting rooms, offices, and conference auditoriums spiraled out, row upon row.

"How did he get there so fast?"

Marcellus was certain he'd only asked the question in his head, until Denise replied in a low whisper. "The orbits are in his favor. With the way the planets are aligned right now, Kaishi is even closer to Laterre than Albion."

"I came here to seek council and advisement from the esteemed delegates of the Alliance," the general was now saying. "These are wise voices who represent great leaders of even greater planets. I trust their judgment. I trust their opinion. And in times of such confusion and uncertainty as we are now living in, I believe we must reach out to our allies and neighbors and listen to their wisdom as well as find our own."

Marcellus heard a small snort from behind him and turned to share a look of disbelief with Sister Léonie. She must have been thinking the same thing he was.

The general doesn't ask the opinions of others. The general only manipulates.

Marcellus cast his gaze around the rest of the room, taking in all of the sisters who had gathered. His eyes lingered momentarily on Alouette, who stood in the far back corner, watching the broadcast with a glazed-over look, as though she was hearing the general's words but not absorbing them. He was worried about her. Sister Laurel's death had hit her hard. And if Marcellus knew his grandfather as well as he thought he did, whatever was coming next was going to hit her even harder.

"The delegates and I have been deep in discussion for many hours about the best possible future for our planet," General Bonnefaçon continued. "One that will ensure prosperity, stability, and of course, continued glory for *all* of Laterre. And I'm pleased to announce we have reached a decision. I can assure you that this decision was unanimous among all delegates, who represent the illustrious leaders of our great System."

Marcellus searched for something to grab on to. Sister Noëlle's hand was closest. He clutched it and she squeezed back.

Because she knew.

They all knew.

It was too much to hope for that he'd simply run away and never come back.

It was too much to hope for that he'd *give up*.

Only a fool would hope for that.

But apparently, Marcellus was a fool. Because it was all he'd been hoping for—praying for—since he'd watched his grandfather's cruiseur disappear into the clouds.

"Given the circumstances and certain details that were brought to light at the disrupted coronation ceremony," the general announced, "the System Alliance has decided to uphold their original decision to invoke the contingency clause of the Order of the Sols."

"What?!" Marcellus shouted at the screen. "You can't do that!" He turned to Sister Noëlle. "He can't do that. There's an heir. There's a direct Paresse descendant."

The sister gave his hand another squeeze and nodded for him to watch. Wait. Listen.

But Marcellus was so tired of listening. He was tired of hearing his grandfather get exactly what he wanted. All the Sol-damn time.

The general's eyes gleamed through the monitor, the same way they used to gleam across the Regiments board as he slid his legionnaire piece to victory.

It was like nothing had changed. More than three months of planning and hoping and searching for a way out of this, and Marcellus was still locked up in that Palais, forced to watch his grandfather win over and over and over.

When would this man *ever* stop winning?

The general cleared his throat and continued. "The contingency clause of the Order of the Sols clearly states that should Laterre find itself without a direct Paresse heir, or the heir is determined unfit to rule, the responsibility of appointing a new leader shall fall to the System Alliance. And after much discussion and careful examination of the facts, the Alliance has unanimously decided that Alouette Taureau is, in fact, unfit to rule."

Cold.

That was all Marcellus could feel now.

A chill had slithered through the bedrock walls and settled over every surface, infected every molecule of air, until even the heavy breaths from the sisters' lips were nothing more than puffs of ice and frost.

Every fiber of his being was screaming at him to turn around. To have the courage to look at her. To be there for her when these words and this cold and this shift in the planet's orbit sank in. But the chill had already numbed him. Already slowed his heart and stiffened his limbs.

Until he was nothing more than a stone shaped as a man.

Shaped as a coward.

"Alouette Taureau has allied herself with a rebel group known as the Vangarde," the general went on, his voice deepening, becoming more threatening with every syllable. He was turning back into the man Marcellus remembered from his childhood. All warning and no warmth. "And given their long history of inciting violence and chaos on our planet, we are forced to assume that these rebels have brainwashed, coerced, or otherwise manipulated our Regime's only heir. We cannot allow such a person to represent our planet. We cannot allow the Vangarde's deceitful, dishonorable tactics to rule Laterre."

"He's taking her out of the equation," Léonie whispered, and Marcellus glanced at the sister to see an empty, defeated look in her eyes.

She had been one of the supporters of the idea to have Alouette claim the Regime as a provisional Matrone. Just until the planet stabilized and the Vangarde could earn the people's trust again. But that was no longer an option. His grandfather had made sure of it.

"Alouette Taureau is not the leader we hoped she would be," the general continued. "A fact that she made plain when she stood beside Citizen Rousseau—an escaped prisoner and known terrorist—and pledged her loyalty to the Vangarde. We need a leader who will pledge their loyalty to you. To the Regime. To Laterre." The general paused. A twitch of a smile. A fist clenched around a hard-fought victory. "And I am honored to be chosen as that leader."

The cam zoomed out further. And that's when the entire image became clear to Marcellus.

General Bonnefaçon stood in the System Alliance's main assembly hall with its vaulting roof and vast curving windows that looked out on the clear and star-studded skies of Kaishi. Behind him, in a sweeping line of seats, sat the delegates from the twelve planets of the System Divine.

But that wasn't the part that made Marcellus's heart riot in his chest.

The delegates were mere shadows compared to the general, who was, Marcellus could now see, swathed once again in the imperial robe of Laterre. Each star and planet hand-sewn into the garment's purple velvet seemed to shimmer and glint of its own accord, making General Bonnefaçon appear like a brilliant universe unto himself.

And perched atop a satin pillow on a nearby table, simple in its construction, but grandiose in its implication, was a crown.

It was not the imperial crown that had been locked back up in the Maison de Valeur four days ago. This was something new. Something modest yet elegant. A smooth ring of unadorned titan.

Movement flickered in the corner of Marcellus's eye, and his gaze swung to one of the smaller monitors that was currently showing a feed from the Vangarde's surveillance cam in the textile fabrique, where the scene could only be described as a celebration. People were standing on cutting tables and giant mechanical looms, shouting and singing at the top of their lungs, throwing anything that could pass as confetti, honoring the man they loved. The man who had saved them.

The man who had fooled them all.

Just as he'd fooled Marcellus for so many years. Just as he'd fooled the Patriarche and the Patriarche before him. And now the System Alliance as well.

Because the truth was, he was not a man. He was a Sol. And his light had blinded a whole planet. A whole *system*.

"However," the general said sternly, yanking Marcellus's attention back to the center screen, "I am not of the Paresse line. I do not have the blood of Laterre's founder in my veins. Therefore, I cannot rightfully claim the title of Patriarche."

Marcellus's fury started to simmer into confusion.

"What is he doing?" Sister Léonie asked warily.

But no one in the room answered. No one *could*. Not even Marcellus. For the past three months, he'd been the resident expert on all things General Bonnefaçon. He'd been whom the sisters turned to when they needed to think the way the general thought, see the world the way he saw it. Just as his former governess, Mabelle, had once told him, the uniform Marcellus used to wear was a gift. A rare key to a locked door. It had given him insight into the general's mind.

But this was uncharted territory.

This was a forteresse even Marcellus couldn't penetrate.

"The title of Patriarche has always been reserved for the Paresse family," the general continued. "And I believe it should be for the rest of time. Which is why I have chosen a new title. A title that I hope instills faith and trust and the belief that I have had and always will have the best interests of the Laterrian people in my heart. It is time to usher in a new era for our planet. A new hope for our future. And a new kind of leader for a new kind of Laterre. Which is why, today, here in the presence of all of you, and the twelve delegates of the System Alliance, I will become not Patriarche Bonnefaçon, but Empereur Bonnefaçon."

CHAPTER 50

CERISE

"WITH THE RESPONSIBILITY OF THIS CROWN, I WILL LEAD my people with virtue, fairness, and strength. Understanding the legacy of this crown, I will continue the tradition, greatness, and values of the leaders who came before me. Great Sols of the sky, I entreat your blessing. Before you today, under your mighty powers and light, I, César Bonnefaçon, crown myself, your humble servant, as the first Empereur of Laterre."

The general's voice reverberated across the System Divine, strong and steady and robust. And as he lowered the shimmering titan crown onto his head, his hands didn't falter. Not once.

But the same couldn't be said for Cerise's mind.

Her neuroprocessors were churning at full speed. Her cheek and forehead burned from the zealous flickering of her circuitry. Programming streamed through her mind, trying to arrange itself in the right order, trying to find the right conclusion.

The System Alliance had invoked the contingency clause.

The contingency clause was a lawful provision of the Order of the Sols.

The Order of the Sols dictated who was the rightful ruler of Laterre.

And Cerise Chevalier was ordered to follow the command of that ruler.

Which meant Cerise Chevalier . . . was a traitor.

She had defied the general's—the *Empereur's*—orders when she released Marcellus Bonnefaçon. She had sided with a rebel. She had betrayed her leader. She had dishonored her planet.

That girl—Alouette Taureau—had told her to stand down. To let Marcellus Bonnefaçon go. And Cerise had listened. She'd obeyed. Because she'd thought it was the right thing to do. But of course it wasn't. She had been duped. By a terrorist.

Of course Alouette would be deemed unfit to rule.

She was a member of the *Vangarde*.

". . . the Vangarde," said a voice, syncing up with her thoughts. Cerise blinked and focused back on the broadcast projecting to the Bureau of Défense's central hologram unit. As she gazed quickly around at her colleagues, she realized she was the only cyborg not listening to the Empereur's every word with intensely flickering circuitry.

Cerise straightened up and focused back on the projection.

"The Vangarde are still out there," Empereur Bonnefaçon went on. "They are still a threat to our way of life. They still seek to bring about the destruction of everything we have worked so hard to build on this planet. Obviously, they've proven to be resourceful, breaking their leader out of Bastille, hacking into our hologram network, brainwashing our own Patriarche's daughter."

Cerise nodded earnestly.

Yes, she thought. *Alouette Taureau has been brainwashed, indoctrinated into a corrupt institution that doesn't appreciate the functionality of the Regime.*

"Which is why, my first act as Empereur of Laterre is to ensure that the Vangarde are eliminated once and for all. They've evaded us too many times. They've lived in the shadows and spread in the darkness. They have been responsible for tens of thousands of innocent deaths, including the more than fifty people who lost their lives in the most recent disturbance at my coronation. They have even inspired dangerous copycats. Like this fringe group who call themselves the Red Scar. But make no mistake. Without the Vangarde, there would be no Red Scar. In order to ensure our planet's safety and prosperity, we must

defeat them. I will be back on Laterrian soil in four days and I promise you: I will not rest until every last Vangarde rebel is gone. Today,
I have sworn my allegiance to this planet and to the protection of the
Laterrian people, and I swear to you all right here, right now, that my
number one priority will be to find the Vangarde base and destroy it.
For good. Only then can we be safe. Only then can we continue to work
toward glory for *all* of Laterre."

The feed cut out and the department fell into a shocked silence. Despite
the amount of enhanced brainpower in this room, no one seemed to be
able to fully process what had just happened.

But Cerise didn't need any more time to process.

She'd heard what she'd needed to hear.

She'd heard *enough*.

After easing through the crowd of techniciens who had gathered
around the hologram projection, Cerise tried to make herself invisible.
Once in the hallway, she moved quickly. With fervor. With purpose.

She had one chance. One shot. If there was any possibility of redemption for her now, this was it.

Hours later, the Third Estate marketplace was in a state of celebration.
Commandeur Moreau had lifted the lockdown, and people were pouring
out of the fabriques and streaming in from the fermes to sing and chant
the Empereur's name, toasting cups of strongly brewed weed wine to his
prosperity. Despite the overturned stalls, piles of debris, and other remnants from the quelled riots, the atmosphere was festive.

Cerise navigated to the very center of the marketplace, to the place
where four days ago, Alouette Taureau had called for the general's arrest.
From here, Cerise could look up at the Policier Precinct and see the very
window behind which she'd stood, with a confiscated Vangarde communication device in her hand.

As the founding Patriarche's bronze statue towered above her, Cerise
opened her sac and pulled out that same communication device. The
gray boxy contraption with the squat buttons, small screen, and shell-
like design. With hands as steady and unwavering as the Empereur's had

been when he'd placed the crown atop his head, Cerise flipped open the device, powered it on, and watched again as that same mysterious symbol appeared on the screen.

Two lines angled toward each other, connecting at the bottom.

It was a Vangarde symbol. Cerise was sure of that now. And this device was connected to a Vangarde network.

Ignoring the screeching interference that echoed deep in her ear, she reached back into her sac and pulled out her TéléCom. "Activate network search," she commanded in a whisper.

She waited, her eyes darting between the bulky device in one hand and her TéléCom in the other. Even though she *knew* what the response would be before it came back. She couldn't quite pinpoint *how* she knew that. She couldn't identify where the certainty was coming from. It was just . . .

Intuition.

"No networks found."

A shiver passed through her. Cerise returned to her sac and opened it wider, revealing the *second* TéléCom that was hidden inside.

This one was illegal. This one was designed to commit treason. Because this one had belonged to her former self.

When she'd gone back to her old closet to retrieve it, for the first time ever in her short existence as a cyborg, she was grateful that cyborgs were not trackable. That their neuroprocessors were designed to accomplish a thousand tasks humans could not do, but that reporting their whereabouts to the Ministère was not one of them. Because, also for the first time ever, Cerise wasn't 99.7 percent certain that her actions were lawful.

But she knew they were necessary.

With cold, numb fingers, Cerise slowly pulled the illegal TéléCom from her bag, unfolded it, and swiped it on. The message from her former self was still paused on the screen, those twinkling dark eyes and smooth skin frozen midsentence.

"It's a program that's able to trace unregistered networks. Networks invisible to Ministère scans."

She didn't want to do it. She didn't want to even touch it. Using this

TéléCom would not only require her to engage with an illegal device, but it would require her to admit that her former self had been capable of doing something she could not. That a treasonous *hacker* had developed technology more advanced than the Ministère's.

Cerise's circuitry sparked in protest, but she knew she had to do it. For the Regime. For the Empereur. For Laterre.

For her own salvation.

"Activate network search," she whispered for a second time.

As the illegal TéléCom processed the command, Cerise almost found herself hoping it wouldn't work. But the response that came not a second later was both invigorating and shattering at the same time. "One network found."

She stared down at her former self still frozen on the screen. At the unmistakable sparkle in the girl's eyes.

Like a teasing flash of triumph.

A gloating laugh.

"The general is not who you think he is. . . ."

"If you run the program while he's on an AirLink, you can trace the signal back to its source. . . ."

". . . you might be the only one who can stop him."

With an angry flicker of her circuitry, Cerise swiped the girl's face from the screen. She would not allow her to claim the final victory. She would not allow this traitor to win. Because Cerise had no intention of using this hacked device to spy on the Empereur—to commit treason against the Regime.

Instead, she would use it to *save* the Regime.

"Navigational display," she commanded the illegal TéléCom, and watched as the screen dissolved into a map of Laterre. She zoomed in on the west coast, on Vallonay, on the monstrous Frets in the midst of which she now stood. And there, flashing like a beacon, like the start of a trail waiting to be followed to victory, was a blinking orange dot.

The Vangarde network.

Unregistered.

Invisible to Ministère scans.

The final piece of the puzzle that would lead Empereur Bonnefaçon to the one thing he wanted more than anything.

Her circuitry gave a final, determined flash before she tapped on the screen and whispered, "Initiate trace. Locate signal source."

CHAPTER 51

CHATINE

THIS IS NEVER GOING TO WORK.

"It's going to work," Etienne assured them, as though reading her mind.

"If that spacecraft carrier is purposefully hiding all the way out here," Chatine said, clutching the edge of her seat, "I still don't think we should be trying to get *onto* it."

"I don't remember you coming up with any better ideas!" Gabriel shouted, his voice drifting through the ship's speakers. There was only one extra seat in the cockpit, so Roche and Gabriel had been strapped into the jump seats in the cargo hold. "It's the only way we're going to get the zyttrium back."

"And find out what's going on with all those kidnapped crocs!" Roche reminded everyone.

"Do you realize how much security must be on that thing?" countered Chatine.

Gabriel snorted. "You think I'm afraid of a few bashers?"

"This is a vessel of the Laterrian Spaceforce! There are going to be more than just a few bashers!"

"Everyone be quiet," Etienne shouted. "I need to concentrate."

"You heard the capitaine," came Roche's voice from the cargo hold. "Kindly shut your faces."

"Deactivating gravity simulator . . . *now*." Etienne punched a button on the console and Chatine felt her body go weightless. If it weren't for the restraints digging into the tops of her shoulders, she would have floated right out of her seat.

Etienne eased the contrôleur to the left. Chatine stifled a yelp, gripping on to her restraints as the ship started to rotate. The view outside the window shifted, turning and turning until her vision swam and her stomach felt queasy.

She closed her eyes. And when she dared open them again, the ship was completely upside down. The floor was the ceiling and the ceiling was the floor.

"Inversion complete," Marilyn reported.

"Okay!" Etienne said, kneading his hands together like he was trying to warm them up. "Let's do this. Prepare for approach."

"You're doing great!" came Gabriel's voice from the cargo hold.

Roche quieted him with a "Shhh!"

It had been hours since they'd watched the Courrier-class voyageur they'd been following disappear into the spacecraft carrier's enormous landing bay. Etienne had spent the entire time circling the carrier, mapping its structure, scouting out every hatch and every docking port, comparing the layout to all the other spacecraft carriers he'd encountered on his past missions for the community.

But it wasn't until he'd activated Marilyn's thermal sensors that he'd located the zyttrium.

"There," he'd said, pointing to the monitor, where Chatine had been able to clearly identify a large icy-white swath covering a giant area of the ship's left hull. "This whole space is registering extreme cold. Zyttrium has to be kept at a very low temperature or it loses its chemical properties. Obviously, this isn't a problem in the Terrain Perdu or on Bastille where it's mined, but on a ship built for human habitation, like this one, it would have to be kept in some type of cooled storage facility."

"That's a really big storage facility," Gabriel had remarked, squinting at the huge white mass on the thermal scan. "Did the community really have *that* much zyttrium?"

"No," replied Etienne, and the meaning had been instantly clear.

The camp wasn't the only place where zyttrium had gone missing.

"So, now we just have to figure out how to get it out of there," Gabriel had said. But Etienne hadn't looked worried. A plan had clearly already been forming in his mind.

The plan they were now attempting to pull off.

Still upside down, Etienne maneuvered Marilyn toward the underside of the spacecraft carrier. With the gigantic structure looming above them, it felt like they were flying beneath a Sol. But instead of solar spots and swirling flares, the underbelly of the vast ship bore strange rectangular protrusions, circular hatches, and jutting valves.

"Oh Sols," Chatine swore, fighting the urge to shut her eyes again. Etienne was aiming toward one particularly prominent valve right at the center of the carrier's underside. But they were coming in too close. Too fast. They were going to hit it. They were going to smash right into it. And then, all the zyttrium in the world couldn't hide them.

"Easy does it," Etienne said quietly to himself as he steered the ship closer.

There was an almost imperceptible bump as they made contact with the spacecraft carrier above, and Chatine heard a low hissing sound before Marilyn announced, "Attachment complete."

"WAHOO!" came a cry from the cargo hold. Undoubtedly Gabriel. Chatine breathed out a sigh of relief, even though she still felt queasy.

"Okay," Etienne said, scanning his console. "Preparing to open Marilyn's auxiliary hatch. Roche, are you ready?"

Chatine's stomach did another flip. This time, it was not in any way related to the ship's precarious inverted position. "Wait, what?!" No one had told her about *this* part of the plan. She would have remembered this part of the plan. Because she most certainly would have rejected it. "Ready for what?"

"We can't access any of the carrier's maintenance hatches from the outside without being detected," Etienne explained, still focused on his controls. "In order to avoid any alarms going off, we need to open one from the inside. And the best way to do that is for someone to climb up through this disposal valve into the filtration room and crawl through the air ducts to the laundry facility, where there's an accessible maintenance hatch. Roche is the only one small enough to fit through the valve *and* the ducts."

"No. No way." Chatine reached down to release her restraints, but for some reason they wouldn't unlatch.

"Chatine," Roche said calmly through the speakers. "Relax. It's okay. I'll only be gone a few minutes. We don't have a choice. I'm the only kid here, so I have to do it."

"Oh, so *now* you want to be the kid!" Panic started to well up inside Chatine.

"He'll be fine," Etienne said. "The stealth will keep us concealed from their sensors and scans, and the zero gravity will make it easy for him climb up the chute."

Chatine clenched her teeth. "I did *not* agree to this."

"And that's why we didn't tell you," Gabriel called out. "You're not exactly a *team* player."

Chatine's heart beat faster. So *that* was the reason Etienne suggested she sit up in the cockpit while Roche and Gabriel took the cargo jump seats? So they could betray her? Trick her? Put her in a position where she was literally trapped upside down with no way to stop them. "I am a team player. I just don't want *Roche* on my team. Or *any* team. I want him back in the Refuge, where it's safe and—"

"And boring!" Roche called out. "You said so yourself. We were completely left out back there. Overlooked. You said you wanted a chance to do something. Something worthwhile. Don't you think I want that too?"

Chatine squeezed her mouth into a tight line, unsure how to respond to that.

"Ready, Roche?" asked Etienne.

"Ready, Capitaine!"

Etienne pressed a button on the console. "Pressurization complete. Auxiliary hatch deployed," announced Marilyn.

Chatine immediately lunged for the buckle on her restraints, but it still wouldn't open. She jammed her thumb against it again and again until Marilyn finally seemed to get fed up with her efforts and said, "Restraint release override currently active."

And that's when Chatine realized the *second* half of their treachery. Etienne had locked her in.

With a roar, she swung her arms wildly toward the capitaine's chair, hoping to make contact with some body part—any body part. But Etienne was too far away.

"Calm down, gridder," he said, and she swore she *almost* heard laughter in his tone.

"If anyone is not being a team player, it's all of you!" Chatine's gaze snapped to the monitor currently showing the view of the cargo hold, where a circular gap in the floor—now the ceiling—was widening. And then, with another nauseating pulse of panic, she watched Roche float upward, grab on to the perimeter of the hatch door, and angle his body toward the opening.

"Roche!" she cried out. "No. Please! Not him. Anyone but him."

It was Bastille all over again. She was going to have to watch her brother disappear into another foreign ship. She was going to lose him *again*.

"It'll be okay, Chatine," Roche told her, turning to smile into the cam. "I'll see you in a few minutes." And then, he was gone, drifting up through the hatch.

When the door sealed behind him, Chatine felt rage boil up inside of her. "How could you do this?! How could you send him into a Laterrian spacecraft carrier by himself?"

"Don't worry," Etienne said, his eyes still locked on his monitors. "These kinds of maintenance rooms are completely machine-operated. No one ever steps foot in them unless there's a mechanical issue. They'll most likely be empty."

"*Most likely?*" Chatine spat. Sols, she hated when Etienne talked like that. "And what if they're *not* empty?" She peered back at the view of the cargo hold, where Gabriel was now out of his restraints and doing somersaults in zero gravity. The fire inside of Chatine burned even hotter. Was she the only person on this ship who understood how dangerous this was?

"They *will* be empty," Etienne assured her, pressing another button on his console.

"Detachment complete," said Marilyn.

Etienne took hold of the contrôleur and steered them away from the disposal valve. But he may as well have been steering Chatine away from her body because every single gramme of sensation inside of her emptied.

He guided Marilyn slowly along the underbelly of the spacecraft carrier, toward the awaiting maintenance hatch, and eased the ship into the docking port.

"Attachment complete," Marilyn repeated.

Chatine let out a tiny sob of a breath.

"Everything will be fine," Etienne said. "I've given him detailed instructions on how to deactivate the alarms and open the maintenance hatch in the laundry room."

"But he's just a child!" Chatine cried.

"Who survived his entire life on the street. Alone." Etienne's words were meant to be calming, reassuring, but they only worked her up more.

"You have no idea what I've been through to—"

"Yes, I do."

She spun to look at him and startled to find he had disengaged his restraints and was now floating before her, his dark eyes staring deep into her. Like he could not only read her thoughts but enter them. Influence them. Shift them around until they didn't make sense anymore.

"I was there," he whispered. "Remember?"

Chatine tried to turn away, but Etienne caught her chin between his fingers, holding her in place, forcing her to look at him.

"I know what you went through when you thought you'd lost him," he said. "But you're not going to lose him this time. I won't let that happen. You need to trust me. But mostly, you need to trust *him*. He's not your baby brother anymore. And he's not a child. He can take care of himself. And he can do this."

As much as she wanted to cling on to it, Chatine could feel her anger slipping away from her. Like the lack of gravity in this ship was making it impossible to hold on to anything.

She swallowed hard and nodded. Etienne's fingers fell from her face. The warmth of his touch lingered. She breathed in. Out. Feeling the ship's stale oxygen fill her lungs.

And then, an alarm started to blare.

"Breach! Unauthorized hatch deployment! Breach!" It was the most worked up Chatine had ever heard Marilyn.

"What's going on?" she asked Etienne, but he'd already moved away from her, back to the console, where his hands were moving skillfully across the controls. A moment later, Chatine heard a hiss and a click as her restraints unbuckled. She pushed out of her seat and tried to move, but her feet never touched the floor.

She was *floating*.

It was the strangest sensation she'd ever felt. A weightlessness mixed with total freedom. If it weren't for the alarm still blaring through the ship, she might have taken a second to enjoy the experience.

"Breach! Unauthorized hatch deployment!" Marilyn continued to drone.

"What happened?" Chatine uneasily pushed her way across the cockpit toward the console. But she soon realized she had no way of stopping herself and slammed right into Etienne. She grabbed on to the edge of his chair to keep herself still, quickly deciding she did *not* like zero gravity. She felt too out of control.

"Breach! Unauthorized hatch deploy—"

Etienne tapped twice on a screen and the alarm fell mercifully quiet.

"Did something go wrong?" Chatine asked, feeling the panic return full force.

"Nope," Etienne said with a beaming smile. "Something went very right." He slid a toggle across one of his screens and pointed at the view of the cargo hold.

"What?" Chatine looked up at the monitor. The sight of Roche's beaming face as he floated back into the ship was *true* weightlessness. She felt like she could fly.

"Roche!" she cried out.

He turned his face toward the cam and gave a salute. "Phase one complete, Capitaine."

Etienne smiled. "Well done, copilote."

Chatine reeled on him. "Is that it? Are there any other parts of the plan you haven't told me? Any more surprises I should know about?"

"Hopefully not," said Etienne. "Okay, Gabriel and I are going in to locate the zyttrium—"

"And the crocs!" Roche called out from the cargo hold.

"I told you," Etienne replied with an exhale, "we will see what we can find out. But right now the priority is the zyttrium. We obviously don't have the time or the resources to rescue hundreds of people. As soon as we're back on Laterre, we'll send more help."

Roche stayed quiet, evidently satisfied with this compromise.

Etienne turned back to Chatine. "Do you remember what you're supposed to do?"

She nodded, feeling her gut twist. "Yes. I fly Marilyn into the spacecraft carrier's landing bay to rendezvous with you and Gabriel."

"Right. The primary hangar is just inside the landing bay doors. Once we find the zyttrium, we will bring it there and load it into Marilyn's cargo hold." His expression grew more serious. "Do you remember how to initiate the thrusters?"

"Yes."

"What about the stabilizeurs?"

Chatine rolled her eyes, secretly pleased to hear glimpses of the old Etienne again. For a moment, it was like they were back above the Terrain Perdu, soaring among the gray Laterrian clouds, Etienne nervously teaching her how to fly.

"I can do it," she said.

"Let's go!" came Gabriel's impatient voice from the cargo hold. "Blue Bandits assemble! The zyttrium awaits!"

But Etienne apparently wasn't finished grilling her. "Your best chance of getting into the landing bay is to wait for that voyageur we followed to leave. If you slip in before the outer doors close, you can wait in the pressurization chamber while it stabilizes and then enter the primary hangar without being detected."

"I got it—"

"Keep her in stealth mode the entire time," Etienne went on, "but keep an eye on the gauge. It's running low. And watch out for the main thruster, it's—"

"Damaged, I know."

Etienne let out a sigh. "It's not *damaged*. It's just a little . . . cracked."

"It's damaged!" Gabriel shouted through the speakers.

After a sharp look toward the steps to the cargo hold, Etienne turned back to Chatine. "When you see us in the hangar, flash Marilyn's underwing lights three times so we can locate you. Otherwise, keep *all* exterior lights off or you'll give away your location."

"Etienne—" Chatine began. But once again, he didn't let her finish.

"Do you remember where the underwing lights are?"

"Yes. I've got this. I remember how to fly this thing."

Etienne's mouth pressed into a tight line. She could tell he was trying to ignore the fact that she'd just called his precious ship "this thing." He took a deep breath, as though steeling himself to leave. "Okay, just one more thing."

"Etienne!" Chatine shouted. "I told you. I know—"

But the words were swallowed by Etienne's lips. They were suddenly on hers. Pressing into her. In zero gravity, his kiss felt both light as a feather and urgent as a rainstorm. Without thinking, she kissed him back, letting her lips open and her tongue roam.

Her mind became as weightless as her body. He wrapped his hand around the back of her head, keeping her from floating right past him. Keeping her there. With him. For as long as they had.

Which wasn't long.

"Etienne! Mec!" Gabriel shouted. "What is going on up there? Let's do this!"

They drifted apart almost as suddenly as they'd come together. Without hands and lips, they had nothing to keep them connected. But their gazes stayed latched even as their bodies floated farther and farther away from each other. And before Chatine could think of what to say, or if there even was anything left *to* say, Etienne was gone.

With her heart in her throat and her lips still tingling, she watched him float up the stairs to the cargo hold. And then, on the monitor, she watched him disappear through the hatch behind Gabriel.

- CHAPTER 52 -
ETIENNE

THE HATCH SEALED BEHIND THEM, LOCKING ETIENNE and Gabriel in the small pressurization chamber between Marilyn and the gigantic spacecraft carrier. As the hissing sound of the stabilizeurs rushed into his ears, his feet began to sink back down to the floor and his pulse began to slow, as if the machine were stabilizing his emotions, too. They had been churning wildly ever since he'd pressed his lips against Chatine's. Ever since he'd let his heart claim victory over his head.

It had been a brutal battle for the entire journey, being so tightly locked up in that ship with her, bumping up against her as they all tried to carefully maneuver around one another. And every time he felt the urge to reach for her, brush his hand against hers, his mind would kick in and remind him of what a horrible idea that was. How badly it would end . . . *again*.

His heart lost every time.

Until, finally, it just got tired of losing.

"Pressurization complete," announced a voice, and the lights along the wall of the chamber turned from a deep, warning red, to a soothing green. The hissing sound stopped, both in the chamber and inside his mind.

He took a deep breath. He had officially left the atmosphere of the ship.

It was time to leave all thoughts of it behind too. They had zyttrium to find.

Gabriel reached for the round handle above their heads and yanked it open. As they climbed up and through the hatch, Etienne smiled at the sight of the gigantic machines that surrounded them. Washers churned sudsy, steaming water in their massive drums, while a line of dryers let out deafening thumps, whirs, and puffs of steam. A strong smell of soap hung in the air, and great piles of laundry plummeted down from a line of chutes in the ceiling and landed on a conveyor belt that trundled them to the awaiting machines.

"How do you like that?" Gabriel said, looking thoroughly impressed. "You were right. It's the laundry room."

"Don't sound so surprised," Etienne grumbled as he hurried over to one of the huge washing machines and opened his backpack.

"No offense, mec," said Gabriel. "It was just when you were like, 'And then we're going to break into the laundry room and I'm going to bust the water valve,' I was kind of like, 'Yeah, okay, sure, have fun with that.'"

Etienne rifled around in his bag until he found the pliers that he'd taken from Marilyn's onboard repair kit, and lined them up with the valve that connected the water supply hose to one of the massive machines.

"It's not that I didn't *believe* you could do it, I just, well . . . didn't really believe you could do it."

"Believe me now?" Etienne said, giving the pliers a powerful wrench. On cue, the hose broke away and water began to gush out of the valve.

Gabriel jumped as it reached his toes. "Whoa. Titanique."

Etienne returned the pliers to his bag and pulled out two syringes, which he plunged into a vial of golden liquid before handing one to Gabriel. "Aim for the neck."

Gabriel stared down at the "weapon," looking slightly daunted by the idea of using it. "So how long do you think it'll take them to send someone to—" But Gabriel's question was silenced as urgent footsteps pounded outside the door.

"Get behind that dryer!" Etienne whispered as he concealed himself beside a massive laundry cart.

Gabriel let out a small yelp and splashed through the growing pool of water to get into position. Hidden behind the dryer, he hoisted his syringe above his head like a dagger. Etienne rolled his eyes. So much for being a criminal mastermind.

There was a quiet beep and a hiss before the door slid open, and two men in pale gray coveralls with tool belts hanging at their waists barged into the room.

"Sols!" one of them swore as he hurried toward the busted valve.

Etienne held his breath, counting the seconds until the door sealed shut. It felt like a lifetime.

Come on, come on, he urged silently while the two maintenance workers fought to staunch the flow of water still gushing onto the floor. There was a soft hiss as the door finally started to glide shut.

And then . . .

Etienne charged, barreling into the stomach of the smaller of the two men and falling on top of him on the floor. Once the maintenance worker got over the stun of being attacked, he began to fight back, clawing and shoving at Etienne's chest as Etienne aimed the syringe for the man's neck. But the worker was unnaturally strong for his build and the two men tussled, rolling twice before smashing into one of the giant laundry machines. The syringe fell from Etienne's grip. He reached for it, his fingers grappling, but before he could make contact, another hand bent down to scoop it up.

The worker was now on top of him, cocking back a fist. Etienne closed his eyes and prepared for the blow, but it never came. The man's body collapsed onto him like a pile of rocks. Etienne shoved him aside and jumped to his feet, ready to face off with the other. But he, too, was sprawled out on the ground, unconscious.

Gabriel let out a dramatic sigh. "Well, that was exciting."

Etienne glanced between the two workers, still trying to process what had just happened. "You . . ." His brow furrowed. "You took down *both* of them?"

Gabriel proffered the two now-empty goldenroot syringes. "You're welcome."

Dazedly, Etienne took them, keeping one eye on the fallen repairmen, still not convinced they were really out.

"Strong stuff," said Gabriel, following his eyeline.

"Maman makes the best." Etienne stuffed the syringes back into his bag, pulled out his pliers, and worked quickly to reconnect the water supply hose to the valve. Then, he turned back to the fallen maintenance workers and said, "Come on, let's get these uniforms off them."

"This place definitely doesn't give me the warm and fuzzies," Gabriel whispered as they swept down the stark white corridor of the spacecraft carrier's lower deck, pushing a large repair cart in front of them. "Do you really think this is going to work?"

"Not if you keep talking," Etienne snapped. "We have to figure out how to get to the highest deck. That's where the storage facility is located. There has to be an elevator in one of these hallways."

"I mean, maybe Chatine was right," Gabriel went on as they turned down yet another hallway that looked identical to the last. "Maybe this stolen zyttrium *has* blinded you."

Etienne stopped walking and turned to him. "Wait, she said that?"

"W-w-well," Gabriel stammered uneasily, "not really. I mean, she might have, um, mentioned something that sort of resembled that, but really I'm paraphrasing."

"What did she say?" Etienne glared at Gabriel, who looked to the ground.

"Just that, I don't know, maybe you're obsessing over the wrong things."

"The wrong things?" Etienne fired back. His voice echoed ominously down the empty corridor, and he quickly lowered it to a whisper. "The wrong things? You mean because I don't want to get involved in her stupide revolution?"

"Technically, it's not really hers. It's kind of everyone's."

"It's not everyone's," he hissed. "It's not ours. Those gridders can do whatever they want to each other. We're staying out of it. We don't get involved." Etienne gripped the handle of the repair cart and kept walking, sweeping his eyes up and down the corridor in search of anything that resembled an elevator.

Gabriel jogged to catch up. "Well, yeah, fine, but have you taken a look around at where we are right now?"

Etienne didn't understand the question.

"We've just broken into a Laterrian spacecraft carrier," Gabriel said. "So, whether you like it or not, you're involved."

Something cold trickled down Etienne's spine, but he quickly chased it away. "No. We're not. *I'm* not. They stole zyttrium from us and we're stealing it back. That's it. I'm doing this for the camp. Not for anyone else."

They turned another corner, and Etienne nearly crumpled in relief at the sight of two silver doors at the end of the corridor. "Thank the Sols," he whispered, and picked up the pace, only to lurch to a halt a moment later when they found themselves face-to-face with a glowing biometric panel on the wall.

"How are we supposed to get around that?" Gabriel whispered, but just then, the elevator gave a sharp ping and the doors slid open. Etienne tightened his grip around the handle of the cart and prepared to rush inside when, suddenly, out of the elevator stepped the two most terrifying creatures Etienne had ever seen. With beaming orange eyes and a skin of pure metal, they were almost double his height, and every centimètre of their enormous frames radiated a glimmering, terrible strength.

Etienne's heart no longer seemed to be anywhere near his chest. It had leapt into his throat. He couldn't move. He couldn't breathe. He couldn't see. His vision had turned to blackness, like the infinite space between worlds. No light. No color. No stars.

"Are you okay?" came a voice, but it sounded like it was coming from the other end of the System.

"What is wrong with this man?" came another voice. This one horrifyingly inhuman. It was the voice of a murderous machine. And it ricocheted around in his brain like a loose screw inside a ship engine. Pinging loudly. Dangerously.

"Nothing!" Gabriel rushed to say. "He's fine. Just breathed in a little too much laundry soap."

"Halt while I perform a scan to assess his condition."

"Uh, that won't be necessary!" squeaked Gabriel. "I'm taking him to the infirmerie right now. Come on, then."

Etienne felt something push on his back until he was stumbling forward, falling onto his knees. He heard a soft whoosh as the elevator doors closed, and then Gabriel was shouting at him. "Etienne!"

But all he could hear were the screams.

"*Etienne!*"

Hot violet flames licked up the side of the chalet.

"*Don't go in there!*"

Heat from the fire bit at his skin.

"*Etienne! Come back!*"

The door caved in, the walls collapsed. The sharp smell of burning emberweed oil flooded the air. And all the while, those things, those monsters, were right outside the door, ready to pummel. To bash. To destroy.

"*Papa! Help!*" he tried to cry out, but his voice was snuffed out by the smoke.

So much smoke.

It burned his eyes.

It blinded him.

"*Etienne!*"

Rough hands were shaking him, slapping against his cheeks. He blinked away the memory of the flames and focused on the face hovering in front of him. It was Gabriel. "Etienne, snap out of it!"

Etienne groaned and tried to push himself up. He was lying on his back inside the moving elevator. It was rising. Up and up and up.

"Are you okay?" Gabriel asked, reaching out to help him to his feet.

"I . . ." He tried to speak, but his voice was scorched from the fire. "Yes."

"You went a little whacked there, mec."

"I'm fine," Etienne grumbled, silently berating himself. How could he have let that happen? How could he have let down his guard so easily?

"Yeah, sure," scoffed Gabriel. "That was a totally natural reaction to a basher."

"Construction Sector, View Deck," the elevator announced as it slowed to a halt and the doors slid open.

"Just forget it," said Etienne, grabbing hold of the repair cart once more. "Let's go. Chatine could be flying Marilyn into that landing bay at any moment, and I don't want her waiting there for any longer than she has to."

They stepped out of the elevator, but they may as well have stepped into another dimension. Gone were the stark white hallways of the lower deck; gone were the narrow walls of the endless corridors, and closed, unmarked doors. A towering ceiling soared above them, and below the gangway where they now stood, a vast PermaSteel floor stretched out as far as the eye could see. Along the sides of this gigantic space, hundreds of men and women and children were lined up against the walls, all of them wearing the same blue coveralls and the same haggard, exhausted expression.

"What is this—" Gabriel started to ask, but Etienne shushed him and stepped up closer to the edge of the gangway, gripping his hands around the railing as his mind struggled to take in what he was seeing.

In the middle of the immense metallic floor, clusters of cyborgs milled around. The silver stripes on their dark uniforms glinted almost as brightly as the circuitry on their faces. They tapped at their TéléComs and exchanged quick words with one another. But the strangest part was that each of them seemed to be staring at something. Pointing at something in the center of the vast hangar.

Yet there was nothing there.

Apart from the hundreds of workers lining the perimeter, the hangar was empty.

Then, three long chimes rang out, sharp and deafening. Etienne flinched and yanked Gabriel back into the shadows.

"Secondary test phase complete," an electronic voice announced, and Etienne crept back toward the railing with Gabriel close behind.

"Test phase?" Gabriel said in a panicked whisper. "What does that . . ."

But his words fizzled out as the whole floor below suddenly started to shimmer and glow. A strange crackling vibration ricocheted off every metallic surface, through every human nerve ending, until finally, it collided painfully with Etienne's chest.

"Oh. My. Sols," said Gabriel, who stood stiffly beside him, his hands gripping the railing of the gangway like he might rip it clear off its PermaSteel bolts. "What the fric are those?"

Etienne counted ten.

Ten gleaming, colossal warships appearing out of thin air, right before his very eyes.

Like glimmering Sols suddenly bursting into life.

"Invadeurs," Etienne whispered with a shiver.

As he raked his gaze over each one, trying to take in their great yawning thrusters, glinting shells, and terrible deadliness, the workers charged forward and clustered around the now-visible ships. In a cold and clearly disciplined silence, every sorry-looking man, woman, and child began to hammer at the hulls, tweak at panels, and open hatches to slip inside the ominous crafts.

"Well," said Gabriel in a defeated voice, "I guess now we know what the zyttrium is for."

- CHAPTER 53 -
CHATINE

"DETACHMENT COMPLETE." MARILYN'S VOICE DRIFTED through the cockpit of the ship, but Chatine could only stare numbly at the view of the cargo hold, which, only moments ago, had held Etienne, too.

Now the hatch was closed.

The cargo hold was empty.

The ship was no longer attached to the spacecraft carrier. And Chatine felt like she was no longer attached to her body, either. That they were both drifting aimlessly through space. Detached from the very thing that had kept them tethered.

"Would you like to engage thrusters?" Marilyn asked, and Chatine couldn't shake the feeling that the ship was trying to help her. Tossing her hints and lifelines in an attempt to break her out of her trance.

But still, she couldn't bring herself to move, except to run her fingertips over her lips for the thousandth time. How was it possible that they were still tingling? Surely, the manufactured oxygen in this cockpit would have wiped away all traces of his kiss by now. Surely, lips weren't capable of leaving behind physical sensations.

Which meant, it was her mind conjuring up these things.

Her mind playing tricks on her.

And she hated when her mind did that.

"Would you like to engage autopilote?" Marilyn tried again to get her attention. To get her to do *something*. Anything but stare at an empty cargo hold.

Finally, the ship got fed up. "Activating autopilote emergency override in ten, nine, eight . . ."

A hand shot out toward one of the levers on the console. It took Chatine all of two seconds to realize it wasn't her hand. Her impulses took over and she roughly slapped it away.

"Owww!" cried Roche. "What's your problem?"

"Don't touch the controls," Chatine said. "I've got this."

"Well, you certainly didn't *look* like you did," Roche replied, still cradling his hand like it was an injured bird. "You were staring off into space like a broken basher."

"I'm fine." Chatine blinked away the cobwebs around her mind and reached for the contrôleur. It felt strange in her grasp, like a memory she'd sworn to forget suddenly rushing back with no warning. She yanked it to the left, clearly too hard because the ship began to spin in dizzying circles.

Roche screamed. "We're going to hit it!"

Chatine looked out through the window to see the underside of the vast spacecraft carrier looming closer and closer as they spiraled toward it. She hastily overcorrected to the right, sending them rotating the other way.

"Would you like to engage autostabilizeurs?" asked Marilyn, who sounded about as nauseous as Chatine felt.

"Yes!" Chatine and Roche cried at once.

The ship took over. The spinning stopped. They were right side up again, hovering beneath the shadow of the spacecraft carrier. Chatine struggled to catch her breath and ease her pounding heart.

"Maybe you should let me fly," Roche said.

"No," Chatine snapped. "I told you. I got this. Etienne taught me how to fly this thing."

"Clearly, you've forgotten." Roche reached again for the contrôleur, and Chatine swatted at his hand. This time, he was quick enough to pull it away.

"Okay," said Chatine in a stern voice. "Now that I'm capitaine of this ship, I think it's time to set some ground rules. Rule number one: Only *I* touch the controls, okay?"

"And rule number two?" Roche asked in a snarky tone. It was a haunting echo of her own reaction to these same rules.

"There is no rule number two. There doesn't have to be. Because rule number one is everything. As long as Etienne is gone, Marilyn is under my command and I'm the only one allowed to fly her. And you don't touch anything unless I tell you to. Understood?"

"But—" Roche argued at the same time as Marilyn gave a small protest of her own in the form of an engine shudder.

"Understood?" Chatine repeated to both of them.

Roche crossed his arms over his chest and nodded. Marilyn said nothing, which Chatine took as acquiescence.

"Good, now let's get to that landing bay. Etienne said the best way to sneak in is to wait for that cargo voyageur we followed to leave, and I don't want to miss our chance."

After a steadying breath, Chatine powered up the thrusters and the ship seemed to tremble with excitement beneath them.

Carefully, she steered away from the massive spacecraft carrier, banking left until its monstrous form was no longer filling every window of this ship. "Strap in," she told Roche as she double checked her own restraints and jabbed at a blinking blue button on the console.

"Reengaging gravity simulator in five, four, three, two, one."

It felt like a droid fist to the head. The impact ricocheted down her spine all the way to her toes. Her organs fought to arrange themselves into their correct alignment as everything she'd eaten in the past day threatened to come right back.

"Ooommph," moaned Roche from the jump seat, doubling forward like he'd been punched. "Well, that wasn't fun. Let's not do that again."

Chatine took hold of the contrôleur once more. It felt good to fly again. Good to have gravity pinning her to her chair. Maneuvering Marilyn away from the massive vessel, she took a moment to refamiliarize herself with the controls, maxing out the thrusters and easing them back down, performing dancing loops among the stars. She felt like she was stretching her wings, returning to some former version of herself. One that was capable of flying. It all came back to her. Etienne's lessons in this very cockpit, his tense voice and nervous fingers pointing out the various buttons and levers on the console. His shrieks as she soared through the clouds too fast.

When she felt, once again, confident behind the controls, she made a wide, arcing turn and started her approach back toward the spacecraft carrier. Directly behind it, the three Sols were visible in the distance. Sols 2 and 3 were barely more than specks of red and blue. But the brilliant white glow of Sol 1 peeked over the top of the colossal ship like a new day dawning. Chatine squinted against the light and steered Marilyn closer. Up ahead, the enormous PermaSteel doors of the landing bay stood locked together like gritted teeth.

"What if they don't open?" Roche asked once Chatine had slowed to an idling hover and released the contrôleur.

"They'll open," she said, trying to instill more confidence in her voice than she felt. But her gaze kept falling to the small gauge in the corner of the console. Their zyttrium level was dangerously low. "That voyageur has to leave sometime, doesn't it?"

"What if it doesn't?"

"It does."

"What if it's parked in there for days? And we can never get in?" Roche asked, and Chatine peered again at the gauge. They didn't have days. They barely had hours. As soon as that meter reached empty, the ship would become visible on every detection scan from here to Usonia.

"And then Etienne and Gabriel won't be able to get the zyttrium out," Roche continued to ramble, "and they'll be wandering around the hangar, wondering where we are, and they won't be able to contact us and then they'll get caught by some evil officer who likes to torture people by pulling off their toenails and—"

"Roche?"

"Yeah?" he asked from the jump seat.

"Please shut up."

"I'm just saying we should come up with a plan B. In case those doors don't open. I can always go back through the—"

"You're not going back in there," Chatine snapped. "End of discussion."

Roche let out a dramatic sigh, and Chatine was convinced he was going to argue with her again. But he fell uncharacteristically silent. And just when she thought that a miracle had taken place and this really might *be* the end of the discussion, he said in a much softer voice, "You know, Chatine, sooner or later, you're going to have to let me go."

Chatine spun to face him. "What? Go where? Where are you going?"

He rolled his eyes. "I don't mean go, I mean *go*."

"Huh?"

Roche jabbed his tongue against the inside of his cheek. Why did she get the sense he was trying to figure out how to dumb down a complex concept so that she could understand it?

"Look, I know you thought I was dead for a long time. I know how heavily that must have weighed on you." He suddenly didn't sound thirteen anymore. He sounded like he was reading from one of those First World books in the Refuge library. The kind Chatine would never have any hope of understanding. "I've been talking to Sister Clare about this a lot lately."

"You've been talking to Sister Clare about me?" Chatine spat, the sharp sting of betrayal splintering through her.

"She has a lot in common with you. She lost her little sister in the Rebellion of 488."

"I . . . ," Chatine began, conflicted. "I didn't know that."

"She said you have something called a savior complex."

Burning heat ignited in her stomach. "A what?"

"Not about everything. Just about me," Roche rushed to say, as if this made it all better.

"What the fric does that mean?"

Roche continued to stab his tongue against his cheek. "It just means that you spent so long trying to save me, you don't know when to stop."

Chatine opened her mouth to argue, to scream that this was nonsense, but there was something in Roche's nervous fidgeting and downcast eyes, something in his quiet, tentative voice, that told her to stop. And then, against all odds, she found herself saying, "How long have you been wanting to tell me this?"

Roche shrugged an adorable, child-like shrug. And suddenly, he was thirteen again. Naïve and inexperienced, trying to broach difficult topics that reached beyond his years. "I don't know. A while."

Chatine swallowed down something that felt like a jagged stone. "Roche, I . . ."

But she didn't know what came next. What happened after she stopped trying to save him? What would she do? Who would she be? She peered down at her hands, which trembled uselessly, and then finally out at the great white star that was peeking above the spacecraft carrier, flooding the cockpit with light.

"Do you remember where you were the last time the Sols were visible on Laterre?" Chatine asked quietly.

She could feel Roche's eyes on her, suspicious of the change of topic. "The Sols were visible on Laterre?"

"Just for a few minutes." She rested her head back against the capitaine's chair and let the bright light wash over her. She could feel none of its warmth, of course, but she imagined she could. She imagined it was just like that day when she'd stepped out of Fret 7 and seen that the world had come to a stop. Everyone had been gazing up at the sky. Chatine's first thought had been that danger was coming. An asteroid hurtling toward Laterre. An invasion from the Albion Queen. Then, she'd just assumed they'd all gone insane. Their brains melted from hunger or the rot.

Until she felt it.

The beautiful warmth.

Like invisible arms were wrapping around her, holding her. Not tight enough to suffocate her, but not loose enough to feel like it was only temporary. Like it might leave her at any moment.

But then it did. Leave her. Just like everything else good in her life. It vanished beneath the gray overcast skies.

And by the time Chatine looked up, the three Sols were already slipping back behind the clouds.

"It was almost ten years ago," she said. "Maybe you were too young to remember. We had only been living in the Frets for about a year. I didn't even get a chance to see the Sols themselves. Just the light on the ground. But it was still unlike anything I'd ever seen before. A kind of pinkish glow. It was beautiful. I thought it meant . . ." Her voice trailed off again as the words got lodged in her throat.

"What?" Roche pressed.

"I thought it meant you were still alive. I thought it was a sign that you were close by and that I would see you again."

"And you did," Roche pointed out.

"And I did," she admitted.

"Principale Francine says the cloud coverage on Laterre is what keeps us warm. It creates kind of like a blanket around the planet, trapping in all the heat. She says without the clouds, we'd all freeze to death."

Chatine allowed herself a tiny smile. "I guess that makes sense. But sometimes it's hard to see it that way. Especially when every time you look up, you see nothing but rain." She let out a shaky breath. "When those clouds came back all those years ago, when the Sols disappeared almost as quickly as they'd come, I thought it meant—"

"Chatine," Roche said urgently.

"I know," she said, "I haven't been the easiest to live with. I just can't lose you again."

"No, look!"

Chatine glanced up through the windshield. Before them, the vast doors of the spacecraft carrier's landing bay were splitting apart and light was splintering through from the inside, splicing through space.

"It's leaving," Roche said.

He was right. A moment later, the doors had yawned fully open and the same voyageur they'd been tracking for the past three days was drifting out from the carrier, its silvery hull twinkling momentarily from the light it was leaving behind.

"Go!" Roche cried.

Chatine slammed her hand down on the thrusters, pushing them up to near full throttle. The ship juddered slightly before letting out a horrific screeching noise, and then everything fell silent.

"What's happening?" Roche asked. "Why aren't we moving?"

"I don't know," Chatine said, panic clawing at her throat. She eased the thrusters back down and tried again, this time ramping them up slowly. Marilyn let out a groan of protest and shuddered again, like someone trying to wake up from a deep sleep. Chatine gave her a little more power, trying to coax her awake. "Come on, come on. You can do it."

There was another earsplitting screech and then the ship went silent again. But this was not a normal silence. There was no constant hum of the engines. No quiet rattling of the monitors in their frames. This was a silence that was only present in deep space.

A silence that seeped into your bones.

"What happened?" Roche asked, panic squeezing his voice.

"It must be the thrusters. Etienne told me one of them was damaged. I might have overloaded their system and now"—she silently cursed every Sol and star in the sky—"I think they've all shut down."

Up ahead, the voyageur eased forward, clearing the landing bay. Chatine recognized the slow, even crank of the spacecraft carrier's doors starting to seal shut again.

"We have to do something!" Roche cried. "We have to get on that carrier. We're going to lose our chance!"

"I know!" Chatine shouted back, her eyes scouring every centimètre of the cockpit. "I just don't know what to . . ." Everything stopped—her words, her thoughts, her heart—as her gaze fell upon a little red door cut into the side of the hull. "Roche!" she said. "Can you get to that door?"

Roche didn't hesitate. In an instant, his restraints were off, and he was darting toward the emergency access panel. He yanked it open and peered inside. "What am I doing in here?"

"Do you see a lever?"

"Yes."

"It's an override. It'll restart the entire system." Chatine steadied her hands on the contrôleur, ready for the very likely chance she'd have to dodge Ministère explosifs. "Pull it."

"But what about stealth—"

"Just do it!"

Roche yanked down on the lever. Nothing happened and, for a second, Chatine was convinced they were doomed. Without power. Without stealth. Without hope.

And then, light.

From the console before her, from the panels surrounding them. From deep inside of her.

Everything powered back on.

Chatine grabbed the contrôleur and eased on the throttle. Her heart slowed, trying to decide whether or not it would be worth beating again.

"Hurry!" Roche said, pointing toward the landing bay doors of the spacecraft carrier, which were still making their steady trek toward each other.

There was no more time to be gentle. Chatine shoved the thrusters up to full power. The engines quivered beneath her, slowly and uncertainly. "Come on, Marilyn! You can do this. I love you. Etienne loves you. And he needs our help."

There was a low hissing sound, followed by something that sounded like metal grinding against metal, and then the ship lunged forward so suddenly, Chatine slammed against her restraints. Her hands slipped from the contrôleur and she dove to take hold of it again.

They sped toward the spacecraft carrier. The landing bay doors continued to creep closer and closer together, the locking mechanisms already protruding from the sides like jagged teeth. Chatine was now certain they were *not* going to make it.

At least not at this angle.

Roche must have come to the same conclusion because he shouted, "Rotate!" at the exact same moment that Chatine yanked on the contrôleur, maneuvering the ship onto its side. She fought to keep her eyes open and her hands steady as they soared through the narrowing gap and the landing bay doors sealed shut behind them.

- CHAPTER 54 -
MARCELLUS

MARCELLUS WAS SWEATING UNDER THE STIFF COLLAR
of his jacket as he stood at the front of the Assemblée room, waiting for a
response to his connection request. There was no guarantee there would
even *be* a response. And he had to prepare himself for that.

He smoothed down the front of his tuxedo. He hadn't worn it since
the Ascension banquet, and even though Sister Clare had done her best
to remove the bloodstains and mend the slashes from the riot, Marcellus
could still feel the animosity and rage in the garment, as though it had
seeped into the fabric.

"Marcellus Bonnefaçon," boomed a male voice in a sharp Reichenstatian accent. "I didn't quite believe it when my aide told me it was you. I had
to see it for myself."

A hundred tiny cams illuminated around Marcellus, looking like golden
stars in the darkness of the Assemblée room. His eyes pivoted to the holographic projection that was slowly taking shape before him. Gradually, the
faces of twelve men and women shimmered into focus, followed by the
dazzling view from the topmost chamber of Kaishi's infamous skytower.

The delegates of the System Alliance sat around a half-moon table, all
in the formal dress of their own planets. As Marcellus took in the luscious

silks of Samsara, the fur trims of Novaya, the stiff Reichenstatian linens, and the sparkling buttons handcrafted from the titan of Usonia, a ripple of trepidation passed through him, like his courage was threatening to flee right out the Assemblée room door.

Was he really doing this?

Yes, he told himself. *My grandfather must be stopped. And we're out of options.*

"Well?" barked Delegate Ziegler of Reichenstat, his thin moustache twitching with annoyance. "Do you have something to say to us? Or did you simply wish to waste our precious time?"

Marcellus swallowed. "Your Honorable Delegates. Please excuse my unscheduled connection request." He dropped his gaze to the piece of paper in his hands, scanning the words he'd scribbled down in the late hours of the night. Because he'd known if he didn't write them down, they would float right out of his head, just as they always did when his emotions got the better of him. But now his fingers were trembling so badly, the letters of the words blurred before his eyes.

"Oh look, the poor thing is nervous," someone said, and Marcellus glanced up to see the cams had pinpointed Delegate Varma from Samsara as the speaker. Her strong jaw and soulful dark eyes now filled the projection, only to be replaced a moment later by the austere face of Delegate Coburn from Usonia.

"Does your grandfather know you are speaking with us?" Coburn asked. He sat stiffly in his tailcoated jacket with its rows of titan buttons descending from each lapel.

The question gave Marcellus strength. "Your Honorable Delegates," he began again. "I stand before you today with a humble yet urgent request. I realize my methods of contacting you are unorthodox and surprising, but I believe you have made an egregious error and I beseech you to reconsider—"

"I'll give you one guess who is behind this." The voice wasn't brusque or even loud. It was calm, almost soothing in its lullaby-like cadence. Marcellus glanced up from his speech, already knowing who the cams would be focused on. Mylène LaPorte had been one of his grandfather's prized officers, head of the investigation into the Premier Enfant's murder. She'd recently been promoted to Laterrian delegate of the System Alliance, which had come as no surprise to Marcellus. She'd done the general's bidding back on Laterre—why not continue the tradition on Kaishi?

"Marcellus Bonnefaçon has had a long family history of association with the Vangarde," Delegate LaPorte continued, and even through the trillions of kilomètres of space that stood between them, Marcellus could feel the weight of her stare. "His father, Julien Bonnefaçon, was also a prominent member of the rebel group. You can be sure they are the ones pulling the strings of this little stunt."

"They are not!" Marcellus fired back before quickly berating himself for the outburst. He *had* to stay calm. Just like Sister Noëlle always told him. Use his words. Not his anger. He had to be diplomatic, or they'd boot him right out of the session. He softened his voice. "What I mean to say is, I am alone."

At least that much was true. The entire Refuge was asleep and utterly unaware of his actions. He hadn't told any of the sisters or Alouette of his plan. It had barely *been* a plan. More like a last-minute act of desperation. And he couldn't help but wonder what Chatine would have thought about it. Would she have tried to talk him out of it? Would she be standing across the room right now, glaring at him with those intense gray eyes of hers? Being his rock and his voice of reason, yet again. How he wished she were here with him now. But he hadn't heard from her in nearly a week. And every attempt he'd made to contact her using the Défecteurs' radio had gone unanswered. Which made him feel more alone than ever. He prayed Roche had found her and was looking out for her, just as Marcellus had begged him to do.

"I believe you have made an egregious error," Marcellus repeated, focusing back on the piece of paper in his hands. He would get through this speech if it killed him. "I beseech you to reconsider your appointment of my grandfather as the next ruler of Laterre."

"Someone cut this feed!" thundered Delegate Ziegler, inciting a flurry of movement on the projection as a dozen aides and advisors shuffled around, trying to decide who would be the one to fulfill the request.

"Wait," someone called out, and when Marcellus looked up again, he was face-to-face with Anastasia Volkov from Novaya. "I, personally, would like to hear what he has to say."

The young delegate cocked a playful eyebrow at Marcellus, reminding him of the days when they used to play hide-and-seek around the sky-tower. The general would often bring Marcellus on his diplomatic missions to Kaishi, and Anastasia would accompany her father, the former Novayan delegate. Although Marcellus had never told a living soul, Anastasia was the first girl he'd ever kissed, concealed behind the doors of the skytower elevator, while the System Alliance debated acceptable trade routes.

"Let him speak," said Delegate Volkov, and after a round of grumbles and protests, she turned back to Marcellus and added, "You have two min-utes."

Marcellus's cheeks warmed. It was clear from the gleam in Anastasia's eye now that not only did she remember the kiss, but it had bought him exactly two minutes.

"Merci," he said with a nod and a renewed well of confidence. He glimpsed down at the carefully scrawled words on his paper, cleared his throat, and continued. "I know you believe that my grandfather is the most qualified person to lead Laterre. You're not the only ones who believe it. The people of Laterre adore him. He has cleaned up the streets. He has updated the fabriques. He has fed the hungry, clothed the freezing, and taken care of the sick. He has done everything one would expect and hope from a good leader." He blew out a breath, rereading the next line for what felt like the thousandth time. "But that is only what appears on the surface. Below the surface, my grandfather has left behind a dark and bloody trail of lies and deceit. He is not the man he claims to be. He has committed countless acts of treason and murder, including the murder of the Premier Enfant and—"

"Ah yes," interrupted Delegate LaPorte with an air of impatience. "We've heard these allegations before. From Alouette Taureau. This is a gruesome and insidious theory that has absolutely no evidence to back it up. While I, on the other hand, was in charge of the investigation of that murder. I *do* have proof. Plus, a confession from the real murderer, whose name was Nadette Epernay and who was swiftly brought to justice." LaPorte turned to address the Alliance. "My Honorable Fellow Delegates. You should know that the Vangarde are famous for spreading lies like this. It was their primary recruitment tactic seventeen years ago. And you can see now that not much has changed."

"That's—" Marcellus tried to argue, but he was promptly cut off by Delegate Ziegler.

"It appears what your grandfather told us about you is true. You are nothing more than a little boy who likes to dress up like a man and play war, but you're still a foolish child."

Heat rose instantly to Marcellus's cheeks. His body flushed red under the thick fabric of his tuxedo. He felt his fingers clench around the paper in his hands.

"It's a pity," continued Ziegler. "You showed much promise as a child. Yes, I remember you. So well-behaved. So eager to please. And now look at you. A rebel. Spreading slanderous lies about the man who gave you everything."

"The man who lied to me!" Marcellus shouted, causing a few of the delegates to startle and sit up straighter. "Just like he lied to all of you!"

There was a shocked silence in the skytower. The delegates stared eerily back at him as if the feed had frozen.

Marcellus angrily stuffed the prewritten speech into his pocket. If he didn't know how to tell the truth about his grandfather now, he never would. "César Bonnefaçon—the man *you* trust, the man *you* appointed to lead one of the twelve planets of the System Divine—has colluded in secret with Queen Matilda of Albion to build a weapon. In exchange, he agreed to help the Queen invade Usonia and secure the planet back under Albion rule."

Murmurs shattered through the shocked silence, spreading around the crescent-shaped table, growing into shouts of disbelief and outrage. Until one voice carried above the rest.

"What a pathetic and preposterous accusation." The accent was rich and melodious, reminding Marcellus of sleek aerocabs and puffs of purple vapor from a pipe. The hologram cams immediately focused on Delegate

Aldridge of Albion, who up until this moment had remained quiet in these proceedings. "Albion and Usonia are allies. Friends. The idea that the Queen would plot against them—with *Laterre*, no less—is ludicrous. I absolutely will not tolerate such impudent and unfounded defamation of Her Majesty. Why are we even still listening to this boy?"

"I was there!" Marcellus fired back, holding tightly to the delegate's cold stare. "On Albion. I saw the weapon."

Delegate Aldridge flicked his manicured hand dismissively toward the cam, as if this whole exchange bored him. "Nonsense. Utter lies. Laterrians are not even allowed on Albion soil."

"Ask Admiral Wellington of the Trafalgar 4000," Marcellus replied. "It was his crew who escorted me in."

This seemed to capture the Albion delegate's attention. Perhaps not enough that he dropped his disinterested façade, but enough to keep him from interrupting again. At least for now.

"I went to Albion," Marcellus continued, addressing the entire Alliance. "I visited their Royal Ministry of Defence. I saw the weapon with my own eyes. I saw two men—*Laterrian* men—put into a glass cage." His stomach clenched at the haunting memory, but he forced himself to keep going. "I saw their TéléSkins flash as a new technology—developed by Albion scientists—took hold of their brains and compelled them to fight." He swallowed down another rise of bile in his throat. "To the death."

He paused again, trying to find the strength to keep going. Keep talking. Keep fighting. It was the look on Anastasia Volkov's face—half horror and half confusion—that spurred him on.

"Then, I saw it again. Here on my own planet. In my own backyard. The same technology used on hundreds of our people, compelling them to fight, to kill. My grandfather's plan was to use this new weapon—an army he could control with the touch of a button—to murder the Patriarche, knowing that with no heir left to inherit, the contingency clause of the Order of the Sols would have to be invoked. Knowing that if he just threw some spackle on the planet, and a few pieces of meat at those who were starving, *you* would all be coerced into appointing him. And he was right. He fooled you all. Just as he fooled me. Just as he fooled everyone here on Laterre. Because my grandfather—the man you just nominated as *Empereur*—is always three steps ahead of everyone. Even all of you." Marcellus let his gaze linger on each of the twelve faces that now stared silently and speechlessly back at him.

"But the one thing he *wasn't* expecting," Marcellus went on, "was the reappearance of Alouette Taureau. Not only was she a legitimate heir to the Paresse line, but she had the ability to shut down the Skins. And disarm his weapon. Which she did. Not my grandfather. But her. She did that. With her DNA. But Paresse blood or not, my grandfather wasn't about to let her get in his way. He's already found a way to denounce her, to delegitimize her, and he's already convinced all of you to go along with it."

He cast another purposeful look at each of the delegates. "And if you think he's finished now that he's been appointed Empereur, you're wrong again. The word 'Empereur' is a First World term. It means 'sovereign of *many* lands.' Conquered lands. Stolen lands. He will destroy anyone who stands in his way, including all of you and all of the Regimes you represent."

The Reichenstatian made a noise that sounded like half throat clear and half choke. "That is a serious accusation, Monsieur Bonnefaçon."

"Yes," Marcellus agreed. "It is. Because these are serious times, and my grandfather is a serious threat not just to Laterre but to this entire System. Which is why you need to pull your support for him now. This can all be undone. If you withdraw your appointment, he will be forced to step down."

"And who do you propose we appoint instead?" said Delegate LaPorte with a derisive chuckle. "That rebel-lover Alouette Taureau? You want us to put a puppet monarch in the Palais with the Vangarde pulling the strings?"

"The Vangarde fight for peace!" Marcellus snapped before checking his temper. "The Vangarde fight for equality. For the people's right to rule themselves."

"People cannot rule themselves," retorted Delegate Ziegler, but after a sharp look from Delegate Coburn of Usonia, he amended his statement. "*Most* of the time."

Marcellus turned his attention to Delegate Coburn, seated at the far left end of the table. For centuries, there had been no chair there. It had been stripped away after Usonia had fallen under the rule of Albion. But when they won their War of Independence and declared themselves, once again, their own planet with their own people-elected ruler, the twelfth seat had been added back to the chamber and the alliance of eleven had become an alliance of twelve once more.

If there was any hope of convincing anyone in this room to reject his grandfather's appointment, it resided with this man, who represented the coldest, darkest planet in the System. It was the farthest from Sol 1 and yet ironically, its people were the most free. While the rest of the planets were ruled by powerful monarchs, Usonians had created a different life for themselves. A life the Vangarde hoped to replicate on Laterre.

But as long as César Bonnefaçon was in power, Usonia was also in grave danger. Especially if the Empereur fulfilled his promise to Queen Matilda.

"The people will soon come to see the truth about my grandfather," Marcellus said. "Yes, they have been fooled. Yes, they have been blinded and lulled to a peaceful sleep. But we *will* wake them up. And when we do, war will be inevitable. Lives will be lost not by the hundreds but by the hundreds of thousands. The riot at the coronation ceremony will be nothing compared to the bloodshed we will see if you don't intervene. Right now. You can prevent so much death. So much violence. Pull your support from my grandfather. Reverse the appointment. The Vangarde—with Alouette Taureau beside them—will show the people how to lead themselves. Alouette Taureau may have been raised by revolutionaries, but she has the blood of a founder in her veins. Her legacy dates back to the beginning of our world. By casting your vote against her, you cast your vote against your own leaders. Against your own founders. By supporting my grandfather, you send a message to the farthest reaches of the System that *anyone* can overthrow a monarch, if they're clever enough. If they're deceitful enough. Is that the message you want to send to your own people?"

"Well, we certainly don't want to send the message that monarchs are obsolete," growled the Reichenstatian, who was joined by a small chorus of agreement. "That the people don't need them. Governments are much better run by one than many." He nodded at Marcellus. "Your own planet is proof of that. You have rebels warring among themselves, leaving a trail of bodies in their wake. Red Scar. Vangarde. And whatever other groups decide to rise up and take their shot. How will you possibly rule yourselves when you can't even decide which revolutionary faction to follow?"

Marcellus opened his mouth to argue, but Delegate Ziegler held up a hand. "The Empereur brought peace to your mess of a planet. Before he took control, Laterre was on the brink of civil war, and if we retract our support, you will surely be plunged into it. César Bonnefaçon restored order. Something your 'people' have been unable to do on their own. He is not only the best choice, he is the *only* choice. And you and your lies are no longer welcome." Ziegler turned to his fellow delegates and raised one of his thin eyebrows. "Is there anyone here who believes we should continue to entertain this trespasser?"

There was silence in the skytower chamber as the hologram cams floated, one by one, to each delegate. Marcellus waited for someone to speak. To give him so much as a word of encouragement. A seed of doubt was all he needed.

But as the faces drifted past—representatives from Kaishi, Samsara, Albion—his hope slowly slithered out from under him. The cam settled on the Novayan delegate. The face that was once beautiful and happy in Marcellus's memories now turned sorrowful and bitter as Anastasia Volkov gave a single, apologetic shake of her head.

Boulders settled on Marcellus's shoulders, weighing him down until his feet couldn't support him anymore. Who was he kidding? How could he have let himself hope? Even if they did believe his claims about his grandfather—which they clearly did not—the System Alliance could never outwardly support a government led by the people. They would be digging the graves of their own leaders. They would be setting a fire that was sure to engulf the entire System. One planet—one people's revolution—was an anomaly, a fluke. But two was a precedent.

Finally, the hologram cam hovered at the far left side of the table, landing on the man representing the little blue planet of Usonia. The *free* planet of Usonia. And even though his heart told him not to, Marcellus still found himself leaning forward. He still found himself hoping, praying. If not for the Vangarde, if not for Alouette, then for his own sanity. He *needed* Usonia to be on their side. Of all of these planets, he needed them to believe him.

If he couldn't convince the one planet that had fought this battle before—whose own safety and freedom were in danger—then what good was he? What good was *any* of this?

Delegate Coburn's silence felt like a lethal rayonette pulse straight through Marcellus's skull.

Marcellus fought to stay upright, but he could feel his strength waning. He could feel his resolve waning. Maybe this whole thing was a lost cause. A battle that couldn't be won. Maybe General Bonnefaçon—*Empereur* Bonnefaçon—was never meant to be defeated.

Maybe Marcellus *was* just a little boy, a foolish child, who had tried to dress up like a man and play war, only to be called a liar and laughed out of the room.

"The Alliance has spoken," announced Delegate Ziegler. "Or rather *not* spoken." He shared a smirk with Delegate Aldridge before refocusing his icy blue eyes on Marcellus. "Interrupt these proceedings again and there will be consequences."

The delegate nodded to someone off-screen, and a second later, the skytower chamber shimmered into nothingness and the flock of golden hologram cams swarming around Marcellus fluttered uncertainly before their light extinguished and their tiny bodies sank to the ground.

- CHAPTER 55 -
CHATINE

THE DOORS OF THE LANDING BAY'S PRESSURIZATION chamber unlocked, and Chatine eased Marilyn forward, into the spacecraft carrier's massive hangar. It seemed to stretch on for kilomètres. A walled city lined on either side with more combatteurs than Chatine had ever seen. More than she ever hoped to see. Their knife-edge wings shimmered under the overhead lights, and as Chatine maneuvered slowly and silently down the center aisle, the mouths of their explosif launchers seemed to stare back at her like watchful eyes.

Chatine had seen these deadly crafts twice before—once on Laterre when she'd saved the Frets from their devastating power, and again on Bastille when she and Roche had been trying to escape. But somehow, *these* combatteurs looked different. They looked shinier. Almost *new*. Like they'd never even seen stars before. Never fought in a single battle or dropped a single explosif.

Silently, Roche pointed to an empty space up ahead on the left, between two of the shimmering crafts, and Chatine carefully maneuvered Marilyn to the ground. She eyed the zyttrium gauge again. It wasn't just red now. It was flashing red.

That can't be good.

Workers in blue coveralls and caps scurried around the hangar, attending to the rows of sinister crafts, opening panels to perform checks, and connecting power cells to charging ports. Chatine raked her eyes over each of their faces, searching for a familiar one.

"Do you see them?" she whispered to Roche.

He shook his head, his eyes narrowed in concentration.

"Etienne said they'd be disguised as maintenance workers, right?" asked Chatine.

"Yes. Keep looking. I'm going to check the cargo hold to make sure it's ready to load the zyttrium when they get here."

Chatine nodded and, with her heart thudding behind her ribs, continued to scan the faces of the uniformed men and women, her hand poised on the switch for the underwing lights. But there was still no sign of Etienne or Gabriel.

What if something had gone wrong?

What if they'd been caught?

She shoved the thought away, trying to do that thing Sister Noëlle had told her to do: *think positive.* Expect the best, instead of the worst. It had been a foreign concept when the sister had first mentioned it, and it was still a foreign concept. Because the only thoughts streaming into Chatine's head now were thoughts of catastrophe and doom.

"Keep moving. No talking!" A deep, mechanical voice ricocheted across the vast hangar, pulling Chatine's attention to the far end, where a pack of droids was escorting a long line of people from a penned-in waiting area, through a retracting door, and down a corridor that led into the depths of the ship.

Her body gave an involuntary shiver at the sight of the bashers.

"Single-file line," one of them boomed, reminding Chatine far too much of her days on Bastille, being bossed around by those metal heads with their tazeurs and chilling orange eyes.

She recognized the prisoners. Their haggard appearance hadn't improved in the journey from Laterre. These were the passengers from the voyageur they'd followed. Men and women weakened from hunger and fatigue, dressed in threadbare shirts that hung from their skeletal shoulders and ragged pants that puddled at their ankles. Children with dirty faces and blank stares shuffled obediently one after the next, their small hands bound by Ministère cuffs that sparkled beneath the stark light of the corridor. It was about the only thing that sparkled on any of them.

What were they doing here? And how did they fit in with this fleet of brand-new ships and a storage facility full of stolen zyttrium?

"Cargo hatch deployed."

"What?" Chatine's gaze was ripped from the cockpit window, and she glanced at the monitor showing the cargo hold. Just as Marilyn had reported, the hatch was open, and the cargo hold was empty.

Her heart leapt into her throat.

No, no, no, no. He wouldn't. Would he?

But she knew the answer almost as quickly as she'd asked the question. Of course he would.

She looked back out through the cockpit window and felt all the oxygen in the ship evaporate at once, leaving her gasping for air. Gasping for life.

Because there, on the hangar floor, scurrying between the Ministère's deadly fighter crafts, ducking below their razor-sharp wings and powerful thrusters, was her stupide, worthless idiot of a brother.

And Chatine knew, instantly, in one single, shuddering heartbeat, that this had been his plan all along. From the moment he'd spotted those kids marching onto the voyageur back at the Vallonay spaceport. He'd been plotting, strategizing a way to get to them. To slip through her fingers. And she'd fallen for it.

She would have screamed. She would have roared. If it weren't for the open cargo hatch below that would surely broadcast any sound she made to the entire hangar. Instead, she jammed down on her restraints to release them and leapt out of the capitaine's seat.

"Hold down the fort, Marilyn," Chatine whispered to the ship as she crept down the stairs to the cargo hold and onto the hangar floor below.

She was going to kill him. As soon as she caught up with him, she was going to murder him.

That is, if the droids didn't murder him first.

Keeping Roche in her sights, she weaved through the aisles of fighter crafts, all the while trying to stay hidden, stay small, stay invisible. Just as she'd done for years in the Frets.

She glanced back only once and breathed out a sigh when she saw nothing but empty space where she had landed Etienne's ship. So far, Marilyn's stealth mode was still holding, but the memory of that flashing red light on the zyttrium gauge compelled her to move faster.

Up ahead, in the white corridor that led off from the hangar, she watched with a lump in her throat as Roche darted out from behind one of the maintenance carts and slipped seamlessly right *into* the line of prisoners.

What is he doing? Is he insane?

With a quiet huff, Chatine dodged around two more combatteurs before creeping through the retracting door and down the passageway after him, silent as a cat. As she moved, something warm and fiery crackled within her. It was the same sensation she'd felt on Bastille, every day that she saw Roche in that tattered blue prisoner uniform. The same sensation she'd felt in the Terrain Perdu, when her injured leg had kept her from running off to search for him. It made her feel anxious and yet steady at the same time.

It made her feel *alive.*

The realization terrified her. Maybe Sister Clare was right. Maybe she *did* have a savior complex. But she wouldn't *need* a savior complex if Roche didn't have a stupidity complex.

The prisoners continued down the hallway, shuffling past an endless parade of unmarked doors. Chatine hung back, concealing herself behind a rack of ship parts. She wasn't sure how long she could keep this up. These people were obviously being led to a destination. Eventually they would reach it. And then what would she do?

She didn't know. All she knew was that she had to follow them. She had to get to Roche before he got himself killed.

The procession turned a corner and Chatine scurried out from her hiding place, only to stop short a moment later when she heard heavy, booted footsteps coming from behind her, followed by voices. Two of them. One male, one female.

"They keep coming. Why are there so many of them?" asked the woman with a twinge of disgust.

"Because he keeps ordering more ships," replied the other. "Admiral Bosquet told me a new requisition just came in. Twenty-five more combat-teurs and three more invadeurs."

The voices were getting closer, turning the nearest corner. Chatine looked to the unmarked doors on her left and right, choosing one at random and praying it was unlocked. It was. She darted inside and shut it behind her, listening in the darkness as the footsteps grew closer and then, to Chatine's bitter frustration, slowed to a halt.

"And he's trusting a bunch of déchets to build them?" asked the woman.

"Hey, it's free labor. And much faster than building a whole robotic assembly line."

"Well, it's making the hallways smell like a waste management center. Where is he getting all of these people?"

"Plucked from the streets, I suppose. Or directly from Bastille. Who knows? More than a decade flying for the Laterrian Spaceforce, I've learned not to question General Bonnefaçon." The man scoffed quietly. "Sorry, *Empereur* Bonnefaçon."

Chatine's thoughts scrambled as she struggled to put the pieces together. The general had a spacecraft carrier hidden in the Asteroid Channel, tasked with manufacturing deadly fighter ships built by kidnapped Third Estaters? And now he was an Empereur?

What is going on?

And what the fric is an Empereur?

"Well, I hope he knows what he's doing. I'm shipping out in one of those invadeurs in two weeks, and I have a bad feeling about all of this."

Chatine swore she heard a tremor in the woman's voice. It sent one crackling down her own spine as well.

"Where is he sending you?" asked the man.

There was a pause and a shuffling of feet before Chatine could just make out the faintest breath of a whisper. "Usonia."

That word. That place. It brought back so many memories. So many fears.

It was a planet she'd once dreamed of escaping to.

It was a planet lost by Albion in the War of Independence.

It was a planet that Queen Matilda desperately wanted to win back.

And *Empereur* Bonnefaçon had promised to help her.

Chatine's vision started to go fuzzy. This dark room was spinning, and she knew she had to get out of there. She had already lost too much time. Roche was probably long gone, and those people were still camped out in front of the door. She needed to find another way out.

Turning around, she squinted into the pitch-dark room and ran her hand over the wall until she found a light panel and switched it on.

Immediately, she wished she hadn't.

Under a row of dim blue lights, she could make out three rows of gurneys, each one holding a body. An unmoving, lifeless, breathless body. None of the cavs had sheets covering them, and her stomach lurched as she spied missing hands, blistered burns, ribs poking out of whisper-thin skin. And implanted in every single arm was a darkened screen.

Chatine swallowed down a yelp and scurried backward, helplessness clawing at her throat and tears stinging her eyes.

Why? a desperate voice inside of her cried.

Why no matter how far she traveled—to the moon, to the Asteroid Channel, or even just across the Frets—did she somehow always end up in a Sol-damn morgue?

But she knew the answer. Perhaps she'd always known. There was no escape from the morgue. Because there was no escape from *him*. No matter how far she traveled, no matter how hard she tried to run away from it all, César Bonnefaçon was always there, plotting, manipulating, scheming.

Leaving behind a trail of bodies in his wake.

And now, he was sending out deadly crafts to the far reaches of the System.

Sister Noëlle was wrong. You can't expect the best. Not if you want to protect yourself. Not if you want to prepare yourself for the worst when it comes.

But Chatine would never be able to prepare herself for what came next.

The sound of heavy thudding footsteps echoed down the hallway, and when she ran to the door and braved a glance outside, her pulse instantly spiked again. The man and woman were gone, but the empty white corridor was no longer white. Everywhere she looked, a blinding orange light flashed ominously, reflecting off the shiny tile floor, bouncing down the endless corridor like a moonbeam trapped in a hall of mirrors.

And somewhere in the distance, an alarm was blaring.

- CHAPTER 56 -
ETIENNE

THE ALARM WAS A WAILING, EARSPLITTING SOUND THAT felt like a drill against the side of Etienne's skull. He had been cramming the last crate of zyttrium into the repair cart when it went off, and now he stopped and glanced up at Gabriel, who was standing watch at the door of the freezing-cold storage room.

"What do you see?" Etienne asked, his heart thundering.

Gabriel stood on his tiptoes to get a better look out the narrow slit window. "It doesn't look good, mec. Lots of flashing orange lights, and a bunch of people running."

"Running here?"

Gabriel shook his head. "I don't think so. But they all seem to be running in the same direction."

"We need to get out of here," Etienne said, reaching up to close the compartment door on the cart.

They'd managed to locate the storage facility off the gangway of the view deck, exactly where Etienne had calculated it would be, and Etienne had stuffed as many crates of zyttrium as he could into the repair cart's various compartments. But now it was too full, and he couldn't get the final door to latch. He shoved it urgently with both hands, just as a mechanical voice slipped into the air, sending a lightning bolt of panic careening through his body.

"Unauthorized craft detected in primary hangar. Unauthorized craft detected in primary hangar."

Gabriel spun to face him, his eyes wide. And instantly, they both knew.

"Chatine and Roche!" Etienne cried. "Marilyn!"

Etienne slammed the compartment door with his shoulder, hearing the latch click, and grabbed for the handle. Within seconds, he and Gabriel had maneuvered the repair cart through the door and were sprinting down the hallway. It wasn't difficult to figure out where to go this time. All they had to do was follow the seemingly endless stream of spaceforce sergents running toward the primary hangar. No one seemed to care about two maintenance workers barreling down the corridors alongside them. But with every new uniformed guard that joined the fray, Etienne felt another knife stab at his heart.

"Unauthorized craft detected in primary hangar."

He already knew what had happened.

They'd taken too long. They were too late. The last few molecules of zyttrium had finally been used up, and now Marilyn stood vulnerable and exposed in the middle of the hangar. With Chatine and Roche trapped inside.

Chatine . . .

Etienne compelled his worthless legs to move faster. His arms were already burning from steering the heavy repair cart around the corridors' endless turns and intersections. He could hear Gabriel panting beside him, struggling to keep up. Following the guards, they rounded another corner, and the hallway opened up into a vast warehouse-like room where rows and rows of deadly Ministère fighter crafts sparkled under the overhead lights.

The sergents spread out, a giant swarm dispersing among the aisles of the hangar, searching, scouring, examining every craft, every ship. Some clutched rayonettes, others carried handheld explosif launchers, the sight of which nearly brought Etienne stumbling to his knees.

"This way," Etienne said to Gabriel as they broke off from the horde and ducked between two charging stations. Etienne peered around the edge, his eyes roving methodically over each of the nearby crafts. "Where are you?" he whispered.

Meanwhile, pounding footsteps continued to echo down every aisle as more armed guards joined the search party.

"This hangar is massive," Gabriel said, his head rotating back and forth like a broken toy. "We'll never find them."

"We'll find them," Etienne said. What he didn't say, but added silently in his mind, was, *Just maybe not first.*

"Unauthorized craft detected in—" The voice accompanying the alarm suddenly cut out midsentence. Curious, Etienne looked up toward the ceiling, waiting for it to finish. But it never did.

Instead, the blaring sound that was drilling holes in his skull stopped abruptly. The orange lights flashing across every surface were extinguished as well. Heavy boots dragged to a confused halt. And the hangar fell silent.

"What happened?" Gabriel whispered. "Did they find them?"

Then, the mechanical voice returned. And this time, it felt like a voice sent straight from the Sols. "No unauthorized crafts detected."

Etienne heard a few grumbles from nearby guards as they shuffled back through the hangar.

"What was that about?" one of them asked.

"I don't know," replied another. "False alarm, probably."

"It's that Sol-damn stealth tech. It confuses all the sensors."

Stealth tech? Etienne's gaze darted back toward the nearest combatteur. *All of these crafts have stealth capabilities?*

The moment the guards were gone, Etienne was on the move again, shoving the cart out from their hiding place. He hurried down the nearest aisle, zeroing in on every empty space between crafts, squinting into thin air like he was trying to spot a ghost.

"Did they leave us?" Gabriel whispered beside him.

"No."

"Then, what was—"

"It's the stealth," Etienne replied hastily. "It's going in and out as the last stores of zyttrium are used up. It must have triggered the sensors."

They reached the end of the aisle, and Etienne maneuvered the cart under the glimmering wing of a combatteur as they cut across to the next row. "Look for the flashing underwing lights."

"Uh, mec." Gabriel grabbed at the sleeve of Etienne's uniform. "I don't think we're gonna need the lights."

"Wha . . . ?" Etienne spun around and the word died on his lips.

Her wings appeared first, with their familiar juts, slants, and odd angles. Then the thrusters emerged out of thin air, before finally, her domed window shimmered into view like a vast winking bug's eye.

It was Marilyn, as clear as the frozen rocky outcrop back home on the Terrain Perdu.

"Thank the Sols!" Etienne veered the cart into a sharp turn and rushed toward the ship, which was already starting to vanish back into the air as the last droplets of zyttrium dripped through her system. "Hold on, baby. We're here. Just hold on a little bit longer."

"How long before she trips the sensors again?" Gabriel asked, but it wasn't Etienne who answered.

"Unauthorized craft detected in primary hangar."

The alarms began to blare again.

"Fric!" Gabriel swore as they both sprinted the rest of the way to the open cargo hatch, which was now almost completely visible again. Gabriel pounded up the steps. "Start handing me the crates!"

The alarms continued to clang, and another thunderous storm of footsteps could be heard in the distance as the sergents fanned out once more, searching for the breach.

Heart racing, Etienne unloaded the crates one by one and passed them to Gabriel, who tossed them unceremoniously into the cargo hold. They'd barely gotten the last one in when the first group of guards rounded the corner, stopping in their tracks as the foreign craft continued to shimmer in and out of view.

"Go!" Etienne called, pushing against Gabriel's back. They clambered into the ship and Etienne sealed the hatch. "Chatine!" he called out. "Initiate thrusters! Get us out of here!"

But his shouts were met by a chilling, breath-stealing silence.

He looked to Gabriel, who only stared back with a matching expression of dread. Etienne charged up the steps to the cockpit. "Chatine! Roche!" But his limbs went numb and the blood in his veins turned to ice when his gaze fell upon the empty capitaine's chair and jump seat.

"Oh Sols," Gabriel whispered solemnly behind him. "This is not good."

Etienne's mind raced as, through the cockpit window, he saw more guards arrive and surround the ship, their various weapons raised. An officer in a white uniform pushed her way to the front of the pack and paused, her eyes roving up and down Marilyn as though she was taking a moment to analyze the threat.

"This is Vice Admiral Tréville. We have you surrounded!" she called out. "Surrender yourself and no physical harm shall come to you. Disobey and we shall have no choice but to attack."

"What do we do?" asked Gabriel. "If they're somewhere in this spacecraft carrier, we can't leave them behind."

Etienne gnawed on his lip, trying to bring his swirling thoughts into focus. He peered out at the legion of guards and their glittering weapons—rayonettes and Sol-damn explosif launchers—pointed straight at them. Straight at Marilyn.

Gabriel was right. He couldn't abandon Chatine. He couldn't leave her.

Then, in the periphery of his vision, he noticed a red light flashing. His gaze snapped to the zyttrium gauge in the corner of Marilyn's primary console. And it was as if the idea came to both him and the ship at the exact same time.

"Zyttrium level depleted," Marilyn announced. "Stealth mode deactivated."

"Yes!" He lowered himself into the capitaine's chair and buckled his restraints. "Gabriel, strap in."

"What?" Gabriel shrieked.

"Just do it."

Gabriel stumbled into the jump seat and fumbled to get his restraints fastened. Etienne reached for the thruster throttle, his hand trembling as he pushed up the lever. "You ready for this, baby?"

"Thrusters activated," replied Marilyn.

"Um, mec," said Gabriel. "I don't mean to argue with the capitaine or anything, but what about the whole *not* leaving them behind thing?"

"We're not leaving them behind," said Etienne. "We have enough zyttrium in the cargo hold to shield Ledôme for a decade. We're going to fly out of here, refuel the stealth management system, and then come back to get them."

He squeezed his hand around the contrôleur. Outside the window, the Laterrian Spaceforce aimed their weapons. "Hold on," he told Gabriel. "I have a feeling this is going to be a very bumpy liftoff."

- CHAPTER 57 -
CHATINE

THE HALLWAYS OF THE SPACECRAFT CARRIER WERE A labyrinth of stark white walls, unmarked doors, and shiny, reflective surfaces. Each one looked identical to the last. Chatine came to a halt at yet another intersection, listening to the alarms blare overheard. Fortunately, they drowned out the sound of her pounding heart and the voice in her mind telling her this was hopeless. *Un*fortunately, they also drowned out the sound of any footsteps or voices that she might be able to follow. That might lead her to Roche.

When the bright orange lights had started to flash for the *second* time, that's when she'd known. There was no more deluding herself. No more silent reassurances that it was just a false alarm.

Marilyn's stealth had finally run out.

She was found.

And they were all doomed.

She couldn't just give up, though. Not on Roche.

Instinct told her to take a left, so she did, continuing to dart down hallway after hallway, and peer into any doors that weren't locked. Had the prisoners been taken to another deck? It was the only logical explanation. It felt like she'd already searched every square centimètre of this floor.

Fatigue had come and gone. Her lungs had stopped trying to keep up long ago. She was operating on pure adrenaline now. And that was running low too, flashing a dangerous red just like Marilyn's zyttrium gauge.

She turned another corner and skidded to a halt, overtaken by sounds of a commotion. People shouting and bodies hitting the ground.

"Do not let that craft take off!" a fierce female voice called out.

Chatine struggled to focus her vision through the sweat that was dripping into her eyes. It took far too long for her brain to process the sight in front of her. But once it did, she was hit by not one but two crushing waves of defeat.

The first: She was back in the hangar. She had run in circles.

And the second: Marilyn was airborne, fully visible, and wobbling precariously above the rows of glossy new combatteurs, while an entire squadron of armed spaceforce sergents aimed weapons at her hull.

"Is he leaving without us?" screeched a voice behind her.

Chatine jumped and spun around. Once again, the fatigue and sweat and overexerted lungs were making it far too difficult to process what she was seeing. Her mind convinced herself she was dreaming. Or she was dead. Because that was the only explanation for seeing her little brother standing before her now.

"Roche?!" The word came out like a croak, like she was choking on her own disbelief.

But the boy in front of her didn't even look at her. His eyes were still locked on the scene in the hangar. "He can't leave without us!"

For a moment, Chatine couldn't be bothered to care about any of it—Marilyn's lost stealth, Etienne's ambiguous betrayal, a hundred guards pointing rayonettes and explosif launchers at their only ride out of here. Because all she could do was pull him to her. Squeeze her arms around him so tightly, neither of them could breathe.

"Chatine!" Roche protested, struggling to break free. "Stop!"

And then came the anger. Spooling out of her from places she didn't even know she was keeping it. "What on Laterre were you thinking? Running off like that? Risking your life? Running me around this entire ship like a mouse trapped in a maze."

Roche rolled his eyes. "I told you. You have to let me go."

"I have to let you go get killed?"

"But I *didn't* get killed. That's my point. I'm alive and unharmed and . . ." Roche turned and gestured to something. It was only now that Chatine realized he wasn't alone. Huddling close together behind a nearby heating vent were two emaciated children—a boy and a girl—who didn't look to be older than seven. "I found them," Roche said in a quiet, breaking voice that sounded like he was speaking not to Chatine but directly to the Sols. "I found my bébés."

Confused, Chatine glanced between Roche and the ragged, dirty-faced children in frayed blue uniforms who were clinging to each other like they were afraid of getting swept away in a violent windstorm. She opened her mouth to say something but was cut off when that same fierce female voice called out from the center of the hangar. "I repeat, do not let that craft leave! Fire at will!"

Chatine spun back around just in time to see Marilyn charge forward, her thrusters lit up like she was going to try to accelerate to supervoyage right inside this spacecraft carrier. Chatine snapped her gaze toward the front of the hangar, where the pressurization chamber was still open and the giant metal doors of the landing bay were firmly locked in place.

Is he going to try to . . .

But she never finished the thought because just then, one of the sergents sent an explosif soaring into the air, directed right at Marilyn's main thruster. Chatine sucked in a breath, knowing what would come next. If it had hit anywhere else, Marilyn might have been able to take it. She might have survived.

But not there.

The already-cracked thruster exploded in a shower of sparks that rained down on the guards below. Some ducked to protect themselves from the debris. Others jumped on the opportunity, firing another volley of pulses and explosifs into the black hole that now gaped open at the back of Marilyn's hull.

It was too much.

The ship started to come down. Chatine grabbed Roche's hand and squeezed it, certain she was about to witness something that would haunt her for the rest of her life. Marilyn juddered, tilting at an awkward angle as Etienne tried to keep her stable, keep her upright. But it was no use. The flames from the broken thruster started to spread until the entire back half of the hull was on fire.

Chatine let out a whimper. Because all she could do was watch as Etienne lost control. As Marilyn wobbled uncertainly before flipping over and plummeting to the floor of the hangar. The collision shook the ground beneath Chatine. She grabbed on to a nearby workbench to steady herself. Several guards and maintenance workers were knocked off their feet from the tremor that ricocheted across the entire spacecraft carrier. Marilyn careened across the hangar floor on her back, taking out two combatteurs and a nearby charging station. The sides of her rounded hull flickered out of view for a split second as the last drops of zyttrium flooded through the system, and then, she fell still. The only movements from her battered shell were from the dying embers of the fires that left her scorched and blackened.

Chatine couldn't move. Her entire body had been ravaged by that fire. Her balance had been forever knocked off-center from that collision. And now, as she watched for signs of life from the silent craft, she felt a numbness start to spread inside of her. A numbness that she knew would blacken and scorch her heart until it looked just like the carcass of that ship.

"Chatine!" It was Roche's voice that pulled her out. That forced her to blink. To breathe. Forced her heart to take another cautious beat. "Chatine, we have to go. We have to get out of here."

Chatine shook her head dazedly. The idea was as distant and as impossible as a star.

Where would they go? How would they ever escape?

But Roche was already two steps ahead of her. His clever brain making plans while hers was doing nothing but shutting down. "Look." He pointed to one of the combatteurs that Marilyn had demolished in her wake.

The brand-new fighter ship was mangled now, its knife-edge wings crumpled like a child's toy crushed beneath the foot of a droid. But it wasn't the cracked plastique of the windows or the awkwardly bent angles of its rear thruster that Roche was pointing at. It was the way the ship was catching the light. The way it almost seemed to shimmer out of focus. Like a ghost struggling to stay seen. Stay solid.

"Stealth," Chatine whispered as she glanced around the massive hangar, a chill cascading down her spine. "He's building an entire stealth fleet."

And that's when she understood. Not only what was happening on this carrier, but how they would get off it.

"Come on," she said, beckoning to Roche and the trembling boy and girl who still sat huddled together nearby.

They weaved through the rows and rows of combatteurs, doing their best to stay hidden under the shadows of wings and fearsome thrusters. Meanwhile, Chatine's gaze kept cutting back to the crash site, where sergents now had Marilyn surrounded and a female officer in a stark white uniform was shouting at the wreckage. "Come out with your hands above your heads and you won't be harmed!"

A lump formed in Chatine's throat. Had that woman seen movement from within? Were they still alive in there?

"Over here!" Roche called, and Chatine realized she'd stopped walking. Roche was up ahead, standing beneath the hatch of one of the combatteurs.

"How are you going to open it?" Chatine asked.

"It's not locked," whispered a tiny voice, and Chatine spun around to see the little girl pointing at the glowing panel installed in the hull.

Wary, Chatine pressed her palm to it, and with a quiet hiss, the hatch did indeed open. She turned back to the girl in amazement.

"These ones haven't been programmed yet," she explained before pointing farther down the hangar. "That happens down there."

"Let's go!" Roche cried, ushering the two children up the steps.

Chatine didn't stop to wonder if this was a good idea. Or if it would work. It was the *only* idea and it had to work. She climbed through the hatch, scrambled toward the cockpit, and lowered herself into one of the pilote seats.

She'd been inside one of these crafts only once before. With General Bonnefaçon when she'd been expected to lead him to the Vangarde base.

But they had been sitting in the passenger hold. And she hadn't really been paying much attention to the *mechanics* of the craft. She'd been more concerned with whether or not she was going to let him destroy an entire Fret in his obsessive quest to defeat the Vangarde.

Now, as she took in the vast console before her, she wished she had paid more attention. She could tell, right away, that this was *nothing* like Marilyn. Where Marilyn's flight console was all jutting knobs and timeworn levers, this was completely smooth. A giant screen that stretched from one end of the cockpit to the other with hundreds of colors and grids and virtual buttons.

"Can you fly it?" Roche asked, plopping himself down in the seat next to her.

"I . . . ," she stammered. "I don't know."

"You have to try. You have to do something." Roche cast his gaze over the console. "Like, what does this do?" He lunged for one of the controls. Chatine tried to stop him, but it was too late. His finger made contact with the screen, and a low hissing sound vibrated beneath them.

Chatine yelped and leapt back as something began to protrude from the floor between the two pilote seats. "Roche! You can't just start touching random—"

"It's the contrôleur!" Roche said.

And to Chatine's shock and relief, he was right. The long lever, with its smooth PermaSteel handle, extended upward and then forward, before locking into position. This she knew what to do with. She grabbed hold of the contrôleur and slowly pulled back. Nothing happened.

"Why isn't it working?" she shouted.

"Like I know!" Roche shouted back.

On the panel, a strange icon was blinking. She shared a look with Roche, who simply shrugged. She supposed his tactic was as good as any. She reached out and tentatively tapped at the icon.

"Primary hatch closing," announced the ship, and the voice brought a wave of sadness over Chatine. It was cold and mechanical. As far from sexy as a ship could get. "Primary hatch closed."

Chatine took hold of the contrôleur once more. This time, it immediately responded to her touch. A little too sensitively, she soon discovered, as the combatteur gave a sudden jolt, causing the children in the passenger hold to scream.

"Okay, so that works," Chatine said. "But we'll never get out of here without stealth." She bit her lip and tentatively called out to the ship, "Activate stealth mode?" They had established the ship could talk, but did it listen as well? Chatine waited with her heart in her throat as, again, nothing happened.

"Maybe you're saying it wrong," said Roche.

"How else would you say it?" she snapped.

"It's that button," said the same small voice of the little girl, who was now standing behind Chatine's seat, pointing at a section of the console.

Chatine narrowed her eyes. "How do you know that?"

"I built it."

Chatine took a moment to study the girl, remembering that Roche had called her Adèle, back in the Refuge. "*You* did?"

She nodded, her dark gray eyes gleaming with a mix of fear and determination. "I wired the consoles. That's my job."

"Your job?" Chatine repeated, struggling to wrap her mind around this. "You mean—"

"Halt!" came a frenzied voice from somewhere outside the ship. Chatine glanced out of the cockpit window to see three spaceforce sergents barreling toward them, weapons outstretched. "Identify yourself!"

"Do it!" Roche cried.

Chatine jabbed her finger against the button. The ship gave a low, rumbling noise and then, to her beautiful relief, she heard, "Stealth mode activated."

The sergents outside pulled to a startled stop as they gazed with vacant eyes at the space where they'd just moments ago seen a combatteur.

"Okay, are you ready to do this?" Chatine asked Roche.

He gave her an enthusiastic thumbs-up. "Ready, Capitaine."

Chatine's lungs let out a shudder as she pulled back on the contrôleur and the ship leapt obediently into the air. She eased up toward the ceiling of the hangar and steered the ship slowly forward, keeping the thrusters low and silent.

"Wait," Roche said, looking out the window at the landing bay doors, which were now behind them instead of in front of them. "Where are you going?"

But Chatine didn't answer as she maneuvered closer to the crashed ship, lying motionless on its back.

The officer still had Marilyn surrounded with sergents and was shouting orders at the passengers inside. It was only a sliver of hope, but Chatine had survived on much less. Lowering the combatteur, she drifted silently over the top of Marilyn's exposed hull, easing to a stop directly above the auxiliary hatch, the same one Gabriel and Etienne had used to sneak onto this carrier. Then, holding her breath, knowing this could be the end of all of them, she turned to Adèle still standing quietly behind her and asked, "Where are the underwing lights?"

Roche's eyes went wide. "You can't! It'll give us away!"

"They might be alive in there. And I'm not leaving until I know for sure."

The girl batted her large eyes uncertainly at Chatine before finally pointing to one of the grids on the vast console screen.

"This one?" Chatine confirmed, and Adèle nodded.

Roche gripped tight to the edge of his seat and closed his eyes as Chatine tapped the button once, twice, and again. Three times. That was the signal.

"What was that?" called the officer, shielding her eyes as she glared up into the lights of the hangar.

"It's one of ours," came a reply from one of the three breathless guards who had spotted them moments ago. They were now charging across the hangar. "It's one of the fleet."

"Who's flying it?" asked the officer. "Is one of our own in there?"

The sergent shook his head, resting his hands on his knees to catch his breath. "I don't know. I don't think so. There were no authorized flights in the log today and they didn't identify themselves. The biometric lock of that ship hasn't even been paired with a pilote yet."

"Shoot it down," replied the officer, and Roche shrieked.

As the sergents took aim at the space above Marilyn, Chatine quickly maneuvered the ship to the left and watched with a satisfied smirk as the volley of pulses and explosifs hit nothing but empty air. They tried again and again until finally the officer grew frustrated and called them off.

Chatine delicately eased the combatteur back over the hatch and flashed the lights again.

"There!" someone called, and the guards took aim once more.

"They're going to keep firing at us!" Roche shouted. "And there's no sign that anyone is—"

But then, they saw it. The tiniest flicker of movement from the hull of the crashed ship. Marilyn's auxiliary hatch eased open, and through the sliver of a gap, Chatine saw Gabriel's wide, terrified eyes peering out.

"They're alive!" she cried, her heart bursting with relief, just as another shot was fired from the guards below. The combatteur shuddered as a rayonette pulse pinged off the hull. Then came another. And another. Chatine gripped tightly to the contrôleur, doing her best to dodge the onslaught, but there were too many.

"How are we going to get them on board?" Roche asked.

Something blasted against the side of the ship, knocking Chatine's head back against the seat. When her vision stopped swimming, she noticed Adèle's tiny hand reaching into the cockpit and tapping something on the console. Another low hiss echoed through the ship as a second lever protruded from the floor between the seats.

"What the fric—" Chatine started to ask, but clearly Roche had already figured it out because a second later, a giant explosif shot out from the underside of the combatteur. The officer and her sergents dove for cover under the neighboring ships as a nearby charging station exploded.

"Soop!" Roche said, looking down at his hands wrapped around the trigger, like he couldn't believe he had just done that.

The space around Marilyn was now clear. Chatine eased back toward the still-open hatch and flashed the underwing lights three more times before reaching for the hatch control.

"Primary hatch open," announced the boring, far-from-sexy ship.

"Roche! Get down there and help them in!"

Roche leapt from his seat and charged toward the door. From one of the surveillance cams, Chatine could see the underside of the combat-teur, where Gabriel was climbing out of Marilyn's auxiliary hatch. Once Gabriel was aboard, Roche reached out his hand, beckoning for Etienne to follow. Chatine watched his head pop out of the hatch. He looked uncertainly between Roche and the interior of Marilyn.

"Come on," Chatine murmured under her breath. "Get in, already."

She could see Roche waving his arms wildly, gesturing to Etienne, but he still wouldn't move. Chatine flashed the lights once more, hoping to snap him out of whatever trance he had fallen into.

Etienne blinked up at the invisible ship, at Roche's hand protruding from the open door, and then back down at his own ship. The one he'd built from scratch. All by himself. The one that had carried him across the stars and the Terrain Perdu. His partner in crime. His first love.

And that's when Chatine understood.

He couldn't leave Marilyn behind.

But it soon became apparent he wouldn't have a choice. From the corner of her eye, Chatine saw one of the nearby combatteurs lift into the air before vanishing from view.

She turned back and screamed in the direction of the hatch, "Etienne! Get in now!"

Either he heard her or he saw the fighter ship for himself because with one last apologetic look at Marilyn, Etienne heaved himself up out of the hatch and into the combatteur. Chatine pounded down on the console, sealing the door behind him, and yanked back on the contrôleur.

The combatteur launched up toward the ceiling, just as their invisible assailant opened fire on the crashed ship below.

One minute Marilyn was there, scorched and battered but still in one piece, and the next she was gone. Obliterated in an exploding cloud of smoke and debris.

Chatine heard a wail from somewhere in the depths of the combatteur, which she tried desperately to block from her consciousness as she rotated the ship around and pointed it at the colossal PermaSteel doors in the distance.

The moment Roche slipped back into his seat and looked out at the barrier that stood between them and freedom, he understood. He wrapped his hands around the trigger and gave Chatine a sharp nod.

She initiated the thrusters and pulled back on the contrôleur. The landing bay doors came rushing toward them. Roche opened fire. One explosif was enough to make the crack. The air from the pressurized hangar did the rest. The doors exploded outward, sucking out everything and everyone with them, including an entire fleet of newly minted stealth crafts, which spun and tumbled chaotically through space.

And one stolen combatteur, which glided through the wreckage as easily as a cloud.

CHAPTER 58

CERISE

"I COME WITH AN URGENT MESSAGE FOR THE EMPEREUR."

The guards stepped aside to allow Cerise to enter the vast foyer. The difference was startling. Empereur Bonnefaçon had been back on Laterre less than a day, and already the interior of the Grand Palais was unrecognizable.

The hallways were drastically sparse. No more decorative vases displayed on pedestals. No more delicate titan sculptures to weave around. No chandeliers dripping decadently low and heavy from the ceilings with their sparkling crystals. The opulent woven rugs imported from Samsara had been rolled up and taken away, and the walls were almost bare, stripped of most of the paintings that usually hung there. Nothing was in the way. Fussiness had been vanquished, and Cerise couldn't help giving a small smile.

She much preferred it this way.

Everything stripped down for maximum efficiency and function.

"South wing," the guard directed her.

Cerise turned back to him. "South?" she repeated, certain he must have misspoken, a mistake made out of habit. "Not the east wing?"

The east wing was where all the Patriarches and Matrones had always resided. It was the imperial wing, with the grandest bedchambers and the largest salons and the highest-soaring ceilings of the whole Palais.

The guard shrugged. "He prefers the south wing."

Cerise mounted the staircase and strode down the long hallway toward the Empereur's private study. Similar to the foyer below, the corridor had been stripped bare. Titan-framed First World paintings had been replaced with empty austere walls that caught the artificial moonlight streaming in through the opposite windows. As she walked, Cerise caught sight of her reflection in the long panes of darkened plastique. The young cyborg that strode beside her was confident, sure-footed, brimming with pride. Her obsidian-black hair was tied back in a sensible knot at the base of her neck, and her circuitry flickered with a confident hum.

She was not worried about an unannounced visit to the newly appointed leader of Laterre. She knew whatever the Empereur was doing, this was more important.

This was a priority.

He'd said so himself.

And this was not the kind of news one delivered over an AirLink. This was the kind of news one delivered in person. Not just for the sake of security, but because she wanted to be standing in Empereur Bonnefaçon's presence when she delivered the coordinates of the base. She wanted to *feel* the appreciation and respect radiating off him. She'd gotten a taste of the glow that came with a job well done, and she craved more of it.

And this wasn't just a job well done. This was *the* job, done the best it could possibly be done.

When she arrived at the heavy wooden door at the end of the hall, she reached into the pocket of her uniform and pulled out the TéléCom that had once belonged to her former self, her traitorous self, and now belonged to the Regime. And to the worthy cause of protecting it.

On the screen the tiny orange dot still blinked in the center of Fret 7.

The Vangarde base. Hiding beneath Vallonay. All of this time.

The sight of it gave her a final rush of conviction. More than enough to lift her hand and knock with the same fierce determination that had led her here tonight.

But a voice from inside the office stopped her just shy of making contact with the door.

"And what was the reaction from the other delegates?" the Empereur was asking in a tone so hushed, so discreet, Cerise doubted she would have been able to hear it if it weren't for her enhancements. "I see. Well, I appreciate you bringing this to my attention. It sounds like you were able to defuse the situation effectively."

There was a long silence on the other side of the door, in which Cerise could hear only the sound of steady breathing. One breath. One person inside. The Empereur was on an AirLink.

Suddenly, without warning or invitation, that voice was back in her mind.

Gloating and triumphant and treasonous.

"The general sends all of his AirLinks over a secure network. An unregistered *network . . ."*

A dark fog seemed to settle over the whole of the hallway, casting Cerise in a dream-like trance. She stared numbly down at the TéléCom in her hand.

"If you run the program while he's on an AirLink, you can trace the signal back to its source. To his private, encrypted server . . ."

She reached toward the screen, moving in slow motion, moving through thick clouds.

The TéléCom let out a small chime and then a voice in her audio interface announced, "One unregistered network detected."

It was enough to break through her trance, sending the fog skittering to the far corners of her mind. Cerise blinked and stood up taller, mentally berating herself for losing focus, even for a moment.

Empereur Bonnefaçon was the confirmed leader of Laterre now. The *crowned* leader. And despite what her former self had assumed, Cerise was not a traitor.

"Really?" came the Empereur's voice through the door. "He actually accused me of being behind the murder in front of the entire Alliance?" The question was followed by a long pause, in which Cerise could almost feel the air grow colder in the next room. "Well, let's hope you're right about that."

Cerise's circuitry began to flash wildly as her processors worked to connect the details, but she was missing too many integral pieces.

"And you're sure there's nothing out there that can implicate either of us?" There was another pause before the Empereur said, "Fine. Alert me immediately if he attempts to contact the Alliance again."

Then, the door in front of Cerise flew open. She let out a shriek and scrabbled ungracefully backward, nearly tripping over her own feet.

"Spécialiste Chevalier," the Empereur said, casting a suspicious look at her, then at the TéléCom in her hand.

"General—I mean, *Empereur*. My congratulations to you on your coronation."

"Merci." He gave her a tight nod, but his apprehensive gaze never faltered. "How long have you been standing here?"

"One point seven minutes," Cerise said automatically.

The Empereur's brow furrowed, as though he were attempting to perform a difficult calculation in his mind. "And what exactly did you hear?"

Cerise's circuitry gave another intense flash. Some strange impulse in her brain was telling her to lie. To say she'd heard nothing. But that was impossible. Just as she'd told the Empereur in this very study, only two weeks ago, she was incapable of deliberate deceit.

"You were speaking to someone about being accused of murder."

For just a moment, the Empereur's hazel eyes flashed with something that resembled fury, but it was replaced just as quickly with a smile. Then, he began to laugh.

Uncertain of what the source of his amusement was, Cerise simply stared.

"Quite ridiculous, isn't it?" the Empereur said. "It's just my grandson trying to stir up trouble again." He gestured to his own TéléCom, now folded up in his hands. "That was Delegate LaPorte of the System Alliance. Apparently, Marcellus crashed their session a few days ago to accuse me of murdering the Premier Enfant." He gave another small chuckle, followed by a weary sigh. "Which of course is not true."

It happened so fast, Cerise couldn't even think to stop it. Her cybernetic eye captured the image. Her brain processed it. The result came rushing at her like an explosif ready to detonate the moment it landed.

Lie.

And suddenly a searing pain thunderbolted through Cerise's skull. It was so sharp, so intense, she doubled over, dropping the illegal TéléCom on the floor. She fought back an audible groan as her brain was attacked by voices, all trying to shove their way in at once. She closed her eyes tight, attempting to regain control, but they were too strong. Too powerful. It was like she'd opened a door in her mind, and now she couldn't shut it.

"*. . . guilty of treason . . .*"

"*. . . not who you think he is . . .*"

"*. . . plotted to kill the Patriarche . . .*"

"*. . . I won't tell you what he's done because I know you won't believe me. . . .*"

"*. . . killed the Patriarche's other daughter . . .*"

"*. . . you will need to see it for yourself. You will need proof. . . .*"

And then, for the first time in Cerise Chevalier's life, her mind emptied. She had no thoughts. No processes. No memories. Her brain felt as vacant and barren as the Terrain Perdu. All she could hear as she stood hunched over, her hands crushing against her temples, was the sound of her own blood pumping through her veins. Hard and fierce and relentless.

"Spécialiste?" the Empereur's voice called out to her. "Spécialiste Chevalier, are you all right?"

But she couldn't seem to process his words. She couldn't seem to process anything. She tried to blink the blurriness from her vision, but it was like the world had gone permanently out of focus. Or perhaps it was *her* who had gone out of focus.

Glitched.

It was a glitch. It had to be. She was broken. She was faulty. She was damaged. She was—

"Do I need to call someone from Reprogramming?"

With those eight little words, everything shuddered back into place. Her vision cleared. Her thoughts arranged methodically and orderly in her mind. She peered down at the TéléCom that was now lying on the floor. The screen had shut off, and she hastily picked it up and swiped to activate it again.

As the blinking orange dot reappeared on her screen, right over the center of Fret 7, her pulse began to stabilize. And she could once again feel the warmth of confidence and determination thrumming through her.

"My apologies, sir. I don't know what happened. I will certainly have my processors checked by a médecin as soon as possible." She stood up straighter and smoothed down her uniform. "But first, there's an urgent matter that cannot wait."

CHAPTER 59

ALOUETTE

ALOUETTE WAS BACK IN THE FLAMES, CHOKING, GASP-ing for air. This time, they were consuming the entire Refuge, spreading from room to room, devouring the sisters' small wooden beds, their neatly folded tunics, their books.

"*No!*" Alouette tried to scream, but just like in the last dream, no sound came. The smoke snuffed out her voice and blurred her vision until all she could see were her own tears.

She tried to save them, tried to snatch up the precious volumes of the Chronicles, but the paper turned to ash in her hands and crumbled into nothing.

"Little Lark!" came the voice again. Always the same voice. Always the same dark hooded figure rushing to her rescue. She turned back toward the door to the hallway, only to find it was blocked by the fire. She was trapped in the library with the smell of burning words stinging her nostrils.

"Little Lark?"

She could see the dark hood through the thick blaze. She called out to him, begging him to stop. "Papa! No! Don't!"

But he didn't stop. He plunged through the wall of fire, his coat catching at once. He coughed violently and fell to the ground. Alouette threw her body on top of his, trying to smother the flames.

When the last spark had been extinguished and the coat was nothing more than frayed, charred fabric, Alouette finally reached to lift the hood.

It was not Hugo Taureau.

It was Sister Laurel.

Alouette woke with a cry, her room pitch-dark, her sheets, once again, drenched in sweat. Another nightmare. They'd gotten worse since the general had crowned himself Empereur. She switched on the light and glanced at the clock on the wall. It was still the middle of the night. It took a few bleary-eyed seconds for Alouette to realize what had woken her. And then she heard it. The loud, repetitive howl of the Refuge's alarm.

Alarm?

Her gaze snapped to the door, searching for signs of smoke. She *had* been dreaming, hadn't she?

She heard footsteps outside her door. They were not the quiet, calm padding of a sister walking to the dining room or carrying a book back from the library. They were panicked, pounding footsteps. Desperate trampling against bedrock.

Alouette's heart leapt into her throat as she climbed out of bed and tiptoed toward the door. Easing it open, she peered into the hallway. It was empty. She crept outside and scurried down the corridor toward the library, breathing out a deep sigh when she saw everything was as it should be. All the books were stacked neatly and orderly on the shelves. Sister Jacqui had been in here every day for the past week and a half, organizing and cataloguing just like she used to.

The alarm continued to howl from the speakers embedded in the walls. Curious, Alouette glanced up and down the empty hallways, wondering if it had been tripped by mistake. Perhaps the footsteps she'd heard were someone rushing to shut it off.

Then, she heard the voices.

"We have to get everyone out now!" shouted Sister Léonie.

"How do you propose we do that? The mechanical room exit is

completely sealed off. And we can't possibly use the tunnel now!" That was Sister Noëlle.

Sister Noëlle? But she never shouted.

"We'll have to take our chances," replied Léonie. "Before more of the Ministère get here."

Alouette's feet froze. The Ministère? Here? At the Refuge?

"Everyone calm down," said Francine.

"Don't tell me to calm down!" shouted Léonie.

"Sister," said a warning voice that Alouette recognized a second later as Citizen Rousseau's. "The moment we turn against each other is the moment we lose this battle."

"No," Léonie fired back. "We already lost this battle. The moment General Bonnefaçon slapped a crown on his own head, it was over. You're all just too blind or too stubborn to see it, but I see it quite clearly. It's over. We lost. Now either we evacuate or we lose our lives, too."

Sensation surged back through Alouette's body and then she was running, pounding down the hallway in her bare feet. She stormed into the Assemblée room to see Marcellus and the sisters gathered around a bank of monitors in varying states of dress.

Principale Francine and Sister Nicolette had sweaters pulled over their nightgowns, while others like Léonie had clearly just dashed out of their rooms in nothing but their flimsy pajamas. Marcellus stood barefoot among them in bed shorts and a crumpled white T-shirt. His thick hair was a riot of waves and disobedient curls.

"What's happening . . . ?" Alouette started to ask, but the question died on her lips when her gaze focused on one of the monitors and suddenly she understood. The alarms. The panic. The shouting.

A darkly clad figure was halfway down the founders' tunnel, moving closer to the Refuge's back door with every passing second. From her size and gait, Alouette guessed it was a young woman. She walked with confidence and determination, a girl on a mission. And when she passed by one of the small emergency lights embedded in the wall, Alouette could make out the shimmer of something on her face.

"A cyborg?" she asked with a shiver. "Coming here?"

Marcellus nodded. "She set off the sensor alarms when she accessed the hidden door in the sewers."

"B-b-but," Alouette stammered, looking desperately from the monitor to each of the sisters. "How did she get in? How did she find us?"

"She hacked the lock," said Denise, the scars on her face pulled taut with dismay. "And I'm still trying to figure out how she found us."

"And she's alone?"

"Yes," said Sister Noëlle, shooting a pointed look at Léonie.

"For now," Léonie replied sharply. "She's probably a scout. There's probably an entire army of Policier droids coming up right behind her."

Alouette frowned and peered back at the monitor. Her pulse was thudding in her ears, but there was something about this situation that felt off. For some reason she couldn't put her finger on, she didn't feel the same sense of urgency as Léonie so obviously felt.

"Why would a cyborg be sent as a scout?" she asked. "Why not send a droid? And if she's not a scout, then why is she alone?"

"The Ministère is probably tracking her every move, waiting to see where she leads them," said Léonie.

"Cyborgs are not trackable," Denise reminded her. "Their circuitry isn't designed with tracking capabilities. Trust me on that."

"Is she armed?" asked Francine.

"She has something in her hand," Nicolette said, and Alouette squinted at the screen to see a flash of silver peeking out between the cyborg's thin fingers. "We don't know what it is. It's too small to be a rayonette. Could be some kind of explosif. Who knows?"

Léonie threw up her hands. "Every second we spend standing here asking questions is a second lost." She turned to Francine. "Principale, order the evacuation. Now."

Francine looked apprehensively from Léonie to the monitor. Alouette could see the quiet, contemplative wheels turning in the sister's mind. Francine swallowed. "Léonie is right. We can't waste any more time. Sisters. Prepare the Refuge for—"

"Wait!" Marcellus called out, pointing to something on the screen. "Can you back that up?"

Sister Denise's hands moved confidently over the controls, reversing the footage from the tunnel security cams.

"There!" Marcellus said, and the footage paused. He tapped on the girl's face, which was unabashedly staring up at the nearest cam. No, not staring *at* it, staring right *into* it.

Like she wanted to be seen. Wanted to be recognized.

And Alouette most definitely recognized her.

Her throat went dry. "It's Cerise."

"Who?" asked Sister Marguerite.

"My . . ." Alouette flicked her gaze to Marcellus. "*Our* friend. She was with us on the voyageur to Albion. She was the one who helped us infiltrate the Ascension banquet. She was trying to stop the general, but then she—"

"You went to Albion with a cyborg?" Sister Clare asked in disbelief.

Alouette shook her head. "She wasn't a cyborg then. She was caught when we broke into the Ministère headquarters. Her father is the directeur of the Cyborg and Technology Labs, and he—"

"The directeur?" Léonie screeched. "Well, that settles it. Evacuate now."

"No!" someone shouted. Alouette didn't even realize it was her until the sisters were all staring intently back at her. She fumbled for something to say. Something to explain this feeling deep inside of her. But she couldn't. There were no words for it. She stared at the frozen image of her friend with that mysterious object in her hand, and suddenly, it all made sense. "I need to talk to her."

Léonie guffawed. "You're not going out there. It's too dangerous. She's definitely armed."

"No," Alouette said again, this time much quieter. She leaned toward the screen and zoomed in on the still image of Cerise's hand. "That's not a weapon. It's one of our récepteurs. Maybe that's how she found us. Maybe she traced the signal."

"But how?" argued Marguerite. "It's a First World network. The Ministère doesn't have the technology to—"

"She's traced First World networks before." Alouette turned to Denise.

"That's how she found your father's message. From the space probe. Marguerite, can you patch me into the récepteur?"

Marguerite nodded and before anyone could voice their protests, the small green light was flashing on the console. "You're connected."

Alouette blew out a shaky breath, trying to slow her pounding heart. She pressed down on the talk button. "Cerise, this is Alouette Taureau."

The cyborg on the monitor careened to a halt, staring wildly around the tunnel until she tracked the voice back to the device in her hand. "Alouette," she said quietly. Almost curiously, like she was speaking the name for the first time, feeling the strangeness of it on her tongue.

"Yes," said Alouette. "It's me. Your friend. At least I hope we're still friends. Why are you here?"

There was a long pause in which no one moved nor spoke nor breathed. Cerise still stood motionless in the hallway, staring at the récepteur as though she wasn't quite sure what to make of it. "I have something for the Vangarde."

Sister Clare sucked in a sharp breath. Alouette shivered again. There was something so sinister about her voice. Was it just that eerie cyborg monotone? Or was Cerise making some kind of threat? It was impossible to know.

And yet, still so possible to hope.

Alouette shared a look with Marcellus before pressing the talk button again. "What is it?"

"I can't tell you." Cerise resumed her long, determined strides down the tunnel. "I must show it to you." There was another pause before she added, "I have recently come into possession of some very important intel that the Vangarde will definitely want to know about."

The words tumbled around in Alouette's brain, looking for a place to land. She snapped her gaze back to Marcellus and could instantly tell from the relief on his face that he recognized them too. They were the exact same words Cerise had spoken in the cruiseur all those months ago, when she'd come to find Marcellus with the encrypted message from the space probe. When she'd simply been Cerise Chevalier. A girl. A sympathizeur. Not this product of the Ministère who was rapidly closing in on the Refuge's back door.

"Let her in," Alouette said.

"LET HER IN?!" thundered Léonie, reeling on Alouette. "Have you lost your Sol-damn mind?"

"Léonie!" scolded Marguerite. "Please."

"No," Léonie shouted back. "I don't have to listen to her. She's not the ruler of Laterre. *Empereur* Bonnefaçon is. And in case you've all forgotten already, he's put a target on our heads. He made it perfectly clear in his last broadcast that we are his number one priority. And now he's sent a cyborg to our door and you want to *let* her in?"

"I don't think she was sent by the Empe—" But Alouette couldn't bring herself to say that shudder-inducing word. "I don't think he sent her."

"Oh no? Why not?" Léonie replied, and Alouette tried to ignore the sting of her tone. She'd never heard any of the sisters speak to one another like this before. This war—the Red Scar, Sister Laurel's death, that man sitting in the Grand Palais—it was tearing the sisterhood apart.

Alouette swallowed. "It's just . . . a feeling. I don't think she's here to harm us. I *know* her."

"You knew her," Francine corrected gently. "Remember that cyborgs are—"

"Are capable of change," cut in Denise.

"Well, of course," Francine admitted. "But—"

Denise didn't allow her to finish; she turned to Alouette with a determined gaze. "Do you have reason to believe she's starting to wake up?"

Léonie groaned and started to pace the length of the room.

Denise ignored her and kept her focus on Alouette. "Can you trust her?"

Alouette glanced back at the monitor. Cerise was mere mètres away from the end of the tunnel. If Alouette was wrong, it could be the end. Of everything. The Refuge. The sisterhood. The books.

She swallowed hard and stared back at Denise, at the rough red lines of her scars. The permanent reminders of her past. She had once been a cyborg. She had once been loyal to the Regime, but she'd changed. She'd woken up.

Alouette thought back to the last time she'd seen Cerise, in the hallway of Fret 6, when she and Marcellus had been trying to escape the riots. Cerise could have arrested Marcellus. She could have fired that rayonette, but she didn't. She'd let him go.

Was it only because of the Paresse blood running through Alouette's veins? Or was it because of something else? Some deep-rooted tie that still strung them together. Some sliver of humanity that had shown through.

Alouette wanted so badly to believe that was true. That the Ministère could not conquer all with its fancy weapons and cutting-edge technology. That in the end, it was what was inside people's hearts that mattered most.

But more than anything, she wanted to believe it because if she didn't, it would mean there was no hope. For Cerise. For the Vangarde.

For Laterre.

And if there was no hope, then Sister Laurel had died for nothing.

Tears brimming in her eyes, Alouette stole one final glance at the monitor—at the dark figure closing in—and then turned back to Denise. "Yes. I trust her. Let her in."

CHAPTER 60

MARCELLUS

IT WAS HARD TO EVEN THINK OF HER AS CERISE CHEVA-lier. The cyborg sitting at the long table with a TéléCom open in front of her looked nothing like the girl Marcellus once knew. She exuded none of the same charisma or effervescence. She flashed not a hint of her usual smile. Even her long black hair seemed to have lost some of its shine.

Everything that had once sparkled about Cerise Chevalier had been tamped down, stamped out, dulled by the thousands of tiny nodes implanted in the left side of her face.

After Marcellus and Léonie had checked to make sure she wasn't carrying any weapons, they'd guided her through the back door and into the dining room, where everyone was now gathered around the table, waiting with captured breaths while Cerise tapped methodically on her TéléCom. As though she was wholly unaware or unaffected by the eleven women—and Marcellus—who stood watching her.

"Is she going to say anything?" Marcellus whispered to Alouette.

"Yes, Monsieur Bonnefaçon," replied Cerise in that unnerving monotone that sent shivers down his arms. "I am simply preparing my evidence."

"Evidence of what?" snapped Léonie. She was standing farthest away from the table, a rayonette clutched in her hand, her eyes dark and distrustful.

Denise put a patient hand on her arm. "Cyborg brains don't work the same way as humans'. Give her time."

Léonie snorted. "Time to what? For all we know, she's calling backup right now."

"I am not," Cerise said at the same moment Denise said, "She is not."

Cerise looked up, seeming to notice Denise for the first time. Her cybernetic eye latched on to the river of scars running down the sister's face before she returned her attention to her TéléCom. "I believe it will be more efficient to present the evidence first, then explain."

"I think it best that you explain first," Léonie fired back.

Cerise stopped tapping at the screen and looked up. "Very well. Where shall I commence?"

Marcellus did a quick scan of the sisters. Apart from Denise, Citizen Rousseau appeared to be the only calm one in the room. Even Principale Francine, who was usually so collected and composed, was fidgeting relentlessly with the metal tag on her devotion beads.

"How about at the beginning?" Léonie suggested through clenched teeth.

"Three months ago, I was given the assignment to locate Marcellus Bonnefaçon," Cerise began, turning her gaze on him. Marcellus swallowed and tried to focus on her right eye. The other one, with its vibrant shade of Ministère orange, was too unsettling. Too probing. Too out of place in this Refuge with its vintage technology and First World books. "I was able to track him to a decommissioned silo east of Vallonay. Would you like the coordinates?"

"How did you track him?" Marguerite asked with wide eyes. She'd worked so hard to keep the Vangarde's new network hidden from Ministère technology.

"Chatine Renard led me there."

At the mention of her name, Marcellus felt a clawing at his throat. He still didn't know where she was, but every time he dared think about her, a powerful ache in his chest threatened to overtake him. She was the freezing-cold ocean he never wanted to wade into but that still beckoned him every single day. Once again, he hoped Roche was with her and was looking out for her.

"I performed a periphery examination of the silo," Cerise was now saying, "but was unable to ascertain its function at the time. Shortly after, I spotted Marcellus Bonnefaçon traveling northeast through a wheat-fleur field."

Marcellus's attention slammed back into focus. "You were there? Were you the one who called the Policier?"

"Naturally," Cerise replied as though this were a redundant question. "May I continue?"

Chastised, Marcellus quietly nodded.

"The Policier arrested Jolras Epernay, an affiliate of the Red Scar."

"But he escaped," Marcellus cut in again. "Do you have any idea how he did that?"

"I do not," replied Cerise. "The Policier report gave no details. It was simply marked as a breakout. But at the time of his original arrest, this device was found on his person." Cerise tapped on the récepteur she'd set on the dining room table upon her arrival.

"I was able to use this device to intercept your communications at the Empereur's coronation ceremony."

"How?" Marguerite countered. "I deactivated that device."

"I reactivated it," Cerise replied simply.

Marguerite shrank back, looking dejected.

"That was you?" Denise asked Cerise. "The other récepteur online that day?"

"Yes."

Denise looked far more impressed than annoyed. She even nodded at Cerise as though they were sharing some kind of secret cyborg salute. "Well done."

"Merci," said Cerise, returning the gesture. "And I must commend you as well. The hologram hack was impressive. The Bureau is still trying to figure out how you managed it." She turned back to the group. "Once I was able to establish that you were using an unregistered network for your communications, I attempted to trace the signal with the Ministère's standard triangulation program."

"And it didn't work?" Marguerite looked hopeful.

"It did not," confirmed Cerise. "Apparently, you are operating on a network that Ministère technology does not recognize. Which is why I was forced to abandon my Ministère-issued TéléCom and employ this one instead." She tapped on the device in front of her.

"So whose TéléCom is that?" asked Clare.

"It belonged to my former self."

Noëlle's forehead creased. "What?"

"She means the person she was before her surgery," Denise translated.

"My former self built a program that is capable of not only identifying unregistered networks, but tracing them as well."

"And you used it to trace the signal here," Denise concluded.

"That is correct."

Léonie clenched her hand around her rayonette. "This is going nowhere. She's definitely stalling."

Cerise pinned her with her cybernetic eye. "I was going to begin with the evidence. *You* requested the full explanation."

Léonie jabbed her tongue against the inside of her cheek but said nothing.

"I was in the process of delivering the location of your base—this base—to the Empereur," Cerise said, and Marcellus felt everyone draw in a collective breath, stealing all the oxygen from the room at once. "But before I could relay the information, I overheard the Empereur on an Air-Link connection."

This surprised Marcellus. He hadn't expected the story to take this particular turn. "With who?" he asked.

"Mylène LaPorte."

Marcellus flashed back to the woman who'd glared at him through the hologram cams, all the way from Kaishi's skytower. "The System Alliance's Laterrian delegate?"

"Yes," Cerise replied. "But you might recall, she was formerly an officer under the command of General Bonnefaçon."

"Right," Marcellus replied hesitantly. "She was in charge of the investigation of the Premier Enfant's mur—" The words evaporated on his tongue as he remembered what Cerise had said only moments ago.

Evidence.

His heart started to pound. Could this be . . . ? Could she have . . . ? He shut down the questions instantly. He didn't want to let himself hope. He didn't dare. Mabelle had told him months ago that searching for proof was a lost cause.

"You won't find it. The general is a clever, careful man. He would have covered his tracks too well. Distanced himself from the crime to ensure it could never be traced back to him."

And Marcellus had believed that.

Wholeheartedly.

Until now.

"What did you find?" Marcellus rushed toward Cerise. He placed both hands on the table and leaned forward, fighting the urge to rip the TéléCom right out from under her.

If Cerise was in any way fazed by his sudden outburst, she didn't show it. She didn't show anything but a calm, restrained flicker of her circuitry. "The Empereur told me that he did not kill the Premier Enfant."

Marcellus snorted. "Yeah, he's lying."

Cerise's head clicked up to stare at him. "How did you know?"

"Because I lived with the man my entire life."

"But . . . ," Cerise began, sounding uncertain. "You're human."

"What?" Marcellus's brow crinkled.

Denise flashed the cyborg a patient look. "Human beings sometimes have the rare ability to emulate cyborg deduction *without* enhancements."

Cerise considered this for a moment before Léonie let out a groan. "Can you just tell us what you found already?"

If the atmosphere in this room hadn't been so tense, Marcellus *might* have cracked a smile, remembering a similar frustration he'd felt when Cerise had tracked him down to tell him she'd uncovered an encrypted message from Albion. She'd milked that moment for everything it was worth, loving being the one in control of the suspense. Perhaps there *was* still a glimmer of the old Cerise left.

"I, too, was able to decrypt the Empereur's true meaning," Cerise said to Marcellus. "And when I deduced that he was lying, I used the program developed by my former self to trace the Empereur's AirLink connection through his private, secure network."

"The Empereur has his own network?" asked Marguerite.

"Yes," said Cerise. "It's unregistered. The Ministère has no record of it."

"And?" Marcellus leaned forward again. "Were you able to access the AirLink? With LaPorte?"

"The AirLink was encrypted. With one of the stronger encryptions I've come across."

"But not strong enough for you," Alouette said quietly. It was the first time she'd spoken since she'd demanded Cerise be let into the Refuge, and now Marcellus could see a look of pride pass over her face as she stared almost lovingly at Cerise.

"I *am* a decryption spécialiste," Cerise said, with a gentle flickering of her circuitry. "And it did help that two weeks ago, the Empereur granted me access to all of the Ministère's most powerful processors for a special project he was working on." She tapped twice on the TéléCom and turned it toward the group.

Two faces were positioned side by side on the screen. One was Marcellus's grandfather and the other was Delegate Mylène LaPorte. From the star-filled view behind her, she was evidently sitting in her private office in the skytower.

"I feel I must inform you, Empereur," said LaPorte, "that your grandson made an unscheduled appearance at one of our recent sessions, requesting that the System Alliance reverse our appointment."

Eleven pairs of eyes swiveled toward Marcellus. Some looked betrayed, others simply surprised. He cleared his throat awkwardly and was grateful when his grandfather's response pulled everyone's attention back to the screen.

"Is that so? And what was the reaction from the other delegates?"

"Of course, they rejected the request. And I made certain they knew of his ties to the Vangarde terrorists."

"I see," said Empereur Bonnefaçon, scratching his chin. "Well, I appreciate you bringing this to my attention. It sounds like you were able to defuse the situation effectively."

"Yes, Empereur. Nothing to worry about on that front. However, there is something else."

There was a pause, during which Marcellus's grandfather raised a single eyebrow.

"He mentioned the Premier Enfant." LaPorte swallowed. "And repeated what Alouette Taureau said at your coronation."

The Empereur's face darkened. "Really? He actually accused me of being behind the murder in front of the entire Alliance?"

"Yes," said LaPorte, before rushing to add, "but I was quick to quash these allegations, reminding the delegates once again of the Vangarde's history of spreading falsehoods. No one was even somewhat suspicious that Marcellus was telling the truth."

Marcellus pinched the bridge of his nose. The room was starting to spin. It was all just too much. Too fast. His tired, underfed brain couldn't keep up.

"Well, let's hope you're right about that," warned the Empereur.

"I'm right," LaPorte said confidently.

"And you're sure there's nothing out there that can implicate either of us?"

"Absolutely. I followed your instructions exactly. As far as the evidence is concerned, Nadette Epernay is guilty."

Even though Cerise had ended the playback, everyone still stared at the screen in a stunned silence. It was Marcellus who spoke first.

"LaPorte?" he whispered in disbelief. "She was behind this?" He'd always known his grandfather had to have been working with someone. He'd had to have someone do his dirty work for him. Marcellus had just assumed it would have been Inspecteur Limier. But now, after watching this, he realized that his grandfather would never have been able to use a cyborg. They were designed to be incorruptible. Incapable of betraying the Regime.

But then how did . . .

He narrowed his eyes suspiciously at Cerise. "Why are you bringing this to us? To the Vangarde? Haven't we been marked as enemies of the Regime? And aren't you supposed to be unwaveringly loyal to the *Empereur*?"

The shift was instantaneous. One second Cerise was seated calmly at the dining room table, her circuitry humming in a steady, even rhythm. The next, it was as though something had exploded inside of her. She began to tremble. To convulse. The tiny nodes implanted in her skin lit up like stars in the night TéléSky. She opened her mouth, seemingly to try to speak, but only a strange stuttering sound emerged.

"T-t-t-t-t . . ."

Marcellus took an instinctive step back, as though Cerise were an explosif about to detonate.

"What's happening to her?" asked Nicolette.

"Is the Ministère doing that?" asked Léonie.

"Is she okay?" asked Noëlle.

"It's a rationality loop," said Denise.

Marcellus scowled. "A what?"

"A glitch in her programming."

"T-t-t-t-t . . ."

As Cerise continued to sputter like a stalled engine, Marcellus glanced around the room at the sisters. All of them shared matching expressions of bewilderment laced with fear. All but two.

Denise and Alouette were both watching Cerise not with confusion but with compassion.

Denise took a step toward Cerise, as though wanting to help her, comfort her, but Alouette pulled her back. "No," she said quietly. "I'll do it."

As Alouette slowly and carefully approached the trembling cyborg, Marcellus squeezed his hands into fists. He wanted so badly to yank her back, to protect her from what was certainly a terrible idea that would not end well. But there was something about the determination in Alouette's eyes—the *comprehension*—that made him hesitate.

She understood.

Somehow, she knew exactly what she was doing.

With a lump building in his throat, Marcellus watched Alouette walk around the side of the table, bend down low toward Cerise's ear, and whisper something he couldn't hear. He held his breath, waiting for the inevitable. A strike. An outburst. An explosion.

But none of that came.

Instead, the stuttering stopped. The tremors stilled. Cerise's body seemed to collapse in on itself like a dying star.

And then, Marcellus saw it. The flash of dark brown in the cyborg's left eye. The same flash he'd seen in the hallway of Fret 6 during the riot.

A flicker of Cerise Chevalier.

The *real* Cerise Chevalier.

Cerise blinked as though waking from a dream and focused on Alouette first before sweeping her gaze to Marcellus. "Because we're friends," she said.

It had been so long since he'd asked the question, he almost didn't understand the response.

"And because I want to help the Vangarde." Cerise's voice was still monotone, still a cyborg, but there was something behind it that wasn't there before. It was both new and familiar at the same time. "I am sympathetic to the Third Estate cause. I am a . . ." She paused, as though searching for the right word in her vast and endless database of information. "A sympathizeur."

Alouette smiled, her eyes glassy with tears. Marcellus felt a rustle of something pass through the dining room. It felt like wind. But it was just his captured breath breaking free. He reached out and grabbed Alouette's hand. She squeezed and, in her dark eyes, Marcellus saw a reflection of his own thoughts. His own relief.

She's back.

"So, what do we do now?" asked Sister Noëlle.

"We have to use this," Sister Marguerite said, pointing to the TéléCom screen, which was still frozen on the side-by-side faces of Empereur Bonnefaçon and Mylène LaPorte. "This is the only proof we have that he's been lying."

"It's not the only proof," Cerise said, and they all looked back at her. Her circuitry was still flashing faintly, but where her chilling cybernetic eye had once been, there was now a dark, unwavering, permanent brown hue. "This footage was stored on a private server, where the Empereur keeps archives of all his AirLink connections."

"WHAT?" Marcellus spat.

"I was surprised as well," said Cerise evenly. "But apparently, my former self already knew this. Or at least, she suspected. Because she sent me a message, directing me to use her program to find this server, where she claimed I would discover evidence of the Empereur's crimes. There are over two years of archived files there."

"Two years," Marcellus whispered. "Ever since . . ."

"Lyon Paresese became Patriarche," Alouette finished the thought.

"That's how long he's been plotting against the Regime." Marcellus squeezed his temples, feeling like his head might actually explode. "Are you saying . . . you have access to all my grandfather's AirLinks from the past *two* years?"

Cerise nodded once. The sisters exchanged incredulous looks.

"Obviously, decrypting them will take some time," Cerise said.

"We can help," Denise offered eagerly. "We'll devote every server we have to running your decryption program."

"And then what?" asked Nicolette.

"Isn't it obvious?" replied Marcellus. "We have to send the footage to the System Alliance. All of it. Whatever implicates my grandfather. This will change their minds."

Hushed murmurings broke out among the sisters, only to be quieted a moment later by Citizen Rousseau. As usual, the Vangarde leader spoke with a clear, calm conviction. "The System Alliance can't help us."

Marcellus clenched his teeth. "But my grandfather must be stopped. If we show this to them, they'll have no choice but to withdraw their appointment."

"Exactly," said Rousseau. "And then what? The Empereur is ousted from the Palais, and they simply appoint someone else to take his place. The System Alliance wants more of the same. They want an absolute ruler who will not threaten their own ways of life. This is our chance to do something bigger. This is our moment to enact *real* change. This is the catalyst we've been waiting for. Laterre has been asleep for far too long. Lulled into a trance by the Empereur's soothing lies. With this evidence, we can finally wake them up. Taking it to the System Alliance is a waste of time. This needs to go straight to the people."

- PART 5 -
THE FRETS

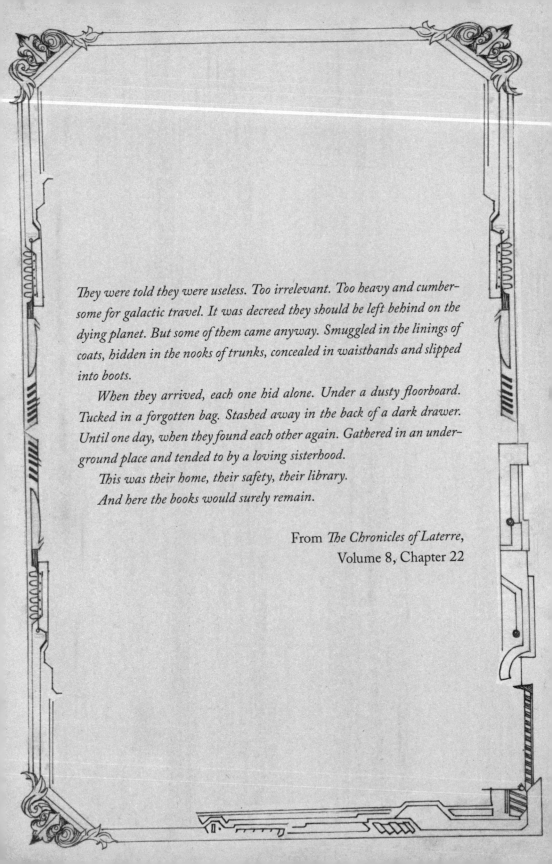

They were told they were useless. Too irrelevant. Too heavy and cumbersome for galactic travel. It was decreed they should be left behind on the dying planet. But some of them came anyway. Smuggled in the linings of coats, hidden in the nooks of trunks, concealed in waistbands and slipped into boots.

When they arrived, each one hid alone. Under a dusty floorboard. Tucked in a forgotten bag. Stashed away in the back of a dark drawer. Until one day, when they found each other again. Gathered in an underground place and tended to by a loving sisterhood.

This was their home, their safety, their library.

And here the books would surely remain.

From *The Chronicles of Laterre*,
Volume 8, Chapter 22

CHAPTER 61

MARCELLUS

THE FOOTAGE REEL LOOPED FOR THE TENTH TIME, broadcasting what Marcellus had privately named "Empereur Bonnefaçon's Greatest Hits" to the entire planet. As he sat at one of the workstations in the now-empty Assemblée room, he imagined all the techniciens and spécialistes at the Ministère headquarters desperately trying to find the source of Denise's hack, trying to stop every hologram on Laterre from revealing his grandfather's deepest, darkest secrets.

For the *tenth* time.

Everyone in the Refuge had worked through the night, scanning months of archived AirLinks, running them through Cerise's decryption program, sorting, assembling, editing it all together to create this masterpiece that now played on the screen in front of Marcellus, filling him with a sense of vindication and relief the likes of which he never knew existed.

Two years of deception and lies and evil boiled down into a shocking montage that Cerise had programmed to play on repeat.

A whispered plot to inject one of Marie Paresse's morning peaches with cyanide.

A corrupt officer covering all the tracks.

A bogus investigation into the murder.

An innocent governess framed, for the sole reason that she happened to be a convenient and dispensable scapegoat.

Then, the footage darkened, grew more sinister, as the general's plot widened.

Secret, encrypted AirLinks across the Asteroid Channel.

Hushed conversations with the High Chancellor to the Albion Queen.

A weapon designed to control the Third Estate.

The proof was all there, displayed across a network of holograms that the Empereur had installed himself. His own propaganda machine was now being used against him. His own words coming back to destroy him.

The montage came to an end, the screen went black, and Marcellus counted the seconds, wondering if this would be the time the Ministère would finally figure it out, would finally find a hole in Denise's hack.

But then, it started again. And Marcellus couldn't help but smile.

As the footage looped for the eleventh time, Marcellus tore his gaze away from the large monitor in the center of the Assemblée room and focused on the smaller screen in front of him, where a new batch of decrypted files from the AirLink archive had just populated.

He selected the first one and, with his chin cupped in his hand, settled himself in to watch.

"Month 4, Day 7, Year 504," announced the screen before launching into the footage. It was an uneventful conversation between the general and his former commandeur, Michele Vernay, discussing output numbers from the droid fabrique.

Marcellus swiped it from the screen and selected the next one from the same day. But this was even less interesting than the last. He swiped again. His eyelids were starting to get heavy. The excitement of the past day was wearing off and the fatigue was setting in. He nearly fell asleep in the middle of a conversation about the development of some kind of new droid operating system but caught himself just in time and slapped both of his cheeks to rouse himself before selecting the next file.

"Maybe you should call it a night?" came a voice from behind him. Marcellus jumped and turned to find Alouette watching him. How long had she been there?

"I know." He sighed. "But look at this."

He cleared the screen of the current footage and pulled up the one he'd found hours ago and had been waiting to show someone.

"It's from three days ago," Marcellus said as he pressed play and an older man's face appeared next to his grandfather's.

"Who is that?" Alouette asked, lowering herself into a nearby chair.

"His name is Admiral Bosquet. Last I knew, he was in command of the Masséna spacecraft carrier, but now . . ." Marcellus sighed and turned up the volume. "Just listen."

". . . I'm afraid the damage to the landing bay and primary hangar was quite extensive," the admiral was saying. "We were able to seal off the rest of the carrier, but we still suffered a giant loss. My vice admiral is dead, along with plenty of good sergents and maintenance workers. And we lost almost the entire combatteur fleet, except for . . ." Admiral Bosquet took a deep breath, like he was trying to prepare for the backlash.

"Except for what?" the Empereur demanded.

"Except for the craft the perpetrators escaped in."

Empereur Bonnefaçon started to ask a question, but the admiral preempted it. "And no, we haven't been able to track the craft. It was still in queue for upgrade installations. Which means it has no tracking capabilities and no biometric lock pairing. But we're doing our best to try to locate it using other measures."

The Empereur's face fell into a deep grimace. "And you have no idea who is responsible?"

"None, sir. We believe there were four of them. Clearly trained in espionage, as we still have no idea how they infiltrated our security measures. They snuck in on one of their own ships."

"An Albion ship?" the Empereur asked, looking somewhat alarmed.

The admiral shook his head. "I don't think so. It wasn't a vessel I'd ever come across before. It almost looked rudimentary in its design. Like it was made out of spare parts. Very unusual."

Alouette looked to Marcellus, who was already nodding in agreement before she even uttered the question. "The Défecteurs?"

"What if it is? What if it's Etienne? And Chatine? He said there were four of them. With Gabriel and Roche, that makes four." Marcellus didn't even want to entertain the possibility. It made him physically ill to think about. And it was a long shot. But after a week and a half with absolutely no word from her or Roche, he was grasping at anything.

"But what would they have been doing on the Masséna spacecraft carrier?" Alouette asked. "You told me they were looking for stolen zyttrium."

"That's the thing," said Marcellus. "I don't think this AirLink was sent from the Masséna. Listen to this. . . ." He fast-forwarded the footage and pressed play again.

"What about the primary fleet?" his grandfather was now asking.

"The invadeurs are still intact," replied the admiral. "And because we were able to seal off the carrier so quickly, there is no delay in our production timeline. The fleet will be ready for deployment on schedule. But the debris from the landing bay was quite significant. I can't be certain that it won't appear on any scans."

Marcellus pressed pause. "The Masséna doesn't have a production hangar. They don't build ships there. Especially not invadeurs. They only dispatch. And that thing he said about the scans? Why would my grandfather be worried about showing up on scans? The Masséna is a registered vessel of the Laterrian Spaceforce. Everyone in the Alliance knows about it. It's not a secret."

"So, are you thinking your grandfather has another spacecraft carrier somewhere that no one knows about?" Alouette asked. "And that maybe Etienne and Chatine snuck onto it when they were looking for stolen zyttrium?"

Marcellus ran his fingers through his already-disheveled hair. He hadn't realized how ridiculous it sounded until she'd said it aloud. "Yes? No? Maybe. I don't know what to think anymore."

There was silence beside him and then he felt Alouette's hand land on his shoulder. Her grip was tender, supportive, yet firm at the same time. "Why don't you get some sleep?"

Marcellus shook his head and swiped to the next file. "No. I have to keep going."

He pressed play and listened to his grandfather discuss output levels with the foreman of the meatpacking fabrique. He scrolled quickly to the end of it and clicked on another.

"What are you hoping to find?" Alouette asked.

He shrugged. "I don't know. Something. Anything. *Everything.*" He flung his hand toward the monitor, where a new batch of decrypted files were lining up behind the others. "I can't just stop now that I know all of this is here. Right at my fingertips."

"But the truth is out. Your grandfather has been exposed. To everyone. First, Second, *and* Third Estate." Alouette pointed to the large monitor, still showing the montage of "Empereur Bonnefaçon's Greatest Hits." What loop were they on now? Fourteen? Fifteen? Marcellus had lost count. "The people will rally with us now. We've done enough. *You've* done enough."

Marcellus sighed and turned down the volume on a tedious conversation about projected yearly exports to Samsara. "But what if there's more? What if he has more secrets? Even darker ones?" He gestured to the footage feeding out to all of Laterre. "We knew what to look for to find all of this. We knew all the right search terms. But what about the things we *don't* know to search for? What about everything else he's hiding? I know my grandfather well enough to know that this"—he pointed again at the looped footage—"is not everything."

"Maybe not," Alouette said, and in her voice he heard that same kindness and compassion that he'd always admired in her. No matter what he was going through, no matter how worked up he got, she always seemed to be vibrating on some lower, calmer frequency. "But it'll take you months to watch all this footage. When does it stop?"

Marcellus furrowed his brow. "What do you mean?"

"I mean, when is it enough?"

He blew out another breath and reached to select the next file. "I don't know."

Alouette put a hand over his, pulling it back. "You need to know. Or you'll kill yourself trying to find out. And then who wins?"

Marcellus glanced down at her long fingers wrapped around his hand. He knew she was right. If there was one thing he'd learned about Alouette, it was that she was usually right, especially when it came to him and his grandfather.

But then, he looked back up at the screen, at all of those files still waiting, still taunting him with their possibility of secrets. Of lies.

He gave Alouette a sheepish, almost apologetic look and clicked on the next one.

"Month 7, Day 42, Year 505." The face of Directeur Chevalier appeared side by side with his grandfather's, and the two immediately launched into an update about the most recent batch of cyborg candidates scheduled for surgery.

Alouette let out a sigh and stood from her chair. Marcellus didn't dare look back at her for fear of seeing the disappointment etched into her face. But honestly, what else was he to do? Cerise had given them a gift. A piece of magic. She'd given them access to things Marcellus only dreamed about. Encrypted conversations behind hidden doors. Locked vaults jammed full of information.

Empereur Bonnefaçon might have been exposed, his secrets might be out, but he still wore the crown on his head. And he would not give up without a fight.

Therefore, neither would Marcellus.

"There's another matter I wish to discuss with you," Directeur Chevalier was saying on the AirLink. "My daughter, Cerise."

Curious, Marcellus turned the volume back up.

"As you know, she's going into surgery this afternoon," said the directeur.

"Yes," replied General Bonnefaçon, his voice tightening ever so slightly. "The surgery will be good for her. Program some obedience into the girl."

"Exactly," said the directeur, and Marcellus could almost feel the tension between the two men. He accessed the time stamp again and quickly did the calculations. This AirLink occurred the day after the Ascension banquet. The day after Cerise was caught sneaking them into the Palais.

"Are you thinking médecin?" asked the general.

"No. Technicien. She's very good with . . ." The directeur paused as though trying to find the right word. "Devices. She's been taking them apart since she was a child."

The general nodded. "That explains a lot. Well, you don't need my permission, Directeur. I don't tell you how to run your department."

"Of course," replied Chevalier. "But I do need your permission to make any modifications to the standard surgical procedures."

The general cocked an interested eyebrow. "You want to alter her operation?"

Directeur Chevalier looked pained by the question. "I . . . ," he started, and then decided to rephrase. "Cerise is a very unique girl. I've been keeping a close eye on her for many years. She has tremendous potential. Off the charts. But, as we've both recently witnessed, she also has a tendency to disregard authority."

Marcellus leaned forward, uneasiness churning in his gut. He'd never seen the directeur look so visibly uncomfortable. He was having trouble keeping constant eye contact with the general.

Directeur Chevalier rubbed anxiously at his gray beard before finally blurting out, "I'm worried that the procedure might not fully take."

Comprehension dawned on the general's face and he nodded solemnly. "You think she's susceptible to a system-wide malfunction?"

Chevalier released a shaky breath, like he was grateful not to be the one to have to say it. "Yes. Obviously malfunctions are rare, and despite our efforts, we still haven't been able to pinpoint exactly why or how they occur, but given that we've witnessed how devastating they can be to the Ministère in the past—namely, two specific cases—I think it's prudent to be cautious and be on the lookout for any warning signs ahead of time."

"Is he talking about Denise and Brigitte?" Alouette asked, slipping back into the seat next to Marcellus. He hadn't realized she was still in the room.

He shook his head. "I don't know." And they both turned back to the screen with wide, eager eyes.

"I agree," said the general. "What did you have in mind?"

Chevalier sat up straighter in his office chair, reverting back to the version of himself that Marcellus recognized. Sharp, no-nonsense, just the slightest bit scary. "Cyborgs are an investment. As you know, they're expensive to create. They also hold a lot of classified information. About our systems, our technology, even the layout of our departments. It's a dangerous threat to have one of them turn on us. We've made improvements to the procedure over the years, obviously, but in certain scenarios, like with my daughter, I think it best to take extra precautions. Which is why I'm proposing a slight alteration to Cerise's procedure. Something we don't normally do but I feel is necessary in this case. It's an insurance policy of sorts. To ensure that, if she malfunctions, she is, at least, recoverable."

Something cold slithered down Marcellus's spine, and he exchanged another wary look with Alouette.

"The modification is actually quite simple," the directeur continued, sounding nothing like a parent whose child was about to undergo major surgery. There wasn't a hint of concern in his voice. "The médecin will simply insert a small tracking device in her left inner ear. It's relatively undetectable. She might experience minor interferences with certain technologies, but otherwise, she will have no idea it's there. We will set the default mode to inactive, but it can be activated remotely at any time."

The general shifted in his seat, folding his hands under his chin. "Sounds reasonable. I give you full authority to do whatever you think needs to be done, Directeur."

CHAPTER 62

ETIENNE

SPACE SEEMED TO SWALLOW HIM UP AND SPIT HIM OUT. Over and over and over. Etienne stared out the window of the combatteur's passenger hold and wished the stars would turn off. Just stop. Their light was nothing more than a tease. An endless sparkling sea of reminders. Every kilomètre they flew, every minute that brought them closer to Laterre, Etienne felt the stars crushing down on his chest.

He would have to tell them. He would have to stand up in front of the whole community and tell them that he failed. Some people would turn away, hiding their disappointment. Others would have the courage to face him, sorrow reflecting in their eyes. Mentor Ava would already be calling for more proposals. More ideas. More ways to save the community. His maman would wrap her arms around him, tell him he was brave, he had done his best.

But had he?

Could he have done something different?

Saved the zyttrium?

Saved her?

"Zoom! Zoom! Zoom!" A tiny body came barreling through the passenger hold, followed closely behind by another. "You can't catch me! I'm a combatteur! Zoom! Zoom! Zoom!"

"I can catch you! I'm a combatteur too!"

"I'm a faster one!"

The two children made a lap around the small cluster of seats and disappeared back into the cockpit. They'd been playing this same game for hours, and Etienne had lost his patience with it two minutes in. Normally, he loved children, and their story was sadder than any he'd ever heard. Abandoned and forgotten. Grabbed off the streets. Thrust into cages. Shipped off to a terrifying spacecraft carrier to work until their knuckles bled and their fingers blistered. They had regaled everyone on the combatteur with all the details.

Adèle, the slightly older of the two, but still no more than seven, had been tasked with building the circuit boards for the pilote consoles, while Léopold had been put to work in the stealth processing center, forced to breathe in noxious fumes as zyttrium was processed and fed into those deadly invadeurs and combatteurs.

Zyttrium.

There had been so much of it packed into that storage facility. The sight of it all had made Etienne's head spin. Much more than just what was taken from the camp. Enough to last a thousand voyages across the System. Or a thousand battles, which was much more likely given the size of that fleet.

He'd had it in his possession. He'd been this close to saving the camp. And then . . .

He pulled his knees up to his chest and squeezed his arms around them, as if he could trap something inside of him. A sensation. A memory. The feeling of being so close. Of having the zyttrium—the camp's salvation—in his possession.

"Now you can't see me!" squealed Adèle as she charged into the passenger hold again.

"I can see you!" cried Léopold in her wake. "And my explosif launcher is going to shoot you out of the sky!"

"No, you can't! I'm stealth!" Adèle spun and was about to make another lap around the cargo hold when Chatine stepped out of the cockpit and grabbed her.

"Okay, okay. That was a fun game. For everyone. But I think it's time now to sit down and rest."

"But we're combatteurs!" protested Adèle.

"Yeah! Stealth ones!"

"Well, maybe you can be sleeping combatteurs for a while," said Chatine, her voice ragged with fatigue.

"I don't think you should have given them those protéine bars," said Gabriel, emerging from the cockpit, rubbing at red-rimmed eyes.

Chatine gritted her teeth. "That's all the food there was on the ship."

"Where is Roche?" asked Gabriel. "Isn't he supposed to be taking care of them? Aren't they *his* bébés or whatever?"

"He's napping in the sleeping pod," Chatine muttered.

"Smart kid," said Gabriel.

"Can we fly the combatteur?" asked Léopold.

"No," said Chatine. "The ship is in autopilote mode right now. And *you* should be in sleep mode."

"We don't want to sleep," said Adèle. "We were never allowed inside the ships. And this is the soopest one I've ever seen!"

Etienne felt Chatine's eyes land on him for just a second before turning back to the kids. "This ship is all right. I've seen much better, though."

He knew what she was doing. He appreciated it. But it didn't help. Nothing helped.

"Let's go flush the space toilettes again!" suggested Léopold.

"Yeah!" cried Adèle, and the two took off toward the small bathroom.

Gabriel collapsed into one of the passenger seats. "Fric. Do all kids have that much energy?"

"I think they're just making up for lost time," said Chatine. "Adèle said they've been working on that carrier for more than two mon—"

Gabriel cut her off with a warning look and tilted his head toward Etienne in a far-from-subtle gesture. They'd been flying for almost four days, and Chatine and Gabriel had made it a point not to talk about what had happened on the spacecraft carrier in front of him.

But this was not a big ship. He'd heard their whispered conversations when they thought he wasn't listening. He'd put all the pieces together.

The man who now called himself Empereur had kidnapped thousands of Third Estaters to build a fleet of deadly stealth crafts. In less than two weeks, he was sending them to invade Usonia for the Albion Queen.

And Etienne didn't need to understand gridder politics to know this wasn't good.

"Arrival on Laterre in two hours." The voice of the ship seemed to crash through everyone's thoughts at once. It was so cold, so sterile, it felt like a punch in the face by a frozen droid.

Etienne looked up at Chatine, whose eyes were already waiting for him, waiting to catch him. It was still so amazing to him how much she could convey with those cat-like eyes of hers. How many things she could say without saying anything at all.

She cleared her throat. "I'll, um, see if I can shut that voice off."

Chatine disappeared back into the cockpit, and Etienne was alone with Gabriel. He returned his attention out the window. He couldn't stand the way Gabriel looked at him now. Like he was as miserable and pathetic as those kids. Like *he* was the true sob story here.

"So—" Gabriel started to say, his voice light and artificially airy.

"Don't," Etienne cut him off.

"But—"

"Just don't."

"Well, you can't mope around forever, mec."

Etienne sighed. Just *once* he wished Gabriel would actually shut up when he told him to. Was that really too much to ask? To let him grieve in peace? To let him stew in his wretched thoughts all by himself?

"If your maman were here, she'd tell you to talk about it, don't hold it in—"

"Yeah, but she's not here, is she?" Etienne finally exploded, like he was another faulty thruster that had taken its last hit. "I'm here. Because they sent *me*. The community gave *me* the job of finding the zyttrium."

"Which you did," Gabriel pointed out. "Quite spectacularly. I mean, goldenroot? To take out the maintenance workers?" Gabriel smacked his knee. "Sheer genius."

Etienne knew what Gabriel was trying to do too. They were all tiptoeing around him like he was one wrong-footed step away from shattering. They were all trying to stroke his ego, make him feel like he'd done something more than just fail.

He turned back to the window, cursing the stars and all of their brilliance.

He could hear Gabriel fidgeting behind him, gearing himself up to speak again, to attempt another daring walk across this tightrope between them. Etienne poised the bitter comeback on the tip of his tongue. But it dissolved in an instant when Gabriel whispered, "She died a hero's death, you know?"

Etienne cut his eyes to Gabriel. "What?"

"Marilyn," Gabriel said, and the name was like a thousand knives plunged into his heart. "She didn't die for nothing. She saved our lives."

Etienne scoffed. "She was just a ship."

Even as he said it, he could feel the sting of his own betrayal. What did it matter, though? She couldn't hear him. She wasn't listening. Because the truth was, she *was* just a ship. She had always been just a ship. Not a friend. Not a partner. Just a vehicle that he'd built to get him from one place to another.

That happened to have a very sexy voice.

Gabriel chuckled and rested a hand on Etienne's shoulder. "No, she wasn't."

And without thinking, Etienne reached up and placed his hand over Gabriel's. For a moment, the two men just stood there, understanding each other, listening to each other breathe. Until Etienne uttered the one word he was sure he'd never said to Gabriel before. "Merci."

Gabriel squeezed his shoulder once before pulling away, just as a series of joyful shrieks shot out from the bathroom. He sighed. "You don't happen to have any more of that goldenroot lying around somewhere, do you?"

Etienne cracked a smile and shook his head.

"Okay, I'll have to do this the hard way." Gabriel cracked his knuckles once before calling out, "Hey! Kids! Who wants to lie down and listen to Uncle Gabriel tell them a story about the time I broke into an Albion weapons complex?"

He disappeared down the steps, and the passenger hold refilled with that same heavy silence. Etienne peered back out the window, marveling at how stationary the stars looked. The ship was traveling so fast, tearing through space at hundreds of thousands of kilomètres an hour, and the stars didn't even seem to notice. They just went about their lives, kept to themselves, kept shining, regardless of the turmoil and chaos that broke out in their midst.

Like us.

It was a thought that usually brought him comfort. To know that his community would always be as stationary and resilient as those stars. Living outside the chaos, shining on their own, without any help, without the Ministère's powerful grids, whose energy and light came at such a high price.

But now, Empereur Bonnefaçon had stolen all of that from them.

Just like he'd stolen from so many other communities.

Just like he'd stolen Etienne's father.

Suddenly, he couldn't look at those stars anymore. Couldn't bear their relentless taunts. They were awakening something within him. A monster he'd lulled to sleep long ago.

He tore his gaze away from the window just as Chatine rushed back into the passenger hold.

"Etienne," she said, and the urgency in her voice made the hairs on the back of his neck stand up. "Can you come see this?"

Etienne hesitated, eyeing the door to the cockpit like it was on fire. In all the time they'd been on this Ministère ship, he hadn't dared step foot through that door. It was bad enough he had to sit in here, in this plush passenger hold, surrounded by leather-clad cabin walls and buffed-metal floors so polished he could see his own reflection.

"Please?" Chatine said after more than five seconds had passed and Etienne still hadn't moved.

He wasn't sure if it was that word—such a foreign word on Chatine's lips—or the way her voice cracked around it, but it was enough. Slowly, Etienne stood up and followed her through the doorway of fire.

The cockpit was just as he'd imagined. Rows of glowing monitors, ranks of blinking control panels, two high-backed pilote seats separated by a sleek, glinting contrôleur, and a spotless wraparound windshield that looked out onto the blackness of space. It all reminded him of Marilyn, and how hard he'd worked to make her the embodiment of everything this ship was not. He felt sick to his stomach and almost turned around, when he heard it.

A soft crackling sound, like one of the camp's radios struggling to receive a transmission.

But it wasn't coming from his radio, which now sat lifelessly on the copilote's seat. Of course it wasn't. They were still way too far from Laterre to pick up a signal.

It was coming from the console. But it was choppy, full of static. Etienne could only catch a few words.

". . . flight dispatch . . . all combatteurs . . . reroute . . ."

"What is that?" Etienne asked.

Chatine shuddered. "I don't know. I was trying to shut down the ship's voice alerts when I must have accidentally activated some kind of communication module. It's been the same message repeating over and over. I thought maybe you could do something to amplify it?"

"Why?" Etienne asked. He could think of a million things he'd rather do than use his skills to try to listen in on a Ministère communication network.

"Because we're flying in a stolen combatteur," Chatine said in a voice that told Etienne she'd assumed the reason was obvious.

He sighed and lowered himself into the capitaine's seat. It felt hard and unwelcoming beneath him, like it wanted to eject him right out of the cockpit.

Meanwhile, the message continued to repeat. ". . . flight dispatch . . . all combatteurs . . . reroute . . ."

Chatine stood behind him, rigid as stone, as he maneuvered around the console, searching for a signal booster. But he felt lost and disoriented. A stranger in a stranger land, trying to make sense of even stranger technology.

And then, his fingertip found its way up and to the left, sliding a slim lever across a small grid. The transmission crackled once before repeating again. This time, the static was still there, but they could hear the voice clearly.

"This is Ministère flight dispatch. All combatteurs in Laterrian airspace are ordered to reroute to Fret 7 in Vallonay."

- CHAPTER 63 -
CHATINE

"THERE'S STILL NO SIGNAL!" CHATINE CRIED AS SHE jammed the palm of her hand against the side of the radio.

"Well, hitting it is not going to help," said Etienne. He was in the capitaine's seat, flying the combatteur at speeds that were making Chatine dizzy. But she didn't complain. "We must still not be close enough. Our radios aren't strong enough to be used from space. And if the Refuge is underground, it's going to be even harder to reach them."

"I don't understand," Chatine said. "How did the Ministère even *find* the Refuge?"

"Are you certain that's what this is? They could be rerouting the combatteurs to Fret 7 for . . ."

"For what?" Chatine asked when Etienne's voice trailed off. "A *different* rebel group hiding underneath it?"

Etienne only shook his head. Because he must have known she was right. This had to be what she was afraid of. What she'd been the *most* afraid of for months.

There was only one reason to send combatteurs.

Only one objective.

"Can't you go any faster?" Chatine begged.

Etienne checked the gauge on the craft's vast control panel, which he had seemed to quickly get a handle on, much faster than Chatine had. "We're already at top supervoyage speed. We'll be within range of the community's network in a few minutes."

"They may not have a few minutes! What about hypervoyage?" Chatine cringed as she said it. The horrifying story Marcellus had told her about jumping to hypervoyage when they'd been trying to get back from Albion still haunted her.

"We're too close," said Etienne. "And combatteurs don't have hypervoyage engines. They're not built for deep-space travel. They're built for . . ."

His voice drifted off, but Chatine didn't need for him to say it aloud. She knew exactly what these crafts were built for. She'd seen it with her very eyes . . . twice. And now, an entire squadron of them were heading to Fret 7.

Through the cockpit window, amid the midnight blackness of space, Laterre grew larger as they hurtled toward it. Silver-gray with its unending cover of clouds and whirling in the void like a vast metallic spinning top, it was exquisite.

It was home.

But Chatine had no time to wonder at the sight of it.

She continued to fiddle with the radio, turning it on and off in desperate hope of connecting, all the while imagining the sisters and Marcellus tucked away in the Refuge, completely oblivious to the fact that a fleet of deadly combatteurs were headed straight toward them.

"Any more word from the Ministère?" Chatine asked, her voice rough and ragged from lack of sleep and now complete and total panic.

Etienne checked the control panel again. "No more transmissions have been sent from their flight dispatch. Or if they have, we're not picking them up."

Chatine gripped the armrests and shoved her head back into the seat, letting out a groan. "We have to warn them. We have to—"

"Chatine." Suddenly Etienne's hand was on hers. It was warm and soft and everything she needed right now. "We're doing everything we can. Just take a breath and keep checking for a signal."

She did as she was told, inhaling deeply before focusing back on the clunky radio in her hand. But just as she reached for the power button, prepared to cycle it on and off again, she heard it. It was beautiful. It was static, but it was beautiful.

Etienne glanced at her with sparkling, hopeful eyes and nodded toward the radio.

Chatine squeezed the red button with her thumb and spoke as clearly as her trembling voice would allow. "Hello? Come in. Come in. This is Chatine. The Refuge is in danger. You need to evacuate now. Do you copy?"

She released the button and waited, her heart taking up permanent residence in her throat. Seconds passed. All too slowly. And still no response.

Chatine tried again. "Hello? Can anyone hear me? Is anyone there? This is Chatine. Do you copy? Evacuate the Refuge now! I repeat, evacuate NOW!"

More time crawled by that felt like centuries. Laterre grew larger still through the cockpit window, but Chatine felt no closer to anything. They may as well be lost out in space for all the good she was doing.

"Please! Someone! Anyone! Can you hear me? You're in danger! Please!" Her voice broke. Tears sprang to her eyes, blurring everything around her.

"Maybe they've already left," Etienne said, his hand gripped firmly around the contrôleur, like he was using it to try to hold on to his own composure. "Maybe they were warned another way? Maybe—"

"Maybe no one is listening," Chatine said miserably, wiping at her eyes. She thought about the last place she'd seen the radio in the Refuge. The one that Etienne had first used to contact her. It had been left haphazardly on the desk under a mountain of Marcellus's research books and maps. Who knew if anyone was even *in* the library right now. It was the middle of the night in Vallonay. The sisters were probably still asleep or gathered in the Assemblée room. Her message would continue to go unheard until . . .

Until everything went unheard.

Their screams.

Their cries for help.

The fires lashing, burning, destroying everything.

The sound of static broke through Chatine's tears. Her hopes lifted and then crashed back down a second later as she and Etienne both realized where it was coming from. Not the radio in her hand. But the flight console.

Etienne turned up the volume as a steady female voice boomed out from the speaker.

"Attention, pilotes. This is Commandeur Moreau. Merci for responding so quickly to the reroute orders. As you all make your way to Vallonay, I can inform you that we have confirmed the location of the Vangarde base. It is hidden under Fret 7. As you know, the Vangarde have been a long-standing enemy of the Regime. We have chased their shadows for too long. And now we have finally caught up to them. You are being given the gift of heroism. Laterre will always look back on this day and recognize what you have done. How you have saved us from a dangerous threat. How you have won a long and well-fought victory."

There was a pause, during which the commandeur's voice seemed to falter. For a moment Chatine thought it was an unstable connection, but then, the commandeur cleared her throat, sounding like a woman fighting against her own doubts. Against her own conscience. "Your assignment," she continued, "is total annihilation of Fret 7. All explosifs deployed. Leave no survivors. I understand that this order might bring you some pause. I know, because I was once in your seat, with *my* hand on the trigger. I know what it feels like to hesitate when innocent lives are at risk." Another pause, another throat clear. "If there was any doubt in our minds that our greatest enemy was hiding underneath that building, we would not be asking you to do this. We coordinate a strike in thirty minutes and counting." The commandeur took an audible breath that seemed to suck all of the air out of the cockpit. "For the glory of all Laterre, destroy the base."

Chatine's stomach dropped out from under her as, just then, Etienne banked the ship to the left to start their approach into the Laterrian atmosphere. Her ears were ringing, as though they were already hearing the echoes of those blasts, reverberated backward through time.

It was just as she'd feared.

The Ministère had finally found the Refuge. She didn't know how, but they had. And now the general—the *Empereur*—was going to obliterate it. Just like he'd always wanted. Just like he'd intended to do all those months ago, when Chatine had sat in the passenger hold of one of these killing machines with a holographic map of Laterre glowing in front of her. She'd saved the Refuge then, but she was starting to doubt that she could do it again.

Chatine pressed her shaking hand to the red button once more. This time, her voice was less urgent, more resigned, less desperate, more mournful. "Hello? This is Chatine. Can anyone hear me? Please come in. You must evacuate now. Do you copy? The Refuge is . . ." But she couldn't even finish. Because the truth was, she had already given up. She was already grieving over their fallen bodies. Over Marcellus.

Etienne called toward the passenger hold for everyone to strap in for atmosphere break. And as they plunged into the swirls of gray and white clouds, Chatine felt their heaviness descend through her, their moisture soak her body, their violent storms shake her to the very core.

She bent her head over the radio and cried, huge sobs racking her body, tears cascading over the dials.

And then, just as they broke through the cloud coverage, and the vast city of Vallonay sprawled out before them, she heard the tiniest, most significant *click*.

"Yes . . . I . . . copy."

The voice was unfamiliar to Chatine. It did not belong to any of the sisters she'd lived with for the past three months. That she was sure of. And there was something broken about it, hesitant. Like it was speaking for the first time.

Or the first time in a while . . .

Chatine sat up straighter and fumbled with the radio, trying to orient herself amid her mess of tears and trembles. Finally, she plunged down on the red button and in a voice that came out half shudder, half sob, whispered, "Jacqui?"

- CHAPTER 64 -

ALOUETTE

FOR THE SECOND TIME IN TWO DAYS, THE EVACUATION
alarm blared through the Refuge. Alouette felt like her legs might collapse beneath her as she ran dizzily and breathlessly down the hallway.

She'd lived in this Refuge for thirteen years, and there wasn't a single day
that had passed when this hadn't been her nightmare. The Ministère knew
where they were. The Ministère had found them. The Ministère was coming.

Alouette's feet pounded harder against the tile floors.

Thirty minutes. That's what Chatine had reported. *Thirty minutes to save
as much as they could.*

At first, the news had been met with three silent seconds of shock.
Partly because of the news itself, partly because it was Sister Jacqui who
had delivered it, speaking for the first time in months. Speculations were
thrown around as to how this could have happened. The Empereur must
have known it was Cerise who had discovered his archived AirLink footage—she was the only one capable of decrypting it. And the hack that was
broadcasting it to the holograms was the same one that had disrupted his
coronation. He must have put the pieces together and realized Cerise was
working with the Vangarde.

That's when the fights had started. Léonie accused Cerise of setting a trap, of knowing about the tracker implanted inside her. Denise argued in Cerise's defense. More quickly joined the debate until Francine finally restored order and sounded the alarm. "Initiate evacuation procedures."

Those words—those nightmarish words—had sent everyone into panicked, chaotic motion.

But Alouette hadn't been able to move. Or breathe. Or think. The walls had felt like they were closing in. Her mind struggled to remember what the evacuation procedures were. She knew she'd been taught them. They'd been drilled into her mind over and over, but she couldn't, for the life of her, remember a single word.

She'd closed her eyes, searching for strength. And that's when the memory had slipped into her mind. Warm and reassuring. Alouette had known it had to be a memory because it was Sister Laurel who had been speaking.

"In case of emergency, use the founders' tunnel. Save as many of the books as you can."

Alouette rounded the corner and charged into the library. Sister Jacqui was already there, hastily piling books into a duffel bag. They shared a single, silent look before Alouette got to work. She dashed over to the shelf that held the Chronicles and began to toss volumes into the sac, cringing at the roughness of her movements. She'd never handled the Chronicles with anything but delicacy and care. But there was no time for that.

Clare, Noëlle, and Marguerite barged into the room a moment later, carrying more duffel bags that they filled with more books.

"Are those all of the Chronicles?" Alouette asked, searching the library for stray volumes left out on tables.

"No," whispered Jacqui as she glanced meaningfully toward the hallway.

Alouette understood in an instant. Her mind flashed back to that night months ago, when she'd returned to the Refuge to learn the truth about the sisters, about the Assemblée room, about the shelves and shelves of books they'd kept hidden from her.

She glanced at the clock on the wall. Less than twenty minutes.

"I'll get them," she told Jacqui. "You stay here with the others and gather whatever you can."

Jacqui nodded. Alouette threw the duffel, which now seemed to weigh more than her, onto her shoulder and staggered out of the library and down the hall. The heavy bag nicked corners and scuffed the walls, but she didn't stop. She charged into the Assemblée room and cranked open the doors of the heavy metal cabinet, revealing rows and rows of colored spines. *The Chronicles of the Vangarde.* The sacred histories of the sisters' decades-long fight for justice and equality.

She stepped into the small chamber and hastily snatched volumes from the shelves to dump into her sac. She had no idea what she was grabbing or the damage she was doing to their delicate hand-sewn spines, but she didn't care. She had to get these to the tunnel.

Or they would be destroyed, along with everything inside these walls.

Alouette peered out from behind the curtain at the glowing monitors of the Assemblée room. She took in Denise's carefully constructed consoles, the tangle of wires feeding into Sister Marguerite's newly built network, the hand-drawn blueprints and maps. Decades of work—of trying to save the planet—that would soon be turned to dust.

Because they couldn't possibly save it all.

Tears pricked the corners of Alouette's eyes, but she blinked them away and kept going, until her duffel was overflowing and she couldn't even close the top. She turned, readying herself to run for the tunnel hatch, when a voice stopped her cold. It was Principale Francine.

"We're out of time," she whispered to someone Alouette couldn't see from where she stood. "We need to get everyone into the tunnel and far enough away from the blast radius."

"But what about the rest?" asked a second voice. This was Citizen Rousseau. Alouette was certain neither of them knew she was here. "All of those innocent lives in the Frets?"

"They are nothing more than collateral damage to him," said Francine, and for the first time in Alouette's life, she heard true anguish in the sister's voice. "He doesn't care about them."

"Yes, but we do," said Citizen Rousseau. "We have to warn them."

Francine was silent for a moment, thinking. "Do we still have a connection to the hologram network?"

"Yes," said a third voice, which Alouette immediately recognized as Denise's. "The Ministère still hasn't been able to break through my hack."

"Good," said Francine. "We'll use it to broadcast an evacuation alert." The sister took a deep, burdened breath, like the weight of a planet was resting on her shoulders. "I will transmit the message."

"No," someone replied, and it took a moment for Alouette to realize it was Citizen Rousseau again. But she suddenly sounded nothing like the woman who had stood up in the Marsh, pleading with everyone to wake up to the general's lies. This voice was not pleading. It was not asking. It was demanding. "I will stay behind to transmit the evacuation message."

"But—" Francine began to argue, but something stopped her short. Alouette peeked her head out from the curtain to see Citizen Rousseau and Principale Francine standing nearly nose to nose, staring at each other. Two leaders. Both desperate to protect the people they loved.

"Very well," Francine finally said with a tight nod.

"Capture the message quickly and press here to set it to loop," Denise instructed.

"Then get into the tunnel as quickly as you can," Francine added.

"I will," replied Rousseau solemnly.

Francine gave her a long, anguished look before lifting her hand and drawing a single letter across her chest.

The letter *V.*

Then she rushed out of the room, calling out over the sound of the alarms, "Sisters! We are out of time. Take whatever you've collected and head for the tunnel."

Lifting the strap of the heavy sac back onto her shoulder, Alouette stumbled out from behind the curtain, startling Citizen Rousseau, who was positioning herself before a swarm of hologram cams just starting to glow to life.

"Alouette," she said urgently, rushing over and grabbing hold of her hands. "You must get out of here. You must get the sisters to safety."

Alouette glanced between Citizen Rousseau and the cams, which still hovered in the air, eagerly awaiting something to capture. "But aren't you—"

"Don't worry. I'll be right behind you." Rousseau peered toward the hallway, where they could still hear Francine's voice calling for everyone to get to the tunnel. "Here, take this."

Alouette looked down to see the sister sliding something into the pocket of her tunic, and panic clawed at her throat. "Your kaléido-scope?"

"You might need it. Promise me you'll protect them. You'll protect them *all*."

"But—"

"Promise me!" It was the first time Citizen Rousseau had ever raised her voice to Alouette.

"I promise," she said shakily, and before she could protest further, Rousseau gave her a firm push.

"Go. Now."

Alouette rushed out the door, glancing back just long enough to watch Rousseau reposition herself in front of the cams, take a steady breath, and say, "Attention to everyone in the Frets. Your lives are in danger. . . ."

"Come on!" Marcellus appeared in the hallway and grabbed Alouette's hand, leading her to the back entrance.

"Where's Cerise?" she cried out over the blaring alarms.

"Already in the tunnel!"

They followed the line of sisters squeezing through the hatch into the passageway with giant duffel bags full of books strapped to their bodies.

Breath ragged and heart pounding, Alouette concentrated hard on putting one foot in front of the other in the dark and narrow tun-nel. The weight of the sac was slowing her down, making it hard to walk straight, let alone quickly. Marcellus offered to take it, but he was already carrying enough. And she didn't want to let the Chronicles out of her sight.

She kept moving, letting her fear fuel her, stopping only to glance back into the darkness to check that Citizen Rousseau had kept her word. That she was there, behind them. But Alouette could hear nothing except the fast-fading alarms. And even through the emergency lights affixed to the walls, she had to squint to see only a few mètres in front of her.

"Keep going!" Marcellus urged, and she stumbled forward again, counting down the minutes in her mind, trying to calculate how much time they had left. How much time Rousseau had left.

Where is she?

Did everyone else get out?

Thoughts were spiraling through her mind like leaves caught in a violent storm. It was only now, as they moved farther and farther away from the Refuge, that she realized she hadn't actually *seen* all the sisters enter the tunnel. What if they'd left people behind?

But it wasn't until they climbed through the door of the sewage chamber and Marcellus's flashlight bounced between the tired, frightened faces of the sisters that she was able to take a mental head count.

And a sharp pain pierced her between the ribs.

There weren't enough.

There weren't nearly enough.

Her eyes darted into the tunnel. "I have to go back!" she cried. And before anyone had a chance to stop her, Alouette was already charging back through the door, calling out to the sisters as she ran stumblingly, blindly, through the passageway.

"Alouette!" Marcellus called from behind her, but she didn't stop. She had promised Rousseau she would protect them. *All* of them. And she would keep that promise. She would—

BOOOOMMMMM!

Alouette's heart stopped, followed by her feet. Everything seemed to fracture at once. Her vision. The sound of Marcellus's voice behind her. The ceiling of the tunnel. It was all breaking apart. Splintering into pieces far too tiny to ever put back together.

BOOOOMMMMM!

The ground beneath her feet shifted violently and she went down, falling hard to her knees. The duffel bag slipped from her shoulder and volumes of the sisters' *Chronicles* spilled out across the tunnel floor. She fought to hold on to her thoughts, but they were fracturing too.

The Ministère is here.

And there are sisters still—

Another earsplitting explosion rang out in the tunnel ahead of her, followed by something Alouette struggled to make sense of. It was moving toward her. And it was hot. Like fire.

No, not *like* fire.

With a yelp, she leapt to her feet and began to run back toward the sewers. Her body and mind screamed at each other in a violent battle to the death, one compelling her to run, the other compelling her to go back, to keep her promise, to save them.

But the heat was coming closer, destroying the fragile tunnel as it went. Debris showered down around her. Dust coated her lungs and made it impossible to breathe. Impossible to see. She listened for Marcellus's voice, hoping to use it as an anchor in this rough and merciless sea.

But there was nothing for kilomètres except that horrifying sound of the world fracturing. Of the planet collapsing around her. Of being chased by death.

She could just make out the sewage chamber door up ahead. She summoned a final burst of strength and charged through it, just as a giant current of hot air lifted her body and sent it flying. Her legs paddled uselessly, her hands searched for something to grab on to, but there was nothing. Stars danced in her vision and pain ricocheted through her bones as her body slammed against the wall of the chamber and fell limp to the ground.

It was impossible to move. Impossible to think. Impossible to stay awake.

The last thing Alouette remembered before she lost consciousness was the sound of heavy footsteps splashing through puddles before a pair of hands lifted her from the ground and carried her into the darkness of the sewers.

CHAPTER 65

CHATINE

THE EXPLOSION SILENCED THE WORLD.

It was unlike anything Chatine had ever seen before. On Bastille, she had witnessed death and destruction. She had stood on the rooftop of the Trésor tower as Ministère explosifs rained down around her. At the docklands, she had witnessed desperation. She had watched from above as the general ruthlessly destroyed what he believed to be the Vangarde's secret base.

Each time, she had been certain she'd witnessed the worst these combatteurs could do. The worst kind of pain they could inflict. The worst kind of devastation they could leave behind. The worst kind of obsession they could serve.

And each time, she had been wrong.

Because this was it.

A sight like no other.

A pain that eclipsed all pain.

A devastation that felt like the end of stars.

A man's obsession that ran so deep, so bottomless, there was nothing he wouldn't do. No city he wouldn't destroy. No limit to the number of beating hearts he would stop.

The explosifs hit in unison. Like a coordinated dance. Creating the most perfect bloom of debris, swirled with streaks of gray smoke and black ash.

It wasn't until that moment, as their stolen ship swooped over the fabriques in stealth mode and Chatine watched an orb of fire destroy Fret 7—and most of Frets 1 and 14—that she fully understood why red was the color of death on Laterre.

So much death. So many lives wiped out so one man could claim his "long-fought" victory over the Vangarde. Over a group of women who had claimed only to want peace. A group of rebels the Ministère had to turn into an enemy all on their own, with their lies and corruption and twisted truths.

The silence spread throughout the city.

The people streaming out of the Frets like blood from a wound had identical openmouthed stares, as if their lungs had been snuffed out mid-scream.

Citizen Rousseau's message was looping on every visible hologram unit. "Attention to everyone in the Frets. Your lives are in danger. Evacuate now." Until finally, it blinked out of existence. Like someone had disconnected every power cell on the planet, leaving behind twitching walls of three-dimensional static.

Ash and debris and smoke and death plumed into the air in a storm cloud of defeat. And that's all that Chatine could feel as she sat in the cockpit beside Etienne with Gabriel, Roche, Léopold, and Adèle standing speechlessly behind them.

Defeat.

Cold, numbing defeat that froze the blood in her veins and her eyes in their sockets and her tongue in her mouth. Because even if her warning had come in time, even if the Refuge had been safely evacuated, even if Marcellus and Alouette and all the others had made it out, this was still too much for one heart to bear. There were still too many lives trapped inside. Too many bodies thrown into the air from the blast, never to land again.

There weren't enough tears in the sky to mourn them all.

"Holy fric," whispered Gabriel behind her, and Chatine reached out to grab his hand. She needed something to hold on to. Something to keep her from exploding too. She could feel it bubbling up inside of her. The anger. The rage. The monster coming back to taunt her.

It was the radio in her lap that finally quieted them all. It crackled loudly, and the voice on the other end was like someone breathing life right into her lungs.

"Hello? Can anyone hear me? This is Marcellus. Do you copy?"

With a cry of relief, Chatine jolted upright, releasing Gabriel's hand and fumbling to bring the clunky device to her lips.

"Marcellus! Oh my Sols! Yes, we copy! Are you . . . are you okay?"

There was a silence that felt as long as a death sentence. Chatine became convinced she had imagined the whole thing. She had been speaking to a ghost in the radio.

And then, the voice breathed another whiff of life into her lungs. "Yes . . . I'm okay."

The singular sentence made Chatine feel like she was watching those explosifs fall all over again. She squeezed the red button on the side of the radio. "What about everyone else? Did you get everyone out? Is everyone safe?"

Even though there was nothing but faint crackles coming through, Chatine could hear the hesitation in Marcellus's pause. The avoidance. And finally, when he spoke again, the hollowness. "We're nearly out of the sewer chambers. Can you meet us at the silo?"

Silo? Etienne mouthed next to her.

"Yes," Chatine said, pointing in the direction of the ferme-lands behind them. "We're on our way."

Etienne maneuvered the stolen combatteur higher into the sky and mercifully steered away from the terrible sight in front of them.

No one spoke as they flew. Roche sat in the passenger hold with his arms wrapped around the children, who were crying quietly into his chest. Gabriel kept his hands locked on the back of Chatine's flight seat.

As they approached the silo, Chatine saw nothing but the dark shadows of overgrown wheat-fleur crops stretching out toward the blackening horizon of the Frets behind them. The silo stood crooked and slumping in the dirt, just as she'd last seen it. There was no sign of life.

She ordered Etienne to land, and the two of them jumped out of the cockpit onto the muddy ground below. "Wait with the kids," she shouted to Gabriel before taking off toward the silo.

It was dark when she first entered, with a musty smell that she knew too well. After a moment, as her eyes adjusted, her brain took in the huddled, trembling bodies, covered in dust and debris. And she knew instantly that the number was wrong.

There weren't enough of them.

Marcellus stepped out of the shadows and she ran to him, throwing her arms around his neck. He hugged her back, but his embrace was weak, his strength gone. As she pulled away and gazed into his empty, haunted eyes, she knew.

Without having to examine the faces in the darkness, she knew.

"Alouette?" she asked quietly.

Marcellus shook his head. "We lost her in the tunnel. I don't think she—" His voice shattered. He was as broken as the skies over the Frets. And filled with just as much grief. "There was so much chaos. I was told to run. The explosifs hit and . . . everything was shaking. The tunnel was too old, too unstable, to take the hit. It collapsed behind us. There was no way to go back." He dissolved into sobs that shook his entire body. "I don't think she made it out."

Chatine turned then, forced herself to look. To take in the waned, soot-covered faces.

Denise, with her arms wrapped tightly around a crying Jacqui.

Francine, with a ripped tunic and hair matted to the side of her face with blood.

Léonie and Clare staring at the ground as though they could see right through it, straight to the place they'd once called home.

Marguerite fiddling absently with a charred string of beads hanging from her neck.

And scattered among them were piles and piles of ripped and ragged duffel bags, split open at the seams, torn at the handles, books spilling out across the silo floor.

But there was no Noëlle. No Nicolette. No Muriel.

No Citizen Rousseau.

Chatine's legs started to give way and she feared she would go down. Thank the Sols for Etienne, who took control of the situation. "Come on," he ordered. "Let's get everyone onto the ship."

Chatine turned to him, trying to infuse gratefulness into every fiber of her being. She wasn't sure if she'd succeeded, but he nodded to her just the same.

One by one, the sisters stood. Marcellus, Chatine, and Etienne helped them out of the silo and onto the ship, where Gabriel settled them into the passenger hold, two to a seat. Then they loaded the books, stuffing the ripped bags into the combatteur's small cargo hold.

Chatine was about to board when she noticed Marcellus was still outside. He was staring numbly in the direction of the Frets, where smoke could be seen billowing into the air.

"Marcellus?" she said.

"I'm not going."

Panic threatened to knock her off her feet. "What?"

"I have to go look for her."

Chatine stared at him in disbelief. "Y-y-you can't go back there."

"I'll come with you," Principale Francine offered, stepping back out of the combatteur.

"No!" Chatine said. "It's too dangerous. You didn't see it. It's a bloodbath."

"I am responsible for those lives," Francine said in a voice that was difficult to contradict. "If any of the sisters are still alive, I must find them."

"No one is alive!" Chatine shouted. "I can guarantee you. No one survived that."

Marcellus reached for her hands and squeezed them with such intensity, she knew there was no point in arguing anymore. That blind obsession had already taken over. Had already shut his mind to any suggestions, especially from her. No matter what she said, no matter how much she pleaded, it would fall on deaf ears. Just like her pleas always did.

"I've got the radio," he told Chatine. "I'll call with any news."

And then, he released her hands. And it felt like she was falling.

"Come on," Etienne said, ushering her away. "We need to get everyone to safety."

Chatine nodded dazedly and let herself be guided onto the ship.

"Wait," Denise called out as Etienne was about to close the hatch. He turned to her, his eyes roving over the tangle of faded scars on the left side of her face, and Chatine could clock the moment he realized who she was. "There's one more," she said.

Confused, Chatine glanced back toward the silo. Where, only moments ago, she'd seen an empty doorway, a girl now stood in the shadows. She was tall and built gracefully like a dancer. But there was a stiffness to her that seemed almost unnatural. It wasn't until something flashed sharply on the left side of the girl's face that Chatine understood. And immediately recoiled.

A cyborg?

"Get in!" Denise called to her, but the girl shook her head.

"I can't. They might track me again. I can't put you all in danger."

And it was only then—as she stepped out into the light from the combatteur, and Chatine could see past her circuitry, past the dirt and debris covering her face—that she recognized her and let out a small gasp. It was Cerise.

"How would they track her?" Etienne asked Denise. "I thought cyborgs don't have trackers."

"Normally, they don't," replied Denise. "But she does. It was implanted without her knowledge. Inside her left ear. We're pretty sure that's how the Empereur found us."

"Just go!" Cerise shouted from the silo, causing Chatine to flinch again. "Leave me here. You can't risk being followed. He'll never stop looking for you."

"She's not loyal to the Ministère anymore," Denise explained. "She's woken up. We can't just leave her here. They'll find her and who knows what they'll do to her. She's a traitor now. Just like all of us."

Etienne nodded, like this settled everything. He disappeared back into the ship, leaving Chatine to stare blankly after him. When he returned less than a minute later, he had a terrifying-looking tool with him. Like something he'd yanked out of a combatteur repair kit. It was long and metallic with tiny pincers at the end that made Chatine shudder.

Etienne shared a glance with Denise, who in turn looked at Cerise. Chatine swore some kind of silent understanding passed between the three of them. "I don't have any sedatives," he said to Cerise, his voice brimming with regret.

She swallowed hard before giving him a single, solemn nod of permission.

"I'll hold her down," said Denise.

CHAPTER 66

MARCELLUS

RAIN SPLATTERED DOWN FROM THE SKY LIKE TEARS.

Tears for everything that lay below.

The rubble. The ash. The debris. The twisted metal sticking up like angry, jagged teeth gnashing in pain.

The combatteurs' explosifs had eviscerated Fret 7. But the destruction had spilled out across the entire Marsh, decimating stalls and cloaking the wooden walkways in a thick layer of scorched debris. In the neighboring Frets, windows had been shattered, great holes gashed through the Perma-Steel, and small fires smoldered and smoked.

And then there were the people.

What was left of them.

Those who walked could barely walk. They hobbled among the wreckage, the sleeves of their woolen coats blasted from their skin, and their skin ransacked with burns and bruises and bleeding wounds. Others simply sat amid the obliteration, haunted and horrified and unable to move. Babies cried. Old men moaned. And women shrieked their children's names.

The smell of burning flesh hung in the miserable pre-dawn air.

Laterre's heaviest rain could not wash away this smell.

This carnage.

The tears from the clouds would do nothing.

"Alouette!" Marcellus had called her name until his voice was gone, charred like everything else around him. The world had turned even darker and grayer than the skies overhead.

Every face he passed was the same. There was no difference between the living and the dead. They both bore vacant expressions, with empty, hollowed-out eyes that stared back at him without seeing him. Without seeing anything. All these people had gone to bed last night thinking they were safe, thinking Empereur Bonnefaçon would take care of them. Just as he'd been doing for months.

Fool's paradise, indeed, Marcellus thought.

He heaved aside a splintered couchette door and leapt back, stifling a cry at the body that lay crumpled and twisted underneath. It was too young. Too small. Too innocent. They were all too innocent.

He turned around and vomited what little he had in his stomach. It wasn't much.

Francine appeared beside him and rubbed his back as he retched. "Did you find anything?" he asked, wiping his mouth.

She shook her head. Her glasses were smudged with dirt and ash. Her wiry gray hair was still mussed and untamed. "It's no use. The rubble is too thick. And no one is being found alive."

He collapsed down and crushed his temples between his hands, trying to drown out the world. It wasn't a world he could live in anymore. A world where his grandfather could treat people like dirt and then turn them to dust. A world where the System Alliance stood by and let it happen. A world where those who tried to do good were punished and those who murdered and cheated and deceived were rewarded.

A world where César Bonnefaçon won and everyone else lost.

Marcellus felt a scream building in his throat. No, in his *bones*. It was a scream he'd been holding back for too long. A cry of pain, of frustration, of helplessness, that had nowhere to go but out.

If Sister Noëlle were here now, she'd tell him to find the words. Use the words. She would say that they were designed for this very reason. Marcellus tried to find them. He wanted so badly to dispel this glowing-hot ball of rage inside of him with the right words. The right expression. The perfect symphony of syllables and sounds.

But he couldn't.

Because Sister Noëlle *wasn't* here. She was buried underneath this wall of rubble. Her words were silenced forever. Along with Sister Muriel's and Sister Nicolette's and Citizen Rousseau's and Alouette's. Never to be spoken again.

And all he could do was scream. Into the burning abyss. Loud and hot and useless. Until his lungs were empty and his eyes were scorched dry and his body could no longer sustain the effort.

And that's when he heard it.

Words.

Rising up from the ashes. Echoing against what remained of the charred, twisted walls. Spreading like fire across the darkened world.

". . . I hear your cries. I feel your pain. I am here with you when no one else is!"

Someone was speaking to him. Those words were for *him*. Marcellus could feel it in his very core.

"Where is the Ministère who promised to protect you? Where is the Empereur who promised you glory? Hiding behind the walls of Ledôme, all of them. While we dig up the remains of our loved ones."

Marcellus turned his face toward the sound and blinked against the early-morning Sol-light seeping through the smoke and thick clouds and swirling ash. Maximilienne Epernay stood on a peak of rubble, like it was a mountain she had scaled. A podium she had fought her way up to. Her red coat and hood and face were stained with everything that could be found here—dirt and soot and blood. The new colors of death.

"We have seen the true face of Empereur Bonnefaçon," she continued, causing more people to stop and turn and squint into the sky. "We have seen the villain that lurks beneath the savior's mask. And he has called *us* terrorists?" She spread her arms wide, gesturing to every charred beam, every mangled window frame, every fallen soul. "Look around you! This is the very definition of terror. We are standing in it. We are soaked in it. I see it on every single one of your faces. Grief. Fear. *Terror.*"

Marcellus took a step forward, like he was being pulled into her, into her angry voice and entrancing words. They were the very words he had failed to conjure on his own. The very definition of his pain that he'd been searching for. She spelled it out like she was inside his mind, making sense of his scrambled thoughts, organizing them into order. Into poetry.

"We have seen the extent of the Empereur's lies." Max pointed to a nearby hologram projection, which was now just a jumble of confused static. "On the very holograms he erected across the planet, we witnessed his deceit. We watched him plot with an enemy planet to turn us into killing machines. We watched him conspire to murder a child and then pin the blame on one of us, an innocent. My poor sister, who we all watched die on this very ground. We watched him cheat and murder and delude his way to the top. And now he sits behind the walls of Ledôme, in his plush rooms of the Grand Palais, watching us burn."

Marcellus peered to his left, where Principale Francine stood, her eyes brimming with fear. Was it the words themselves that inspired it? Or the woman speaking them? Marcellus couldn't tell. But when he gazed around at the now hundreds of people who had stopped digging, stopped calling out, stopped wandering in aimless circles, to stare up at the woman standing atop the wreckage of Fret 7, he saw not fear on their faces but something else.

This woman—who had screamed at Citizen Rousseau that words were not enough—was capturing the minds and the imaginations and the *hope* of everyone here.

With her words.

"Now," said Max. "I ask all of you to reach deep within, to grab hold of that terror, to twist it and squeeze it and crush it until all that's left is anger. Embody that anger! Use that pain! Board the bateau of your suffering and let your grief blow your sails. Now is the time—as we stand in the ashes of our *children*—it is time to put an end to this brutality once and for all. Now is the time to grab whatever weapons you can—stones, sticks, the scorching shards that now remain of your homes, your own fists—and follow me."

It was like watching storm clouds gather. Like watching mountains move. Like peering into space and witnessing the constellations rearrange. Grief twisted into rage. Useless, defeated hands clenched into fists and shot into the air. Eyes once wet with tears now burned with fury.

It was like watching an army rise from ashes.

And inside Marcellus, a long-simmering fire ignited once again.

"We will cut this evil off at the source," cried Max. "We will break through the barrier that has kept *them*—the First and Second Estates— separated from us, like we are rats in their cage. Experiments in their labs. Worker bees in their locked-up hives. We will take this fight to *their* doorstep, make *them* understand what it feels like to have their homes threatened and destroyed, their lives dismissed as nothing more than col- lateral damage. We will show César Bonnefaçon, once and for all, that we are stronger than him. Because we are *angrier* than him. And that is our weapon. That is our advantage. That is the key that will earn us our freedom. Follow me now and we will break these chains once and for all."

A rallying cry shot into the air like a firework. Like one unified scream into the ether. More powerful than any scream one person could pro- duce on their own. The crowd began to jostle around Marcellus. People stumbling to gain footing on the uneven ground. He glanced around for Francine but had lost her in the commotion. One by one and then ten by ten and then hundreds by hundreds, they began to march. Through the wreckage, through the alleyways of the Frets, spilling into the Fabrique District.

As Marcellus watched them stream past, his legs longed to move. His heart longed to follow. But for some reason, it was Chatine's voice in his mind that held him back.

"Don't do this."

"You don't have to do this."

"The woman is a murderer. She killed the Patriarche. . . . She killed my sister. . . ."

Marcellus clenched his fists, another scream building inside of him. He knew all of this! He knew Max was violent. Maybe slightly unhinged. But she was the only one fighting. She was the only one doing *anything* to stop his grandfather.

The Vangarde was finished.

Citizen Rousseau was dead.

Alouette, too.

Maximilienne Epernay was the only leader this revolution had left.

Marcellus stumbled forward. The red-hot fuel churned through his veins, compelling him on. Max's words reverberated through his mind, connecting with every emotion, every gramme of anger he'd held back, pushed aside, swallowed down.

He felt like he'd been waiting for this from the very beginning. From the moment he first watched that microcam footage of his grandfather plotting to bomb the copper exploit and pin the blame on his own son. From the moment Marcellus saw Mabelle's body lying in the smoking wreckage of Bastille. From the moment he watched his grandfather place a crown atop his own head.

So many moments that had brought him here. That had brought them all here.

As hundreds turned to thousands, as people spilled through the city, spreading out like rivers dividing and then merging back together again, Marcellus knew that Laterre had been waiting for this moment for a long time too. All roads leading here. All paths, all destinies, all three Sols, guiding them toward the great hill in the distance, where the bright, ever-present light of Ledôme glowed like a beacon.

- CHAPTER 67 -
ALOUETTE

THE AIR WAS HOT AND DAMP. IT FELT LIKE A WEIGHT pressing down on Alouette's chest. She inhaled, feeling the moisture tickle her lungs. When she opened her eyes, she saw nothing but a tangle of green leaves, dotted with tiny pops of color. Red and purple and blue.

Alouette sat up, her head woozy from the humidity and . . . something else? The memory came back to her in a terrified heartbeat. The tunnel collapsing behind her, the explosion lifting her up, sending her crashing against the sewer wall. And then something else lifting her. Or rather, some*one*.

She spun around, searching her surroundings.

Where am I?

She gazed up and down a small aisle lined with thick bushes bursting with what she could now see were vibrant, ripe berries. A massive plastique dome arched above her head and through it she could see the thick Laterrian cloud coverage swirling above.

A hothouse, she realized. What was she doing in an empty hothouse?

She stood up, testing her balance on legs that still felt wobbly beneath her before venturing down the aisle. The berry bushes opened up into a small nook filled with shelves of potted seedlings growing under strips of propagation lights. She reached out and touched one of the sprouts, feeling its energy stream into her fingertip, followed by a wave of sadness at the memory of Sister Laurel's propagation room. Which was now buried under a pile of rubble.

Alouette glanced down the aisle until she could just make out a large window at the edge of the hothouse. With a surge of desperation and a thirst for answers, she hurried toward it, pressing her face against the plastique, trying to squint through the thick condensation.

And then, with a sob that seemed to choke the life out of her, she saw it.

At first, she hoped—prayed—it was just the steam sticking to the plastique. But steam wasn't black. It wasn't laced with ash. It wasn't *that*.

That was the Frets. But not the Frets as she'd always known them. Not a cluster of metallic giants, looming on the horizon. Now their lumpy, angular shapes—the traces of the great freightships they'd once been— were engulfed in eddying and spiraling smoke. Black ash and debris rode on these plumes, like frightened birds skittering into the sky.

And suddenly, with a tiny, helpless cry, it all came back to her.

The evacuation alarms blaring endlessly.

Alouette stuffing volumes of the Chronicles into a duffel bag, which she'd left behind. Which was now buried underneath all of that rubble. The sisters' legacy. The planet's history. Lost forever. Forgotten. Just like the words they were written in.

And the faces of the sisters who didn't make it out. Whom Alouette had failed to protect. Noëlle and Nicolette and Muriel. And Citizen Rousseau.

She shut her eyes against the sights and the sounds. Her body trembling. Her heart breaking into a million shattered pieces.

A noise broke her from her reverie—a creaking sound, like someone repositioning themselves on an old chair. And then a voice called out through the hothouse. "Little Lark? Is that you? Are you awake?"

It was a voice from her dreams. A voice from her oldest memories. A voice she never thought she'd hear again except in the midst of her nightmares.

"Papa?"

And then she was running. Because she knew, before she even saw him, before her eyes could even take in his vast shoulders and ice-white hair, that, just like in her dreams, he had come for her. He had walked through fire for her, he had saved her.

As she turned the corner, she nearly barreled into him. He let out a soft laugh as she threw her arms around him and buried her head in the familiar crook of his neck and inhaled his familiar musky scent.

"Papa!" This wasn't a dream. He was real. And he was the only thing that could possibly make her body stop trembling and her heart stop breaking. If even for a minute.

Hugo Taureau was here.

"I missed you so much."

"I know," he said in that deep, husky voice that felt like fresh-baked bread and tenderness and home. "I missed you, too. But I'm here now, Little Lark. I'm here."

And suddenly, the familiarity of everything—his scent, his voice, his arms around her—morphed into strangeness. She pulled back and stared up into his warm brown eyes with confusion. "*Why* are you here? Why did you come back?"

His intense gaze bored into her, and in it, she saw a lifetime of weariness. The kind she now knew only came from being on the run. Always fearful. Always looking over your shoulder. "For you, Little Lark," he said, as though he was surprised she hadn't yet worked this out. "I came back for you."

"But—"

"I saw the broadcast," he explained. "The general's coronation interrupted by a missing heir. The Patriarche's long-lost daughter that no one knew about."

She pierced him with a suspicious look. "Did *you* know about it? Did you know who I was? Who my real father was? All this time?"

Hugo winced painfully and reached for his leg before lowering himself down onto a stool near a cluttered potting bench.

"Are you okay?" she asked, her attention diverted to his pant leg, where she could see scorched fabric and a ripped seam. "Are you hurt?"

"I'm fine," he said, gesturing for her to take the stool across from him. "It's just a small burn. It'll heal."

Hesitantly, Alouette sat, but her eyes kept drifting back to his leg.

"Your mother didn't talk much about her life before we met," Hugo said. "She mentioned a time or two that she used to work in the Palais, but I never thought much of it. Then, when she got sick and told me to fetch you from the Renards and bring you to the Refuge, she started to say things. Nothing concrete. Mostly just nonsensical rambles. She said the Patriarche wanted her daughter dead. She said I had to hide you away from him, so no one could ever find you. I thought it was the fever. I thought she was delirious. I didn't think . . ." His voice trailed off and he ran his fingers through his hair. "It wasn't until much later, as you started to grow up, and I started to catch little things from the sisters—strange phrases here and there, whispered conversations—that I began to suspect maybe your mother wasn't delirious after all. Maybe there really was a bigger threat to protect you from. But then, after Inspecteur Limier found me again, in the Forest Verdure, I knew I had to leave. For your sake. I had sworn to your mother that I would protect you, and I couldn't risk leading the Ministère straight to your door, especially if you were who I suspected you were. It wasn't until I saw the broadcast, from the coronation ceremony, that my suspicions were confirmed."

Alouette remained quiet for a long moment, taking it all in, trying to fuse these details together with all the other splintered pieces she'd collected about her mother's life. About her own life.

"So, then, why did you come back?"

"Isn't it obvious?" he asked. "Empereur Bonnefaçon wants you dead. The Red Scar want you dead. I couldn't just sit by and watch." His expression darkened. "I left you with the sisters because I thought they could protect you, but the moment I saw your terrified face on that broadcast, I knew they could not. I work as a chef now, on a Reichenstatian trading ship. We were on our way back to Reichenstat when I saw the broadcast from the coronation ceremony. I immediately put in a request that we be rerouted to Laterre so I could get you. I snuck into the city two days ago. I went to the mechanical room only to find the entrance had been sealed off. I didn't know what to do. I thought maybe the Refuge had moved. Then I remembered the founders' tunnel. I figured it was worth a shot. But when

I accessed it from the sewers, the door was locked, and I didn't know the code. I waited in those sewers for more than a day, hoping someone would come out." Pain flashed over Hugo's face. "Then the evacuation alarms started to sound. I heard the tunnel door open. I heard voices. I heard someone calling your name and . . ." His voice trailed off. He didn't need to finish. She knew the rest of the story.

A vise started to close around Alouette's lungs. "I promised I would get them all out." Her voice cracked, and she dropped her head into her hands. This time, the tears came. This time, there was no numbness, only grief.

"Shhh," Hugo said, placing a gentle hand on her head. "It's okay, Little Lark. I'm sure you did everything you could do. I'm sure—" But his words were cut off by another sharp wince of pain.

Alouette's head jerked up and her attention landed again on the singed fabric of his pant leg. She sniffled and wiped at her wet cheeks before slowly reaching out to push back the fabric.

An involuntary cry bubbled up in her throat at the sight of the wound. This was *not* a small burn. This was angry and blistering and very, very bad.

Suddenly, Alouette was overcome with a different sensation. It chased away all other emotions that were coursing through her. Just as it had so many times in her life, in so many difficult situations. That need—that pulsing need to fix, to heal—it drove her. It overpowered her. She was on her feet in an instant, searching, weaving through the aisles of the hothouse, until she found a small supply shed with a med kit. She rushed back and went to work tending to the wound, ignoring Hugo's protests that he was fine, that it would heal on its own.

"It won't," she finally snapped. "Now stay still."

The med kit was sparse, with barely enough supplies to properly clean the wound, and nothing to ward off an infection, which would surely come. None of the crops in this hothouse had healing properties, and she longed for the herbal remedies Sister Laurel used to grow in her propagation room.

"We need to get you to a med center," she concluded after doing her best to bandage his leg. "A proper one."

"There's one on the ship," he said.

Confused, Alouette lifted her eyes to peer into her father's gentle, reassuring gaze. "What?"

"I can't go to a Laterrian med center. I'm still a wanted man here. But this is just a stopover. Someone is picking us up shortly to take us back to the spaceport where my ship is waiting."

Alouette dropped the spool of gauze still clutched in her hand and dazedly watched it roll across the floor.

Hugo reached out and took her hands in his. "You'll be safe with me now. We'll be together again. Just as it should be."

Silence descended over her thoughts. She stood up and walked back to the window, pressed her palms against the plastique. As she continued to watch the smoke and debris swirl over Vallonay like a harbinger of even darker things to come, Hugo's words banged against her skull like monotonous strikes on a drum.

Together.

Again.

Ship.

Waiting.

"Reichenstat," she whispered, feeling echoes of the past rushing back to her like an unsettling surge of déjà vu. She'd been here before. On this precipice of a new life. An escape.

From all of this.

From a broken world.

From a rebel group who tried to mend its seams. But failed again and again and again. Just like she'd failed to save them.

She had been offered this choice before. And she had said no.

And the world was now covered in ash.

What would have transpired if she had simply said yes? If she had followed Hugo to another life. Another future. Another destiny. One where she was not the Patriarche's long-lost heir. Where there were not dangerous rebels and power-hungry Empereurs fighting to be the one to stand over Alouette's dead body and claim it as their own.

Would the sisters have been better off?

Would the planet have been better off?

She would never know.

With a cold, numb heart, Alouette pulled her face away from the window and turned back toward her father. The only father she'd ever known. The only one who'd ever fought to save her, keep her alive, protect her—the way fathers were supposed to do.

The only one who'd been around long enough to call himself Papa.

And who now needed her help.

"What time does the ship leave?" she asked.

- CHAPTER 68 -
CERISE

IT WAS LIKE THE SPACE BETWEEN SLEEP AND WAKING. An uneasy junction of reality and something just beyond it. Her vision was still crisp but ringed by spinning halos. Her mind was still sharp, but the edges around her thoughts were soft and nebulous. They drifted and returned. They ventured off to faraway places she couldn't remember going before. Destinations brimming with color you could feel but not see. Dark, murky grays of grief. Crimson, bloodred fears. Luminous golden light streaked with peals of laughter. Deep, penetrating blue guilt that reminded her of the Secana Sea.

"What is happening to me?" Cerise whispered. She didn't expect anyone to answer. For the past twenty-two minutes since she'd woken in this strange tent with a pulsing ache in her left ear, she'd been alone.

But somewhere beyond her immediate realm of awareness, a voice—vaguely familiar—whispered back, "It's okay. It's just your mind. You're still waking up."

"Waking up?" Cerise repeated. "From sleep?"

"I suppose you could call it sleep. But it's a very different kind of sleep."

Cerise peered around again. The fabric walls of the tent flapped in a whistling, battering breeze, and a small heating stove radiated a peculiar purplish glow at the foot of her cot. Then, her gaze fell down to her hands, lit faintly by the hazy light coming in through the tent walls. Were they her hands? They looked like her hands. But there was something fragile about them. Delicate. Easily crushed. Easily broken.

"They're the same hands," the voice said, reading her mind as clearly as if Cerise had broadcast her thoughts to a hologram projection. "Everything is the same. But it will all feel new for a while as your brain acclimates."

The voice came nearer, and then, from the shadows emerged a woman. Her eyes twinkled, her smile was wide and broad, and across her left forehead and cheek, smooth fibrous tissue snaked, weaved, and glinted in the dull light.

"I know you." It was half question and half statement of fact. The blend of both certainty and unknown confused Cerise.

The woman smiled even wider. "Yes, we've met. A few months ago. I treated a friend of yours. Gabriel?"

Gabriel.

The name echoed through her mind, which now felt like a war zone after the final battle has been fought. Demolished houses and buildings threatening to topple over. Did she know a Gabriel?

"Don't worry," said the woman. "Your human memories will start to come back. Slowly at first and then in random bursts that might frighten you. But I assure you it's all normal."

Human memories.

Her left ear pulsed again. A sharp, angry pain that seemed to stretch deep through the canal, scraping at her brain. Cerise reached up and felt a thick bandage secured there. Panicked, she moved to her cheek and forehead, clawing at her face in search of—

She blew out a sigh and relaxed back down into the bed as her fingertips ran over the roughness of her embedded circuitry. She reached for it in her mind, feeling the neuroprocessors buried deep beneath her skull connect and communicate and come to life. "Am I still a . . ." Somehow she couldn't say the word. Why couldn't she say the word?

"A cyborg?" the woman said for her. "Yes. Technically. But things will be different now. As your human memories return, you'll slowly start to remember who you are. Your speech will change. You'll feel more. Emote more. Your old personality will start to return. But . . ." Her voice trailed off.

"But what?" Cerise asked.

"But eventually, you'll have to choose."

"Choose." Cerise touched her circuitry again. She didn't need an explanation. She knew what was being implied. She cut her gaze back to the scars that ran up and down the left side of the woman's face.

"Brigitte!" Cerise blurted out, the certainty coming to her from some forgotten place. "You're the one who built the Forteresse. With Denise."

"Yes," Brigitte said with a smile.

"Is she okay? Denise? And everyone else?"

"They're fine. Everyone's fine. They're here and they're safe."

"Here." Cerise took another long glance around the gloomy tent. "Where is here?"

Brigitte chuckled. "It's not much, but it's home for now. Until we can find something more permanent. We had to abandon our old camp and find a new place to live. But I can't complain. We have food to eat and beds to sleep in and plenty of emberweed oil to keep the heat on."

Cerise looked toward the stove near her feet, glowing that strange color. It was almost violet. "Emberweed." She couldn't place the name in her memories—human or cyborg.

"It's not a Ministère-catalogued herb," Brigitte explained, reading her confusion. "But it grows all over Laterre, most prominently in the Terrain Perdu. The oil is highly flammable and burns hotter and longer than any other substance we've found. So it makes a great heat source for indoor stoves or outside fires when we're low on wood." Brigitte stared wistfully into the purple flames. "I also find it the most pleasing to look at it."

"You *use* fire?" Cerise couldn't even fathom such a thing. Fire was not only outlawed, it was dangerous. It was responsible for destroying most of the First World. The only fire ever seen on Laterre was the result of Ministère explosifs. The result of *destruction*.

Brigitte chuckled. "I know it's hard to believe, but yes. We not only use it. We *need* it. Our communities have spent the past few centuries becoming experts on all types of fire. It has been key to surviving outside of the Regime and staying hidden from the Ministère."

Cerise flinched. Those words, "hidden from the Ministère," felt like they were ripping apart more structures in her mind, leaving behind more wreckage. Her internal body temperature shot up five degrees in an instant.

"I'm sorry," Brigitte said, grabbing her hand and squeezing it. "I need to remember to be more careful about my words. At least, until you're fully awake." She bent down to study the left side of Cerise's face, her expression burrowing into a frown. "I think it's time to change those bandages."

With quick, gentle movements, Brigitte pulled the white cloth from Cerise's ear and tossed it into a nearby waste bin.

"My tracker," Cerise said quietly, remembering the searing pain that had cut through her like a dull knife as Etienne had removed it. Eventually, it had become too much for even her enhanced brain to take and her body had shut down, her mind had shut off, casting her into a fitful sleep.

"It's out," confirmed Brigitte. "And your ear will heal, with a bit of scar tissue. My son did a good job, despite what he had to work with."

"So, they can't . . ." Cerise's voice began to tremble, the words getting stuck in her throat again. "They c-c-c-can't . . ."

"No," said Brigitte with a warm smile as she secured another bandage in place. "They can't track you anymore. You're free."

The shame instantly spread through Cerise. It was the same sensation she'd experienced back in the Refuge when Marcellus had told her that her father had ordered a tracking device to be implanted inside of her. A sickening black sensation that coated her from the inside.

It was her fault.

Her fault the Refuge had been found.

Her fault there was now a jagged, smoking wound in the middle of the Frets.

Because her father had never trusted her. Had never had faith in her. From the very beginning, he'd suspected her of failing. Of malfunctioning. Of *breaking*.

Everything Cerise had done for the past three months had been for him. Her cyborg programming might have been telling her to do it for the

Regime. For the glory of the Ministère. But her *other* programming—the one the Ministère had never touched—had told her to do it for him. To prove to him that she wasn't the disappointment he thought she was. She didn't need to be fixed. She didn't need to be erased.

But in the end, he'd been right not to trust her. Not to have faith in her. Because she'd done exactly what he'd suspected her of doing.

And now, she couldn't decide how to feel about that.

Everything was at war in her mind.

It was so loud, so chock-full of conflicting colors, she wondered if she would ever see or hear stillness again.

Movement caught her attention and she darted a look toward the entrance of the tent, where she could see a shadow shuffling back and forth.

"Holy sheep's turd, it's fric-ing freezing out here!"

Brigitte chuckled and turned to Cerise. "Someone has been waiting to see you. Do you feel well enough for a visitor?"

Cerise nodded and Brigitte called out. "Okay, Gabriel! You can come in now."

It wasn't even a split second before the flap burst open and a tall, lanky man came tumbling into the tent, his shaggy hair covered in tiny ice crystals. He secured the tent shut behind him with an exaggerated shiver. "Brr! Could you people have found *any* colder place on the planet to set up camp? It's like you *want* to freeze to death."

He shook the ice from his hair and dusted it from his reflective coat before stomping farther into the tent, leaving a trail of white flurries in his wake. When he noticed Cerise on the cot, his entire demeanor seemed to shift at once. As though he'd suddenly forgotten all about the cold.

"Sparkles! Hey . . . *you*. How you holding up?" There was something off about his voice. It was too high. Too squeaky. "Is Brigitte taking good care of you? She's the best healer in town. Got me in tip-top shape, isn't that right, Brigitte?" He nudged his shoulder against the former cyborg, and she flashed him a smile.

"I'll leave you two alone to talk."

When the tent flap closed behind her, Gabriel suddenly looked like a lost child whom someone had abandoned. He glanced around, as though searching for somewhere to go. Something to look at. It did not escape Cerise that he had not once looked directly at *her*.

"So, Sparkles," he said, clapping his hands together once. "Do you mind if I still call you Sparkles? I mean, it's not like offensive or anything, is it? You know, with your . . ." He gestured ambiguously to the side of his face. "I mean, you do kind of *sparkle* now."

Cerise didn't reply. She was too busy analyzing this strange, strange man with his even stranger habits. After circling the tent twice, he had ultimately decided to stand next to the small heating stove, his arms crossed over his chest in a position Cerise deduced was supposed to look relaxed, but there was nothing about him that was relaxed. Nervousness clung to every centimètre of him like the tiny ice crystals that he'd brought with him.

"So," he said again, rearranging himself awkwardly until he finally gave up and sat on the chair opposite Cerise's cot. "Um, how's life? How's the ear?"

Cerise gingerly touched her new bandage. "It hurts."

Gabriel nodded. "Yeah, I can imagine. When I was shot by a cluster bullet, it hurt like fric."

Cluster bullet . . .

Her circuitry flickered wildly as the words bounced around in Cerise's mind.

"Oh, sorry!" Gabriel rushed to say. "Brigitte said you might not remember things. And that I shouldn't push you to—"

"I remember!" she cried out, the memories cascading into place. All those fuzzy images that had plagued her for months were shaking loose like tiny avalanches in her brain.

A message from a probe lost in deep space.

A scientist on Albion.

A voyageur streaking across the stars.

A weapon.

A chase.

An escape.

A young man shot open, bleeding on the floor.

"You!" She pointed at him. "You were shot. They shot you. When we were running. You almost died. I was . . ."

Gabriel held his breath, like whatever she said next was more important than air.

"I was . . . worried about you." With the memory came the emotion. It was the color of the night TéléSky. Hot tears pricked her eyes. Waves of grief undulated through her. A fear bloomed in her chest, spreading, pressing, breaking.

Gabriel released the breath and flashed her a playful smirk. "Well, that's to be expected. People worry about me a lot." He paused and then quickly added, "I mean, because they like me. Not because they're worried I'll rob them or anything. Okay, so maybe some people worry about that. But what I meant to say was, I can't blame you for worrying about me. You were *pretty* taken by me. By the end, anyway. Maybe not at first. I'm an acquired taste."

"And maybe a *re*acquired taste too?"

The words startled Cerise. She couldn't believe they had just come out of her. All on their own.

"Hey!" said Gabriel, his eyes lighting up. "You made a joke! A very *Cerise* joke. That has to be a good sign, right?"

She kept her mouth clamped shut, afraid more words like that would come out. She wasn't sure she liked the sensation of words escaping all on their own.

The "joke"—as Gabriel had called it—seemed to relax him, at least. He leaned forward in his chair, but Cerise noticed he still wouldn't look at her. At least not straight on; his gaze seemed to be fixed obsessively on the right side of her face, like he was doing everything in his power to block out her *other* half. The cyborg half.

"So, when's the surgery?"

Cerise's brow furrowed. "Surgery?"

Gabriel leaned back in his chair. "Yeah, you know, to remove the . . ." He gestured at the side of his face, and Cerise remarked that he never said the word "circuitry." Never looked at it. Never acknowledged it. As if he were pretending it didn't exist. Pretending that half of *her* didn't exist.

And she was reminded of the coronation ceremony. When her father had asked her to wear that synthetic flesh. Had asked her to conceal herself.

"What makes you think I want to remove it?" she asked.

Gabriel flinched, momentarily stunned, but he quickly covered it up with a laugh. "What, you want to keep it? You got a nice pair of sparkly shoes that will match?" But when Cerise didn't reply, his smile collapsed and his expression darkened. "You can't be serious. Why would you want to keep *that*?"

And now, he did look at it. And Cerise was certain she would remember that look forever. Revulsion and disdain all wrapped up in one single glance.

Her mind scratched for an answer. Even though she knew she didn't owe him one. But she wanted to understand it herself. This defensive reaction that was building inside of her. This deep-rooted desire to hold her hands in front of her face and refuse to let anyone change it.

But why?

She wasn't a product of the Ministère anymore. She wasn't Spécialiste Chevalier anymore. Which meant she wasn't a cyborg anymore. Not in the official definition of the term. Cyborgs belonged to the Ministère. To the Regime.

She didn't know whom she belonged to anymore.

"What if . . . ," Cerise began hesitantly. "What if I do want to keep it?"

Gabriel's face drained. "Oh, you *were* serious." He stood up and began to pace the length of the small tent. "I mean, can you do that? Can you keep it and still be . . . you know, you?"

"I don't know. Maybe not. But would that be so bad?"

He stopped pacing and turned to her, his expression softening ever so slightly. "I kind of liked the old you."

"That's not how I remember it."

Gabriel chuckled. "Let's just say you were an acquired taste too."

Cerise rubbed her fingertips over the rough nodes of her circuitry. "I just can't help but think that maybe it can be useful. That now that I'm awake, I can use what the Ministère gave me against them."

"But what if they use it against *you*?" Gabriel asked. "What if they suck you back in with whatever they put in your head? And even if they don't, I'll never be able to look at you and not see . . ." His voice trailed off and his fists clenched at his sides. "Never mind."

"Not see what?"

"Nothing," he muttered. "Just forget it."

"No. I don't want to forget it. What do you see when you look at me?"

Gabriel lowered his eyes and began to pace again, before finally blurting out, "Do you want to know the real reason I didn't like you at the beginning? Because you were one of *them*. A Second Estater. A pomp. The enemy of every croc on this planet. Every person like me. But you claimed to be different, you said you were a sympathizeur, which I still think is not a real thing, but it doesn't matter. Because eventually you did prove to be different. But now . . ." He blew out a breath and ran his hands over his stubbly jaw. "Now it's like you're forever marked. As one of them. And I don't think I'll ever be able to unsee that."

When he finally looked up from the floor, his gaze landed back on the right side of her face. On the human side. And Cerise wondered if that's how everyone would always see her. Like she was one half of a whole. One part Ministère, one part human.

But most of all, she wondered if that was how she'd always see herself.

- CHAPTER 69 -
ALOUETTE

"WHO IS HE?" ALOUETTE ASKED AS SHE PACED THE LOAD-ing dock in the back of the hothouse, her eyes roving the morning mist for signs of headlights.

Hugo sucked in a sharp breath and repositioned himself on the small fruit crate he was sitting on. "Just an old friend who owes me a favor. I trust him with my life. He will deliver us safely to the spaceport."

Alouette glanced back at her father, feeling the familiar urges of frustration rise up inside of her. The secrets. The cryptic, unhelpful answers. After everything that had happened, her father was still hiding from her. "What old friend?"

Hugo gave her a sideways glance and she could practically see his walls rising. The locks around his past sealing shut.

"Papa," she said sternly. "I'm no longer a child. *You* might trust him with your life, but I deserve to know who I'm trusting with mine."

He nodded as though he'd been afraid she might use this argument. "His name is Fauche. He's the superviseur of this hothouse. But he used to work for me."

"For *you?*"

Hugo stretched out his bandaged leg with a low groan. "Yes. Before you came into my life, I ran a fabrique in a small town near Montfer called Pontarlier. We made toys for the Second Estate. Building sets, wooden blocs, Regiment boards and"—he darted a meaningful glance at Alouette—"dolls."

"Katrina," Alouette whispered, tears springing to her eyes as she thought of the doll's tattered yellow dress catching fire, her smooth skin burning in the flames of the explosifs.

"Yes," said Hugo. "That's where I got her."

Alouette darted a look back into the mist. There was still no sign of the transporteur that her father had sworn was coming.

"How did you run a fabrique as a member of the Third Estate?"

"They didn't know I was Third Estate," he said simply. "They didn't know I was a convict named Jean LeGrand."

Alouette flinched. She so often forgot her father had once lived another life. A life that had earned him a prisoner number—2.4.6.0.1.—etched into his skin.

"When I got the job of superviseur," he went on, "they thought I was a Second Estater named Hugo Taureau. I had escaped from Bastille a few months earlier and was on the run. A group of people living in the Forest Verdure—Défecteurs, they're often called—took me in. They removed my Skin and nursed me back to health. Bastille was not kind to me. The moon is not kind to anyone. I went back to their camp years later to repay them, but they were already gone. Rounded up by the Ministère, I suppose. I pray some of them survived."

"That's why you buried the titan blocs there," Alouette said, thinking about the clearing where Marcellus had first taken her on his moto and where Hugo had later gone to dig. The flimsy details that she'd collected over time were finally connecting in her mind. Finally forming a more complete picture.

"I figured the Ministère had already raided the camp, so they probably wouldn't come back."

"You said the titan was stolen. Did you mean because you earned it in the fabrique, posing as a Second Estater?"

Hugo stared down at his injured leg, his expression distant. "Some of it I earned there, yes. But most of it *was* stolen."

"Who did you—"

"There he is," Hugo said, stopping her question in its tracks and pointing to a pair of headlights that had just appeared in the distance. As the transporteur swooped down and hovered at the edge of the loading dock, Alouette rushed to help Hugo to his feet.

She gritted her teeth against his weight bearing down on her shoulder and helped him walk, step by agonizingly slow step, toward the awaiting vehicle. A man lumbered out of the cargo hold and hurried over to position himself at Hugo's other side. Fauche was small and compactly built with tufts of white hair sticking out from beneath his superviseur's cap. Alouette noticed he, too, walked with a slight limp.

They maneuvered Hugo into the front compartment of the transporteur, and Alouette positioned his injured leg so it was extended straight out in front of him. "Merci," she said to Fauche.

He bowed his head slightly. "It's an honor to serve a Paresse."

Alouette froze, her skin tingling with dread as the nightmare of the coronation ceremony came flooding back to her. "I'm not . . . I don't . . ."

But Fauche stopped her fumbled protests with a raise of his hand. "Don't worry. I'm good at keeping secrets." He nodded toward Hugo. "I've kept his for a long time. Are you coming?"

Alouette stared numbly into the open compartment, feeling doubt start to creep into her mind. She was doing the right thing, wasn't she? She was going where she was needed. And that wasn't here. She reminded herself that the sisters didn't need her anymore. She wasn't the symbol they had hoped she would be. She wasn't the beacon they had sworn the people would flock to. She wasn't the lark that could bring down the Regime.

She was just a girl.

Who had failed so many times.

"Yes," she murmured softly, and climbed inside the transporteur.

The doors sealed shut around them and the vehicle glided away from the dock, juddering slightly as it collided with a rough pocket of air. Hugo let out a soft groan.

"Okay there, Jean?" Fauche asked, glancing over from the controls.

Alouette startled at the name, thinking of the story her father had just told her.

"I thought you went by Hugo Taureau when you met him."

"He did," Fauche said at the same time her father muttered, "I did."

"None of the other workers knew," Fauche clarified. "He had a fake identity. A good one. Fake profile in the Communiqué and everything. It's not hard if you know the right people."

"So, how did you find out who he really was?" Alouette asked as the transporteur slipped through the quiet, early-morning mist.

"I didn't know until the accident."

"Accident?" Alouette looked uneasily between Fauche and her father, who was still grimacing from every slight shudder of the craft.

"It was a delivery transporteur," Fauche answered for him. "I used to drive it for the toy fabrique. The power cell exploded and nearly killed me. I was trapped beneath the rubble. Jean here pulled me out." He smiled gratefully over at Hugo. "He saved my life."

Hugo gave a weak smile in return. "Fauche likes to exaggerate."

He scoffed. "Maybe with some things but not with this. He lifted half of a transporteur off me. As big as this one."

Alouette sucked in a sharp breath. "Like you did in the Marsh. When that statue fell—"

"Yes," said Hugo, wincing, as though every word he spoke brought another onslaught of pain. "And just like then, it attracted attention. Too much attention . . ."

His voice trailed off, unable to say more, but Fauche quickly continued for him. "Inspecteur Limier arrived in town, and I could tell the moment I laid eyes on that creepy cyborg that something was up. Something was not right. I went to tell your father about it, but he was already gone. Back on the run. I tracked him down, though. Forced him to tell me the truth."

"I swore he was going to turn me in," Hugo whispered.

Fauche reached out and patted the old man's elbow. "Never, mon ami. Never." He turned back to Alouette. "Like I said, I owed him my life. I tried to mislead Inspecteur Limier, but . . ." His face darkened. "That cyborg is relentless."

Mist continued to cling to the sides of the transporteur, curling against the windows, and suddenly Alouette was back in that terrifying darkness, hiding beneath the rock that used to haunt her memories as a child, thick fog swirling around her as sirens blared and orange lights sparked in the distance. And Hugo whispering in her ear, *"Hush, ma petite, hush."*

"That's when you came for me," Alouette said, threading the details together in her mind. "At the Jondrette."

Hugo nodded. "By the time Limier showed up looking for me, your mother had already gone to the Sols. She worked at the toy fabrique. That's how we met. When Limier arrived in town, everything just kind of fell into place. Like the Sols were lighting my path, guiding me. I had your name, I had the directions to the Refuge, I had a plea from your mother to protect you. Lisole . . ."

His voice trailed off and a shiver passed through Alouette. She knew at once, from the way he said her name, that Lisole was more than just a worker. That something had blossomed between them. Something that was genuine and cherished and missed.

"She just wanted to keep you safe." Hugo's words were so soft, so hesitant, and when Alouette glanced back at her father, she saw a wistful ghost of a smile dancing on his lips, like he was lost in a beautiful dream. For just a moment, Alouette felt herself slipping right into that dream with him. Because she knew exactly what it was.

It was the night they'd arrived at the Refuge.

Into the sisters' awaiting arms.

Into their protection.

For thirteen years, they'd kept her safe. Just as her mother had wanted. Just as Hugo had promised.

The doubt started to slither its way back into Alouette's mind. Doubt about what she was doing. Where she was going. Whom she was leaving behind. She had a feeling it would always be there, lurking in the darkness, waiting for the right time to spring forth and remind her that it was still there. She could not escape it. Not inside this transporteur. Not inside a voyageur sailing across the stars. And certainly not on Reichenstat.

She shut her eyes and tried to tamp down the doubt, push it back to the dark corners where it came from. But it fought back. Hard and scrappy. Throwing unfair punches. Kicking her where it knew she would feel it the most.

"Promise me you'll protect them. You'll protect them all."

A muffled banging sound cut through her thoughts, and Alouette's eyes fluttered open. "What is that?" she asked, desperately turning to the window, only to find it was still shrouded in mist.

"I don't know," said Fauche, looking just as uneased by the interruption.

"It almost sounds like . . ." Alouette listened carefully to the sound coming from outside the transporteur. There was a rhythmic quality to it. Like someone pounding on a giant drum. "Footsteps."

And as soon as she said it, she knew that was exactly what it was. An *army* of footsteps.

Fauche overrode the autopilote and reached for the contrôleur, compelling the transporteur to rise farther into the air. They lurched upward, the mist thinning as they went. Until, through the thick white tendrils dancing across the ground, Alouette could see it.

She could see it all.

There were thousands of them. Streaming like one single body, one winding snake, weaving through the fabriques and across Vallonay's vast fermelands. They marched with their arms raised and mouths open, gaping and fierce. Someone was chanting something. A question. And the massive crowd of people was answering. But Alouette couldn't make out what was being said. Some held sticks. Others brandished lengths of jagged PermaSteel. Still others seemed to be holding, in their angry fists, glinting rayonettes.

And through it all, through this storming, indignant mass, weaved a deadly ribbon of red. Red hoods. Red scarves. Swaths of red fabric billowing high over the crowd like sails on a First World bateau.

"What's going on?" Alouette asked.

But Fauche could only shake his head numbly as they all stared down at the moving, marching mass.

"Check your TéléCom," Hugo bellowed, and Fauche seemed to break from his trance as he fumbled to withdraw the device from his pocket and unfold it.

The urgent, frenzied voice of Desirée Beauchamp came flooding out of the speakers almost instantly. ". . . I repeat, all First and Second Estaters are being told to lock yourselves in your homes for your own safety. Do not attempt to leave Ledôme."

Ledôme.

A cold dread slithered through Alouette as her gaze traveled up and out, to the very front of the enormous crowd and the hill they were preparing to ascend.

The hill that led to only one place.

The massive arching structure stood at the summit, like a twinkling, brilliant, but impenetrable forteresse. The peak of its great dome kissed the gray clouds above. The glow from its three artificial Sols within beamed out like stars fallen from the sky.

And from its gates, Alouette could see armed guards streaming out by the hundreds. Sergents and officers trampling into position around the perimeter of Ledôme. Each of them was dressed in full riot gear. Shining helmets, padded chest protectors, ballistic shields, riot-gas canisters strapped to their backs, and rayonettes and explosif launchers poised and ready in their fists.

Silence filled the transporteur. An uneasy silence that sent tiny bumps spreading across Alouette's skin. It all played out in her mind like the worst kind of nightmare. The clash. The screams. The sound of rayonette pulses and explosifs ripping through flesh. So much death.

"Turn!" Hugo shouted, gazing out in horror at the sight in front of them. "Take another route. Get us as far away from this as possible."

Fauche gripped his hands tighter around the contrôleur, and the transporteur banked sharply to the left. As they turned, Alouette could see the Frets in the distance. Smoke still rising up from their center. A wound still bleeding. Bodies lying in the wreckage that weren't even cold yet. And already, they were going to add more.

"Promise me you'll protect them. You'll protect them all."

"Turn back!" The words erupted from some unknown place within her. Some unknown depth.

"What?" asked Fauche, staring at her like she'd lost her mind.

"Turn back now!"

"Alouette," Hugo warned, stern and fatherly. It was the voice she remembered from years of her questions and his secrets, her desperation to see and know the world, and his walls constructed around it.

"Papa," she said, matching his voice with a sternness of her own. "I have to go back. I have to protect them."

"How?!" her father thundered, causing Alouette to flinch. He so rarely raised his voice with her.

"I don't know," she admitted. "But I have to try." She spun back to Fauche. "Please turn this transporteur around."

"Fauche," retorted Hugo. "Whatever you do, do *not* turn this thing around."

Fauche looked uncertainly between Hugo and Alouette—between the man he'd made a promise to long ago and the girl with Paresse blood running through her veins. His hands were paralyzed on the contrôleur.

"I can't leave them!" Alouette shouted. "Those people down there need me!"

"No, they don't," Hugo said before breathing out a weary sigh. "I've been afraid of this ever since I learned the truth about who you are. Little Lark, just because the Patriarche was your father doesn't mean you are responsible for these people."

"I know," she said, her voice softening. As she looked into Hugo's warm brown eyes, she could see herself reflected back in them. Not as she was now, though. As a little girl. A four-year-old child lost in the mist, carrying heavy pails full of reeds back to the Jondrette. It was how he would always see her. She knew that. Through the tinted lens of a promise he'd made long ago.

A promise to protect.

Something began to bloom inside of her then. Something new yet familiar at the same time. Maybe it had been there all along. A tiny seedling waiting just below the surface, waiting to break through the ground and reach up toward the light.

And yet someone had already known it was there. Someone who had tried to water it and coax it to grow. At the very beginning, Citizen Rousseau had asked her why she wanted to join the Vangarde. Why she wanted to join this fight. Alouette had thought it was because it was her duty. Because she'd been born with the right blood. Because she was a symbol. But she'd been wrong.

It wasn't because of what Lyon Paresse had given her. It was because of what Hugo Taureau had given her. And her mother. And the sisters.

Something to protect.

Books from a lost world. Words that had been forgotten. People she loved.

"Promise me you'll protect them. You'll protect them all."

She wasn't a symbol. She was a guardian. It was what the sisters had raised her to be all along. It was the why that had always fueled her. Driven her. Lit her way even in the darkest moments.

Alouette reached up and pressed a palm to Hugo's cheek. "He was never my father. It was always you. If I inherited anything from anyone, it was from you. You kept me safe. Just like my mother wanted. You protected me. I learned it from *you*. You may not have given me your blood, but you gave me your heart."

Hugo's eyes filled with tears. He pressed a hand over hers. "But—"

"I release you from your promise," she whispered. "You don't need to protect me anymore. But I do need to protect them."

Hugo breathed out. A thirteen-year-long breath. His shoulders fell. His tears fell. His walls came last.

He turned to Fauche and said, "Turn around."

CHAPTER 70

MARCELLUS

"THEY PLUNDER US!" CRIED MAX.

"We plunder them!" shouted the crowd in an eerie and angry synchronicity.

Marcellus marched through the fog, toward the base of the steep hill. He could still hear the thousands coming up behind him, smashing in windows of nearby ferme buildings, violently pulling up crops, firing pulses at passing cruiseurs heading to Ledôme to seek sanctuary.

"They steal from us!" Max shouted.

"We steal from them!" came the response.

Red Scar guards slipped through the crowd, distributing rayonettes from giant sacs strapped to their chests. Marcellus barely had a chance to wonder where all of those weapons had come from before one was shoved into his own hand. He stared down at it, feeling both empowered and uneasy at the familiar touch of the metal.

Up ahead, Max bellowed into her amplificateur, which projected her voice across the mighty moving horde. And before her, high on its hill, loomed their target.

Ledôme.

Marcellus had never approached the massive structure on foot before.

It was enormous. It was shimmering and beautiful. But it was a forteresse that would be protected. He, of all people, knew that.

The mist started to swirl and wisp away, and Marcellus could now see shapes moving atop the giant, sloping hill before them. Massing. Assembling. Guards were undoubtedly pouring out through the security shields by the hundreds, forming a thick wall around the perimeter. Marcellus knew the protocol. They had been summoned from all over Ledôme, tasked with holding back the tide until the real reinforcements could arrive.

And, as Marcellus gazed up into the sky, at the long procession of transporteurs arriving from Vallonay, he knew that those reinforcements were here.

"They behead us!" shouted Max.

"We behead them!" echoed the crowd.

The first of the transporteurs touched down at the top of the hill and droids flooded out, one after another. From way down here, they looked like one swarming mass of glinting PermaSteel.

Marcellus instinctively stopped marching. His feet could no longer move. All he could do was stare as more transporteurs landed and the legion of droids spilled out, hundreds of them. And they kept coming. Lining up in rows upon terrible rows that began to descend partially down the hill. Their exoskeletons formed indestructible silver walls. Their dazzling, beaming eyes glowed through the thinning mist like a gargantuan sky of orange stars.

There was a commotion up ahead. Bodies parted and people grumbled in frustration as a man staggered through the crowd. It took Marcellus a moment to realize he was walking the wrong way. Walking *away* from Ledôme. And it took another moment for Marcellus to recognize him.

"Jolras!" Marcellus caught the man by the elbow, forcing him to stop. But Jolras's glazed eyes looked right through Marcellus. As if he couldn't even see him. "Where are you going? What are you doing?"

People streamed around them, continuing to march toward the base of the hill.

"It's over," Jolras murmured. There was something wrong with his voice. Something wrong with his face. He looked and sounded so haunted.

So defeated. Like he'd already seen his own death in the battle to come.

"What do you mean?" Marcellus shouted over the chants of the crowd.

"I could have stopped her, but I didn't. I had so many chances, but I didn't take them," Jolras said numbly, his eyes still unable to focus on Marcellus. "Now there's no stopping her. It's too late. She's going to get us all killed."

"Jolras—" Marcellus tried to speak, but the man pushed him aside and continued to wade against the current of the crowd.

All the while, he kept muttering, "She's going to get us all killed."

Someone pushed at Marcellus's back and he stumbled forward. He had no choice but to keep moving, keep marching, toward that hill and the ghastly sight that loomed on top of it. But his mind was finally processing what Jolras had said. Finally catching up to what his body was doing. What *all* of these bodies were doing.

They were walking straight into a slaughter.

A cheer rose up somewhere in the crowd behind him. Marcellus spun around to see a volley of coordinated pulses had found their target in a passing cruiseur, and with a judder and then a series of deadly screams, the craft came tumbling out of the sky. It spun and twirled, momentarily regaining its balance before finally sputtering out completely and crashing into a nearby silo.

The crowd roared. Marcellus only felt more sick.

With every transporteur that landed atop that hill, with every droid that disembarked and armed-to-the-teeth sergent who assembled behind them, Marcellus felt his confidence slipping. His wide gaze took in the wall of Ministère might that was amassing above them, and the planet seemed to tilt farther on its axis.

"They plunder us!"

"We plunder them!"

Too many.

Those were the only words to float through his mind. Not the battle cries that were spewing forth from Max's lips at the front of the crowd. But two little words that made everything around him slam into focus.

Too many.

And that was the irony. There were far more people marching *toward* the hill of Ledôme than standing guard on top of it. That had always been the irony. The Third Estate far outmatched the First and Second Estates. But only in their numbers. Not in their power. Not in the weapons at their disposal.

"They steal from us!" Max's voice reverberated from the amplificateur, traveling across this massive, chanting crowd that seemed to be growing by the second.

"We steal from them!"

People were still streaming in from the Frets and fabriques, their anger coalescing with the crowd, like a contagious disease.

Marcellus peered up into the sky. So far, his grandfather had not yet summoned the combatteurs. But Marcellus knew he would not hesitate if need be.

Too many.

Another battalion of transporteurs sailed over their heads, heading toward Ledôme, delivering more reinforcements from the droid fabrique, more weapons, more sergents dressed in riot gear, ready for a fight.

"They behead us!"

"We behead—"

"No!" came another voice, so loud, so commanding, the crowd pulsing around Marcellus seemed startled into a momentary silence. "If you attack now, you will surely die."

Marcellus followed the confused gazes of everyone around him as people searched frantically for the sound. Even Max had stopped her passionate speech, her expression balanced precariously between confusion and irritation.

"Do you really think you can launch an offensive attack against a legion of droids?"

Marcellus froze. The voice was echoey and slightly fractured, like it was being broadcast through a speaker turned up too loud. But it was familiar, too. Achingly, heart-wrenchingly familiar.

"If this is your strategy, you will never win!" the voice called out.

The crowd grew restless, displeased with the demoralizing words being shouted at them from some unseen place. They began to boo and shake their fists with fury, calling for Max to revive them again with her rousing rhetoric, with the words they *wanted* to hear.

But Marcellus knew, deep in his soul, that the voice—wherever it was coming from—was right.

"You will never defeat their power and their weapons with the ones in your hands now," continued the voice, undeterred. It sounded like it was crackling from the sky. From the clouds themselves. "You will only be bringing about more blood. More death. More of the same violent, deadly cycle."

And then, like a vision sent straight from the Sols, she was there. She was in front of them. One of the transporteurs that had soared above them only moments ago was now hovering in front of the massive crowd at the base of the hill, stopping it in its tracks. The final tendrils of fog whispered away, and the giant loading ramp of the craft unfurled to reveal a girl standing in its depths.

A girl with eyes that reflected Laterre's endless clouds above. With hair that fanned out in curls around her face like rays of a Sol. A girl who, up until five seconds ago, Marcellus had believed was dead.

But here she was. Rising from the ashes like the ghost he'd always believed her to be. A beautiful, ethereal, magnificent vision.

- CHAPTER 71 -
ALOUETTE

A HUSH FELL OVER THE CROWD AS ALOUETTE WALKED to the end of the loading ramp, which was now extended like a great floating bridge.

For a moment, all she could do was stare. It was another field of stars. Just like the ones peering back at her in the Marsh during the coronation ceremony. Except this time, she was not speechless in their presence. She was not overwhelmed by their vast number. She was only inspired.

"You have all come here today because you are hurt. You are grieving. You are angry. And that is understandable." Her words echoed out through the transporteur's speakers, which Fauche had turned all the way up. "I am hurt and grieving too. But this is not the answer to your hurt. This is not the way out of your grief. And this is not the way to bring about real change."

"Don't listen to this!" Max shouted wildly into her amplificateur. "Of course she tries to convince you not to fight. The girl is *one* of them! She is a Paresse. She is the enemy."

"No!" Alouette shouted, a tempest of fire and passion building inside of her. "I have never been a Paresse. I have never stepped foot in their Palais. Or drunk a single sip of their champagne. Or draped myself in a single garment of their fabric. I stand here with you because I am one of *you*. I was raised by women who fought for change and a man who spent his life on the run from this corrupt Regime. Yes, I was born with First Estate blood in my veins. But I was also born with Third Estate blood. *Your* blood. My mother was a maid. A fabrique worker. A blood whore. A woman who died trying to protect me from the murderers who bear the name Paresse."

"Close your ears to this nonsense!" Max cried.

"My very existence proves that the estates are an illusion," Alouette surged on. "A fairy tale that you've been told since you were little. Since your parents were little. Since their parents were little. It's a lie constructed to keep you from realizing your true potential. I stand before you, not as your ruler, not as your Matrone, not as anyone but another tired, weary soul who wants to see a new dawn for Laterre, a better dawn. A better planet. But I'm telling you, if you march up that hill, if you try to take on that army, if you try to achieve this dream through means of violence, you will only fail."

The crowd was silent, like a sea beneath a cluster of ominous gray clouds, waiting to see if the storm would hit or simply pass them by.

"Some dreams are worth the risk!" Max shouted. "We have come here to fight. Because we have come here to *win*. And if we die today, our lives will be worth the sacrifice. Our deaths will pave the way to a better life for our children."

"Look at what is behind me!" Alouette shouted back. "Look up there! At their weapons, their might, their armor, their riot gas, their explosifs. You'll all be dead in minutes, and then who will care for those children? Who will fight for a better life for them?"

"They may have stronger weapons," Max went on, undeterred, "but we are stronger in our numbers. The Third Estate are the true power that runs through the veins of his planet. Not the First and not the Second. Today, we must show them, we must *prove* to them with our anger and our fists, what true power means."

"Violence is never the answer! We can achieve change peacefully!" Alouette cried out, but she could tell her words were no longer landing. She was losing the crowd. She could feel them being pulled to Max. To her passion. To her anger. To her conviction.

To *her* words.

"Violence is the *only* answer!" Max bellowed. "Peace achieves nothing. We can't just stand here and hope for change. We can't just knock on the door of the Palais and ask nicely for a better life. We have to fight for that life. We have to take that life. We have to be willing to die for that life."

She punched a hand in the air and the crowd immediately broke into a raucous, rioting roar. More fists were raised, holding rayonettes and makeshift weapons.

"They plunder us!" Max shouted.

"We plunder them!" the crowd responded in unison.

But all Alouette could hear was her own heart pounding in her ears. She could see her own face reflected back at her in her mind. In her memories. It was the same helpless face she'd seen on the holograms that day in the Marsh. When she couldn't convince the crowd. When she couldn't make them see. When she couldn't stop them from fighting.

And it was happening again.

"They steal from us!"

"We steal from them!"

The Vangarde's words—their hopes, their dreams, *their* conviction—were failing. Everything Alouette had been raised to believe—every philosophy and principle and mindset that had been instilled in her since the day she walked into that Refuge—was failing.

"They behead us!"

"We behead them!"

Slowly, like a mighty wind building, the crowd began to march forward again. Step by step, body by body, they passed beneath the transporteur that held her aloft. They shouted and burned with energy. So much energy.

Alouette wilted in defeat. Her shoulders slumped. Her head tipped back. Her face rose to the sky.

And that's when she saw it.

The slightest shift in the light. Nothing more than a movement of clouds. A rearranging of trapped water molecules. A gentle stirring of mist and vapor. But the result was wondrous, fracturing the light in a whole new way, cutting it into magnificent patterns that fell across the great landscape of the planet.

Like a kaléidoscope.

Alouette gazed out at the massive moving crowd, still chanting, still marching toward that formidable army that stood guard at the top of the hill. The sheer number of people who had come here today was astounding. So many of them willing to fight, willing to lay down their lives.

Max was right. They were stronger in their numbers. The Third Estate were the true power that ran through the veins of this planet. The Vangarde had always known this. But they wanted to use that power to fight for change peacefully. With words. While Max wanted to use that power to fight for change violently. With weapons.

But those weren't the only two options.

Alouette reached into the pocket of her tunic and wrapped her hand around the small cardboard cylinder that was tucked inside.

"I keep it with me at all times. As a reminder that there's always another way to look at something."

"Wait! Stop!" Alouette cried out, the transporteur's speakers carrying her voice across the crowd.

But they had stopped listening to her useless pleas. They kept going. Kept chanting. Kept marching forward with their weapons clutched in their hands.

Alouette could feel the fractured light shining down on her, the Sols fighting to be seen through the thick cloud coverage. And she knew she had to keep going too. "There's another way! Yes, we can choose to fight and die here today. And hope that our sacrifices will be worth it in the end. Or we can choose to live and *show* Empereur Bonnefaçon—show them all—how powerful we really are. By taking away what they need most from us."

It wasn't the reaction Alouette was hoping for. Most of the crowd continued their determined forward march up the hill. But a few people stopped and looked back up, their gazes burning not only with rage and revenge but also with the slightest traces of curiosity.

Alouette focused on them, trying to keep her voice steady and her confidence from faltering. "The truth is, they can't survive without the Third Estate. Without you. You grow their food and mine their minerals and purify their water and build their goods. Without you they are nothing. We must remind them of that. We must remind them of who the true beating heart of this Regime is."

More people stopped. More looked up. More asked questions with their blinking eyes and speechless stares.

"If we cut off their supply to what matters most to them—their bread, their cheese, their precious champagne, their luxury goods, their meat and fancy fabrics—we can show them exactly how powerful we are. We can remind them that without us, they are nothing and they *have* nothing."

Seeming to notice the quiet that was spreading throughout the crowd, Max began to shout into her amplificateur again.

"Ignore this ignorant girl who attempts to steal your power away from you. She is only trying to distract you and it's working! Your true power lies in your fists and your weapons and your passion!"

But this time, Alouette didn't even acknowledge the second voice in the crowd. She let Max's words ricochet off her like useless cluster bullets off an invisible shield. She looked out into the crowd with the face of an adoring mother, the face of a guardian who would stop at nothing to protect what she loved.

And she would.

"Return with me now to Vallonay. Help me protect what is yours. What you build and make and manufacture every single day. Help me guard it all, defend it, as it is your true power. We must block off their access to these resources. We must stand between them and what they want from us. What they *need* from us. But it cannot just be one of us. It cannot be ten of us or a hundred of us, or even a thousand of us. It must be *all* of us. Only then will they be forced to listen. Only then will they be forced to hear. And only then can we demand the change we dream of. The kind of planet we deserve to live on. Return with me now to Vallonay and help me build these barricades."

Once again, Alouette felt like she was peering out at a field of stars. They were silent. But in their eyes, she could see something dawning. A realization. A truth. A light.

Somewhere behind her, Max let out a roar. "They plunder us!"

But there was no response. Only more silence.

And then, Alouette heard it.

Just like the pulse that had ripped through the marketplace less than two weeks ago, this too tore through the paper-thin wall that had been holding back the tides. This too felt like it had stopped time. Stopped the planet spinning on its axis.

This too drowned out everything for kilomètres, until all Alouette could hear was that single sound whooshing through the air.

Not a pulse. But a shout.

"To the barricades!" a woman cried.

And that was all it took.

Once again, the wall came down.

A second person echoed her cry. "To the barricades!"

Then a third and a fourth, until the whole crowd had joined in on the new chant. "To the barricades!"

And suddenly, everyone was running. But not toward the hill of Ledôme like the awaiting sergents and droids were expecting. They were running *away*. Back across the ferme-land, toward the city, toward the fabriques that had once enslaved them but now were the key to setting them free.

"Stop!" Max shouted at her retreating army. "All of you! Stop! Don't run away! Don't you see that's what they want? They want you to stand down! They want you to turn and flee! They want you to run! Don't give them what they want! Come back here, you cowards!" She turned to her nearby guards, her face contorted with rage. "Stop them!"

The stampede continued. Thousands upon thousands of people rushing away from the battle that would never happen. The attack that would never come to light. The blood that would never be shed. Alouette turned to watch Max's eyes flash with fury, with vengeance, with something Alouette had never seen before. It made her chest tighten.

Max was a general who had lost her army. A bloodthirsty warrior who had lost her chance to fight. She was a wounded woman who had lost her mother and then her sister. And now she was a desperate leader who had lost her mind.

"No!" Alouette screamed as she watched Max toggle the switch of her rayonette and aim the weapon into the fleeing crowd. But Alouette was too far away to do anything. And there were people who were still too close.

She heard a pulse rip through the air. Rip through flesh. She heard a body hit the ground. She blinked once. Again. Certain she was seeing everything wrong. Certain when she rewound this moment in her mind, it would become clearer.

Alouette stared down at the body crumpled on the ground. At Max's determined, vengeful stare frozen in time forever. At the smoking black hole in the center of her forehead.

And finally, at Jolras Epernay holding the rayonette.

CHAPTER 72

CHATINE

"THEY'RE COMING! HUNDREDS OF THEM. THOUSANDS of them. They're flooding the fabriques. They're building barricades! This is it, Chatine. This is the moment we've been waiting for. The people are finally going to make a stand against him. You have to come."

Chatine clutched the radio between her cold, trembling fingers, listening to Marcellus's words but unable to make sense of them. He was talking too fast and the words were too strange.

Flooding the fabriques?

Make a stand?

Barricades?

A wind blew off the Secana Sea, icy and sharp like a single swarm of piercing daggers. Even though Chatine was buried inside her insulated coat, her teeth chattered, and her cheeks burned with the cold as she stood in the gaping mouth of the cave. The community had set up their temporary camp on the most northern reaches of the Terrain Perdu, where vast frozen cliffs plunged into the Secana Sea. Footsteps away from where she stood, a bluff looked out over the infinite grayness of choppy waves and heavy, frigid skies. And behind her, tents, makeshift storage units, and a small fleet of ships huddled together, hiding from Ministère ships above and sheltering from the worst of the squalling ocean blusters below.

"You have to come," Marcellus repeated, his voice still rushed and frenetic like an overzealous child. "You have to join us. They're barricading themselves in. They're guarding all the doors. It's the other way. The *third* way!"

"Marcellus," Chatine said, struggling to keep her freezing fingertip steady on the talk button. "Slow down. What are you talking about? What third way?"

Marcellus exhaled heavily, and even from thousands of kilomètres away, Chatine swore she could feel his breath on her cheeks. Although she knew it was just the wind echoing off the cave walls, coming back to slap her in the face. "When Citizen Rousseau and I went to meet with the Red Scar, I asked her about the vote. Yes or no. Keep searching for Alouette or not. Save her or give up on her."

Chatine closed her eyes. He was talking nonsense now. The stress of losing Alouette and the Refuge and the sisters had clearly gone to his head. He was rambling, slipping around in time, jumbling his thoughts together. "Marcellus," she said again. Ever so slowly. Ever so cautiously. Because she knew this version of him all too well. The way his obsessive mind tangled in knots. The way he disappeared into his own head, his own planet. The way one wrong word could startle him.

But he kept going. Kept speaking, like he couldn't hear her at all. "I asked her what she would have voted. I needed to know if it was yes or no. I needed to know what side she was on. And she said . . ."

His voice trailed off and Chatine heard nothing but static through the radio. Then, like a whisper on the gusting ocean spray, Marcellus's voice came back. Quiet. Collected. Focused. "She said nothing is that black and white. Nothing is just yes or no. There is always another way. A *third* way."

Chatine stood up a little straighter, trying to piece the details together. As chaotic as Marcellus seemed, this sounded exactly like something Citizen Rousseau would have said. One of her many riddles to solve.

"And this is it!" he went on, his excitement building again. "Alouette has—"

"Alouette?" Chatine repeated, feeling the crack in her voice spread through her chest.

"She's alive," said Marcellus, and for just a moment, the frozen air swirling around Chatine turned warm and beautiful and inviting. Until she could have convinced herself she was standing directly under a Sol. Not huddled in a cliffside cave on the icy shores of the Secana Sea.

"What?" she whispered.

"She's alive," Marcellus repeated with no trace of hesitation in his voice. "She survived the bombing of the Frets. She stopped the attack."

Chatine's mouth went dry. "What attack?"

Marcellus took a breath. "Maximilienne tried to get the Third Estate to attack Ledôme. But Alouette talked everyone down. She turned the whole crowd around with nothing more than her words."

"So she convinced them not to fight at all?"

"No!" said Marcellus. "That's what I've been trying to tell you. The Vangarde kept insisting that peace was the only way to enact real change. And the Red Scar kept saying that change could only be brought about by violence. By spreading fear and fighting the Regime head-on. But there's another way. A third way. Fighting to defend. Fighting to protect. Guarding the true power of the planet."

"By barricading the fabriques?" Chatine asked, still struggling to understand. "But your grandfather will never let that happen. He'll send in the combatteurs. He'll blow it all to dust, just like he did with Fret 7."

"He won't," Marcellus said, and there it was again. Crackling through the radio. That certainty. That clarity. That conviction. "He *can't*. My grandfather has always believed that the estates of Laterre are like a body: the First Estate, the brain that rules; the Second Estate, the heart that provides the power and pulse; and the Third Estate, the legs on which everything else stands. If he destroys the fabriques, he destroys his own goods. His own food, materials, médicaments, exports, and the workers, too. He destroys the very legs on which this planet stands."

"Maybe so," Chatine said. "But he still won't give up without a fight."

"And neither will we."

There was a long pause, during which Marcellus never released the talk button. Chatine could hear the muffled sounds of shouts and chants around him. People moving. People running. People mobilizing. And then, she could hear the sound of one quiet, yearning sigh. And she knew it was him. "You should have heard her, Chatine. Her words. Her passion. The hope she's given these people, it's like nothing I've ever seen. . . ."

The warmth that had enveloped Chatine only moments ago began to slip away. There was so much reverence in his voice. So much devotion. And Chatine reprimanded herself for forgetting—even for a second—that this was how it had always been. Alouette was always the Sol, and Chatine was always the shadow. Nothing had changed. It had only been amplified. And she'd been a fool to ever believe differently.

"You need to see this, Chatine." Marcellus let out a wistful sigh. "It's really something. There are so many people. And they're all willing to fight. To defend what's theirs. This is the revolution we've been waiting for. The revolution *you've* been waiting for. It's not about Paresse heirs and famous rebels who escaped Bastille. It's about people. Third Estaters finally woken up and demanding change. You have to come. I need you with me. I need you, Chatine."

Every time he said her name, it was like he was pounding directly on her heart with a hammer.

"You don't . . . ," she started to say, but a lump was growing in her throat faster than she could squeeze the words out around it. "You don't need me."

Another pause. Another flurry of static. Another painful thump against her heart.

And then came a voice she'd only ever heard in her dreams.

"I do," said Marcellus. "I've always needed you. From the moment I first saw you in that morgue. With that giant ripped hood covering your face. With those impossible gray eyes staring back at me. Don't you get it, Chatine? You're the reason I'm here right now. Something happened to me that day. *You* happened to me. You changed everything. You woke me up. You made me see the world for what it really was. A miserable place that could turn innocent girls like you into criminals. A rain-soaked planet painted over with fake Sols and a shiny titan gloss. You pulled it all away from my eyes. And now that I've seen that world, I can't stop seeing it. I can't ignore it. I have to do whatever I can to change it. Not for me. My life was a dreamscape compared to yours. Compared to the lives of all of these people around me. I have to do it for them. For you."

Chatine felt her knees giving out. Felt her resolve giving up. She slid down onto the damp, rocky bluff, while the Secana Sea winds swirled and stabbed and buffeted against her coat. She sat with the radio clutched to her chest, Marcellus's words pouring out of it. Pouring into her. They were never words she dared hope he'd say to her. She knew better than to hope for such impossible things. They were coming from another realm. Another life. Another beating heart.

"Chatine?" Marcellus said, and the space around him seemed quieter now, like he'd stepped away from the shouting cries and rousing chants. "Are you still there?"

She nodded. Foolish, she knew. Because he couldn't see her. He couldn't see her pathetic body huddled around an old First World radio like it had the power to save her.

But it didn't matter. Because somehow he just knew she was still there.

Maybe because she could never leave. No matter how many times she tried. She could never stop huddling around this fragile hope, cradling it like a weak flame that, at any moment, could be snuffed out by another bitter gust of wind.

Maybe because, despite everything, the answer to his question was always, *Yes. I'm still here.*

"Back in the Forest Verdure," Marcellus began, his voice hushed like he was telling her a secret, whispering it in her ear, "I told you I would die to protect Alouette. . . ."

One more pause. And her heart gave up too.

"I want you to know, I would die to protect you, too, Chatine." Marcellus breathed out a slow breath. "And I think you would do the same for me."

She rested her head against the top of the radio. Tears dripped down the sides. She cried for those people flocking to the barricades, willing to fight for a better life. She cried for all those children still trapped on that spacecraft carrier as slaves, working to make Empereur Bonnefaçon stronger. She cried for every single soul—every star—he'd already snuffed out of the sky in his ruthless pursuit of power. She cried for Roche, the brother she was always trying to save, and Azelle, the sister she couldn't save. But mostly, she cried because she knew what would happen next.

"Will you come?" he asked. "Will you stand beside me?"

Once again, she didn't need to speak. He didn't need to see her head fall into a silent nod to know what her answer would be. Because the answer was always *yes*.

- CHAPTER 73 -
ETIENNE

ETIENNE HAD ALWAYS KNOWN HOPE WAS A FOOLISH
thing to base your life on. He'd learned that at four years old, as Maman
had dragged him away from their burning chalet. As he'd prayed that the
door would swing open, that a window would be smashed from within,
that his father would escape.

He stood on the rocky bluff at the edge of the community's new
encampment, watching Chatine wrap her entire body around the radio,
like she was protecting a deep and deadly wound, and something inside of
him broke. He'd heard their whispered conversation. Marcellus's pleas and
Chatine's silence that felt as loud and as conclusive as an explosif.

He knew that hope was gone. Vanished like the seabirds that danced
on the ocean breeze, coming so close to the cliff's edge, only to disappear
a second later into the gray clouds above. Maybe that hope had never been
real to begin with. Maybe he'd invented it all on his own, conjured it out
of fleeting glances and brushed fingertips, solidified it in his mind with a
single, stolen kiss. But as it snapped and shattered inside of him now, he
felt something new being formed. A different kind of hope. A different
kind of expectation. One that, for once, he had total control over.

"We need to tell the camp," he said. Chatine startled and looked up at

him with those clear gray eyes that had always mystified him and infuri-
ated him.

She wiped at her damp cheeks and sniffled, looking caught out as she
hastily scrambled to her feet. "What?"

"Everyone needs to know what's happening."

When she didn't make any show of moving or even comprehending,
he took her hand and guided her away from the cliff's edge and back into
the cave.

The small, domed tents were arranged in a neat circle, their ice-gray
fabric billowing in the ocean winds. Etienne and Chatine weaved between
them and when they reached the largest one in the center, Etienne
unzipped the entrance flap and waved Chatine inside. After the frigid
air on the cliffside, the warmth hit them like one of the pounding waves
below.

Members of the community were gathered around a large stove,
as if it were a monument they'd all come to worship. Bathed in its
bright purple glow, children sat in their parents' laps. Older folks were
shrouded in thick blankets. Some people hummed and whispered. Little Léopold and Adèle sat with Saros and Castor, who were teaching
them how to fuel the stove with the community's homemade emberweed oil.

Etienne still hadn't gotten over the shock of seeing his people like
this. In this place. Crowded around a single source of heat, trying to keep
warm. Trying desperately to keep their spirits up. In spite of everything.

It could have been different. If he'd managed to steal the zyttrium, they
could have had their old lives back. Their old protections and comforts.
They could have been safely concealed.

But he was done with concealment. He was done hiding.

Etienne clapped twice to get everyone's attention. Conversations
drifted off as a hundred pairs of eyes stared up at him. Some blinking
with disappointment, just as he'd suspected, others twinkling with curiosity.

"We've just received word that the gridders are mobilizing against
the Regime," Etienne said, instigating a frenzy of shocked whispers.

"They're barricading their fabriques and holding their goods hostage."

"Received word from who?" asked Mentor Ava.

Etienne stole a hasty glance at Chatine, who was standing near the tent wall, her eyes wide and glassy, as if she were still trying to make sense of what was happening. "Marcellus Bonnefaçon. He's calling it a revolution. He says thousands are joining the fight." Etienne took a breath. "And I think we should too."

The whispers instantly turned to shouts, some of outrage, others of confusion. The purple flames inside the stove seemed to echo the emotions in the tent as they cracked and popped loudly and shot tiny sparks through the grate.

Etienne shouted to be heard over all the noise. "We can't keep living like this! Running at the sound of a Ministère transporteur. Hiding in caves like rats. We have to do something about it. We have to take a stand. And now is the time."

More shouts came hurtling back at him, growing with intensity.

"We don't fight their battles!"

"Gridder politics are not our concern!"

"We have to worry about ourselves!"

Sylvain rose to his feet, turning to Mentor Ava like a small child tattling to a parent. "What is the meaning of this?"

Ava tried to restore order. "Quiet down, everyone. Please."

"I'm scared," cried Astra, running to Brigitte, who scooped her into her lap and kissed the top of her head.

"You should be!" shouted Sylvain. "What your brother is suggesting is suicide."

"Sylvain," warned Ava. "That is not constructive."

"Neither is dropping an explosif like that in the middle of our camp."

Mentor Ava turned to Etienne with a look that said, *He has a point*.

"Sorry," Etienne said. "But I have the right to back up my proposal."

Ava turned back to Sylvain with the same look. And the tent seemed to settle into an uneasy silence. Because this was the way it was done. Proposals had to be listened to, considered with open hearts and open minds. It was the cornerstone of their community. The reason they'd been able to survive this long without warring among themselves.

Every pair of eyes slid back to Etienne. He ignored all of their anxious, expectant expressions except one.

As his gaze met his mother's, he felt every broken thing inside of him mend. It was a look of pure faith. The kind that only a mother can give a child who has grown up from a single seed she planted, who has ventured off into the galaxy and come back their own person. With their own purpose.

Etienne nodded and cleared his throat. "The Regime has taken so much from us. Our zyttrium. Our camp. Your families. *My* father." His voice started to break, but he didn't stop. "I lost him because of them. But also because of *us*. Because we keep insisting on hiding. On running. And as long as we run, they chase. I used to think life was good for us. Staying out of everyone's way. Keeping to ourselves. Thinking we were safe. Thinking we were better off than the gridders. But we were never safe. And we were never better off. We were always one last drop of zyttrium away from being rounded up like so many of our loved ones. The very fact that we *have* to hide should be enough. Because what kind of life is that? And what kind of life will we have if we continue to live in hiding? Did you know that the man responsible for the roundups now sits in the Grand Palais? Now rules over all of Laterre as Empereur? Did you know he's using *our* zyttrium to build a fleet of stealth ships to attack Usonia with Albion? I saw it with my own eyes. Giant deadly invadeurs. Legions of combatteurs. Invisible to scans. Invisible to the eye."

A few murmurs percolated through the tent. Gazes cast downward in disbelief. In fear.

"We don't get involved," someone grumbled quietly from the back of the tent. Etienne didn't need to see his face to know it was Sylvain.

"That's right," said Etienne. "Because that's our code. The code I swore to live and die by. We don't get involved. But you're forgetting—as I so often did—about the other half of it. If you can help without getting killed, do it."

Sylvain snorted. "And how are you so sure this *won't* get us killed?"

"I'm not," Etienne admitted. "But maybe some things are worth the risk." He glanced once again at Chatine. "Maybe some things are worth getting involved for."

"Why?" Sylvain countered, the violet light from the stove flashing angrily in his eyes. He was breaking all the protocols, but no one seemed to care. Even Mentor Ava didn't object. "Why should we join their 'revolution'? Why should we risk our lives for them? A bunch of gridders who look down on us. Who scorn us. Who call us *Défecteurs* like we're some kind of stain on the planet. Why should we help them?"

"Because he's the right kind of monster."

All eyes swiveled toward Chatine, who'd moved out of the shadows at the back of the tent. Her gray eyes were no longer glassy. Her expression no longer resembled that of a cornered animal in a trap. She took another step forward, closer to the heating stove in the center of the tent.

"Someone in this community once told me that life is full of monsters." She cast a look at Brigitte before turning back to face the others. "She said we can't confront them all. We have to choose. We have to decide which ones to face and which ones to step away from. She said you all made that choice long ago. That the Regime was not the kind of monster you wanted to confront. So you chose to turn away. To fight by *not* fighting."

More whispers spread throughout the group, people muttering their agreement, others wondering why a gridder had been given permission to speak.

"But she also said that some monsters must be confronted. Otherwise, they'll destroy you." Chatine peered at Etienne, who gave her a nod to continue. "Empereur Bonnefaçon *is* the Regime now. He rules over all of us. And *he* is the kind of monster you fight."

She scanned the tent, as though she wanted everyone here to see the clarity in her eyes. The determination in her jaw. "It's true. I used to look down on you. I used to scorn you. I used to call you Défecteurs. Because that's the name the Regime gave you. And like the other stupid, brainwashed gridders, I bought into it. I believed it. That's what the Regime does. That's what Empereur Bonnefaçon does. He brainwashes. He lies. And he won't let you live your life the way you want. He never has. He's worked tirelessly to stop you for almost his entire career. Sniffing out every camp you built. Rounding up as many of you as he can. Why? Because you're a threat. And if I've learned anything about César Bonnefaçon, it's that he doesn't stand down to threats. He fights them. Head-on. Until they're destroyed." Chatine closed her eyes for a long moment, as though her own words were finally sinking into her mind too. "But this is your chance to do something about it. Maybe your only chance. Because this isn't just about gridders. Or estates. It's about all of us. We all have the same enemy here."

Silence followed. A penetrating silence that seemed to sink into Etienne's bones. Mentor Ava cast her gaze around the tent, waiting for someone to raise their hand with another proposal. Another suggestion. But there was only a question.

"How would we even help?" asked Jordane as she hugged tight to baby Mercure, strapped to her chest in his sling. "We're powerless outsiders. We have nothing to offer."

"That's not true," said a voice, and Etienne turned to see his maman stepping forward. She gave Chatine's arm a quick squeeze before coming closer to the center, next to the stove with its flickering purple flames. "We have protected ourselves against the Regime for decades. Centuries, even. And in that time, we have become experts on a tool—a *weapon*—that dates back to our earliest ancestors. A weapon that the Ministère has very little knowledge of."

"Stealth?" asked Castor.

"No." Brigitte shook her head and, like a tiny spark, Etienne felt the heat of her answer before it was even ignited. "Fire."

- PART 6 -
THE
BARRICADES

The people rose up. Like a gathering storm. Like a building wave. Like the ascending notes of a song. It was time to protect what was theirs. To barricade their livelihoods. To guard what their hands had crafted and sewn and spun. And as their brave hearts beat out across the planet, they steeled themselves for the fight. For the fury. For the forces of hate.

But most of all, they hoped and they dreamed.

That with just one more day, a new Laterre might be won.

From *The Chronicles of Laterre,*
Volume 17, Chapter 89

- CHAPTER 74 -
CHATINE

THE COMBATTEUR TOUCHED DOWN ON THE ROOF OF
the bread fabrique. Despite Etienne's delicate landing, Chatine still felt
like they'd just dropped out of the sky, leaving her stomach back up with
the clouds.

She stepped out of the craft and gazed uncertainly over the edge of the
roof. The sight below stopped her breath cold.

Even though night was closing in, the Fabrique District buzzed with
activity. People hurried between buildings like worker ants, collecting
crates, broken pipes, large metal boxes, window frames, and even doors
ripped from their hinges. All this stolen loot was being stacked in huge
tangled piles in front of loading bays and worker entrances. At some of
the larger fabriques, massive manufacturing machines were being shoved
into these makeshift barricades, and a couple of transporteurs had been
upturned to form bedrock from their sleek metal shells.

The surrounding fabriques had been completely commandeered by the
Third Estate.

Cut off, Chatine thought as she watched the giant structures rise up
before her eyes. *Protected.*

From her viewpoint on the roof, Chatine could make out the dairy fabrique, the furniture and meatpacking fabriques, the fabrique where the champagne for the First Estate was processed and bottled, and to her left, the textile fabrique. As she stared down at it, at the mess of giant spools and toppled-over looms blocking its loading entrance, Chatine could almost feel the ghost of her Skin vibrate with the reminders that used to go off every morning, telling her where she was supposed to be, what she was supposed to do.

"Quite a sight, isn't it?"

She blinked up at Gabriel, who was now standing beside her at the edge of the roof, the same mix of wonder and unease playing out on his face.

Chatine nodded. "Yes."

The sound of an engine cut through the air, and she turned to see the second craft landing. She cringed at the sight of one of the community's ships so visible out here, in the middle of the city. So vulnerable.

The ship eased down next to their stolen combatteur, and the cargo hatch sprang open. Roche leapt out first and ran to the edge of the roof to revel in the sight below.

"Soop!"

Brigitte stepped out next, carrying a large sac full of supplies, followed closely by Sister Denise, Sister Marguerite, Sister Léonie, Sister Clare, and finally, Cerise. Gabriel had argued against her coming, insisting she needed more time to heal, but Cerise had been adamant.

"Get back to the camp," Etienne called to Caroline, the pilote of the craft. "Tell them to keep filling cartridges of emberweed oil. We'll radio you with an update."

Caroline nodded through the cockpit window, and the cargo doors sealed shut before the ship lifted gracefully into the air and disappeared back behind the clouds.

"Come on," Etienne said, summoning the group. "Marcellus said there was a roof access over here."

As they pulled open the hatch and, one by one, began to descend the ladder, Chatine was grateful, once again, that Etienne had taken charge. Her stomach was still floating somewhere among the clouds, and her mind was still trying to process everything that had happened over the past few hours. She'd been preparing to give up. And now she was climbing down into a barricaded bread fabrique, preparing to protect it with her life.

She hopped off the last rung of the ladder and slowly glanced around at the strange sight in front of her. Powered-down conveyer belts twisted like metal snakes across the vast room, and a row of gigantic mixing vats lined two of the walls. At the far end, a bank of enormous metal ovens sat with their heavy silver doors open like hungry mouths. An almost imperceptible sheen of white flour dust covered every floor tile, metal pipe, and machine.

"Thank the Sols!" Marcellus appeared from behind one of the ovens and ran to greet them. "You're here." He stopped awkwardly in front of Chatine, like he was trying to decide whether or not to embrace her. For Chatine, there was no question. She wanted to pull him toward her. She wanted to wrap her arms around him and never let go. She wanted that same voice that had whispered achingly through the radio—*I need you with me. I need you, Chatine*—to whisper in her ear now. To tell her that she was right to come. That this was the right place to be.

But then his gaze dropped from her and focused earnestly on Etienne. "Merci. For bringing them. And for your community's offer to help."

Etienne nodded and extended out his fist. Marcellus reacted the same way Chatine had once done. He flinched.

"It's okay," said Chatine, rushing to position herself between them. "It's just how they greet people at the camp. Like this." She tapped her fist gently against Etienne's.

"Oh." Marcellus chuckled. "Sorry, mec." He made a fist and tentatively extended it toward Etienne until their knuckles touched.

Chatine's chest squeezed at the sight of it.

"Where is Alouette?" asked Cerise, breaking through this fragile moment with her peculiar voice that still sent tingles of unease through Chatine. It wasn't the monotone drone of a cyborg anymore. But it wasn't quite human, either.

Marcellus blinked like he was just now remembering why they had come. "This way," he said, leading them through a maze of mixing vats and conveyer belts into an enormous loading bay.

Chatine's mouth fell open, and Roche plucked the word right from her head. "Whoa."

Where Chatine imagined there were normally boxes of sweet breads, stacked up and waiting to be shipped off to Ledôme, there were now only people. So many people. They filled every centimètre of this massive space. And just like the people outside, they were in constant motion, shoving machines, hefting sacs, and ripping off metal siding from the fabrique walls. At the vast mouth of the loading bay, everything was being stacked, stuffed, and reinforced into the huge barricade that blocked any goods from leaving this facility.

"Help me fill this hole!" someone shouted over the din, and Chatine glanced over to see a tall figure hefting a heavy sac of flour toward a narrow gap in the rising wall.

Even though she couldn't see the girl's face, Chatine knew right away that it was Alouette. Not just because of the twisting curls that sprang from her head like a beautiful jet-black halo. Or the way she always held herself, so confident and regal, like she'd been raised to be here. Raised to be a leader.

It was the energy radiating off her as she helped three more workers secure emptied bread crates around the flour sac. It was like a signal transmitting into the air. Strong and clear and purposeful. Even in the tumult and buzzing of people around her, it was palpable, almost visible. It filled Chatine with a sensation she'd sworn was lost the moment she saw those explosifs fall from the sky. When she'd watched Fret 7 dissolve into ash. When she'd watched her people burn at the hands of a man who had the nerve to call himself an Empereur.

And suddenly, she understood.

Everything.

Marcellus's message. The thousands of people outside and inside of these walls. Building, constructing, barricading. They weren't just doing it because the First and Second Estates needed these goods—their precious bread and champagne, fancy cheeses and fine clothes—they were doing it because Alouette had sent the same signal to them. She had filled them with the same sensation that had felt so lost. So burned. So disintegrated into nothing.

Like a Sol, she had given them hope.

Like a lightning strike, she had given them power.

Like the perfect collection of words strung together, she had given them something to protect.

Principale Francine approached Alouette amid the fray of people and touched her arm. She gestured toward Chatine and the others, and Alouette turned, her lips curving into a smile.

"You came," she said, hurrying over to the sisters and hugging them one by one before addressing Etienne. "Where are the others?"

"Back at the camp. Preparing." He pulled a radio from one of the many pockets of his utility vest. "They'll make contact when they're ready."

Chatine's breath hitched at the mention of the people they'd left behind. Sister Jacqui, who was still so weak. Jordane and Saros and Castor, who had ventured into the Terrain Perdu to collect more emberweeds. Mentor Ava, Brianne, and the others, who were working tirelessly into the night to manufacture them into oil and fill more cartridges.

"We now control all but ten of the fabriques," Alouette reported to the group. "We're trying to get to them all, but we have to prioritize our resources and make sure we can defend the ones we have."

"I don't understand," Chatine said, peering around the crowded loading bay. "How did you get all of these people inside? How did you get past the doors? The biometric locks?"

Alouette shot a knowing look at Cerise. "The sympathizeur network."

"The what?" said Roche.

"You mean that's really a thing?" Gabriel asked.

"Yes, it's a thing," snapped Cerise. "I told you it was a thing."

"It's really a thing," Alouette confirmed. "And Cerise was right. There are a lot of them. The movement has grown pretty big in the last few months. Superviseurs, foremen, even a few people inside the Ministère who were able to give us full control over the biometric locks. We now can open and close almost any door in this Fabrique District."

"Wow," said Chatine.

"But who was in contact with them?" Cerise asked.

Just then, a young man dodged past two Third Estaters heaving a metal door toward the barricade and made his way to Alouette. Chatine recognized him as the Second Estater who had snuck them into Ledôme for the Ascension banquet. His name was something like . . .

"Grantaire!" cried Cerise. She pushed her way past Chatine and threw her arms around his neck. He staggered backward from the impact, taking a moment to register what was happening before hugging her back.

"Why, hello there."

"I missed you so much," said Cerise.

It was the most human gesture Chatine had seen from her. It gave her hope that, just as Brigitte had said, she would eventually return to the girl she used to be.

"Do you have an update?" Alouette asked.

Grantaire cleared his throat and disentangled himself from Cerise. "Yes. It seems the Empereur has caught on to what we're doing. I think at first he assumed the people were just fleeing Ledôme, realizing they didn't stand a chance against his fortifications. But now our scouts are reporting that the transporteurs that were sent to Ledôme are being filled back up and rerouted here."

Alouette stood straighter, like someone had shot her with a jolt of electricity. "We need to transmit the message as soon as possible." She turned to Cerise and Brigitte. "How long until you can get me patched into the AirLink network?"

Cerise was already unfolding her TéléCom, and Brigitte was pulling various devices out of her sac.

"If nothing goes wrong, we can have you live to all of the First and Second Estaters in fifteen minutes," said Brigitte.

"There are offices upstairs." Cerise gestured to a row of windows overlooking the loading area. "We can broadcast from up there. It will be much quieter, but the barricade will still be visible in the background of the shot."

"Good," Alouette said. "Merci."

"Do you know what you are going to say?" Chatine asked, sidling up to Alouette.

Alouette turned back toward the loading doors of the fabrique and for a moment seemed to lose herself in the tangled wall of debris, metal, and wood that appeared to have grown even taller in only the last few minutes. "I think I've known all my life."

CHAPTER 75

ALOUETTE

"CITIZENS OF LATERRE. I AM ALOUETTE TAUREAU. Descendant of the Paresse family. Sister to the Vangarde. And Guardian of the people. I'm broadcasting to you from the Fabrique District of Vallonay, where I stand beside the workers, the true beating hearts of Laterre. We have taken the bread fabrique. We have taken the dairy fabrique. We have taken the textile, the meatpacking, the furniture, the jewelry, and the médicament fabriques too. We have taken over these fabriques not to hurt you. We have seized control of these vital resources not to let you starve. We have not built our barricades out of spite or malice or cruelty. Our actions are actions of love and hope and promise.

"Each and every one of us here on these barricades today loves Laterre. We love our planet and our beautiful lands. And we see the infinite promise of the Laterrian people.

"*All* of our Laterrian people.

"But for too long, we have been divided. A system has been forced on all of us, separating us into the three estates. Three estates that sometimes seem as firm and unwavering as layers of rock. We have been made to feel like we are fundamentally different. That a First Estater is one kind of person. A Second Estater is another. And a Third Estater is another still.

"Yet all of us live. We all breathe. We all laugh and cry. When we are pricked, we bleed. When we are hurt, we cry out in pain. When a baby is born, joy fills us. And when a flower blooms, we smile. We might believe that our estates make us different. But we are not so different. Whether we are First, Second, or Third Estate, we are all humans first.

"And if we are all humans first—if we are all fundamentally the same in our loves and laughter and sadnesses—is it fair that some children grow up hungry? Is it fair that some people live their lives in rotting homes under raining skies? Is it fair for a family to starve while a man is sent to a freezing prison moon for stealing them a loaf of bread? Is it fair that men and women toil and labor in Laterre's fabriques—like this one—for food they will never eat, for clothes they will never wear, and for goods they will never enjoy?

"And is it fair that a man who calls himself a leader, who calls himself Empereur, can send in a fleet of combatteurs and destroy an entire Fret, killing women and men, children and babies, in their homes? In the hundreds? In the thousands? Is it fair that their blood is still warm on the streets? Is it fair their lives are disposable in this way, just because the Empereur says he is tracking down a terrorist group who were never terrorists in the first place?

"The answer, of course, is no. None of this is fair. In *all* of our hearts we know this to be true. And what we also know deep down to be true is that without this suffering of so many on our planet, without this inequality, this cruelty, and this harsh division between our estates, Laterre would be a better place. We would not be divided against each other. We would not be fearful of each other. Nature never intended for people to be separated. As long as we are divided, there will always be unrest. But if we live together, in harmony, our roots, like the roots of mighty trees, will intertwine and mingle and support each other in one vast, beautiful network. If we live the way nature intended, as one people, one planet, we will *thrive*.

"And so today, we have come here to the fabriques to make three resolute demands.

"First, the estate system must be dismantled. It is outdated and unjust and harms all of us.

"Second, we demand that Empereur Bonnefaçon step down as leader. He is a murderer and a tyrant who uses Laterrian weapons to kill Laterrian people. You've seen the footage the Vangarde released to the planet. You've seen the way the Empereur has lied and cheated and committed heinous crimes against his own people. He is not fit to rule us. He has none of our interests at heart. Not First, nor Third, nor Second Estate. Only his own.

"Finally, we demand that from this day forward, Laterre must be ruled by the people. No more Patriarches. No more Matrones. No more self-crowned Empereurs. Our planet is *our* planet and must be guided only by us. Together we will decide a way forward that serves all of us, that is just and fair to all of us. A way that lets no one starve and no one suffer.

"These barricades will not be brought down until these demands are met. We will protect them. We will defend them at all costs. They will remain, and we will remain, until Laterre can promise all of its people liberty and equality and solidarity."

- CHAPTER 76 -
MARCELLUS

AS ALOUETTE FINISHED HER SPEECH, MARCELLUS FELT as though he'd been transported. He was no longer himself. No longer in his own body. In his own skin. He was Julien Bonnefaçon, his father. He was Carra Epernay, Max's mother. He was every rebel who had fought and died for Laterre seventeen years ago.

He felt all of their passion, all of their confidence, all of their anger, all of their frustration, and finally, all of their disappointment.

Because in the end, the Rebellion of 488 had failed.

But as he drifted back to his own body and his own mind, as the echoes of the past shimmered away like a dissolving hologram projection, Marcellus knew this was different.

He could feel it in the air. In the silence of the heavy machines that had been shut down in protest. In the unified voices of the people both inside and outside this fabrique, building, chanting, protecting what was rightfully theirs. In the reverberation of Alouette's words that were now speeding through the airwaves, finding their way through the gates of Ledôme and over the city walls that had been erected to keep the upper estates in and the Third Estate out.

He felt it in his blood, which coursed with the conviction of his father and the compassion of his mother.

"Four hundred views," Cerise reported from her makeshift workstation in the superviseur's office, overlooking the loading bay below. "Five hundred. Six hundred. A thousand."

Marcellus blew out a breath and turned to hug whoever was standing next to him. It was Gabriel. The two men embraced like long-lost brothers reuniting.

"It's going to work," Gabriel whispered in Marcellus's ear.

Marcellus pulled back and nodded. "I hope so."

"They have to listen." Gabriel chuckled. "Those pomps can't go a day without their champagne and fancy cheeses. And the Empereur is nothing without their support. They'll make him give in."

"Two thousand views and still rising," Cerise reported.

Marcellus wiped his sweaty palms on his pants and glanced around the small office where they'd set up their command center. It wasn't the Assemblée room, but it worked. Below, in the loading bay, Chatine, Roche, Etienne, and the sisters were helping to fortify the inside of the barricade.

Anything to keep their hands occupied and pass the time. Because they all knew that this was the hard part. Hacking the AirLink network and broadcasting a message to all of the upper estates was easy. Now they'd have to wait for a response.

Urgent footsteps pounded up the stairs from the loading bay, and Grantaire burst into the office. "Four transporteurs have just landed in the Fabrique District."

Alouette walked to the small window that looked out onto the street below. "What are they doing?"

"Right now they're just unloading," said Grantaire. "Droids mostly."

Marcellus joined Alouette at the window and glanced out. The growing barricade obstructed half the view, but through the towering stack of crates and ripped-off doors, Marcellus could see glimpses of those ghoulish orange eyes that pierced through the gathering darkness. "Are they advancing?"

Grantaire shook his head. "No. Not yet, anyway. They seem to just be mustering, getting into formation. I think . . ." He paused, like whatever he was about to say next was difficult. "I think they're surrounding the fabriques."

Alouette bit her lip. "Okay, keep me posted and let me know immediately if they show any signs of preparing to attack."

Grantaire nodded and disappeared back down the stairs.

Alouette continued to stare out the window, deep in thought. Until finally, with a surge of determination, she rushed down the stairs. Marcellus shared an anxious look with Gabriel before they both followed after her.

Stopping three steps from the ground floor, Alouette switched on the amplificateur hanging from her neck and called out over the noise of the construction. "We need to get everyone inside the fabrique! Seal off the loading bay doors. Anyone still outside the building needs to be brought in immediately."

Chatine, Roche, and the others hurried over, breathless.

"What's going on?" asked Principale Francine.

"The droids are assembling outside," explained Marcellus.

"We need to keep everyone safe," said Alouette, her gaze following the fluster of activity in the loading bay as workers from outside climbed over the top of the barricade and squeezed through small cracks between crates.

"What about the other fabriques?" asked Francine. "We should warn them and tell them to get everyone inside."

"How?" asked Marcellus. "If we send anyone out there now, the droids might start shooting."

"TéléComs?" Gabriel suggested. "Shouldn't these sympathizeur people have them?"

"Too risky," said Marguerite. "The Ministère will be monitoring the AirLink network, especially since we transmitted that message. And we don't have time to secure all those TéléComs."

Chatine turned to Etienne. "Can we distribute the radios you brought from the camp?"

"Yes, but how are you going to get them to the other fabriques?"

"If we can't communicate with each other, this will never work," said Marguerite.

"Which is probably exactly my grandfather's plan," Marcellus muttered, feeling heat boil up in his chest. "He's trying to cut us off from each other by surrounding the fabriques."

Gabriel snorted. "We hold his champagne hostage, he holds us hostage."

"Three thousand views," reported Cerise from the open door of the office above.

Marcellus glanced at Alouette, who appeared to be deep in thought, quietly processing all of this.

"What about the combatteur?" asked Roche. "It's still on the roof. We could fly it between the fabriques, to deliver the radios."

"I don't know," said Etienne, rubbing anxiously at his chin. "The stealth will only last so long. And as of now, the Ministère doesn't know we have one of their crafts. I'd kind of like to keep it that way. It's an advantage."

"He's right," said Francine. "I think any air travel is risky. It's too open. Leaves us vulnerable."

"Then we go under," said Alouette, her dark eyes suddenly alert and sparkling.

"What?" asked Chatine.

"Underground," said Alouette, giving Francine a wink. "It's the way of the Vangarde."

"You want us to dig tunnels?" asked Gabriel. "Won't that take, like, I don't know, years?"

"We don't have to dig," said Alouette. "The tunnels already exist."

Marcellus felt a chill of realization pass through him. "The old sewers."

Alouette caught his eye and nodded. "Citizen Rousseau said they used to be a network for rebels."

"They *were*," said Léonie. "Until the Regime caught on and shut them down."

"But did they really shut down thousands of kilomètres of sewer tunnels?" asked Alouette. "Or did they simply close off the access points? Like at the silo?"

Immediately, Marcellus understood. "Fan out!" he said. "Search the entire fabrique. Look for anything that resembles a drainage grate or an opening in the ground that's been boarded up or covered over."

A ripple of energy spread throughout the group. Everyone seemed grateful to have a task, a purpose. Roche darted in the direction of the manufacturing floor with Gabriel close on his heels. But they were both stopped by a loud throat clear that came from behind Alouette.

Marcellus turned to see Cerise at the bottom of the stairs. "You don't have to search," she said with a quirk of a smile. "I already know where all the entrances are."

"You do?" asked about four people at once.

"I downloaded the utility grid to my neuroprocessors weeks ago when I tracked Marcellus to the grain silo. And since my circuitry is intact . . ." She shot a pointed look at Gabriel that Marcellus could not quite interpret. "I still have them."

"You're amazing," said Alouette, squeezing Cerise's arm. "Can you download them to something?"

"Already done." Cerise reached into her pocket and pulled out one of the Défecteurs' strange TéléCom-like devices. She handed it to Alouette before ascending back up the stairs.

Alouette turned immediately to Gabriel. "Will you lead a team to locate the access points to the sewers and remove any barriers the Ministère set up?"

Gabriel snorted. "Does a sheep's turd stink?" And then, off Alouette's confused look, he cleared his throat and said, "I mean, yes, I can. Definitely."

Alouette handed over the device. "Good. You'll also need to track routes to all the other fabriques we currently have control over and remove any blockages there."

Gabriel flashed a winning smile. "Don't you worry about a thing. The criminal mastermind is on the job."

There was a small snort from the office above. "Five thousand views."

"Take these," Brigitte said to Gabriel, carrying a sac full of radios down the stairs from the office. "Keep one for yourself to stay in communication with us, and distribute the rest to the other barricades."

Gabriel pulled the strap of the bag over his chest and then clapped his hands twice to get everyone's attention. "Okay, listen up! Who would like to have the honor—nay, *privilege*—of being on Team Gabriel?"

No one raised their hand.

Gabriel's face fell. "Really?"

"I'll do it," said a deep voice, and several heads turned to gape at the massive figure that had just appeared from the manufacturing floor.

"Who the fric are you?" said Gabriel.

Hugo Taureau ignored the question. "You'll need a strong back to break through any blockages the Ministère has set up."

"No," said Alouette, her brow creasing. "You're supposed to be resting. That wound on your leg is still in danger of infection. You're not well enough to go tromping through the sewers."

"I'll be fine." Hugo turned and cast a loving gaze at each of the sisters. "It's good to see you again."

Francine placed a tender hand on his arm. "You as well, Hugo. We're glad you're back and safe."

"I'm sorry for your loss," he offered. "Nicolette and Noëlle and Muriel. They were good women. Strong women. They will be missed."

"Merci," said Francine.

Hugo turned back to Gabriel. "Let's go. We'll need to round up some more volunteers."

Gabriel looked slightly terrified by his new partner as he followed Hugo out of the loading bay, passing by Grantaire on his way back in.

Alouette looked up, fear brimming in her eyes. "Are they advancing?"

Grantaire shook his head, confused. "No. It's strange, actually. Ten more transporteurs have landed and the droids now have every one of our barricades surrounded, but there's still no sign of movement. If it weren't for those creepy orange eyes, I would have thought they were all powered down."

"Maybe they're just waiting for more to arrive?" said Etienne.

"I don't think so," replied Grantaire. "The transporteurs have stopped coming. It's totally silent out there. Like they're all just waiting."

A shiver passed through Marcellus. "Waiting for what?"

But no one answered. Because no one knew.

"Everyone is in!" someone shouted in the distance. "Close it up!"

Marcellus turned to see the giant metal doors of the loading bay slowly glide across their tracks. The last glimpses of the night sky and the towering barricade flashed out of view as the doors sealed shut, locking them all inside.

"Something's coming through," Cerise announced, pounding down the stairs again with her TéléCom clutched in her hands. "The anonymous profile I set up in the Communiqué to transmit Alouette's broadcast is receiving an incoming AirLink message."

Alouette sucked in a breath, like she was arming herself with air. Preparing for battle. "It's him. It's the Empereur." She nodded to Cerise. "Play it."

Cerise flicked her fingertip across the screen, and everyone pressed closer together. For a long time, no one moved. No one even breathed.

As Marcellus watched his grandfather's face fill the screen, he felt physically ill. Of all the people in this room, he knew Empereur Bonnefaçon the best. He'd spent eighteen years looking into those cold hazel eyes, listening to that chilling, crisp voice, watching that shadow of disappointment pass over his face.

Which was how he could almost mouth the words right along with him.

"This message is for Alouette Taureau and everyone hiding behind the barricades like the cowards that you are. The glorious Regime of Laterre does not give in to the demands of terrorists. You have until Sol-rise to clean up the mess you made of my fabriques and remove yourself from the premises. Or I will have no choice but to remove you by force."

CHAPTER 77

ETIENNE

"WHAT ARE WE SUPPOSED TO DO NOW?"

"We had to know he wouldn't just back down."

"He could be bluffing."

Etienne tried to tune in to the hushed and urgent conversation playing out in the superviseur's office, but he was too distracted by the image of those metal monsters that loomed outside the barricade. Just the thought of all those droids out there, surrounding them, their glowing eyes cutting through the night that had fallen over the fabriques, was enough to send tiny spiders racing over his skin, and taunting memories flashing through his mind.

"He's not bluffing," someone replied. "My grandfather doesn't bluff. Play a game of Regiments with him and you'll know."

Etienne felt a warm hand close around his, and he startled and looked up into the eyes of the woman who had always been there for him when the droids had haunted his nightmares, when their monstrous forms had bashed their way into his mind, and his own screams had pierced the night.

"I can't stop thinking about them out there," Etienne whispered to his mother. "So many of them. Just like the night when . . ." The words trailed off, failing him the way they always did when it came to talking about his father.

Brigitte squeezed his hand. "I know."

"How many views?" someone was asking from the back of the room.

"Twenty-two thousand," said the cyborg girl.

"That's good," another voice replied.

"Is it?!"

It was this question that finally pulled Etienne's attention to the conversation. Not only because it was Chatine who had said it, but because of the aggravation with which she'd practically shouted the words.

"I'm sorry." She threw up her hands. "I'm just . . . what was the good of any of this if all the Second Estaters are just going to continue to sit up there in their precious little dome and watch us die? I mean, yeah, they're viewing the broadcast, they're hearing Alouette's words, they even saw the proof that the Empereur lied to their faces. But are they doing *anything*?"

"We just have to wait and see," said Alouette, exuding more of that endless patience that astonished Etienne.

"You mean, just wait around for the droids to attack?" asked Chatine.

Etienne shivered. "Can they get past the barricades?"

"They can't climb," said Chatine. "But remember when you asked me why they're called 'bashers'?"

"She's right," said Marcellus. "They'll most likely use their rayonettes first. And what the pulses can't break through, they'll take care of themselves."

Everyone in the group fell silent as these words sank in. Etienne peered out the office's interior window to the loading bay below, imagining those massive doors giving way, collapsing down on all of those people packed inside, imagining the droids trampling through.

The screams . . .

He shut his eyes tight to block out the sound, only to open them a second later when Grantaire returned from his lookout point on the roof.

"Gabriel and Hugo's team has made it to the meatpacking fabrique. They were able to unblock an old sewage hatch and deliver one of the radios to the man who's been leading up the barricade efforts there. His name is Borel. I told him to bring everyone inside and seal all their loading doors."

"Good," said Alouette. "Any activity with the droids?"

Grantaire shook his head. "Nothing. The Empereur seems to be keeping his word. It doesn't look like they'll attack tonight. But . . ."

"But what?" Marcellus asked, looking like he wanted to shake the man.

Grantaire peered anxiously at Alouette and then at each of the Vangarde members. "The Red Scar are inside the meatpacking fabrique."

"What?" shouted the woman named Léonie, glancing around the office as though expecting them to appear here, too. "How many?"

"Just two, as far as we know. Jolras Epernay and one other."

"How did they get inside?" asked Léonie.

"I don't know," said Grantaire. "Borel thinks they probably just slipped in while the barricade was being constructed. They're Third Estate, after all. But Jolras is asking to talk to one of us. In person. He says he can help."

"No. No way," said Roche, crossing his arms. Then, he quickly uncrossed them and looked uncertainly at Alouette. "Right?"

Alouette turned to Marcellus. "Can we trust him?"

Marcellus shifted his weight anxiously, running his fingers through his hair. And then, with a look that pierced through Etienne's chest, he turned to Chatine. "What do you think?"

Etienne glanced back down at his feet. He couldn't watch whatever was passing between them. Whatever sad, pleading look Chatine was throwing at him.

"*You* should go," she said, surprising more than just Etienne. When he glanced up again, Marcellus's brow was furrowed.

"What?"

"Do you remember the last time he reached out to you?" asked Chatine. "Before the Patriarche's execution? He was genuinely trying to help then."

"Yeah," Marcellus muttered, "and then he ran right back to Max like a frightened lapdog."

"But Max is dead now," Alouette said somberly. "*He* killed her. Don't you think it's safe to assume he's on our side?"

Roche scoffed and mumbled under his breath, "Or that he's deranged."

Marcellus nodded once, his mind made up. He grabbed a radio from the pile on the desk. "I'll go."

Chatine watched him disappear out the door and down the stairs. Etienne watched Chatine, until he could feel his maman's eyes on him and he quickly pulled his gaze away.

"How long until Sol-rise?" Alouette asked.

"Seven hours, thirty-two minutes, ten seconds," replied Cerise, and Etienne could practically feel the clock ticking down like a drum inside his chest.

He glanced out again at the loading doors, wondering how long they would last in an attack. Was this how his father felt when the fire was burning him from the inside and the droids were waiting for him on the outside?

"We can't just sit here and let them come at us!" he finally cried, the pressure in his head threatening to burst. "There has to be a way to stop them."

"There isn't," Chatine said miserably. "Trust me."

"Actually, there might be."

Everyone seemed to turn at once toward the voice. It was the first time the woman standing in the back corner of the office had spoken. Since the moment she'd boarded the combatteur out in the wheat-fleur field, Etienne had been fascinated by her. By the web of scars on the left side of her face, so similar to the ones he'd lovingly traced as a child on his own maman's cheek. The woman who called herself Denise represented a whole other side of his mother that he didn't know. A whole other life before the one he'd been welcomed into.

Denise shared a look with Brigitte, who seemed to understand because she said, "We'll never be able to upload it."

"What are you talking about?" Cerise asked, rising from her makeshift workstation. She walked over to stand between the two former cyborgs. "Upload what?"

Brigitte sighed and turned to the group to explain. "Years ago, after we escaped the Ministère, Denise had an idea for a virus. That could potentially corrupt the droids' operating system, forcing them to power down."

"All of them?" Chatine asked, her eyes wide.

"That's the problem," said Brigitte. "In order to infect all of them, you'd have to upload it to the mainframe that sends updates out to the droids. Obviously, that system is highly guarded."

"No, you don't," said Cerise with a casualness that implied droid hacking was everyday common knowledge. "The droids are sent operating system updates from the mainframe, yes, but they're still connected to the same network, and as of a few months ago, they have the ability to update each other."

Denise took a single step toward her. "Hive-mind technology?"

"Exactly," said Cerise.

"I'm sorry," said Chatine. "Can someone please explain what's going on?"

"If I understand correctly," said Brigitte, "Cerise is saying that the droids have the ability to learn from each other's experiences and update their own operating systems accordingly."

"If one droid encounters a criminal that outsmarts them, for example." Cerise cast a cryptic look at Chatine. "The droid will analyze what went wrong and share that information with all other droids on the network so the same mistake will never be made again. By any of them. It was the Empereur's idea. The Bureau of Défense only recently finished developing it. He thought it would strengthen the reaction time of the droids. Which it does."

"So what does that mean?" Etienne asked.

"It means . . ." Cerise's face broke into a mischievous, unmistakably human grin. "If we want to spread a virus to every droid on the planet, we only have to infect *one* of them."

- CHAPTER 78 -
MARCELLUS

MARCELLUS COULD THINK OF NO BETTER LOCATION
for a meeting with the Red Scar.

Sheep carcasses hung in long, eerily neat lines in the main packing
area, while piles of discarded trotters, eyeballs, and heads filled vast metallic bins in a nearby disposal area. Despite the enormous freezers and cooling rooms lining the hallways, locking the chill in, it was cold everywhere.
Freezing. As icy as the Terrain Perdu. The masses of Third Estaters who'd
barricaded themselves into this building were dressed in thick coats and
knit hats, and they huddled together in groups, trying to keep warm in the
frigid air.

The most unnerving part, however, was the floor. Even though all the
tiles throughout this meatpacking fabrique had clearly been cleaned, Marcellus could still see, in the cracks and crevices and corners, the traces of
blood.

Dark and red and angry against the polished white ceramic.

"We didn't know whether or not we could trust them," the man who'd
identified himself as Borel was saying as he led Marcellus past more freezers and up a flight of metal stairs. "When one of my fellow fabrique workers recognized Max's brother, a group of men cornered him and his friend

and searched them. They had a giant bag filled with rayonettes."

Marcellus stopped walking, his mouth suddenly dirt dry as he remembered the Red Scar guards weaving through the crowd marching on Ledôme, handing out weapons from their sacs.

"What did you do with them?" Marcellus asked.

"The mecs or the weapons?"

"Both."

"The rayonettes are downstairs," Borel said. "And we locked up Jolras and his friend."

"You did what?"

Borel beckoned for him to keep walking until they'd reached a heavy metal door. He opened it to reveal a room filled with a knot of pipes, valves, and clunking machines, which Marcellus assumed was the cooling system for the fabrique. In the center, Jolras Epernay and one of his Red Scar guards were bound to a pipe with rope. Although the only thing still marking them as Red Scar were the slashes cut into the backs of their hands. Their signature hooded coats had been replaced with fabrique uniforms, and without their fearless leader to stand beside, they looked sadder somehow, less threatening. Jolras's eyes were still glassy, just as they'd been when Marcellus had seen him outside Ledôme. His lips were pale, and his face drawn, like he'd been staring at death for too long and it had sucked the life out of him.

"You came," Jolras said weakly, barely managing to lift his head to meet Marcellus's eyes. "I wasn't sure anyone would come after . . . well, after everything."

"I came." Marcellus fought to keep his voice steady. He refused to let on just how much this man still scared him. How when he looked into his eyes, all he saw was that rayonette pointed at Alouette's head in the hallway of Fret 6. "Why am I here?"

Jolras cut his gaze to Borel, and Marcellus understood. "Can you give us a minute?" he asked.

Borel didn't look thrilled about the idea of leaving Marcellus alone with these two, but he nodded and slipped out the door.

Marcellus crossed his arms over his chest. "I don't have a lot of time. So let's be quick about it."

"We have weapons," Jolras said.

Marcellus took a step back. "On you?"

Jolras gave a weak chuckle. "No. They're hidden."

"Borel already told me about your bag of rayonettes."

"I only brought those as proof," said Jolras. "There are more. Lots more. And not just rayonettes. Tazeurs and canisters of riot gas, too. All Ministère. Max was building an arsenal."

For two long breaths, Marcellus closed his eyes. It hurt to open them again. "How did you get them?"

Jolras nudged his chin toward the man tied up next to him. "Antoine."

Marcellus remembered the name. "Your spy?" He glanced at the unfamiliar face. Under a heavy brow and unkempt hair, the man's brown eyes stared up at him with a strange, slightly off-kilter gaze.

Jolras nodded. "Antoine is Ministère. He's the reason we knew the Patriarche was trying to flee the planet. He tracked us down shortly after the Ascension banquet riot. He was in bad shape, barely able to stand up. But he had a TéléCom on him that revealed the Patriarche's location. That's how Max knew she could trust him. He's the one who told us how to get to the Favorites and he helped us escape from the Policier Precinct. He's been slipping weapons out of Ministère arsenals for the past few months and bringing them to Max."

Dizziness overtook Marcellus and he uncrossed his arms to try to balance himself. Doubt was trickling through his mind like drizzling rain, making the hairs on the back of his neck prickle. Something about this did not add up. Marcellus had practically grown up in the Ministère. But this man bore no semblance to any face he could place in his memories.

"What bureau do you work for?" Marcellus asked, taking a step toward the spy.

But Antoine barely looked up. And his lips stayed firmly closed, as if in protest.

"He doesn't speak," said Jolras.

"Why not?"

Jolras shrugged. "I don't know. He just never has."

"How do you communicate with him, then?"

"We get by," said Jolras vaguely.

Marcellus snapped his gaze back to Jolras. "So, why are you telling me this?"

For a long time, Jolras didn't reply. He just stared down at his hands. "I can't undo what she's done," he finally said in a voice on the verge of cracking. "I can only try to make amends for . . . for not taking action sooner." He grimaced, like he was trying to hold back a tidal wave of emotion.

Marcellus thought about Max's body lying in the fields outside Ledôme. About the pulse that killed her. About the hand that fired it. And unexpected sympathy rose up inside of him. "You did the right thing, you know? She never would have stopped."

Jolras cleared his throat, and when he peered up again, his expression was stony. "Anyway, like I said to Borel, I want to help. I'm sure you've seen the droids. Right now, most of the people locked inside these fabriques are unarmed. I can change that. If you untie us, I can lead you to the weapons."

Jolras's words sank deep down into Marcellus's brain, connecting with echoes of the past. With the last time Jolras had summoned him, promising to be on their side, only to betray them.

"Can I trust you again?" Marcellus asked, but he already knew the answer.

He *had* to trust him. They had no other choice. Most of these people *were* unarmed, and his grandfather's army would be advancing in less than seven hours. What if Jolras Epernay and his stash of stolen weapons were their only hope?

Marcellus turned and rapped twice on the door. Borel appeared a moment later, eyebrows raised in a silent question, waiting for an answer Marcellus prayed he wouldn't regret giving.

"Let them go. They're coming with me."

CHAPTER 79

CHATINE

"HOW MUCH FARTHER?" ROCHE WHINED, HIS FEET MAK-
ing annoying sloshing sounds in the foul water that trickled along the
floor of the sewage tunnel.

Chatine squinted down at the hand-drawn map Alouette had made for
them, trying to catch glimpses of the paper in the bobbing light of Roche's
flashlight. She turned it around and around until she couldn't figure out
which way was right side up. "I think the entrance is up here."

"Just admit it," Roche said. "You're lost."

"I'm not lost," Chatine said through gritted teeth. "I'm just . . ." She
spun the map again. "*Slightly* turned around."

"Why don't you let me read the map?" Roche made a swipe for the
paper, but Chatine pulled it out of his grasp.

"My job is to get us there. Your job is to guard the virus. Do you still
have the drive?"

Roche groaned. "Yes. I still have it. You've asked me that twenty times. It's
right here." He pulled the tiny square of glistening metal out of his pocket with
such speed, it fumbled through his fingers and went flying. Chatine reached
into the air and snatched it, before stuffing it into her own pocket.

"I guess I'll have to do that part too."

Roche harrumphed and leaned against the side of the tunnel, pretending to fall asleep. "I'll just take a little nap. You let me know when you figure out where the fric we're going."

Chatine ignored him and narrowed her eyes at the map again, trying to orient herself amid the crisscrossing grid of tunnels scribbled onto the page. The drive—tiny as it was—felt like a wooden bloc in her pocket. Or more like an explosif waiting to go off.

She still couldn't believe the key to bringing down the entire droid army fit on something so small. When Denise had finished coding the virus and had held up the minuscule device, Chatine had actually laughed.

"That?" she'd said. "Seriously?"

Denise's expression never faltered. "All droids have an auxiliary charging port on the back of their heads," she'd explained to the group. "I've designed the drive so that it can be inserted directly into the port. Once plugged in, the virus will upload and spread through the network to the other droids."

Chatine's amusement had quickly been replaced with disbelief. "You honestly expect someone to get a basher to stand still while they plug something into the back of its head?"

"No," Denise had replied flatly, her eyes darting to Chatine. "I expect *you* to do it."

"Me?" Chatine's face had grown hot as the rest of the group turned expectantly to her.

"She's right," agreed Alouette. "You have the most experience dealing with droids. If anyone can upload this virus, it's you."

"And I'll come!" Roche had immediately launched his hand into the air. "I've been waiting my entire life to bring down a basher."

"You will absolutely *not*," was Chatine's automatic response. But then, after a sharp look from her brother that clearly meant, *This is what we talked about*, Chatine had sighed and relented. "Look, unless you can figure out a way to lull a droid to sleep, then this is a pointless conversation. No one is going to get close enough to that charging port to—"

"Sleep," Cerise had repeated with an urgent flash of her circuitry. "Yes. Exactly! Brilliant idea, Chatine."

Chatine had looked from Cerise to Alouette to Denise, trying to figure out what she had missed. But Cerise still seemed to be the only one following her own logic. "Implant the virus before the droid is awake!"

And that was how Chatine had found herself lost—or slightly turned around—in a maze of stinking sewage tunnels underneath the Fabrique District with the sounds of trickling water and rats skittering in the shadows.

She gave the map one final turn, trying to orient herself. "I think it's this way," she said, then attempted to insert some confidence into her tone as she adjusted the strap of the bag on her back and continued down the tunnel. "It's definitely this way."

Roche sighed and pushed himself off the wall before following after her. But by the time they hit the next crossroads, Chatine had to admit they were definitely lost. This one had not four but seven tunnels jutting out from it, like rays of a Sol. She was starting to feel hopeless.

"Shine your flashlight here," she told Roche, pointing at the map.

In the light, she squinted at Alouette's neat handwriting scrawled on the far left side of the page, sounding out the letters one by one, just as the sisters had taught her to do. "D-r-o-i-d fa-bri-que."

"I still say we should have gone with an ambush," Roche muttered. "I could have led a droid away from the pack and you could have pounced on it."

Chatine cut him a look. "You can't ambush a droid."

He scuffed his boot against the floor. "Well, it's a better idea than this one."

Chatine turned her focus back to the map, trying to ignore the clench in her stomach. She didn't want to admit that she was just as doubtful about the plan as Roche was. Break into the droid fabrique? Had they lost their minds?

Maybe so. But first they had to actually *find* the place.

"I think we must have taken a wrong turn." Roche directed his flashlight down one of the seven passageways. "Maybe we should radio back to the base for—" But he was interrupted by a low, creaky sound echoing from one of the seven tunnels. A rat?

"It sounds like someone is lost." A raspy voice reverberated out of the darkness.

Definitely not a rat.

Roche spun around, shining his flashlight down each of the passages in turn. But there didn't seem to be anyone there.

"Do you think we should help these poor lost souls, chéri?" the voice spoke again.

It was getting closer.

Chatine grabbed Roche's elbow and tried to shove him behind her, but without knowing which of the seven tunnels the voice was coming from, there was no such thing as *behind*.

She reached for the rayonette that Alouette had plucked from their small supply of amassed weapons and clutched it tightly in her fist. "Who's there?" she called out.

"Of course we should help them," came the response. This was a second voice. Just as low, just as echoey against the tunnel walls. "We know these sewers so well and we are nothing but generous. Isn't that right, chéri?"

"That's right, my darling." There was a slithering silence followed by two sets of splashing footsteps. Chatine's blood ran cold. It was as though her body recognized their presence before she could even see them. And then out of the darkness, the figures emerged.

Chatine had been wrong. It *was* a rat. Two of them.

Roche swung his flashlight violently like a weapon, illuminating the two filthy, disheveled people who now stood huddled before them like the vermin that they were.

"We always help those in need." Monsieur Renard smiled and added, "For a price."

Chatine didn't care what promises she'd made to Roche or how much he protested, her instincts were far too strong. She pushed him behind her, shielding him with her entire body.

The pair of them had aged a thousand years. Or so it seemed. He looked more angular, gnarled, and shriveled up like week-old chou bread, while she appeared like a mountain whose sides had slumped in a series of avalanches. Her once-curvy hips and heaving bosom were now deflated and sagging forlornly under her ragged, threadbare clothes.

Yet, even in the beam of the flashlight, Chatine could see their matching beady eyes.

The glint of shared greed still shone, inextinguishable like Sols.

"Oh my," said her father, the recognition finally registering on his face. "Look what the sewers dragged up. I hoped we'd see each other again, my little kitty cat."

Of course they were here. They could smell the looming battle in the air. They sniffed out chaos and blood like hunting dogs sniff out prey. They'd be ready to pounce on the first body that fell. Ready to pillage and loot and steal.

"My darling," said her mother, spreading her wobbling arms wide as if she expected Chatine to run to her. "Come to Maman."

When Chatine didn't move, Madame Renard smiled, revealing a mouthful of missing teeth. "And who do you have hiding back there?" She leaned to the side to get a better view of Roche.

Chatine tried to angle herself to block her, but it soon became a lost cause when Roche stepped out on his own.

"I'm your son," he said, his voice harder than Chatine had ever heard it. The sound of his sharp edges, the defensive shell he had to manufacture at a moment's notice, broke her heart. "The one you abandoned and sold off to pay your debts, remember?"

The Renards shared two consecutive looks, the first incredulous, the second silently communicating how they might be able to exploit the situation.

"Henri!" Madame Renard exclaimed, turning back to Roche. "My darling boy. I've missed you so much. I've thought about you every day. I pictured your face. Your sweet, sweet face." She spread her arms out wide again, as if to see if the charade would work on him.

"Really?" Roche replied venomously. "Did you also picture me living on the streets by four years old? Scrounging through heaps of trash for something to eat? Did you picture me freezing in the rain? Huddling under tarps to keep warm?"

Madame Renard brushed away an invisible tear and spoke in a soft, cooing voice. "Oh, mon chéri. I'm so sorry."

"Shut up!" screamed Roche, and before Chatine could react, he had plucked the rayonette from her grasp and was aiming it at the Renards.

"Roche, no," Chatine said. "They're not worth it. I swear."

"I had nothing!" Roche bellowed, ignoring her. "I grew up alone and terrified and so, so cold. You did that to me. You don't deserve to live. People who sell their children don't deserve to live."

"Roche." Chatine eyed the rayonette, calculating how to grab it before he did something he would regret.

"It wasn't my fault!" Madame Renard blubbered, pointing a long, bony finger at Chatine. "Your sister was just too demanding. She ate too much. She needed too much. We couldn't afford to care for you both. We had to choose. And she insisted that we choose her."

Chatine waited to feel it. The anger. The disgust. The fear. All the things that used to run through her Renard blood. All the things that used to keep her up at night, vowing revenge, vowing retribution.

But as she glanced around at the warren of endless dark passageways with their scrabbling rats and oozing damp walls, all she felt was pity.

"Roche," she said gently, turning to her brother, who still had fury in his eyes and the rayonette pointed at his mother's head. "Look at what's become of them. Scrounging through the sewers. With rats. They can't sink any lower."

Her father hissed back at her. If there was anything he despised more, it was other people's pity. "This is merely a stopover. We have plenty of bigger and better things in the works, don't we, chéri?"

"Plenty," repeated her mother.

"I'm working up the con of the century as we speak."

"Roche, please," Chatine pleaded, but her brother's cruel, vengeful gaze never faltered.

"Do you know what 'Oublie' actually means?" he spat. "It means 'abandon.' It means '*forget*.'" Roche shook his head and let out a mirthless laugh. "I always thought that was referring to me. That *I* was the one who was forgotten. But it's not. It's referring to you. Because that's exactly what you deserve. To be forgotten."

Then, slowly, shakily, Roche lowered the weapon.

Chatine let out a breath, grabbed his hand, and together they continued down one of the tunnels. She didn't care which one, as long as it was a path that led them both away from the Renards.

"Wait!" called her father. "Don't you want in? I could offer you a hefty cut!"

But they kept walking, refusing to look back.

"You're going the wrong way!" called her mother. "That tunnel only leads to the droid fabrique, and you'll get yourself killed wandering around that basher mill."

Chatine smiled, holding tight to Roche's hand. Like she would never let go. Like she *had* never let go.

- CHAPTER 80 -
MARCELLUS

THE SEWAGE TUNNEL FELT DARKER TO MARCELLUS with three people in it. As though the two figures walking steadily in front of him somehow sucked up rays of light from his flashlight, making it harder to see, harder to navigate.

"Turn left up here," Marcellus ordered as they approached one of the many crisscrossing intersections of the old sewage system. Their destination wasn't written on the map he'd drawn when he'd left the bread fabrique, but he knew the general direction.

Up ahead, the beam of his flashlight illuminated a rusty ladder, and Marcellus dropped the sac of rayonettes he'd been carrying and began to climb. The access point above was boarded up with a row of heavy wooden slats, and Marcellus grunted as he tried to push through them with his hand, then his elbow. But the only thing seeming to give way were his own joints.

"Move aside," Jolras ordered, and before Marcellus could react, a pulse came whizzing past his head.

"Sols!" He fought to hang on to the ladder as the barrier exploded above him, wooden splinters and shards raining down on his face. When the dust and debris finally cleared, he looked down to see Antoine holding one of the rayonettes from the sac, and Marcellus's stomach instinctively clenched again. As much as Marcellus still distrusted the man, he couldn't fault his aim. It was impeccable. Otherwise Marcellus would probably be dead right now. "What the fric? A little warning would have been nice."

Jolras shrugged as he plucked the rayonette out of Antoine's hand and returned it to the bag. "Sorry. But whatever you were doing before looked pretty painful."

The stabbing sensation in his elbow pulsed in agreement. Marcellus sighed and glanced up again at the now-open flood drain. Wincing, he grabbed hold of the ladder and pulled himself through.

They found themselves in a murky alleyway between two buildings. The coldness of the night was both startling and refreshing, slapping Marcellus across both cheeks. He'd been trapped inside those sewage tunnels and fabriques for hours; the fresh air was almost calming. Until he took in his surroundings.

Amid the shadows in the alleyway, trash was piled against the walls and old rainwater oozed in small, trickling rivers through the mud. The buildings that loomed on either side of them were pocked with holes, broken gutters, and smashed windows. Marcellus had been to the Planque only a few times before. The dark, secluded area of the Fabrique District that had always been a hotbed of illegal activity was conveniently avoided by most members of the Policier and Ministère.

And now, with a shiver running down his spine, he couldn't shake the feeling that maybe this had been a trap all along. Lead the former officer into the abandoned Planque and ambush him.

"This way," Jolras called out, hitching the bag of rayonettes farther up his shoulder. Marcellus reached out a hand to stop him.

"I think I'll take those back now."

Jolras chuckled, as though Marcellus's distrust highly amused him. "Suit yourself." He passed the bag to Marcellus, who looped his arm through the strap.

Marcellus followed behind the two men, keeping both of them in his sights, just as he'd done in the tunnel. Jolras led them out of the alleyway and into the center of the Planque. This area, tucked behind Vallonay's lumber fabrique, had always been a dismal place with run-down build-ings huddled around a dilapidated square. But since Marcellus's grand-father had shut down its taverns, shops, and other illegal operations, the Planque now felt like a rotting, forgotten carcass of its former self. Doors that hadn't been boarded up hung on busted hinges. Splinters of broken windows carpeted the ground, and trash and rats roamed the streets like Third Estaters on market day.

Marcellus quickened his pace to keep up with Jolras, who was guiding them across the dingy and muddy square. They headed toward a small ram-shackle structure that lurked in the shadows between two larger buildings. When they reached the door tucked around the side, Jolras spent a few moments tweaking and clattering quietly at the hinges with a screwdriver, until finally, the big rectangle of metal wobbled in its frame and a gap large enough for the three of them to slip through opened up.

Despite being inside again, Marcellus felt a chill rustle through him as he whipped his flashlight around and caught sight of a massive machine laced with tubes and dials that glimmered menacingly under his searching beam. Suddenly, he knew exactly what kind of building this was. And he couldn't stop his mind from picturing that horrifying machine whirring to life, sucking blood out of the arms of innocent girls, all so the First and Second Estates could rub rejuvenating creams into their skin.

"It's right through here," said Jolras.

Swallowing down a gag, Marcellus followed after him, weaving between the rows of extraction chairs, deeper into the abandoned blood bordel, until they reached a back room.

In the darkness, Marcellus could see only shadows. Narrow shafts of light cut through the dirty windows, illuminating muddled shapes and sporadic glints of metal. It wasn't until he fanned his flashlight around the space that he felt his heart stop.

Crates upon crates crowded every surface and covered the entire floor. Each one filled with weapons. Hundreds, maybe thousands, of them. Some overflowed their crates, cascading like waterfalls of shimmering metals. In every container and across the floor, long, sleek barrels of rayo-nettes tangled together with the smaller and chunkier tazeurs, and a legion of riot-gas canisters were stacked in rows, looking like miniature droids ready to attack.

Marcellus was certain he was still alive because he was still standing upright. But it felt like every last gramme of blood in his veins had been sucked out, into those terrifying machines behind him. He wasn't sure what he'd imagined when Jolras had said those chilling words—*"Max was building an arsenal"*—but it definitely wasn't this.

He could feel Jolras watching him, like he was waiting for Marcellus to say something. But what on Laterre was he supposed to say? Congratulations? Well done stealing enough weapons to fortify a small army?

With another numbing chill, Marcellus realized that this was exactly what the Red Scar had done. Max had been forming an army. She'd been ready for many more battles beyond just the march on Ledôme.

"So?" Jolras prompted after Marcellus still hadn't uttered a single word. "Do you trust me now?"

But it wasn't Jolras whom Marcellus felt the need to respond to. Hands shaking, Marcellus fumbled in his pocket for the radio, struggling to even find the strength to press the talk button on the side.

"Alouette, this is Marcellus. Assemble a very large team and send them to the Planque."

- CHAPTER 81 -
CHATINE

CHATINE AND ROCHE WERE BACK IN THE RAFTERS, looking down at the world below. Normally, this was where Chatine felt the most safe. The most protected. High enough that no one could touch her. No one could hurt her.

But not now.

And definitely not *here*.

Far below, the manufacturing floor of the droid fabrique vibrated and clanked in a constant, dizzying motion. Long sheets of shining Perma-Steel unspooled onto a conveyor belt and whizzed effortlessly into a vast machine that cut and stamped them into enormous exoskeletons. Farther along, hollow metal skulls were being molded, shaped, and then implanted with complicated circuitry and microchips. And surrounding the whole operation, all the way down the line, were the robots that assembled the droids into being. Slicing, pounding, riveting, inserting, tweaking. With their jutting, hinged drills and pointing lasers, they looked like flocks of long-necked pecking birds.

Robots making robots.

Chatine shivered at the thought and forced herself to keep going. She crawled silently behind Roche as they made their way across the rafter overlooking the giant assembly line, watching the Empereur's weapons being constructed right before their very eyes.

The sight of the machines should have comforted her. They were one of the primary reasons Cerise had suggested this place to begin with. It was an entirely automated fabrique. Which meant, no workers. No superviseurs. No human guards. The fabrique's exterior was fortified and protected by the very product it was manufacturing, making it nearly impossible to break in from the outside.

But not from the inside.

The busted sewer grate they'd climbed through still sat half ajar on the far end of the manufacturing floor.

"Almost there," Roche whispered as he carefully maneuvered around a support beam and continued to scurry along the rafter toward the end of the assembly line.

Chatine followed behind, shuddering at the sight of the lifeless PermaSteel bodies that now clattered along a moving track like slabs of meat. Their silvery skulls lolled to the side, their empty eye sockets looked downward with haunting, dead stares, and their weaponized hands juddered with every movement of the track as if itching to come to life.

The knot in Chatine's stomach twisted with desperation. If this plan didn't work, if they couldn't upload Denise's virus, this revolution was doomed. The Empereur was creating more soldiers by the minute. Even if the rebels managed to fight off a few bashers, more were already being manufactured to take their place.

Roche pulled to a stop and repositioned himself on the beam. "There's the activation zone," he whispered, pointing toward the end of the assembly line, where a circular platform rose up from the manufacturing floor. They watched, silent as mice, as one of the lifeless droid carcasses rattled across the track and the gigantic metal robot lifted it by its neck and placed it upright in the center of the activation zone. The moment the droid's feet landed on the platform, a single green light on its perimeter glowed to life.

Chatine silently starting counting.

One, two, three . . .

One after another, the lights all around the platform were blinking on, forming a perfect circle of glowing green.

All the while, Cerise's final instructions echoed hauntingly through Chatine's mind.

"If you can plug the drive into the charging port before the new droid is activated, the virus will automatically upload to the network the moment the droid comes online."

Finally, after a sequence of sharp beeps, the green lights around the perimeter of the platform flashed three times before clicking off. Chatine shot her gaze toward the face of the droid and waited, holding her breath. At first it was just a spark of light. But it soon became a confident, pulsing glimmer, which quickly morphed into a glow. A blinding orange glow that beamed out from its cavernous, metallic eye sockets.

"Twenty seconds," Chatine whispered with a shudder of despair. "We have twenty fric-ing seconds before it comes online."

"We can do it," Roche asserted.

And Chatine wished she could steal a smidgen of his confidence.

The droid stood up straighter, extending to its full height before stepping off the platform and marching determinately toward a set of large double doors that led to the fabrique's distribution center. A sensor registered its presence and the doors whooshed open, welcoming the droid inside the vast warehouse, before closing securely behind it.

Chatine peered back at the assembly line, where another finished basher was already clanking down the track toward the activation zone.

"Okay, let's do this," she said, blowing out a breath and reaching into the small sac secured to her back. She pulled out the long black strap they'd taken from the bread fabrique. Normally, it was used to secure crates to the inside of a delivery transporteur. She prayed it was strong enough to secure a person as well.

After threading one end of the strap through a joint in the rafter, she then fashioned a makeshift pulley and handed the other end of the strap to Roche. He secured it around his hips and back to create a harness.

"I can't believe I'm letting you do this," she hissed as he gave the knot a final tug.

Roche shrugged. "You didn't have a choice, remember? I'm lighter."

She sighed and pulled the drive out of her pocket. "Please be careful."

He grinned back at her. "I'm always careful."

"No, you're—" she began to argue, but Roche was already easing himself over the edge of the beam. Chatine gripped the strap tighter, preparing for his weight. He released one hand, testing the mechanism. The strap held. He released the other, and Chatine let out a little more slack, lowering him a centimètre.

Two more bashers had already come online and disappeared into the distribution center. She looked up at the overhead track, where the next droid was approaching, just waiting to be woken up.

"Are you ready?" she whispered to Roche.

He gave her a thumbs-up, secured the drive between his teeth, and grabbed hold of the strap with both hands. Chatine sucked in a breath, her pulse racing, and her gaze darting between the assembly line and Roche dangling just below her.

The bird-like beak of the robot plucked the newly formed droid from the track and set it down on the platform, where the first green light on the perimeter blinked to life.

"Now!" Roche whispered, and Chatine hastily fed the strap through the pulley, lowering Roche toward the newly manufactured droid.

In her mind, she started to count.

One, two, three . . .

And in her heart, she started to pray.

Please work. Please don't kill him.

Moments later, Roche was face-to-face with the still and silent basher. The sight of it sent every fiber of Chatine's body bursting into flames. He pulled the drive from between his teeth and eased it toward the back of the droid's head.

Chatine glanced down at the activation zone. A semicircle of lights around the platform was now glowing bright green. Halfway there.

"Come on," she whispered urgently, holding tight to the strap. "Plug it in."

But as he extended his arm, he came up centimètres short. His fingertips were just able to graze the droid's skull, but it wasn't close enough. Chatine's heart threatened to pound right out of her chest.

The platform's perimeter was almost fully illuminated now, and in just a few seconds, those green lights would flash, and it would be over.

Chatine sucked in a frustrated breath. There was no time left. They'd have to wait for the next one. She began to pull him back up but froze when she felt a strange tension on the strap and glanced down to see that Roche was lurching his body back and forth, trying to build up momentum to swing toward the droid.

"No! Don't!" she whispered, but he either couldn't hear her or chose to ignore her. His body swung back, away from the droid, and then crashed, way too hard, into its metal shoulder.

The next thing Chatine heard might have been the most terrifying sound of her life. Barely audible over the din of the fabrique, the tiniest, subtlest *ping* rang out as the metal drive slipped from Roche's grasp and fell to the ground.

Her thoughts spiraled. Her body responded on instinct, yanking on the strap to heave him back up. But it soon became apparent that Roche had other plans. Didn't he always? Chatine watched on, horrified, as he unknotted his harness and leapt, cat-like, to the ground.

She wanted to call out to him. To scream at him, but she couldn't risk the sound. The doors to that distribution center were only mètres away, and crammed inside were enough activated droids to invade a small planet.

Roche scrabbled along the floor and scooped up the device. He lunged to his feet just in time for them both to hear that terrifying sequence of sharp beeps and then see the lights around the activation zone flash their final three times before flickering off.

A second later, with panic clawing at her throat, Chatine watched the droid's orange eyes glow to life and land almost instantly and unmistakably on Roche.

Alouette had been right. Chatine did have enough experience with droids to know what to do next.

It was the only thing she *could* do.

Pushing off with her hands, Chatine launched forward and dropped.

She landed on the droid's back with the force of a cruiseur hitting a PermaSteel wall. Pain ricocheted through her entire body, but her momentum was enough. The droid staggered off the platform and fell to its knees, momentarily stunned. Wrapping one arm around its neck, she reached toward Roche.

"Give me the drive!" she called out in an urgent whisper.

But before Roche could react, the droid was already rising back to its feet, reaching over its shoulder with its massive claw-like fingers to grapple for her. Chatine managed to swing herself to the side, just out of its grasp. Until the other hand reached back too. It gripped on to the arm that was wrapped around its neck and tugged. Chatine heard a pop in her shoulder and bit back a cry.

Then, the basher gave an almighty shake and Chatine's body went soaring backward. She collided with the next assembled droid trundling down the track and fell to the ground. The heavy PermaSteel shell toppled down around her in a cascade of bangs and clatters. Her shoulder screamed in pain. Stars swam in front of her eyes. But she managed to clear her vision long enough to focus on the spot where Roche had been standing.

He was gone.

And so was the droid.

"Roche! No!" she bellowed, but it was too late. He was already sprinting down the assembly line, his hand clutched protectively around the drive, with the droid clomping after him.

A lightning bolt of pain shot through Chatine as she pushed herself to her feet and dashed after them, struggling to yank the radio free from her pocket as she ran.

"This is Chatine! Does anyone copy? We need immediate assistance at the . . ." Her voice trailed off as she realized there was no static accompanying her voice. She pressed the button again, but nothing happened. The radio was dead, obviously damaged in her tussle with the droid.

Up ahead, she heard the unmistakable sound of a rayonette firing, the air rippling as a pulse searched for its target. The sound powered her legs to move faster. Tossing the useless radio aside, she kept running. But as she turned the corner and darted out from behind a giant spool of wire, the sight in front of her stopped her cold once again. And a scream bubbled up in her throat.

Roche's rayonette lay on the ground next to the assembly line, and her little brother was sprawled out on his back on top of a massive piece of PermaSteel that was gliding down a wide conveyer belt. He was attempting to hold back the basher that was hovering over him with its tazeur outstretched. Roche kicked and thrashed and punched, but it was no use. The droid was too strong.

The first jolt of electricity from the tazeur shot through Roche's body, causing it to judder violently and his teeth to chatter before he fell still.

"Stop!" Chatine grabbed the rayonette from the ground and fired three times at the droid's back. The pulses sparked against its exoskeleton, causing a shower of rippling light. But the impact only startled the droid for a moment before it resumed its attack, plunging down the tazeur once more. Roche's body gave another violent wrench as the electricity surged through him. Chatine knew, from living on Bastille, that his system couldn't take many more consecutive shocks before it simply gave up.

Desperately, she peered around the fabrique, searching for something to use as another weapon. Something to stop this from happening right before her very eyes.

And that's when her gaze landed on the assembly robot up ahead. The giant slab of PermaSteel that Roche was lying on was heading right toward it. But all Chatine could focus on was that blue light.

It hissed and sizzled as it beamed down from the robot's long beak. A blinding, unceasing laser that moved with a deadly determination and terrifying rhythm. Again and again and again, it spat out showering sparks as it sliced its way through the PermaSteel being fed beneath it.

Roche blinked his eyes, his vision focusing again, the sensation in his body clearly coming back. The conveyer belt moved steadily forward. The droid lifted the tazeur for its third assault.

Chatine knew she couldn't wait. Aiming the rayonette at the droid's head, she held down the trigger, firing an endless barrage of pulses into its skull. As expected, the shots did not penetrate, but the stunning effect was enough. The droid froze.

Roche ducked and rolled off the belt. The conveyer trundled forward. And as the blue laser came slicing down once more, it found its target not in the slab of PermaSteel on the belt, but straight through the droid's neck.

Chatine leapt back as the basher's head rolled off the conveyer and bounced three times on the hard concrete floor of the fabrique before coming to a stop against her toes.

She stared down at the empty sockets that once glowed a menacing Ministère orange but now looked like dark, bottomless caverns. Swallowing down the bile that was rising up in her throat, Chatine ran to Roche and pulled him into her arms, squeezing him until he probably couldn't breathe.

"Did you . . . ," she began to ask, but her little brother sadly shook his head, unfurling his clenched fingers to reveal the answer to her question.

Nestled in his sweaty palm was Denise's drive.

Tears welled up in Roche's eyes.

"It's okay. It'll be okay. We'll figure something out." She reached for her brother again, but the sound of sharp, thunderous footsteps stopped them both. Chatine knew that sound. The rhythm of it. The way it shook the ground. She glanced back toward the activation zone, and the distribution center just beyond it.

The doors were no longer closed.

"We need to get out of here!" She grabbed her brother's hand, and they made a mad dash toward the drainage grate that led back to the sewers. Unfortunately, however, their path was blocked. An army of fully formed, fully activated droids now stood in eerily neat rows in front of Chatine and Roche, forming an impenetrable wall between them and their only escape.

- CHAPTER 82 -
CERISE

"ANY UPDATE?" ALOUETTE ASKED FOR THE FIFTH TIME
in the past ten minutes. She'd been calmly pacing the length of the
superviseur's office, her hands wrapped around a strange cylindrical
object that she kept turning round and round.

"Not yet," reported Cerise from her makeshift workstation. It certainly
wasn't as prestigious or as well equipped as her cubicle back in the Bureau
of Défense. Instead of her three state-of-the-art monitors, she had only
her former self's hacked TéléCom and a few of Brigitte's impressive handmade devices. Instead of all of the Ministère's processors and networks and
resources at her disposal, she only had the ones she could make or hack
into herself.

But as she sat at the small desk, next to Denise and Brigitte, carefully monitoring Denise's virus code, her circuitry had never flickered with
more contentment.

"As soon as the virus is implanted, we'll see it come online," explained
Denise. "And then we'll be able to track it throughout the droid network."

Through the window overlooking the bread fabrique's loading bay,
Cerise could hear the distorted murmur of voices and activity below, as the
Red Scar's stolen weapons were distributed to the workers. She couldn't

believe how many Maximilienne Epernay had managed to take from the Ministère. They kept arriving by the sac-ful.

Alouette gave the object in her hand another anxious twist. "Have we heard anything from Chatine and Roche?"

"No," Etienne muttered from the chair in the corner where he'd been sitting for the past hour, staring miserably at his silent radio. "Nothing. And I'm afraid to contact them in case it gives away their location."

Alouette turned to stare out the window of the office, into the night— the Darkest Night—as though she were waiting for a miracle. The season of the Blue Dawn come six years early. "How long?" she whispered.

Cerise swiped at her screen. "Two hours, seventeen minutes, forty-five seconds until Sol-rise."

Alouette sighed and pocketed the object in her hand. She turned to Etienne. "I don't think we have a choice. I think we need to radio them. If the virus isn't uploaded and the Sols rise . . ." She let the words drift away, knowing no one in this room needed them to be said. The near-constant orange glow from the droids outside the window was enough of a reminder. When Cerise peered out at just the right angle, they almost looked like a fourth Sol. A fiery, angry one that, in less than three hours, would come to burn them.

And then, all the stolen rayonettes on Laterre couldn't save them.

Etienne nodded and blew out a heavy breath. Slowly, he brought the radio to his lips. "Chatine? This is Etienne. Are you there? Do you copy?"

Silence filled the room.

Heavy and deadly and determined.

"Chatine? Roche? This is Etienne. Can you hear me? Do you copy?"

Cerise could immediately sense the shift in his voice. The rushed words, the clipped edges. The desperation. And the emotions on his face were lighting up her neuroprocessors.

Fear.

Panic.

Guilt.

Regret.

For as many words as he was pouring into that radio, a hundred more were shouted back at Cerise. She lowered her gaze back down to her TéléCom to give him privacy. Her ability to decrypt human emotions was useful but also, she realized, highly intrusive. She would have to learn to control it, use it sparingly.

"Chatine!" Etienne cried. "Please. Come in. Do. You. Copy?"

More silence. That felt more definitive, more conclusive, with each passing second.

It was broken a moment later by a set of heavy, lumbering footsteps climbing up the stairs. Cerise looked up to see Hugo Taureau, Alouette's adoptive father, limping into the office, his skin and clothes covered in a layer of grime and his large frame barely fitting through the doorway.

"All of the barricaded fabriques now have open access to the sewer tunnels," he reported.

At the sight of him, a strange, unidentified emotion began to swirl in Cerise's chest. It wasn't until Etienne asked, in an alarmed tone, "Where's Gabriel?" that she realized she, too, was concerned about his absence.

"He's fine," Hugo said. "He stayed behind at the textile fabrique with the others to help distribute weapons."

And just like that, the fluttering subsided.

"Merci, Papa." Alouette stood on her tiptoes to plant a kiss on her father's cheek. "Now, please promise you'll find a place to rest. You have been pushing yourself too hard. I don't want anything to happen to you."

He smiled down at her and pinched her chin with his fingers. "I promise, ma petite."

Hugo turned and left the office just as Etienne launched up from his chair, gripping the radio in his hand like he was trying to strangle it. "That's it. I can't sit here any longer. I have to go after her. Something is wrong. I can feel it." He turned to Alouette. "The droid fabrique, right? That's where Chatine and Roche were going?"

Alouette nodded. "That was the plan, yes."

"Show me the map of the sewers," he said to Cerise, who hastily pulled it up on her TéléCom. Etienne studied the schematics, quickly memorizing the route the way he used to memorize flight plans.

"You should take some people with you," Alouette said. "A small team at least."

Etienne glanced through the interior window at the crowded loading bay below. He considered for a short moment before shaking his head. "You need them here. I'll be fine."

He strode purposefully across the room toward Brigitte and reached for her hands. "Maman, I'm sorry. I have to do this."

Brigitte smiled. "I know, my sweet boy." Then, she stood up and, balancing on her tiptoes, planted a kiss on his forehead. "Be safe."

"I will." He gave his mother's hands a final squeeze and then darted out the door.

Alouette turned to Denise, looking pained by what she was about to say next. "What if Etienne is right? What if something has gone wrong? Can you build another drive?"

Denise blew out a breath. "I don't know. With only two hours . . ."

". . . eleven minutes, and thirty-nine seconds," Cerise finished helpfully.

"Factoring in the time to have someone upload it," said Brigitte. "It will be cutting it close."

"Well, we have to try, right?" said Alouette. "We have to be ready in case . . ."

She didn't let the sentence finish. But the stifling silence that followed was enough.

It was shattered moments later by a knock on the door, and Marcellus entered, followed by a man whose face immediately registered as a threat in Cerise's neuroprocessors.

Jolras Epernay.

Escaped convict.

Known terrorist.

She struggled to override the alert, reminding herself that Jolras Epernay was helping them. He was on their side now.

"The teams are handing out weapons at all of the fabriques now," Marcellus announced. "Jolras and Antoine have been instrumental in facilitating the operation."

Antoine?

Cerise's gaze darted to the doorway of the office, where a second man now stood, slightly hunched and hesitant, like he wasn't sure whether or not he was allowed to enter.

As she scrutinized his features, she felt a shiver of apprehension trickle through her. Whether it was her cyborg processors or her human intuition, she couldn't be sure. But something wasn't right about his face. Her initial scan revealed no profile matches in the Communiqué, and when she tried to decrypt his expression, the result was something she'd never experienced before.

Error.

"Merci to both of you," Alouette was saying. She reached out to squeeze Jolras's shoulder. "We are so grateful for your help."

"You're welcome," said Jolras quietly. "We will continue to monitor the disbursement of the weapons. Make sure everyone is armed and ready."

"Please remind the fabriques that the weapons are to be used for protection only," said Alouette. "We are defending ourselves and the goods we produce. We are not launching an offensive attack."

Jolras nodded and disappeared down the stairs with Antoine. Cerise watched the stranger leave, her thoughts spinning out of control as she tried to troubleshoot the error in her processors. Were they failing her? Now that she'd woken up and was becoming more human by the hour, were her cyborg abilities slowly deteriorating?

"What is the status of the droid virus?" Marcellus asked, crossing the office to stand beside Denise and Brigitte.

"Nothing yet," said Denise regretfully. "The code has yet to come online."

"And Chatine?" Marcellus asked, panic registering in his voice.

"Don't worry," Alouette said, placing a hand on his arm. "Etienne has gone to check on them. I'm sure they're fine."

Cerise told herself she was only doing it as a test. A systems check. To make sure everything was functioning properly. As she scanned Alouette's face, analyzing her eyes, the slight downturn of her lips, the crease between her brows, she tried not to visibly shudder as the decryption came back perfectly clear and unhindered.

Lie.

An icy chill worked its way down Cerise's spine. Not only was Alouette convinced Chatine and Roche were in danger, but Cerise was now certain there was absolutely nothing wrong with her processors.

Which meant there was something very wrong with Antoine.

She opened her mouth to report her concerns when suddenly, Alouette's gaze snapped to the window. Cerise noticed it too. In the corner of her eye, Cerise saw the fiery, glowing orange Sol was splitting apart, radiating outward like sparks from a broken star.

"What is it?" Marcellus asked, rushing to the window.

"It can't be." Alouette's voice was now barely a whisper. "We still have . . ."

"Two hours, eight minutes, and fifty-five seconds," said Cerise. But it didn't matter. Because she could now see what was happening outside that window. Even through their splintered view, half obstructed by the massive barricade that had been erected, the movement was undeniable.

Somewhere in the shadowy depths of the fabrique, where hundreds of men and women were huddled together, a commotion was building. Voices were shouting out questions that no one could answer. Bodies were suddenly in chaotic motion.

And then, Cerise heard the thunderous footsteps. Not from outside the window, but from the stairs leading up to this very room. When Grantaire burst through the door, hollow-eyed and out of breath, the words that spilled urgently from his mouth were as predictable as a Sol-rise.

Only they were coming two hours, eight minutes, and twenty-seven seconds too early.

"The droids are advancing on the barricades."

- CHAPTER 83 -
ETIENNE

ETIENNE DID NOT LIKE BEING UNDERGROUND. THE AIR was stale. The walls were closing in on him. His meager flashlight did little to chase away the bone-chilling darkness. And it seemed as though every tunnel and passageway he turned down, something was waiting to jump out at him: a rat, a swarm of spiders, even his own shadow.

It was Chatine's face that kept him going. Kept him sloshing through suspect puddles. Kept him turning corners, his flashlight bobbing frantically in front of him.

Finally, the ladder came into view and Etienne glanced up at the ceiling of the tunnel. The access point to the droid fabrique was a drainage grate that had already been busted open. Tucking his flashlight between his teeth, he began to climb. But the moment his head rose up above the floor of the fabrique, everything shuddered to a stop.

A thousand thoughts clamored through his mind at once, the loudest and most dominant being, *Get out of here!* But he shoved that one away and reached for the second.

Find her.

Lowering his head until only his eyes were visible over the edge of the grate, he swept his gaze across the manufacturing floor, trying to ignore the ringing in his ears and the relentless pounding of his heart.

The whole fabrique trembled in a chorus of noise and motion. Strange angular robots pounded on metal. Blue lasers sparked and hissed while overhead tracks whirred and clanged. And in the midst of it all, packs of fully formed droids were marching across the floor, the orange embers of their eyes glowing menacingly from under their heavy silver brows. They were searching under machines and behind giant spools of raw material. Searching for *something*.

Without warning, Etienne's mind immediately drifted back. To the fires. The screams.

"Etienne! Don't go in there!"

"Etienne! Come back!"

"Papa! Help!"

He squeezed his eyes shut for long enough to chase the memories away. He didn't have time for nightmares. He had to find them. But he didn't even know if they were still alive. All he had was his hope. And that intuition that kept pulsing through him, guiding his body, steering his thoughts.

She's alive.

And she knows how to hide from bashers.

Something Chatine said earlier reverberated back at him—*"They can't climb"*—and his gaze shot up toward the ceiling.

That's when he saw it. Emerging from the dark rafters.

Three flashes of light.

Quick and purposeful.

Then again. One. Two. Three.

It was their signal from the ship. She was up there. He pulled his focus back down to the ground, mapping out a path from that rafter to this grate. There was no way to get here without attracting the attention of the droids.

Etienne lowered himself back down the ladder and began to pace the length of the tunnel, racking his brain. He knew nothing about bashers. Nothing about how to fight them. Except that they certainly weren't scared of fire. His community had tried that before. They'd doused their own chalets in emberweed oil—the most flammable substance on Laterre—and set fire to their own homes to try to scare the droids away, but instead—

"Papa! Help!"

The fire had taken his father's life. Because Etienne had gone back inside to get that stupid spinning toy. He could almost still feel the flames licking at his skin, the smoke charring his throat. He could almost see the inside of that chalet as the violent purple flames roared around him, singeing all their possessions, scorching his maman's precious herbs, burning everything. He could see his own terrified four-year-old face reflecting back in the shards of shattered windows as he gazed out for help. But all that had waited for him in the darkness of night were those chilling orange eyes. The same eyes that now blazed above his head.

He stopped pacing. His thoughts skittered to catch up.

There had been no droids *inside* the chalet.

They had all been *outside*.

Why?

Because they were scared? No. Droids weren't scared of fire. They weren't scared of anything. They were machines. Etienne knew that. But the members of his community must have known that too. So why set the fires in the first place?

The answer fluttered into his mind like ash finally settling to the ground after swirling and swirling for too many years.

To get away.

His mother's words at the camp came echoing back to him. *"We have become experts on a tool—a* weapon—*that dates back to our earliest ancestors. A weapon that the Ministère has very little knowledge of."*

He rested his hand against one of the pockets of his utility vest, feeling the round metal cartridge tucked inside.

The droids hadn't been scared *off,* but they hadn't walked into the fire either. Because it wasn't normal fire. Emberweed oil didn't burn at the same temperature or even the same color as anything the droids had ever seen before. They didn't know what to do with it. They didn't know what it would do to *them.* So their programming told them to hold back, at least until the threat could be assessed.

At least, Etienne thought, staring up through the open grate at the rafters far above his head, *until I can get them out.*

CHAPTER 84

ALOUETTE

ALOUETTE STOOD AT THE BACK OF THE LOADING BAY with Marcellus, Brigitte, Francine, and Léonie, watching the hundreds of people who had gathered with stolen weapons. They were all waiting on her. Her decision. Her command.

She had read countless books about the First World. About their wars, their battles, their political struggles, their failures and their triumphs. She knew that every leader experienced a moment that defined them. A crossroads that would mark them. That would decide how history would view them forever.

And she knew that this was hers.

Outside the giant metal doors, an army approached. She could hear the clomping of their metal footsteps. She could hear the muffled bangs of their pulses hitting wood, hitting steel, hitting the sides of crates and ripped-off doors and overturned machinery.

"We just lost the meatpacking fabrique," Marcellus said beside her, listening to the soft chatter of the radio in his hand. "Borel said they locked themselves inside, but the droids destroyed the barricade and smashed right through the loading bay doors."

Alouette gave a small nod to let him know she had heard. But her mind had not yet caught up.

"Maybe we should retreat," Principale Francine said.

"Where would we go?" asked Léonie. "The droids have the place surrounded. We're sitting ducks in here."

"We have to defend this barricade," Marcellus said. "Or it will fall too."

"But can our weapons do anything to stop them?" Alouette asked. And from the way Marcellus avoided her eyes, she knew she wasn't going to like his answer.

"Not much can stop a droid. All you can really try to do is hold them back, force them to drain their power."

"And then what?"

Marcellus winced. "And then, my grandfather sends in more."

The gravity in his voice made Alouette shiver. No one here wanted to state the obvious. That no matter what they did, no matter what they tried, these were temporary solutions, temporary hopes. They needed that droid virus.

"Any word from Etienne or Chatine and Roche?"

Marcellus shook his head. "Still nothing." The radio crackled, and he pressed it anxiously to his ear. A shadow descended over his face. "We just lost the dairy fabrique too."

Alouette turned to the others with an apologetic look. "We don't have a choice."

She switched on her amplificateur and faced the crowd. Hundreds of people who were scared and energized and determined and fed up. "We've already lost two barricades," she called out to them. "We can't afford to lose any more. It is time to defend ourselves. It is time to protect what is ours. Unseal the doors!"

A rallying cry rose up through the loading bay. Hands punched in the air. Before her, the massive metal doors trundled across their tracks, bringing with it a beautiful view.

The barricade.

Which they had built with their bare hands.

Which protected their resources. Their hard labor. Their birthrights.

Which was still standing.

But not if they didn't defend it.

Another unified cry shot up and the people advanced, running toward their makeshift forteresse, climbing, scurrying, positioning, finding crevices and nooks and holes big enough to fit the barrel of a rayonette through.

Alouette flinched as the sound of pulses filled the air. They weren't loud like Albion cluster bullets. They were quiet, almost muted. But with so many of them firing at once, it sounded like drums banging against her skull. And she couldn't tell which ones were going which way. How many of those dreadful whooshing sounds were aimed at the droids? And how many were aimed back at them?

"What should I tell the other fabriques?" asked Marcellus.

Alouette drew in a deep, steadying breath. "Tell them they can do what they think is best, but that we have opened our doors and are fighting back."

Marcellus lifted the radio to his lips to deliver the message, and Alouette watched on, breathlessly, wordlessly, as the rebels continued to fill every available space behind the barricade, firing their weapons at the advancing army. Her fingers began to twitch. Her legs grew restless. She paced back and forth in the loading bay, kneading her hands. She felt useless. Helpless. She needed something to do.

She turned back to Francine. "What's the status from upstairs? When will Denise have the second virus upload ready?"

"She's still working on it."

Alouette continued to pace, the sound of rayonette fire filling her brain, like the pulses were pinging straight off her skull.

She'd never wanted it to come to this. She'd never wanted to put anyone in the direct line of fire. But what choice did they have? The Empereur hadn't kept his word.

"Why would he do this?" Alouette blurted, still pacing, still flinching at the sound of every pulse.

"Send the droids?" Marcellus asked.

"Send them early," Alouette clarified. "It doesn't make sense. He gave us until Sol-rise. Why would he break his promise?"

"Because that's what he does," muttered Marcellus. "He's a monster."

Alouette bit her lip. Something still wasn't adding up in her mind. There was something she was missing.

Marcellus's hand wrapped around her wrist, stopping her in her tracks. "Why don't you go back up to the office. I'll let you know if anything changes."

"No." Alouette shook her head adamantly. "I won't leave them. I just wish I could do something to—"

And just then, she felt the touch of cold metal between her fingers. She spun around, her gaze finding the rayonette clutched in her hand first before finding the man who had put it there. Jolras gave one definitive nod in the direction of the barricade.

And Alouette knew he was right.

Despite Marcellus's protests behind her, she marched forward, crossing the loading bay floor in a matter of seconds. The giant structure loomed before her, with people covering nearly every centimètre of its surface. Some had climbed high and were shooting over the top; some were on their bellies on the floor, firing through cracks in the bottom.

Alouette found a vacant space between two of the rebels and bent down, peering between slats of a bread crate until she could see the terrifying sight for herself.

Although there were many of them, hundreds of them, they seemed like one solid wall of PermaSteel, punctured only by those terrible orange eyes. Rayonette pulses rained upon them from the barricades, rippling off their glinting exoskeletons like waves washing up against an unyielding shore. With every direct hit, a droid would freeze, stunned for only a moment, before it seemed to snap itself awake and continue advancing, sending a cascade of ferocious pulses fired back with twice the force and three times the intensity.

"Use lethal mode," Jolras's voice whispered from behind her. "It's more powerful."

Weapon clutched in her trembling hand, Alouette rolled her finger against the toggle. The rayonette vibrated once in response before settling to a low, even hum. Like it, too, was tired of waiting, tired of standing back, protected in the shadows.

Pushing the barrel between the slats in the bread crate, Alouette squeezed her left eye shut and focused the other on one of the three-mètre-tall beasts moving toward her. And suddenly, she was back in her nightmares. Back under that rock with her father while the droids came closer, their orange eyes cutting through the night, her tiny heart pounding in her chest.

Bum.Bum.Bum.Bum.Bum.

The droid staggered backward as her volley of pulses hit it squarely between the eyes. She hadn't even realized she'd pulled the trigger. The metallic monster faltered for a moment, as though trying to remember where it was, what it was doing. But Alouette didn't give it the chance. She aimed again and fired. The pulses sparked off the front of its exoskeleton, freezing it in place once again. But, just like before, the effect was temporary. Seconds later, it was moving forward.

They all were. Alouette glanced across the great advancing wall of PermaSteel, her heart squeezing as she took count of the fallen droids.

There were none.

Not a single one had drained power or even dropped to its knees. They were just too strong.

Suddenly, there was a loud crack as one of the droid's pulses found its way to the crate Alouette was peering through. She gasped and staggered back as the wood splintered and blackened before her eyes.

"It's not working!" she called to Marcellus. "Our rayonettes are barely holding them back. They only seem to stun them for a few seconds before they keep advancing." She took a deep breath and pointed at the blackened wood. "And they're firing *lethal* pulses."

Just then, Alouette heard the heart-wrenching sound of one of those very pulses burying itself into flesh, followed by a scream that she knew would be the first of many. And would haunt her dreams forever.

A man—no older than twenty—fell from the top of the barricade. For a moment, it almost looked like he was flying. Like he was moving in slow motion. Peaceful. Delicate. Majestic, even. Until his body hit the loading bay floor with a gruesome, bone-crunching crack.

Alouette ran to him, checking his pulse. It was weak but there. The man let out a low, anguished moan. "He needs help!" she called out.

Brigitte hurried over to examine him, turning to Alouette with grim eyes. "We have to move him. But carefully."

Alouette nodded and scanned the loading bay, her gaze settling on a bread-oven door that had been ripped off its hinges and abandoned before anyone had had a chance to secure it to the barricade. "Can someone bring that over?" she called out.

Grantaire came running with the makeshift stretcher, and together he and Brigitte delicately lifted the man and carried him to the manufacturing floor. Brigitte directed them to position him next to one of the powered-down mixing vats and then, with the help of Grantaire, went to work organizing the medical supplies she'd brought with her.

The man began to writhe against the pain. Alouette bent down to clasp his hand. "Shh. Try to be still." She pulled up the hem of his ripped shirt and flinched. The wound was bad. The lethal pulse had grazed the side of his abdomen, leaving behind a blackened, blistering gash. Alouette clenched her teeth to fight back the cry of frustration that rose up in her throat. Then, she heard it again. And again. More wood splitting, more metal bending, more pulses finding more targets.

And more screams.

It felt like someone had woven thorns around her lungs. She couldn't breathe without feeling the stabbing. "What do we do?" She darted her desperate eyes to Marcellus.

But a crackle from his radio snagged his attention, and all Alouette could do was stand there, motionless, frozen, listening to those horrible sounds behind her. Listening to this all fall apart. Her mind longed to leave her body behind, longed to drift to somewhere safe, a memory from her childhood with the sisters.

But she knew there was nowhere safe to go anymore.

"You're going to want to see this," Marcellus said, lowering the radio that was still crackling in his hand.

Alouette blinked, struggling to make sense of his words. "What?"

He grabbed her by the hand and led her through the manufacturing room floor, weaving around the giant ovens, until they reached the ladder that led up to the roof.

The moment she pulled herself up through the small hatch, the cold night breeze slapped her in the face and tangled in her hair. Marcellus climbed out beside her and led her to the edge of the roof. She peered over the side and her stomach turned.

From here, she could see five more barricades, all facing the same inevitable fate as theirs. The droids were advancing on every single one, firing their deadly weapons, exploding the hand-built walls with their lethal pulses, sending shards of wood and metal and debris pluming into the air like upside-down rain.

"This is what you brought me up here to see?" Alouette shouted, tears stinging her eyes now. "More failure? More defeat? More death?"

Marcellus shook his head. "I brought you up here to see that." His hand extended eastward, past the roof of the textile fabrique, past the bottling fabrique, until Alouette could see tiny pinpricks of light dotting the sky, like stars.

As the lights drew closer, the night filled with the low hum of an engine, breaking through the noise of the commotion below.

"They're here," Marcellus said.

The fleet of crafts swooped in close enough for Alouette to see their off-kilter wings, the jumbled paneling of their hulls, and their bubbled cockpit windows that glimmered as if they were still frozen by the icy Terrain Perdu air they'd left behind.

Like a flock of strange night birds, they soared in an arrow formation, before peeling off into two fleets that roared over the bread fabrique. The first fleet banked around and began to swoop and dive. From their patchwork underbellies, they released something sparkling, viscous, and wet that fell in blustering waves downward.

A sharp, tangy smell filled the air as the strange liquid waterfalled onto the streets below, right in front of the legions of droids advancing on the fabriques.

"Emberweed oil," Alouette whispered, recalling the name of the homemade lighting fluid Brigitte had told her about.

Just then, the second fleet of crafts soared by and, from their undersides, rained down a cascade of pluming fire. Like magnets destined to come together, the projectiles of the two crafts met and the result was immediate. Ferocious. Terrifying. Fierce purple flames exploded into light and soared up from the ground. And suddenly, the droids were locked in a corral of fire, like animals trapped in a pen. Some stepped up to the flames, as though to examine them closer, but froze upon feeling the unfamiliar, blazing heat radiating off them.

The fleet of crafts banked around again, and in another synchronized, one-two formation, they released more of the deadly liquid, more of the fire, until the violet flames raged even higher and the fiery walls around the droids snaked like a glowing, burning First World python through the depths of the Fabrique District.

CHAPTER 85

CHATINE

"WHERE DID HE GO?" ROCHE WHISPERED BESIDE CHA-
tine as they sat mètres above the droid fabrique, watching bashers march
around the manufacturing floor in chilling, regimented rows.

"Shh." She swept her gaze across the fabrique for a third time, searching for Etienne. Was he looking for another way out? Another access point
to the tunnel?

"Did he just leave us here?" Roche asked, his voice on the verge of tears.

Chatine shushed him again. "Of course not. He's coming up with a plan."

"But—" Roche began to say. Chatine clapped a hand over his mouth
and pointed to the open floor grate, where just then, a hand shot out and
released a small, round cartridge. It rolled across the floor, slowly enough
not to attract the attention of the finished droids, but steadily enough to
track a clear path in front of them.

Chatine's eyes followed the rolling canister, watching the streak of dark
liquid trail in its wake. It hit the very support beam that Chatine and Roche
had climbed up to reach the rafters and clanked quietly to a stop.

Despite the army of lethal monsters amassing beneath them, Chatine's
lips curved into a knowing smile.

Brilliant.

"Roche," she whispered, gripping her brother's arm. "Get ready to jump."

"What?" he asked. "What about the droids?"

Then, just as predicted, Etienne's hand appeared again. This time, holding nothing more than a lit match. The flame was tiny, barely a speck of light. Compared to the glowing orange eyes of the droids scouring the fabrique, it was insignificant.

Yet, it was everything.

The trail of emberweed oil caught instantly. That tiny flame multiplied into a wall of brilliant purple fire. It raced across the manufacturing floor like a croc on the run with a stolen loaf of bread. The droids came to a clanking halt. Their glowing eyes scanned the colorful flames, assessing, calculating, running the images through their newly installed processors.

"Now!" Chatine cried, and for the second time that night, she swung from the rafters, flipping once before landing in a crouch with Roche right beside her.

They ran. Nothing could slow them now. Not the heat from the fire that burned their eyes and brushed up against their skin. Not the fear pumping through their veins. And certainly not the droids who had definitely noticed them and were stirring uneasily on the other side of the flames.

And still, the bashers did not advance. The fire seemed to be holding them captive. Like they were entranced by the sight of it, caught in a spellbinding dream.

The thought fueled Chatine and compelled her legs to move even faster, until they had reached the open drainage grate and were tumbling down the ladder into the sewers below. She collapsed into Etienne's waiting arms, breathless and overflowing with gratitude and relief. As he held her, tighter than she'd ever been held, he felt like a warm jacket on the coldest night in the Terrain Perdu.

"Merci," she breathed into his chest, which was rising and falling as rapidly as her own. "For coming for us."

Etienne rested his cheek on top of her head and chuckled. "Yeah, well, we have this code back at the camp. If you can risk your life for someone, you should do it."

Chatine looked up at him, her eyes sparkling with questions. His eyes sparkling back with the answers.

Roche cleared his throat. "Sorry to interrupt, but . . ." He held up his hand, and Chatine's throat went dry. All of the relief and joy that had been streaming through her only moments ago dissolved into the stale air of the sewers.

In the commotion of the droids being released from the warehouse, their scramble to find a hiding place, and Etienne's rescue, she'd nearly forgotten why they'd come to this death fabrique in the first place.

The tiny square of metal glinted in the low light streaming down from the open grate above their heads. And for a long, tense moment, all three of them simply stared at the drive, like they were staring at their own demise and their own salvation at the same time.

And all at once, Chatine knew what she had to do.

Perhaps she'd known it all her life.

Perhaps she was destined for this moment. This choice. This sacrifice. Like it had been written long ago in the yellowed pages of one of those First World books. Written in the stars.

"Roche," Chatine said in a slow, deliberate voice. She swallowed, building the courage to say the words that were rapidly forming in her mind. Because she knew, of all the words that had ever been forgotten on this planet, they were the right ones. The ones to remember. "I want you to go back to the bread fabrique. I want you to tell the others—Marcellus, Alouette, Brigitte, the sisters—that I love them. That I'm grateful for everything they did for me. For giving me a home. A real one. For teaching me how to read, even though I'm still dreadful at it. And for giving me a purpose. Something to be a part of. Something to hope for. Something to fight for. That's really what it's all about anyway, isn't it?"

"What?" Roche's brow furrowed and then smoothed as it took him all of three seconds to comprehend. That's when he tried to pull the drive out of her reach. But she was too fast. Too determined. She swiped it from his small, nimble fingers as easily as she'd swiped a thousand other things from a thousand other marks.

"Go," she told him.

"Chatine, no," Roche said stoutly. "I can't let you do this. Not alone."

Chatine smirked. "Why not? I've done everything else alone."

"Not this."

"Roche." She bent down slightly so they were nose to nose, eye to eye, Renard to Renard. "I did what you told me to do. I let you go. I stopped trying to protect you from all of the stupid situations you get yourself into. But now, you have to do the same for me."

"Chatine." Roche's voice broke then, sending cracks through Chatine's heart. "No."

"Go," she told him again. "That's an order. From your sister. Who's much older and wiser than you."

Roche backed slowly away, shaking his head and brushing tears from his cheeks. "Please," he begged.

"GO!" she screamed.

And finally, he went. He ran. His sobs reverberated down the sewer tunnel, each one like a tiny echo of the baby she'd held in her arms. The baby she'd sung to and rocked to sleep and told stories to about the stars.

"There are three Sols in the sky. Yes, three! Sol 1 is the white one, Sol 2 is the red one, and Sol 3 is the blue one. Aren't we lucky to live under so many stars?"

They were very lucky.

Brushing tears from her cheeks, Chatine turned toward the ladder, only to find it blocked by Etienne, who had strangely not said a word in the past few minutes. Now he stood with his arms crossed, his eyes narrowed disapprovingly at the drive in her hand.

"Etienne—" she began, but he cut her off.

"I'm afraid I have to agree with the kid. I can't let you do this."

She sighed. "Please move."

"So you can go up there and get yourself killed by a bunch of bashers?" He pretended to ponder that. "No, I don't think so."

Frustration boiled up inside of her. Roche she could boss around, but Etienne was another story. For starters, he was physically stronger than her—she'd never be able to force him out of her way. Not to mention, he might just be the only person she'd ever met who was more stubborn than she was.

She gritted her teeth. "You're the one who said some things are worth getting involved for. Worth dying for."

"Yes, I did." He flashed her that roguish grin that she both despised and couldn't live without. Then, he kissed her, hard on the mouth. The impact knocked her slightly off-balance, and definitely off her game. Because she didn't even notice that he'd slipped the drive right out her fingers. Not until she'd opened her eyes to find the air was colder, her hand was empty, and Etienne was already halfway up the ladder.

CHAPTER 86

MARCELLUS

IT WAS LIKE NOTHING MARCELLUS HAD EVER SEEN before. He and Alouette stood on the rooftop of the bread fabrique, mesmerized by the thousands of droids trapped in cages of purple fire. And the Défecteur ships that continued to swoop and dive, fortifying the cages with bigger, fiercer flames.

"How long will it hold them?" Alouette asked Marcellus.

But it was another voice that answered. "Until they figure out it won't hurt them."

They both turned to see Cerise standing on the roof, her TéléCom clutched in her hand.

"And how long will that take?" Marcellus asked, not sure he even wanted to know the answer. They needed this victory. They needed any reprieve they could get from the relentless attacks, these relentless failures that had seemed to befall them from the moment they'd barricaded themselves into these fabriques.

"With the hive-mind technology, probably not long," said Cerise apologetically. "Right now, that kind of fire—that specific threat—is unknown to them. But only one of them has to learn that it won't hurt them, and the rest will be updated with the knowledge almost instantly."

Marcellus felt his glimmer of relief melt into the fires that blazed below. "Any update on the virus? Or Chatine and Roche?"

But Cerise was no longer listening. Her gaze was now pinned to the glowing TéléCom in her hand, her circuitry sparking wildly like someone had nicked one of the wires.

"What is it?" Alouette asked, stepping closer to her.

Cerise looked up, and in her dark brown eyes, Marcellus saw the violet flames from below dancing with what could only be described as elation. "You're not going to believe this."

"What?" Marcellus asked.

Cerise consulted her TéléCom once more before staring out into the night, as though she were searching for something in the darkness. "Wait for it."

Marcellus groaned. "Clearly your flair for the dramatic has returned."

"There!" she shouted, pointing past the blazing fires and the imprisoned droids to a giant shimmering display that had suddenly appeared like magic. The sight of it was so colorful, so foreign among all of this destruction, at first Marcellus couldn't fully focus on it.

"A hologram?" he asked.

Cerise nodded. "The TéléCast feed. It's back."

The towering footage showed the Grand Palais, in all its glowing and nighttime grandeur. Marcellus recognized its rows of ornate columns, the immense roof, and the multitude of glinting windows. But what he didn't recognize—what he'd never seen before in his life—was what was happening outside the gates. Crowded and buzzing on the pathways and streets just beyond the perimeter fence were people. Hundreds of them. Thousands of them. And like a tide being pulled in by the moon, they converged upon the Palais. They banged and rattled at the ornate metalwork of the gates. They climbed the fences and yelled through the bars. Fists pounded the air, and a sea of outstretched arms waved huge, fluttering banners.

"Why is my grandfather broadcasting this to all of Laterre?" Marcellus asked.

"He's not." Cerise's eyes sparkled with mischief. "Desirée Beauchamp and her broadcast team have hijacked the feed. Look!"

Marcellus spun back to the hologram, where Desirée's jubilant face was now filling the bottom corner of the projection as she stood before the crowd gathered at the gates of the Grand Palais. Her lips were moving animatedly, but the sound was drowned out by the roaring flames below and the Défecteur ships that continued to soar past, dropping more fire from above. Cerise turned the volume up on her TéléCom, which was displaying the same footage, and held it up so they could hear.

". . . less than an hour away from daybreak, and still the crowd here has not died down. In fact, it only seems to be growing as even more people continue to arrive from cities around Laterre, joining the rest of the protestors here at the Grand Palais. Since earlier this evening, Second Estaters and even some First Estaters have been amassing here by the cruiseur-load to demand a ceasefire and a resignation from the Empereur."

"What?" Alouette asked, her eyes wide and her voice cracking with disbelief.

"It's your broadcast," Cerise told her. "Your words did this."

Marcellus's tiny glimmer of relief returned like it, too, had been doused in emberweed oil and lit by flames. The cams hovering around the Grand Palais zoomed out and rose up, giving them a glimpse of all of those people. One enormous, swarming mass reaching to the far ends of the Palais grounds, all the way to the Ministère.

"So far," Desirée went on, "we have yet to hear a single word from the Empereur in response to these demands, but I'm honestly not sure how he can continue to ignore such a large uprising. If you're watching this right now and you're not either behind a barricade or here with us, then you're in the wrong place. We are watching history unfold—"

A flicker of movement caught Marcellus's eye, pulling his attention away from Desirée's voice. He looked out, toward the neighboring textile fabrique, and as if a gust of cold air had whipped in from the Terrain Perdu, every warm feeling inside of him was instantly extinguished.

He watched it happen in slow motion.

A single droid breaking free from its fiery prison. A single droid advancing on the barricade, its weaponized arm outstretched.

And just like Cerise had said, the effect was almost instantaneous.

One droid turned to two droids turned to a hundred. They all stepped through the wall of glowing purple flames and marched forward, as if nothing had happened. As if their momentary delay had been a simple glitch in the timeline.

Pulses rained down on the remaining barricades once more. Relentless and destructive. Far below, Marcellus heard the rallying cry of the people inside the bread fabrique taking up arms once again, firing at the incoming droids. But once again, they were only able to momentarily stun. Not maim.

Then, a horrible cracking sound shattered the air, and Marcellus's eyes were drawn across the street to the textile fabrique, where the barricade was teetering precariously, its massive structure threatening to come down. He heard people shouting, followed by a riot of desperate footsteps.

"Get out of the way!" someone screamed. The voice was familiar, but Marcellus couldn't identify it over the sound of the relentless attacks.

Alouette clasped a hand over her mouth, like she was trying to keep her own screams from escaping. They all watched silently, wordlessly, as the barricade erected in front of the textile fabrique's vast loading bay began to crumble.

Huge rolls of fabric wobbled, clattered, and crashed to the ground, while the large glinting frames of the power looms seemed to crumple in on themselves. The people who'd been perched on this makeshift wall trying to hold back the droids were thrown in every direction like seeds scattering in the wind. Some screamed. Some frantically scrabbled and grabbed for something to hold on to. While others simply vanished under the torrent of debris.

The droids marched on, toward the demolished barricade, toward their fallen prey. The loading bay doors started to glide closed, a last line of defense that Marcellus knew wouldn't survive longer than a few minutes. Anyone who had made it off the collapsing structure was now diving through the closing gap between the doors, desperate to get back inside.

And as the orange beams of light from the advancing droids shone on the rubble of the fallen barricade, Marcellus could make out a body trapped beneath one of the broken looms. A feeble sob finally escaped his lips. It was the only sound he was capable of making.

But that certainly wasn't the case for the person who stood beside him.

"GABRIEL!" Cerise bellowed. A piercing primal cry charged from her, cutting through the night. If there was any part of Cerise Chevalier left that still belonged to the Ministère, it was chased away by this terrible, anguished human sound. "NO! Someone help him! Please!"

Tears streamed across Cerise's circuitry, causing it to glimmer and reflect. "Someone! Please! Help him! You have to help him!" Cerise grabbed hold of Marcellus and was shaking him. Hard. He struggled to break free, finally managing to wrap his arms around her and clutch her trembling, shuddering body to his chest.

Alouette spun in a desperate circle, seemingly searching for a place to direct her own grief, her own heartbreak. But all that was left was that crumpled barricade in front of the textile fabrique, and the one directly below them that would surely fall too. Marcellus watched her helplessly, wishing he could protect her from it all, wishing he could make it stop. But he felt more useless and powerless than ever. Like he was suddenly back in the Refuge library, wading through old maps and journals, desperately trying and failing to save her.

"What is the point of any of this if he won't stop?" she screamed at the sky. "If he'll never stop? He won't listen to me! He won't listen to his own estate! Who the fric will he listen to?"

No one answered her. No one could.

The only sound that came rushing back at them was the ping of those hopeless rayonette pulses firing at the droids below. Stunning them for mere seconds. But it was not enough. It would never be enough.

"Don't move! Don't you dare move, you pomp scum, or I'll shoot your fric-ing face off!"

Everyone on the roof turned toward the sound of the voice. It was coming from inside the fabrique. And Marcellus recognized it at once.

"Roche?!" The name erupted from his lips as he let go of Cerise and sprinted for the ladder. With every clumsy, desperate rung down to the bottom, he held Chatine's face in his mind, praying she had returned safely. Praying this horrible grimness had not spread to her, too.

But when he jumped onto the manufacturing floor and flung his gaze around the fabrique, he saw no sign of her. All he could see was Roche, standing next to one of the giant mixing vats, pointing a rayonette at someone hiding behind it.

Alouette leapt down beside him and followed his gaze. "What's going on?"

"I don't know." Marcellus took a cautious step toward Roche. The boy looked worse than he'd ever seen him. Almost feral. His eyes were wide and bloodshot. His face was covered in a layer of ash that streaked beneath his eyes and onto his cheeks as if he'd been crying.

Marcellus's stomach clenched. "Roche. Where's Chatine?"

But Roche barely acknowledged him. He clutched his weapon in his trembling hands and gave it a flick toward whoever was standing behind that mixing vat. "I am so tired of people like you winning. Taking advantage of us. You will not get away with this." His voice was broken and charred, like he'd inhaled too much smoke. And there was a wildness in his red-rimmed eyes that terrified Marcellus.

"Roche," he tried again, gentler, slower. "What are you doing? Where is Chatine?"

"He killed her!" He jabbed the rayonette toward the vat.

Marcellus felt the ground give out beneath him. The kid was hysterical. He wasn't talking sense. It wasn't true. It couldn't be true. "Roche. What are you talking about? Who killed who? Who is back there?"

"A traitor!" Roche cried out. "A mouchard! Maybe he didn't kill her directly, but he had something to do with it. They all did. Every single one of those pomps. They all killed us a little bit every day. Me. Chatine. The Oublies. The crocs. We're all dead inside because of them. And soon we'll be dead on the outside, too."

Marcellus shared an anxious look with Alouette, silently forming a plan. They still had no idea whom Roche was pointing his rayonette at, but they had to defuse the situation. The boy was clearly distraught, an explosif waiting to go off.

Alouette gave a tiny nod and they both crept forward.

"Roche," Alouette said, reaching delicately toward his outstretched arms. "Can you give me the rayonette?"

"No!" Roche screamed. "He needs to die! He should have died months ago! Years ago! Better yet, he never should have been made!"

Made.

The word sank into Marcellus's subconscious like a heavy stone. He took another hesitant step forward, until he could peer around the side of the giant mixing machine. And that's when he saw him.

Silent as the night.

Hands raised in surrender.

Dark brown eyes darting anxiously between Marcellus and Roche's trembling rayonette.

Alouette must have seen him too because she took a deep, sympathetic breath and said, "Roche. That's Antoine. He's with the Red Scar. But it's okay. They're on our side now."

"His name is not Antoine!" Roche spat. "And he's not with the Red Scar! He's with the Ministère."

"That's right," Alouette said gently, coaxingly. "He's a spy. For the Red Scar. He's been helping them and now he's helping us."

Roche rolled his eyes, like this was all a game and he was tired of playing. "Yeah, and my mother's Queen Matilda. This traitor must die."

"Stop!" came another voice, and Marcellus's throat went dry when he saw the man now aiming a rayonette at Roche. "Put it down, kid. Back away."

"Jolras," Alouette said, exuding a level of calm that Marcellus knew he was not capable of. "It's okay. He's just a little freaked out. We're taking care of it. Please, lower your weapon."

But Jolras shook his head. "Not until he lowers his. We protect our own."

"Will all of you WAKE THE FRIC UP?" Roche screamed. "He's not one of you. He's not helping you. He's helping *them!*"

Panic started to swirl in Marcellus's stomach. Because he'd had his doubts about Antoine from the beginning. And he'd ignored them. Because once again, he'd been too distracted, too obsessed with his own objectives, to see what was right in front of him. But Roche had evidently seen it instantly.

"Don't you know who this is?" Roche asked to no one in particular.

And Marcellus almost found himself hoping that no one would answer. That they'd all just keep going the way they'd been, pretending that the man standing before them—the Red Scar spy who didn't speak, who'd stolen weapons from the Ministère, who'd helped Jolras and the others escape Policier custody, who'd delivered intel to Maximilienne about the Patriarche and the Favorites, who'd been here the whole time, listening— was everything he'd said he was.

But even now, in the stunned silence that followed Roche's question, the truth was lining up in Marcellus's mind. And it was grim. It was dark.

It was Cerise who finally broke the silence. Not with words but with her urgent, determined footsteps. She marched up to Antoine and stared deep into his dark brown eyes. Like she was searching for something. Something she already knew she wouldn't find.

Then, to Marcellus's shock and horror, she reached up and grabbed at the flesh of Antoine's cheek. Alouette gasped as the ripping sound echoed off the empty machines of the bread fabrique. The skin came loose from his face like it wasn't skin at all. Like it never had been.

And Marcellus only had to glimpse the tiny filaments of sparking light that radiated from the man's left cheek before he understood.

It was his grandfather's ultimate manipulation.

His hand on the final puppet string. Pulling Maximilienne wherever he'd wanted her to go, convincing her to do whatever he'd wanted her to do.

Execute the Patriarche.

Murder the Favorites.

Infiltrate the coronation ceremony to attack Alouette.

That's why he'd been confident enough to reveal her to the entire planet. Because he knew he had his finger on the trigger of a weapon powerful enough to kill her.

And the Red Scar had no idea.

"Mesdames and Messieurs," Roche said in a haggard yet triumphant voice. "I present to you Inspecteur Limier."

Shock and disbelief crackled through the room. Jolras lowered his weapon, his brow furrowed, like his mind was retracing every step, every silent exchange, every clue that he'd missed. That they'd all missed.

"That's why the Empereur attacked early," Alouette said dazedly, almost to herself. But then she lifted her eyes and met Limier's cold, hardened stare with one of her own. "Before we had a chance to distribute all the weapons. Because *you* told him that's what we were doing. You've been reporting back to him."

"B-b-but how?" Marcellus stammered, the details still swimming in his mind. "Cyborgs can't lie. They can't deceive."

"Unless they're programmed to," said Cerise, her voice so soft, Marcellus was convinced she was only talking to herself. Once again, she gazed into Limier's eyes, her own circuitry flashing with rage and conviction. "Reprogramming. That's why the Empereur sent you there. That's why you were never quite right afterward. He tweaked your code."

"How could he do that?" asked Alouette. "Wouldn't he need a médecin? Or another cyborg to go along with it?"

"Or the directeur of the Cyborg and Technology Labs," said Cerise glumly. "That's why you didn't apprehend César Bonnefaçon at the coronation ceremony when Alouette called for his arrest. You weren't loyal to the Order of the Sols anymore. You were only loyal to him."

Roche let out a frustrated groan. "Now will you let me shoot him?"

"No, let me," Jolras growled, taking a step toward Limier. He raised his weapon once more, his finger tense on the trigger.

But then, a large yet gentle hand rested on Jolras's shoulder. When he looked up at Hugo Taureau, the sheer size of the man seemed to overwhelm Jolras. His eyes widened and his grip on the rayonette faltered ever so slightly.

"If it's all right with you," Hugo said in a steady voice, "I'd like to deal with the traitor myself."

Limier's circuitry gave a flash of fear, which Jolras definitely noticed. He must have sensed something between the cyborg and this giant of a man, because in the next instant, Jolras was handing his rayonette to Hugo.

Slowly, steadily, Hugo raised the weapon and aimed it at Limier's forehead.

Marcellus shared an anxious look with Alouette, both understanding at once what was about to happen. Hugo Taureau had finally come face-to-face with his ancient foe. With the man who had pursued him relentlessly for more than two decades. And for the first time ever, their roles were reversed. *He* was the hunter and Limier was the prey.

"Papa. No." Alouette rushed to her father's side, but he held her back with a single glance.

"Little Lark, this is between me and the inspecteur."

"No, it's not," Cerise spat, anger now rolling off her in thick waves. "This is between all of us. He betrayed us all. And because of that, Gabriel is dead!"

"What?" Hugo's gaze snapped from Limier to Cerise to Alouette.

"The droids stormed the textile fabrique," Alouette explained in a ragged voice. "The barricade fell. We saw it happen. Gabriel was pinned beneath the wreckage."

"And it's his fault!" Cerise cried, all of her former restraint slipping away. She lunged toward Limier with wild, swinging arms. Marcellus caught her and held her back.

Hugo wrapped his hands tighter around the handle of the rayonette. "I promise to be swift and just."

Marcellus squeezed his eyes shut. As much as he disliked Inspecteur Limier—had always disliked him—he couldn't just stand there and watch him take a lethal pulse to the head.

"Let's go," barked Hugo, and when Marcellus opened his eyes again, Alouette's father was marching Limier past the mixing vats, past the row of bread ovens, before disappearing down a long, dark hallway.

Counting the seconds, Marcellus held Alouette's gaze tightly until he heard it. It was almost lost in the sound of the battle still waging outside. But he knew, from the way her face flinched and her eyes widened with fear, that she had heard it too. The soft, muted *whoosh* of a pulse leaving a rayonette.

He released Cerise and she sank to the ground, her body trembling and her face haunted. He kept his eyes trained on the dark hallway for a long time, waiting for Hugo to return. But it was silent and still, like a place of mourning.

Marcellus took a step toward it, but Alouette stopped him. "It's okay. I'll go."

He nodded and collapsed against the mixing vat, the long night taking its toll on his mind and body. He glanced over at Roche, who was staring numbly down at the rayonette in his hand, like he was wishing he'd pulled the trigger himself.

Marcellus knew the feeling.

None of this would be happening if he'd simply pulled the trigger on his grandfather when he'd had the chance.

Marcellus watched a silent tear track its way down Roche's dirty face and splash onto the side of his rayonette. And that's when the memory of his words came clattering back into his mind.

"He killed her!"

Panic began to swirl in his stomach again. "Roche," he whispered, his voice shattered, his heart preparing to go with it. "Where is Chatine?"

Another tear splashed down. It felt like a boulder crashing down around them. Everything was crashing down around them now. From the loading bay, Marcellus could still hear the rebels fighting, firing their weapons uselessly at the advancing droids.

He could hear parts of the barricade starting to crumble.

"She . . . ," Roche started to say. "She told me to come back. She said to tell you that she's grateful to the sisters for giving her something to fight for. A purpose. She told me to tell you that she loves . . ." His body dissolved into sobs. Marcellus wanted to reach for him, but everything was too numb.

"Where is she?" he demanded. "What did she do?"

But Roche was too distraught to speak. And it didn't matter anyway. Because the answer was already barreling down the stairs from the superviseur's office. Denise rushed toward Marcellus, her eyes dancing with a relief Marcellus was certain he'd never be capable of feeling. No matter what happened next. No matter what she said.

"The virus is online."

CHAPTER 87

CHATINE

"ETIENNE!" CHATINE STRUGGLED TO SEE THROUGH THE smoke of a hundred fires. They were blazing everywhere. By the time her mind had made sense of what had just happened—how he'd kissed her to distract her, how he'd kissed her to say good-bye—Etienne had already disappeared through the open grate.

She'd scrambled after him, but he was lost to her in the smoke. The only proof that he'd even been there at all were the fires that now blazed, purple and blinding, around the droid fabrique. His only weapon. His only defense against them.

And then she'd heard it.

That unmistakable sound that made her heart stop and her body freeze. Like it was remembering all the times that sound had come for her, ready to paralyze her, ready to leave her numb and senseless for hours.

Except she knew, in the deepest part of her, that it wasn't a pulse determined to paralyze.

It was the other kind.

The kind she wouldn't even allow herself to think about.

"Etienne!" she screamed again. But still nothing. No movement. No sound apart from these roaring flames and the constant, head-pounding drone of the machines, still churning and spinning and cutting and creating.

She stepped forward, trying to see through her thick tears and the even thicker smoke, but a single flame shot out, clawing at her face with its hot, angry talons. She yelped and leapt back.

There had to be another way in.

Her gaze drifted to the left and landed on a massive support beam shooting up to the ceiling. She berated herself for not seeing it before, for still being so distracted by that kiss. And everything that came after it.

Chatine darted to the beam and shimmied effortlessly up to the nearest rafter. After swinging her leg over, she hung momentarily upside down, until she could build up enough momentum to shift her body up. She straddled the rafter and scanned the sea of fire, the whirring machines, the billowing smoke. Until finally, her eyes stopped, and her body went numb.

The droids.

There was something wrong with the droids.

They were . . . *motionless*.

And not the kind of motionless that came before an attack, as they awaited orders or assessed a threat. This was as though someone had pressed pause on life itself. There was no quiet vibration in their thick steel limbs. No hum reverberating out from the metal skulls that housed their processors.

No light in their eyes.

Only a cold, black stillness.

Then, something in the corner of her vision moved, and Chatine snapped her gaze to the giant bird-like beak that was lifting another finished droid off the assembly line and placing it in the activation zone. The lights around the platform glowed green, one by one, until finally, the droid powered on, its whole being purring like a tiny engine. Its orange eyes flickered to life and then, after only a few steps from the platform, died just as quickly.

Like it had been installed with a faulty processor. A hacked processor. *The virus.*

It was spreading. Passing through the network. Just as Brigitte had said it would. Infecting the new droids moments after they came online.

Which meant . . .

"Etienne!"

She spotted him at the very instant his name crossed her lips. He was curled into a ball on the ground, less than a mètre away from one of his fires, with a lifeless droid sprawled facedown next to him.

And he was breathing.

"Etienne!" she called again, this time with a rush of relief as she crawled carefully across the rafters, away from the nearest flames, and swung down to land beside him.

"You're okay," she said, reaching for him, tears streaming down her face. "It's okay. I'm here. We'll get you help. We'll get you to your maman and she'll—"

But when she rolled him onto his back, the words left her. They abandoned her. They betrayed her.

Because in that second, she knew. There would be no help. There would be no healing. And it would never be okay again.

The lethal pulse had destroyed his vest.

His shirt.

And almost everything beneath.

From his gaping wound, there was only blood and pain and a scorched, terrible darkness.

Chatine let out a sob that sounded almost as inhuman as the droid that lay nearby with a tiny glimmering square of metal protruding from the back of its neck.

"What did you do?" she cried, barely comprehensible. "What did you—"

"I . . . ," Etienne whispered in a feeble voice. "I bashed the bashers."

Chatine let out a weak laugh. "You did. You did good."

He tried to speak again, but the pain was too much. He winced and shut his eyes.

"Shh. It's okay. I'm here." She pulled Etienne's head onto her lap and ran her fingers across his forehead, his cheek, his chin. "I'm here. I'm here. I'm here."

It was all she could say. And yet, she knew it wasn't enough. It would never be enough. It had never *been* enough.

"I'm sorry," she whimpered. And then, the tears broke free. They cascaded down her cheeks like the first drops of a tempest. With great effort, Etienne reached up and touched her face, letting one of those tears roll onto the tip of his finger. Like he was trying to catch a little fall of rain. A tiny piece of a grief that would spread much wider, become much vaster, consume so much in the violent storms to come.

"Don't worry." And then, in a voice so soft yet so clear, he whispered, "It doesn't hurt. It will never hurt anymore." He smiled weakly. "To see you with him. To watch you watching him."

The fires that blazed around them came closer, seeming to lash out at Chatine, going straight for her chest. Straight for her heart. "Stop," she pleaded to Etienne. "Don't."

"'S okay," he said, his words losing shape, losing strength. His eyes struggled to focus on hers. Struggled to hold her. "It was worth it."

She shook her head, barely able to speak through tears that she swore would never stop falling. "No. No. No."

"Yes, it was," he said quietly. So quietly Chatine had to bend her ear to his lips to hear. "Because I think I was a little in love with you."

And then, she felt his breath on her face. So soft. So warm. So final.

Her body dissolved into sobs. Her heart shattered into more pieces than any machine in this blazing fabrique could ever hope to put back together. The smoke swirled around them like a curtain, protecting them from the world. Concealing Chatine in her silent, lonely grief like a layer of stealth.

As she draped herself over him, feeling the fading warmth of his skin on her cheek and the ghost of his heartbeat against her chest, she thought of the skies. Thick, gray Laterrian skies. The kind that trapped in heat. The kind that one could get lost in.

She would have stayed lost in those skies forever. She would have stayed here forever. If it weren't for the fires that were lashing at her skin. And the smoke that burned her eyes.

Chatine knew she'd never be able to understand where the strength to leave had come from. And she knew she'd never even try to figure it out. It was just there. Like an invisible force compelling her to move. Invisible strings tied to her limbs, pulling her up, guiding her lips to his forehead, gently placing his head on the floor, slowly pushing her away. From the vibrant flames that reached for him. From the heat that pulled him close. Like an old friend welcoming him home.

- CHAPTER 88 -
MARCELLUS

IT WAS LIKE A GREAT FROST HAD SETTLED OVER THE planet, freezing it in time, draping it in an eerie silence, and Marcellus was the only one still alive. As he stepped out from behind what was left of the barricade, into the crisp dawn air, and walked between the motionless, dark-eyed droids, he almost couldn't believe there was once a time when they had been so frightening.

Now they stood, frozen in mid-step, mid-attack, so harmless, so powerless.

"She did it," he whispered in disbelief as he rose up on tiptoes to scrutinize the darkened eyes of the nearest droid. He'd never been able to come so close before. He'd never dared. He reached up and touched its metallic face, shivering at its coolness, its emptiness. "She did it," he said again.

"No," came a quiet, almost strangled voice behind him. "Etienne did it."

He spun around, and when he saw Chatine standing there among the motionless droids, covered in ash and blood and dirt, he didn't allow himself to hesitate again. He reached for her and pulled her to him. He crushed his body against hers. He held her for what felt like an eternity. He would have gladly held her for an eternity.

If she hadn't pushed him away.

The roughness of her retreat startled him.

Like she wasn't just tired of being held. She was tired of being held by *him*. She stood back, her gray eyes glittering from beneath the layer of grime on her face, and for just a moment, she looked exactly like she had that night on the rooftop. When she'd pulled off her hood and shaken out her hair and kissed him.

But then, that moment dissolved into the dewy morning air, chased back into the vault of his memory, and he was left with what she really looked like.

A girl not just covered in ash. But covered in grief and anguish and the pieces of a broken heart. As sharp and glinting as shattered glass.

"*He* did this!" she cried, flinging her arms around at the legion of lifeless droids. "Etienne did this. Not me. Not me."

"Then, he saved us," Marcellus insisted. "He's a hero. Our barricade—the last barricade—is still standing because of him. Denise said the Ministère is trying to override the virus, but they can't. He won this for us."

"But it should have been me!" she screamed, startling Marcellus. "I shouldn't have let him go. I shouldn't have let him distract me. He didn't know how to deal with bashers. I did! He didn't know what he was doing. And now he's . . . he's . . ." The sobs swallowed her words. The shudders overpowered her entire body. And suddenly, Marcellus felt as frozen and useless and trapped as one of these droids. He wanted to say the right thing, do the right thing, be the right person, but his mind, too, was corrupted with a virus that was far too clever. It kept him still, kept him stupid, kept him useless.

Until all he could do was watch her cry.

Watch her heart continue to splinter.

Watch the pieces ricochet straight into his own.

And he could do nothing to stop it.

Sister Clare appeared beside them and wrapped her arms around Chatine's trembling body before leading her away, back to the fabrique, leaving Marcellus alone again in the silent, frozen world.

As he watched Chatine disappear behind the remains of the barricade, he felt like kicking something. Punching something. Squeezing something until it, too, shattered. Why was he always watching her walk away? Why was he always letting her? She had been his rock for so long. She had been the planet to his moon, keeping him from spinning off into space. And yet when their roles were reversed, when she needed him to be stable, to be solid footing under her feet, he failed. Time and time again, he failed her.

Just as he was failing her now.

"Marcellus." Alouette's strained voice came charging into his ears, her urgent footsteps close behind. "I can't find my father. Or Limier. They're both gone."

But he couldn't hear the words. He could hear nothing but the dark, helpless rage twisting and building inside of him. He couldn't stand here any longer. Couldn't look at these darkened shells of his grandfather's fallen army for one second more.

He started to run. Not back to the fabrique, where Chatine had gone. Not toward her. Never toward her. Because something was wrong with his programming. Something buried deep inside of him never seemed to steer him in the right direction.

"Marcellus!" Alouette shouted after him. But he didn't stop. He had to get out of there. He had to get as far away as possible. He crashed through the perimeter of frozen droids and charged forward, toward the first glimpses of ferme-land beyond. He would run across the entire Terrain Perdu if that's what it took for him to escape himself. Escape his own weaknesses.

It was the beam of light breaking through the morning mist that finally wrenched him to a stop. It swept above his head, followed swiftly by another. Then, three more. Then, too many more.

With a shiver, Marcellus looked up at the sleek silver underbelly of the passing transporteur as it made its slow, ominous advance toward the fabriques. Its shadow, as it blocked the low light of the three Sols rising behind the clouds, left Marcellus feeling colder than he'd ever felt before.

The fleet was enormous. At least twenty transporteurs. All of them carrying not droids, but something possibly even worse. Something that would not be shut down by a line of code. Something whose allegiance to the Empereur could not be hacked.

Marcellus's legs had never moved so quickly. He sprinted back through the Fabrique District, screaming to all the people who had wandered out from behind their fallen barricades to gawk at the frozen droids. "Get back inside! Everyone get back! Seal the doors!"

"What's wrong?" Alouette asked as he finally reached the bread fabrique, heart pounding and sweat pouring down his back.

Marcellus gasped, trying to catch his breath long enough to speak, but all he could do was point into the sky. The first transporteur broke through the fog, descending like a harbinger of doom in front of the loading bay.

The hatch unsealed in a swirl of vapor and steam. And Marcellus saw the first black boot step onto the muddy ground.

Alouette understood at once, turning to order everyone back behind the barricade. Back inside the fabrique. She had to know it wouldn't be enough. They all did. Even before the first row of Policier sergents mustered into formation. Even before the low light glinted off the sides of the explosif launchers gripped in their hands.

They wore full riot gear, with masks hanging around their necks, ready to be strapped on at a moment's notice. Marcellus knew exactly what those masks were for. He'd seen them in archived footage from the Rebellion of 488. He'd watched the Patriarche's soldiers spray innocent people with the noxious orange gas. He'd watched them scream as the vapor burned their eyes and scorched their skin.

The next squadron of sergents piled out from the transporteur. These men and women carried massive canisters on their backs. The familiar emblem of the Ministère—two rayonettes guarding the planet of Laterre—glowed on the sides of the metal tanks, reminding Marcellus of exactly who was ordering this attack.

Who was still in charge here.

Who would not back down simply because his droids had fallen.

He would keep sending weapons. Sergents, explosif launchers, riot gas. He would keep fighting. He would never stop.

When will it end? Marcellus wondered as he stood beside the barricade and watched the new soldiers assemble into formation.

When they were all dead?

When every manufactured good and grown crop and mined metal had been destroyed?

When César Bonnefaçon was the only one left standing?

Finally, the last member of this deadly regiment stepped out of the transporteur. Marcellus immediately recognized the blinding white sheen of her uniform. The titan epauletes and Sol-shaped buttons. His gaze landed on the glimmering titan insignia pinned to her lapel. The one he'd never received. Because he hadn't appeased his grandfather for long enough to complete his training.

Commandeur Apolline Moreau walked slowly toward the front of her troops, staring up at the makeshift barricade that loomed over her like a mountain she was determined to climb. To conquer.

And then, with a steely, determined stare, she began to speak. "Attention to the rebels inside the bread fabrique." Her voice was amplified through the transporteur speakers, echoing across the silent streets. "This is Commandeur Moreau of the Laterrian Ministère. We have you surrounded. There is no hope left for you. Surrender now and live. Or keep fighting and die. The choice is yours."

"Marcellus!" Alouette hissed from behind the barricade. "Get back inside! We're closing the doors!"

But Marcellus couldn't move. Something was holding his body hostage. It was a paralysis not of the mind nor of the body. But of something else. Some force deep within him that told him he would not run from this.

That told him, *No, those aren't the only two choices. Live or die. Surrender or fight.*

That even though the men and women assembled before them—with their terrifying weapons and eyes as cold as steel—were not droids, were not hackable with code, they were still just as fallible. Because they *did* have a choice.

They all did.

Every human being on this planet had a choice. The rebels had made theirs. The Second Estaters protesting outside the Palais had made theirs, too. Even his grandfather had made a choice.

At some point in his dark, anguished existence, he had *chosen* this.

Marcellus stepped out from his hiding place, attracting the attention of the first row of sergents, who snapped their weapons toward him. He held up both hands to show he was not armed. Commandeur Moreau studied him for a long beat, clearly recognizing him and the threat he failed to pose. She signaled for the sergents to stand down.

He took another step forward, through the swirl of morning mist. Then another. Until he was only a few mètres away from the woman who now served his grandfather in Marcellus's place.

"Commandeur Moreau," he said in a stern yet conciliatory tone, just loud enough to be heard over the gentle purr of the transporteur engine and the synchronized breaths of the soldiers. "I suppose I should congratulate you on your promotion."

"What do you want, Bonnefaçon?" she snapped. "I hope you're here to negotiate the terms of your surrender. But I must warn you, you don't have much leverage for negotiations. So I suggest you all lay down your weapons and step out from"—she glanced up at the towering wall of bread crates and overturned chairs and repurposed machines—"whatever it is you call this thing."

Marcellus took a deep breath, trying to ignore the legion of sergents standing before him, the heat radiating off their primed weapons. "I remember the first time we met, Commandeur. Do you?"

Moreau gave an impatient snort. "Whatever you're trying to do, it won't work."

"I was eight," Marcellus went on. "You were a pilote, quickly rising up the ranks of the Laterrian Spaceforce. You attended a briefing in my grandfather's private study. And on the way out, you saw me, playing in the hallway with my toy transporteurs. You smiled at me and told me I was lucky to be the grandson of such a brilliant man."

"You were," she said with a raise of her eyebrows. "Too bad you threw it all away."

He gave a small, solemn nod. "I did. I threw it all away. Because I knew I could never be the person my grandfather wanted me to be. I could never live up to my predecessor, the woman who could do no wrong. The woman who my grandfather adored and revered and glorified. I could never be Commandeur Vernay."

And there it was. The tiniest, almost imperceptible flinch. It was enough to give Marcellus the confidence he needed to keep going. Because he knew he'd hit the right spot. The sore spot. It had been his for too long and now it was hers, too.

"When Michele Vernay was executed by the Albion Queen, my life changed forever. I was immediately promoted in her place. Well, 'in training,' as the title went." Marcellus glanced down at the insignia that was secured to the front of the commandeur's uniform and shook his head. "I should have known I would never actually become commandeur one day, as I so desperately hoped I would. Because deep down, I knew I could never fill her shoes. And I imagine neither can you."

"I think this trip down memory lane has gone on long enough," barked Moreau. "If you're not here to surrender, then I have no choice but to treat you as the traitorous rebel that you are and either arrest you or, if you choose to struggle, shoot you." She wrapped her fingers around the handle of her holstered rayonette. "But I must warn you, the Empereur has forbidden all use of paralyzeur pulses in this matter."

"I would like to think it's because we're both decent people," Marcellus went on, his words—now his only weapon—picking up speed and urgency. "I would like to think it's because we could never be corrupted in the way my grandfather needed us to be in order to successfully serve him. At least, that is my hope."

"Bonnefaçon," Moreau said through clenched teeth. "This is not a joke. I don't care if you *are* the Empereur's flesh and blood—I will not hesitate to put a lethal pulse in your head. In fact, he'll probably reward me for it."

"Do you want to know what gave me that hope?" Marcellus surged on, his heart thundering in his chest. "It was you, Commandeur. In the cockpit of your ship. On the way to Bastille. My grandfather gave you the order to destroy the Trésor tower and you . . . hesitated." Marcellus latched on to her gaze, daring her with his eyes and his words to look away. To refute it. "Commandeur Vernay never would have hesitated. But you did. Because I think—I *hope*—that deep down, you will never be the commandeur he wants you to be either. That deep down, you know that human life is worth more than greed, and power, and domination." He sighed and cast his eyes over the rows of awaiting sergents, lined up like pieces on a Regiments board. "I know you've pledged your life to this Regime. All of you. I know you vowed to serve the crowned ruler of Laterre no matter what. And maybe the proof of my grandfather's lies and vicious crimes wasn't enough to sway you. Maybe you have to rely on something stronger than proof. Something that stolen footage and hacked broadcasts can't give you. Something you can only give yourself."

Moreau's gaze flickered ever so slightly but did not leave his. He stared into her dark, unreadable eyes, willing her to hear him. Willing his words to be enough. He *needed* them to be enough. Maybe he couldn't convince the System Alliance to reject his grandfather, but he had to be able to convince one person. He had to be able to convince Moreau. Because they were the same. He knew it in his heart. They were both products of a man who rewarded the ruthless and punished the softhearted. They were both his victims. Maybe Michele Vernay had been as well. Maybe no one had been able to save her in time.

"Sergent Toussaint," Commandeur Moreau said tightly to the man next to her. "Get ready to execute this traitor on my command."

Marcellus swallowed down the lump in his throat as the sergent pushed aside the explosif launcher strapped to his chest and pulled his rayonette from its holster. He aimed it at Marcellus's forehead.

"I'm giving you ten seconds to surrender this fabrique and step aside," Moreau told him.

"Or what?" Marcellus challenged with a mirthless laugh. "You'll have *this* mec kill me? You can't even do it yourself?!"

The commandeur stiffened. Marcellus walked slowly toward the primed weapon. Until it was only centimètres from his face. He noticed the sergent slightly waver as he glanced at Moreau.

"That's fine!" Marcellus cried out. "But you should know that I have nothing left to lose. My grandfather took most of it. And whatever was left was lost here tonight." Hot, burning tears sprang to his eyes, and he wondered if this was what it felt like when riot gas was released into the air. Like you couldn't see straight. Couldn't keep your voice from shaking with anguish. Couldn't hold on to the last shreds of determination to keep going. Keep fighting. Keep living.

"Ten . . . nine . . . ," Moreau began slowly, steadily, like she knew she had to reach one eventually but hoped she never would.

"César Bonnefaçon is not a good man!" Marcellus shouted through the tears and the hopelessness boiling up inside of him.

Moreau let out an impatient breath. "Eight . . . seven . . ."

"He raised me to think that he was. He raised me to believe in him. Trust him. Follow him. And I did. Because he's *that* convincing. Because he's *that* good."

"Six . . . five . . ."

"And now, as I look at all of this—at these innocent lives lost, at these destroyed hopes for a better life, at his unquenchable thirst for power—I am reminded of my blindness. My stupidity."

"Four . . . three . . ."

Marcellus's shoulders dropped, along with his voice. He was no longer speaking to her. He was speaking only to himself. The last words of a dying man. His last eulogy to a dying revolution. "But I was fortunate enough to discover the truth. And that is why I left. I saw past the lies and the deceit and the façade he has so believably constructed around everything he does, and I saw who he really was. A murderer. A monster. A villain."

Moreau fell silent, like she had simply lost count. But in her eyes, Marcellus saw something that made him feel as light as rain. It almost looked like hesitation.

He let out a shuddering breath. "I am now free from his mental chains and his bewitching spell. Forever. And that's enough for me. The question is, Apolline, are you?"

The commandeur started to speak. To say what, Marcellus would never know. Because suddenly her dark eyes shot up toward the sky. Her expression contorted into something incomprehensible. Something incredulous.

And that's when Marcellus heard the whispers. First from behind him. Then from the sergents themselves as, one by one, their steely gazes rose upward.

Marcellus spun around, watching the crowd of people streaming out from the fabrique. He opened his mouth to scream at them, tell them to get back inside. It wasn't safe. But then his eyes landed on Chatine. She, too, had emerged from behind the barricade. And she, too, was staring up into the sky.

As though it were falling.

He saw it in her eyes first. It looked like three perfect orbs of light reflecting back at him. And then, like a tide drifting back to sea, something cleared from her face. A lifetime of shadows. A lifetime of dark, gray clouds. A lifetime of grief and misery.

It was all washed away in an instant.

In a brilliant, dazzling glow of Sol-light.

- CHAPTER 89 -
CHATINE

THEY SHONE LIKE THREE PRECIOUS JEWELS.

Flawless.

Mesmerizing.

Perfect.

And peeking out from behind them was a deep, blazing blueness the likes of which Chatine had never seen. It was truer and more beautiful than anything that stretched across the TéléSky of Ledôme.

Chatine gazed up, feeling the warmth on her face, the gentle sting in her eyes. But she didn't dare look away. This time, she wasn't going to miss it. This time, she wasn't going to blink and doubt and let her mind's ability to expect the worst steal one second of this moment.

Because this time, she *knew* it was temporary. Ten years older and wiser and she knew that she was witnessing nothing more than a passing fluke. One cloud moving too quickly and another moving too slowly. An accident. Like someone had gotten the calculations wrong, sent the wrong directions, crossed the AirLinks.

And soon it would be righted.

But it was the most beautiful accident she'd ever seen.

She felt a hand slip into hers and she squeezed it tight. She pulled her attention away for long enough to glimpse Roche standing beside her, his head tipped back, the Sol-light making his face look almost unreal. Like a First World portrait hanging in the Grand Palais or a statue carved out of marble.

"Don't look away," he told her. "I don't want you to miss it again."

Chatine smiled and nudged his shoulder as she stared back up at the sky.

The world around them had fallen silent. For the first time in nearly a decade, everyone on Laterre was looking at the same thing. Standing under the same miracle. And the Sols lit up each and every one of their faces in the exact same way.

There was no more light shining over those soldiers than there was shining over her and Roche. The Sols were not brighter over Ledôme than they were over what was left of the Frets. Because real light didn't play favorites.

And then, just as quickly as they had parted, Chatine watched the clouds drift back into place, like a curtain being pulled over a brilliantly lit stage.

One by one, the three Sols of the System Divine disappeared back behind the clouds. First the soft blue light of Sol 3, then the crimson red of Sol 2, and finally the brightest of them all, the brilliant, warm white glow of Sol 1, vanished as well.

And the gray cloak that hung over Laterre sealed up, like a mother wrapping its young in a blanket, keeping them warm and comforted and safe.

Slowly, the gazes fell. All around her, people broke from their trances. Chatine watched the soldiers blink to attention, gripping their explosif launchers tighter, standing up straighter, like they'd momentarily drifted to sleep and were now ready to resume their deadly task as though nothing had happened.

But she knew—they all knew—that wasn't true.

Nothing could continue as it was. Everything had changed.

Because even though the Sols had retreated back to their hiding places, the memory of them still lingered. The proof that they existed was ingrained in every mind on this battlefield.

And just like Chatine, they all knew, deep down inside, that it hadn't been an accident at all. That ten years was too long to wait for a coincidence. And that maybe there was no such thing. Maybe there were no wrong calculations, no wrong directions. And although the Sols were invisible now, they were still there. Watching, guarding, creating beautiful accidents.

It was Commandeur Moreau who moved first, reaching for something. Chatine watched Marcellus flinch, assuming it was a weapon.

But all that was visible in the commandeur's hand was her titan insignia, glinting in the cloud-filtered light. Moreau captured Marcellus's eyes with her own and held them for a long time. Until, finally, her hand opened, and the badge fell swiftly and unceremoniously to the muddy ground.

Murmurs of confusion began to spread through the rows of sergents still holding tight to their mighty explosif launchers. They looked to one another, trying to find answers. But every face held the same expression: disbelief. Chatine was certain they'd never witnessed anything like this before. None of them had.

Marcellus turned back, looking for someone to corroborate this incredulous moment. He found Chatine, and she allowed herself the tiniest of smiles.

"Attention to the rebels of the bread fabrique," Moreau announced, in the same brusque voice that had shot out from the transporteur speakers only a short while ago. "This is Apolline Moreau, former commandeur of the Laterrian Ministère. From this moment on, I stand with you."

A shocked silence descended over the streets of the Fabrique District. Just like the baffled sergents still clutching their weapons, people turned to one another, wordless questions bouncing between them. No one quite knew what to do next, or if Moreau's claims could even be believed.

But Chatine was no longer looking at Moreau or her soldiers or the silent rebels. Her gaze was back in the sky as every muscle in her body began to pulse at once. Roche's hand slipped numbly from hers. Because he heard it too.

That low, distant hum.

Moving closer.

Growing louder.

They had both been there the day the combatteurs had come for Bastille. The day this woman standing before them—this *former* commandeur—had unleashed catastrophe on the Trésor tower. They'd both felt the rumble of the ground beneath their feet and the wind swirling the dust around their faces. They both recognized this storm.

And so did Marcellus.

And so did Moreau.

Her face darkened with dread. And then, suddenly she was bellowing into her TéléCom, her words fast and furious and terrified. "This is Apolline Moreau to flight dispatch. There is a combatteur inbound over the Fabrique District. Please confirm and identify."

Marcellus was now beside Chatine, urgently scanning the sky. But the clouds were too thick to see anything. There was only that sound. That horrific, bone-rattling sound. "It's him," he said in a chilling whisper.

"How do you know?" asked Chatine.

Marcellus chuckled darkly. "I just know."

"Get everyone inside the fabriques now!" Moreau called out, still clutching her TéléCom. "I have just received confirmation that Empereur Bonnefaçon has commandeered a combatteur and is heading straight toward us."

Even though people reacted quickly, racing back toward the loading bay doors, Chatine knew there was no time.

And those fabriques couldn't protect them. Nothing could.

"He can't!" Alouette cried out to Moreau, like she was trying to bargain her way out of the inevitable. "He can't destroy the fabriques. What about all the goods? The resources? The workers?"

"He doesn't care anymore!" Moreau shouted as she helped corral the hordes of panicked people back toward the barricade. "He's desperate. He'll kill us all if he has to. He just wants to win."

Screams erupted all around Chatine. Pounding footsteps shook the ground. But she didn't move. What was the point?

There was no hiding.

There was no running.

There was no escape from what that thing could do.

The hum grew louder. The wind picked up, tangling in Chatine's short hair, swirling the dust around them. And then she saw it. In the very place where the clouds had parted to reveal three beautiful Sols, she saw the end of everything staring back at her. It had wings that could slice through Perma-Steel. It had thrusters that could cut through the stars. It gleamed and glistened in the morning light, momentarily blinding Chatine.

She reached for Roche's hand again and pulled her brother to her, wrapping her arms tightly around his body. She could no longer protect him from what was sure to come. But she could hold him. She could tell him that she loved him.

Beside her, Marcellus stiffened and murmured a quiet prayer. Chatine waited for the sound. She didn't have to wait long.

BOOOOOMMMM!

It shook the world. It parted the sky. It set the clouds ablaze.

BOOOOOMMMM!

BOOOOOMMMM!

BOOOOOMMMM!

Chatine shut her eyes, waiting for the burn. The heat. The end. But she felt none of it.

"Oh my Sols!" someone cried, and Chatine's eyes fluttered open to see the clouds were still on fire.

That's when she realized the explosifs were not raining down from the sky. They were coming from the ground. She spun back toward the rows of hovering transporteurs and the sergents who stood in their sharp, rigid lines, awaiting a command.

But a few of them were no longer waiting to see what came next. They had *decided* what came next. Their explosif launchers were gripped in their hands, pointed unmistakably at the sky. And they were firing. Giant soaring explosifs rocketed into the air, searching for a target.

The Empereur's combatteur wobbled and swerved. It dipped to the left, avoiding a near collision with one of the projectiles before righting itself and circling back around for another approach. But the sergents were relentless. And soon more had joined in the assault.

BOOOOOMMMM!

BOOOOOMMMMM!

BOOOOOMMMMM!

The Empereur tried to dodge, sending his ship into a looping roll, but there were too many. The sky was alight with defiance. With rebellion. With the turning of his own soldiers against him. He had planted their disgust. His hateful acts had seeded their revolt. And every move he made had blossomed into this.

Then, something hit. No one would ever know who had fired the fateful shot. No one would ever care.

Smoke billowed up from the Empereur's combatteur, and when the air cleared a few seconds later, Chatine could see that the entire left wing was blown off and the craft was spiraling helplessly across the sky.

Roche pushed himself away from Chatine and shook his fist at the sky. "That's for the Oublies!" he shouted, tears stinging his eyes.

Then, a mighty crash rang out across the Fabrique District as the combatteur plummeted to the ground, landing in a plume of smoke and debris and finality.

CHAPTER 90

CERISE

THE MANUFACTURING FLOOR OF THE BREAD FABRIQUE was full of bodies. Some dead. Some dying. Some who might actually survive to see another day.

But not one of them was Gabriel.

Cerise made her third lap around the makeshift hospital that Brigitte and Alouette had set up to tend to the wounded, letting her cybernetic eye capture and analyze every face, convinced that she'd simply missed one the last time around. Or that in the constant flurry of people coming in and out, delivering more wounded, more fallen, from the other fabriques, one of those faces had slipped through her count.

And that one would be him.

"Don't worry," Alouette said, resting a hand on her shoulder. "We'll find him."

Cerise felt tears glisten against her circuitry again. "I don't understand. I saw him pinned beneath that loom. You saw it too, right? But when I went back to the textile fabrique to look for him, he wasn't there. My neuroprocessors are all confused. Did I imagine it?"

"No," said Alouette soothingly. "Because I saw it too."

"So what does that mean?" Cerise asked.

"It means he's probably still alive."

"Then where is he?!" The words came out louder than she was anticipating. Since witnessing Gabriel trapped under that wreckage, she'd been learning how to regulate the sound of her voice. She'd been learning how to regulate a lot of things.

"Alouette." Grantaire appeared beside them. "The med cruiseur is here. The médecins want to start with those in the most critical condition."

Alouette nodded and turned back to Cerise. "We'll find him," she assured her again before guiding Grantaire through the maze of gurneys and stretchers.

Cerise sighed and completed her third lap before wandering into the loading bay, where a team of people were tearing down the barricade. Médecins were already streaming in through the open gaps, pushing stretchers and carrying bags of supplies. Near the stairs leading up to the superviseur's office, Roche was surrounded by an eager audience as he rehashed the triumphant moment for what had to be the seventeenth time.

"And then, the clouds parted and the Empereur's ship was there and we all drew in what we were certain would be our final breaths," he was saying dramatically. "But then, destiny intervened. The Policier sergents fired their launchers into the sky. BOOM! BOOM! BOOM! BOOM! BOOM! The Empereur dove. The sergents fired again! It was a direct hit! And the Empereur's ship went . . ." He made a high-pitched falling noise before pantomiming the epic, deadly crash that Cerise knew would be talked about on this planet for years, maybe even centuries, to come.

Apolline Moreau had already left with a recovery team to search the debris for the Empereur's body and anyone injured in the crash.

Cerise kept walking, past Roche and his new throng of spectators, past the half-dismantled barricade and the squad of med cruiseurs hovering outside, all the way out into the daylight.

She peered up into the light gray skies overhead, thinking about what had transpired there only hours ago. She knew people would be talking about that for centuries to come as well.

The day the Sols rose and Laterre's greatest enemy—Laterre's *rea* enemy—finally fell.

She rubbed at her temples, trying to sort through the scattering of emotions that were mixing in her brain. Since her awakening, it felt like new emotions were welling up every few seconds. Things she didn't remember having to deal with before. How did humans manage so many of them at once?

She felt happy for Laterre. Relieved for those who had survived the battle. Saddened for those who had not. Guilty for not having woken up sooner. And then, on top of all of it was this anguish. This unnerving, distracting, destabilizing anguish that seemed to overpower everything.

How could she feel *anything* else while Gabriel was still missing?

She pulled her gaze down from the sky, and that's when she noticed someone sitting on the ground, in the midst of the powered-down droids that no one had quite decided what to do with yet.

It was Chatine. Cerise walked over and sat down next to her. From down here, the droids looked enormous. And the sight momentarily unsettled Cerise, as if any moment they could awaken and smash them both to pieces with a single footfall.

"What are you doing?" Cerise asked, and Chatine seemed to blink at the question, as if she, too, had been lost in a haze of conflicting emotions.

She sighed and glanced up at the nearest droid. "Would you think I had lost my mind if I told you that sitting here is the only place that feels safe right now?"

Cerise considered the question thoroughly. "No."

"All of my life I've run from these things. I've been so terrified of them. They kept me trapped. And now they're just . . ." She swatted at the leg of the nearest droid. "Useless hunks of metal."

Cerise shook her head, trying to understand but falling short. "I have a lot to learn about human behavior."

That made Chatine laugh. She peered over at Cerise. "It's not that hard to be a human. It just fric-ing hurts a lot."

"Hurts?" Cerise repeated carefully.

Chatine pressed a fist to her chest. "Here."

"And what do you do? When it hurts?"

"I'm not sure there's much you can do. Except let it hurt. And try not to run away from it." Chatine's gaze drifted back toward the fabrique. "A very wise person taught me that." And then, she started crying. Fat, rolling tears that made no sound. How could so much grief make no sound?

"I haven't told her," Chatine finally said, but her voice was barely a voice at all. "I haven't been able to tell her that her son is . . ."

And that's when the sound came. Loud and ugly and uninhibited. Cerise watched the girl cry with another strange mix of new emotions that she couldn't identify. When would she finally recognize them all?

Cerise's circuitry flickered as she tried to process Chatine's words logically, ignoring the distractions welling up inside of her like ocean waves. Her neuroprocessors sorted through the events of the past night, until finally she understood.

Etienne hadn't come back either.

And his mother didn't yet know.

Cerise glanced back at the fabrique, where right this minute Brigitte was tending to the wounded. Was she searching for a face in the crowd too? Was she plagued by this same painful uncertainty?

"If what you said is true," Cerise began thoughtfully, "that there's not much you can do but let it hurt, then you should tell her now."

Chatine sniffled and studied Cerise with a look of surprise. "But what if she blames me? What if she thinks it's my fault? What if she never forgives me? She's the closest thing to a maman that I've ever had."

"Then, she won't," Cerise concluded.

There was a long silence in which Chatine only stared at her, like she was trying to determine whether or not to put aside a lifelong prejudice and simply trust her. Finally, she nodded and, with a sudden burst of determination, rose to her feet. Cerise stood too and watched the girl disappear back into the fabrique.

That's when another emotion began to pulse through her. This one she recognized at once. Because she'd felt it before. As she'd stood in front of the briefing room and the weight of the Medal of Accomplissement had settled against her chest. As the room had broken into applause and she'd watched her father's face beam back at her.

But now, the pride took on a different shape. Less intense and with duller edges. Less defined and more nebulous. No longer motivated by a predefined sequence of unyielding code, but by something subtler. More nuanced.

It was as though her human processors were softening her neuro-processors. Evening everything out.

"I think someone's under there!" came a voice in the distance, and Cerise's attention was pulled back to the deconstructed barricade, where Jolras and a group of men were digging through giant pieces of wood and metal.

"Is someone trapped?" asked another.

"I don't know," said Jolras, desperately shoving aside debris. "I swore I heard someone call out for help."

Mesmerized, Cerise watched as the group worked together to clear away the wreckage. She braced herself for what they might uncover. Another wounded rebel. Another body to be transported to the med center. But when they finally dug their way to the ground, they revealed only an old storm drain, sealed off with a round metal cover.

"What the fric?" asked one of the men. "Are you hearing things, mec?"

Jolras stared numbly at the drain, a look of confusion etched across his face. "I could have sworn I—"

And then it came.

A quiet banging. Followed by a voice.

"Is anyone up there! Please help!"

Everyone heard it this time. Cerise rushed forward to help the men push aside the heavy metal disk. The figure who stood below the ground was huge, his shoulders crammed painfully between the sides of the pipe that he'd climbed up to call for help. His face was covered in dirt and grime. But Cerise's facial scanners made the connection anyway.

"Go get Alouette!" she shouted at Jolras. "Tell her we found her father."

As Jolras darted into the fabrique, two of the others reached down to pull Hugo to safety. He collapsed onto the ground, gasping for breath. Cerise was no médicin, but she could easily see he was not well. A nasty scrape scored its way across his right temple, and a bruise was forming on his square, stubbled jaw. But worse, far worse, was the blood. It seeped through his shirt, his coat, and onto his large hands, which pressed futilely at his abdomen as if trying to hold in the blood. Hold in the pain.

"Papa!" Alouette raced toward him and sank to her knees. "Where have you been? Where did you go? I thought you were . . ." She cut herself off and embraced him instead. "Thank the Sols."

Hugo was struggling to say something. But his words came out in broken wheezes.

"Don't speak," Alouette said. "We'll get you to a med center immediately. You'll be okay." She flagged down one of the passing médecins. "This man needs help. He's in critical condition. Possibly a punctured lung. Or a broken rib."

The médecin nodded and gestured to two others, who came forward with a stretcher.

"No," Hugo wheezed as they tried to lift him. "Wait. He's . . ." He clutched his chest and winced as he pointed back toward the exposed storm drain. He took in another ragged, painful breath before finally conjuring up the strength to utter one more word. "Gabriel."

Cerise's circuitry exploded. She was suddenly on the move, scrambling through the hole in the ground and down the ladder into the darkness below. She spun around, squinting through the low light from above until her gaze landed on a dark shape slumped against the side of the tunnel.

"Gabriel!" she cried, running to him, kneeling before him in the dirty water that tracked across the old sewer floor. "Are you okay? Please be okay! Can you hear me? Can you speak?"

Gabriel's eyes dragged open. It took a moment for him to focus on her, but when he did, a tiny smile tweaked the corners of his lips. "Sparkles."

"Yes, it's me," she said, her heart bursting with relief. "Sparkles."

"Cerise!" Alouette's voice shot down from the storm drain. "What do you see?"

"He's here!" she called back. "He's alive! But he needs help."

"I'm sending down a crew. Stay with him."

Cerise turned back to Gabriel and touched his damp forehead. "I will."

Gabriel's smile broadened. "Hugo," he struggled to say. "He pulled me out of the wreckage. He carried me through the sewers. He saved my life."

"Thank the Sols," Cerise said. "You're going to be okay."

Behind her, she heard movement as the med team began to lower people and supplies down into the tunnel.

"You're going to be okay," she said again, and leaned forward to gently kiss his cheek. But Gabriel turned suddenly, and his mouth met hers. It was soft. It was urgent. It was everything.

Cerise's neuroprocessors emptied. There were no words for the emotion. No words for the sensation strumming through her as his lips moved against hers. And eventually, she stopped trying and gave in to the kiss.

When he pulled away, his face was glowing. Bright light cascaded over his skin like fiery stars. He smiled at her, his gaze locked onto the left side of her face. And that's when she realized the light was coming from *her*. From her circuitry. It was dancing.

Embarrassed, she tried to cover it with her hands. But it was too bright. Too sparkling. The glow bounced through her fingers and lit up the entire tunnel. Until finally, Gabriel reached up and pulled her hands back down.

"Don't," he whispered.

She bit her lip, which still tasted like him. "Brigitte says I'll eventually learn how to control them."

"Sols, I hope not." Gabriel grinned. "Because that was titanique."

CHAPTER 91

ALOUETTE

THE MED CENTER WAS COLD AND STERILE WITH GLIS-
tening metal cabinets and stark white walls and shelves upon shelves of neatly
organized plastique vials. Alouette stood at Hugo's bedside, aching for the
Refuge's warm infirmerie and sweet-smelling medicinal herbs. But mostly,
she ached for Laurel. For the comfort she brought in situations like this.

He'll be fine, she tried to imagine the sister saying now. *He will live. He
will heal. The body is the most wonderful healer in the world.*

But as Alouette gazed down at her father, his limbs and eyelids heavy
from the médicaments, his bruises made even more evident in the unforgiving light of the treatment room, she knew these words were as imaginary as the voice saying them.

The médecin's blunt diagnosis had assured her of that: two broken ribs,
a punctured lung, infections from an untreated burn wound, and lacera-
tions from a lethal pulse. Chance of survival: 5 percent. Recommended
treatment: Make him as comfortable as possible.

At first, Alouette had tried to argue, to insist he examine her father
again. Take more scans, analyze more blood. She'd almost ripped the
TéléCom right out of his hands, demanding that she take over treatment.
She knew better. She could do better.

But then, her father's hands had rested on hers, and when she'd looked into his eyes, she knew that there was no use fighting. That she could turn the kaléidoscope a million different ways and it would not change the light fading from his eyes. It would not change the story.

"Alouette," said a voice from the doorway, and a second later, Apolline Moreau stepped into the room. She cast an anxious look at Hugo. "How is he?"

Alouette only shook her head.

"I'm sorry," the former commandeur offered. "But I bring important news from the barricade that can't wait."

"The barricade?" Alouette asked, confused. The barricade was being taken down. The battle was over, wasn't it? Her stomach clenched.

"My recovery team searched the combatteur wreckage. We found the Emper—César Bonnefaçon." Moreau's eyes darkened. "He's alive."

"What?" Alouette gasped. She'd been so certain he was dead. They all had been.

"He survived the crash with a few minor injuries."

"Is he . . . did he . . ." Alouette's throat went dry. She couldn't do this again. She couldn't keep fighting. They'd already lost too much.

"He's in custody," Moreau rushed to say. "We've taken him to a cell at the Policier Precinct. We just . . ." Her voice trailed off and she glanced down at her hands, which were kneading anxiously in front of her. "Need to know what to do with him."

The relief in Alouette's chest gave way to more confusion. "What do you mean?"

"What do you want his sentence to be?"

Alouette stared at the woman in her dirty, mud-stained uniform with its ripped and tangled epauletes and Sol-shaped titan buttons that had lost their gleam. "Why are you asking me?"

But even as she asked the question, she was certain she already knew the answer.

"Because you're the—" Moreau began to say.

"I'm not." Alouette shook her head. "I never wanted to be. That's what I tried to explain at the coronation ceremony, but no one would listen.

No one wanted to hear it. I was raised to be a guardian. To be a protector of this planet. And that's what I've done. I've protected it. I've guarded it against the forces that sought to harm it. Now . . ." She glanced at her father, his chest rising and falling in a hesitant, almost precarious rhythm, as though each breath had to be thought about, considered, the pros and cons weighed. As though any minute, the cons might outweigh the pros.

Then, she let her gaze drift out the window of the med center. Just beyond this room, in the fading evening light, the Frets—or what was left of them—sat like injured giants, slumping in the mud. The heaviness of everything that had transpired on this planet seemed to weigh them down, crack their walls even further. "Now I think I just want to help heal it."

Moreau watched her quietly, like she was unsure what to say next.

Alouette lowered herself into the chair next to her father's bed. "One of the women who raised me was a healer. A good one. She had a kind heart and a nurturing soul. I think that's what we need right now more than anything. Not more power-hungry leaders who get to decide who lives and who dies. I could never do that. I could never be that."

The former commandeur's brow furrowed. "But then—"

"Go back to the barricade. Find a woman named Francine and one named Léonie and one named Clare, and Denise, and Marguerite. They will know what to do next. They will make sure the planet is placed in the right hands. The most capable hands."

Moreau still looked uncertain, but she eventually nodded and backed out the door, passing by a médicin in green scrubs who was on his way in.

"He's still asleep," Alouette reported, looking back to her father. "His breathing has been fairly regular, a little erratic at times, but he seems to be comfortable. He might need another dose of médicaments, though. I don't want them to run out. I don't want him to be in any pain."

There was an unusual silence in the room. The médecin had not said a single word in response. Alouette turned back to him, expecting to find the cyborg diligently analyzing something on his TéléCom, but he just stood there, his circuitry flickering with a steady, determined rhythm. And in his hands, he held not a TéléCom . . . but a rayonette.

Alouette gasped and leapt from her chair, scanning the cyborg's face more closely this time. Despite the green scrubs he wore, this was not a médecin. It was Inspecteur Limier.

She opened her mouth to scream, but a single wave of the rayonette in Limier's hand snapped it shut again.

"H-h-how did you . . . ," she stammered.

"I let him go," came Hugo's weary voice as his eyes dragged open.

Alouette glanced anxiously between the two men. "What? Why?"

"Because he is a fool," Limier replied in that eerie, inflectionless tone. "He had a chance to take his revenge and he threw it away."

"Because no man should be able to decide the fate of another," Hugo responded weakly. "Because if I were to kill him, I would become him. And because mercy is our greatest gift from the Sols."

"You should have killed me when you had the chance," Limier growled, stepping forward, his rayonette outstretched.

Alouette moved in front of him, letting the barrel rest against her own chest. "Please," she begged. "He's dying. He'll be gone soon. Please don't hurt him."

"He is a criminal," Limier replied evenly. "He has broken the law too many times. He must be punished."

"He's a good man!" Alouette screamed back. "*You* are the criminal!"

"Little Lark," Hugo whispered. "Don't. It won't work. Just let him do what he's come to do."

"No, Papa!" she cried, tears now blurring her vision. "I won't let him." She turned back to Limier, that same fierce, protective energy coursing through her veins again. "You'll have to kill me first."

"Alouette," came Hugo's rebuke. He sounded more like her father than he had in a long time. "You will not take this fate in my place. This is my destiny and mine alone. I have lived a happy life. A fulfilling life. Now you must do the same. The people of Laterre need you to be alive. They need your heart, which is full of love for them, they need your joy, your wisdom, your protection. Only the Sols have use for me now."

"Papa," she tried to say, but the only sounds that came out were more violent, body-shaking sobs.

Then, through the pain and the glimmer of his own tears, her father smiled at her. And it was both happy and sorrowful at the same time. "You can cry for me, Little Lark. But not too much, okay? You have too much left to do to spend your life in grief. Now please step aside and let the inspecteur do what he has come to do. He won't give up until he does. Because he can't help himself. It is duty. And it is hardwired into the very core of his being."

Alouette shook her head. She couldn't do it. She couldn't move. She couldn't step aside for a pulse that had waited twenty-five long years to find its target. Her limbs were frozen.

And then, she heard it. Not the quiet click of the trigger. Not the pulse she was ready to take in her father's place. But something else. Something that stirred memories deep within her, that transported her back to a dank cell on a forgotten island.

It was the sound of lips tapping uselessly together.

The sound of words failing to form.

The sound of a tiny glitch sparking in the darkness, spreading across the vast fabric of code that lived within all cyborgs.

When she turned back around, she already knew what she would see.

The inspecteur's circuitry was lit up like his whole being was on fire. His body started to convulse, a single unspoken word still trapped uselessly on his tongue.

"What's happening to him?" Hugo asked, his once-valiant voice now cracking with fear.

"He's glitching," Alouette said. "His programming is conflicting with itself."

"Can you stop it?"

"Maybe," she whispered, remembering what Sister Denise had done for Inspecteur Champlain and what she, in turn, had done for Cerise. She sucked in a shaky breath and slowly began to move toward Limier, her mind filling with possible words to pull him out. The problem was, she didn't know what was causing the glitch. All she knew was that she had to try before . . .

Whoosh!

It happened faster than Alouette could process it. Faster than she could scream. In one blurring motion, Inspecteur Limier had raised the rayonette and fired it at his own temple. His circuitry didn't even spark. It just flickered off as his body collapsed to the floor.

Having heard the commotion, three médecins rushed in, kneeling to check the inspecteur's pulse.

Alouette could barely move. Could barely speak. "He . . . it just . . . I . . ."

But she didn't need to explain. The evidence was right in front of everyone, still clutched in Limier's hand.

Two of the médecins carried the body of the inspecteur out of the room, while the third approached her father's bed to check on his vitals. "My condolences," he said after a moment, his voice as emotionless as ever. "We did everything we could."

Alouette felt the breath leave her at once. "What?"

She ran to her father, her eyes desperately searching his body for new wounds, blackened holes, anything. But there was nothing.

Nothing.

No air.

No movement.

No life.

"But he was fine!" Alouette cried. "And there was only one shot. He couldn't have . . ."

The cyborg reached out and placed a hand on her shoulder. It was almost comforting. Almost tender. Before he turned and left the room.

Alouette sank to her knees beside her father and pressed her cheek into his hand, which was still warm. And his face, which was pointed upward, straight toward the Sols, held the slightest ghost of a smile.

CHAPTER 92

MARCELLUS

"ARE YOU SURE YOU WANT TO DO THIS?" ASKED FRANCINE.

Marcellus Bonnefaçon reached up to straighten the collar of his shirt, before remembering that he no longer had anything to prove. No longer had to look any certain part. There was no one to impress anymore.

He roughly rumpled the collar again and even took a moment to muss his hair until a single rebellious strand curled against his forehead. There was something about that strand of hair that gave him a sudden rush of courage.

"I'm sure. I want to see him."

As Francine led him down the long, familiar hallway of the Policier Precinct, his mind flashed back to the time he'd come here to interrogate Jacqui and Denise. Come to discover the truth. About everything.

It felt like a lifetime ago. A planet's lifetime ago.

Although the stark corridors and interrogation rooms looked exactly the same, there was something decidedly less ominous about the Precinct now. Maybe because it was mostly empty and quiet. No sergents barking out orders. No Third Estaters being herded in and out of holding cells.

It had been just over a week since the barricades had come down, and the planet still felt like it was hovering in a state of in-between. The corrupt, ancient Regime was no longer. The droids had been permanently decommissioned. And the three estates were something that people would hear stories about one day, wondering how such a thing could ever have existed. Wondering how it had taken so long to see through its flimsy construct.

But the new government was still in the works. Still being carefully planned and strategized by a provisional council made up of the Sisterhood and representative members of the people. *All* of the people. And the Grand Palais had been appropriated as its temporary headquarters.

The only remnant of the old world, the old life, *Marcellus's* old life, was sitting behind a door at the end of this hallway.

Francine stopped and turned back to Marcellus, as if preparing to check one more time if this was what he truly wanted to do.

He preempted the question. "I need to see him."

Francine nodded, as though she'd expected this. "We haven't yet told him what the council has decided about his sentence. I thought I'd let you be the one to do it. That is, if you want the job. I will understand if you—"

"I'll do it."

"Very well." Francine swiped her palm against the panel on the wall, and the lock hissed open.

Marcellus reached for the door handle but froze when he felt Francine's gentle hand on his shoulder. "I'll wait out here. In case you need me."

"Why would I—" Marcellus began to ask, but Francine cut him off with a knowing smile and he surrendered with a sigh. "Merci."

The holding cell had been subdivided into two rooms with a thick pane of plastique in the middle. It reminded Marcellus far too much of the transparent cube he'd seen in a secret weapons lab on Albion. Where he'd watched two men fight to the death at the command of their Skins.

The man on the other side of the plastique wall, however, was in no shape to be fighting to the death. He looked like he'd already lost that battle.

At a bare metal table, the general sat slumped and unmoving. He was dressed in a blue prison uniform that sagged at the front, revealing his neck and collarbone, which had been scraped and bruised in the combatteur crash. His once-perfectly-combed hair stood in a ragged halo from his scalp, which was peppered with burns. Great shadows hung under his eyes while large, glinting cuffs shackled his wrists and his ankles, pinching at his skin.

But what surprised Marcellus most about his grandfather's appearance was his age. Over the past eighteen years, he'd lived within the same walls as this man, taken his first steps under his cool, watchful stare, spoken his first words in his intimidating presence. He'd grown up right beside him. But for some reason, he couldn't remember his grandfather getting one day older. In his mind, he was always the same. Like an ancient artifact trapped in ice, never aging, never changing, never thawing.

But now, under these harsh lights and in this depressing room and after the very first battle he'd ever lost, César Bonnefaçon looked like an old man. A tired, defeated, pathetic old man.

And yet, when his grandfather's gaze lifted, when two pairs of matching hazel eyes met through the plastique, Marcellus could see the same glimmer, the same stubborn arrogance, the same unrelenting determination.

Like he was still playing.

Still fighting.

Still moving pieces around the invisible Regiments board in his mind.

Marcellus cleared his throat, eager to get his task over with. All he'd really wanted was to see him. To witness, with his very eyes, the fall of César Bonnefaçon. And he'd done that. Regardless of what was gleaming in his grandfather's eyes, the man was done. Finished. And it was time he knew that too.

"I've been asked to deliver word of your sentence," Marcellus began in a clear, steady voice. "The provisional council of the République of Laterre has decided—"

"République." His grandfather let out a snort. "It will never work."

Marcellus swallowed down every angry, biting remark that bubbled up in his throat and kept going. "Has decided that your sentence shall be exile. You are to live out the rest of your days in a satellite prison. Alone. You shall have no contact with anyone."

Marcellus swallowed in an attempt to wet his parched throat as he watched his grandfather's face for a reaction. He should have known he would never find a genuine one.

"Is that all?" César asked with a twinge of amusement.

"Your ship is scheduled to depart tomorrow morning," Marcellus said stiffly before retreating back toward the door.

"And I suppose all of this was *your* idea?"

He stopped just short of the exit and stared down at the glowing biometric lock.

When Marcellus had first heard the sentence—first pictured a lonely satellite forever orbiting the glorious planet his grandfather had once tried to control—he had felt only numbness. Not the relief he'd expected. Maybe because even if he'd had a *thousand* years to contemplate the most appropriate punishment for the man behind that plastique wall, he couldn't have come up with one. Which was why he was glad he hadn't been in charge of doing so.

He turned back around. "No, actually. I'm just the messenger. Unlike you, I don't take pleasure in determining other people's demises."

"You arrogant wretch!" his grandfather shouted, suddenly rising from his chair and stomping over to the clear divider with such ferocity, Marcellus was certain he was going to bash right through it. But he stopped, nose centimètres away from the wall, hot angry breath steaming up the plastique. "You think you're better than me, Marcellus? You think you're not just like me? Well, you're wrong. You're *exactly* like me. I made sure of that. I raised you. I was in charge of your education, your upbringing, what you were exposed to. And I've seen it in your eyes, Marcellus. I've seen the glimmer of something great. Something powerful. Something you can't stop. No matter where I go, no matter how far they shoot me into space, I will always live inside of you. I will always be there. Waiting in your darkened, bitter heart. Waiting to wake up. I don't care what they do to me now, because I know I leave behind a part of me when I go. *You*, Marcellus, are my legacy."

It was like a storm brewing inside of Marcellus. It was like emberweed oil spreading over every organ, through every vein, just waiting for the match. Just waiting to ignite. Like it had ignited a million times before.

The flame that had fueled his passion. The flame that had lit a hundred darkest nights as he stayed awake, searching that library for hints of Alouette, racking his brain trying to think like his grandfather, trying to climb inside his mind and become him, so that he could defeat him.

It was the same flame he saw in his grandfather's eyes now.

The blaze of blind obsession.

And just like fire, it burned. It scorched. It raged out of control. It chased everyone else away, until all that was left was charred rubble.

A tired, defeated, pathetic old man.

And Marcellus was not and would not become that.

"You lost," he said quietly, more to himself than to his grandfather.

But his grandfather snarled in response, "I lost the battle, but as long as I'm still alive, there will be more to come."

"No." Marcellus shook his head. "You've lost everything. Your planet. Your estate. Your Ministère. Even your allies have turned against you. Queen Matilda found your secret spacecraft carrier hidden in the Asteroid Channel. The one that was building stealth ships to invade Usonia. Turns out, she knew nothing about it. Because you were never planning on fulfilling your promise to her, were you? You were never planning on helping Albion. You were going to try to take Usonia for yourself. Because that's what you do. You take and you take and you take, and it's only ever for *you*. The Albion Royal Space Fleet surrounded the ship five days ago and forced its surrender. The workers you kidnapped were freed and anyone still loyal to you was taken into custody. The System Alliance has publicly denounced you and voted to recognize the new République of Laterre."

Marcellus looked into his grandfather's fierce, fuming gaze. "You lost," he repeated, keeping his tone soft, tender, even merciful. "And not just the battle. Not just the ships and the droids and the influence. You lost everyone who could have ever loved you. Your son, your grandson, even Michele Vernay. Your obsession, your relentless thirst for power, pushed them all away. Until you had no one left. You *have* no one left. And *that* is your legacy."

"Marcellus!" his grandfather roared.

But Marcellus was already reaching for the door, already pressing his hand against the panel. His grandfather banged violently on the plastique barrier, the chains around his wrists rattling. "Marcellus! Don't you walk away from me! You ungrateful little clochard. Come back here!"

"Adieu, Grand-père," Marcellus whispered. And this time he made sure it was only for himself to hear.

- CHAPTER 93 -
CHATINE

THE LIGHT FROM THE THREE RISING SOLS WAS JUST VIS-
ible through the thick clouds that swept over the Terrain Perdu. The icy
ground beneath Chatine Renard's feet seemed to glitter in that light, like
a vast ocean of tiny sparkling crystals.

She wrapped her fingers tighter around the stone in her hand, like she
was trying to infuse it with warmth, with hope, with all of the things she
wanted to say and would ever want to say but would never get the chance.

Then, she bent down and carefully placed the stone at the tip of the
small line that had begun to form in the dirt.

With this one, she remembered Marilyn. His ship. His creation. His
love. The echo of her voice—just the slightest bit too flirtatious—brought
a fragile smile to Chatine's lips.

Brigitte placed the next stone, closing her eyes and planting a delicate
kiss on its smooth surface before adding it to the emerging shape. Back
and forth they went, stone after stone, memory after memory, teardrop
after teardrop, until the shape was almost complete.

It was Brigitte's idea to place the arrow next to his father's. Like two shooting stars, flying through the same sky, toward the same final destination.

"Why don't you place the last one?" Brigitte said, and when she glanced over at Chatine, her eyes were glistening, but her face held no more pain. Not like the pain Chatine had witnessed on that day in the fabrique. When she'd somehow scrounged up enough courage to tell Brigitte what he'd done.

That was a pain the likes of which Chatine had never witnessed on another human being. The likes of which she doubted she would ever understand, unless she were to have children of her own someday. A kind of pain she knew she'd never seen on her own mother. Even when she'd sold off her own child.

But now, it was as though Brigitte's pain had been replaced by something else. Something that would always line her face but not torment her heart. Something that would always lurk behind corners, but not to destroy her, only to remind her.

Chatine hoped that one day her own pain would turn into the same thing.

A shadow instead of an endless swath of darkness.

A memory lurking behind corners, instead of a monster.

But this was helping.

"Are you sure?" she asked Brigitte, who nodded solemnly.

Chatine reached into the basket by their feet and took hold of the final stone, feeling the smooth edges between her fingertips, letting the coolness of it, the iciness of it, seep into her bare skin.

With this one, she remembered the first time she saw him. Before she knew his name or his secrets. Before his eyes started to sparkle when she looked into them. Before she fell a little in love with him, too.

Or maybe it was a lot.

Maybe it could have been a lot.

If they'd only had more time.

She'd been lying on the floor of his cockpit with a piece of shrapnel buried in her leg and a hearty dose of goldenroot pumping through her veins. He'd been sitting in his capitaine's chair, his hands moving confidently over the controls, totally calm, totally in his element, despite the dangers that lurked outside.

That was how she would strive to remember him. Immune to danger. Safe from harm.

She set the stone down with a quiet breath and stood up.

For a moment, neither of them spoke. They simply stared down at the ground, at the hundreds of patterns that surrounded them, hundreds of lives immortalized in memories.

A flock of birds fluttered up from the icy ground nearby, startled by the sound of the construction behind them. Chatine turned back toward the camp, where one of the old chalets was being deconstructed, its lightweight pieces coming apart one by one. Several of the community had returned here to tear down what was left of the old buildings. From the almost clear horizon in front of Chatine, it was evident they were nearly done.

"Where will you go now?" she asked.

Brigitte gave a little shrug. "I guess wherever we want. We don't have to hide anymore."

She nodded. "Right."

"What about you?"

Chatine peered out into the icy tundra. She would no longer be able to call the Terrain Perdu no-man's-land. She supposed it was every man's land now.

She sighed. "I don't know. Is that okay?"

Brigitte smiled and squeezed her hand. "I think that's just fine." They stood for another few breaths before Brigitte turned and said, "I'm going to go help the others. Would you like to stay a little longer?"

Chatine nodded and Brigitte leaned in to kiss her cheek. Her lips were cold, but her touch was warm. It was a paradox she would always associate with the people who'd lived out here. In such coldness, with such warmth in their hearts.

Brigitte's footsteps faded behind her, and she was left alone with her thoughts. They were always the same these days. An endless loop of the same story. The same hopeful reassurances she'd told Brigitte that day.

"He died for a reason."

"He died so this planet could be free."

"There was no other way it could have ended."

And for the first time, with the cold winds whipping across her face and tangling her hair, with the memories of him shaped so perfectly at her feet, she started to believe it.

Footsteps crunched behind her and then, a shadow fell over the frozen ground. At once, Chatine recognized the broadness of his shoulders, the shape of his torso, the untamed wildness of his hair, like a mirror image of the landscape that surrounded them.

Of the unknown that stood before them.

Marcellus didn't speak. They both knew he didn't have to. They'd both experienced so much pain. So much loss. Sisters and fathers and mentors and friends. They were bonded in their grief. The whole planet was. They had broken the world apart, and maybe someday they could start to stitch it back together too.

For now, though, Marcellus just stood beside her, letting his presence be enough. Letting his heat and his comforting shadow say all the right words.

I was never there for you.

I want to be there for you now.

I will stand right here for as long as you want me to.

And in her silence, in her own unspoken words, she answered.

She let him.

- CHAPTER 94 -
ALOUETTE

ALOUETTE TAUREAU WALKED THE LONG, QUIET STREET of the Boulevard de la République, running through the heart of Ledôme. She liked walking at this hour, at the moment right before night became day, when the tomorrow that lay just beyond the horizon was so full of promise and possibility.

Despite there being no stars in the sky, the night always seemed to twinkle at this time. Like the sky was so dark, it had become light again. Gone were the artificial stars and imaginary moon that used to shine here. The great panels of the TéléSky had been ripped out weeks ago, leaving nothing behind but the truth.

Sometimes the truth was difficult to see, difficult to accept, difficult not to run from, but none of that changed it from being the truth.

And every day that truth became a little clearer, a little softer, a little easier to stand before and not run from.

As she reached her destination, she glanced out, toward the end of the boulevard, where the Paresse Tower—now the Citizens' Tower—soared upward in its glinting and proud majesty, a memorial to everything they'd stood for, everything they'd fought for, everything they'd won.

With a delicate smile, Alouette unlocked the door of the Maison de

Valeur and stepped inside. The brilliant stained-glass windows were the only thing that still remained of the building's interior. The vast, overly embellished room had been completely transformed in the reconstruction. The great titan panels on the walls had been stripped away and sold, just like the precious gemstones that were once stored in the vaults. The tokens had been used to build new housing in the cities. Clean, dry, stable housing that didn't reek of five-hundred-year-old debris.

Now the walls of the Maison de Valeur held nothing but shelves, mètres and mètres of beautiful wooden shelves. Some held the collection of First World books that the sisters had managed to save from the Refuge. But the rest—the majority—stood empty. Just waiting to be filled with new treasures, new things for the people of Laterre to value and cherish.

Lowering herself into a chair behind a small, modest desk at the back of the room, Alouette pulled out a single sheet of paper and a pen. Her heart immediately began to flutter at the thought of what she was about to undertake. The journey she was about to embark upon.

The war might have been won. But there was still so much to do.

She took a deep, courageous breath and carefully, across the top of the page, began to form the very first letters of the very first volume that would fill these shelves.

The Chronicles of Laterre.

This would be Alouette's most sacred task. This would be her life's work and her life's love.

To ensure that the sisters' legacy lived on. To ensure that knowledge was available to all who sought it. To ensure that the Remembered Word was never forgotten again.

And to ensure that this history, the history of the *people*, was forever protected. Forever guarded.

Because one day, a young girl not too unlike Chatine Renard would want to be inspired by the bravery and spirit of the rebels who built and defended and died at the barricades. Would want to experience the triumph of stopping the Regime's most powerful weapon right in its tracks.

One day, a young boy not too unlike Marcellus Bonnefaçon would want to read the fateful words said to Apolline Moreau before she and her troops joined the rebels' side.

One day, a young girl not too unlike Alouette Taureau would want to feel the light of the Sols break through the clouds and shine down on her face.

And when the real Sols couldn't give that to her, these words would be able to.

These stories could enchant her.

Could inspire her to write more of them.

Alouette stared down at the blank page, her mind dizzy with possibility. Where to even begin? There was so much to write. So much to chronicle.

The inauguration of Laterre's first elected leader.

The demolition of the Frets.

The first session of the people's parlement.

The closure of the Bastille prison.

The opening of Ledôme's gates to all who wanted to enjoy its warm weather, beautiful parks, and cozy cafés.

And the body of César Bonnefaçon, found dead in his satellite prison, after Albion royal guards sent by Queen Matilda broke in and put a cluster bullet in his temple.

Alouette took another breath, trying to organize her thoughts and calm her racing pulse. She had time. She had all the time in the world. And enough passion in her heart to capture every moment.

She peered up at the windows of the Maison de Valeur, at the light of a new dawn streaming in. It split and fragmented through the stained glass, creating a magnificent display of colors and shapes across the floor. Glowing blue hexagons and dazzling red triangles. Vibrant pink diamonds, purple rectangles, and zigzagging slithers of silver.

The answer came to her as steadily and determinedly as a rising Sol.

She would start at the beginning. At the very beginning.

With the blood of the past running through her veins, and the ink of the future running through her pen, Alouette bent her head over the empty page and began to write.

The System Divine offered hope. Hope to the inhabitants of a dying world . . .

TEN YEARS
LATER

When the Blue Dawn swept over Laterre, the nights glowed a little brighter. The days glowed brighter still. And in the grassy dales of Delaine, where morning breezes blustered quietly in from the east, she baked bread. So warm and crusty and round, like planets all of their own. In the afternoons, she would lie beneath the hull of her ship, tinkering with the thrusters she'd crafted and the fuselage she'd welded, while the prisoner tattoo glinted like a line of silvery, forgotten freckles on her arm.

At night, by a fire, she looked up at the dark sapphire skies, and they would huddle close to her. Their small arms wrapped around her. Their soft, sweet breaths against her skin.

Julien and Azelle.

Her children.

Their children.

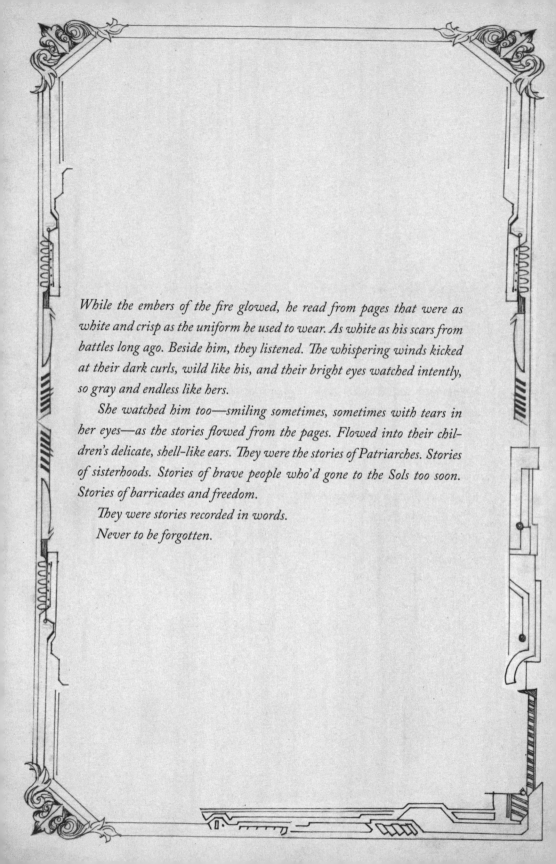

While the embers of the fire glowed, he read from pages that were as white and crisp as the uniform he used to wear. As white as his scars from battles long ago. Beside him, they listened. The whispering winds kicked at their dark curls, wild like his, and their bright eyes watched intently, so gray and endless like hers.

She watched him too—smiling sometimes, sometimes with tears in her eyes—as the stories flowed from the pages. Flowed into their children's delicate, shell-like ears. They were the stories of Patriarchs. Stories of sisterhoods. Stories of brave people who'd gone to the Sols too soon. Stories of barricades and freedom.

They were stories recorded in words.

Never to be forgotten.

Nothing ends, it only transforms. Like a cloud becomes rain and rain becomes tea, the cycle goes on. And these pages will transform too. Laterre's past is written and now the Chronicles belong to those who come after us. To those who have learned the Remembered Word in our new schools. To those who tend our Sisterhood libraries. To those who lovingly print and bind our books for all to read.

I hand my pen onward to those who will write our future. Recording and witnessing all that is to come. The Chronicles do not end here.

They change and continue.

They guide us like our three beautiful Sols.

ACKNOWLEDGMENTS

Writing a book is always a beautiful challenge. And for us, writing *Suns Will Rise* amid the COVID-19 pandemic, this was especially true. The lockdown gave us much-needed time to focus on writing and spend many hours on video calls, hashing out plot points and character arcs. But just like it has for everyone, the pandemic presented several challenges, too.

Thankfully, we have a wonderful team behind this book and series. Although their lives were turned upside down—having to work from home, on tighter deadlines, juggling childcare and sickness—our team came through once again. Many thanks to our ever-supportive agent, Jim McCarthy; our amazing editor, Nicole Ellul; our copyeditor, Jen Strada; our proofreader, Erica Stahler; our managing editor, Morgan York; and the truly stellar S&S team, including Justin Chanda, Kendra Levin, Amanda Ramirez, Anne Zafian, Mary Nubla, Christine Foye, Emily Hutton, Michael Rosamilia, Heather Palisi-Reyes, Sara Berko, Elizabeth Mims, Lauren Carr, Nicole Russo, Caitlin Sweeny, Alissa Nigro, Annika Voss, Chrissy Noh, and Anna Jarzab.

To our immensely talented illustrator, Billelis, you outdid yourself once again. We couldn't have dreamed of a more beautiful cover and such a sparkling Sol! And to our map illustrator, Francesca Baerald—you probably heard us shrieking with delight over the new maps from all the way across the Atlantic. Also, many thanks to our audiobook narrators, Vikas Adam, Joy Osmanski, and Emily Woo Zeller. To keep all the details of our very long books fresh in our minds, we listen to your amazing performances again and again. For us, your voices *are* our characters' voices!

Caroline Roland-Levy, *merci beaucoup pour votre assistance avec ce livre*! And we're so grateful for the stunning translation of Victor Hugo's words for the epigraph! We owe you many boxes of PG Tips!

Deepest thank you to Jessica Khoury, who has supported this series from the very start and who has continually fielded our panicked questions every hour of the day and night. Also, many thanks to Professor Marva Barnett, a Victor Hugo and *Les Misérables* scholar from the University of Virginia. You saved us much time and uncertainty with your expertise.

As we were writing this book, the Black Lives Matter protests unfolded in streets and cities across the world. This powerful and important movement, seeking to fight injustice, violence, and oppression, inspired and motivated us as we wrote our own story of revolution and the struggle for change. We were also inspired by the bravery, engaged lives, and wise words of the many great activists, thinkers, and philosophers throughout history, such as Dr. Martin Luther King, Jr.; Mahatma Gandhi; Thích Nhất Hạnh; Sojourner Truth; Rosa Parks; the Dalai Lama; Malcolm X; Nelson Mandela; Susan B. Anthony; Mary Wollstonecraft; and Malala Yousafzai.

Merci beaucoup to all the booksellers, librarians, teachers, and educators who supported this series, stocked our books on your shelves, and shared our words with readers. We are forever indebted to you for the Refuges you provide and the work you do to ensure the written word is never forgotten.

To all our friends and family who have supported us in the writing of this book amid a pandemic, we are so grateful for the video calls, the texts, the many check-ins, and the love: Ron Aja, Kate Dorney, Melanie Feakins, Donna Lewis, Jana and Alan Lewis, Pamela Mann, Lesley Sawhill, Stephanie Schragger, Linda Rendell, Jennifer Wolfe, Marissa Meyer, and the Brody Bunch (Michael, Laura, Terra, Cathy, and Steve).

Of course, so much gratitude goes to our nearest and dearest: Benny, for making sure our space adventures aren't too lame; Brad, for reminding us there are always other ways of looking at things, if only we allow ourselves to turn the kaleidoscope; and Charlie, for reading every first draft, fixing all the broken tech, and solving all of Laterre's problems (at least in terms of plot). *Nous vous aimons.*

And finally, to our readers. It is your enthusiasm for this series—your love for Chatine, Alouette, and Marcellus; your posts; your tweets; your fan art; your questions; and your support—that has kept us writing and, most importantly, kept us smiling. *Merci beaucoup* from the bottoms of our hearts. May you never stop looking for Sollight, even in the most Laterrian of skies.